The Advent of the King

Fletcher King

Bloomington, IN Milton Keynes, UK

authorHOUSE™

AuthorHouse™
1663 Liberty Drive, Suite 200
Bloomington, IN 47403
www.authorhouse.com
Phone: 1-800-839-8640

AuthorHouse™ UK Ltd.
500 Avebury Boulevard
Central Milton Keynes, MK9 2BE
www.authorhouse.co.uk
Phone: 08001974150

First published by AuthorHouse 7/28/2006

ISBN: 1-4259-1493-4 (sc)

Library of Congress Control Number: 2006900565

Printed in the United States of America
Bloomington, Indiana

This book is printed on acid-free paper.

This work is dedicated to the
Lord God, the Father, the Son, and the Holy Spirit
and to His glory forever.

ACKNOWLEDGEMENTS

I would like to thank the following people who have given so graciously of their time, knowledge, expertise, and support so that this work could come to fruition.

James Adame
John Adame
Margaret Adame
Michael Allen
Father Hugh Assenmacher O.S.B., Subiaco Abbey, AK
William S. Bonds
Gary Brown
Lynnea Brown
William E. Brown, M.D.
Ed Chenoweth of the British Library in America
Jason Coats
Melissa Gay Cooksey
Rick Diamond
Linde Evans
David K. Fletcher, M.D.
Martha I. Fletcher
Fr. Gus Tharappel, M.S.F.S.
Mary Jo Hoch
HM3 Troy C. Humphries USNR
Marlee May
Leslie Neill R.N.
Barry W. Rath, Ph.D.
Ron Roberts
Rev. Canon Jack Russell
Douglas Seiters, Ph.D.
Rev. Stephen B. Stine
Father Joseph Strickland
Connie Tennison R.N.
Carol Thomas R.N.
Rosa Thomas
Richard Walker, British Library
Stan Watson
Sharon Woodrow

CHARACTERS

Christian Oengus Tillo Cuthbert - King of Speyron
Acrida - serf-born seer, a.k.a. **Cinsara**
Olbert - alderman, advisor to the King, Palace Steward and Exchequer (green)
Dewain - alderman, advisor to the King, and Palace Chancellor - (crimson)
Grey - alderman, advisor to the King, and Palace Chamberlain (blue)
Paschal - alderman, adviser to King, Commander of King's Forces (gold)
Felix - alderman, adviser to King, Commander of Palace Watch (blue and green)
Van Necht - alderman, warlord, and Queen's Royal Guard (black)
Tate - court fool to previous King of Speyron
Bennet - a monk
Filberte - previous King of Speyron and Christian's father
Herryck - King threatening to invade Speyron
Deidre - aunt of Acrida
Roe - uncle of Acrida
Albern - knight and vassal to Lord Van Necht
Geoffrey - knight and vassal to Lord Van Necht
Kaithryn Genevieve - cousin and ward of King Christian
Ean - a knight in the service of King Christian
Eldwin - a knight in the service of Lord Olbert
Ecktor - young knight in service of Lord Olbert
Adamson - a prisoner of the King
Jebedye - long time seer for the royal family
Father Poll - parish priest, prisoner of the King
Aldric - Lord Van Necht's steward
Mae - wife of Aldric
Roderic - King of Fors
Elise - runaway niece of King Roderic
Leander - brother to Elise, nephew to King Roderic
Thormonde - Elise's father, brother to King Roderic
Eamon - Bennet's father
Fenton - rebellious vassal of Christian
Bishop Gildas - Bishop of Speyron, seated at Magnushamlet
Julius - Bishop's secretary

Avar - Bishop's secretary
Hunfred - Abbot of St. Brychan monastery
Desle - senior confessor at St. Brychan monastery
Huntingdon - alderman over Brackenbach village
Brackenbach - Acrida's village
Allerd - outspoken serf in Brackenbach village
Perran - knight of King Christian
Reynaud - an alderman in Gaulia
Ardo - knight of Lord Reynaud
Gage - knight of Reynaud who trained Christian in arms
Ita - previous fiancee' of Christian from Ria
Cedd - the King's valet
Boisil - the King's cook

MONKS:
Cai - an oblate
Quintus- an oblate
Selby - young novice
Balfrid - novice
Esterwine
Swithbert
Lubin
Septimus - novice master
Oskitell
Trumwin
Caedmon
Patricus

Kingdoms:

Speyron	Gaulia
Bonaqua	Ria
Caldignis	Multimbria
Fors	Grenad

St. Brychan's - monastery in the eastern mountains of Speyron
St. Benedict's Abbey - largest abbey in Speyron

Other Lords:
Manton - father-in-law to Paschal
Walfrid - Lord in NE of Speyron
Aistulf - Lord in ENE of Speyron

1

No one in my family had ever met a king: I was the lucky one, and all because my mother had cut out my female parts.

In the same year that our kingdom was blessed by the birth of Prince Christian and I was two years old, my mother held me down and sliced open my belly with a large cooking knife. No one can say what she took from my body or what she put in its place, but one thing was certain: the act that took but a moment to carry out changed my life forever.

Because of it, I was shunned in the village of my forefathers on the lands we were bound to. Other children were wary of me because my mother was said to be a witch; but their parents feared that I was some sort of monster to have survived such a gory ordeal. Needless to say, I turned out solitary, peevish, and sullen. My aunt who raised me called me "Acrida" because of my bitter disposition and my sharp tongue.

Such my life would have been, but when I was eleven years old, I began to experience strange dreams in which I was shown things to come and happenings that occurred far away from me. My uncle was anxious of my gift and the new trouble it was sure to bring. My aunt was unconcerned though; she had said simply that if the dead had chosen me to talk to, there was little anyone could do about it.

Never did we imagine at the time what affect my dreams would have on our lives.

I was presented to His Grace, Christian the Fair, King of Speyron, when I was a score and five years of age. Awakening me out of a sound sleep, knights invaded our hut on the village edge and yanked me from my bed. Despite my screams, they dragged me barefoot and wearing nothing other than my undertunic out of my uncle's hut into the cool darkness of waning night. Outside in the distance at the heart of the village, barking dogs, shouts of confusion, armed knights with lighted torches, and frightened villagers and livestock were everywhere.

Ignoring my cries for help and my protests, the knights pulled me by the hair to where a very young boy and a man with the beginnings of a dark, scraggly beard, both as tousled as myself, sat miserably silent on the ground, tied together. They were not from my village.

"Mercy, Sir Knights! What have I done? Why do you take me?" I pleaded.

"Silence, Woman, or we will tie up your mouth!" one of the knights answered as he began tying my wrists together.

Stunned by his response and overwhelmed with panic, I could not even cry. Did they intend to sell us as slaves in a foreign land? Terrified, I stood looking about for help, as the other knight bound my ankle to the ankle of the captive man.

Where was Lord Huntingdon? I wondered. Did he even now sleep undisturbed in his tower? Did he know of this attack on his lands?

As soon as I was bound, the knights ordered the man and boy to their feet and then ordered us to move, and fresh panic surged through me. Twisting around in the direction of our hut, I looked desperately about for my aunt and uncle, but was shoved forward by the guard behind me. I could not see my aunt anywhere in the dim moonlight, but I caught a glimpse of my uncle among our neighbors. He stood neither protesting nor resisting my capture as they led me away.

As we went through my village, we passed more knights searching other huts. What could they be seeking? I wondered.

Then we joined a great force of knights and carts in the common of the village. Three youths on horseback were watching the commotion apart from the knights by the light of the many burning torches.

One of the youths sat upon a large, shining, snowy-white horse. His blond hair which hung loosely about his shoulders shone like gold even in the limited light. One of the knights approached him on foot and bowed.

"He will not be pleased, for we have found no weapons," a knight walking past us said to another.

"Why would we? Sheep do not have the spirit to fight or rebel."

I wondered at his words. Were these raiders not only seeking slaves but other items of value to sell? Whoever they were, they were ill-informed. Brackenbach was the smallest and poorest of villages on all of Lord Huntingdon's lands. There was very little, if anything, of value here.

The knight was correct. Even from a distance, I could see the noble youth was irritated by the report from the knight. He made a gesture of irritation and suddenly dismounted. His two companions dismounted quickly after him, and the three of them strode boldly toward the nearest huts.

They entered the first hut followed by two knights. There was a crash with accompanying wails. Squawking chickens flew out the door, and the squealing of a sow filled the air as it escaped the hut. Then there was nothing for a long moment. After a few minutes, the youths exited the hut, cursing and empty handed.

Then they entered the hut beside it. The other knights watched in silence. There was no crash this time, only the sound of shouts and cries of panic and despair from the people and livestock within.

The young warlord came out of this hut bringing a girl with him. I knew her by sight; she was about fourteen years old and engaged to be married in the spring. He pulled her by her brown, curly locks and handed her to a knight.

"Take her. She will have the honor of serving in our hall. Even if we find no weapons, the journey here will not have been wasted."

Who was he and why was he searching for weapons here? Our village had barely adequate numbers to farm enough food to live.- We did not even have a proper smith. Why would he think we had weapons?

The knight led the weeping girl away. Her mother cried, and her father held his wife, but they made no move toward their daughter. I watched as stunned as the rest as the youths went through the other homes and took the most beautiful young girls of my village away from their wailing parents and protesting husbands, all the while laughing among themselves as if it were some jest.

The last hut, however, was Allerd's. He was the hardest working farmer in our village and the most outspoken at the manorial court. He followed his redheaded daughter and the youths out of the hut, carrying a homemade spear. The warlords' knights were behind him almost immediately, but they kept their distance.

"Release my daughter!" Allerd ordered.

The blond youth only stopped his tread for a moment. Having caught sight of the spear, he pulled the girl in front of him like a shield and smiled while his companions drew their swords.

"We knew someone must have a weapon in this village," he said lightly, as if it were all sport. "We will make a pact with you. You show us where your village has hidden the rest of its weapons, and we will allow this girl to remain here."

"We are farmers here. We have no arms."

3

"As you wish- no arms, no daughter. We will make certain she is well cared for."

"You have no authority to take her," Allerd answered.

"No authority? Do you not know Us?" he laughed. "We are Christian, King of Speyron!"

I gasped and blinked, astounded as the rest of the village. This was the first time I had ever seen our young, 'golden-haired' king as I had heard him described by travelers passing through our village. The rumor was that the youth was quite handsome.

All of the villagers stepped back then and went obediently to their knees. Allerd made an awkward, short bow, but then spoke boldly.

"We are the serfs of Lord Huntingdon. None can be removed from his lands without his consent. Take her or any of us, and you break faith with your vassal, Lord Huntingdon."

"You are learned in the law," King Christian said with some surprise. "Very well."

Then he turned and called to a horseman a little away from him, "Lord Huntingdon, thy King has need of these women. Do you give your consent that We should take them?"

My heart skipped a beat as I and the rest of the village turned to see among the King's knights an elderly man on a horse mostly concealed by the darkness. I was startled to see our gentle master, exhausted from many years of life as well as the late hour, nod his head and give his consent.

Chuckling, the King turned to take the girl to the cart where the other girls were being loaded. Allerd, however, neither lowered the spear, nor stepped aside to allow the King to pass.

"I would rather my daughter were dead than living in your palace of sin and wickedness."

"Very well," King Christian said with a shrug, drawing a blade from his belt and putting it to the girl's throat.

The girl's mother screamed, and Allerd seemed momentarily surprised, but he did not relent.

"Kill him," King Christian said, without taking his eyes from the man.

My heart pounded in my chest as the knight standing behind Allerd thrust his sword into his back. Allerd caught his breath and paled. The daughter's screams echoed her mother's as Allerd fell to his knees and then slumped to the ground. As the knight freed his sword from Allerd's back with a cruel jerk, Allerd's wife was beside him in the dirt, crying pitifully as she attempted to cradle her dying husband's body in her arms.

"Their home, burn it," King Christian added coolly, not relinquishing the wildly struggling and wailing girl in his grasp.

He turned away then and smiled as he shoved his prize into the arms of a knight who took the raving girl to a cart where the other girls sat weeping. Allerd's younger children were pushed aside while the men with torches set fire to their little home that had been considered so fine by their neighbors.

Terrified, I watched the hut burn. The yellow and white flames leaped high into the dark sky, lighting the faces of Speyron's wretched people and the blood of a good man as it dyed the ground black in the dark. The King did not look back as he mounted his pale horse. He gave the order to depart and led his men and prisoners away into the darkness.

2

After marching to dawn and then all day, we did not stop at dusk as I had expected. After sunset, the knights had simply lit torches and continued on. When we finally arrived long after dark at a large wooden tower, I was disappointed to learn that this was only the home of another vassal and not the end of our journey. The knights hastily made camp within the wooden fence that surrounded the tower while the King enjoyed his vassal's hospitality inside. Some of the knights simply lay down and went to sleep on the spot, allowing the alderman's servants to tend to their tired horses. Others sat up with the fires that were built and talked quietly while they waited on their food.

Still tied together, we prisoners lay exhausted on the ground, huddled close together for warmth in the crisp, autumn night air. With feet and body aching, I rested in the darkness remembering the day. By midmorning, I had no longer known where we were or whose lands we were on. Our route had seemed endless and undirected as we bypassed some villages and stopped and searched others.

As the day had continued, what occurred during a village raid no longer shocked me. I watched indifferently with the other prisoners as the knights rummaged through another hut, scattering belongings everywhere, or beat and threatened a few more helpless peasants until they turned over any weapons that they knew of, or a knight led another beautiful girl to the cart. In truth, I began to look forward to the raiding of a village, for it was the only time we prisoners were allowed to sit down and rest for any length of time. The King usually stopped his forces at the village well, and while the knights searched the villages, the guards and servants watered the horses and prisoners.

On every set of lands, the King sent word to his vassal of his arrival. And like Lord Huntingdon, the nobleman came and greeted the King cordially, only later to sit upon his horse, mutely watching the King's men disrupt the peace of his lands and bully his peasants.

The King was definitely looking for weapons. In a few of the villages, the knights did succeed in finding some, but usually they were the wares of a smith who claimed he was making swords for the knights under his alderman. A few peasants were even found with remnants of old arms that their fathers or grandfathers had used long ago when neighboring lords had been at war. Regardless of their condition, the knights seized the weapons and heaped them into a cart with the rest.

I wondered again what the King wanted with me. Not counting the girls in the cart, he did not take many prisoners, which made his selections all the more curious. The middle-aged man, the child, and myself were the only ones until the addition of a parish priest in the afternoon. The knights took the holy father right out of the alderman's castle where he had been working on the lord's accounts. The noble lord had followed the knights out of the castle and demanded an explanation, but after a few words with the King, he allowed the priest to be removed without any further objection.

The three of us prisoners had not actually spoken to each other. Earlier that day, I had tried speaking to the man, but he only ignored me. The child was fearful of me also, though I know not why. When the priest joined us, though, he immediately began to recite the Paternoster and the Ave Maria, and we said it with him too, quietly. After a while of walking, however, our prayers all died out as weariness overtook us.

Toward evening, the knights took a wild man from a forest. At first, I thought him a hermit who was too holy to live in the world; then I saw the way he raved and fought and fell upon the ground without warning. He had not bathed in a very long time, and he looked like a hairy animal dressed in the tatters of a monk's habit. He had bits of leaves and sticks and filth in his beard and unkempt, matted, oily hair, and he smelled so foul that he attracted flies, which would in turn light upon us. With the way he scratched himself and the many scabs on his skin, I suspected he had more than fleas on him as well.

It had taken some time for the knights to subdue him. Barefoot and confused, he sputtered, drooled, and ranted wildly about bad fruit, stuttering over the same words again and again until finally the guard hit him on the back until he was blessedly silent. He was tied to the rest of us, and then we continued to cut and toughen our feet on the rocks, sticks, and rough terrain on the way to the next village.

The King and his companions had remained on their horses for most of the entire day, overseeing the activity with an air of boredom. How many days had they been at this? I wondered. And what could be so important about finding weapons in a few villages that it required the King of Speyron to attend to it personally? But, by the end of the day, I was just as bored and indifferent as everyone else, wanting only some food, more water, and to get wherever we were going so this ordeal would be ended.

Finally now, we had stopped, and while the knights made camp, we prisoners had quickly eaten the portion of day-old bread we had been given. The girls in the cart were permitted to walk around some while they ate, but they were closely watched.

It was a very quiet camp. The sound of buzzing bugs, crackling fires, and horses champing hay mixed with the soft murmur of the conversations of the men around the fires. I had worried all day that the knights would make sport with us captives once we stopped for the night. Even in Brackenbach, women and girls had to take care when Huntingdon's household visited the lands, for our small village had no brothel, and the knights, if drunk or bored, would rape any girls they could catch and overpower. To my relief, however, the King's knights took no interest in any of us.

I glanced at my companions. Only the child was sleeping. I longed for sleep too, but, like the rest, I was too frightened. I watched his peaceful expression and even breathing, enviously. How frantic his mother must be. Did she know that the King had taken him? Was she even now searching for him?

The wild man beside me suddenly reached out and snatched at something in the darkness. I watched him carefully open his fingers revealing a large insect. Gripping the bug in his foul fingers, he popped the wiggling morsel into his mouth and chewed it up greedily. I held my breath and thought for a moment I was going to be sick. I rolled over onto my other side with my back to him and closed my eyes.

"At last!" came the voice of our guard near us.

In the dark, I had forgotten him. As I looked in his direction, I heard the sound of dried, fallen leaves crunching underfoot as another knight approached, bringing with him the smell of freshly roasted meat. My mouth watered, and my stomach ached and growled its complaint.

"What took so long, Ralf?" our guard asked.

"Complain not to me, Tomas. The meat was not ready."

"The King was made to wait upon his meat? Why, I am surprised he did not order the cook's head set upon the gate."

Sir Ralf laughed, handing our guard a chunk of roasted meat and some bread.

"The lord of the castle seemed to fear it could befall him as well! He offered his apologies repeatedly."

"Nervous, was he?"

"Aye, very. 'Twas a very reserved table."

"No drinking and dancing, eh?"

"No," Ralf laughed again and shook his head.

"How about some good wine to wash down the meat?" came a third voice approaching from the dark.

"Ean!" our guards chuckled. "What have you found?"

"Just two young knights of this household who have graciously offered us the remains of a hogshead of their lord's private stock of wine."

"Well, bring it here, Man! We will not refuse their generosity!"

Our guards threw out the drink in their horn cups and held them out for the young knights to refill.

I watched the two youths, one chubby, and the other, tall and lanky, serve our guards. The men tasted the drink and complimented it.

"Sir Ean tells us you were at Fenton's castle this summer when it fell," the tall one said.

"Aye, we were there with Lord Van Necht for two months laying siege to the castle," Sir Tomas replied, sitting down to eat his meat.

"Is it true what they say?" the chubby one asked almost in a whisper. "Did the King really execute Fenton's elder son in front of him *after* Lord Fenton had already surrendered the castle and sworn fealty to the King?"

"Aye, 'tis true," Sir Ralf answered. "'Twas a surprise to all. He ordered the lad's throat slit right there, in front of Fenton, Lady Eleanor and the entire household."

The hair stood up on the back of my neck.

"Monstrous!" the chubby youth exclaimed.

"The King did not believe Fenton sincere," Ralf added.

"I did not care for his manner either," Sir Tomas said. "After his castle fell, Fenton carried himself too proudly. He stood before King Christian and grudgingly asked forgiveness."

"Aye, he swore his allegiance haughtily."

"Not a wise thing to do," Ean chuckled.

"Aye," Ralf agreed, "but that changed when he saw his son's throat slashed before his very eyes."

"Aye, the whole household was aghast," Tomas said. "The lad's mother and nursemaids screamed and crowded about the dying boy, soaked in the rain of his blood."

"Lord Fenton himself was so stunned, he could not speak," Ralf said.

"That changed too when the King summoned the second son," Tomas added.

"The second son!" the youths gasped.

The blood in my veins turned cold.

"Aye! The child was brought forward and a knife held to his throat next. The household was terrified; the blood-soaked women fell at the King's feet weeping and begging for the boy to be spared even as the blood continued to spout out of the first born."

"What of Fenton? Did he not beg for his son's life as well?" the tall youth asked.

"Aye! Fenton groveled on the floor with the women in tears, pleading for his remaining son's life! He begged the King's pardon. He swore allegiance. What did he not promise?"

"'Twas a pitiful sight!" Tomas admitted.

"Aye, but he managed to satisfy the King," Ralf continued. "King Christian spared the boy. Then he ordered the execution of Lord Fenton and had the man's head hung on the gate of his own castle!"

"God's bones!"

My heart pounded wildly as I listened.

"Lady Eleanor returned to her parents with her son, did she not?" Sir Ean asked our guard.

9

"Aye."

"And Lord Grey holds the lands in trust for the King until the King awards them to someone else?" Sir Ean verified again.

"Aye, I believe that is so," Tomas answered.

"God's wood!" the young knight exclaimed again. "You speak so calmly! The King sacked the castle of his own noble vassal and put him to death with his eldest son, -and you speak of it as if it was nothing more than the execution of a peasant!"

"King Christian had no real choice," Ean shrugged. "Fenton had broken his allegiance."

"No choice?" the youth asked. "Could he not have shown mercy? Perhaps only banished him? Fenton was defeated, and his castle and lands taken back by the King."

"Fenton broke his sacred oath of vassalship. Should he not have paid with his life?" Tomas asked.

"Perhaps, but to execute a lad of noble blood, an innocent, who had no part in his father's offense-"

"The King did show mercy, for he spared the rest of Fenton's family and his household," Sir Ean argued.

"That is mercy?"

"It is a rare mercy for *this* King."

"God's eyes!"

"Lord Fenton not only broke his vow of allegiance to his King," Ralf argued, "but he refused to acknowledge King Christian's sovereignty! There is nothing graver!"

"Aye, 'tis one thing when a vassal does not pay his taxes to this king; 'tis another when he encourages other vassals to revolt-" Tomas added, "-telling them the King's excommunication has released them all from their oaths of fealty!"

I had forgotten about that. King Christian's excommunication had been announced so long ago.

"-Aye, and telling them the kingdom is cursed on account of the King and that they should all join him in rebellion!"

I raised my eyebrows.

"Fenton said all that?" the tall youth asked.

"Indeed! He came out and proclaimed it all to Lord Van Necht and all of us knights who had come against him," Sir Ralf said.

"So Fenton was making alliances with other vassals," the chubby youth said.

"Aye, to control the north of Speyron."

"Aye, it is as I was saying," Ean replied, "King Christian had little choice but to execute Fenton once he refused to acknowledge his sovereignty and began acting as if there was no king at all."

"-As if *he* himself was king- or was planning to make himself one."

"For so great an offense, Fenton was lucky to die quickly, and his wife and child and the knights in his household were all lucky to be spared at all," Ralf said.

"Aye," Ean agreed, "and with Fenton and his elder son's deaths, King Christian sends a very clear message to his subjects: Be loyal and do not offend, lest blood spill, both innocent and guilty."

They were all silent then.

"What do you think he wants with these vermin?" the chubby youth asked, glancing at me.

"I know not," Ean answered. "The girls in the cart will go to the King's bed. I do not have any idea what he wants with this odd group though. I just know their names were on the parchment."

My heart skipped a beat and then pounded rapidly. I rolled over again, my stomach tightening with fear. I shut my eyes and whispered an Ave Maria, hoping sleep would come and rescue me from my fear. I could not sleep though. Instead, I began remembering the early days of my visions.

Deidre and Roe were the only family I could remember. After my mother died, they took me in and raised and loved me as their own child; their five surviving children were long grown, married and working other lands of Huntingdon.

Aunt Deidre was a wise, outspoken woman and an opposing figure next to her slim and meek husband. Uncle Roe was a simple, hard working, quiet man. In fact, he was so quiet that it was easy to forget that he was present in a room, for he hardly spoke a word, no matter what the discussion.

When I was eleven, instead of getting my monthly blood like other girls my age, I began having dreams that came true. They were strange, confusing dreams with often scary images, but in time, they began making more sense to me, and I realized I knew what was going to happen before it did.

In my village, few of the villagers would even speak to me when I was a child. Watchful mothers did not allow their children to play with me. Few of the children would talk to me for more than a moment, but only when their parents or older siblings were not around, and usually only to tease me about my mother.

When I began having visions, I shared what I had dreamed with whomever would listen. First I told one girl, and then she brought two more to hear, and on, and on, until there was a large group of children listening. They thought what I said was strange, and me too. But when what I predicted happened, I instantly became a novelty among them, and someone to be feared and respected.

I had revelled in my new status, but not for long. The children could not keep it to themselves. The girl told her mother, and after the beating she received, she did not come near me again.

Word quickly spread through my village. After that, the villagers and their children shunned me even more than they had before. Our parish priest scolded me for communing with spirits and demons. He gave me a penance, and I had not even gone for confession! Then Uncle Roe reprimanded me. He told me after what had happened with my mother, I was a fool to bring more trouble on myself. He told me I could tell Deidre about my dreams, but that was all.

As the villagers would have nothing to do with me, I had no real choice in the matter. But when I was about thirteen, I had a new opportunity. Lord Huntingdon's entire household arrived in the late summer from his other manor lands for the season. The neighbor woman had come over that day to tell the latest gossip heard in Huntingdon's hall, as her daughter was taking a turn working as a servant there. She had just arrived, and seeing her, I suddenly realized that it had been someone of Lord Huntingdon's household that I had dreamt about the night before. The neighbor was describing a scandalous servant from another of Huntingdon's villages- a young girl with small, delicate features, who had not been a nursery maid for yet a year.

"Greenish eyes-" I commented, while I worked at grounding flour.

"Aye-" the woman commented without looking up, "Well, the girl two days ago-"

"Her baby was born dead; it would have been the lord's fifth son," I said, hardly concealing my pride and glee at being able to show off my abilities.

The neighbor stared at me, stunned, as I beat her to her news.

"How did you hear that already?" she asked me.

I suddenly had not had an answer.

"And the girl has never said who the man was," she added, giving me a suspicious look. "-And Lord Huntingdon has never dallied with other women or his servants as some married noblemen are prone to do. It is not well for you to speak such a lie."

"'Tis not a lie! He has not lain with his lady wife in over two years, nor will he again! The lady has had her last child by him. Lord Hun-"

I do not know if my words or insight surprised my aunt because I never saw her face. But everyone was astonished at my uncle's sudden appearance out of the shadows of our hut. He slapped me down in mid-sentence before I knew what was happening. I was dumbfounded as he proceeded to drag me outside the hut and there, whip me soundly.

When he stopped, he gripped my shoulders in his huge hands.

"Do you not have any sense in your head, Girl? You know how they feel about you! Do you want your end to be like your mother's?"

"No!" I had sobbed.

"You will bring the death of us all! If you must have these visions, keep them to yourself, for they are nothing but trouble! They will bring nothing but trouble! -And *never* tell everything you know!"

Of course, the gossip told everyone what I had said, so that even the friendliness that had existed between the neighbors and my aunt and uncle cooled. Likely word reached Huntingdon himself as well.

And as I had predicted, Lord Huntingdon and his wife had no more children; the lady died a year later from a fever. The villagers regarded me with even more suspicion after that, and a rumor began to circulate that I had actually put a curse on Huntingdon's wife. After that, the village children did not even dare come near me even to tease me.

From then on, I became a silent witness of my visions and the foretelling they promised. And I tried to learn to be a quiet observer of people like my uncle, for in a violent and unsure world, the quiet, humble man was often left alone.

I jerked awake, panting, my heart beating rapidly. Looking around in the darkness, I swallowed hard and remembered where I was and what had happened. I told myself that I was safe, as I always did, and wiped my sweating forehead with my sleeve. Carefully, I took a deep breath and relaxed, as I remembered my dream.

The woman had been there. Her frail frame was covered with sagging, weathered flesh that hung from her bones like wet clothes hanging to dry on tree limbs. Her wrinkled skin was tanned dark and freckled, and she had the odd look of a young woman in an old body. She wore a short headrail with her hair tucked up sloppily inside it except for a few sparse, brownish-gray, disobedient strands that hung in her face. Her gown had no color and was short, the jagged ends only going down below the knees. In every dream, she wore shoes of some sort.

She walked and talked very quickly in my dreams, speaking in a kind of gibberish. She would talk to the air itself or at nothing in particular, hardly ever looking at me directly. She mumbled so rapidly that I could hardly ever make out what she was saying to me. Only occasionally would I catch a word or two, sometimes only part of one. But no matter how often I pleaded with her in my sleep to wait or slow down, she never did.

Tonight, she had been adamant- yelling at me. She kept talking about sand. She had said the word three times and was very impatient with me when I did not see her meaning.

"Yunstd?" she had asked, which was her word for 'Do you understand?'

I shook my head asleep. She was talking too fast and mumbling under her breath. I could hardly hear her, much less make out the words. I was sweating as I pleaded with her to repeat herself. She shook her head and yelled to the side, not looking at me, "Lizn!"

She gestured once, and she suddenly turned her back to me and began walking very fast. I hurried to follow her, but I could never keep up. Already she was way ahead in the distance. Finally, she stopped, and we stood in a place where all was sand and dead trees as far as the eye could see. I looked around. There was no water anywhere, and it was very hot.

"Where are we? In a desert?"

Her answer was a long series of words that I could not make out.

"Where?" I asked again.

She glared at me as if I was a simpleton, but when she repeated it this time, I managed to get, "Wehn gonywerr. Samplac. Werte samplac. Yunstd?"

I looked at her, confused. What did she mean we were at the same place? I looked around the landscape that was empty except for a few leafless shrubs and trees here and there. All was still. The faint sound of birds only filled the air. It was hot under the bright sun. I was thirsty now, and the sun was blistering my face. There was not even a breeze.

But as hot as I was, the middle aged woman was cold. She had on a long cloak then and was wrapping it around herself.

She pointed to a small shrub a little ways from us, and I went in the direction of her gnarled finger. Three birds were perched in the bare limbs, singing contentedly.

"Lcathz sin sa ra."

I looked back at the old woman, and in so doing, was suddenly at her side again. The old woman, wrapped in her cloak, was pointing in the distance now. Something was happening. A large crowd of people all in a line were meandering through the sand, winding up and back, as they journeyed. When they neared us, I saw a young man with golden hair leading them, and I knew it was the King. He paused for a moment, stopping the procession that was following him, and seemed to listen for a moment. The song of the birds was quite clear. The King left the long trail of people, and as he moved toward the brush, I became suddenly frightened, more frightened than I usually was when the old woman visited my dreams.

Suddenly, the crowd of people was gone, and it was only the King looking at the birds in the bush. My heart was beating frantically in my chest as I watched the King, dressed richly in all his heavy, dark purple clothes, reach into the shrubbery and pluck out a small black bird; it chirped calmly in his hand. He looked at it closely for a moment, examining its eyes as it tweeted, and then he suddenly bit the creature's head off. Blood spurted from the bird's headless body onto the King's fine clothes and ran down his hand and fingers. I screamed.

The old woman began to mutter rapidly again as the King spit the head from his mouth and threw the dead body to the dry ground. Then he reached into the brush and took the next bird. Unable to cover my eyes, I watched him in complete terror, as he bit off the head of every bird in the brush. Then all was silence except for the sound of the old woman's gibberish.

I turned away from the sight of the bloody King and the discarded heads and bodies of the birds that lay on the dry earth. With my heart beating frantically, I looked back to the old woman in her ankle high leather shoes who was wrapped in her cloak as if she were going to freeze in this hot, empty desert.

"Take me away from here!" I pleaded.

I did not know if she had heard me at first. She was talking rapidly to the midair again, but she suddenly turned her dark, ringed eyes on me directly as she rambled and simply shook her head.

3

After three and a half days of walking, we finally arrived at the palace of Speyron's King. We were not alone. Early that morning, we had taken the main road and were suddenly met by many more travelers journeying there.

The palace was like nothing I had ever seen! Lord Huntingdon's tower was a common hut compared to this place! The walls of the palace first came into sight at midmorning, but we did not arrive at the palace gate until afternoon, after a long, hard trudge up a very steep hill.

The great stone wall that surrounded the palace seemed to continue forever- like a road that disappears into the horizon; and it enclosed such a huge breadth of land that it was able to contain the entire village inside it. Outside the walls, the large fields were nearly ready to be harvested.

The great gate was open wide, and the small groups of people gathered there stopped talking to observe our approach curiously. As we passed through the massive, wooden gate at the entrance, a pair of skulls that had been nailed into the left wall glared sightlessly at us.

Inside the walls, people were everywhere- all sorts of people. There were nobles and knights, commoners, peddlers, and foreigners- all mixed together selling, buying, or trading their goods and wares in a marketplace along the road. Carts full of grain grown in other villages had been brought here to be sold. To the left, a crowd of knights was gathered around a smith, trying out swords. Other knights were checking the quality of leather at a tanner's shop. To the right, women were haggling with a long bearded, foreign peddler in strange garb over the price of his goods. Groups of children ran, laughing, down the road, weaving in and around the various people. Vendors lined the entire way to the entrance of the palace with their wares: different kinds of dye, cloth, dyed cloth, shoes, cauldrons, earthenware, knives, fresh produce, fish, beads, honey, ale, chickens, swine, sheep, cows, and oxen- and more. There was much to see, and the roar of it all filled my ears.

I was so enthralled by all the people and all the wonderful things they had to sell or trade that I at first did not notice the huge, open structure that towered above everything until we stood right before it. I had never seen anything like it. It resembled a giant, open shelter of sorts, but crafted of stone. The roof and left and right walls were of solid, light gray stone, and four, immense supports of the same stone stood where we entered and at the far end. Even the floor was made of the same stone, and its smooth, polished texture felt good to my sore, bare feet.

"What is this?" the little boy among us suddenly asked.

"The entrance to the royal palace and courtyard-" the guard among us answered.

"Why is it so big?"

He laughed.

"This palace was built by the Romani. They were great builders. They wanted to impress our forefathers whom they had conquered, so they built this huge palace of marble and stone columns. Now, come inside and sit down."

I sat down on the shady, marble floor, grateful for some relief from the pain of my tender, swollen feet. I frowned, examining the blisters and cuts. The soles were black with dirt, manure, blood and bruising. I did not even know how I had made it this far barefoot. I had cut my left foot deeply yesterday and had been limping on it ever since. My feet, ankles, and legs were scratched, skinned, and bruised from walking through all sorts of rocky, brushy and prickly terrain.

As we rested in silence, we were again brought water, while most of the knights were dismissed. The knights took away the weapons they had collected from the villages, and some stable boys came and collected the horses of the guards who remained with us. The girls, destined for the King's bed, were unloaded out of their cart and pushed into a line near us. There we all waited inside the grand passageway as passersby regarded us with interest.

I wondered where the King was. He had left the march early this morning. Was he here already or had he stopped at some other place with some other business?

After I had my drink, I turned my attention to my fellow prisoners again. I was still tied to the man with the dark, scruffy beard. He was a little younger than myself with quick moving eyes. I could not tell from his dress if he was a slave, serf, or a freeman. He talked to the boy sometimes, or the priest, but he never spoke to me. I had asked him his name a few times, but he would never answer. It was as if I was not worthy of a reply. Daily along the journey, he had asked the guards where we were going, what was to be done to us, and why we were taken, but the guards would tell him nothing. And everyday, he had continued to pester them until they threatened to beat him if he was not silent.

The little boy sat with his arms around his bent legs, resting his forehead on his knees. His ragged braes exposed his scratched and bloodied ankles and feet. His pale skin seemed even paler against his startling snow-white hair that hung untended in his eyes. I had noticed after I was first captured that along with being extremely quiet for a child his age, the boy was marked with different colored eyes: one blue, the other green. Throughout this ordeal, I had been affected by his lost expression and sorrowful gaze; I had longed to reach out and comfort him, but he had recoiled from me and instead had turned to the priest for solace.

The priest, Father Poll, sat beside the boy. He was pudgy, and his hair was shorter than anyone else's; and his hands were pale, soft, and unused to hard labor. His everyday clothes, not much better than any freeman's, were torn and soiled with dirt and dust from the journey.

On the other side of him, the hairy, wild man sat on the stone floor tracing the lines in the marble stone floor with his grubby finger. He seemed unaware of where he was or what was happening around him. He smelled worse today, so much so that I had thought earlier that I might be ill if I was confined too close to him, but there was little possibility of actually vomiting since there was so little in my stomach.

Beside him sat the oldest man I had ever seen. He had almost no hair on his head, and his skin was terribly wrinkled from a life too long, but he had a very long beard, which was unusual, for the custom of the men of Speyron was to shave daily. He looked about, squinting, and sniffing the air and wrinkling his nose. He wore layers of rags and sat there stroking the long staff he carried which was knotted and carved with some sort of design. His eyesight was very poor, and he was so frail and unsure of foot, he had stumbled and tripped from the moment the knights took him out of his hut this morning. Clearly, it would have been impossible for him to keep pace with the rest of us, so the knights had put him in the crowded cart with the girls.

After a while, we heard music above the bustle of the vendors and customers, and it drew our attention to the far side of the entrance. The boy stood up and moved as close to the other side as his restraint would allow him, to see what was happening.

"Quick, Father! Come see! What is that?"

We all rushed to stand up to see at what the boy was pointing.

This wondrous entrance did not lead directly into the King's palace, but actually opened out into a large grassy area. At the center stood a large, stone jar which continuously poured three streams of water into a large, circular, stone trough below it, around which even more people and vendors peddled their goods.

"I know not, My Son. But it is a wonder," Father Poll replied.

"'Tis called a 'fountain'," the old man among us said, pointing his gnarled finger. "The palace has many such wonders."

I raised my eyebrows.

Around the fountain, the vendors were selling jewels, shirts of mail, silver goblets, casks of wine, horses, saddles, and all sorts of items that could rarely be found in any peasant village that I knew of in Speyron. Here, noblemen, knights, and ladies in their fine clothes laughed and talked and examined the goods, while a group of minstrels played a merry tune nearby.

"Sit down!" our guard ordered again.

We sat back down in the center of the stone entrance where the activity on both sides of the entrance could be viewed, and we waited again, occupying ourselves as we watched the people.

Gradually, the sun began to set, the vendors put away their wares, and the people went away. A pair of torch lighters went around lighting the many torches that were secured to the outer walls of the palace, and they lit the torches in the entrance where we waited as well.

Still we waited, and a single bell began to peal, summoning the people to the church. Groups of men, women, and children hurried down the road toward a building in the distance, but just out of sight. Some men and women came from inside the palace itself, passing beside us in the stone entrance, and then heading down the road out of sight.

Then it grew dark, and we still waited. I shivered in the cooling autumn air as I examined what was left of my tattered undertunic which had snagged and ripped on almost every bush and stick from Brackenbach to here. I scratched some of the itching, oozing scabs on my legs; my exposed knees, calves, and ankles had been bit by every insect and scratched by countless brush along the way. I covered my legs again with the tunic and looked at the other prisoners, each of us lost in thought and exhaustion.

"Get to your feet!" a new guard yelled, abruptly. "Stay close together as we go through the courtyard into the palace!"

They ushered us through the now empty courtyard, past the fountain, toward the palace that glowed in the torchlight. The palace was built entirely of stone and formed a square of sorts with the courtyard as its center. Directly in front of us was a long, large building lined with many enormous columns. At its center, stairs led up to another column entrance that resembled the large one we had waited in for so long. To the left was a long building with smaller columns and doors every few feet. To the right was a wall, but you could see the top of a building behind it.

Leaving the courtyard, we climbed the stairs and went through the columns through a great wooden door that had a guard posted on each side. We entered a corridor that was lit well with torches and was also lined with thick columns that were part of the wall that reached a high, arched ceiling. The sheer height of the ceiling dwarfed us and made me feel even more insignificant than I already felt. As I limped behind the man in front of me, I noticed the many servants scurrying about, all wearing clean clothes, talking and smiling, and in good spirits.

The guards led us through another door into a beautifully decorated chamber with a very high ceiling. I marveled at the colors and designs. On the long right side, the wall had been painted with a group of hunters riding through the fields with elongated dogs racing at their feet. On the opposite wall, beasts not of this world pulled a speeding chariot; the driver of the chariot had just snatched a maiden away from her startled companions.

But as splendid as the colors of the pictures were, neither of these painted scenes could compare with the simple beauty of the floor that with its black and white stones formed an intricate design. In the center of the floor, the stones formed a circle, and inside the circle was a picture of a wolf giving suck to two boy babies.

"This is the King's Audience Chamber," the old man said with a nod. "I have been here several times in my younger days."

Directly opposite to the entrance of the chamber was a finely carved chair set with jewels. Behind it at the far wall was a staircase that gave way to a landing. A pair of knights were on the landing, talking and laughing as they watched us enter the chamber. Two wooden doors on the landing were open, and I could just see another knight on the parapet outside.

A long table stood near the left wall. As we came in, two men near the table were speaking with their backs to us: one looked to be about my uncle's age; the other in his late thirties. They were both dressed in rich, heavy clothes. The older man wore dark green, and the younger wore crimson.

"Stop here," our guard instructed us, leaving us in the center of the circle.

As I looked around, the chamber was quickly filling with lively young knights, most of them no older than the King; they flirted, joked, and smiled at the three or four maidservants who bustled about the room, serving drinks.

"Well, these are a fine-looking group," came a loud voice behind us.

I turned around and saw an old man in worn, commoner's clothes. He appeared to be about the same age as the nobleman in green. He wore his long, gray hair tied back from his head. He was gulping down a drink from a silver goblet as he walked and gesturing toward the girls who had followed us into the chamber with a pink rose he carried.

"They will all make fine, fine royal concubines," he added, his speech slightly slurred.

The noblemen looked around to the old man for a moment and then went back to their discussions.

I raised my eyebrows. Was everyone welcome to attend audiences of the King? Even the drunken, palace gardener?

Then King Christian entered, striding into the chamber toward the two lords, and everyone bowed low.

I swallowed. The King was handsome; in fact, he was striking. The youth was of average height, with broad shoulders and a smooth complexion. His hair was the color of gold and just brushed his shoulders. He had recently bathed, shaved, and wore clean clothes of costly purple. He even smelled sweet. And his smile made my heart skip a beat.

The King was trailed by two, noble youths of similar age. One was a freckled redhead dressed in gold fabric. The other was a dark blond lad adorned in bright blue and green.

"Take these girls out of here," King Christian ordered the guards. "Take them to their chamber and bath."

"Some of these are real beauties-" the old man with the rose suddenly called out.

The guards bowed and ushered the girls back out of the chamber.

"They will look much better, though, when they are cleaned up- and their spirits- are absolutely- crushed-" he continued, making an odd gesture with the cup in his hand.

One of the knights near him smiled, but glancing at the King, he quickly put on a straight face again.

"From slavery-" the old man finished.

Hearing the comment, the King's gaze fell on the old man. The old man, however, did not recoil from his obvious glare. Instead, he stood his ground and smiled a charming smile.

"But what has a woman need for free choice, after all?" he said. "That is the gift given by God to men."

"Again, he is back," the King muttered.

The old man smiled.

"Indeed I am. Out of love for you, Sire, I have come-"

The knights snickered.

"Love! Ha!" the King's companion in blue and green snorted. "More like free food and wine."

"Thy King does not love thee, Old Man," the youth in gold told him coldly. "Nor does thy King crave thy love."

"How is it, Tate," King Christian asked, "that after setting you out repeatedly and making known to all that you are unwelcome, We have but to leave Our palace but a few days and when We return, We find you here again?"

Tate smiled and shrugged.

"Sire, the live fox makes it his business to know where the curs are, as well as the chickens."

Then the old man bowed a deep, reverent bow while the knights chuckled around him.

King Christian made a gesture of irritation as he went over and sat down on his throne. His two young companions followed and stood near him. I watched curiously as the old man, rather than depart, went over to the long table where already a place had been made for him by the knights.

"Tell me, did you choose these girls yourself, Sire?" Tate asked. "I hope-" and he began to take another swallow of his drink, "-No, actually, I wonder, if these girls will have a better sense of direction-"

All eyes were on the old man.

"-than the girls Your Grace keeps already. I suppose they do not have what one might describe as a refined sense of direction, else they would have found their way home already.-"

Who was this commoner? I wondered. And how was it that he dared to speak so boldly to this King, seemingly without fear of reprisal?

"What I mean," he continued, "is that you would think that if they had - just a little sense, they could find their way around the palace. The concubines quarters are-" and the man put his thumb and forefinger together to demonstrate, "-only a small portion of the palace."

"Oh, what is your point, Fool?" the nobleman dressed in crimson asked.

"My point, Lord Chancellor Dewain, is: there she was-" the old man began in a grand manner, as if he were a bard about to tell a story of old.

The King, who with his companions was being served a drink at his throne, however, failed to ignore the old man's words and now watched him carefully.

"Last night, as I lay in my bed fast asleep-"

"What bed do you have, Fool?" the redheaded youth in gold called out.

The commoner laughed.

"Funny you should ask, My Lord Paschal."

The youth immediately frowned as the youth in blue and green snickered with some of the knights.

"There she was-" Tate continued, "a vision, wearing, wearing... Why, I do not remember what she was wearing at all."

He took a sip of his drink.

"It matters not," he told the nearby knights with a wink and a smile. "She was not wearing it for long."

The men at the table smiled as well as the serving women.

"Oh, but she was young. Her skin was incredibly smooth, and her breasts -round."

And then the old man looked at the old serving woman who was refilling his goblet and smiled.

"Not that I mind age or wrinkles.-"

The woman smiled back at him with playful, raised eyebrows.

"But she was young, and her hair was dark-" he said, and then paused as he noticed the King's angry stare, "but it might have been light, for it was dark in the chamber. And seeing her undress before me,

I asked, 'Who are you?' And she replied, 'Dear Me!'" and the old man laughed out loud, as all around him chuckled.

"'Dear me! I thought this was the King's chamber-'" he voiced dramatically.

The hall erupted in laughter.

"'What?' said I. 'Does this look anything like the King's bedchamber? Or I- the King?'"

The knights along the table were all trying not to laugh and were hiding their grins behind their hands.

"And then I thought better of it and said, 'Never mind. The King is gone- touring his kingdom or something. Do you wish to leave a message for him?'"

Then the old man smiled and winked.

"And she did."

The chamber erupted in unrestrained laughter, even among the noblemen.

"You dared to bed one of my- Our women!" King Christian suddenly yelled in outrage, slamming his cup down.

His angry outburst lessened the mirth, but did not totally dampen it.

"Sire, a rose in bloom begs to be plucked!" Tate shrugged with a wicked grin, smelling the flower in his hand. "And I would be a fool indeed to send away a young, beautiful, naked woman, disappointed, on the pretense that she had made several wrong turns down a few corridors. Why, it would have been unchivalric, even a dereliction of my duty as your subject not to have at least tried to stand in while you were away. But, fear not, I do not think she was disappointed. No, I am certain she was *nearly* as satisfied had I been of royal blood, like yourself."

The guards, the nobles, and even the servants were holding their sides as they laughed uncontrollably while the King reddened. Only his two companions were equally unamused.

"If We only knew which one it was, We would have her strangled at once!"

"Aye!" his companions agreed.

The room quieted again.

"And my ears, my poor ears," Tate continued. "I thought I would go deaf."

"Deaf, eh? Now I know which ones you must have sampled. A few of those accursed girls will wear out your ears with their begging and weeping for peace and to be allowed to leave," the King muttered.

At this, Tate laughed hard and shook his head.

"No! It was I, Your Grace, who was begging for peace last night, and she crying 'Oooo, oooo, oooo' like a baying hound leading the pack on the hunt."

King Christian was stony silent as the whole room laughed again at the description. I could not help but smile myself.

"Why do you not go away and die, Old Man?" the King snarled spitefully.

"Well," Tate replied with a grin and a shake of his head, "with many more nights like last night-"

There was another accompanying roar of laughter.

"I must remember to bolt my door at night now, lest death come for me again, naked and beautiful. Next time I may not have the strength to survive her."

"Sounds like a wonderful way to meet death," said the nobleman in green with a smile.

"Oh, I agree, My Lord Olbert, but I have no desire to die so young myself."

"Enough!" King Christian said, and the chamber quieted. "We have tolerated your presence and spared Our wrath countless times, Atateo, because of our cousin's fondness for you. But, beware, Old Man, Our tolerance is at an end."

Tate smiled, but remained silent in his place along the table with the knights.

4

With order finally restored to the hall, the two, older aldermen approached the King and bowed, and King Christian immediately began to rebuke them.

"Here *they* are, Ministers, those you claim are riling the people against Us!" he declared firmly, gesturing towards us. "Now We will hear no more of this nonsense from you!"

My heart skipped a beat at this. Was I so accused?

Both noblemen immediately began to protest, and the King's voice boomed over both.

"Enough!"

"Let them be executed and their heads hung on the wall, but let us not waste a moment more on them!" the youth in gold argued loudly.

My heart raced in panic as the advisers in green and crimson both shouted him down, immediately renewing their arguments.

"Execute them, Paschal?" the King replied in clear amusement. "'Twould make a better example to simply cut out their tongues and send them back where they came from."

"Well and good," Lord Paschal shrugged with mirth.

Fearful and numb, I listened as the noblemen continued arguing our fate, but they spoke so low and quickly that, as hard as I tried, I could only catch part of what they were saying. The rest of the Court casually turned back to their own conversations as the King and his counselors quarreled.

The alderman in crimson was shaking his head, insisting, "Your Grace, they must be questioned. It is essential."

The lord in green kept his hands clasped in front of him; and he smiled while he spoke. His voice was certain and calm.

"With all respect, Your Grace, neither am I saying that our kingdom is under a curse, nor that any of these *persons* have cursed the kingdom. Yet all the signs suggest…"

My heartbeat quickened. I could not hear all of his words, but the King was clearly irritated by them, and his reply echoed throughout the chamber.

"So you have said, Olbert, repeatedly! We have heard nothing else for weeks!"

The two men replied immediately, talking in turn again very quickly: first the one in crimson with huge gestures, then Lord Olbert with his calm but persistent demeanor, but I heard nothing of what they said.

"Olbert, you know well of the King's fondness for children, and we all are deeply grieved by the reports that so few children have been born to our people of late. But King Christian is not to blame for it," Lord Paschal in gold replied.

"Aye, speak to the priests!" the King said with a shrug. "They are to blame! It is the Church that teaches the people that swyve is sin on any nights but Monday, Tuesday, and Thursday, and not even then, if it be a feast day."

26

"Your Grace-" Lord Olbert continued, but was interrupted by the nobleman in crimson who said all too loudly:

"My Liege, there have been none among the royal concubines!"

His statement ended all other conversations in the audience chamber. All eyes were on them. The King flushed red; his companions were immediately silent. Lord Olbert covered his face momentarily with his hand and looked away. The alderman in crimson swallowed and grew pale.

After an awkward silence, the nobleman said, "My apologies, Your Grace, if my words have offended thee."

King Christian did not reply, staring stonily at the man like an angered, deadly snake, waiting to strike. The entire Court was utterly silent, as everyone waited for the King's response. For a moment, I thought the King might actually hurt the man, for he was clearly provoked.

"So you blame God. Is that it, Dewain?" King Christian finally asked, his voice sharp with open hostility.

It was obvious to me that although Lords Olbert and Dewain were trying to keep the mood in the audience chamber civil, King Christian plainly did not like either of them, and both were aware of this. These two ministers exchanged glances and made some reply that I could not hear.

"This is ludicrous, Sire. The kingdom is not cursed," Paschal said. "We should be preparing for war, not-"

"Superstitious simpletons," the King muttered, rising from his throne.

He testily snatched a golden goblet from the serving woman who offered it to him and drank deeply.

At this point, another gray-headed, elaborately dressed nobleman, this one in blue, approached the men and bowed.

"Your Grace, I have word from the border."

The King frowned as he took the offered parchment from the man and stepped away from the ministers to look at the message. Lords Olbert and Dewain gathered around the new arrival and began to talk to him quietly. Lord Paschal and his companion gestured for a servant to refill their cups.

The King, having examined the parchment, slowly crumpled it in his fist. Staring ahead into space, oblivious to the crowd around him, he walked idly over to staircase and went up the stairs onto the landing and looked out of the open, wooden doors into the dark night, sipping his drink. Everyone was quiet, waiting.

In the silence I could hear faint singing coming from outside.

With my feet aching, I turned to look at the other prisoners and was surprised to see that they were already sitting on the floor. I was the only one still standing, but I quickly sat down beside them.

"Olbert, what is going on at the church at this late hour?" King Christian called down from the landing.

"I believe it is the special service," Olbert replied. "The priests requested permission to hold a votive mass to pray for children for the families in our kingdom."

"At this hour?" the youth in blue and green asked.

"The priests did not wish to interrupt the villagers' work by having it before sunset."

"And you *allowed* it?" Paschal replied in a voice that was mocking.

"I saw no reason to deny it," Olbert replied calmly.

"No reason? What of the King's will?" Paschal remarked.

"Aye!" the other youth chimed in. "The priests already have an allotted time of day for their daily Mass!"

"You know well the King surely would have denied it had the priests petitioned him directly!" Paschal finished.

"Aye, you know well how the King feels about-"

"Indeed, but I was attempting to act in the King's best interest," Olbert answered calmly, "yet if I have offended my liege lord, I beg My King's pardon."

"Where is the wisdom, Olbert," the King spoke from the landing, "in encouraging the people to pray?"

The hush that fell upon the chamber was overwhelming; no one breathed. All eyes were on the King. My heart skipped a beat, and Father Poll made the sign of the cross.

"We are the King. The people owe their loyalty to Us. How will they learn this if We encourage them to put their trust in superstition? How will they learn obedience and devotion to Us if We encourage them to divide their allegiance between Us and the Bishop? Only confusion and trouble can result from allowing the people to put their hopes in myths and things that can not be seen."

The King turned back to his dark view then. Lords Olbert and Dewain were frowning, but no one made any reply.

I looked around to see if anyone else was struck by the King's irreverence. At seeing my fellow prisoners, I wondered if they had even heard him. In the torch lit chamber, they looked like phantoms, the shades of what once was. A chill ran up my back as I noted their listless appearance. The face of the boy was particularly pale and drawn, skull-like, with dark circles of weariness around sunken eyes. The old man and the commoner sat mutely upon the floor; their faces, sober and expressionless, revealed nothing of their thoughts.

Father Poll was visibly sweating, and he was whispering quietly to himself: "Be strong in your faith and fear not." Despite his words, he looked terrified and defeated.

Only the wild man seemed himself. He lay on the stone floor, his eyes closed peacefully in sleep.

As I glanced about at the knights that lined the room, I noticed some were staring at me -or my exposed legs, including Tate. I looked away and pulled my scratched, bare legs up more under the tunic.

Having delivered some drinks to the knights, a young maidservant walked past me, and I grabbed at the bottom of her skirt.

"Have mercy! I was taken from my home days ago," I said as quietly as I could, my voice cracking from not being used in days. "Please give me something to cover my nakedness. I beg it of you!"

She was alarmed that I addressed and touched her, and she looked quickly at the noblemen to see if they had noticed. The advisers had actually heard me, and they turned to look upon us. The girl abruptly pulled away to scurry out.

"Bring her something to wear, Girl," Lord Olbert ordered.

I saw the King's young companions give the minister an insulting look, but they did not argue. The girl curtsied and hurried out.

She returned in a few minutes with a plain gown and a long, worn, headrail to cover my head. She dropped the items beside me and left. I stood up and turning my back to the majority of men, I pulled the gown over my head. It was a bit short for my height, but I laced and tied it up the front quickly. I put the headrail on my head, concealing my disheveled hair. Then, I sat back down quickly.

While I had been dressing, the King had descended from the landing.

"Very well, Ministers, let us begin and be done with this," he remarked impatiently, as he sat in his large, ornate throne again.

He took out of his belt a piece of parchment, unfolded it, and looked it over. He smiled and shook his head.

"A priest, a madman, a serf, a witch, an old man, and last, a child: after a week's march through Our kingdom in search of Speyron's most determined rebels, this is all We have found. -And very few weapons among their fellow peasants as well."

"I anticipated as much days ago, if you will remember, Sire," Lord Paschal commented.

King Christian folded up the parchment again. Then he smiled and looked sharply at the older noblemen.

"However, We return to Our very own palace to find it *infiltrated*," he continued, glancing at Tate, "and Our will set aside like an empty cup. Beware, Advisers, We are not so blind that we do not see that the real dangers to our throne lie much closer than our borders or even outside the palace walls and in far better disguise than these miserable creatures."

The murmur of the assembled Court was loud in the hall as the three older noblemen began to object.

"Enough! Interview them if you will, You Curs, -but bark at Us no more!" the King shouted over them all. "Our patience is at an end!"

Satisfied, the older ministers bowed quickly and approached us. Lord Dewain went to Father Poll, asking him his name and where he was from.

"I am Adamson," said the bearded commoner, grabbing at the feet of the adviser in blue. "I am a loyal man of Speyron."

The blue minister gave him a unkind look, while a guard pulled him off the adviser.

"Art thou yet among the living, Jebedye?" Lord Olbert asked, squatting down beside the old man.

"It seems so, My Lord."

"'Twas over score years ago since last I have seen you, and you were so great with age then," Olbert told him kindly.

"Indeed, I was last summoned to Court to speak to the Queen when King Christian was great in her womb."

"Are you certain this is the child from Rothshire that we have heard so much about?" the adviser in blue was asking the guard.

"I am certain, My Lord, that he is from Rothshire," the knight replied.

"He wants your name!" one of our guards called loudly.

"R-r- r- r-re p- p- p- pent!"

"No! I have asked your name only!" Lord Dewain argued.

"Your name!" the guard demanded, shaking the wild man roughly to get an answer.

"M- m- my n- n- name is n- n- not im- im- im po- portant," came the very loud reply. "On- Only the n- n- n- n- name of G- G- God is im- im- im- p-portant. R- r- re- re- pent and s- s- save your- your- yourself f- f- fr- from de- de- de stru- struction!"

Lord Paschal and the other youth smirked, and the King sighed with irritation.

"On second thought," he interrupted, "let Us just kill them all and be done with this. This is more trouble than it is worth!"

"Patience, Sire," was Olbert's gentle reply.

The King sighed again and picked up his cup.

I watched the advisers talk to the other prisoners for a moment, waiting for one to speak to me. Gradually, my gaze drifted back to the handsome king who was talking to his two companions near him, his beautiful smile entrancing me.

They finished their drinks and held out their golden cups for the servant to refill. The King drank deeply from his refilled cup and glanced at me.

"If you continue to stare at me, Witch, I will order your eyes put out."

I blinked at him, not understanding, and then my heart pounded wildly as I realized he was addressing *me* -and as a *witch*. Horrified, I stared at him, watching as he and his companions laughed.

"God's eyes," Lord Paschal said, "she is ugly! Are you even certain she is a woman, Sire?"

Then they laughed again.

"No, I am not certain. Nor do I know if she is a witch or if one just looked upon her as a child," the King answered smugly.

I frowned and looked at the floor.

"They say a witch has both male and female parts and lies with the Devil," the youth in blue and green added.

"If she has both parts, Felix, the Devil may have her," the King answered.

Even the knights at the table laughed at this.

"And even if she proves to be woman, I still would not chance it. 'Tis a danger to cuckold the Devil," Lord Felix replied.

"I would make the Devil a cuckold-" Paschal began.

"I have!" Tate boasted to the snickers of the knights around him at the table.

"I would make the Devil a cuckold as well-" King Christian said, "but not with a witch. For if a witch looks on a man, it will make his yard shrivel up; 'twill make a child ugly and an old man blind."

His companions nodded in agreement at this.

Despite myself, I was on the verge of tears. I had never been fair, nor liked, but most of the people in my village were too afraid of me to hurl insults to my face. I turned away so they could not see how they hurt me. Still they continued.

"How shall you test her, Sire?" Lord Felix asked.

"I shall not, but perhaps later we shall devise something for our sport. Perhaps we shall use her to bait a bear."

My heart skipped a beat and pounded so loudly that I missed what was said next that caused the laughter that followed. I looked gloomily around; it seemed like the whole chamber was laughing at me.

"Witch!"

I looked at the youths.

"Witch!" King Christian called, an amused smile on his face. "We wish to know if your husband is simpleminded. Or is he a cripple or perhaps some deformed creature- something so altered by nature that his condition may not be worsened by looking on you daily?"

This was followed by a new fit of laughter.

And despite the peril of my predicament and my shame, I felt my temper well up within me. However, in spite of my anger, I had nothing to say.

"What? No answer?" he laughed.

"Sire, I believe she hath no husband," Lord Paschal suddenly said.

I went pale at his words.

"Aye, surely he is dead already," Lord Felix said into his cup.

"Perhaps," Paschal continued, "but it is unlikely that any family-even peasants- would allow their son to call a witch 'wife', no matter how desperate their choices, for-"

"I am not a witch," I suddenly answered, my heart pounding wildly in my chest.

The entire Court seemed to be muttering.

"You are mistaken," replied the King. "You are a witch, as was your mother."

"No."

"The village caught her practicing her dark craft. She only escaped capture and arrest by drowning," Lord Felix added.

"My mother was not a witch. She was only -confused," I answered angrily.

"Confused? Aye, your mother was so confused that she mistook the Devil for her lover," King Christian replied with a laugh.

"You were not born yet, I think."

"Ooo-" the youths laughed.

The Court grew quiet at my boldness. All eyes were on us now.

"That would make you the child of the Devil," the King smiled, undaunted.

My jaw set as I glared at him. He was toying with me, and that made me even angrier than I already was. And though I knew it would not help me, I answered him.

"Do you really think a witch would allow herself to be chased by a crowd, Sire? If my mother was a witch, she would have escaped capture either by transforming herself into a tree or the like, or by changing her pursuers into toads. Either way, drowning would not have come into it."

The King raised his eyebrows at this. The Court was absolutely silent as they listened to every word.

"So you are not a witch either, then?" Lord Paschal said.

"No. If I was, I would have turned you all to pigs by now- and *eaten* you!"

The Court gasped, and a few spectators crossed themselves. But one man laughed. I turned to see Tate at the table, shaking his head as he chuckled, nearly spilling his cup.

"Just like a commoner-" he explained. "A highborn witch would have turned us all to hind, or maybe pheasant."

The Court chuckled at this, and even the King and his companions smiled.

"We shall see in good time," the King said to me coolly, rising from his throne then.

"Cousin!"

There was a child's giggling behind us accompanied by a woman's voice.

"My Lady, the King is occupied now!"

We all turned to see a young girl who looked about ten years old with long golden hair running into the chamber, followed by an old serving woman.

"Cousin Christian!" she laughed and slowed to a trot as the knights in the room all bowed as she passed.

On first hearing her voice, the King had looked up, and upon seeing her, he smiled widely. The girl wore a long scarlet gown that was decorated with white embroidery. As she walked along the length of the table, she paused in front of the drunken, old commoner and kissed his cheek.

"Greetings, Uncle."

Tate embraced the child warmly, but chided her, saying, "Lady Kaithryn, I am not your kinsman."

"My maid says you have relations in every household in the kingdom."

The entire Court hooted at this.

"Oh, she did, did she?" he answered, glancing at the child's maid merrily.

"If this is so, then we must be related also," the young girl told him with a smile.

"Methinks thy maidservant overestimates the truth, My Lady," he replied good-naturedly.

The girl giggled and tugged his long, gray ponytail playfully, and then continued on her way to the King.

As she reached him, he smiled and embraced her.

"How now, Cousin?" he asked.

"Christian, I am glad you have returned. I missed you. It has been so dull without you."

"I missed you, too."

"And now my maid would put me to bed, Cousin, though I am not tired. I want to stay up and hear about your journey."

"Right she is. 'Tis long past time you were in bed, but I will see you tomorrow."

The girl frowned.

"Very well, Cousin, kiss me goodnight," she instructed.

King Christian embraced the girl heartily and kissed her on the forehead, saying, "Heaven's angels guard your sleep, Kaith. Sleep well."

"Goodnight Cousin," she replied, curtseying, and as she turned, her long gold hair that hung loose down her back swished sideways.

As she went, the advisers bowed to her. She paused again before the old man once more.

"Uncle, will you come see me to bed?"

"I will come readily, My Lady," Tate answered with a smile, giving her the rose.

The knights hooted again.

The girl smelled the pink bloom, and smiling, continued to the door where the maid collected her to take her to her bedchamber.

"Was there ever such a sweet child as this?" King Christian asked.

"Indeed, Sire, your cousin is a treasure," Lord Dewain said.

"A sweet child-" Lord Felix agreed.

"I was not like that at that age," Lord Paschal said. "I was a rascal to my tutors and servants. Ah, and what of it? They deserved no better."

The King and his companions laughed.

"A child for not much longer," Lord Olbert observed. "The bud of childhood is blossoming into-"

"We grow bored with this business, Lord Ministers," the King announced then. "The questions can wait. Come, let us show our guests around Our fine palace."

Without further discussion, the King drained his cup and handed it to a servant, then headed for the chamber doors with his two companions close behind him. Although clearly exasperated, the three ministers managed to smile and join with the rest of the Court which bowed to the King as he passed.

I heard the King's voice in the corridor, asking, "Our new possessions? Have you made a place for them among Our other beautiful women? I wonder which beauty I shall sample tonight? Perhaps the one with chestnut-colored hair."

The guards ordered us to our feet and shoved us toward the door, and we followed the procession of knights, ministers, and servants out of the audience chamber. Everyone followed the King down the corridor, except for Tate, who went in the opposite direction, presumably to see the young lady to bed.

5

I do not know why the King showed us the palace. I had expected our *excursion* to consist of either a visit to the dungeon or the tower. It was just the opposite; the King showed us the feasting halls, the baths, a few of the many guest rooms, the servants' quarters, and more, all the while talking about the palace's history. He must have been drunk- or perhaps he was simply proud of where and how he lived, and he wanted us to see just how poor and pathetic our lives really were. The journey through the palace had just this effect on me, if not on us all.

Jebedye had been correct. The palace was full of wonders. I was amazed by its size. It housed three garrisons of knights and the Palace Watch, the Court, and the palace servants, and there were still empty chambers to house many more.

And there were more beautiful things here than I had ever dreamt existed in one place. Every room was clean, decorated, and well-lighted with windows. A few of the chambers were decorated with sculptures of half-clad women or of soldiers and horses; some were carved out of the very stone of the walls. In both feasting halls and several of the rooms, scenes had been painted on the walls depicting nymphs at love or men at war. Every bedchamber we saw contained a large bed with a lumpy feather mattress on a wooden frame, and some chambers had fur hides covering the floors.

It was all marvelous to behold, but none of it could compare with what they called 'the bath'. The palace had, not one, but four baths, one at each of its four corners, and each with a wall painting and a spectacular stone floor. The bath itself was made up of five chambers: the first was a chamber for undressing; the second was a room for washing; the next contained a stone vat that was set into the floor, large enough to hold a score of men. It was filled with heated water for relaxing in; the next chamber had a similar size vat in the floor filled with cool water; the last chamber was heated also and contained benches for resting.

In the north section of the palace, to the right side of the audience chamber, there were, among other rooms, offices of the King's advisers. These offices contained chairs with velvet cushions and finely carved tables.

On the left side of the audience chamber was the grand feasting hall, where the knights took all their meals and the King, too, when he desired the company. It was a very large chamber with long tables and rows of benches where many of the King's knights were presently eating, drinking, and carousing while minstrels played a merry melody. The food being served here smelled wonderful, making my mouth water, and my stomach pang from emptiness.

Turning the corner, the north section of the left wing housed the kitchen for the great hall and the bath used by the King's garrisons and body guards. Each knight had his own bedchamber on the first floor of the palace in the left wing.

I had noticed already that the servants of the palace were not only well-dressed, but seemed truly happy. When I saw their quarters, I knew why. Each servant had his own bedchamber on the second level of the palace. The servants also had their own kitchen, bath, and hall in the south left wing of the palace. The hall where the servants ate was decorated in such a grand manner that any villein here would have considered himself with a birthright. The luxuries enjoyed by the lowest born servant here were finer than those reserved for Lord Huntingdon. What a small, horrible shack my family and I lived in compared to this place! Truly, this palace was fit to house a king!

We were not shown the right wing of the palace. We were told, however, that the King's chambers and bath were located in the north section. The south end of the right wing housed the chambers and bath of the King's advisers. We were also not shown the chambers of the royal concubines, but we were told that their accommodations were equal to those of the servants and the knights.

King Christian told us that all that we had seen had been originally built by the Romani to house the governor and his soldiers when they had occupied Speyron long ago. He told us that his great grandfather had built on to the palace behind the north, right wing, adding a tower and two more long halls, though he was not certain of the reason. The addition lacked the decoration and splendor of the main palace and had fallen into disuse years ago.

As we went back through the courtyard to return to the audience chamber, a great, thunderous voice overwhelmed us, halting everyone: *AMEN!*

Turning in the direction of the sound, my heart pounded fast, and chill bumps covered my arms, back, and neck from the sheer power of the word. How many people had gone to Mass? I wondered, for the sheer number of worshipers saying the response was so great that the one voice they created was like a thunderclap.

"They sound serious," King Christian joked. "Yet, methinks it is long past time for them to disperse."

The frowns on the faces of the older advisers were unmistakable as the King changed direction and walked briskly toward the main entrance of the palace with Lords Felix and Paschal and the torch-bearing knights close at his heels. The older advisers shook their heads, mumbling, and hurried after them. Our guards pushed us along as well. Thus, we too went through the courtyard, past the stone fountain, and back through the main column entrance where we had waited for so long earlier in the day, and hurried down the road after the rest.

"What the devil is he planning?" our guard grumbled.

"I know not. I doubt any of them will see the dawn, -and he is showing them every trinket in the palace."

My heart leaped into my throat, hearing this.

"Have you ever seen the King toy with anyone as long as he has with these wretches?" the guard asked the other.

"No, but nothing the King does surprises me anymore- especially when he is out for sport."

Up ahead, the small church was lit brightly against the blackness of the night. Every torch and candle the church owned must have been lit to fight off the darkness, while the booming responses beckoned Heaven.

The doors of the church stood open wide, and there was a great throng of people gathered outside on the steps and beyond, participating in the service from there, for all the people could not get inside.

When the mass of faithful, however, caught sight of their King approaching, they quickly stepped away from the doors. Immediately they were on their knees in respect, many clinging together in silence, not daring to look up. King Christian ignored them and walked directly up the steps into the church, neither pausing to bow in reverence, nor to cross himself with holy water. His personal bodyguards and Paschal and Felix were close at his heels. We, too, followed, but our guards held us together on the top step at the door. I peered over a shoulder to get a look into the church.

The church itself did not look like the church in my village, although it had the familiar rood, screen, and altar. The air inside was warm and reeked of burning candlewax, sweet incense, and body odor. The church was packed with families; people were standing shoulder to shoulder, their attention rapt by the priest's prayers over the host at the altar which could just be seen through the lattice of the dividing rood screen.

As the King proceeded forward, Paschal and Felix stayed at the back of the church. King Christian made his way farther inside the nave, and as the people recognized him, immediately they stepped aside with a gasp and, crossing themselves, knelt to the ground. The sea of worshipers parted quickly down the center of the church all the way to the rood screen. The change in their mood was immediate and noticeable.

On the other side of the screen, the assisting priests near the altar were staring at the King, and the priest behind the altar looked up, and catching sight of the intruder, stopped his prayer and set down the silver chalice he held in the air. For a moment, no one moved or spoke as the King and the celebrant priest confronted each other.

The abrupt quiet uncovered an argument between the old advisers who were behind us in the dark. I stepped away from the other prisoners a little so that I might hear them better.

"Me? He never listens to me! You go after him!" Lord Dewain was saying with great agitation.

"It is too late anyway, Olbert. You see, they have stopped the Mass already," the nobleman in blue said.

"Grey, we still must retrieve him before he makes it any worse than it already is," Olbert said.

"Then I suggest you make speed," Grey replied with a shrug. "We will all have to go."

"Why must we all go? It was you who started all this, Olbert! You gave them permission!" Dewain said.

"Very well," Olbert answered.

"I tell you true. I know not how much more of this I can endure!" Dewain said.

"This is no time for your sniveling, Dewain!" Grey answered.

"It matters not what we advise or if we do at all," Dewain continued, ignoring the criticism. "The King does as he wills! There is no restraint in him! His own excommunication for killing that priest has not lessened his desire for mischief at all!"

"Of course not. Did you expect otherwise? Thou knowest the King is a slave to his passions and has not the gift of prudence."

"Grey, stop thy tongue," came Olbert's voice again.

"You two whine like old men," Grey continued. "Do you not realize what opportunity has been granted us? Were Christian other than what he is, we would have nothing more than our appointments, and at most, the King's ear.

"But because the King is rash and irresponsible and wholly unfit to rule, we will profit, for the tide that goes out must eventually come back. Right now, while the King's position is strong, he ignores our wise counsel and dotes on his arrogant and foolhardy companions. But before much longer, he will feel the instability of the branch that he has climbed upon. Then he shall be afraid, and he will hunger for our words. The King shall have sleepless nights, and we- all that we dare dream of. We must only remain in his favor while we wait for the tide to change."

Before I could hear more, I was shoved closer to the other prisoners. Inside the church, the celebrant priest was speaking to the King as the frightened faces of the faithful looked on.

"Sire, you must remove yourself at once! You know well it is forbidden for you to worship with us."

King Christian's laugh shattered the quiet.

"Fear not, for We come not to worship."

"You must still retire from this holy place, Sire. The Mass can not continue until you depart!"

"So much the better," the youth replied, crossing his arms.

At this point, nothing more was said. The priests stood their ground, and the King- his. The worshipers, still on their knees, watched the exchange, hardly breathing. Finally, the King spoke.

"Go home."

The King had spoken the words quietly, but the effect was as if he had screamed them. The frantic commoners leaped for the door, pushing and shoving and yelling, tossing us prisoners back outside down the steps. I was amazed by their reaction, my heart skipping a beat and then pounding rapidly. The women were screaming and crying and clutching their children close to them. All was panic and confusion, as though the Devil had followed them to church.

The guards held us tightly together and pushed us, against the swell of people, back up the steps and inside the doors of the church, lest we escape into the crowd that was nearly trampling us. In the commotion, Jebedye cried out as he fell and again as the guards grabbed him roughly back up; and the wild man was stuttering "bad fruit" rapidly over and over again. The guards pushed us forward toward the middle of the nave.

The King continued to stand his ground, facing the priest, oblivious to the panic around him.

"Put out the light," he ordered the knights near him.

"You have disrupted the Mass!" the priest complained hotly. "-The Mass that Lord Olbert, in your absence, gave us special permission to sing."

"Indeed We have! 'Tis a pity, but We feel that all the singing and chanting will keep Us awake."

By then, the older advisers and a few more guards had managed to enter the church as well and were going to the King's side. The two assistant priests had started chanting eerily, as knights, following the King's order, went about the nave and into the sanctuary itself extinguishing the flames from the several candles. The remaining peasants continued to flee the church as quickly as possible.

"We might have granted you permission had you approached Us personally on this matter. We might have allowed it, perhaps, during some other part of the day, when it would not have disturbed Us."

One of the knights approached the King then and whispered in his ear.

"What?!" he questioned the man.

The knight nodded.

"What is this?" King Christian demanded, turning back to the priest. "Do you know what the penalty is for breaking the King's law?"

"Sire, your presence in this holy place is forbidd-"

"*Our* presence? This is *Our* kingdom. This is *Our* palace. This is *Our* church. No, *you* are the guest here and must obey *Our* laws."

"What is happening?" Jebedye was asking behind me.

"I know not," I answered, my heartbeat quickening.

"And you know," King Christian continued, "that under Our father's own edict, there are to be no orders on royal lands, neither monks nor nuns. It was forbidden long ago."

Two knights approached the King then with a young nun between them in the mostly empty church.

"Oh, no-" our guard moaned under his breath, crossing himself.

"Woman, when did you arrive here- on the palace grounds and lands of your King?" he asked. "And from what convent did you come?"

The nun was but a girl, and her answer was very meek.

"I was born on these lands and have lived here all my life, Sire. I have not yet gone to a convent."

"What!" the King demanded, turning back to the priest. "Dare you celibate the King's own peasants?! This will not be endured!"

"Sire," the priest argued back, "it was *her* wish, and the taking of holy vows is-"

"Is against the order of nature! To which it was outlawed on royal lands by Our father! What hypocrites you are! You complain about the lack of children being born while you celibate the people!"

The King grabbed the nun's arm and dragged her through the opening of the rood screen into the chancel to the altar. He stood before it while the priests on both sides of him spoke at once.

"It is forbidden for you to be here!"

"You must leave at once!"

Clearly furious, the King made no reply, but stood resolute, staring at the altar table with its shiny vessels and holy food.

Suddenly, with a fierce motion, King Christian grabbed the plate that held the broken Body of the Christ and slammed it violently against the wall. Then he turned and shoved the remaining holy vessels off the altar savagely, sending the cross, the book of prayers, the chalice, and three of the burning candles to the floor with a great clatter.

Astounded, everyone gasped and crossed themselves in horror. My heart pounded wildly at what I had just witnessed. The blessed hosts were strewn about all over the floor. The cruets lay on their sides as well, pouring out their holy contents of divine Blood and water.

"Bbb -ad Fff- rruuit! Bbb bbb bbba ddd! Fffffffff-"

"Christ save us!"

"Ruin! Ruin! Woe to us!" Jebedye called out mournfully.

The startled priests were immediately on their hands and knees, frantically gathering up the scattered and broken hosts, eating them quickly. They licked up the consecrated wine from the very floor and the crumbs from the bread that were too small to be picked up.

Numb, I watched the scene in horror as the remaining peasants screamed and fled the church in terror. While the priests scurried about the floor and the nun collected the holy objects, the altar- still partially dressed in its white linens, seemed itself to bleed as the spilled wine streamed down it to the floor.

King Christian watched the commotion around him, mute and still.

Suddenly, he seized the nun again. He yanked her to her feet and shoved her face down onto the altar, -the book and cross toppling out of her arms onto the floor again. He forced her feet apart with his boot and began to untie his braes with one hand while the other arm held her down.

My heart skipped a beat and then beat madly as I realized what was to come. Surely, this could not be happening! Surely, the King would not dare to do this, not here! Not on the holy altar! Surely, there must be a limit! He must be in jest! Surely, the priests would stop him! Surely, they could appease him- somehow.

"Where is your god now?" he was asking her. "Will your *king of heaven* come down and save you? *I* am your King. This is *my* kingdom. Cry out to me for mercy, and you shall have it."

I gasped and looked at the priests. They were as amazed as the rest of us. Clutching the holy vessels and the broken host tightly, they backed away from the altar and began to chant loudly words that I did not recognize.

Chanting! That was all! But what should I expect from them? Exactly what power did they have to stop the King? After all, who was the Bishop or even the Pope to this young man? Indeed, what was a priest, but a man in special robes that spoke of how things should *not* be or of what was permitted in the Kingdom of God? In the end, this was King Christian's kingdom, and we only flesh and blood mortal, and he might ravage and kill us at his whim.

Lord Dewain was beside him at the altar then, speaking quietly, but the King waved him off. Lord Olbert approached him next.

"Your Grace, have mercy on your people. This is a holy place. God will destroy our kingdom for certain if you defile His sacred altar and His house any further."

"Olbert, you are hopeless in your devotion to superstition!"

Then Lord Grey spoke.

"Sire, not here," he smiled. "If you would have this woman, we can arrange for her to be brought to the palace."

And the King stopped and looked at him and laughed cruelly.

"Grey, I have no desire for this woman. Know you not that the wench has no hair?"

He pulled off her veil then, throwing it to the floor.

The nun, seemingly the very embodiment of the Holy Virgin in the flower of her youth and the purity of her faith, uttered not a word in protest to the humiliation that she suffered. At the sight of her uncombed, shorn hair, the tears rolled down my face.

I understood then the extent of his hate. It was hopeless. We were at the mercy of a king who was intent on shaming us, killing us, and destroying all that was holy and good. There was no one to save us, not the Bishop or the Church. Perhaps God Himself might save us; but even now God was allowing this youth to commit so great a sacrilege.

"Oh, Ruin, Ruin, Ruin! Our poor, wretched Speyron!" Jebedye was weeping.

"Heaven help us!" our guard muttered.

Father Poll behind me was saying the Ave Maria.

"B-b- ba- bad f-f-fr-fruit! B- b- ba- bad fr-fr-fruit! B- b- bad fr-fr-fruit-"

"Your Grace," Lord Olbert tried again. "Is this really necessary? The Mass has ended."

"Aye, and there is so much to attend to this night- and with you being so tired from your journey," Lord Dewain added.

The King gave him a look, but then after a moment replied, "You may be right. There is much business to attend to this night."

The advisers smiled. The King looked around at the knights present.

"Sir Perran, come here," he ordered.

The young knight approached and bowed.

"*Here*, in Our place, take this woman- you with a few of Our men. Bring her to Us later, and We shall check your work."

I stood amazed as the rest.

The knight stared at the King, but his hesitation only lasted for a moment; then he bowed again. The knight walked behind the King and put his hands on the back of the woman's neck. The King stepped back, retied his braes quickly, then stretched, and went back around to the royal ministers, who stood dumb.

"Let us depart," he said.

He looked back at Sir Perran, who was pulling up the heavy skirt of the nun's habit. Then King Christian walked back through the screen past us prisoners to the doors. As he passed them, Lords Paschal and Felix bowed with amused grins and followed him out of the church. The guards hurried us out of the church after them, leading us from one horror to meet the next.

6

Shoved along in the darkness from behind, I shuffled back to the palace, amazed and weeping. I entered the audience chamber in a daze, not seeing or hearing anything distinct, for the horror of what I had just witnessed made me numb to what my own fate would doubtless be.

Surely we would all die at the King's hand, but I only wanted it to be done quickly now. I no longer desired to live. The terror for me was no longer the promise of death but the threat of continued life where God and everything sacred and important to me would be stripped away, violated, destroyed, or defiled. Nor did I want to live to bear any of the other unimaginable terrors the King could devise for us.

Back in the center circle of the audience chamber, our guards forced us to our knees in a line. Readily, I fell to the floor and wept in despair. Above me, I heard the ministers approach and the mocking words of the King above me, "What is this? What is this? Ministers, Our guests seem-"

The King stopped his insult short and was silent. I raised my head off the stone floor and looked to see what was happening.

The King was staring at us prisoners with a questioning look on his face. I glanced at the other captives and realized that, except for the mad man who continued muttering about bad fruit, there was not a dry eye among us.

King Christian was disconcerted by our demeanor, and I realized that our agony had somehow *embarrassed* him. I watched him frown and turn away from us.

"What is this about *bad fruit*? Did the man eat some?" Lord Paschal asked.

He and Lord Felix laughed.

"The rest of you are no longer needed here," the King told the knights and servants. "In fact, everyone may retire except for Our advisers and Our personal guards."

As the chamber began to empty, the King told a passing servant, "Girl, bring them some water -and Us more drink as well."

The girl smiled and curtsied to the King and left the chamber. Another servant entered the chamber, bowed, and then approached the King and whispered to him.

The King frowned.

"He has been waiting all day?"

"Aye, Your Grace."

"Very well, show him in now. We will not want to be troubled about it in the morning," King Christian mumbled.

The servant bowed and left.

"Dewain," Paschal said sarcastically, "if you are really intent on questioning these prisoners, you should send for a clerk. This opportunity likely will not come again."

Lord Dewain nodded and grabbed the arm of a passing servant, ordering him to summon the palace cleric.

"He is abed already, My Lord," he reported.

"Rouse him! This is important!"

Another servant returned then and announced, "Your Grace, the ambassador of Fors."

A man with dark, curly hair, dressed in elaborate, but strange clothing bowed grandly at the doorway and then walk carefully around us to approach King Christian. He was followed by a servant carrying a small chest.

"Your Grace!"

"Ambassador! You flatter Us with yet another visit," King Christian responded politely to the visitor who bowed deeply before him again and then handed him the gift.

"Your Grace is such a magnanimous host that one can hardly endure being away from thy royal hospitality," he spoke with a thick accent.

King Christian smiled.

"There is always a place for King Roderic's most valued ambassador at Our table."

"Thou art too kind," the foreigner replied with a smile.

Christian opened the chest and held up a large jewel to the light.

"'Tis remarkable!" Christian smiled. "Truly, King Roderic is too generous! Give him Our thanks."

"Of course, Your Grace."

"May we presume that King Roderic's niece has not yet been found and recovered?" King Christian asked, while returning the jewel to the chest and handing it to a nearby servant and then sitting down in his throne.

"Alas, Your Grace has surmised the heart of the matter. We have heard, however, further accounts of the Lady Elise residing within

Speyron's borders, and King Roderic fervently wishes to send a company of trusted men to bring her home."

"How large of a company?"

The ambassador to Fors shrugged and smiled.

"No more than a garrison, I should think, Sire, for one woman."

"Ah-" King Christian said with a nod. "Surely, so large a number would not be wise. If Roderic sends so many knights to retrieve his runaway niece, word of their approach will surely reach the lady, and she will escape again."

The ambassador smiled as did King Christian.

"Furthermore," Christian continued, "We fear that foreign knights on Our soil would needlessly alarm Our people and might in turn unnecessarily endanger the lady's rescuers. It would be better for Us to make inquiries about the lady for your king. You may tell King Roderic that We will send word immediately if she is discovered."

The ambassador smiled again and seemed to be about to reply when King Christian nodded at the servant who suddenly appeared at the ambassador's side, waiting to escort him out of the chamber. Seeing that his audience was over, the man smiled and bowed again and then quickly left. King Christian shook his head and rolled his eyes.

"How long have they been searching for that woman?" Felix asked.

"For some years now," Dewain answered.

"Clearly, she is either dead or simply does not wish to be found," Felix replied.

"This is some ruse that Roderic is using to try to move troops into our kingdom- though what his exact purpose is remains a mystery," Paschal added.

Grey approached the King and smiled.

"Still, shall I instigate a search for the lady, Sire?"

"Certainly not," King Christian replied, with a wave of his hand.

The minister in blue smiled.

"Is it wise, Sire, not to at least make an attempt at seeming to aid them? Though his true desires are unknown, Roderic is powerful, whether he be an ally or an enemy."

With a gesture, the King shrugged.

"Very well, Grey, if you actually have some time to squander on this matter, you may make some inquires by letter to the convents in Speyron. As for Ourselves, We pledge personally to lay hands on each royal concubine to make sure the lady has not concealed herself among them."

Paschal, Felix, the bodyguards, and the King all laughed.

"As you wish, Sire," Grey answered with a small bow.

A girl returned with more wine and goblets for the King and his companions. Another girl arrived after her with a bucket and gave each of us a dip of water from a hollowed gourd. A sleepy, disheveled clerk arrived shortly afterward. The servants retrieved a chair from the wall and set it down at the end of the long table. Another servant carried in some parchment and some ink and a quill. The cleric quickly bowed to the King, who waved him off, and then the man took his seat. He took some of the parchment and began to make markings with the quill and ink.

Then King Christian took the parchment from his belt and turned his attention back to his prisoners.

"Although Our wise and worthy advisers have filled Our royal ears with accounts of your crimes against Us-"

My heart beat quickened.

"Crimes? What crimes?" Adamson was immediately calling out.

The guard behind him struck him into silence.

"That is the very heart of the matter," the King continued. "For months now We have been warned of the treachery planned by Our own people. Mutterings of rebellion have been heard in all parts of the kingdom, designs have been made, and weapons hoarded by the lowest serfs to depose Our authority and rightful rule of this kingdom. -We are told there are sections of the kingdom that are too perilous for Us to travel."

I stared at the King, wondering what he was talking about.

"The coming insurrection is said to be the result of the people listening to the treacherous words that have come from each of your lips. Thus, you have been arrested and removed by Our order."

This was not true! I had never spoken a word about him! I had never given him a thought before he snatched me out of my home four days ago!

"Tis a lie!" Adamson was calling out. "Never have I spoken against my vassal lord or my king."

He was struck from behind again by the guard.

"Fear not," King Christian answered. "For the situation sounded so dire and immediate that rather than send a garrison to collect you as We would normally have done, We have seen to this matter personally. Your King himself has witnessed where you all come from and the conditions in which you live. We have conducted a very thorough search of areas of the kingdom rumored to be sown with the seeds of rebellion, where piles of arms were supposedly so numerous that every peasant man, woman, and child could be outfitted with a weapon and a spare."

How had such absurd tales come to the King's notice? I wondered.

"We found nothing of the kind in truth," King Christian told us.

"All the search managed to do," Lord Paschal said, "was to frighten the peasants, irritate the King's vassals, and make our most gracious King look the fool."

"To which, if anyone had dared laugh, the King would have murdered them on the spot-" the guard near me mumbled under his breath.

"Therefore," the King continued, "We have concluded from this unfortunate farce that the fears of our advisers are wholly unfounded and their advice is the trivial, needless worry of fools."

"But, Sire!" the older advisers began.

"Thus," King Christian continued, "after Our ministers have had their fill of questioning you, you will all be released."

It was hard to tell who was more surprised, we prisoners or the King's advisers and guards. It was so unexpected that I hardly believed I had heard the words. With my heart pounding excitedly, I looked around the chamber. Even the cleric had looked up from his writing momentarily. Among the prisoners, Adamson was laughing and weeping in relief, and Father Poll was crossing himself and thanking God and the Saints. The older advisers had immediately surrounded the King, and they were all presenting their arguments at once.

"But Your Grace has not heard them speak!" Lord Dewain argued.

"Your Grace, we are not recommending their deaths," Olbert said.

"You should detain them indefinitely," Lord Grey said, "so that they can not continue to incite the people against you."

"We see that Our royal breath is wasted on you three. What have We been saying for the past month? It matters not what gibberish anyone hears them speak, for who would believe them? No one can speak for God, unless it is God's own sovereign representative, which would be Ourselves."

"Aye, and even if they were to speak in favor of insurrection, only a fool would be moved to action by the likes of them!" Lord Felix added.

"Still, Sire, would it not be wiser to reserve your decision to free them until after you have heard what they have to say?" Olbert answered calmly.

The other two senior advisers agreed with him; and they all continued to caution the King against freeing us until, finally, the King ended all discussion.

"Very well, if you believe so strongly that they are a danger to Our sovereign authority, then show your evidence. Prove they not only are desperate rebels, but have the gift of foresight. Prove they can tell the future!"

The blood drained from my cheeks as I suddenly understood why I had been taken. My uncle had been right.

The three advisers hesitated for a moment, but then turned and looked at us. No one said anything for a moment.

Lord Grey turned back to the King and smiled.

"Sire, there is really no need of troubling yourself any longer over this matter. If you prefer, your advisers will question the prisoners at length and discover the dangerous parties while Your Grace attends to pleasanter distractions."

"We would hear them speak this treachery for Ourselves, Grey. Go ahead! Ask them something!" King Christian demanded. "Ask them anything!"

"Where is King Roderic's niece?" Lord Felix offered.

"Why does Roderic wish to send troops into our kingdom?" Paschal suggested.

"Sire-" Grey began.

"What? Can you not even ask them a simple question?" King Christian criticized.

He rose from his throne and pushed aside his advisors.

"You three really are useless," he said to them in disgust.

"Hear the words of your King. If you wish your freedom and to return to your homes, you must give answer to *this question*: Where is Roderic's niece?"

We stared at the youth.

"Let us begin with you, Adamson. You are so eager to speak. Where is she?"

Adamson looked blankly at the King, and then at the advisers and shrugged his shoulders.

"Speak!" the King demanded.

"Not with her family?" he offered meekly.

"Not with her family! Well, Ministers, there is no doubt in my mind that this man has the gift!"

The older advisers cringed, but Paschal, Felix, and the guards chuckled. The King moved to the boy next.

"Where is the lady, the niece of King Roderic?"

"My Lord King," the child answered, "I have never heard of her."

The King made a gesture and moved on to the priest.

"Well, Priest?"

"Sire, I have not the gift of prophesy."

"That was not the question."

Father Poll shook his head.

"I have never heard of her either, Your Grace, but if she has not entered a convent to assume the religious life, then I suppose she might be with her husband."

"Brilliant!" the King laughed. Then he turned to me and said, "What have you to add?"

My heart was already beating fast, for I had never heard of her either.

"I know nothing, Your Grace, about her."

The King laughed.

"Of course not! And you?"

The wild man was staring at the wall, not seeming to heed what was being asked. Thus the King stood right before him and yelled loudly.

"King Roderic's niece! Where is she?"

The man slowly shook his head and answered, "N-N-Not not- t-to your-your b-b-bed."

Upon hearing this, King Christian threw his head back and laughed hard.

"I am so relieved to know this! -What about you, Old Man? Do you know where she is?" he asked impatiently.

"Am I finally allowed to speak?" Jebedye asked.

"Only to answer the question," Christian snapped.

"Aye, I know where the Lady Elise resides. Indeed, she is in Speyron- in the northern lands where even now she sews a shirt for her beloved."

The few in the chamber began whispering, and all eyes were on the ancient, withering man who sat on the floor clutching his cane.

"Where, exactly?"

"I know not whose lands she resides on, but fear not, she will be discovered by Christmas, and Roderic will generously reward the finder, for he values the lady highly."

The King and the remaining Court were impressed.

"Tell us, is it because he values the girl so highly that he wishes to send an entire garrison here?"

"No, that is because he values Speyron highly."

"In what way?"

"I know not, Your Grace."

I marveled at the old man who spoke so confidently and with such authority. Truly, this man was a seer. Although I saw the shadow of the future in my dreams, I was moved by how clearly someone else could see it.

"You see, Your Grace-" Lord Dewain began.

"It is a pretty story. But I shall not believe it is a gift of foreknowledge lest at Christmas the girl is discovered as he has said," the King said.

The guards whispered among themselves, and Lord Grey said something to Lord Dewain.

"Why are there no children being born?" Lord Olbert asked suddenly.

"That is not the sort of question for a seer, Olbert," Paschal complained.

"He is correct, Olbert," King Christian answered. "I do not think they can answer that question. The boy is barely of an age to know how children are begat, and the blind man is too old to remember. And she-" the King said gesturing toward me, "I am certain she has no idea."

Then he laughed with his companions. I bristled at the jest.

"Although I am no seer, perhaps I can answer, My Lords," Father Poll began, his wavering voice revealing his nervousness.

King Christian gestured for the man to rise, so the priest carefully got to his feet.

"Over score years ago, if My Lords will remember, there was an aged monk in the kingdom who foresaw that a time would come when the women of Speyron would all become barren. He often quoted the holy scriptures that say, 'Ephraim's glory shall fly away like a bird- no birth, no pregnancy, no conception!' and 'Blessed are the barren, and the wombs that never bore, and the breasts that never gave suck!' It seems that all that has happened is a fulfillment of his prophecy."

"Another seer!" Paschal said with a gesture of exasperation.

"Sounds like the one we need," Felix said. "Why was he not arrested? Where is he?"

"He died years ago," Jebedye answered quietly.

"To simply say that it fulfills a prophecy spoken long ago does not explain why it has happened," King Christian argued.

Father Poll, clearing his throat, answered quietly: "God can not abide sin, Sire, and he requires all people, even those who do not know Him, to live righteously. From times of old, God has humbled the mighty and unleashed His wrath against kingdoms and their inhabitants whose acts have offended Him. Storms, floods, droughts, famines, plagues, war, and barrenness are all ways He chastises us.

"-He did not even spare His chosen people, but allowed them to be conquered and enslaved when they fell into sin. And even the sin of a single man can bring an entire country low: Witness how Pharaoh's pride cost every Egyptian their first born son."

"So you are saying-" King Christian said, "that 'God' has been so offended by someone's sin in Speyron that He is withholding fertility from the women in the kingdom."

"That is my belief," Father Poll answered.

The King looked at him sourly and waved his hand in exasperation.

"What absurdity!" Paschal answered with disgust. "Why would 'God' want to curse Speyron more than say Gaulia, Multimbria, Bonaqua or even Fors? Is not sin everywhere, after all?"

This time, there was no answer from Father Poll, nor from any of us. Perhaps a braver soul would have instructed the youth to seek the answer in the church where the King had left a few of his knights, but not us captives, for our release was too near at hand to risk speaking the truth.

After a momentary silence, Lord Dewain said, "Sire, this man may be ill."

The wild man during the last question had slumped onto the floor and lay on his side, drooling and mumbling to himself.

"Hmm- so it would seem," the King replied, unconcerned. "So, Priest, you have said that you are not a seer. Grey, why was it that he was named?"

"There have been reports that in his church, during his sermons, he has incited the people against his King," the counselor in blue replied.

"No!" Father Poll denied, shaking his head.

"Is that so?" King Christian answered, sitting down on the throne again. "You realize that it is a very grave matter for anyone to speak against the anointed sov-"

"My Lords, I regularly speak out against sin-" the priest interrupted, his voice atremble, "-the sins of the people in my parish as well as those of my vassal lord. It is true that I have preached against the numerous sins of the King, just as I have written letter after letter to the King himself about them. For, as you know, the unrepented sins of all the people, including the King, rest on the head of the Bishop. And lest the sinner is moved to make correction, the Bishop will have to answer to God for it at Judgment Day.

"But *never* have I encouraged the people to rise up in rebellion against their anointed King, no matter what his faults!" Father Poll finished, wiping the perspiration from his forehead.

"A convenient answer," Paschal said.

"Lord Dewain, do you remember His Grace receiving such a letter from Father Poll as he describes?" Lord Olbert asked.

"I do not precisely recall," Dewain answered, "for the King receives ten such letters daily."

The King smiled and picked up his cup again. Lords Paschal and Felix laughed with the knights.

"You need not trouble yourself with further letters, Priest, for it seems that everyone in the kingdom who can write sends letters denouncing Our actions and recommending correction," the King instructed.

"Furthermore, consider this suggestion: In future exhortations to your parish, speak more about your own sins and less about Ours. You will be less likely to have your intentions confused by Our vassals and subjects this way."

The knights snickered at this comment, but Father Poll bowed slightly, saying quickly, "I see the wisdom of these words, Sire."

"Otherwise, We have heard enough from you, Priest. You have Our leave to go."

Then King Christian gestured to one of the guards.

"Show him out."

My heartbeat quickened with surprise and hope.

The older advisers looked like they wanted to protest, but they said nothing as a guard cut the ropes that bound the priest's ankles to the other prisoners and escorted him out of the chamber.

We looked back to the King, excited, when the priest called out from the door.

"Your Grace, you have shown me mercy. I pray that you will have mercy on your own soul. God loves you. He does not want to condemn you or anyone to eternal damnation. Reach out to Him and turn from the evil path that you walk before it is too late."

"Go!" the King answered coldly, "while you are able!"

Father Poll said nothing more. He bowed and quickly turned and went out of the audience hall, the doors shutting behind him.

7

y heart raced. I saw my opportunity then, as we all did. I *could* get out alive! I would just tell them I knew nothing, and then I could be on my way back to my home. The priest was already free; I might be next! Please, let me be next, I prayed silently.

King Christian sent another knight to retrieve more wine, for he and his companions had already drained the new pitcher. Then he rose from his throne and approached us.

Adamson was suddenly on his feet, and, jerking me forward with him, threw himself at the youth's feet.

"Please, Most Royal King, spare my life!" he began. "I have been most falsely accused! Never have I spoken against you! Nor am I a seer! Those of my village who accused me are liars and knaves!"

King Christian smiled, and then chuckled, for the man had so firmly wrapped his arms about the King's leg that the two guards could not remove him without the risk of unbalancing the King. He made a gesture for the guards to stand back while the man continued to plead for his life.

"Thou art my King- and I- your loyal subject! I have a wife and family who need me. Please, have mercy!"

I was appalled by the sight of the desperate man begging for mercy at the foot of the youth. This king was not worthy of such supplication. I watched, sickened, as King Christian gloated over the humiliating display, smiling and patting the man on the head like a dog.

"You see, Ministers, they want to be obedient," he commented smugly. Then he told Adamson, "That is enough."

Adamson released his grip on the King then, and the guards immediately pulled him back to his place among us captives at the center circle.

The King looked at his parchment again and went over to where the ministers stood and began to confer with them. The ministers were shaking their heads, and then the King gestured to one of the knights to approach.

"When we marched through the village, the reeve handed him over," I heard the knight say.

As they talked quietly among themselves, the wild man, having been unbound when Father Poll was released, began to wander around the audience chamber muttering to himself.

After a few more minutes of conference, the King returned to his throne.

"Adamson, You are not on Our list and, therefore, are neither accused of being a seer, nor of provoking the people against Us."

In relief and excitement, Adamson was standing again, thanking God and the King. King Christian smiled.

"Do you know why the reeve of your lands handed you over to Our authority?" he interrupted.

Adamson smiled and shrugged.

"No, Sire, nor the new charge against me, for one villager or another is always bringing an accusation against me. It happens so often, in fact, that the lord of the manor will no longer hear the charges."

"For what cause do the villagers do this?"

"No true cause, Sire. The villagers are simpletons and envious of me, and the reeve is no just man."

King Christian raised his eyebrows.

"I have only tried to help myself," Adamson quickly added. "The villagers surely have all done the same- or they would have, if they had been clever."

"Your Grace," the knight said, "the reeve claimed this man to be a most disagreeable fellow, a man who did not count the day well spent unless he had bested someone or quarreled with them."

"'Tis not true!" Adamson declared.

The King raised his eyebrows again.

"It is clear to Us, Adamson, that you are an argumentative fool. Obviously, your continuous quarrels have exasperated the reeve, rankled your manor lord, and vexed your neighbors until they want no more of you," King Christian surmised.

"But Sire!" Adamson began to argue.

The King shrugged his shoulders.

"Very well, take him out. Put his head on the wall."

"What?!" Adamson gasped. "No!"

I stared, aghast, my heart pounding loudly in my chest. Lords Paschal and Felix smirked.

"The choices you make have consequences," King Christian told him.

"But Sire, the villagers-"

"We would sooner feed you to Our dogs for sport, Adamson, than listen to you prate on about the petty squabbles and jealousies of your accusers. Therefore, you have Our leave to die."

"Mercy! I will make amends! I will-"

"The time for making amends is past. On the short walk out of the audience chamber to the place of execution, think on how you could have lived in peace and charity with your neighbors."

A guard walked over and cut the man's legs free of the ropes, even as Adamson was weeping in terror and anguish. Without delay, the two knights grabbed Adamson by the arms and the back of the neck of his shirt and dragged him backward the few feet to the audience hall doors, the chamber resounding with his desperate pleas for mercy the entire time.

Once again the doors were shut, the hall was silent, and all eyes were on the King.

"Four left, and only the old one for certain is a seer," Lord Paschal said.

"-And that one We always have known of," King Christian said with a yawn. "Come, now, Ministers, shall we not set the rest free and retire to bed?"

My heart skipped a beat, then raced, but the three older advisers made it clear that they wanted to continue, so the King urged them to finish it.

"We know you three are seers, just as Jebedye is. There is no use in denying your abilities; unlike the previous two, we have confirmed reports about you," Lord Dewain began. "We have questions for you, and if you answer well, you may be rewarded."

"Really, Dewain," Paschal complained, "the King has already agreed to their freedom. What further reward should they expect?"

Dewain frowned at the young nobleman.

"Indeed, My Lords, shall we not proceed?" Grey added irritably. "The dawn will arrive in a few hours."

"Aye," Felix agreed with a yawn.

"Tell us-" Olbert began and then hesitated.

"What glorious future do you see for King Christian and Speyron?" Felix finished impatiently.

There was a momentary silence.

"I see-" began the old man.

"Not you, Jebedye. Let these others speak first," Grey ordered.

The chamber was deathly silent now as I looked first at the ministers and then at the King. The image of the King haphazardly leading a multitude of people in the midst of a barren desert was fresh in my mind again- as well as the headless birds. I swallowed and looked at the other three prisoners. The wild man was tracing the hunting dogs in the wall painting with his finger. Jebedye and the boy were sitting silently on the floor.

"Why do you not answer?" King Christian asked, surprised.

Looking at him again, I saw that the response he had expected from us was that he would have a long and prosperous reign ahead of him. Our silence, however, had not only upset him, but frightened him. He was glaring at us.

"You will speak!" he ordered, angrily.

"Come now," Lord Olbert began again with a soothing tone of voice and pleasant smile. "Give us answer. What of King Christian?"

The chamber was stirred by a terrible voice then.

"B- b- b- bad fr- fr- fruit."

Lord Paschal rolled his eyes, sighed, and shook his head.

"D- d- d- de- de- destruction," the wild man managed, staring at the wall.

Chill bumps covered my arms, and I shivered, for his voice was grating.

"What?" King Christian asked in surprise.

"Re- re- re - re- p- p- pent -wh- wh- while y- y- y- you are- are a- a- able!"

And after looking momentarily at the wild man, King Christian put his head back and laughed.

I was astonished at his laughter. I looked at the others in the room to see their reaction to his jovial attitude. The guards and all of the royal advisers were quite pale and subdued, even the youths.

The wild man seemed unaware of the laughter. He turned to the knight near him, stood on tiptoes to look the tall man in the eyes, and then called out suddenly, "Re- re- repent!"

The King laughed again and was joined by the uneasy chuckles of some of the Court.

Then the wild man moved to a manservant, looked him intently in the face, and said again, "R- re- p- pent!"

Then he did the same to the serving woman beside him, calling for repentance. Then he approached each of our guards, looking them each over, and then commanding them to repent. Next, he walked past Jebedye and the child and squatted down before me.

The man, covered in dirt and filth, his matted oily hair hanging limp down his back, looked me evenly in the eyes for a long moment, seeming to scrutinize my very soul. The intensity of the gaze of his dark eyes scared me and made me shiver more.

"R- R-Re p-pent!" he suddenly called out in his raspy voice, showering me with his foul breath.

My heart pounded rapidly in my chest, and the hair on the back of my neck stood on end.

He got to his feet again and went to the knights at the table and each of the King's advisers. One by one, he peered into their eyes and commanded them to repent in a very loud voice. Although most were startled, even unsettled, the King himself only laughed.

"Even you, Olbert! Tut, tut! What have you been hiding from the rest of us?" he jested.

The wild man even made his way to the cleric, and bending very near the man's ear, screamed as loud as he could, "Re- re- re- pent!!"

The cleric jumped back, nearly spilling his ink.

The wild man approached Lords Paschal and Felix as one and commanded them to repent as well. Lastly, he stood before the King.

"Rrrrr-pent wh- wh- whillle yyyy- yyou are are aa- aaa- able.."

The King only chuckled, saying with crossed arms, "You are quite mad, Fellow."

"Aye, methinks *he* should repent of his stench," Paschal said, waving his hand before his nose.

"Aye!" the King and his knights and companions laughed.

Frowning, Olbert quickly asked, "Are all the women in Speyron truly barren?"

"Olbert, not again with that folly!" King Christian complained.

"-Aye, ev- ev- every wa- wa- one," he managed. "B- b- b- barren."

"Forever?" Lord Olbert asked.

"Re- re- re- re p- p- pent or- or- or- Sp- Sp- Sp- Speyron is d- d- d- doomed. G- G- God w- w- w- will w- w- wipe a- a- away our ki- ki- kingdom- ..."

The cleric was hanging on every word of the man in order to mark it down. As I listened to him sputter on so slowly, I realized how tired I was. As we listened, a servant arrived with more wine and began pouring it for the ministers. All the while, King Christian continued to chuckle throughout the wild man's attempt to speak while wiping his face on his sleeve and trying to regain his composure. The rest of us stared at him, wondering what the jest was.

"-there w- w- will b- b- b- be n- n- n- no mem- memory of- of- it. As- as-as if- if it- it- h- h- h- had n- n- n- never ex- ex- existed. As- as- as if- if w- w- we h- h- had n- n- never b- b- been b- b- born."

The sound of the King's laughter was nothing more than breath now; his entire body shook with mirth. Was he drunk? I wondered.

"G- G- G- God w- w- will br- bring th- th- the pr- pr- proud l- l- l- low."

"Do you want to hear something- really absurd?" the King managed to ask between fits of laughter, "that God should choose *this man* to speak for Him."

The King went into another fit of laughter while the tears rolled down his cheeks.

"How ty- ty- ty- typical!" he roared.

His companions laughed too. The guards and counselors smiled weakly and looked at each other.

"Y- y- you kn- know a- a- tr- tr- tree- by its- its -its fruit. A- a- a- tr- tr- tree w- w- w- with n- n- n- no fr- fruit w- w- w- will be cut o- off!

"If- If Sp- Sp- Spey -r- ron is -is -t- t- to -sur- sur- sur- vive, it- it- it m- m- must ha- have a- a- n- n- new k- k- king."

The wild man's comment only sent the King into further glee; his face turned quite red, and he gasped for air as he held his sides.

After a few minutes, his laughter gradually began to subside.

"Please, some mercy for your King!" he succeeded in saying finally, though he still chuckled. "The royal ear needs rest. If you ministers wish to question this man further, do so out of Our presence. Otherwise, he is free to go."

"Silence," the knight nearest the babbling wild man ordered, shaking him roughly until he complied.

"You will set him free?" Paschal stammered. "After what he just said?"

"But this is just the kind of talk that breeds rebellion," Lord Grey complained.

"This is the kind of talk that causes fatigue-" King Christian answered. "The man is clearly mad. No one in their right mind would believe him. He is no threat to Us."

"But mad or not, this man has spoken against you, his anointed King," Paschal complained.

"You are too severe, Paschal. Fortuna has robbed him of his wits. For this, should We deprive him of his life? Besides, We rather like this man, as one likes a dog that chases its own tail. Perhaps We shall make a place for him here at Court- for he makes Us laugh."

The advisors and knights were all speechless as they regarded the King.

"Sire-" Grey began.

"Now We will hear from the witch," King Christian said, at once silencing any further protests.

My heart skipped a beat and then raced. I wondered briefly if I should tell him about my dreams at all and the little I understood about them; yet the last dream I had had was a warning to me to remain silent.

"'Acrida', is it not?" Lord Dewain asked.

I carefully stood up.

"Aye, My Lord."

"Acrida, do you divine the future through the ancient arts or do you conjure spirits?" he asked.

"Neither. I am a true woman of the Faith. I see Mass daily. Ask the priest of my village.- And as I said before, I am not a witch! -Nor a seer. Nor have I ever spoken against the King. Who accuses me of this?"

The advisers crossed their arms.

"Your village declares you are a witch and the daughter of a witch and that you can foretell the future. Lord Huntingdon has heard tale of you. The parish priest believes it so also."

I stared at the noblemen in surprise.

"So I ask again, do you speak to spirits?"

I swallowed quickly.

"I am not a witch, and I do not conjure, -but sometimes I see things in my dreams that come to pass."

"Dreams! Ha!" snorted Lord Paschal.

"She is only a threat if she sleeps. Let us confine her to the tower and forbid her to sleep ever again," Felix declared.

"Aye, We could do that," the King smiled.

I looked at them, horrified.

"So why have you not given answer to any question put to you this night?"

I swallowed again, my palms sweating.

"I have not the ability of Jebedye to look into the future to discover the answers that you seek. What I see in my dreams comes unbidden, unasked. I have no control of what is shown me. -I have never dreamt about the King," I finished quickly, glancing at the two guards who moved nearer to me.

"A very safe answer," Paschal commented.

"Aye," King Christian agreed. "We do not believe you."

My heart skipped a beat, and my palms were wet with sweat.

"'Tis true," I lied.

"We know something about women, particularly peasants," King Christian said smugly. "You do not ramble on thoughtlessly as an innocent does, but like a deceiver, you choose your words cautiously. Some of what you say is, no doubt, true, but you are concealing more. Now, We ask again: what do you know about the future of Our reign?"

"I know nothing about your reign, Sire."

"She is not much of a seer or a liar-" Paschal smiled.

"Nor much of a dreamer either," Felix jested.

"So you will not give answer?" the King asked.

"I have nothing to say."

I saw the older advisers frown. I stood mutely then, wondering if I should have at least tried to appease them.

The shock of pain to the back of my head and the force behind the blow sent me to the floor. I lay face down on the stone, dazed by the pain. I had barely caught my breath before I was pulled to my feet, another blow landing on my face. Wailing, I put my hands up to protect my cheeks and ears, only to have the punches land in my belly. Doubled over, I gasped for air as the wind was knocked out of me. I fell to the floor again, and they kicked me repeatedly in the back and on the legs.

"Mercy!" I cried.

They stopped suddenly.

"Will you speak now?"

"I know nothing! -Why do you beat me?"

I heard laughter then.

"Because we can!" Paschal taunted.

"There is really no need of this," a different voice called. "The King has already declared his intent to let you go. You must only answer the question."

I was going to die here- or worse.

The guard kicked me again in the back.

"Owh! Aye, I will speak," I managed, gasping for breath through my tears, my entire body throbbing with pain. "Only tell me what you wish to hear, and I will speak it!"

"What we wish to hear?"

"Should not a seer already know both the question and the answer?" Paschal joked.

"Tell us the future of Speyron!" King Christian commanded again.

"I do not know it!" I cried miserably and then howled painfully as the guard kicked me again.

The blows began once more. One knight kicked me in the belly and then the nose. I whimpered and wept from pain as one stomped the side of my face and my shielding arms over and over while the other stomped on my legs and my sore feet. Then they kicked me repeatedly in the back and knees and legs until I wet myself. They pulled me up off the floor by my hair then and threw me with all their might against the hard wall again and again.

"That is enough," the King finally called out. "You are getting blood on the wall."

"-And making her uglier than she already is," Felix added with a laugh.

The men stopped hitting me and let me fall to the floor.

"We will move on, Witch, but you will not be released until you speak."

They were not going to release anyone else, I knew.

It was quiet in the audience chamber again. I lay on the cool stone floor, panting and tasting blood in my mouth. My head was pounding from the pain. I could not breathe out of my nose. I carefully opened my eyes, but could only open one, and its sight was fuzzy at best. The chamber seemed darker than it was, and I only saw blurs of color. I was against the right wall. The ministers, the King, and the prisoners were all still in my view. The wild man was being held still and quiet by a guard to my right. In front of me, the child, still in the center circle, had climbed into the arms of old Jebedye during my beating. The King was talking privately with the advisers again.

I prayed to God then that He would accept my repentance and receive my soul and those of the other prisoners.

Finally, Lord Olbert turned back to us.

"Child," he said to the young boy. "How old are you?"

"This many, My Lord," he said, holding up his fingers.

"Well, five years old. Practically grown already," the minister replied. "Do you know what I have heard about you? I have heard that you know the future. Is that true?"

"They tell me so," the boy replied.

"Will you tell me the future?"

"Aye," the boy answered simply, "but if I get it wrong, will the knights beat me also?"

Lord Olbert chuckled, replying, "I think not."

The boy pushed himself out of the old seer's arms and rose to his feet. He stood before the minister in his tattered clothes, his little, pale face was almost as white as his hair.

He seemed to be about to speak, but then he stopped and asked, "What should I say?"

I saw the King smile.

"Tell us about King Christian. Do not be afraid," Olbert coaxed.

"My mother told me never to fear anyone but God, the Creator of all things."

"Is that so?" Olbert replied.

"Aye, but she was afraid," the boy answered.

"Of what?" Olbert asked.

"Everything. -And the King."

"Oh."

"My mother was afraid for me the day the King and the knights arrived. We were hiding in the field, but they found us. She was crying and held on to me when the men tried to take me away. The King told the knights to kill her," the boy said sadly.

There was silence in the room. I winced.

"She, I guess, is in Heaven now."

"Aye," Olbert agreed in a compassionate voice.

"I suppose Mother should have done as she had spoken and not have been afraid. But I will not be afraid. I will tell you what God tells me, as you bid."

The boy looked around then.

"I usually stand on something."

The ministers looked at the King who shrugged; one of the knights carried a chair to him, and the boy climbed up in it and stood with a brave face.

"Oh, Most Wretched People of Speyron!" the boy called out, nearly shouting, as if he was speaking outside to a large group of people. "Fear not as I tell you that from where the sun rises every morning and goes away from every day," making a large gesture over his head with his hand, "a man will come-"

The King was already chuckling.

"This looks practiced," Paschal commented.

"-and be such a king and rule us so that this kingdom will not know itself from what it was before. It shall be a new kingdom with a new king!"

The boy stopped speaking and frowned at the laughing youth.

"Pray, continue," Olbert urged.

The boy glanced at the minister and then went on.

"-For God has heard the wails of His people and has had His fill of *our* King."

King Christian's laughter grew louder.

"And- and-" the boy put his hands on his hips. "Stop laughing! Stop laughing!"

"We are sorry," the King managed after a moment, "do continue."

"Now I can not remember where I was!" the boy complained.

The Court laughed heartily at this.

The boy then began to cry. He stomped his foot angrily.

"I am not going to say anymore!"

"Oh, no, do not stop! You are doing so well!" Olbert consoled, rushing to the boy, who had climbed off the chair.

"Really, please, go on. We will try to control Ourselves," King Christian said.

The boy got back on the chair, and with a defiant look and an irate tone, he said, "In the war to come, no help will come to Speyron from Gaulia, or Bonaqua, or-" and he paused, "oh, aye, Caldignis."

The chamber went into another fit of laughter.

"Stop laughing!" the child raged. "This is serious! I have not made a jest! King Christian! Soon you will know fear and regret! Soon you will wish for death as you wash the floor with your tears!"

The child's tone had changed now. The words flowed out of him wrathfully and unrehearsed.

"The enemy will come sooner than you expect, and our kingdom will know misery as it has not known! No man will be able to save our kingdom from this invader's army! You will be forced to accept help from those you hate and to make an alliance that tastes bitter to you!"

The entire Court was mute at these words; only the King laughed.

"You will reap grief, oh, Terrible King, as you come to see yourself as others see you, and as you destroy those things you hold most dear! *You will reap grief!*"

The boy was quiet then, his chest heaving.

After these final words, the smile fell slowly from King Christian's face. He swallowed and was silent.

"Olbert, We have heard enough from this boy," he said. "You may stop now, Boy."

The boy jumped off the chair, wiped his enraged face and went and sat by the old blind man. The only sounds in the hall were the quick scratch of the clerk's quill and the low murmuring of the Court.

The King rubbed his eyes and shifted in his throne again, frowning.

"Make this last one quick, Grey. We grow weary of this nonsense."

"Aye, Sire."

"Jebedye-" Grey began.

The feeble, old man struggled to his feet and leaned on his cane.

"Am I finally to be heard?" he asked testily. "Do you, Your Grace, not know who *I* am? I have been the Court Seer in Speyron for three reigns. Allow an old man to explain to Your Grace the proper way to summon a seer:

"One sends a messenger and an extra horse to retrieve him, or if the seer is aged, as I am, one sends the royal litter. One sets a chair by a fire for him and offers him food and good wine. One does *not* have his knights tear him from his home, take him prisoner, and force him to march -nor ride in a prisoner cart- to the farthest castle possible begrudging him food, rest, and water!

"I am outraged at the way I have been treated- and for no cause, since I have *always* come when I was bidden! However, I can hardly be surprised since the last time I was here, I prophesied to your mother when you were large in her womb that you would be remembered better than all the other kings before or after. I see it comes true every day. You, King Christian, are the most foolish and reckless king I have ever heard tell of. And you do not need a seer to tell you that if you do not amend, you will not rule long!"

The King laughed sharply at this remark.

"And who are we to be laughed at? I might ask. Are we Cassandra that you should laugh at us so? And yet, Sire, Cassandra was correct every time!"

"Ha-" the King replied.

"And for that matter, who are we to be beaten and tortured? We either have the information you seek or we do not. Often, as the woman said, we can not control the sight that has been bestowed on us."

The King said nothing, but only crossed his arms.

"Now let me see if I understand what has been happening for the past few days," he continued. "You have gathered all the rumored seers in Speyron presumably to discover if we are saying anything that will rile the people into revolt against you. Fear not, Sire, the peasantry are too concerned with their crops to give us or you any thought whatsoever. In fact, the harvest was so poor last year, that most of the people are relieved about the lack of children since there are less mouths to feed, but they too have taken notice. It is the nobles that have complained about the lack of children being born, since it means that there will be less workers in their fields in the years to come, and they are rightly concerned."

"For the last three years, there have been no live births in Speyron. And this past year of the three, there have been no pregnancies."

I marked his words, astounded. I thought the lack of pregnancies was peculiar to my own village; I had no idea it was happening throughout the kingdom.

"You have been on the throne for a little more than three years. -Do you really need a seer, Sire, to tell you it is not coincidence?"

The Court was startled into silence; the King only smiled angrily.

"Very well. It is not a coincidence," Jebedye continued.

My heart pounded at his boldness. Surely, he was the first bird in my dream.

"It is the work of God, and only He can remedy it. If you repent, likely He *may*."

Lords Olbert and Dewain and some of the knights and servants were crossing themselves.

The King sniffed and picked up his cup again.

"Still you scoff!" Jebedye railed. "Your kingdom is in peril, and still you will not heed!"

"Heed what?" Christian asked hotly.

Jebedye slammed his cane against the floor.

"God has raised you up to be king, and you regard Him and His works with scorn! This affront will not stand! God will not be mocked!"

"I am king because I am son of Filberte and his only blood! It is my destiny to be king! I was born to it!" King Christian yelled back.

"Even so-" Jebedye spat, "it is *God* who has brought you safely to this harbor-"

"Jebedye!" Lord Olbert interrupted. "Lord Grey fears the peasants will either revolt or join with our enemy. What say you?"

The old seer turned toward Olbert.

"When Herryck and his army come, My Lord, it will be the King's vassals that will be sorely tempted to take up arms to follow him, not the peasants. Some will support Herryck. Others will not give their support to either of them.

"The boy is right," he continued. "No help will come to Speyron in her hour of need. Gaulia will not help us, for they fight their own invaders that come by the sea. Caldignis can not, for Herryck has them under his boot."

The looks on the faces of the King and his companions were pure amazement, and the knights and the servants were all speechless.

"Sire, you wonder whether you should trust your advisers. You should heed some more than *others*, but, regardless, you can not rule Speyron without some help, some advice. And you will not rule for long if you do not begin taking an interest!"

"Enough!" King Christian interrupted.

"Mind your tongue, Old Man-" Lord Paschal began.

"Dare you to scold your king?" Felix warned.

"I do! The lives and well-being of a people have been entrusted to you, King Christian," Jebedye continued, "and you are bound to protect them all as any lord is. There is nothing more complicated than ruling a kingdom; it is not a game. You are playing at it like a child. It is long past time to put childhood behind you!"

"We said 'Enough'!" the King warned, his face reddening.

"You doubt your decision not to pay Herryck the tribute money he demands, but, Sire, it is the best decision you have made."

King Christian and the young advisers seemed startled by this comment, looking at each other in surprise.

"The peace your father bought from Herryck funded his armies to move against neighboring kingdom," Jebedye continued. "In truth, Herryck has his eyes set upon Speyron now, and no amount of money will keep him out. Therefore, be not tempted to buy peace, for if you do, Herryck will betray you, seize Speyron, and put your entire line to the sword. -You must be willing to fight him to the bitter end!

"Your father had a stomach for pleasure, not for work or war, but he was a shrewd man. Your parents sent you to Gaulia to train in arms hoping that under Lord Reynaud's tutelage you would become grounded in the Faith and would grow in character and honor as well as master swords and warfare. But your flagrant disregard for honor and God proves that it was all for naught!"

All in the hall gasped. Christian was on his feet.

"Say more and face the consequences!" the King snarled, throwing his cup at the old man.

The cup missed him and rolled across the stone floor.

"No! You have summoned *me*, and *you* will hear it all!" the old seer replied. "It is yet unclear who will win the war. With the right ally, Herryck may yet be defeated, -but you will not prevail in your war against God! Tonight you have gone too far, King Christian! You will come to rue this night a hundred fold!"

"You will rue it!" Christian yelled back. "I will rip that beard from your chin with my bare hands!"

Jebedye stared straight through the youth as if he was not even there.

"Peace is at an end in Speyron; nothing can change that now. But, fear not, Boy, your time as king is not yet ended. You will live to see all that has been predicted here- and more. Through pain, fear and grief, you will live to see a new king rule where once you did, and you will come to see life from the perspective of those who have nothing."

Lords Olbert, Dewain, and Grey all laughed nervously and glanced at the King who was clearly not amused. Lords Paschal and Felix, equally offended, stood incensed beside their King.

"Have you anything else to say before you die, Old Man?" the King snarled through clenched teeth, as he grabbed the sword from the knight nearest him.

"Have my words ever proven false that I should pay with my life? Take my life, Sire, and you will only have more innocent blood on your hands!"

My heart pounded loudly in my ears, and the three older advisers were suddenly around the King, trying to calm him.

"Spare him, Sire!"

"Sire, have mercy!"

"Where has your merry mood gone?"

The guard nearest the old man began to unsheathe his sword, but then stopped and retrieved a heavy one that lay on the table top.

"Truly, death is my greatest wish now," Jebedye continued spitefully. "For I have lived in this good kingdom too long already. I have seen Speyron when she was great, and then I saw her brought low by a slothful and intemperate king. I can not bear to watch as she is lost completely by his reckless, self-indulgent, dishonorable son."

The King suddenly screamed, running at the man. My heart pounding wildly, I saw only a blur of motion as the King swung the sword. The old man's head bounced on the floor and then rolled; the body fell to the floor. The boy screamed, and the advisers gasped and cursed, and the blood spattered warm on my face and in my uncovered hair.

"We- will- hear- no- more!" he shouted as he continued to attack the fallen body with his sword with all his rage.

As the boy wailed, I watched in terror as the King hacked Jebedye's body furiously. The older advisers looked on numbly.

Finally, breathing hard, the King stopped and turned, bloody sword in hand.

My heart skipped a beat, then raced at the sight of him. The youth was covered in red, spattered blood; his blond locks dripped scarlet. His deadly gaze moved to the crying boy then, and then to me, and last to the wild man.

"It seems things are not going as well in Speyron as We thought," he finally said, frowning. "Perhaps you were correct to fret of these troublemakers among Our people."

"Sire-"

"Kill them all!" King Christian instructed the guards.

"No!" the advisers protested.

The child shrieked and then was silent, and I felt new, warm blood spray me from where the wild man had been standing, the odor of feces and urine suddenly strong in the hall.

Rough hands grabbed me up by my hair then. I whined as new pain shot through my body.

As I felt the cold blade against my throat, I braced and chuckled. Was this the end? I laughed harder. Was this the end to my miserable life? With blood burning my one seeing eye, I forced myself to laugh louder.

"Hold-" came a voice. "Why do you laugh, Witch?"

My guards nudged me.

"Because you could have killed me days ago and spared me the walk," I muttered through my swollen lips.

The King and his advisers stared at me.

"Wait, Sire! Their deaths can not serve you!" Olbert pleaded. "Nothing can stop a prophesy once it has been spoken! It is already ordained after God tells the seer, no matter if the seer speaks it or not."

"Spare her, Sire! Killing her will not serve you! What these seers know, told or not told, will occur! You may cut out the tongue, but that does not change the message!" Dewain argued desperately. "If you kill her, you will make the voice indistinguishable! You will not know what is to be until another seer is born to tell you!"

The King stood there, his hands in fists, scowling at me. He glanced at the old advisers and then at his companions. In agony, I watched him with my partially seeing eye.

"Kill me," I muttered indifferently, my anger emboldening me. "You are already the blindest man in the kingdom, for you can not bear to see the truth."

"What?!"

"No, Sire!"

"Spare her!"

"Kill me!" I dared him. "Kill me and condemn yourself to darkness. We will be the first of your entire kingdom you lead to death and ruin."

"No!" the advisers yelled again.

The guard looked at the King for direction. King Christian himself walked over to me and stared hard into my swelling, bleeding face, his blue eyes regarding me coldly. Then he hit me so hard that I reeled backward and hit my head again against the wall. Everything went black for a moment; when I woke, my head ached so painfully I thought it might burst. Too weak to move on the stone floor, my tongue hurt, and I tasted fresh, salty blood in my mouth.

"I want her watched night and day," the King was saying. "And get these bodies out of here. Get some servants in here to clean this place up."

"Immediately, Your Grace, but most of the garrison have been drinking since they returned, -and almost all of them are afraid of witches."

I heard the King sigh in exasperation.

"I think the tower would be adequate to hold her in her present condition," Lord Grey said.

The King thought for a moment and then suddenly laughed.

"No, We shall send her to Van Necht," he laughed again. "We are confident he will be up to the task."

Felix snorted.

"Van Necht?!" Paschal laughed. "What sport! If only we could be there to see it!"

"Aye, send her to Van Necht, but make certain to instruct him not to kill her," the King said.

8

In the faint glow of predawn, when only the birds know that the sun will arrive directly, a lone man sat in the cool breeze listening to the steady sound of horse hooves plodding up the road. Lord Van Necht, a man of war for too long, was up early, even during this time of peace, feeding his fire with kindling while he waited. He stirred the bright orange embers of the fire, wondering what news the riders would bring at this hour. A rebellion somewhere? A summons to the King?

In a little while, the rider was in sight, and the whinny of the approaching horse was answered by the neigh of his own charger. Van Necht rose to his feet as the knight guided his horse toward the fire and greeted him.

"Greetings, My Lord. You are astir early."

"What grave errand gives you cause to ride through the moonless night, Sir Knight?"

"An errand of the King. He sends you a prisoner to guard."

The warlord raised his eyebrows.

"What prisoner of the King could not wait until day to be brought?"

"A fair question, but I have not the answer, My Lord."

He dismounted his damp horse and walked to the pack animal behind it.

He cut a rope and shoved the large bundle off the animal's back. The load hit the ground with a thud and a low moan, and the pack animal, free of its burden, shook off and snorted.

Lord Van Necht looked at the bundle for a moment. The prisoner was bound in a coverlet and smelled distinctly of war.

"This wench is entrusted to your care now, My Lord."

The warlord looked back at the knight in surprise.

"A woman? -What happened? One of the King's concubines try to poison him?"

The knight laughed.

"In truth, I know nothing about her. I was only instructed to deliver her to you to guard. The King instructs that you may use her however you please, though be sure no real harm comes to her, for he may wish to summon her again in the future."

"Why was she bound so?"

"I know not. Perhaps they feared she would escape me on the journey here," he shrugged.

Van Necht raised his eyebrows.

"Will you stop by the fire awhile?" he asked.

"No, I will be on my way to the village for a bed- if I may have your leave to go, My Lord."

"You have it," Van Necht answered.

The courier bowed and remounted his horse and returned to the road, pulling the pack horse behind him.

Van Necht watched him ride off and then looked back down at his prisoner. Kneeling down, he examined the ropes that were wrapped tightly around the bundle. Certainly the King had not chanced an escape attempt.

Pulling his knife from his belt, Van Necht cut the ropes and peeled back the coverlet. His nose immediately scrunched as it was assaulted by the strong odors of urine and body odor. He reached out and clutched a mass of dark, oily hair and pulled the head up to his view.

It had been a woman. Her blackened, bruised face was swollen out of shape and was decorated with dried blood. Both eyes were swollen shut. Her mouth was gagged, and her hands were tied. As Van Necht held the limp head in his hand, he heard a dim, low moan escape from the creature.

It would be light soon enough, he thought to himself. He reached down and picked up the thing and brought it to the fire; then he moved upwind and waited for light.

The shock of cold water brought Acrida back to consciousness. Besides pain, her first awareness was that she was very, very cold and wet, and then the astonishment of being completely wet. Her eyes would hardly open so she could see nothing distinct. She did not know where she was or what was happening, but realizing her body was actually immersed in cold water was enough to alarm her. Was she drowning? Had she fallen off the horse as they crossed a stream?

The sound of slow moving water was loud in her ears. She instinctively moved to right herself, and, in doing so, she realized that the water was very shallow, for she was actually sitting on the bottom. Shivering, she moved slowly to crawl out of the water, hoping she could guess where the embankment was. She was suddenly and violently pushed back under the water by some unknown force. Panicked and gasping desperately for air, Acrida splashed in the water wildly to right herself again and struck out instinctively at what was attempting to drown her.

Her tied hands were immediately pinned down, and she fell into the cold water again, her knees scraping on the rocky bottom. She was trying to scream now, but although she was no longer gagged, she was quite hoarse, and the fight had already worn her out. She felt a rough hand rubbing her back then, and it was at this point that Acrida realized that her clothes were gone. Horrified, she tried to get away, but to no avail; but when an arm brushed the side of her face, Acrida found it with her teeth.

She heard her captor curse, and then her head was immediately shoved under water. She released the arm and struggled then to get her head above water, but the hand on her neck, holding her down, was too strong. As she struggled, her aching body weakened even more. Suddenly, her captor pulled her up. She barely had time to take a breath before she was suddenly shoved back under the water. When she was pulled up this time, she was coughing and spitting water, gasping for breath.

Again the rubbing began, and now, too weak to fight, Acrida sat still. However, when the hand began to rub her breast, she started to fight with renewed strength. Her captor stopped rubbing her abruptly.

Acrida then felt a strong hand pressing firmly on the side of her neck, choking her. She immediately was struggling to breathe and was pushing blindly against the hand, but the pressure remained. She began to feel lightheaded. Then there was nothing.

9

Mae was concerned with how much care the lass required. It had been three days since Lord Van Necht had brought his prisoner to her to tend, and her improvement had been slow.

From the looks of her, the steward's wife had thought the woman was just starved and exhausted, besides having been severely beaten. However, the prisoner had remained unconscious for so long on the first day that she had feared that her condition might be more serious than she knew how to tend, but, gradually, the lass had begun to wake for short periods of time.

Mae had kept cool, damp rags on the woman's bruised face to try to ease the swelling and had applied salve and clean linen to her cut and swollen feet. Whenever the stranger awoke, however briefly, Mae had been able to get her to drink a little water.

The second day, the young woman stayed awake for longer periods, and Mae managed to get a little broth down her. The lord called at their home twice a day to check on his prisoner's recovery, prompting Mae to silently wonder who this stranger was and how she had angered the King.

On the third day, the prisoner's color was markedly better. Mae had sat her up, leaning her limp body against a wall of pillows. When she woke, Mae encouraged her to take a swallow of water. This time, Acrida took the horn and gulped down the contents on her own. Mae fetched an entire pail of water, sitting down beside her. She handed her a full horn and watched as her patient quickly drank it.

The steward's wife refilled her horn again, and Acrida sipped on the water slowly now. Acrida's left eye was still swollen shut, but the right eye began to blink slowly, and she turned her head taking in her whereabouts. She wondered briefly where she was and where her aunt and uncle were.

"Where -?" Acrida paused, the tone of her own voice sounding strange to her. "Where am I?"

"Shh-" the woman whispered soothingly. "You are safe now."

Suddenly, the events of the past week came back to Acrida in vivid images. She shuttered and peered at the kind-looking woman beside her.

"Who are you?" she asked.

"I am Mae. What is your name?"

"Acrida," she muttered.

Acrida could faintly hear voices, and as she peered around the dimly lit room, she saw two men watching her from the far side of the room. She did not recognize either of them. One was short and chubby, and the other was taller and broad shouldered. She looked about the room, noticing its organization, the benches and a large table.

Acrida wiped her nose on her sleeve and noticed then that it was not her tunic that she wore. This shirt was clean, and it was a different texture than the course weave of the woolen tunic she had been wearing for days. She examined the fabric that covered her legs and noticed then, that it was not a gown that she wore at all; she seemed to be actually wearing braes.

As she repositioned herself on the pillows, her head began throbbing, and the room began to rock and then to very slowly turn. Acrida balanced herself with one hand on the bed and clutched her head with her other. Her head ached with an intense, dull pain; she moaned and shut her eye.

The woman got up, passed the men, and left the room. After a moment, she was back again. She handed a bowl of steaming broth to Acrida who took it in both hands and inhaled. She could not smell anything. She blew on the broth and waited for it to cool before tasting it.

"Why am I here?" Acrida asked quietly.

"The lord brought you so that I might tend you. That is all that I know."

"The lord? Which lord?"

"Lord Van Necht."

Fresh images of the slaughter at the palace came to mind, and Acrida winced, seeing again the King hack at the body and the sprays of blood. She heard the wails of the child and watched again as the bodies of the others fell.

She moaned. What was the King intending with this? She was *not* safe here. If she could get home, perhaps her aunt could hide her or help her run away. But she had to go now- while the King or this lord thought she was too ill to escape.

"I have to go- get home -before they kill me," Acrida mumbled.

"Now, now, Girl," the woman was coaxing, "drink your broth, and you will feel better."

Without another thought, Acrida pushed the bowl back into the woman's hand and moved to get out of bed. Mae turned toward the door and gave the men a look, even as her wincing patient was struggling to stand up. Acrida's feet and legs hurt immediately, but she still managed to limp a few steps before she lost her balance and fell to the rush-covered floor while the room spun wildly around her.

Without even knowing what was happening, Acrida found herself lifted back upon the bed and sitting up again, and a very large man standing above her. His expression looked fierce to Acrida, so fierce, in fact, that she knew that he was going to strike her. She looked miserably at him with her one good eye, awaiting the blow. The blow did not come, however; he was gone as suddenly as he had appeared. Acrida wondered if he had been there at all or if she had merely imagined him.

The woman handed her the soup again and watched carefully as Acrida drank it. The broth had little taste besides salty to her, but it was warm down her sore throat.

Two days later, Acrida felt much better. She was no longer dizzy, and her feet and body ached much less than they had. She sat at the table trying to comb the knots out of her tangled hair while Mae kneaded dough for bread. It was a beautiful day, and the warm sun streamed through the open door and through the one window onto Acrida's back, soothing her strained muscles.

She thought that tonight she would try to make her escape. In truth, she hated the thought of leaving, for the steward's wife and family had been very kind to her. However, she dared not stay. Who knew what this Van Necht would do to her. And even if she survived him, eventually would not the King send for her again? No, she had to go.

Acrida looked out the open door. She had been able to open her left eye the day before, but was seeing much clearer out of it this day. From where she sat, she could just see Mae's lively children laughing and playing among the other village children outside the cottage. Acrida watched them wistfully for a long time.

"You have fine children. You have been truly blessed."

"Aye," Mae agreed with a smile. "They are healthy and strong, and a handful at times. Their father spoils them, I fear."

"I can see how that would be easy to do," Acrida answered sadly.

Mae observed her guest's expression with curiosity, wondering again who she was and why she was the prisoner of the king. Over the past few days, she had not been able to draw any information out of her; and Acrida had volunteered nothing.

"*Acrida.* -That is an unusual name," Mae smiled again. "What is your baptismal name?"

"'Cinsara', but it has been a long time since anyone has called me that."

Mae nodded.

"Childhood nicknames seem to stay with a person. You had a sharp tongue when you were young, I suppose?"

Acrida made no reply. There was silence for a moment, as she decided to ask what she had been asking herself repeatedly for the last few days.

"Why am I here?"

"I know not."

Acrida frowned in frustration.

"There must be a reason why the King sent me to your lord. What do you know about Lord Van Necht? Is he an executioner for the King? An expert in torture?"

Mae raised her eyebrows at first and then chuckled. Seeing the questioning look on the young woman's face, she wiped her forehead and sat down.

"An executioner? Hardly, -but a man loyal to his king and to his oaths, and certainly a man not to be crossed," she answered plainly. But seeing the grave look on Acrida's face, she added, "Fear not. I know not of any time that he has done harm without first having cause. He is a fair man, respected and admired by his equals and by his vassals. We are fortunate to have him as lord here."

Acrida sighed and looked back outside.

"However," Mae added with a smile, "Van Necht is quite a *different* sort than the usual nobleman."

"How so?"

"In many ways. -He does not hold himself high above us commoners, for one thing. He does not go about the village in rich clothes wearing golden rings. He does not dally with the daughters of his vassals or his serfs. He has not made war against the neighboring lords, nor does he ignore the plight of the old, the weak, or the poor. In many ways, he lives the simplest of lives: virtuous, quiet, and just. It is a pity that he is so seldom here."

"Why is that? Has he other lands?"

"No, Lord Van Necht is one of the junior commanders of the King's forces, and his duty calls him away much of the time. He spent the entire summer in the north of Speyron laying siege to some rebellious lords' castles at the King's bidding. He just recently returned home a month or so ago."

Acrida went cold, placing the name then.

"He also bears the title of the Queen's Royal Guard- except that there is no queen at the moment. When the King does take a wife, we will likely never see Van Necht since his presence will be required at Court."

"Does his wife make complaint about his long absences?" Acrida asked.

"His wife is dead," Mae said quickly. "But while she lived she made no complaint about them. -Nor he, for that matter."

"How did she die?"

"The lady died in childbirth some four years ago."

"The child?"

"Aye, it too."

"And he has not remarried?"

"Not yet-" she muttered under her breath.

"Perhaps he has not yet recovered from his wife's death-" Acrida mused.

Mae laughed out loud.

"He has never recovered from her life!"

Seeing the odd look on Acrida's face, Mae added, "Take my word for it, Lass, the lady was a very ill-tempered woman. -And she ruined a good man."

"What do you mean?"

"Lord Van Necht's dislike of women is known of far and wide. He will not abide the presence of our sex in general now. It is a rare thing for him to even speak to a woman at all any more."

Acrida thought about this for a moment.

"Perhaps this explains why I recover in your house and not in his castle."

Mae snorted.

"Aye, more than you know. Van Necht does not live in a castle. He stays in his war tent."

Acrida's forehead wrinkled in confusion.

"He has all those responsibilities and titles, and he has not a castle to call his own?"

"In truth, I believe it is the 'warlord' in him," Mae answered. "He is away so much, and when he is in the field, he lives in a tent anyway," she shrugged. "And he really has not had the time to oversee the rebuilding of a castle since the old one burned down."

Acrida was impressed. Lord Huntingdon was considered a just lord in Brackenbach, but if his castle burned down, he would have every subject he could spare rebuilding it no matter what the weather or the time of year.

"Did they ever find out what started the fire?"

"Lord Van Necht set the place to flame himself."

"He burned down his own castle?"

"Aye."

"On purpose?"

"Aye."

"Why? Had it been captured by an enemy?"

"No, he was just angry at his wife."

"What?!"

"Aye, he does tend to act rashly when his temper is riled," the gossip admitted.

Acrida raised her eyebrows.

The women were silent for a moment.

"Anyway, I am certain all will be well," Mae continued. "Just remember not to anger him- for there are limits to his patience. -And, of course, do not mention his wife. 'Tis still a sore topic."

"What is your meaning?"

"Oh, you are so much recovered now that he is coming to collect you tonight."

Acrida felt the blood leave her cheeks, her heart pounding wildly, as the woman spoke these words.

10

crida had been anxious all the rest of the day as she waited for her captor to collect her. Finally, he had arrived in the early evening after the steward's family and she had already eaten the evening meal.

Upon meeting him, it was apparent to her that Lord Van Necht was the most unusual nobleman she had ever seen. She would not have been able to tell that he was a nobleman at all if the commoners had not shown deference to him. He was a man in his mid-thirties with brown hair and of average height. He was thick with muscles and very quiet. He did not smile at anyone. His clothes were of the same fabric as any freeman's, plain and functional, the sleeves rolled up high upon his arms. He wore no rings or jewels of any kind, and he carried no sword. He had simply put her on his great black horse and led it on foot to his camp, not speaking a word to her the entire way.

His camp was in a secluded area down a path far from the village. Although he lived in a tent, the sheer size of it clearly indicated his authority and position. The circular tent was as large as her village church, and a black pennant fluttered in the autumn breeze from the top of its center pole. The horse's corral was a little away from the tent.

As she looked around, a chill ran up Acrida's spine. Except for a white hound, no one came to greet them at their arrival. There were no servants preparing the nobleman's evening meal, nor tending the smoldering fire, nor setting out feed for the horse. There was no one in sight. There was no one even within shouting distance. Was it possible this alderman lived completely alone, without even a servant to wait upon him? she wondered.

He pulled her off the horse and sat her on the ground, then unhurriedly unsaddled the charger. He led the horse into the corral and put out feed for it. Then he picked up the saddle and took her by the arm and led her as she limped into the tent.

As he held open the door of his tent so that she might enter, the sun sank low in the horizon, coloring the sky in pinks and blues. Wearing the tunic, gown, and headrail that Mae had given her, Acrida's heartbeat quickened more as she realized that she was very apprehensive about being alone with this man.

The tent was empty except for crates of supplies. There was not even a table or a bench. The inside of the tent was divided by a wall of flaxen curtain that extended from one side to the other. Van Necht set the saddle down near the door of the tent, and then he and the dog went through an opening in the curtain near the center pole. He returned momentarily with some bundles of fur and spread them out onto the floor, fur side up.

"Let out your hair," he ordered. "It gets cold at night."

Acrida blushed, but obediently removed her veil and began to unweave her plaited hair.

"Take off your gown and give it to me," he added.

Acrida looked at him in alarm, but his face held no expression. She tried not to panic. So far he had not even truly looked at her. There was no cause to think that he desired her.

Acrida unlaced the gown quickly and pulled it over her head, careful not to let her undertunic come off with it. She gingerly folded up the gown and handed it to the nobleman. She watched as he threw both the gown and veil through the opening of the curtain that halved the tent.

She nervously began combing her long, thick, black hair with her fingers. She tried to ease her fears by recalling the good things Mae had said about this man. -Yet, she was not the daughter of a farmer on Lord Van Necht's lands. He was not her alderman; and she was not his serf. And had not the King intended evil for her, after all?

Van Necht went over and opened one of the chests by the tent door and began rummaging through it. Trying to calm herself, Acrida looked around, examining the many chests, baskets and sacks of various items that were stacked against the tent walls.

Her observations were abruptly interrupted by a brush against her shoulder. She looked up, startled to find him beside her again, as his swift, strong hands grabbed her arms.

Acrida panicked. Shrieking, she attempted to jerk herself away from him, but could not free herself.

"You do not want to start this now-" he warned.

Acrida was overwhelmed by fear. Crying distraughtly, she kicked out at him, all the while attempting to lurch free from him; she received an intense pain in her arms for her trouble and a tightening of her captor's grip. She yelped in pain, but the warlord's face was only a stern, emotionless mask. Weeping blindly, by instinct alone, she sunk her teeth into his left arm and was rewarded with the release of her hands. Immediately, Van Necht had a hold of her hair and yanked her head away from his arm.

The pain on her scalp was too sharp to ignore, and Acrida gave up. Van Necht pulled her to the fur and shoved her down on her back. He pressed his knee into her stomach, and he pinned her arms down firmly above her head with his hands. Utterly helpless beneath the bulk of his powerful body, she avoided his gaze, trying her hardest to stop crying, but she failed miserably.

Van Necht regarded his prisoner irritably, as he glanced at the bite mark in his arm. She had not managed to break the skin, but it had been close. What the devil was wrong with her? he wondered. One minute she was calm; the next, she was raving and fighting. Was she touched with madness? Observing her tears, his anger grew. She had started it, not him. He certainly was not going to lose a minute of sleep over this.

"If *this* is the way you want it, I will oblige you," he told her, roughly rolling her onto her belly.

With a knee in the small of her back, he pulled her arms down and tied her wrists behind her back with a small piece of rope.

Acrida continued sobbing as she awaited the inevitable. When Van Necht finished tying her hands, she felt him take hold of her feet. To her surprise, she felt the rope loop around her ankle and then winced as he tied it tightly to the other one. Then Van Necht bent her knees and tied his prisoner's feet to her wrists with more twine. Then he pushed his prisoner on her side, covered her with another fur, and then went through the opening of the curtained wall.

Acrida rocked and squirmed in order to get off her hair that she was laying on and, therefore, pulling. She took another deep breath and tried to calm herself, whispering a quick prayer for protection and mercy. Then she waited, straining to hear what he was doing on his half of the tent. After expecting his return for a long time, her heartbeat slowed to normal as she realized that he was not coming back.

She could see nothing but the darkening tent wall. Vaguely in her mind, she connected the few sounds she heard with what she thought were the lord's final preparations for bed. Finally, it was quiet in the tent and completely dark inside and outside. Acrida stared into the black for the longest time until finally she fell asleep.

The head of Jebedye rolled across the floor, blood streaming from the gaping, severed flesh. His eyes opened and blinked at me. His whiskered lips moved and formed the word very clearly: *coward!*

I looked away from the head, only to see the boy's head frown at me in disappointment.

"Shame! Shame!" the hairy, wild man was muttering over and over again as the drool emptied out of his mouth trailing over his matted beard into a pool on the bloody, stone floor.

Hearing a laugh then, I looked around and saw the blood-drenched, blond-headed King in the distance coming toward me with his unsheathed, bloodied sword. Overcome with fear, I cried out and ran frantically for the door. I had to escape! I had to get out before he murdered me!

The King's guards were occupied with other duties; I could slip out. The doors were wide open, and pairs of knights were carrying maimed bodies out of the chamber.

I approached the door then; still no one noticed. But as I tried to get out the door, I was pushed out of the way by even more knights. I tried again and again to flee, but failed. The doorman looked at me and said calmly, "There is no escape for you."

Alarmed, I watched the steady line of knights as they walked by the corpses of the seers. They went, instead, to the far end of the chamber, behind the throne, and picked up one of the many fallen bodies, one man taking up the shoulders, the other grabbing the feet. Although the knights carried off the dead steadily, no matter how fast or how many they took, there seemed to be more waiting to be removed.

With my heart beating hard in my chest as if it too were trying to flee, I turned around and looked again at the bodies of the prophets and their heads.

"There is no escape for you!" said the boy's head and then the wild man's. I looked around, and Jebedye's head said the same thing. I turned my back to them, looking around for another door to escape from, and there in the middle of the chamber stood my Uncle Roe.

The sight of him filled me with joy! I ran to him and hugged him.

He pulled me away from him and said with his familiar, gentle smile, "Child, I tried to warn you," then gestured toward the main doors.

"What?" I asked.

I went back over to the chamber doors again, saying to the doorman, whom I now recognized as Lord Van Necht standing with his arms folded, "I do not belong here. Let me go."

He said nothing, but pushed me aside roughly as two knights approached the door. The body they were carrying caught my attention, with its plain, woolen gown and long black hair.

"Wait!" I called.

The knights stopped for a moment, and I peered at the face of the body.

It was I!

My heart pounded wildly in my chest as I examined myself. My face and lips were pale, and dried blood was on my forehead and hair. Suddenly my eyes opened and looked at me with a hollow, dead stare.

"Coward!" I told myself.

I screamed as I watched them carry my body out of the chamber. I looked about the hall at all the death, and screamed again, pulling my hair out of my head in large handfuls. I paused and looked at the long mass of hair in my hands and then carefully placed my hand to my scalp, feeling the bald spot easily with my fingers. I screamed again, but no one noticed.

From the corner of my eye, I saw one of the knights sitting on the stone floor, rocking. I turned and looked closer, and the knight rocking was actually the woman. I ran to her side, clinging to her, weeping in terror.

"Save me! Spare me, please!"

"Cnot. Yrtimzcum."

"I do not want this!"

The old woman did not stop her rocking, or even look up. She was sewing a black cloth. She was dressed in a mail shirt with short boots and a long sword at her side.

"Why are you wearing armor?"

"Whezurs? Yulneet heronth feld."

"What?" I asked, looking around. "We are in the palace, not outside."

But the audience chamber had changed. It was still the same room, but the walls to the left and right of the woman were gone. Instead, to the right and to the left, there was only open country as far as the eye could see.

"Wasr fotn onenlos her. Hrie, timgoz."

"But I do not know what to do!"

At this the woman grunted and laughed and gestured to the left.

It was a horrible view. The line of knights continued to carry out the blood-covered bodies, but they were collecting them now from what remained of a charred castle and taking them to be burned in a large fire. Other knights were removing the armor from the bodies and anything else of value before throwing them into the fire. The sun was setting, and the sky was hazy from the black smoke. From the sheer number of bodies strewn about, it looked as though the burning detail would continue long into the night, possibly until morning. Women and children were kneeling over some of the dead that had not yet been collected, crying distractedly. One such corpse wore familiar green robes of office. A little away, a tall, large-bellied man with grayish hair and a beard was celebrating with his bearded knights.

I looked back at the old woman who was threading her needle.

"Can nothing be done to avert this?"

The old woman made some odd movement of her head and gestured to the right.

On what had been the right side of the audience chamber, there was now a peaceful view of commoners beginning their work in far away fields just as the sun was rising. The sky was brilliantly colored in yellows and pinks. The only sounds were of singing birds and lowing cows.

"I do not understand. What must I do?"

"Ponthem thway."

"Who?"

"Tcing!"

"No!"

"Ay!"

"No, I will not!"

"Yill!"

"This will not help!" I argued. "He will not listen to me! He will kill me!"

"Wearez urfath?"

She shook out what she was sewing then and showed it to me.

"It means nothing to me!" I screamed. "You are sewing my death shroud!"

"Ponthem thway," she said again.

"No! I will not! I will keep silent and live!"

"Sin sa ra-"

"No! I will not hear you!" I shouted.

I covered my ears and refused to listen. I screamed and screamed to drown her out. I would hear no more. I would listen no more.

I felt rough hands grab me. I opened my eyes, and two knights were trying to pick me up and carry me out with the rest of the dead.

"Wait! I am not dead!" I cried.

"Rouse yourself!"

The one had me by the shoulders, and the other grabbed up my feet. Despite my struggles and cries, they carried me out into the corridor where a knight with a long spear stabbed each of the abandoned corpses that lay in a huge pile in the corridor.

"Wake! Wake! The King needs soldiers! Wake and rise! Take arms!"

The knights who carried me suddenly threw me in the pile with all the other bodies. The smell of the rotting flesh filled my nostrils and sickened me even as the spear tore my skin, and the shouts to rouse and rise echoed around me.

Van Necht grabbed the knife under his fur mat and bolted upright. He looked around to find what had awakened him out of a sound sleep. The new scream coming from the other side of his tent answered the question. With the point of the knife, he lifted up the curtain and peered out at his prisoner. Not only was she screaming, but in writhing and fighting against her nightmare, she had knocked her coverlet off and somehow had managed to get one foot loose. With his heartbeat slowing, Van Necht put the knife back in its place and noticed it was raining.

She shrieked again and then whimpered.

"Rouse yourself! You are dreaming!" he called loudly.

To his irritation, she did not wake. He could hear her twisting about in her ropes as she whimpered in her sleep.

"Wake! Wake, I say!"

Again this accomplished nothing. Van Necht groaned and relinquished his warm bed. Wrapping a fur around him, he got to his feet in the cool night air and went through the opening of the curtain. He knelt down beside her, grabbed her by the shoulder and shook her.

"Wake! You are dreaming!"

Van Necht shook her hard then, and the definite register of pain jolted Acrida free of the dream's images. With her heart still pounding rapidly, Acrida blinked and shivered in the cold, slowly remembering where she was and why she was bound in this uncomfortable position.

"God's mercy, you are hard to rouse!"

Acrida looked blankly at Van Necht and wondered briefly why he was waking her up so early; it could not be near dawn yet. Then the memory of the terrible, vivid images in the dream returned to her suddenly, and she was once again very afraid.

Satisfied that he had awakened her, Van Necht pulled the fur coverlet back over her and returned to his half of the tent and his bed. He yawned and stretched and then pulled up his own coverlets. As he shut his eyes and began to drift off into sleep again, he heard the fresh sound of sobs. He ignored it; but the crying grew louder.

"If you do not want to sleep outside, you will control yourself!" he warned.

He rolled onto his side, his back towards his prisoner and pulled his pillow about his ears. He could still hear every whimper.

"Did you hear me?"

His question was answered with a moment of silence and then more weeping.

"God's wood! Go back to sleep, Woman!" Van Necht swore crossly.

"I cannot," she blubbered.

"Why not?"

"I am afraid," Acrida whined softly, as her nose itched from the new tears running down it which she was unable to wipe away.

"Of what? A dream?"

"Aye!" she answered with fresh crying.

As the sobbing continued, Van Necht's irritation grew. What could be the matter with her? he wondered. More importantly, how was he going to get his sleep?

Van Necht frowned as he considered his options: a gag would stop her words, but he would still have to endure the sound of her sobbing, he reasoned. On the other hand, his vassal, Sir Albern, said there were two sure ways of stopping a woman's tears -but there was no way *he* was going to *talk* to her for half the night. The other option was beneath his dignity.

The warlord resolved to ignore her, pulling his pillow more snugly around his ears. She would eventually quiet.

After enduring several more minutes of sobbing that showed no sign of lessening, the warlord got to his feet in exasperation, wrapped his fur coverlet back around himself once again, and grabbed the knife. If she revealed to anyone that he had done this, he would kill her, he promised himself.

Acrida heard him get up and the curtain open, and she whined, her heart beating fast. He was going to put her outside. She felt him cut the twine that bound her feet to her hands. She moaned as she stretched out, the relief flowing to her legs, back, arms and neck. There was no part of her that was not sore now.

He cut her ankles apart and then, in one motion, yanked her to her feet, which immediately gave out from numbness. Van Necht held her up and cut her wrists loose as well.

"Oh, please have mercy, My Lord! I- I have been through so much! -Please do not put me outside in the rain!" she wailed, her crying making her words almost incomprehensible. "I shall surely become ill!"

Van Necht made no reply; and to Acrida's surprise, she was not dragged toward the tent door, but through the slit in the curtain. Realizing she was headed to the alderman's bed, she began to panic anew.

"My Lord, not this! I was mistaken! I will be well outside! I would not want- to - to keep you awake any longer!"

It was only at that moment that Acrida noticed that Lord Van Necht was quite bare underneath the fur that he had wrapped around himself. She was so overcome with fear, in fact, that she immediately began to resist.

Lord Van Necht yanked the woman's arm up behind her sharply and pushed her forward in front of him.

"Owh-" Acrida complained, as the tears continued down her face.

"I do not know what is amiss with you," Van Necht said with hostility. "And I do not care. Your presence will not deny me a night's sleep."

He shoved her before him onto his fur bed on the ground. He pushed her down on her back and covered her up, and then he sat down beside her, pulling his coverlet up to his waist.

Acrida wanted to run, make a break for the door, fight and scream all at once, but would not allow herself, for fear of making it worse for herself. Mae's warning not to anger the alderman above all else was foremost in her mind. It was too late now, she knew; he was already irate, and she knew if she made him angrier, he might kill her in his fury.

She was so close to him that she could feel his warm, naked, flesh against her, and the air she breathed was fragranced with his scent. Her heart pounded violently; she swallowed hard and wiped her wet cheeks.

The first thing Van Necht noticed was that she was very cold. He leaned over and placed his hand on first her foot, and then moved it under her tunic, up her calf, noting the coldness of her skin.

Acrida trembled at his rough touch as she continued to weep, clutching her arms firmly around her.

"Be silent! Thou art more trouble than thou art worth!" he told her testily. "Peace, I say!"

Sobs shook Acrida as she gave into her despair.

Van Necht decided another coverlet was needed and grabbed an extra one that was lying nearby on the floor. He spread it over her feet. Then he lay down and roughly turned Acrida on her side and pulled her backward into his muscular chest and then draped his arm over her. He pushed his knee in-between her legs only to be rewarded by new sobs from his prisoner. This only further infuriated Van Necht.

"Stop weeping like a maid!"

Acrida gasped and cringed, but wiping away her tears, she said nothing, awaiting what he would do.

Satisfied with her silence, Van Necht added crossly, "If you wake me up again, I will give you cause to wail! Take me at my word!"

To her relief, he did nothing more.

After a long moment, she swallowed and took a deep breath, though her heart still pounded loudly in her ears. She was completely unsettled with the intertwining of their bodies and with the man's hand resting on her breast as it did, but she dared not move lest she disturb him. As she waited for him to fall asleep, she could feel his breath in her hair.

As her heartbeat slowed, she wondered, now that she was untied, if she could escape him once he was asleep. She would be very cold, however, without any shoes or her clothes. And how far could she get with her feet still so sore, and in the dark, without knowing the area? It was risky to even try, for if she moved at all, it might well wake him.

Well, at least she was no longer confined in that uncomfortable position, she thought. To try to calm herself further and to keep from thinking of the frightening images of her dream, she made herself listen to the rain and wonder what her aunt and uncle were doing. She thought back to what they usually did as they prepared for bed- talking about something they wanted to have or trade for or what they would own if they were a rich lord and lady. "A fine black horse," she could hear her uncle saying. He had always wanted a fine, black horse...

It was long after dawn when Acrida awoke. She was alone. Her head ached, and she was initially startled by the strange surroundings. After a moment, she remembered where she was and what she had dreamt the night before and what had happened with the lord. Realizing that she had completely mistook the man's intentions with her, Acrida was overcome with embarrassment. She wondered how she could face her captor. She did not have to think long, for Lord Van Necht entered the tent and the curtained area at that moment with the dog and handed his prisoner her gown and veil and some bread to eat. Then he went back out of the curtained area.

She cringed internally as she pulled the gown over her head and quickly laced up the front. She braided her hair and covered her head with the headrail. She could hear him rolling up the furs where she had been tied the night before.

The silence was uncomfortable for Acrida. Deciding that she had better apologize to him, lest he find further fault with her, Acrida began, "My Lord, forgive me for last nigh-"

"Can you sew?" he cut her off shortly.

"Sew? Aye, My Lord," she answered, surprised by the question.

"I have a whole stack of shirts and things that need mending. You can do that today."

"As you wish," she answered quietly.

She heard him leave the tent then. Frowning, Acrida picked up the bread and bit into it.

11

$\mathcal{A}$crida sat outside in the sunshine near the fire, needle and thread in hand, carefully sewing up the holes in the shirts and woolen braes. By habit, she checked the seams of each shirt and reinforced any that seemed to threaten to come apart. The warlord was sitting beside her with his tunic sleeves rolled up, sharpening and oiling his knives and swords and oiling his horse's tack. They had not said a word to each other the whole morning.

Out of the corner of her eye, she watched Van Necht's large biceps as they flexed methodically in the rhythmic process of sharpening each of his many knives. In the hours that came and went, Acrida guessed that the nobleman was probably thirty-seven or thirty-eight and in excellent health. His skin was tan from being outdoors, and he had rich brown hair with slight curls at the end that fell about his very muscular shoulders. His midsection was slim and a contrast to his very broad shoulders. He was the embodiment of power, suitable for a military commander and one whose title was the Queen's Royal Guard, she decided.

Compared to other men, his face was not so inviting; he had a strong jaw-line, and his face held a constant, very grave expression on his features. After trying to imagine him as a child, Acrida decided that Van Necht must not have had the angelic good looks that the King surely had had in his childhood- the kind of looks that will keep a mother from beating a wicked child when that child begins to charm. She suspected that Van Necht was punished every time he had done anything wrong; thus, he probably did not tolerate disobedience from anyone else either.

It was nearly noon when he finally broke the silence.

"Cinsara-" he said tentatively, as if he was testing the sound of the word in his ear.

Acrida looked up from her stitching.

"-An unusual name. -Mae told me," he added.

"No one but my mother ever called me that."

"How did you come to be called 'Acrida'?"

"I was prone to angry moods when I was a child. They were unpredictable. I have since grown out of them, but the name remained."

Van Necht raised his eyebrows only, without looking up from his work.

"At what were you angry?"

"Everything."

The warlord glanced at her. She returned to her sewing.

"My mother died when I was very young," she explained hesitantly. "My aunt and uncle raised me, but our village never let us forget the particulars surrounding my mother's death. -It is difficult for a child to live in such a place."

Van Necht sort of nodded in assent as he examined the straightness of one of the blades.

"Whose lands?"

"Lord Huntingdon's."

She was quiet then as she waited for him to press her for more details, but he did not.

Finally, he spoke again.

"Have you been to the King's bed?"

Acrida was so startled by his question that she pricked her finger, but then wondered whether it was the question or the matter-of-fact way he asked it that she had reacted to. She squeezed the finger noting the large drop of red blood that appeared. She looked at the lord sharply and rubbed the blood on her tunic sleeve.

"I would sooner die," she replied.

Van Necht looked at her in surprise.

Seeing his reaction, Acrida amended her words quickly.

"I mean, no, My Lord. The King would not have one such as me."

He regarded her curiously.

"What do you mean?"

"The King has an entire cart full of young girls for his bed, My Lord. He certainly does not need-" and she was shaking her head then.

"You are one of his servants then- and have displeased him?"

"His servant? No. I am a subject of Speyron, a serf to the lands of Lord Huntingdon- and innocent of wrong doing. In that way have I displeased the King," Acrida answered while returning to the sewing, the bitterness clear in her voice.

"I do not understand you rightly," Van Necht replied. "If you are neither his concubine nor his servant, how did you come to the King's notice? -And if you are innocent, why does he detain you? -And if you have not been to his bed, then why did he deliver you to me?"

Acrida's heart skipped a beat and then pounded. She did not look at the warlord as she asked, "The King has sent you -his concubines before?"

"Aye, presumably his best courtesans -though I found most to be *disappointing.*"

Acrida's stomach tied in knots at the nobleman's words, and she answered very quickly without looking at him.

"I know not why I am here, My Lord. Days ago I was taken from my village in the middle of the night and marched for four days to the palace."

"Most of the King's concubines are acquired in such a way."

"I was there to be questioned."

"For what purpose?"

"I know not -whether it was for the suspicion that I was encouraging simple folk to rise against their king- or for the crimes of my mother-" Acrida answered swiftly, silently rebuking herself for telling this stranger this much.

Lord Van Necht studied the young woman's face carefully, knowing by the way she refused to look at him that she was hiding something.

"Were you the only one to be questioned?"

"No, there were four men and a boy."

"Where are they?"

At this, Acrida looked at the warlord sharply.

"One was released. The others are quite dead, My Lord, as I, no doubt, shall soon be."

Van Necht's face was expressionless. He made no reply as he returned to sharpening a blade.

His lack of response angered Acrida.

"We were all innocent! -But that is the way of it in Speyron, is it not? The innocent suffer and die, and the wicked prosper! I have never spoken against the King, but allow me to do so now! Perhaps you will tell him, and he will order my execution that much sooner, if you do not prefer to carry it out immediately yourself!"

Lord Van Necht listened to his prisoner's response mutely, but was impressed at the passion in her voice and the anger and anguish that was apparent in her black and blue face.

"Our King is not God's chosen representative as everyone claims! King Christian is the Devil's man, and we, the villeins of the Devil, too! For as we commoners serve our manor lord and as his vassals have sworn their allegiance to him, as your vassals have sworn to you, so you aldermen have sworn allegiance to Christian. And King Christian is clearly the vassal to *the dark one!*"

The hair on the back of Van Necht's neck stood on end at her words.

"King Christian is a knave!" she declared. "I hate him and despise him and wish him ill! He is the killer of the innocent and the defiler of the sacred!"

So angry was Acrida now that tears began streaming down her cheeks.

"Oh, would that I were able to snuff out his life with my bare hands half as easily as he killed the others!"

She said no more, wiping her tears away with her sleeve. She threw the shirt she had been sewing back on the pile and got to her bruised, swollen feet, limping a few steps before she stopped.

As her anger subsided, Acrida's face flushed red as she silently reprimanded herself for not minding her tongue. In truth, this was a good way to get beaten again, if not killed immediately. In fact, her words might have already condemned her. She glanced nervously to her captor to see his response.

Nothing came immediately, however.

"Did the King kill another priest?" he asked at last.

"What?" Acrida asked, caught off guard again.

"You said the King was 'the defiler of the sacred'. What did he do?"

"You ask that so indifferently," she replied quietly.

"Well?"

Acrida shook her head and flinched at the memory.

"No. He did not kill a priest."

She faltered as the memory of that terrible event came back to her. Immediately, the sound of the people screaming as they fled the church and the look on the faces of the priests, the nun, and the knights were vivid in her mind. Once again the tears welled in her eyes; she pressed down the memory and the approaching flood of tears by taking a deep breath.

"What did he do?"

Acrida swallowed.

"You will not believe me."

"Speak. I know of many of the acts of King Christian and King Filberte before him."

The tears ran rapidly, but silently, down her face. Acrida shook her head again, bitterly.

"The church at the palace-. Do you know of it?"

"Aye."

Van Necht saw his prisoner's darkly bruised face contort as she spoke and noticed how her hand covered her eyes as if trying to shield herself from the memory. It was clear to him that her treatment at the hands of the King had hurt her deeply; her spirit in many ways was more battered and bruised than her body.

"King Christian interrupted Mass and sent the people home."

Van Necht raised his eyebrows.

"But that was not enough for him-" she continued.

Van Necht watched as the tears poured down her cheeks.

"There he discovered a girl who had taken holy vows and-"

Van Necht sighed inwardly, guessing what had happened.

"I do not know the King," she was saying between sobs, her voice hollow. "He was angry about the nun, but-"

"He added her to his concubines, I suppose," Van Necht cut in, sensing how upset his prisoner was becoming.

"No-" she answered, vividly seeing in her mind the King throw the hosts against the wall, the wafers flying everywhere, then watching him shove the other holy vessels off the altar. "He -attacked-"

"The priests?"

"-The Corpus Christi. -He desecrated- the blessed -*Corpus Christi!*" she cried.

Van Necht's heart skipped a beat. His prisoner had been correct; this was difficult to believe.

"He- he - laid his hand on the most sacred *Body of our Lord* and *threw* it against the wall! *As if it were nothing!*"

In her rage, Acrida was weeping uncontrollably then and laughing.

"-And still he was not content! Still he was determined to- to desecrate the church and altar further!"

She wiped her face with her sleeve and sobbed more, as she once again saw the King uncover the head of the nun and ridicule her.

"The King took this nun to the altar and- and- and- now it is all defiled!"

Van Necht raised his eyebrows and watched as his prisoner dropped to her knees, laughing and screaming in fury.

"Oh, God! God! God! Where are You that You allow this?"

She, with her arms wrapped about her, wept with her face in the dirt.

"King Christian *swyved* a nun on the altar?" he asked incredulously, marveling at the audacity of the King.

He had heard many terrible deeds of this young man and been a witness of a few himself, but all the others paled in comparison to this. He wondered if this could be true.

"No," Acrida answered with a laugh, "the King was not satisfied with his own damnation. He - he ordered some of his knights to do it."

These words left Van Necht chilled to his very core. He sat mutely as his prisoner gave herself to fresh weeping, all the while throwing fists of dirt onto herself, while asking God repeatedly why this was allowed to happen. As Van Necht observed her, he shivered as he concluded, among other things, that his prisoner's misery had brought her to madness.

12

Van Necht sat stirring the fire. It was another dark, cloudy autumn day, an omen of the cold winter that would come. This kind of day made all variety of creatures sleepy.

He rubbed his eyes and looked at the hound to the right of him. The dog lay on its side, eyes shut in deep slumber. The lord patted its side. Startled, the dog jerked awake; however, once seeing that the danger was only its master, it flopped its tail twice, yawned widely, and lay down again to sleep. Van Necht sighed in disgust.

The lord yawned and stretched and stared blankly at the dancing, orange flames of the fire, listening to it pop and crackle. He could do with a nap himself, he admitted. It was not the fear of his prisoner escaping that hindered him getting a full night of rest, but the woman's persistent nightmares. He had given up having a bed to himself, preferring to keep her close at hand so that he might wake her immediately when she began to cry out in her sleep. Also, his close proximity seemed to soothe her as she was able to fall asleep faster after a nightmare, which meant he did too.

Across from him, Van Necht's prisoner sat sewing quietly. She had finished mending his shirts and braes two days before. In an effort to keep her busy, Van Necht had found some tawny-colored cloth tucked away among his things and had bade her to make him a shirt using his old ones as a pattern. As he watched her, he wondered again who she was and what the King intended to do with her.

From all outward appearances, she looked like any other peasant woman. Her hands were rough with calluses, and her arms were thick and muscular from work. The skin that was not bruised on her face, neck, and arms was tan from the sun, and her nails were dirty. She had probably been working in the fields before all this had started, Van Necht thought. She also wore her hair in the style of an unmarried woman although she was quite old.

Perhaps she was a widow, Van Necht considered. She never made mention of a husband, nor of children, although she should have had some surviving children by now.

Although he was loathed to admit it, Van Necht did find her less annoying than most women. First, and most importantly, she was quiet. Most women complained constantly, and others talked on and on just to hear themselves chatter, and then there were the gossips.- Cinsara, however, seldom spoke unless he addressed her.

As he looked at the discolored flesh of her still swollen face, Van Necht tried to imagine what she had looked like before the beating. But even this was difficult because her usual features were so distorted or obscured altogether. Even her blue eyes were hardly noticeable among the purple and yellow of her bruised skin.

At least her hair had not come under attack. It was long, smooth, and thick- and as black as a night with no moon. She kept it braided and concealed under her veil as propriety required, although she loosed it every night before they went to sleep as he bade her.

She was also rather tall. All in all, she would have had a satisfactory form except that she was disadvantaged by small breasts. Except for the breadth of her hips and length of her hair, she could almost have passed for a boy, Van Necht supposed, particularly since at present, she was so thin, which he concluded was the result of her ordeal with the King. It was really a wonder that she had not become seriously ill.

"My Lord, this is ready to try."

Van Necht looked up to see Acrida standing over him proffering the shirt. He stood up and in one motion pulled the tunic he was wearing over his head, revealing his brawny chest, shoulders, and arms which were marked by a few scars that affirmed his profession as warlord. Acrida handed him the shirt and looked away. Van Necht noted her manner and the modesty it communicated.

He slipped the shirt over his head and held out his arms. The garment was well cut and sewn. There was plenty of room to move his arms. Acrida approached him then and marked the length of the sleeves with a bit of soap.

"My Lord, what length do you wish it?"

Van Necht pointed to just above the knee and observed with amusement as Acrida, purposefully avoiding his front, moved to his side and marked the spot on the side seam.

"You are talented," Van Necht remarked.

"No, My Lord."

"Have you worked as a seamstress for Huntingdon?"

"No, My Lord. There is nothing special about my skill that would mark me worthy to be in his service."

"You sew for your husband and family then?"

"I make my uncle and aunt's clothes, My Lord," she replied. "I have no husband."

"Why is that?"

Acrida cringed internally and tried to think of an answer he would find suitable.

"In my village, there are many daughters of marrying age and few sons," she told him simply.

"Oh," Van Necht replied with a nod. "Have you considered a match with someone from a village on neighboring lands?"

"My family is very poor, as is the entire village. Few have the means to pay the formariage fees to Lord Huntingdon for such a match."

Van Necht hesitated for a moment, considering her words, and then took off the shirt and handed it back to her. He turned and put on his original tunic again, exposing, as he did, his back to his prisoner.

As he turned back to her, he saw by the startled look on her face that she had seen the unsightly, twisted scar on his back. The startled look transformed into a pained expression before his eyes.

"It does not hurt," he told her.

"Forgive me, My Lord. I-" she said quickly, embarrassed that he had noticed her stare.

"It was a grave wound; it would not heal for the longest time."

Acrida turned away from him and hurried back to her spot and quickly searched for her needle. Van Necht frowned.

"No, forgive me!" he said bitterly. "I should remember to keep myself covered in front of women lest my nakedness repulse them."

Acrida looked back at him, surprised.

"My Lord, you mistake me. I was noting the seriousness of the scar only and was trying to fathom what it was to receive such a wound as that must have been and then to return to fight in other battles again and again. -How brave you must be, My Lord. You are so much braver than anyone I have ever known."

Her soft words caught Van Necht off guard, and his sarcasm left him immediately.

"When I saw your scars," she continued nervously, "I was not thinking them repulsive, but how much pain you must have experienced in battle when receiving them-" and Acrida, filled with self-consciousness, said no more, quickly turning away to return to her sewing.

Although Van Necht longed to hear what she would say next, he left her at peace, contemplating her words. His attention was shortly distracted as he noticed a man walking up the path from the village. In a little while, the man had arrived at the fire, with a bow to Van Necht and a concerned glance at the black and blue, bruised face of the woman who was sewing.

"Good day, Lord Van Necht."

"Good day, Father."

Acrida glanced at the wiry, little man with curiosity.

"I have not seen you at Mass of late, My Lord."

"Aye, you have not."

"Well, I will not see you there some days to come, I fear."

"How is that, Father?"

"This time the King has gone too far! -I just received word. His Grace the Bishop has put all of Speyron under interdict!"

Lord Van Necht sighed and frowned.

"When I heard this, I asked, 'What has he done this time?' Do you know what he did this time, My Lord?" the priest asked with some passion.

Van Necht had no time to reply.

"He disrupted the Mass and *desecrated* the Sacraments and the altar in the church at the palace! *The Sacraments!!* The very precious and innocent Body and Blood of our Savior that was broken and shed for our deliverance!! And at *his own* church! The church where he himself was baptized! The church where his mother and father and grandfather and great grandfather all heard Mass and received Holy Communion! It is unbearable! What can be said of such a man as this?!"

Van Necht sighed again.

"So, by the order of the Bishop, there will be no more Masses, nor any sacraments administered to the people of Speyron! Furthermore, His Grace the Bishop has forbidden all burial! We are to reap the benefit of seeing the rotting bodies of our neighbors eaten by curs and rats."

Van Necht sighed and rubbed his forehead. This could not have come at a worse time.

"And the stench-" the little man continued.

"What are your instructions?" Van Necht interrupted. "Will you remain here?"

"My Lord, the priests have been instructed to flee their posts in areas where they fear reprisals from the King. Since there is no reason to believe that the King will retaliate against the Church here, I am inclined to stay and suffer among my flock- and continue to look after your lordship's accounts."

Lord Van Necht nodded his head.

"Very well, Father."

After a few more avid complaints, the priest took his leave of the alderman and headed back up the path toward the village. Van Necht then turned to check on his prisoner only to find her wearing a grave expression as she stared off into space, rocking back and forth with her arms wrapped tightly around her.

13

In the bright, cool, crisp midmorning, the three riders trotted up the road under the splendid, colored canopy of the changing trees. As they entered the bustling village, they slowed their horses to a walk, and the inhabitants momentarily paused their varied activities to observe the strangers.

Two of the riders wore shirts of mail and swords under their cloaks; the other man wore expensive clothes of dark crimson fabric underneath a long, crimson mantle which fluttered in the breeze. The villagers returned to their work, concluding at once the noblemen had come to see their alderman.

"'Tis a lively place," said the younger of the two knights, noticing the many cottages and huts along the road and the many people busy with their work.

"It only seems so because there is no castle about, Sir Ecktor," Lord Dewain replied. "One does not notice the activities of serfs in the shadow of a tower."

"Have they begun to gather the supplies to rebuild Lord Van Necht's castle yet?" the young knight asked.

"Not that I have heard tell of," answered the older knight. "In fact, I do not know if there are any current plans to rebuild."

"Really?"

"That is my suspicion also," Lord Dewain agreed. "For the servant household have all built homes in the village now. I believe the steward lives in the large cottage down the way."

"His servants have to come daily all the way from the village to wait upon him? How is that convenient?" Ecktor asked.

Dewain cleared his throat.

"They say Lord Van Necht detests all company and will not even suffer a servant to wait upon him."

"No castle or servants? How does he survive? -And what of his guests? Surely he does not turn them away," the young knight protested.

"Van Necht ordered an inn of sorts to be built right after the castle burned. The former castellan of the castle is the caretaker. Any guest of the lord stays there," Lord Dewain answered.

"Aye, there it is," replied the older knight, pointing to a building on the road, beside the empty, village stocks. "Right near the church and that tavern."

"Do we have time to stop?" Ecktor asked, eyeing again the symbol for ale that had been placed outside a few of the huts along the road.

"Not this time," Dewain smiled.

After passing through the village, the riders followed the road that eventually led to a path through a large, open field.

"Sir Eldwin," began the youth, "what precautions must we take with this sorceress? They say you must bind a witch's hands so that she can not cast a spell; blindfold her so she can not put the evil eye on you, and tie down her mouth so that she cannot speak evil against you."

"-But that is no different from the usual management of a wife," Sir Eldwin said with a robust laugh.

The youth and the Chancellor chuckled.

"Thou art a wit! But in all seriousness-" Ecktor continued.

"Yet-" Eldwin said with a smile and wink to Lord Dewain, "none of those precautions is said to hinder shape-shifting."

"God's Wood! I forgot all about it! To be completely safe, we *must* knock her unconscious before we take her back to the castle!"

Dewain smiled and shook his head.

"I do not think that will be necessary, Sir Ecktor."

"We should have brought more knights!" the youth continued. "How will the King put her to death if she should escape us? We will surely be made to answer for it."

"No worries!" Sir Eldwin laughed. "We will tell him it was *your* fault she escaped- and *your head* can hang upon the wall!"

"God's Mercy!" the youth swore, crossing himself. "God's Mercy!"

"Calm thyself, Lad! I jest with you only!" Sir Eldwin laughed.

"'Twas not amusing!" the youth complained.

After a little while, the riders came upon a clearing on a rise. There the huge tent stood with its black banner flapping in the breeze. A campfire smoldered before the entrance. To the right, a black horse grazed inside a corral, but the riders saw no one.

"It is as you say-" Ecktor marveled, crossing himself, "he lives entirely alone."

"Lord Van Necht!" Sir Eldwin called out. "My Lord!"

The fall breeze whistled through the trees in response.

"Where could he be?" Lord Dewain murmured.

"The witch has likely already murdered him-" Sir Ecktor answered.

Dewain gave him a look and then gestured toward the tent.

The youth jumped off his mount and ran and entered the tent; he soon came out reporting no one inside. Eldwin rode his horse past the tent up onto a slope. He saw the lord down by the side of a stream gutting fish.

"Lord Van Necht!" he called with a wave, then he signaled to Dewain.

The horses sauntered down the hill. Van Necht rinsed his hands in the stream and wiped them on his tunic before standing up. The men stopped their horses in front of him and dismounted, the knights bowing.

"Lord Chancellor Dewain, welcome," he said.

"Good day, Van Necht."

"Sir Eldwin, Sir Ecktor, it is good to see you again."

"Likewise, My Lord. We are relieved to see you in such good health. Has your prisoner been much of a burden to you?" Sir Eldwin asked.

"She was hurt when she arrived here. She is much improved but still is not herself."

"Cure her, did you?" Sir Ecktor laughed. "A wasted effort since the King will surely execute her."

"Do you bring her death warrant?" Van Necht asked.

"No. Grey, Olbert, and I wish to speak with her again," Dewain said with a smile. "We were going to send these two trustworthy knights, but they would not come to retrieve her by themselves, so here am I, also."

"Methinks one of you would have been enough, but perhaps 'twas wise forethought, in her current state of madness," Van Necht said.

"What? Are you certain?" Dewain asked with real concern.

"Madness, too?" the knights marveled.

"Aye."

"Surely additional precautions must be taken now!" Sir Ecktor said. "She *must* be knocked unconscious!"

"In truth, I do not think she will prove a danger to you, for she has clear moments in which she seems as any other woman; other times, when her grief overtakes her, she behaves in the most unnatural fashion."

"Where is she, My Lord, and the boy and I will retrieve her," Eldwin said.

"At the camp. Did you not see her when you rode up?"

The three men looked at each other.

"No, My Lord, there is no one there."

The pleasant expression fell from Van Necht's face.

"Not there?"

"She must have gotten loose. To what did you have her tied?" Sir Ecktor asked.

"Nothing," Van Necht answered irritably, walking up the hill past them.

"Nothing! -Did you not take any precautions?!" the young knight stammered.

"Precautions against what?"

"Lord Van Necht," Dewain called from behind him, "am I to understand that you have allowed a prisoner to roam wherever she pleased, unsupervised, and while plagued with madness?"

"It will not be *my* head upon the wall after all-" Sir Ecktor whispered under his breath.

Van Necht did not answer. In truth, he had relaxed his guarding of this particular prisoner for the simple reason that for the several days that she had been in his custody, she had never made any attempt to flee. In fact, she seemed to feel *safe* in his company, but from what, Van Necht was still unsure.

Today, she had wanted to wash the clothes that she wore, and he had given her some soap and bade her, not only to wash them, but to bathe in the stream as well. He had even given her a fresh tunic, braes, and wraps of his own to wear while her clothes dried. The last time he had seen her, she was going back up to the tent to lay out her wet clothes.

As the three men walked their horses back up the hill to the camp behind Van Necht, Lord Dewain's stomach began to churn. The Chancellor forced himself to be calm. Her escape was only a temporary delay, he knew. No one could actually escape from Van Necht, he reminded himself; he was too skilled in the arts of war. It was only a matter of time before she was discovered. -However, if Van Necht was correct and the lass had gone mad, all of their plans could be ruined.

Van Necht scanned the camp and cursed. They were correct; she was no where to be seen. He went inside the tent and not finding her there, he began looking around to see what was missing.

All the blankets and furs were there. The bread was still in its basket. Even the leather water sack was there. Either she was very dull and had tried to get away without any provisions or else she was not going very far. How long had it been since he had seen her? Maybe an hour?

He came out of the tent, saying, "She is still lame. -She can not walk very long without stopping to rest."

He looked at the two knights.

"Ecktor, you go that way," he pointed, "and Eldwin, you go that way. I will go-"

"No, Your Lordship. Not me. I am not going to hunt a mad witch by myself," Sir Ecktor answered.

"A what?" Van Necht stopped to look at him.

"A witch. She is a witch," Ecktor repeated.

The look of genuine surprise on the normally expressionless face of Van Necht could not be mistaken.

"Did no one tell you, My Lord?"

Van Necht looked at the young knight in disbelief and then at Dewain. The look on the Chancellor's face confirmed the allegation immediately.

"Van Necht-" Dewain began, raising his hands as he tried to calm him.

The Chancellor knew well of the warlord's temper and already saw the dangerous expression on the man's face.

"A witch?" Van Necht snarled. "I have been guarding a *witch*? I have spent the night -several nights, *unprotected*, with a witch?"

"You did not-?" Sir Ecktor immediately asked. "-Not with her!"

Suddenly, Lord Van Necht grabbed the Chancellor by the neck of his clothes, clamping his other hand on his throat. The expression of fear on the face of Dewain was echoed on the faces of the surprised knights. Carefully, Eldwin and Ecktor tried to pull Van Necht off Dewain before the Chancellor was seriously hurt, but the warlord was unaffected by their efforts. He continued to squeeze the Chancellor's throat, threatening to crush it in his mighty hands.

"Why was I not told?" Van Necht asked Dewain through clenched teeth.

"Van Necht- I do not know why you were not informed!" Dewain answered barely above a whisper, gasping frantically for air under the lord's grip. "But we are not certain she is a witch. She has denied it, and she has done nothing- no spells or anything."

Seeing some truth in what he said, Van Necht slowly let go of the alderman, though his anger was far from quelled. While the Chancellor tried to catch his breath, Van Necht tried to control his temper.

Van Necht immediately understood the circumstances then. It explained why she had been bound so strangely when she arrived. No wonder the King had not wanted her for himself- or dared to have her, for that matter. He wondered briefly if she had done anything to him while he had slept. He definitely should never have brought her to his bed or even into his tent for that matter. He should not have allowed her access to anything. -Heaven only knew what spell she had sewn into his shirts. He would have to burn them all now.

He should have kept her tied up, he berated himself. If he had had any idea that she was a witch, he would have kept her tied up the entire time- and as far away from himself as possible.

But then he began to remember her nightmares, the multitude of bruises on her body, her copious weeping, fatigue, hunger, and her miserable expression. His gut had told him there was nothing to fear from her, and his gut was seldom, if ever, wrong.

Well, witch or no witch, he was responsible for her, and she was clearly not here.

"Let us just find her. We will split up- but if you see her or any evidence of her, yell loudly, and I will collect her myself."

"I will not go into the woods!" Sir Ecktor said quickly.

"Then I will search them-" Van Necht answered disgusted.

The youth nodded and walked in the direction of the lord's horse, crunching through the tall, dying grass. The older knight went back in the direction of the stream. The Chancellor turned and walked back toward the road. Van Necht walked quickly away from the tent toward the woods.

"God's Eyes!" the young knight suddenly swore, crossing himself at once.

The other three men turned abruptly towards him.

"What is it?"

"She has shape-shifted! Heaven help us!" Sir Ecktor yelled, excitedly looking around him.

Van Necht and the others looked at him incredulously.

"Look! Here are her clothes!" he added, holding up the damp gown. "We will never find her now!"

"Keep looking!" Van Necht ordered, shaking his head irritably, as he entered into the shade of the protective, orange and yellow trees.

Ignoring the cows that regarded her suspiciously among the timber a little away from her, Acrida examined the moist bark of a tall tree and noticed the mold growing on its side. A few feet away from her the white hound sniffed at some fallen leaves and then snapped at a bug.

Acrida hobbled along further carefully allowing her nose to guide her. She examined the sprouts on the ground. A few, withered, brown stalks still stood above the dirt and leaves in the intermittent sunlight. She knelt down and grasped the largest set of sprouts firmly in her hand and pulled slowly. The dirt moved, and she pulled out the bulbous root of the plant. She raised the bulb to her nose. The pungent odor made her wrinkle her nose. She pulled up another one, placing it with all the other leaves she had picked in the pouch created by the ends of the tunic that she held. Then she summoned the dog with the gesture of her hand and got up and hobbled back the way she had come.

Hearing dried leaves crunch underfoot to the right of her, Acrida turned and saw Van Necht coming to meet her. The dog left her side and trotted to its master, wagging its tail.

"How now, My Lord? I have a surprise for you-" she called with a shy smile.

Heated and angry, Van Necht bristled. In his mind, he could easily imagine what sort of 'surprise' might be in store for him, thinking quickly of the sort of poisonous plants the woman had had time to gather.

As he neared her, the smile fell from her face as she saw he was sticky with sweat and dirty from walking through the woods, and his expression was fierce.

When Van Necht reached her, he grabbed her veil and the long black braid it covered and yanked her down to her knees in front of him. Acrida shrieked, realizing too late that she had done something to anger him. She immediately began to plead in a voice of panic, but before she could say anything substantial, his free hand struck her bruised face soundly, and she was knocked flat to the ground.

Van Necht reached down to snatch her up again, but Acrida, desperate and afraid, held herself to the ground, crying, "Forgive me, My Lord! What have I done?"

"I- trusted you!" Van Necht snarled.

He grabbed her by her hair again and struck her exposed ear forcefully. Acrida fell over, shrieking, and at once tried to crawl away from him now as fast as she could, but the warlord had her, and he struck her again mercilessly. She raised her arms to protect her head.

Van Necht, in a fury, climbed on top of her; straddling her, he rolled her over to face him, preparing to strike her again. The terror in her eyes, her tears, and the bloody lip momentarily lulled his anger, and he was in control again. He took a deep breath and looked away. On the ground beside them lay her headrail, wild garlic, and bits of leaves.

Van Necht took a deep breath and ran his hand through his hair and looked at a startled cow in the distance. She had not been trying to escape, and perhaps she had no intentions other than gathering garlic and other herbs for dinner. He considered again the possibility that she had intended to feed him a poisonous plant- but even he doubted that.

He looked down at her again, noting her face, distorted from crying, and her terrified eyes, not daring to meet his gaze. As he moved, she shied, expecting another blow.

She smelled of soap and perspiration. Despite the knowledge that she might be a witch, Van Necht had to struggle against the urge to take her, for fighting quickened his blood in more ways than one.

He climbed off of her wordlessly and bent down and picked the veil and his prisoner up, and with her over his shoulder, he carried her back to the camp, leaving her collections behind.

As the blood rushed to her head, Acrida's head pounded painfully as he carried her. She blinked at the tears and berated herself for not trying to escape, for trusting him, for believing him a descent man, for believing she was safe with him! God only knew what he was going to do to her now!

The dog led the way back to camp wagging its tail. Once in the clearing, Van Necht called loudly to the others, who were still in sight.

As the three men headed back toward the tent, Van Necht, having set Acrida down, watched her as he wet a rag with some water. He tossed it to her. She took it and wiped her eyes and wet cheeks and dabbed it on her bleeding lip.

Angry and bitter, she sat in silence as the knights approached. When she saw the Chancellor in his crimson clothes of office, however, Acrida's demeanor changed immediately. For a moment, she could not take her eyes from the color. Then, without thinking, she was on her feet, fleeing back toward the woods. Her sore feet shot pain through her body, but she ignored it.

Lord Van Necht was temporarily startled by the flight of his prisoner; then like a hound after a hare, he was instantly running after her. The others stood amazed as they watched Acrida trip over a log, land in a bush, and still get back to her feet, limping, screaming at the top of her lungs, even while the warlord pursued her.

Acrida's heart was beating violently, and despite her screaming, she could hear him behind her. As she neared the forest edge, a tremendous weight hit her on the back as the lord fell upon her. Acrida collapsed under him, hitting the ground again, the breath knocked out of her. Gasping for air underneath his weight, her only thoughts were of escape.

"Let me go!" she wailed in despair. "Please, let me go! I have done nothing!"

Having stopped her, Van Necht was on his feet again, breathing hard. He grabbed the back of the tunic and braes she wore. But Acrida had caught hold of a pair of young saplings near their root and refused to be pulled from the earth.

"Do not take me back! No! Kill me here, but return me not to the King!"

Lord Van Necht sighed and, gritting his teeth, pried his prisoner from the ground. In one smooth motion, he had his prisoner over his shoulder again, her head keeling toward the ground. She wailed dizzily, and the blood pounded around her ears again. Confined in his grasp, Acrida began to cry like a disturbed woman while her captor carried her back to the men. He set her down on the ground, and she rolled on her side, continuing to whimper.

The three men regarded her hesitantly. Could this be the same woman who had spoken so boldly to the King almost a fortnight before? Van Necht was correct; she was clearly mad, and her spirit seemed wholly broken.

"God's eyes! Look at her clothes!" Sir Ecktor suddenly said, crossing himself. "She shape-shifted into a man!"

Van Necht and Dewain gave the youth a tired look.

Lord Chancellor Dewain walked up and squatted down before her.

"How now, Acrida? What is all this? You have nothing to fear. It is not the King who summons you, but the King's counselors. I assure you, you are in no danger."

His words were met by laughter.

Dewain glanced at Van Necht and then at the two knights. Nor did Acrida's laughter cease, but continued on unchecked.

"I speak the truth. The other advisers, Lords Olbert and Grey, and I need to talk with you again. Something has happened. Do you know what it is?"

Acrida's stomach continued to twist painfully at the thought of returning to the palace.

"I do not know, nor do I care!"

"We want your counsel, Acrida."

"Mine?" she answered. "Very well, avoid the King and flee Speyron! Otherwise, I have none to give."

"It is not wise to jest in such a way," Dewain warned.

"Believe you that I jest? Thou art doomed! Help yourself, for I can help you not!"

"We believe you can. We believe the King will listen to you."

"Ha!" she laughed hard.

"Truly, you are the first to speak so boldly to him and survive his wrath- besides King Filberte's old jester. It is important that we get King Christian to listen to what we are trying to tell him."

"So why do you not employ the Court Jester to tell him?"

"Alas," he answered, "Tate was a very good jester to King Filberte, but upon the King's death and His Grace's coronation, King Christian shunned him. Thus, the King has no fool, and Tate has lost his position. The King tolerates Tate to live, but that is all."

"So to the point, My Lord, would you make me the Court Fool? Frankly, there are others better suited for the position," she said defiantly, sitting up and wiping her face.

Van Necht raised his eyebrows at the comment. The knights smiled.

"For now, just come to Court and speak with us.-"

Acrida laughed bitterly.

"I see! You would not even afford me the little protection that the Court Fool receives for bad jests! Your meaning is clear to me, My Lord! You want someone to whom the sword may fall, and it will make little difference. If you employ me to give the King bad news, then he will order my death, not yours or the other advisers."

A slim smile crossed Dewain's features.

"You are a clever lass, Acrida. Make it work to your advantage," he said, getting back to his feet.

Van Necht stepped a short distance away from Acrida and gestured for Dewain. The Chancellor went over to him.

"She told me that four of the others that were brought in with her were executed and one was set free," he said quietly.

"It is so. The King brought in all those rumored to be seers in the kingdom. He released one of the two that had not the gift and killed the others."

"Does she see the future?" Van Necht asked.

"Those in her village say so."

"Why did the King spare her?"

"Olbert and I begged for her life."

"Even so, think you she will be of use to you in her present madness?"

"Perhaps, for she is fearless and does not crumble under the King's gaze! She dared speak her mind to him! She was even bold enough to refuse to answer his questions, even though he had her beaten!"

"*She* - fearless?" Van Necht questioned skeptically.

"Aye, truly, Van Necht, have you not noticed?" Sir Eldwin added, "This woman has bigger bullocks than the manor bull."

"I have noticed nothing of the kind."

"Well, Van Necht," Sir Eldwin concluded with a teasing smile, "perhaps you have *bewitched* the witch."

The other men smiled. Van Necht looked dryly back at them.

"We had better be on our way," Dewain said. "Is she well enough to ride?"

"Do we dare risk putting her on a horse by herself?" Sir Eldwin asked. "What if she flees with it?"

"Better to knock her unconscious and tie her to a pack horse."

"T'would be wise to have her ride with someone else," Dewain said.

"Who?" Sir Eldwin asked.

"Not I!" said Sir Ecktor.

"Forsooth, my horse is already winded from the journey here. I think we shall travel too slow if she rides with me, My Lord," Eldwin said.

Lord Dewain simply smiled and mounted his own chestnut horse. The three men turned then and looked meaningfully at Van Necht.

"Van Necht, you must accompany us anyway. After all, she is still in your charge," Dewain added with a shrug.

Van Necht turned silently, went into his tent, and returned wearing his sword and belt and carrying a bridle and a saddle. He had known all along to what conclusion these three would come.

He quickly caught his large, black horse. Its coat and mane, bleached reddish-brown by the sun, was already thick for approaching winter. He saddled it and led it out of the corral.

Then Van Necht walked over and pulled Acrida to her feet. She jerked her arm away from him and straightened her tunic. Van Necht handed her the headrail that had fallen off her head in the woods.

Acrida covered her head, irritably. He had beaten her, she reasoned, only to impress these men. She did not want to be near him at all, and now she was going to have to ride double with him.

Van Necht stood by the horse's neck and held the tall horse still. He took hold of Acrida and shoved her into the saddle gracelessly. Then he put his foot in the stirrup and pulled himself onto the horse just behind the saddle. The horse stepped forward at the added weight, and the four horses walked toward the village.

"Hold on to the mane and do not clamp your legs around the horse," he directed.

Acrida could smell the lord's scent, and it made her angry. Her back was against his chest as it was, and their legs touched; and it all made her seethe, but she remained silent.

After they had gone through the village, the group began to lope to make better time. Van Necht, with one hand in front of Acrida holding the reins, reached his other hand around her waist to keep her from falling off. That was the last straw for Acrida, and in one swift movement, she rammed her elbow into his abdomen with all of her might. The blow caught the lord off guard. He sharply leaned back and pulled up on the reins.

The horse stopped. The other three riders stopped also. Grabbing her veil and hair, he pulled her face back close to his and said in a very controlled manner:

"Woman-"

"Take your hands off me, You Bastard!"

Van Necht was not a little surprised at this remark.

"Ah, I see she has found her tongue," Sir Eldwin remarked, nodding with amusement. "You should have heard her at Court."

Van Necht tightened his grip on her hair and said, "I shall touch you as it pleases me. Strike me again, and you will regret it, I assure you."

"Why seek an excuse to beat me?" she snarled. "You delight in it so."

"You have yet to sample my wrath, Woman. Mind you do not provoke my fury lest you are prepared to meet it."

Acrida made no reply. She knew Van Necht was as good as his word, and if she made him any angrier, he would beat her again, this time in front of these men. Van Necht let go of her hair abruptly and repositioned his arm around her, and she forced herself to tolerate his touch in silence.

"Aptly named, is she not, My Lord?" Sir Ecktor chuckled.

"Aye, she makes good the petition of men to be allowed to cut out the tongues of women," Sir Eldwin answered.

Van Necht nudged the horse forward into a walk then.

"Truly, she might make a good wife for the Devil-" Sir Ecktor added cheerfully.

Van Necht was silent, still amazed by Acrida's change in nature.

"I prefer a soft woman," continued the young knight. "One that is soft in tongue, temperament and body."

"That is not a rare combination," replied Lord Dewain. "The King's cousin, Lady Kaithryn, may well turn out that way. I have not yet heard the lady raise her voice in anger. If you would yet marry well, Lord Van Necht, she may be the very one for you."

"Hmph!" Van Necht scoffed. "I have married well before, and neither the marriage nor the "marrying well" was well for me. Speak no more of marriage. Besides, there must be a score or more between the lady's age and mine. By the time she was grown to womanhood, I would be too old and blind to enjoy her."

The four men laughed again.

14

The saddle was a source of support, but Acrida still bounced along unbearably at any rate other than a walk. Unfortunately for her, they rode the majority of the way to the palace at a fast trot. The only thing that kept her from falling off the horse was the lord's secure arm about her waist.

After explaining the correct way to sit a horse and then repeatedly ordering her to relax, Van Necht finally gave up on the woman whose apprehension alone at returning to the palace was enough to cause her to be tense. Thus, Van Necht endured her bouncing in silence as did the horse, its ears laid back against its head in irritation. By the time the riders reached King Christian's palace, Van Necht, Acrida, and the horse were all sore and exhausted.

Groups of peasants stood together in the fields outside the palace walls, hardly minding the herds of sheep and cows that grazed among the remaining stubble in the harvested fields. The serfs engaged in conversation as they watched the great influx of travelers on the road coming to the palace. Neither did Acrida notice the idle peasants, nor the great throng of people traveling the road with her, for with the palace looming overhead, her stomach had tightened again painfully in fear.

As the sweating horses reached the top of the steep hill and approached the main gate, Acrida recognized the head of Adamson on the left side of the gate beside the two skulls that had been there previously. She looked away quickly, but was suddenly confronted by the faces of the three seers. The heads of the wild man, the child, and old Jebedye, hung in unending silence on the wall on the right side of the gate.

Acrida screamed and recoiled so violently that she fell off the horse into the dust on the ground. Startled, the horses jumped away from her and began to pitch and rear.

Even the pain of hitting the ground was not enough to distract Acrida. She simply could not tear her eyes from the horrible sight, despite herself. The ashen and filth covered expressions of her former companions sagged in perpetual misery before her. Flies entered and exited their empty eye sockets, nostrils, and open mouths; each of their tongues hung beside their heads, nailed into the stone of the wall.

Having finally gotten control of his exited charger which was bucking and kicking out at everything around it, Van Necht once again glanced back at his prisoner who sat raving in the middle of the road. Despite the other two knights' shouts, the danger of the rearing, pawing, frantic horses, the growing crowd of people around them, and Lord Dewain's annoyed complaints, Acrida was not responding to anything. Van Necht inwardly groaned and dismounted his dancing charger, handing the reins to a bystander.

Realizing that if he grabbed her by the arm she might very well bite him, Van Necht squatted down and very cautiously picked his prisoner up. In his arms, Acrida gradually stopped screaming and simply howled and wept in agony. Van Necht carried her swiftly inside the gates, through the throng of people, and up the remainder of the way to the palace entrance. There, among the columns, he set the weeping woman down again. After waiting several minutes for Lord Dewain, the alderman noticed that her tears had slowed and that she had gone back to rocking and staring off into space.

"Is she well?" came the voice of Dewain from behind them finally.

He was accompanied by two serving women.

"Does she seem so?" Van Necht answered irritably.

"Can she walk?"

"I think so."

"Come. Bring her then."

The servants went to either side of Acrida and helped her to her feet. The five of them walked through the courtyard and up the steps into the palace corridor. They walked past the audience chamber and entered a door that led to a small chamber.

Acrida looked around sharply, suddenly noticing she was no longer outside, although the last thing she remembered was riding on Van Necht's horse to the main gate and seeing the additional decorations there. She was sitting at the end of a long table, and a servant beside her was applying a damp cloth to her forehead and cheeks. They had covered her hair with another headrail, and this one covered her head securely.

Lord Olbert in his green sat opposite to her. Lord Dewain sat to the left of him. Lord Grey, dressed in blue, sat opposite to Dewain. The three advisers each wore a large, golden necklace and several rings, and a silver and gold buckle on their expensive belts. Lord Van Necht, who sat nearest her, seemed out of place in his plain tunic, worn leather belt with horn buckle, and lack of jewelry.

Acrida recognized the chamber as one of the private offices at the palace. The table was covered with an embroidered cloth of fine linen. Rather than benches, chairs surrounded the table, each with a scarlet, velvet cushion. Parchments, quills and ink, and many scrolls were scattered over the table. As she glanced at her surroundings, Acrida watched curiously as another servant refilled Lord Dewain's goblet, not with mead or wine, but milk from a pitcher.

"...we should have anticipated it," Lord Olbert was telling Van Necht. "But *that* night was so chaotic, we did not even consider what the consequences could be-"

"Other than that the Bishop would discipline the King once he received word of the incident-" Dewain cut in.

"But we assumed that the priests would redirect the people to an alternate location the next morning, and Mass would be sung as usual until the Bishop arrived to consecrate the altar again," Olbert continued. "The next morning, however, the people came to hear Mass and found the church doors boarded up; and there was no priest present to instruct them or to explain anything."

Van Necht raised his eyebrows.

"We feared that the priests were all dead," he continued. "-You know the King's temperament."

Van Necht nodded.

"We did not find dead priests, thankfully. We discovered the church stripped and vacated. The priests took every icon, relic, and vessel they could carry with them when they left."

"All the palace clerks were gone as well," Dewain added.

"We immediately dispatched a messenger to Bishop Gildas at Magnushamlet. When he arrived, the Bishop had already departed, but the messenger did find one of his clerks on the road to Gaulia."

"This is the worst possible time for an interdict," Dewain complained between large swallows of milk.

He perused a curling parchment and then handed it to Van Necht. Van Necht glanced at the writing and then set the scroll back on the table. The parchment curled back on itself and then rolled down the table, coming to rest in front of Acrida.

Acrida quietly picked up the scroll, unrolled it and curiously looked at the inked characters in their varying heights and shapes.

"Well, My Dear, you seem to be feeling better," came the pleasant voice of Lord Olbert.

Acrida quickly looked up to see the four men observing her. She swallowed nervously and replaced the scroll back on the table guiltily.

"Can we get you anything?" Olbert asked pleasantly. "Some wine, perhaps? Or something to eat?"

He nodded to a servant behind her. The young man stepped forward and, smiling at her, placed a silver goblet in front of Acrida and filled it with wine. Then he stepped away.

Acrida looked at the expensive goblet dubiously, fearing that someone would yell at her or knock it away in jest if she actually attempted to reach for it. But as no one laughed nor made a move towards her, she gingerly took the chalice into her hand. The silver was cool to the touch and heavy. She cautiously put the precious cup to her lips and tasted the wine. It was the sweetest and strongest she had ever sampled.

"Is it to your liking?" he asked, rising from his chair.

Lord Olbert was older than the other two advisers, and he had a kindly face with deep wrinkles and soft, brown eyes to go with his thinning, gray hair.

"Perhaps we could get you something else if you prefer."

She shook her head once in the negative and wiped her mouth on her sleeve.

"'Acrida', is it not?" he asked in his soothing tone of voice. "I do not believe that you were ever formally presented to us. I am Lord Olbert, Palace Steward, and for the moment, Royal Exchequer also. You already know Lord Chancellor Dewain. This is Lord Grey, the Royal Chamberlain," he said, gesturing to the nobleman in blue. "We are the King's advisers, along with Lord Felix who is Commander of the Palace Watch and Lord Paschal who is Commander of the King's Forces."

Lord Olbert walked over to her side and picked up the scroll.

"You were looking at this. It is the edict the King received from the Bishop. It reads: Let it be known on this- the twenty-ninth day of August in the year of our Lord Eight Hundred and Eighty-two, that-"

"Really, Olbert! How you coddle the woman!" Lord Grey interrupted with irritation. "What need hath she to hear the writ? It is enough to tell her that Speyron is under interdict and that that means that no one in the kingdom can receive the sacraments, nor can Mass be sung."

"I know what it means," Acrida answered sharply.

Grey smiled and gestured toward her, saying, "See! She even knows what it means."

Acrida guessed that Lord Grey was slightly younger than Olbert. He had a penetrating gaze. He too had gray hair, and his ears seemed large.

Lord Dewain was closer to Van Necht's age. And although his hair was not gray, the Chancellor was already balding. He also had dark circles under his eyes.

Olbert returned to his seat at the opposite end of the table.

"Did you foresee the interdict?" he asked curiously.

"No."

"No matter," Grey said quickly.

"Have you had any visions of the future of the kingdom?" Dewain asked.

She sat mute, determined not to answer anymore of their questions. She picked up the cool chalice instead and took another sip of wine, blinking away the memories of the dead at the burning castle in her dream as well as the sight of the seers' heads on the wall.

"It matters little if you have not," Grey added with a pleasant smile.

She glared at the men, her anger growing.

The advisers glanced at each other in the uneasy silence that followed.

"Are you certain you do not want anything? Some bread-" Olbert asked again.

"Aye, I want something!" she told them hostilely. "I want to know what you want of me!"

The royal counselors smiled slightly as they glanced again at each other.

"Leave us," Dewain instructed the servants.

The attendants bowed and left the chamber, shutting the door behind them. Once they were gone, Dewain cleared his throat.

"Acrida, the King-"

"The King still requires the services of a seer- one that can best prepare him for the war to come," Grey interrupted impatiently.

Acrida looked at the alderman in blue for a moment and then laughed out loud incredulously.

"A seer! Why, no, My Lord! The King has three such seers permanently attached to the palace already! -On its outside wall! He has no need of another, nor do I have any desire to be among them!"

"Acrida-" Lord Dewain began.

"No, My Lord!" she told him angrily. "It was useless bringing me here. I will do nothing that helps you or the King!"

The chamber was silent as the men regarded her.

"You do not even know what you have to do," he replied.

"I care not!"

"Tsk, tsk! Such temper! Where is your gratitude to us for begging that your life be spared?" Grey scolded.

"Do you expect gratitude, My Lord, when you continue to put my life in peril? Do you expect gratitude when likely you were the cause that I came to the King's notice at all?"

Grey smiled slightly at her.

"Did *you* not tell the King *I* was speaking against him?!" she raged. "Were *you* not the ones who told the King that my village would rise in rebellion?! What debt of gratitude is owed to you for *lies*?!"

Olbert cleared his throat.

Grey only shrugged.

"My spies must have been misinformed about your village."

She glared at the smug Chamberlain.

"You say you will not help the King," Olbert said. "What of the kingdom or your family? Do they mean nothing to you?"

"It is true that Speyron has many plights to face," she said with a shake of her head, "but it is not in my ability to solve them, My Lords. As for my family, we are serfs. Likely we will remain serfs no matter who is king or whether Speyron falls to invaders or not."

The aldermen frowned.

"Acrida, we understand your reluctance," Olbert replied mildly.

"Do you, My Lord? Has the King ever ordered your death? Have you felt the cold blade at your own throat and by chance alone been spared? Do you fear not only for your own life, but for your entire family, should you displease the King?"

Although Acrida did not see the affect of her words, Van Necht noticed the drawn expressions of the silent advisers.

Acrida laughed then in frustration, her face mirroring the anguish she felt.

"Would he order you and your noble-blooded family put to death for sport? Because, after looking into his eyes, I know he is capable of putting me and my entire family to the sword as a *jest*. -Just because I am lowborn does not mean I value my life or my family's life any less than you do yours!"

The noblemen were all silent, frowning.

"I was in his presence but a few hours," she continued, "but I clearly saw his black heart. -After all of the terrible deeds he has committed, how can you be blind to his true nature?"

"On the contrary, we see King Christian's nature quite clearly, as we saw King Filberte's before him," Grey replied.

"Then why do you continue in his service?"

"He is still the King," Grey added with a shrug. "Without loyalty, the kingdom would be in chaos."

"You know very well, Acrida, that we noblemen have sworn an oath to serve the King," Olbert said. "We are bound to fulfill that oath no matter how outrageously our anointed king behaves or how distasteful we find that behavior. Dishonor would come upon us and our families if we did anything else."

"We think of the kingdom, as you must," Dewain explained. "Speyron is more important-"

"No," Acrida interrupted, "I must think of my *soul!* The Church commands us to avoid the company of excommunicates, and for good reason! My Lords, how will God judge me if I aid an excommunicate and a murderer of the innocent?"

"It is not our wish that King Christian do any of his subjects harm. We have advised against every cruelty that the King has authorized," Olbert answered.

"Likewise, when you advise him, you will be working to curb the King's cruel nature as well, not aiding him in committing atrocities," Dewain added.

Acrida crossed her arms in silence, shaking her head.

"It is folly to even try! The King will not hear me! He will laugh, make jests with his companions, and cut my throat at his first whim!"

"There is that risk," Grey spoke then, "but if you are a clever lass, you will work to convince the King of his need for your counsel long before he picks up his knife. Once he considers your advice invaluable to him, you will find your life protected by the King at all costs rather than toyed with."

"We need you. Speyron needs you," Dewain said. "And whether he knows it or not, King Christian needs you."

Acrida frowned as she considered this. No one had ever needed *her* before.

The advisers whispered to each other as Acrida stared at the table, thinking. Van Necht watched her curiously.

Gradually, she began to shake her head.

"-I can not," she muttered. "The Bishop commands-"

"Acrida-" Grey told her firmly, "despite the wishes of the Bishop, if the King desires your services, you have no choice but to serve him."

"But the King does not desire my services, My Lord," she answered quickly, "for he does not believe in oracles. -And you noblemen may not detain me here either, for I am bound to Lord Huntingdon's lands, and *by law*, you must return me there in good time."

The ministers smiled a tight lip smile as they noted the woman's grasp on the truth of the matter. She was clearly no simpleton. Van Necht sat quietly, listening to the reply with interest. He had never heard a peasant woman argue with a nobleman so confidently.

Lord Grey locked his eyes on Acrida's then and asked very calmly, "Woman, who will enforce that law if we choose to break it? Do you think Huntingdon will raise arms against *us* over the loss of one serf due his lands?"

Acrida's blood chilled at his words. The chamber became uncomfortably silent again as she realized how ruthless and powerful these men truly were and how hopeless her situation actually was. Even the laws of the land were of no concern to them -lest someone was willing to stand against them to enforce the laws.

There was no help to be had for her, she realized. She was not only at the King's mercy, but at the mercy of every person above her lowly station.

Lord Grey leaned back in his chair again, picked up his silver goblet, biding his time. Acrida stared again at the table, considering every option she could think of. When she finally spoke, it was with moderation and no hint of disrespect.

"My Lords, I am not certain what use I can actually be-" she said with a frown. "I have not the abilities of Jebedye. My view of the future comes to me in dreams. I have no control over what is revealed to me. If the King desires to know something that I have not been shown, there is nothing I can tell him."

"We are not so concerned with your deficiencies as an oracle," Grey answered. "If the King asks you something that you do not know, we will make the necessary allowances for you. You need not fear that."

Acrida was silent again considering this information with a frown. She hated the King. She despised him. She did not want to serve him. She wanted to see God's vengeance rain down on him, not help him avoid it.

Finally, Lord Olbert spoke.

"You realize that the King would compensate you for your loyalty, of course."

These words drew her attention.

"How? As he rewarded Jebedye and the others?" she asked sarcastically.

"He will free you from the land, I am certain," Dewain answered.

Acrida looked at him unimpressed.

"That is a beginning, but hardly worth the risk that I take."

The ministers exchanged smiles.

"Would the King raise her to a higher station?" Dewain asked the others.

Grey shook his head.

"Methinks not. But he might bestow lands on her husband."

"I am not married," Acrida said quickly.

They were all silent for a moment, and then Olbert rose and walked about the room.

"Rather than speculate on what the King will or will not do for you, perhaps it would be more prudent to ask what you desire. Anything that you desire that is in our power to grant or entreat the King for, you will be awarded."

Acrida was silent, her mind racing. No one had ever offered her anything that she wanted before. What did she want? More than anything else? Besides to return home to her aunt and uncle?

"Aye, everyone has a price," Dewain said quietly. "A herd of sheep? A cottage of your own, perhaps?"

As she considered the secret desires of her heart, Acrida finally acknowledged the one thing she longed for more than any other, though she had never dared to speak it.

"A child. I want an infant."

"What?!" Van Necht said.

"What?!" the ministers echoed, not sure they had heard correctly.

"A child? You can not be serious!" Dewain stammered.

"This is nonsense!" Grey reprimanded.

"We will get you a husband. He will get you a child," Olbert replied.

"No!" Acrida interrupted. "You would make me answer to two masters then- a troublesome husband and the King."

Van Necht raised his eyebrows.

"I just want the child."

"You dare not make such a request to the King! -Lest he take you at your word and drag you to his own bed, trying to oblige you!" Dewain said, flabbergasted.

Lord Grey laughed at this remark, and Acrida's air of self-confidence abandoned her immediately. She had not considered this possible result.

"But there are no children being born in Speyron now," Olbert protested. "You know as much. Are you saying you wish us to *steal* you a foreign child?"

Lord Grey laughed again. All eyes turned to him.

"Fear not, My Lords, she speaks in jest, I am certain," he explained. "What a joker you have turned out to be, Acrida! Here, you had us convinced of your wisdom and now you make this demand? But can anyone expect anything else from a woman? Talent is wasted on your sex!"

"Grey!" Olbert chided, giving the Chamberlain a scornful look.

"She is ridiculous, Olbert! We will grant her anything, and she wants a baby. -That is a peasant for you. Breeding is all they ever think about."

Acrida blushed, but her humiliation managed to give rise to anger again.

"You do not believe me?" she asked hotly.

"No, I do not," he replied, "nor do I think that you believe it."

"Then, by all means, speak my true desire," she challenged.

"Very well," Grey responded with amusement. "I have observed the way you have looked around the palace, and you do not impress me as a woman who wants to raise some foreigner as your bastard child, particularly in a crowded, stinking, peasant hut, while you work in your lord's fields during the day. No, truthfully, you do not want to return to that miserable village you are from or your pathetic life there."

Acrida went pale as he spoke these words.

"It is so clear what you want. You want all of this," Grey said as he held his hands out. "You want the fine clothes of the softest, brightest cloth, and the tasty meals that are prepared by others; and you want good wine, not watery ale. You want to live here- in the palace in such luxury as you have never imagined.

"But even more than this, when you speak, you want *everyone* to listen. When you enter a room, you want to be noticed. When you are unhappy, you want someone to tremble."

Then Grey paused and turned to look directly into her eyes.

"Do not toy with me, Lass. You will do as we bid for one reason alone and without any need of reward- and that is because, more than anything else, you crave the King's ear. You are finished with being the cur that howls outside the palace gates. It is true. Admit it."

Acrida shuttered inwardly, looking away from Lord Grey. The Chamberlain in blue saw her nature as clearly as her aunt did, and it frightened her. She could not find the words to argue or even speak. She looked about the chamber with its beautiful furnishings again. She looked at the silver chalice before her and at the bright crimson, blue, and green clothes of the King's advisers, and at the fine, embroidered cloth on the ornately carved table. It was all marvelous to behold.

The aldermen exchanged slight smiles again. Van Necht watched her with serious interest.

"It is nothing to be ashamed of," Grey continued after a moment. "You were simply born in the wrong station. But we can get you a place here, and all that comes with it. We need only to ask the King."

Acrida nodded her assent without looking at him.

"We will address His Grace about it today. But, first, you will seem more *able* in your new position if you support the advice we give the King, particularly concerning issues that you know nothing about."

Acrida hesitated for a moment, then replied.

"What do you want me to say?"

The advisers smiled at each other.

"Just be in agreement. Any explanation will do. -Give any reason you like."

15

Once the King's advisers had obtained Acrida's promise of cooperation, they left the chamber and proceeded to the King without any further delay, not even allowing her to change into a gown.

"Should we send for Paschal and Felix?" Dewain asked anxiously.

"Lord Felix accompanied the garrisons on the overnight hunting expedition," Olbert answered. "As for Paschal-"

"Let us not give further encouragement to our opposition-" Grey added quickly.

Wishing they had given her some time to prepare or at least to collect herself before bringing her before King Christian, Acrida walked nervously behind the ministers whispering an Ave Maria, while Van Necht followed at the rear.

The ministers walked down the corridor and stopped a servant that was hurrying down the way.

"Where is the King? Did he go hawking with his cousin?" Dewain inquired.

"No, My Lord, the King is in his chambers."

The group continued around the corner to a door where two knights stood standing guard and a few servants stood talking, including the King's valet. They bowed to the advisers and to Van Necht.

"If the King is engaged, we can return later," Lord Olbert said immediately.

"His Grace has instructed that he will make himself available should his advisers come about some business or his cousin ask for him," one of the knights answered.

"Will he not be angered if we disturb him?" Dewain asked.

"I should think not, My Lords," the valet replied. "The King has been in high spirits all the day."

Lord Dewain turned and smiled at the other advisers and Van Necht and then nodded to the valet. The manservant knocked on the door and then opened it slightly, calling out, "Your Grace, your ministers are here."

A moment passed before there was a reply.

"Send them in."

The servant opened the door wider then, and gestured for the noblemen to proceed. The advisers, Van Necht, and Acrida all entered the chamber; the valet entered the chamber behind them and closed the door.

The chamber actually joined a series of connected rooms which together formed three parts of a large square around a central courtyard. Each room had a door that opened onto the private courtyard at the center. A high wall bordered the other end of the quadrant.

The advisers walked directly to the right of where they had entered to an open door that led into the royal bedchamber. The far wall of this elaborate room was painted with Venus, rising out of the foam of the sea. On another wall, naked nymphs were being pursued by aroused satyrs. The courtyard door for this chamber stood ajar, allowing the late afternoon sunlight and a slight breeze into the chamber. An enormous bed was positioned opposite to the door.

On the edge of the bed, the handsome, blond King, naked except for a gold ring on his finger, sat wrapping himself haphazardly in a purple robe. Beside him on the bed lay a young girl of about fifteen years with long, light brown hair who was weeping bitterly. The neck of her yellow gown and undertunic hung down about her waist, exposing her breasts. The skirt of the gown had been pulled up past her hips, baring her legs which the girl at present held together tightly.

To the left of the bed near the courtyard door was a couch of the old Romani style. A dark-haired woman, perhaps in her twenties, lay silently on her back on the couch, her legs splayed wide apart, as the young Lord

Paschal continued to lunge between them. On her face was a look of detached boredom as she waited on the redheaded youth to finish.

The King smiled and greeted his advisers.

"Greetings, Lord Ministers! Are you about business or have you come to join us?"

He pulled the young girl up to a sitting position in front of him and wrapped his arms about her waist, his hands cupping and playfully squeezing her breasts as he bent down and began to lick and nuzzle the girl's ear. Her body shook as more sobs escaped her.

"Your Grace, we did not mean to disturb you!" Lord Dewain said quickly.

Red-faced with embarrassment, Dewain and Olbert covered their eyes and turned away from the sight, moving to withdraw from the chamber immediately.

"Bide a while! You are not disturbing us," King Christian replied. "Paschal and I have spent the better part of the day very pleasantly. Paschal with an old favorite, and I- with a *honest* woman. For this one claimed adamantly that she was a maid," King Christian said with a laugh, "and -she *was*."

"Your Grace-" Lord Grey began, seeing that once again the young men's lack of propriety had left both Olbert and Dewain at a loss for words, "we had a matter to discuss with you, but we will withdraw until-"

"No, stay. As pleasant of a distraction as this was, a king must look to the affairs of his kingdom. State your concern."

Then taking the girl's jaw in his hand, he turned her face to his and kissed her mouth. When he parted from the kiss, the girl's countenance was a picture of disgust and loathing as she endured his touch. He noted her hateful look with amusement.

"You need not carry on so," he told her, smiling sweetly at her as he wiped away one of her tears with his thumb. "Your maidengear is well lost. You will never recover it again no matter how you seek it."

Noticing that the advisers still had not begun to speak, he glanced back to the men. The look of unease was so evident on Olbert and Dewain's faces that King Christian thought they might bolt from the chamber at any moment. He chuckled and sighed, but without further ado, he shoved the girl forward off the bed onto the floor.

"Very well. Get you back to the concubine's quarters. After a bath, you will be well," he told her.

Still crying, the girl was on her feet immediately, pulling her gown up. She clasped it tightly to her chest with one hand, for the laces in the back were broken and the undertunic was torn. Wiping her face, she fled past the advisers and Van Necht and Acrida to the door which the valet held open for her. Once outside, one of the guards followed the running girl back to the chambers of the concubines.

As the King watched her run out, with her long, brown hair flapping behind her, he smiled as he tenderly touched the red scratch on his arm.

"She has spirit," he said. "I will have to summon her again soon."

"Perhaps, Sire, you will grant us an audience when you have had time to dress-" Olbert managed, still averting his gaze away from Paschal and the other concubine.

"Really, Olbert, we are all men here!" King Christian replied with another laugh.

Lord Olbert cleared his throat and took one step backward, making a gesture toward the outer chamber. The King's gaze followed the motion and came to rest on a woman near the back of the chamber. Acrida's discolored features stared back at the King with a look of cold-blooded hatred.

King Christian immediately covered himself completely with his purple robe.

"Withdraw at once! You may await Us in Our study!"

The vassals bowed and backed out of the royal bedchamber and shut the door. The valet gestured for the visitors to proceed to the opposite chamber, to the left of where they had entered.

This chamber contained several chairs and a table with several candles. Olbert sat down as did Acrida and Van Necht as they waited on the King. Lord Dewain began to pace nervously at the far end of the room with his hands behind his back. While the valet lit the candles, Grey went to the open door that led into the courtyard and, pretending to shiver in the cool air, shut the door securely.

It was not long before King Christian emerged from his bedchamber, dressed in a purple tunic with extensive silver and green embroidery, and braes and leg wraps of the same brilliant, purple color. Lord Paschal followed behind him dressed in his golden tunic and braes. The older concubine emerged also, dressed as well in an unlaced red gown with her dark hair hanging loose. She walked nonchalantly out of the chamber and was escorted back to the concubines' quarters.

As the King entered the small study, the advisers and Van Necht all stood up and bowed. With palms sweating, Acrida curtsied quickly as the King's cold gaze fell upon her.

"Lord Ministers-" King Christian stated with a tone of warning, "if you value your appointments here at Court- you will never bring that witch into Our bedchamber or privy chamber again. Is that understood?"

The three counselors were surprised, but quickly agreed, making their apologies. While they groveled, King Christian noted the witch's appearance with curiosity. Van Necht had cleaned her up and dressed her in a large tunic and braes and wraps that were no doubt his own clothes. How great was Van Necht's distaste for women! the King smirked. The man could not even suffer the sight of their gowns!

"And how is it that the witch has found her way back to Us already?"

"Perhaps Van Necht grew weary and *withered* from watching her night and day," Paschal snickered.

Christian stifled a laugh.

Van Necht looked at the youths evenly, showing no emotion.

"Forgive us, Sire, but we summoned her here," Olbert said quickly.

"Did you?" Christian asked with an air of hardly concealed annoyance.

"Aye, Your Grace," Grey and Dewain said also.

"Why does that not surprise Us?" King Christian muttered irritably. "For what cause, Ministers?" he asked quickly.

"We wished to consult with her regarding her visions-" Grey answered. "After all, it is our duty as your advisors to be prepared with all the information Your Grace may require."

A sarcastic smile crossed the King's lips.

"We are fortunate to benefit from the great loyalty and dedication of Our counselors. -What formidable enemies we would make," he added coolly, "if fate had not put us on the same side."

Olbert and Grey glanced at each other. Dewain frowned as his stomach tightened painfully.

"Cedd, we will have our dinner now," Christian told the valet abruptly.

The servant bowed and left the chamber.

"So, Lord Ministers, you summoned the witch so that *you* could speak with her again. But what cause have you to bring her back into Our presence?" he asked as he took his seat at the end of the table.

Paschal took the seat beside him on the long side of the table.

"Sire-" they all began at once, and then Lord Olbert continued.

"Sire, we feel that although over the years our advice has proven to be both wise and indispensable to your father King Filberte as well as to Your Grace, we can only speculate what future events will take place. However, we feel that with the upcoming war with Herryck, it is necessary to utilize every advantage available to us. Thus, we believe it is in your best interest to take counsel from the last seer that Speyron has."

"How extraordinary, Ministers! One moment you fear the influence of the seers among our people and the next- you desire the King to heed their every word," Paschal complained.

"Her visions could mean the difference between life and death, a speedy victory or a long, drawn out engagement with the enemy-" Dewain asserted.

"Aye, and besides, it is well known, Lord King, that Herryck employs augers when he makes his battle plans," Grey added.

King Christian was silent as he considered this information, but still wondered what these men were really plotting.

"You really believe the witch's dreams will prove that valuable?" he asked after a moment.

"We do, Sire," they answered.

The King looked at Acrida doubtfully again.

"So, you are prepared to speak at last," he said.

Olbert saw her glare coldly at the King.

"She has agreed to share the future she sees in her dreams with us," the Royal Steward said hastily, "provided that she is rewarded-"

"Rewarded?" Paschal scoffed. "Since when do we compensate women, Olbert?"

"Aye, she is rewarded already, methinks," King Christian agreed, his gaze falling on her again. "She lives, and- *she walks.*"

Acrida's heart skipped a beat and then raced at these words and at Paschal's accompanying chuckle. She swallowed and glanced at Lord Grey.

"Think you that that is not reward enough? Here, Van Necht," the King added with a quick wave of his hand, "break her legs."

Acrida went pale, her heart pounding in her ears, and Van Necht frowned mutely as he rose from his chair. Dewain and Olbert stared at the King, aghast; only Paschal laughed in delight.

"Forgive me, Sire, but this simply will not do-" Grey said with a practiced, courtly smile, as he gestured for Van Necht to wait.

"Sire, this woman is your subject, not your enemy," Olbert interrupted. "Is there a reason why you should not compensate her honorably for her unique services as you compensate- your cousin's tutors?"

Seeing the looks of dismay on the faces of his advisers, as well as the frown on Van Necht's face, King Christian sighed. This was a mirthless bunch. They detested all sport. He shrugged his shoulders and gestured for Van Necht to sit back down.

"Very well, what sort of reward do you think appropriate for a witch, Ministers?" he asked.

"I am not a witch."

The advisers sent her a warning look.

"And I have a name-" she said, ignoring the looks, but remembering her place, added quickly, "Your Grace."

The advisers glared at her again.

"Of course you do," the King replied dryly.

He looked at Dewain, who whispered in his ear.

"Acrida-?" King Christian repeated. "What kind of a name is 'Acrida', anyway?" he asked testily.

"A fitting one-" the advisers and Van Necht all mumbled.

"Sire," Olbert interrupted, "since Acrida will be serving Your Grace in the capacity as a minor- as it were, adviser-"

"Adviser? Are you in jest?" Paschal interrupted, looking indignantly at Acrida and then the other ministers. "She will be no adviser!"

"Paschal-"

"If not an adviser, what will she be when she offers her counsel to the King?" Dewain asked.

"This is outrageous!" Paschal argued. "A woman can not be trusted in such a position! Women by their very nature can not keep a confidence, Sire! If we speak freely in front of her, the entire kingdom will know the substance of our plans in a day!"

Acrida and the ministers gave the youth a cold look.

"Lord King, if she advises you, it is only fitting that she should be rewarded for her service and as such an appointment demands," Olbert continued firmly.

"What?! This is madness!" Paschal declared incredulously. "You would not only have the King actually appoint a *woman-* as a royal advisor, but, further, you would have him bestow on her what he has so generously bestowed on *us*? King Christian will be the joke of the Continent!"

"Your Grace, actually-"

"Sire, I protest! She is a witch!" the redheaded youth continued to fume. "Will you make this woman- whose loyalty is still in question- and a witch too, your vassal? Will you bestow lands on her as well? Does she even have a husband? The law does not permit lands to be bestowed on unmarried women, and I cannot see any man marrying a witch, not even if it is their King's will!"

"We know the law, Paschal," Grey answered irritably.

"You are all mad! You, Witch, no doubt, have put a spell on them!" Paschal declared.

"May we speak, Sire?" Olbert asked.

King Christian smiled, amused at his friend's discomposure, and gestured for Olbert to come forward. At this point, Dewain and Olbert approached the King and whispered in his ear.

Red-faced, Paschal rose from his chair, shaking his head, and walked over to the courtyard door and opened it. He stood in the doorway with his arms crossed angrily, observing the sunset. The faint but distinct sounds of cheering drifted into the chamber along with the cool, evening breeze.

Van Necht looked toward the courtyard momentarily. Acrida heard it too, but paid no heed to it since the advisers and the King did not seem to notice.

"Oh? And what did you have in mind?" the King answered.

The two men continued to whisper so low that no one else in the chamber could make out their words.

"Is that all?" Christian laughed. "Very well, Acrida. You will serve Us as an adviser, and you will not speak about what is discussed, or you will reap the *consequences*. In return, We will grant you freedom from the land and make you a place in the palace in the servants' quarters."

Acrida looked at the King and advisers.

"That is not acceptable," she said bluntly.

Olbert and Dewain looked at her in surprise.

"Not acceptable?" King Christian repeated in amazement.

"Not acceptable?!" Paschal echoed, whirling around to face her.

"The King is being very generous to someone of such humble birth," Grey told her.

"It is not my low birth that is of service, My Lord. I will not be looked on as the equal of a maidservant or a cook. If that is how you regard me, then I say get the palace cook to foretell for you. Get the King's valet to advise him. He does not need me."

"In that, we are in agreement!" Paschal retorted.

"What is it that you desire?" Christian asked, amused.

"I want- I want my own chamber- away from the servants! I want fine clothes, and my meals cooked for me, and someone to brush my hair and help me dress. And I want to go where it pleases me, and I want to choose the company I keep!" Acrida demanded nervously. "-And my family shall be freemen as well!"

There was silence in the chamber as the King and all the noblemen marveled at the woman's audacity. Finally, King Christian laughed, paused, then laughed again.

"You hold your value in too great a regard, methinks," he told her. "Very well, so it shall be as you have asked- *if* you prove your worth. You will have a chamber of your own in the ministers' quarters, but, know this, Witch, you will *never* be in *my bed*."

The King chuckled smugly again; the advisers smiled, and Acrida went pale. She was so stunned by his remark that she could make no retort. Could the King be so vain that he actually believed her desire was to be near him?

Cedd entered the chamber then, followed by two kitchen servants carrying trays.

"Finally!" Paschal said, returning to his chair beside the King at the table. "I thought I was going to have to go to the kitchen myself! And, Cedd, find out what all that cheering is about!"

The first servant set the platters of bread and roast goose down before the King and bowed, then with a gesture from the valet, left the chamber to make the inquiry. The other servant placed trenchers, knives, and golden chalices before the King and Lord Paschal. While the servant filled the chalices with wine, the King pulled a leg off the bird and bit into the meat, and nodded with approval. Paschal took the other leg.

"Boisil's seasoning is perfection," he commented.

Paschal agreed, the juice from the bird running down his chin and fingers. Acrida swallowed hungrily and looked away from the food.

"Anything else?" King Christian asked as he ate.

"Your Grace, this is the latest estimate on the location and number of Herryck's troops from our present sources," Grey reported, handing a parchment to the King.

King Christian wiped his hand on his tunic, and then took the document. He read it and passed the parchment to the young adviser in gold as he took another bite from the leg.

"There is no new information here, Grey," Paschal commented with annoyance. "Why do you continue to tell the King the same thing daily? Do you think he hears you not the first time?"

King Christian put down the leg and picked up the bread, ripping it into two pieces.

"Paschal-" Grey began.

"It is as I have told you," the youth interrupted. "It is not yet mid-September! Herryck, if he attacks at all, will come in the summer, or late spring at the earliest! There is plenty of time to make the necessary preparations."

"But as His Grace knows, Herryck now controls more territory than we do," Grey argued. "He has more troops than we do. He-"

"Aye, but the situation is not as dire as you fear!" Paschal reiterated. "You forget that Herryck has been at war for the last twenty years. His kingdom and people are weary of battle. Our people are fresh. The kingdoms that support him have not recovered from his last campaigns against Caldignis. His original troops have been whittled away- dead or wounded, and have been replaced by mercenaries- mercenaries which will be too expensive to hire for an extended campaign. What is more- mercenaries are unreliable on the field; they are less likely to fight to the death as a man whose home and freedom are threatened. The other half are troops gleaned from the kingdoms he has conquered. If Herryck sends newly sworn soldiers from Caldignis or other kingdoms against us that have previously been our allies, their hearts will not be in the fight."

"Even so, Paschal, from the development of this week alone-"

"What development?" the King asked, taking a bite of the bread.

"Sire, the edict from the Bishop," Olbert reminded him quietly.

"Oh- aye, the interdict-" Christian said. "Methinks the situation is not as dire as you believe, Olbert. It is what We wanted- Speyron free from the interference of the Church. The Bishop has obliged Us."

Acrida frowned.

"But, Your Grace," Olbert replied, "the people will be lost without the Church.-"

With a wave of his hand, King Christian dismissed the objection.

"The Church needs us much more than we need it. After all, can there be a Church without people? No. The Church needs us and our tax money. The Church can not afford to hold Speyron in contempt for too long. And without their tithes, the village priests will be begging in the streets before long."

"Your subjects, Sire, feel differently than you do," Dewain answered. "They depend upon the Church, not only as a source of comfort in this life and of promise of the next, but as an assurance that next year's crops will be plentiful-"

"Aye, already there is talk of starvation among the peasants because the interdict prevents the priests from blessing the fields and the village's livestock and chickens," Olbert added.

"Hmph-" Paschal remarked, "I should think that they would be whining about not being able to bury their dead." Then he shrugged his shoulders, adding, "And they say *we* are barbarians!"

King Christian smirked.

"We have given this some thought," the King said. "In the end, We believe this interdict will work to Our advantage, for Our people, who are quite innocent in all of this, will not understand why they are feeling the brunt of this punishment. Therefore, We have decided We will not force Our people to observe the interdict. The dead will be buried. The priests, if We find any, will sing Mass and administer all the sacraments, or they will be declared outlaws and imprisoned in the tower."

"Very shrewd, Sire," Paschal grinned. "For if they are declared outlaws, their property may be confiscated."

"Of course," Christian answered with a curt smile.

"You believe that the allegiance of the priests could be turned by such measures?" Olbert asked.

"I believe that the Church may find interdict very difficult to enforce. When given the choice and the right monetary persuasion, more than a few individual priests may find it in their best interest to bend to Our wishes.

"And if not, given a long enough time without Masses or priests, if the Church should return to Speyron, it may well find that the people no longer have any use for it. In the meantime, the people will have to be satisfied with praying over their own hens."

"Will you issue an edict of non-observance for the entire kingdom, Sire?" Dewain asked.

"No, Our vassals may observe or not observe the interdict on their own lands as amuses them," King Christian shrugged.

Lord Paschal chuckled at this and took a swallow of wine.

"If Your Grace has any vassals left.-"

King Christian's eyes were on Grey then.

"What is your meaning?"

"Sire, the interdict, like your excommunication, in effect releases your vassals from their oaths of allegiance. You may have difficulty getting them to even acknowledge you now."

"Aye, if we hope to raise a substantial army, you will have to make peace with the Bishop immediately, Sire," Olbert replied.

"Aye," Dewain added, "before Herryck has time to make the most of it-"

Christian slammed his goblet onto the table, interrupting the nervous adviser.

"Acknowledge Us?!"

"As their king-" Grey said.

"And why is that, Grey?"

"Your actions have caused the interdict. Like excommunication-"

"Exactly!" Christian argued hotly. "We have been excommunicated for two years now for killing that priest, and excepting two, Our vassals have remained steadfast-"

"And what have you asked of them?" Grey interrupted.

"Forgive me, Sire, but although loyal to your father, your vassals are largely untried in their allegiance to you. The interdict will give them just the excuse they need-" Dewain explained meekly, "if their intentions are to- *forsake* you in the upcoming war."

"Forsake him?" Paschal repeated, setting his bread down.

Olbert continued for Dewain who had begun visibly perspiring.

"In good times, Your Grace, all men will claim loyalty to their king because they risk nothing in their support. But it is in times of crisis, when demands are placed on that fealty, that a king quickly learns whom of his subjects are truly constant and whom are steadfast in word only."

"We know this," Christian answered, unconcerned.

"Thus," Olbert finished, "it would be wise not to give any vassals, whose allegiance is unproven at best, any *legitimate* cause to withdraw their support- which this interdict clearly provides them."

"It would hardly be *legitimate!*" Paschal argued.

Christian made a gesture for Paschal to be calm.

"Very well. Has anyone been sent to the Bishop to find out his demands?" the King asked, cutting into the breast of the goose and removing a large chunk of meat with the tip of his knife.

"He has already left Speyron. We have sent messages, but we have received no replies as yet," Dewain answered.

"To Hell with him then," Christian said, biting into the morsel. "Send some money from the treasury directly to him. -Match the amount that my father sent when he was excommunicated. It worked for him; it will work for Us."

"Sire, it is not so simple either to relax an interdict or an excommunication," Lord Olbert said, "as Your Grace's father understood. Concessions must be made. You will have to formally recognize the authority of the Church and-"

"Never!" King Christian said flatly, picking up his cup. "If some of our vassals withhold their support for this cause, We will have to continue to build an army without them. But, fear not, Ministers, We will remember their betrayal!"

"Sire," Olbert began, "even if all of the vassals in your realm uphold their oaths, the sheer number of men needed to fight Herryck's army may prove impossible to enlist. Free men will not be easily persuaded to risk their lives for honor or the kingdom if they are afraid they will die with their sins on their head. Our people are very devout, and the fear of eternal damnation alone could bring defeat to the realm."

"No doubt, many will be deterred from fighting at the prospect that their bodies, after falling valiantly in battle, will be the food for wolves and other wild beasts-" Dewain added quietly.

"Perhaps initially, Lord Ministers," the King replied calmly, "but war makes practical men of us all. When war comes, all this will matter little. When given the choice of fighting or becoming enslaved to foreign invaders, free men will not stand by idly. They will not hesitate to fight to defend what is theirs."

Lord Olbert closed his eyes and shook his head, not believing what he was hearing.

At this point, Cedd cleared his throat. The King glanced over to him and saw a young knight of the Palace Watch standing in the doorway, waiting to be recognized beside one of the King's bodyguards.

"What is it, Sir Knight?"

"Your Grace!" he said while bowing, hardly able to contain his excitement. "Sire, with Lord Felix away, I command the Palace Watch. I report now some people have assembled at the entrance of the palace!"

"Some people?"

"Aye, peasants for the most part, about two or three score perhaps; they have torches and are yelling and talking loudly. Several of the palace servants are frightened already."

"Take care of it," King Christian answered with a wave of his hand.

"Immediately, Sire," the knight answered with a bow; smiling, he left the chamber almost in a run.

The King's bodyguard remained just inside the door of the chamber.

"Was there any other matter you wished to discuss, Lord Vassals?" the King asked, holding his chalice out so that the servant might fill it again.

Lord Dewain, after glancing momentarily at the others, cleared his throat and meekly said, "We think, -um, we believe it would be advisable for you to send the Lady Kaithryn to a convent in the south of Speyron."

The King stopped in mid-chew and looked up at Dewain.

"Send Our cousin away? Whatever for?"

"And to a convent?! Why would he want to do that?" Paschal asked.

"Mainly for her safety. Your Grace," Olbert answered hastily, as Dewain was already disconcerted.

"Aye, we discussed it and-" Dewain continued.

"When did *we* discuss it? Sire, I was never part of such a discussion, I assure you," Paschal added quickly.

"Safety? Exactly what is she in danger from, Lord Minister, that We can not protect her? Has some threat been made against her?" Christian demanded.

"Sire -"

"Indeed, what danger? I have heard of no threat against the Lady. This is absurd!" Paschal said.

"Your Grace, it is simply a precaution," Olbert tried to explain.

"But who would wish her harm?" Christian asked. "Lady Kaithryn is a sweet child-"

"Sire, I am certain no one would purposely wish-" Dewain began.

"If you harbor even the slightest suspicion that the Lady Kaithryn's life is in danger, even within Our own palace walls, we will have guards accompany her everywhere!" King Christian answered adamantly. "We will restrict her visitors and her exercise to the most secure confines of the palace! But We will not hear of her leaving! She is the only cheer in Our mediocre day!"

Acrida raised her eyebrows.

"There have not been any direct threats made against thy cousin, Sire," Grey answered.

"Then why the concern?" Paschal demanded.

"-But if there were, surely you must realize that such restrictions on her life and freedom would wear heavily upon her disposition," Dewain said.

"But there are no threats!" Paschal argued.

"Aye, children need interaction with other people and other children. At least at a convent she would have the company of girls similar in age which she does not enjoy here even now," Olbert added.

"Aye, and at a convent, she could be protected and supervised without the involvement of armed knights accompanying her everywhere," Grey finished.

The King was silent, momentarily lost in thought.

"Your Grace?"

"Something is amiss," King Christian answered simply. "You say you know of no threats against Kaithryn's life, yet you would still separate me from my cousin, my only family, to ensure her safety. Speak plainly. What is thy reason?"

"Sire," Olbert began soothingly, "I do not mean to alarm you, but if Herryck's troops were to lay siege-"

"She would be much safer here than at some convent!" Paschal insisted.

King Christian ignored the ensuing argument between Paschal and the other three advisers. He continued instead to seek the meaning behind the ministers' words, for he perceived that they were not telling him something.

He frowned after a moment and interrupted the men.

"Verily, Ministers, you are not concerned with my cousin's safety or comfort, but only with the royal line. It is not your intention to send my *cousin* away, but my only *living* relative- lest we are both murdered in one battle."

The advisers were silent then, embarrassed by the truth.

Vaguely, the sound of distant chanting filtered through the chamber. Both Acrida and Van Necht glanced at the door, straining to make out the words.

"Have you old men no confidence in the future of our King whatsoever?" Paschal began chastising. "True, Christian is young, but also wise. You disgrace him with your lack of confidence! Your place is not at his side, but in the tower with all the other faithless, cowardly trait-"

"On the contrary," Grey cut in, "it is not traitorous to be afraid! I fear for the safety of us all -even here at the palace! If the serfs rise up here-"

Olbert looked at Grey in confusion.

"The serfs at the palace are no threat," Olbert said.

"How do we know that?" Grey asked ardently. "Are the peasants here different from the serfs throughout the rest of Speyron? Do they want children less? Do they-"

"Now you are saying We should fear Our own palace serfs?" the King asked incredulously.

"If I may be direct, Sire," Grey said, "-due to your infamous and irreligious behavior, you have lost favor in your people's eyes."

King Christian raised his eyebrows and smiled slightly and seemed to be about to laugh, when the adviser continued.

"For some time now, I have witnessed the people's patience for your antics decline. Your vassals are- exhausted with explanations and excuses."

King Christian was chuckling now.

"Everyday, I hear reports of how the peasants grow less submissive to the desires of your loyal vassals because of it, while other vassals already scorn your authority with flagrant disregard for the obligations and taxes owed to you."

"What reports?!" Paschal demanded. "Which vassals?!"

Acrida looked up, surprised, not only by Grey's accusation, but by the words of the chant that was growing ever louder.

"Sire, there have been no rumors of your serfs or the palace servants-" Olbert began.

"Now that the Church is against us," Grey continued, "I fear, not only Herryck's approaching army -but a rebellion by the people!"

"Rebellion!" Christian sneered. "You can not be serious! No more about rebellion! Can you worthless advisers speak of nothing else? *'Beware! The peasants will be up in arms!'*" he mocked.

"If you are afraid of rebellion, you are afraid of shadows!" Paschal added vehemently. "The peasants will not rebel, Lord Ministers. As long as their bellies are full, dogs have no heart for fighting!"

Acrida, quite pale, stared at the King and Lord Paschal as if they were madmen. Could they not hear the chant? She looked at Olbert, Dewain, and Grey; they did not seem to hear it either. Van Necht, who had risen from his seat, had gone to stand in the dark courtyard itself.

"Sire, I am absolutely grave about this matter!" Grey continued firmly. "For your cousin's welfare as well as for your own, and, as distasteful as it is for me to speak it, for the preservation of the royal line, you and the Lady Kaithryn should no longer-"

Without warning, King Christian hurled his knife against the wall and jumped to his feet.

"How?! How, I ask you!" he shouted. "We have searched their homes! The peasants have no weapons! We have questioned and executed those suspected of turning the peasants against Us with their talk! What will the peasants fight armed knights with? Sticks and sickles? They would have to be mad to try it!"

Acrida's heart pounded hard in fear at his outburst.

"We did not search the peasants *here,*" the King's bodyguard mumbled under his breath.

Paschal glared at him. The knight frowned and remained silent.

"Your Grace, ask not how!" Dewain answered. "When armed with courage and righteous fury, peasants need no other weapons!"

The King whirled around to face him and threw his chalice at him, slinging wine everywhere. Then he yelled at the servants that were attempting to clean up the mess.

Paschal stopped eating and cautiously observed Christian. The King was breathing hard, his hands in tight fists, as he held himself back from beating the servant or Dewain from spite. Everyone else, knowing the King's temper, kept well at a distance, still, and silent.

We Want A Priest! We Want A Priest! We Want A Priest!

The advisers and the King looked at each other in astonishment and then glanced toward the courtyard. For a long moment, they listened to the chant.

"Can the Church mean that much to them?" the King asked finally.

"Aye, Your Grace, it does," Grey replied.

The chamber was quiet and still as the group listened. Then, outside, the chanting stopped abruptly.

"Witc-" King Christian began, and then caught himself. "-Acrida, have you foreseen a rebellion of Our subjects?"

Acrida went cold in surprise at the question.

The nobles all turned their eyes to the woman, and Grey gave her a slight nod. Acrida swallowed and looked at the advisers and then looked at the King she hated. She had been granted a great many things this day. It would be unwise for her to disappoint anyone lest she lose everything, yet it would prove deadly to lie to the King.

"No, Sire, I have not been shown a peasant rebellion in my dreams. *But* that does not mean that it will not come to pass."

"Oh, she will be a great help to us!" Paschal snapped with an irritated gesture of his hand. "She has not foreseen it, but that does not mean it will not come to pass. With insight like this, the palace cook *could* be your equal!"

Acrida flushed red at the criticism, but Grey, Olbert, and Dewain only smiled quietly, their eyes communicating that she had answered well.

"The Lord Ministers think we should send Our ward and cousin Lady Kaithryn away to a convent for her protection. Have you foreseen that her life will be endangered if she remains here with a few guards?"

Acrida saw clearly he was expecting the same noncommittal reply. The three, older advisers looked at her expectantly, trying to signal her with their eyes to agree. She decided that she had better say something meaningful- for her own sake.

"Sire, Lady Kaithryn's safety may be insured by several armed guards-"

"A-ha!" the King celebrated with Paschal.

The other three advisers were visibly horrified.

"But what kind of life is that for a young girl?" she continued.

The King stopped his revelry and regarded her closely.

"What is your meaning?" he asked shortly.

"What type of lady will your cousin become, Sire, if instead of women she is in the daily company of brash, common-speaking men?" Acrida asked calmly. "What type of example is that for a young girl of such high expectations?"

The King and the advisers raised their eyebrows at these words.

In the quiet of the chamber, the sounds of renewed chanting outside were barely audible.

"I have heard that there is learning at the monasteries and nunneries; perhaps they will teach her if she goes," Acrida continued.

"She reads already," the King answered shortly.

Acrida smiled and fought down the urge to ask King Christian if he thought his cousin should be reared by the Devil. Instead, she asked:

"Do you believe, Sire, that your palace is the proper place for a young girl to be raised? Your own activities, I would say, are not the games of children. -And children see everything, and they hear even more- even though their parents try their best to shield them. Think about it. How long do you think it will be before your cousin starts asking questions-about your concubines, or why there is no Mass for her to hear?"

Even Paschal had to yield to these arguments.

"I was taught by example," Acrida continued. "Truly, if your cousin is to be a lady of virtue and charity, she must have these for imitation."

The King listened intently. In the past two and a half years that his cousin had lived at the palace as his ward, he had never considered this.

"We believe you are correct," he said softly after a long moment. "Do you agree, Paschal?"

"I concur, Sire."

"Very well, Lady Kaithryn shall leave Us as soon as We find a suitable convent to take her," King Christian announced.

The King's ministers and the servants in the chamber smiled, awed by how the witch handled the King. Van Necht was equally impressed with how wisely she had spoken and without a hint of the loathing he knew she felt for the King.

King Christian took a new goblet of wine proffered by a servant, and the three older advisers began to whisper to each other.

Olbert nodded.

"Sire," he said, "we also need to speak to you of taking a wife."

"You speak of it all the time," Paschal muttered.

"Very well, Olbert, whose wife do you want me to take?" the King jested.

Paschal grinned with the King.

Shouts, accompanied by harrowing screams, suddenly infiltrated the chamber from outside, overwhelming the chanting.

"What is happening?" Acrida asked with alarm, as she went to the open courtyard door.

"I should think that the answer would be obvious," Paschal replied with curt unconcern, "especially to a *seer.* -Shut the door if it distresses you."

Acrida frowned but pulled the door shut, leaving Van Necht outside.

"Sire," Olbert said, with a stray glance toward the courtyard, "it is not wise for you to disregard your situation. Partially we are to blame for presenting these issues in less than the grave manner which attends them."

"If anything, Minister, you consistently make the situation graver than it actually is," Paschal told him sourly.

"Do you have a recommendation for a bride?" King Christian asked pointedly. "We presume that you wish to make an alliance with a kingdom that will support us against Herryck."

"At the moment, it may be difficult to obtain a betrothal when Speyron is facing imminent attack, Your Grace. Most rulers will want some assurance that after the war the marriage will not be annulled and their daughter put aside when it is convenient to do so," Dewain said.

"It is well they should, for no such assurance has ever existed, as you well know!" Christian laughed. "Many a king on the Continent has expanded his holding by changing wives every few years. It is as customary as changing one's clothes."

"And certainly as necessary!" Paschal added, raising his cup to the King's; then the two laughed and drank.

"Your Grace! We are in earnest!" Olbert admonished.

"As are we!" Paschal replied.

"Fear not," the King replied, "I will marry tonight, tomorrow, whenever- if only Our trusted counselors would come to an agreement on whom the bride is to be. As for myself, I can only declare that the lady, whomever she is, will want for nothing. She may even have her choice of my concubines as companions," King Christian finished with a grand gesture.

Paschal snickered into his wine.

"Surely, Your Grace is in jest," Olbert replied, horrified.

"Indeed, We are in earnest, Olbert. Now, do Our trusted and seasoned advisers have a recommendation or not?"

Olbert hesitated but then was silent. He turned away from the smiling King, stroking what was left of the thin, gray strands of hair on his balding head.

"I thought as much," Paschal quipped.

"The immediate question is what kingdom will suit our needs and has a daughter available," Dewain added.

"Have you not even determined that?" Christian asked with annoyance. "You three ministers are quite useless!"

"On the contrary, Sire, I have already sent out inquires to every kingdom that we consider an ally as well as those we do not, Sire. I simply have not received any replies as of yet," Lord Chancellor Dewain replied.

"But there is much to consider besides troop numbers-" Olbert added.

"Aye," the King agreed, "like the size and wealth of the lands she brings with her."

The King and Paschal chuckled again.

"Actually, Your Grace, my concern is one of fertility," Olbert answered.

"Why? I thought only the women in Our kingdom were cursed with desolate wombs."

"Aye," Olbert replied, "so it begs the question: If we bring in a foreigner to be queen, will she become barren like the rest?"

King Christian blinked at this, surprised.

Grey, Dewain, and Olbert immediately began discussing the matter between themselves.

"Why all this concern with begetting children? We should be directing our energies toward more important concerns!" Paschal interrupted. "Ministers, this barren curse, if it exists at all, can not endure forever. The King is young! He can get heirs even after he is an old man! -Besides, the sooner the King has a son, the sooner that son will be after the throne for himself!"

"Not every prince that wears the crown wears it long!" Dewain snapped at the youth. "And King Christian has a responsibility to his family and the ancestors that came before him to prepare for that contingency by getting heirs without delay!"

"How dare you suggest the King's reign will be brief!" Paschal swore.

"I am suggesting nothing!" Dewain retorted. "You heard the prophecies, as did we all. You heard them speak of 'the new king that comes from the East'."

"The 'King from the East'! Really, Dewain, you are so gullible! You will believe anything!" Paschal chided.

Dewain flushed red.

"Not one of those seers mentioned anything about King Christian having a lengthy reign!" Dewain fumed.

"Well, none of the seers mentioned him having any heirs, either! Regardless, it has no bearing on this war!"

All eyes in the chamber were on the two arguing noblemen now.

"No bearing? Paschal! Stay your arguments, You Foolish Youth!" Dewain demanded hotly. "Are the powers of perception and reason elusive to you? Can you not see that there is a mighty enemy, powerful and hungry, chomping at our borders, ready to consume us as he has consumed our neighbors? Do you not see that the entire future of Speyron precariously resides in this very palace? Lo! There sits our King- without brothers or sisters or nephews or sons! He is alone in the world except for his cousin who also resides in this very same palace! Do you not see that if they die, Speyron is lost? If we fail in the war against Herryck-"

"We will not fail!" Paschal shouted back.

"Hear this? The youth is a seer as well, My Lords!" Dewain called sarcastically to the others in the chamber. "He says we will prevail in this war, no matter what! We need not fear! We need not prepare! -God's eyes, I waste my breath pleading reason to a child!"

Olbert cleared his throat, warningly, but the two youngest advisers did not heed him.

"If the King marries and begets a son, will this drive Herryck from our borders? No! Will this keep his cousin safe? No!" Paschal shouted, his face reddened with anger. "This will not save Speyron!"

"There sits Speyron!" Dewain shouted back, pointing toward the King. "Christian is the symbol, the very embodiment of Speyron! Our home, our borders, our people, our land- is just as any other kingdom's! The only thing that distinguishes one piece of land from the next is the person who speaks for that land, the person who rules that land! If King Christian dies without an heir, without providing for the future of his land, the kingdom of Speyron will pass away with him!"

Acrida stood listening to the words of the Chancellor, quite moved. She understood then why he served a base king so loyally.

"Thus, it is imperative that the King marries and begets a child immediately! Any child- male or female!" Dewain continued hotly. "At this point, a drooling, crossed-eyed, slew-footed bastard of a concubine would be agreeable, if we had one! -The kingdom will have a better chance of enduring after the war if there is an heir of the royal line behind which loyal subjects may rally!"

Everyone stared at Dewain in stunned reticence. Lords Olbert and Grey covered their faces with their hands. Even Van Necht had come in from outside to watch. The servants and bodyguard all took a cautious step backward. Looking around, Dewain swallowed as he realized what he had said and that everyone had heard him. Visibly wincing, he turned toward the King and mumbled.

"Forgive me, Sire, if my words-"

It was too late. The King was clearly offended. The youth rose from his chair, his hands in fists, his expression, fierce and deadly, as he glared at the Chancellor. The hushed tension in the chamber was only offset by the loud and copious shouting and commotion outside.

"Shut that door," Christian finally said.

Van Necht complied immediately.

"Dewain, you are an ill-tempered man," Christian began coldly. "When Our father was king, he referred to you as his Prophet of Doom because no one could ever speak a hopeful word without you adding your foreboding, trepidation, or criticism, unbidden. He tolerated your company because he tolerated everyone's company. But he never liked you, nor your fellowship."

Dewain was very pale and swallowed nervously.

"Clearly, you fear that We will die in this war without an heir," he continued coldly. "But what is that to you, if you find yourself banished? Will any other kingdom endure your continuous cynicism or your anticipation of misfortune?"

The entire gathering stood stunned. Dewain was ashen and speechless with alarm. He fell to his knees before the King.

"Forgive me, Your Grace! I have never intended to give offense- to Your Grace or your beloved father! -I forget myself sometimes. I-"

"Silence!"

The Chancellor said no more, but remained on his knees before the King.

"Sire," Olbert said, stepping forward, "have mercy. Dewain has served you faithfully as he served your father. He-"

"Perhaps, Olbert, but We have not the patience enjoyed by Our father, and the royal ear grows long weary of the Chancellor's *never-ending, morbid prattle*- as well as with all Our advisers' *constant arguing!*"

No one dared to speak then. Acrida's eyes were on the advisers, wondering at this turn of events.

The muffled sounds of commotion were just barely audible in the chamber.

After a few minutes of silence during which his temper had time to lull, King Christian spoke again.

"Chancellor, if you can remain silent and avoid annoying Us for the rest of the day, you may very well, not only remain in the kingdom, but retain your position."

The Chancellor in crimson rose from the floor, bowed hastily, and retreated to stand by the wall beside the valet.

The King sat back in his chair and crossed his arms sullenly, his gaze drifting to the witch.

"Acrida- *some* are not confident that We will win this war, nor that We shall even survive it. What say you?"

Acrida swallowed nervously.

"My Lord King, I have neither seen your death nor the end of the war," she replied simply.

Paschal smirked while shaking his head in disgust.

"Would you like to review the other prophesies, Sire?" Grey quickly cut in, pulling some parchments out of a leather pouch he had brought with him. "Lord Olbert and I have been studying them."

Christian shrugged indifferently.

"I suppose."

"Forgive the interruption, Sire, but when are the garrisons due back from their hunting expedition?" Van Necht suddenly asked.

"Late tomorrow," King Christian answered without turning around.

Van Necht made no reply as he went out the courtyard door, shutting it behind him, the growing uproar outside once again drawing his attention.

Olbert and Grey fumbled through the parchments and passed certain pages to the King and Paschal.

"Pardon, Your Grace," came a breathless voice.

Everyone looked to the chamber door to see the temporary Commander of the Watch with more of the King's bodyguards, all with swords unsheathed. The knight did not wait to be recognized by the King before speaking again.

"Sire, it is a riot! My men are unable to control the mob! There are too many of them, and there are too few of us! For your safety, you must abandon the palace at once! -Withdraw to a safer location until we can send for reinforcements!"

"What?!"

"God in Heaven! I feared as much!" Grey was exclaiming, as he rapidly gathered up the prophecies and stuffed them back into the pouch.

"Leave the palace? Are you mad, Man?" Paschal asked, pushing past Acrida to the courtyard door and opening it.

He went out into the darkness where already Van Necht had climbed to the top of the wall and was observing the situation for himself.

"You do not have enough men to handle two or three score peasants?" King Christian demanded crossly, on his feet now.

"Sire, there are many more now! More than a hundred, possibly two hundred!" the knight replied.

"Two hundred?!"

"All my knights are hunting with the garrisons-" Dewain said in horror.

"Mine, too," Grey admitted.

"Where did they all come from?" Paschal was demanding as he returned from outside.

"Sire, there is little time!" the knight was pleading. "The mob is trying to break into the main corridor, and I do not know how much longer we can hold them back!"

"You must come away now!" the King's bodyguard said.

"This can not be happening!" Christian stammered in disbelief.

"It is as he says," Van Necht answered, striding in from the courtyard with sword in hand and Acrida at his heels.

"Where is Our cousin?" Christian asked. "We will not leave without her!"

"I have sent for the lady and her maid already, Your Grace."

Van Necht was at the young King's side then, ushering him towards the door of the study. Cedd met the King at the door with his hooded mantle and a sword. Christian took the sword and belted it around his waist as he led the way hurriedly out of his chambers into the corridor, his advisers, bodyguards, and servants following.

In the corridor, the shouts and cries of panic echoed down the stone walls and columns. After turning the corner, the group was met by the guards that had been sent to collect the Lady Kaithryn. She and her maid already wore their cloaks.

Running down the corridor, clutching extra swords, Sirs Eldwin and Ecktor hurried to join the group.

"My Lords, the main entrance is blocked! There is a throng of people in the courtyard! You will never get through them!" Sir Eldwin reported as he quickly handed a sword to each unarmed nobleman.

"Are we trapped?" Dewain asked, alarmed.

Behind the knights, the sounds of struggle were even louder.

"The other way-" the King instructed, and the group turned and headed the way they had come.

As the group approached the right bend in the corridor that would lead to the King's and counselors' chambers again, Lord Olbert paused.

"Wait!" he called out.

The King stopped. The Royal Steward stood in the dimly lit hallway, feeling the stone on the left wall with both hands. Sir Ecktor was immediately by his side.

"What is he doing?" Paschal asked.

"If I remember correctly-" Olbert mumbled. "There it is!"

"What is it?"

His hand found a loose stone, and hidden behind it, an old, rusted, iron ring. He stepped aside, and Sir Ecktor pulled on the ring, but nothing happened. Sir Eldwin and Van Necht were immediately beside him too, helping him, and the old, forgotten, hidden door opened, screeching as it scraped against the stone of the floor.

"Get a torch!" the Watch Commander told one of the guards.

The man retrieved the nearest one from its holder on the corridor wall. Holding the torch far in front of him, he peered into the blackness behind the door.

The door opened into a long, dark, narrow passageway full of thick cobwebs. The floor and stone wall were peppered with bugs. With the unwelcome disturbance of noise and light, the rats immediately scurried away.

"Quickly! Go in!" Van Necht commanded.

"But where does it lead?" the knight was asking.

"It matters not! We can conceal ourselves in here if need be," Eldwin answered.

Bending over, the guard knocked the cobwebs away and proceeded to enter the musty passage. Ducking down, the rest of the group followed quickly, cursing the dust, spiders, and vermin as they went while wrestling with the sticky cobwebs that they met.

"Shut the door behind us!" Van Necht called.

Kaithryn's maid swallowed hard as she held her charge's hand. Please let them not be discovered, she prayed. And please let them not be trapped in here.

"Ugh-" Acrida complained, as her bare feet crunched on what she could not see that was both cool and gooey.

"Lord Olbert, where does this lead?" Sir Ecktor asked.

"If I remember correctly, there should be another door at the end that will put us somewhere near the old additions."

"How ever did you know about this?" Paschal asked, hurrying down the passageway after Christian.

"Tate showed me this passage long ago when we were both youths at the palace. He knows of many more."

"That explains much," Paschal muttered.

As they hurried down the passageway, they turned a corner and continued on until another wall ended the short trek abruptly. They could hear the sounds of commotion near them. As the knights and Van Necht busily felt the walls for another door, the rest of the group anxiously waited, hoping to breathe fresh air. The men found the door and with great effort forced it open. The group followed them through the doorway to the smoke-tinged air of outside.

With the roar of fighting in their ears, the group stood momentarily astonished at the ensuing chaos before them. In the growing darkness of falling night, they were surrounded by fighting. However, they were only about thirty yards from the royal mews. The mews, though, was under attack as well. A few of the Watch were there, trying to help the stable hands fend off a group of rioters and keep the horses from being stolen or injured. The younger stable boys were busy putting out the small fires that had sprung up from the torches the rebels were carrying and fighting with. Although there were far more rioters than stable boys, the rioters were having little success approaching the horses that were already rearing and neighing with alarm in their stalls.

Van Necht immediately headed for the stables, as the King and the Commander of the Watch closely followed with the rest. As they neared it, they were able to see the main gate. Usually the massive, wooden gate remained open day and night, but the Watch had closed it once the fighting had begun to prevent more from joining the rioters and to keep the rebels from escaping. However, the gate's closure now trapped both the rebels and the King inside the walls of the palace.

"Commander!" Van Necht shouted above the clamor. "You must take some of your men and secure and open the gate! And we need more of your men here at the stables until the King and his ward are safely mounted!"

The commander nodded and yelled some instructions to the guards that had accompanied them. Then while the other guards went to summon more of the Watch to reinforce the stables, the commander and the knight with the torch hurried off toward the main gate.

At the mews, Van Necht ordered the stable hands and boys nearest him to bridle the King's horse quickly. The lads, recognizing the noble group, ran to retrieve the bridles for the horses, abandoning the remaining fires to burn as they would.

The excited horses, however, would not cooperate. They reared, kicked out, and pawed at their familiar handlers as the boys tried to corner the beasts in their stalls in order to catch them.

"Hurry! Saddle Lady Kaithryn's horse now! We have not much time!" Van Necht yelled behind him.

Then dodging one peasant's rod, he broke the weapon in half with one blow of his sword. The man, startled, quickly ran off.

Acrida, seeking some way to help, picked up the water pails that the boys had dropped and looked about for the cistern of water. Dewain and Olbert joined her, showing her where the small stone fountain was, and the three worked to douse the few, small fires before they spread.

The maidservant held the young Lady Kaithryn closely to her. By the flickering, scattered torchlight, they watched the desperate attempts of the stable hands to still the frenzied horses so that they might bridle and saddle them. It was very dark already; the sky was overcast, and they could not see the moon either.

King Christian, with bloodied sword in hand, stood near the stable boys that were working to saddle his cousin's gelding, engaging any rebel that threatened to deter them from their work. The rioters, seeing themselves out matched, quickly retreated before they joined the dead men at his feet.

Seeing the activity at the stables and realizing that the King must be trying to make his escape, more rebels began to rush the mews. This throng was met by some of the Watch who were coming to fortify the stables. As these knights formed a barrier with their shields, a veritable wall of men, Van Necht, the King, Paschal and the King's bodyguards only concerned themselves with defending their space from those that broke through the line of the Watch.

Lord Grey calmly stood against the side of the mews with his arms crossed, observing the chaos about him with interest. Olbert, Acrida, and Dewain, with their work finished for the moment, came to stand next to him.

"Well, Grey," Olbert said, "you were right about the peasant rebellion after all. You will prove yourself prophetic yet. But how did you know?"

Grey smiled.

"Now, Olbert, I can hardly reveal my confidant and keep him in my employ."

"Perhaps the King is correct," the Steward smiled. "What have we need of a seer when we have you and your army of spies? For if the Bishop of Roma went to Hell, you would know it before the Devil himself."

The pair laughed at this.

The stable hands had finally gotten Lady Kaithryn on her horse and were trying to help the maidservant to mount her horse, but the rest of the horses were hardly more than bridled.

"Enough! Disregard the saddles!" Van Necht ordered, shoving the old, hefty serving woman into the saddle indelicately. "Take the King his horse!"

The stable boys obeyed immediately. The King was brought his snorting, neighing, rearing horse, unsaddled, and Christian, grabbing the mane, slung himself onto its back. It took him only a moment to gain control of the excited, white charger. Cedd ran up to the King and handed him the hooded mantle that the youth had dropped. Eight of his bodyguards and Paschal had also mounted their horses, and the gate was open now as well.

"We ride south!" Christian shouted, fastening the mantle around him. "Van Necht, We shall await you and the others at Wodenfeld!"

From the back of his charger, the King could see that although the great gate was open, the street was flooded with people, some fighting the Watch, some fleeing. Beyond the line of the Watch, it was a good three score yards or more to the main gate, and he was unsure that his cousin could ride through the people without getting pulled from her horse.

"You Four!" he shouted, pointing to the mounted knights near him. "You stay with Kaithryn!"

Then he turned to his valet.

"Cedd! Tell the boys to let the other horses out! And hurry!" Christian ordered.

The valet nodded and shouted the instructions. With the help of Cedd, Eldwin and Ecktor, the stable hands began to open each stall and shoo the horses out into the turmoil.

"Van Necht, get the Watch out of the way!" Christian shouted.

At once, Van Necht relayed the order to the Watch that were still fighting to keep the throng of peasants from approaching the mews. The guards immediately broke their line and retreated to the side, allowing the rebels to pour forward toward the stables.

The rebels screamed in terror as they were met by the first of the escaping horses. Some of the horses met the crowd and stopped, immediately rearing and kicking at the people, but most of the frightened, bucking horses headed in a run for the main gate, trampling anything unlucky enough to be in their path.

As a large group of the freed horses passed him, Christian held back his own mount no longer. The stallion bounded in the direction of the gate with the crowd of horses and with Paschal and four bodyguards following closely beside him. Lady Kaithryn gingerly turned her whinnying horse toward the gate also, but the gelding, seeing the mass of screaming, falling, and running people before it, took one step forward and stopped, despite the girl's frantic urging. At once, Van Necht appeared and whacked the horse smartly on the rear with the flat of his sword. The gelding lunged forward and followed the other horses toward the gate with the child holding on tight, the maidservant and the four knights riding near her.

Hearing the wild neighs and then seeing the loosed devils bearing down on them, the panicked people screamed in terror as they cleared the way before the coming equine flight. Mixed in with the herd, the King and his companions rode unimpeded out the palace gate. Once at a safe distance, the riders turned the mounts southward, riding into the darkness at a fast gallop.

Seeing them safely away, Van Necht turned his attention back to the mews.

"You did not release all the horses, did you?" he asked Cedd.

"No, My Lord. One of the boys is getting your charger now."

"Good."

Van Necht turned to see that Olbert and Grey had not left with the King. And behind them, almost cowering in the shadows, was Lord Dewain.

"Lord Ministers, you must get mounted!" Van Necht said as he strode past them.

"I must get some things," Lord Dewain was saying, looking back in the direction of the palace.

"It is too late for that now! Get to a horse!" Van Necht replied.

The stable boy arrived with a palfrey then. Grey did not wait for a saddle, but mounted the mare and dug in his heels. The road was still somewhat clear except for the few bodies in the dirt. Grey quickly steered around the bodies that were moaning pathetically and those that were silent; then he was galloping through the open gates.

"Olbert, we must go!" Sir Eldwin shouted, bringing his lord a horse.

Sir Ecktor was already mounted and was holding onto Eldwin's horse.

"I am glad you were here today," Olbert told Van Necht as his knight helped him get mounted.

Another boy arrived with a palfrey for Dewain, and Van Necht helped him quickly put the saddle on it.

The shouts of the rioters indicated that the fighting had renewed, and more people returned to the road and the gate entrance, actively fighting with the Watch. Van Necht helped Dewain onto the gelding while Eldwin mounted his horse. Olbert and Dewain bade Van Necht farewell, and they started at a trot for the gate with the two knights.

The road between the mews and the gate was filling rapidly again, before the aldermen. Olbert's horse, a tall bay, negotiated around the people without pausing and exited the gate while Ecktor and Eldwin, closely following him on either side, slashed at the rebels with their swords.

However, a group trapped Dewain, managing to stop his horse and grab its reins. No amount of shouting or threatening could make the angry peasant rebels release the horse and clear the way. Several members of the Watch, seeing the Chancellor's peril, charged the group with a roar and prevented the nobleman from being pulled from his horse and murdered. With his horse freed, Dewain immediately urged the palfrey forward. Although one of the rebel's spears ripped into his arm, he kept going, oblivious to everything except the safety that waited beyond the gate.

"Your horse, My Lord! Your horse!" a stable boy yelled, hardly able to hold on to the black, snorting, excited charger.

Van Necht had stopped giving orders and was now searching for something inside the mews. He broke off the search immediately as he saw that his high-strung stallion was going to be away from the lad in a moment or two.

"Get to safety!" he yelled to the boy, while taking the reins and climbing into the saddle quickly.

Seeing more rebels rapidly pouring toward them, the boy nodded and fled swiftly in the other direction.

Van Necht, from the higher vantage point, was able to see clearly the surrounding grounds. He moved his horse a little away from the mews, ignoring the fighting that encircled him.

The rioters surged toward him, and the horse immediately kicked out, knocking one man to the earth and then kicked him again in the head. As more rebels approached, the charger reared, pawing furiously, and then kicked out with its powerful back legs again as more men rushed it from behind. The peasants fell to the ground, dazed and hurting.

Van Necht continued to hold his mount in place as he scanned the area around the mews, the crowd of people in front of him and then around the surrounding wall. A rebel ran up and grabbed at his reins, but Van Necht felled the attacker with a kick to the face that broke his nose. The next fighter approached on the right, swinging a burning torch, but Van Necht batted the stick out of the man's hand with his sword, sending the torch flying, and then he stomped his foot into the man's chin, snapping his neck. The man crumpled at the foot of the horse, which struck him with its front hoof for good measure.

Then Van Necht spotted her. Acrida, only a few yards away from him, was beside a small fountain, trying to avoid the blows of both the rebels and the guards that were fighting each other near her. Clearly she had no idea of where to go, for fighting was everywhere.

Out of the corner of his eye, Van Necht caught the motion of a spear coming toward him from the left. Instantly, the warlord pitched his sword into his left hand and grabbed the spearhead with his right, yanking the weapon from the surprised man. Then he slammed the pole against the man's head, breaking the shaft. The man collapsed to the ground and was stepped on by the horse.

"C'sara!"

He shoved the spearhead with what remained of its shaft into the chest of a rebel that was running at him with a raised dagger.

"C'sara!" he called again, as his horse reared and struck two more approaching rebels with its front feet.

On hearing her name above the roar of the fighting, Acrida looked toward the sound and saw Van Necht on his horse. He gestured for her to step up on the side of the stone base of the fountain.

Looking around at the fighters, and at the guard that was working to drown a rioter in the water, Acrida quickly complied.

Although still surrounded by struggling people, Van Necht urged his horse forward. The charger did not hesitate. The horse straightway bounded through the people and on top of them rather than resist its master.

Once beside the fountain, Van Necht firmly halted his black horse that pawed one foot anxiously and impatiently. Acrida took hold of Van Necht hastily, and he, grabbing a handful of clothes, pulled her up behind him.

She was barely on, when Van Necht nudged the horse toward the gate. She clung tightly to his waist and put her cheek to his back as the horse charged forward through the fighting rebels, knocking them down. Van Necht and Acrida promptly arrived at the gate and then disappeared into the peaceful darkness, leaving the boisterous pandemonium of the palace behind them.

16

𝕬crida stood a bit wobbly on her feet. She had already been sore from the morning ride to the palace; but now, as she and Van Necht stood under the night sky allowing the horse to rest, her entire body ached. Finally, she sunk down in the high, fading grass of the lonely meadow and squeezed her legs tightly together, holding them there with her arms; she was rewarded with a little relief.

The charger itself was wet with foamy sweat and continually snorted, nostrils flaring. With its muscles twitching erratically, it reached down and grabbed a mouthful of weeds and chewed them greedily.

Van Necht opened and closed his sore right hand that was growing stiff. The hole from the spearhead went all the way through his palm, but the warlord had failed to notice that he was even hurt until a little while ago. The bleeding had mostly stopped already. He pulled up his tunic and ripped off part of the fabric at the bottom. He wrapped the material carefully around his hand and then tied a loose knot with his left hand and teeth.

After calculating how much farther they needed to travel, Van Necht turned to regard the woman lying in the grass. She had once again lost her headrail, and a thick strand of her long, black hair had escaped its braid.

Van Necht plucked a tall weed. He had never encountered a woman like her. In front of the King and his advisers, she was capable and outspoken, with the courage of a lion- or a fool, just the opposite of almost everyone else. But she was completely different away from Court: quiet, uncomplaining, and vulnerable -when she was not completely mad with grief.

Lying on her back, Acrida looked at the dark sky and then closed her eyes. Half of her wanted to fall asleep right there, and the other half never wanted to sleep again. She relaxed to the peaceful sound of the crickets and other insects and the sound of the dry grass waving in the cool, autumn, intermittent breeze.

"-I am sorry about this morning."

Acrida opened her eyes and turned to regard the alderman in surprise.

"You should have told me where you were going. -That you wanted to explore the area," Van Necht said and then hesitated. "It was bad luck that Lord Dewain arrived when he did."

He threw the weed top as hard as he could then, but it went only a few inches forward and then floated to the earth.

"No, forgive me, My Lord," she answered then. "I was wrong to go out of sight when you had been so kind and trusting of me. You made me see that. I am sorry I made you look remiss in your duty in front of the Chancellor."

Van Necht frowned as he thought back again on the search that morning. At first, he had been surprised and embarrassed when he could not find her; then, he had become anxious about what Dewain would tell the King. And, of course, he had been completely surprised by the tidings that they believed her to be a witch. -That was when he had become angry.

But it was the search that had really done it. He had searched for her for so long in those woods that he had begun to fear that something had befallen her. By the time he had found her, he had been furious with her- not so much for wandering off, but for making him care so intensely about her well-being.

But he had cared, and he had cared again tonight- so much so that he had sought, found, and rescued her in the middle of a riot- one in which she was most likely in no real danger, while shirking his real duty at the side of his King. The realization was irksome to him. The lord threw another weed fiercely.

Acrida watched Van Necht's face and wondered both at his words and at his expression that suddenly exposed some turmoil with which he struggled. Had a noblemen ever apologized to anyone of lower station before? She could not remember one tale of Huntingdon ever doing so.

"There is something I must know-" he said abruptly. "Are you a witch?"

She smiled.

"No, My Lord. I am a woman of the Faith."

"But the King believes you are a witch."

"Aye, but the King's belief will not make it so."

Van Necht picked and threw another weed top as he considered these words. He wanted to believe her. Until he learned different, he would believe her, he decided.

"We had better go," he said. "We will walk a while."

He offered Acrida his good hand. She took it and was pulled to her feet. The two led the horse southward.

159

17

While the guards watered the horses, King Christian leaned against a tree and continued to watch for the others to arrive. He and the group had ridden straight to Wodenfeld and found it deserted as they knew it would be. Wodenfeld was an old cottage that was surrounded by shallow woods and fronted by a large meadow. Hidden from the main road that passed by two hundred yards away, the cottage was a good place to go when one wished to be overlooked.

The cottage, no more than one large, dusty chamber, had fallen into disrepair from neglect, but it still had most of its roof, its table and benches, and some old, moth-eaten woolen coverlets. It had never had much more, as Christian remembered, for this cottage had been one of the 'hunting lodges' his father had utilized in his roaming debaucheries. When Christian had returned from Gaulia with his spurs, he had accompanied his father and his courtiers on some of those jaunts, but he had not been back since his father had died.

The King blew into his hands and rubbed them together; it was growing quite chilly, and they were keeping a cold camp tonight lest a fire give away their position to any rebels that might be searching for them. At present, there was no sign of anyone approaching, neither friend nor foe. All was darkness around Christian, and melancholy had replaced his excitement.

At first, the rebellion at the palace, his escape, and the tactical response that was necessary occupied his thoughts, but as the night passed, Christian found himself pondering instead the anxieties voiced by his advisers.

The old advisers believed that his kingdom and throne were in jeopardy. Christian thought their fears were absurd and groundless. The possibility that his rule was at an end was inconceivable to him, but the unthinkable was already happening around him. If anyone had told him that his own subjects, his own serfs even, would riot and run him out of his palace, he would have laughed at them. In fact, Grey *had* told him, if only today, and he *had* laughed. Yet, it had happened.

But why were the people rioting? he wondered. And how had things become so dire- so quickly? Could the uprising really have been in response to the interdict? Did the priests really hold that much sway with the people? Were the peasants really that superstitious?

And what would have become of him or Kaithryn if they had been taken? Would they have been held for ransom or simply murdered where they stood? These questions only made Christian's humor more morose.

He thought back over the past month, trying to recall if there had been any warning signs he had overlooked. There had been nothing- except the foreboding of his advisers and the vague predictions of a 'new king' from the supposed 'seers'. Could those madmen have spoken true? Was he destined to be deposed? But why? He was not doing things very differently than his father had. Why was his reign the one fated to end prematurely?

Christian frowned. If the 'seers' were correct, and he was to be overthrown, then what was he to do? Would it not prove futile to endeavor to remain king? After all, how does one take up arms against fate? Why even risk his life fighting or going to war at all? Would it not be wiser to take his cousin and simply flee the kingdom? If the people did not want him as their king, let them have Herryck! The people would soon appreciate his own benevolent rule after a few months of Herryck, for the conqueror reportedly governed his own vassals and subjects with an iron hand and taxed them heavily.

Christian sighed at these thoughts. Who was he attempting to deceive? He was king, and he desperately wanted to remain so. He had been born and raised for the crown, prepared for it, and trained to defend it. During the last year of his father's life, Christian had patiently appeased the old man while he bided his time, anticipating the day when he would finally rule. He was not ready to give it up. His crown defined him! Without it, he was no one, -nothing! He could never willingly give it up!

The situation could not be this hopeless! Christian told himself. There had to be a way to keep his crown and kingdom safe. He considered his options with a frown. He had known for months that he would have to 'get into bed with another kingdom' in order to secure the troops that Speyron needed to repel Herryck's attack, but he still felt it would make him appear as a weakling.

It was too late to be concerned about appearances now, he admitted. His prestige had already suffered a serious blow by the events of this night alone- perhaps irreparably. For what kingdom would want to align itself to a country where the people were in rebellion against their anointed king? -If word of this farce did not encourage Herryck to invade, nothing would!

Shivering, the youth wrapped his cloak more securely around him. Perhaps it was the stress of his present situation, or the recent talk of marriage prospects, or just simple melancholy, but the memory of his first betrothed came to his mind then. Christian had not thought of her in years.

He had been just fourteen years old when he received word in Gaulia that Princess Ita, to whom he had been betrothed since early childhood, would soon be traveling to Speyron to take her place as his wife. The match had been made with the poor, neighboring kingdom of Ria and had obligated the two countries to be stronger allies. Princess Ita was the youngest and only unmarried daughter of the royal family. The few lands the Princess would have brought with her as dowry would not have amounted to much, but his father had never been interested in expansion. Filberte had always enjoyed easy, expensive living, and these lands would have provided new moneys for the treasury without much effort.

At the time, Ria had recently come under attack by Herryck, and the nation needed military support to hold off the invader. Thus, they had sent the Princess to be married, even though both she and he were still quite young.

He, of course, had not known any of this at the time. He had simply been informed that he was to return to Speyron because his bride was coming, and soon they would be married. He had remained in a state of nervous excitement on the entire journey back home. He had never met the girl, but had heard that although she was not greatly handsome, she had a merry way about her. Christian smiled as he remembered how he had looked forward to meeting her. He remembered thinking back then that what his family really lacked was a sense of humor.

He recalled all the preparations that had been made for the wedding feast. Much food and much entertainment had been prepared. On the day she was to arrive, he had been filled with excitement. He had not gone hawking with his father and the Court, but had stayed in and made a hundred plans instead.

Later as evening set in and it was growing dark, his mother and the advisers had worried that the Princess had not arrived. He had worried also, but had tried to conceal it, for his father detested brooding. When he retired to his bedchamber, he sat up with a candle and read his Latin lessons, expecting at any moment to be interrupted with the announcement of her arrival. However, when he awoke at dawn with his head on the stack of parchments, he found she still had not arrived, but his father had sent some riders to locate the entourage and to find out if the party had been accosted by bandits.

A few hours later, a Rian messenger had arrived. Apparently, the Princess had been sick of late. Her parents had believed her recovered and had dispatched her to Speyron. During the journey, however, the entourage had been caught in the cold, spring rains, and the Princess had become ill again very quickly. The entourage could not travel any further without the fear of compromising her health, so they had taken shelter at some tavern somewhere.

Christian recalled how the King, the Queen, the Royal Physician, some of the Court, and he had all traveled up to the tavern together. Arriving by early evening, the physician had gone in to see the Princess first, and he and his parents had sat by the tavern fire and waited. His mother, trying to comfort him, had told him in her gentle way not to worry, that it was probably just a cold, and the marriage feast would have to be postponed a few days, but nothing more.

After seemingly the longest time, the physician finally had emerged from the chamber and told him he could see her. As he approached the door, he had overheard the physician tell his parents that she was gravely ill. The words had shaken him, but he had come all this way to see his betrothed, and having stowed up his courage, he entered her room.

The chamber had been quite dark, lit only by a few candles. Her ladies had curtsied when he entered, and he saw from the dim light that they were weeping. The delicate creature on the bed was pale and thin, a mere shadow of a real girl. Her arm had red marks on it from where the leeches had sucked. Her breathing was loud and labored. Her eyes were weak, but at seeing him, she had managed to smile.

Back then, the sight of a person so ill always turned his blood to ice, and Christian remembered how frightened he had felt. He had had to fight the urge to flee the room, shaking in terror. But she had held out her hand, and he had forced himself to take it.

"I am Prince Christian," he had managed to say.

Her raspy breathing had accompanied a very low, rough voice. She had managed to answer in a whisper, "I am so happy to finally meet-"

A fit of coughing followed by gasping for air ended her words. Her ladies had surrounded her bed again, but there was nothing anyone could do.

The King and Queen had come into the room then and introduced themselves. His mother had taken her hand and kissed it. After a moment, his father had excused them from the chamber and drew them out into the main room in the tavern.

Very quietly, his father had told him, "Christian, we are leaving."

"Leave? We cannot leave," he had replied.

"Christian, that girl is gravely ill. We cannot allow the Heir of Speyron to become ill also. The Queen may stay with her -if she feels she must."

He had looked at his mother, and she had concurred.

"But should we not bring her back to the palace with us?" he had asked. "We can not leave her in this tavern! Surely, she deserves better!"

"Aye, she deserves better, but she will not make it to the palace. And it is better to die in a warm tavern than it is to die on the road," his father had told him abruptly.

"She is going to die?" he had asked, his voice precariously wavering as he had fought to keep from crying.

His father had given him a disgusted look and walked off. His mother, sensing his pain, had embraced him immediately, but Christian had pushed her away because he knew his father did not approve of weakness.

"Go with your father," his mother had said, and he had, without looking back.

As they mounted their horses, his father had said, "I am outraged that the King of Ria should send such a sickly child to be the wife of a future king! I have never seen such a frail girl in my entire life!

"Do not grieve, Christian! This is for the best! Be grateful that you did not marry her, for if she had not become ill now, she would have surely done so in the near future. I doubt she would have even lived through childbearing -or if she had, she surely would have given you a sickly child as well. No, this is for the best!"

The Princess had died two days later. They sent her body back to Ria without troops. He had returned to Gaulia, and Ria had fallen to Herryck sometime thereafter.

The whole experience had been painful for Christian, but he had learned two valuable lessons. His father had taught him that few people would be worthy of a king's attention, and those who had the privilege of keeping company with a king or serving a king, had serious duties to uphold to retain that privilege. He had also learned that people would take advantage of a king if he allowed them, but a strong king was never taken advantage of.

"Are you well, Cousin?"

Christian looked around, and seeing his ward standing beside him, wiped his watery eyes with his sleeve and said with a forced smile, "Aye, Kaith, I was just thinking."

"About the uprising? Do not be anxious about that, Christian. We will be back home soon."

"Oh- not that. I was thinking about Princess Ita, who would have been my wife and your kinsman if she had lived."

"Oh."

"Aye, she would have been a fine mother to you now," he said, "and a much better example for you than I have been."

"Cousin, speak not so," Kaithryn replied, a little distressed at the low-spirited state of her cousin.

She embraced him and kissed him on the cheek. He smiled, sniffed and hugged her securely to him.

"I love you, Cousin Christian, the most except for my dead mother. I love you more than anything."

"Aye, but will you love me when I am no longer king?" he muttered with a sarcastic laugh, fighting the tears that were welling up within him.

"Not king? Of what do you speak, Christian?" Kaithryn asked. Then she added quickly, "You will always be my king, no matter what befalls us. And I will always love you."

Christian hugged her again and rocked her in his arms gently. How dear she was too him. It would be terribly difficult to be separated from her. He had never realized how empty his life had been until she had come to stay at the palace as his ward. But after this night, he had no doubt of the necessity of their separation.

After a moment, he let go of her and looked at her directly. Even in the dark, her long hair was shiny gold.

"A word, Kaithryn. I have decided to send you to a convent."

"A convent? Why?"

"Your tutor has left, and I wish for you to continue your stud-"

"Please, Cousin, do not send me away! I cannot bear it! You could get me another tutor at the palace, or wherever you are! I need not go to a convent!"

"Truly, Kaith, I think it best for you, -and you will be around other girls your age."

Lady Kaithryn looked away, frowning.

"When?"

"Immediately."

She sighed.

"I abide by your will, Cousin," she replied, "but I would have more diversion wherever you are."

King Christian smiled and took her hand.

"Perhaps you can come and visit me again after I marry. We will have feasts, dancing, and merriment every day. And I will show you off to suitors and arrange your marriage as well."

She smiled at this.

"Do not choose too soon, Cousin. Do not choose my husband until you are certain of what he will look like when he grows up."

They both laughed and then began to examine the stars that were out.

"My tutor had just begun teaching me of the stars when he left."

"Well, and what can you tell me then?"

"Very little. We had just started. But I know why their positions change in the sky during the course of the year."

"Why is that?"

"Because-" Kaithryn replied with a smile, "the stars, the sun, and the moon revolve around *us*."

"Aye, that is correct," Christian replied.

They looked at the stars, and Christian pointed out the different constellations to her and told her stories of how each one was named until her maid came and told them Kaith's bed was ready.

18

"They will answer for this, Sire!" Paschal stormed as he paced.

The bodyguards were nodding in agreement with the young adviser, but King Christian made no reply, his expression solemn and cold.

Earlier Lady Kaithryn and her maid had retired to bed inside the cottage, and now the King and his advisers and bodyguards were gathered in a small circle outside in the darkness to discuss the next course of action. Sirs Eldwin and Ecktor had already been dispatched to notify Lord Felix and the hunting party of the situation.

"Nor should we delay, Sire, in avenging your honor! Send the garrisons directly there and retake the palace tonight!" Paschal urged. "Smite the curs tonight!"

"Let us not act rashly," Grey argued. "'Twould be wiser to send the garrisons to the palace in the daylight. In all likelihood, we will meet little or no resistance tomorrow after tempers have had time to calm. -More lives will be spared."

"Spared?! I want a river of rebel blood to run through the street!" Paschal yelled. "Let us quell this rebellion at once before any more damage is incurred!"

"We do not even know how many rebels there are for certain," Olbert said. "It would be reckless to send the garrisons in unprepared."

"Sire, this *uprising*- if it can be called that-"

"'*If it can be called that*'? What would you call it, Grey? A friendly gathering?" Paschal demanded.

"I am only saying it could not have been planned out," Grey continued.

"Why do you say that?" Paschal asked.

"Because we escaped too easily," the King answered for him.

"Exactly, for all we know," Grey continued, "this '*uprising*' might have initially been nothing more than a drunken altercation of a few men that was bungled by the incompetent Watch."

"*Bungled*, say you?! *Incompetent*, say you?!" Paschal fumed.

"Aye!" Grey accused.

"It is unfortunate that Lord Felix is not here to defend the Watch's performance or his own training and supervision of them!" Paschal said. "And once again, Chamberlain, you malign the competence of one of the King's ministers when he is not present to defend himself!"

"I meant no such slight towards young Felix," Grey replied sweetly.

"Thou art a silver-tongued liar!" the youth replied angrily. "-But condemn *me* before the King in my absence, and I will come after your head!"

Grey smiled and turned his back to the youth.

"Ministers- please," Olbert interrupted, "if we could return to the matter at hand."

"Of course," Grey said evenly. "As I was saying, when the effects of the drink wear off, the guilty subjects will no doubt be stunned at what they have done, -ashamed even."

"Indeed!" Paschal added sarcastically. "I wager that the guilt-ridden culprits are all gathered at the church at this very moment to make their confession!"

"Little good it will do them," Dewain mumbled under his breath.

Acrida smiled.

"You tell a pretty tale, Grey, but it is only speculation!" Paschal continued hotly. "Sire, all we know for certain is that the Watch was overwhelmed by a mob of rebels; nothing more. For all we know, the fighting continues even now! Or perhaps the fighting has ended, the Watch is dead to the last man, and the rebels have penetrated the palace and are presently looting it! -Perhaps the street is full of peasants- all reveling on royal provisions! We do not know! But one thing I *do* know: *Now* is the time to act! Now!!"

Grey sighed dramatically and gestured to Olbert to take over.

"Paschal," Olbert began, "we all feel abused after what has happened, but we should not overreact."

"Overreact?! You, Dewain, and Grey have warned us for months that the peasants were only seeking a convenient time to revolt! Now that your fears have been confirmed, why do you plead for restraint? Now is the time for requital! Now is the time to teach them *all* that disloyalty will not be tolerated from anyone!"

"You mistake me, Paschal, if you believe I wish this offense to pass unanswered," Olbert answered.

Even by the dim light, Acrida could see that the elder adviser was exhausted.

"But if we send the garrisons there tonight," Olbert explained, "who knows how many more innocent lives will be lost? How many serfs who had nothing to do with the uprising will be mistook for rebels? How many loyal palace servants will be harmed? You must think of them also."

"Olbert is correct, Paschal," Grey argued. "If you send the garrisons to avenge the King's honor tonight, innocent lives will certainly be lost. If too many are lost, the King will not have enough serfs to work his fields."

"He can buy slaves!"

Both Olbert and Grey threw up their hands in exasperation.

"Besides, if we wait until light, the rebels surely will have fled! It is unacceptable that these rebels might escape justice!" Paschal fumed.

"If the rebels do flee, it will be simple enough to deduce who is missing, and the identities of the rebels will be known," Grey answered gently.

"Only if the rebels were among the King's own serfs!" Paschal argued.

"Who else would they be?" Grey asked.

"I know not!" Paschal shrugged. "The palace is visited everyday by travelers and traders from other villages and other kingdoms. The rebellion could have been incited by anyone. It could have even been Herryck's men in disguise!"

The entire assembly was quiet then. Dewain sat beside Acrida and Van Necht on a log, not daring to offer an opinion. In the ensuing silence, the forest sounds were loud around them.

Paschal eyed the King nervously, wondering if he was losing ground with him.

"What say you, Van Necht?" Paschal suddenly asked.

"About what?"

"What do you think should be done?"

"It is not my decision," the warlord replied simply.

"Even so, Van Necht, surely with your vast military experience you could advise the King on the wisest and most expeditious course of action."

"The King has not asked for my advice."

The young alderman made a gesture of annoyance. Olbert smiled.

"Well, *I* am asking: What do you believe will happen if we send the garrisons tonight?" Paschal asked with annoyance.

"It depends if the garrisons can breach the walls," Van Necht replied casually with a shrug of his shoulders. "If the gate holds and the rebels can make a stand inside the walls, the fighting could last for days or weeks. The garrisons may have to lay siege, waiting for the palace provisions to fail and starvation to begin. While they wait, those garrisons will have to be supplied.

"If the garrisons can breach the gate, the village, enclosed as it is within the palace walls, will be defenseless against them. The merchants' shops and the peasants' homes will likely be burned to the ground; the women will be violated, the men put to the sword, and anything of value will be kept by the knights. The people, or what is left of them, will be without shelter and utterly broken."

Acrida's heart skipped a beat and then raced at the description. It was not only Van Necht's words that turned her blood cold, but the ease with which he spoke them.

Paschal was nodding in approval.

"And-" Van Necht added, "in the confusion of the moment, you can not expect a knight to stop fighting to determine who is a loyal palace servant and who is a rebel. They will all look and sound much the same in the dark and commotion."

There was silence after these words were spoken. An owl hooted in the trees above the group.

"That would be unfortunate-" Christian finally said, getting to his feet, "but acceptable."

Acrida went pale.

"Your Grace, I beg you, do not do this!" the Royal Steward reiterated strongly. "You have more than four score men and women in your service at the palace in some capacity or another! I can assure you that they had no part in any of this! Please do not jeopardize their lives!"

"How do you know they had no part in it?" Christian retorted.

"Your Grace, if there were any servants whose loyalty or service was in question, as Palace Steward I would well know of it," Olbert insisted.

"Perhaps you have been deceived, for I was certain that everyone, both palace servants and serfs, were all perfectly content before this night!" Christian answered angrily. "Now I do not know what to believe! Now I trust nothing!"

"Still, Sire, if you punish all for the wrongdoing of a few, it will be seen by many as unjust!" Olbert added.

"If I do not take back my palace immediately with a show of force, I will be perceived as a coward!" Christian answered hotly. "Not only by my own vassals and people, but by the entire Continent!"

"Aye!" Paschal agreed. "You have already said, Ministers, that some vassals are sorely tempted not to support the King against Herryck! If he does not answer this rebellion swiftly, those vassals will surely be encouraged in their disloyalty!"

"Ride to intercept the garrisons and send them directly to retake and secure the palace," King Christian ordered the nearby guard.

Acrida stared in horror at the King, as the guard bowed and went to retrieve a horse. She looked at Dewain. Could no one say anything to dissuade the King?

"You should understand, Your Grace," Olbert said quickly, "that if you unleash your knights on your own serfs, they will never forget it."

"Aye, this action will only further estrange your subjects' love-" Grey added.

"They have estranged mine!" the King yelled. "And my honor will be avenged!"

It was more than Acrida could bear. Angry now, she could be quiet no longer.

"Your -*honor*?" Acrida said, standing up.

The King's hostile eyes were then on her.

The advisers were momentarily dumbfounded at what they realized she was about to say. Dewain grabbed Acrida's wrist in warning, but she wrenched it away from him. Van Necht's heart skipped a beat, then raced as he saw the ominous look of displeasure on the King's face. He was going to end up breaking her legs after all, or worse.

"Acrida!" Olbert called, quite alarmed, and signaled for her to be silent, but she would have none of it.

"Must not a man be *honorab*-"

Acrida was abruptly interrupted in mid-sentence as she was yanked back down and her mouth firmly clamped shut by Van Necht's hand. Everyone looked at the usually reserved alderman in surprise as he held the woman fast and mute despite her struggling.

"Forgive me, Sire," Van Necht said with perfect composure. "I know thou hast cast thy favor upon this woman, but my ears cannot bear the onslaught of a sharp tongue, and once this shrew gets started, it takes the threat of a beating to subdue her."

Olbert and Dewain breathed in relief. Paschal and the guards chuckled. The King still looked quite miffed. Acrida was furious and continued to try to twist out of Van Necht's grasp.

"Forgive her, Van Necht," Olbert spoke up hastily, sending the warlord a knowing look. "She has had a long day, and the woman is clearly- fatigued."

"If she is that tired, she should retire to bed," Paschal said contemptuously. "After all, *her* advice is not needed at the moment."

The King agreed. He glared at her angrily with crossed arms, wondering once again why Olbert, Dewain, and Grey valued her visions so highly. Had she foretold something of which he had not been informed?

With a nod from the King, Van Necht stood up to take Acrida into the cottage. In so doing, he loosened his grasp on her only for a moment, and in that instant, she was free from him.

"If you send your knights against your own defenseless servants, thou hast not a soul!" she shouted angrily.

"Hush, Woman! The decision has been made!" Dewain said quickly.

"How is it 'acceptable' for your serfs to be attacked, brutalized and killed, when you know not with certainty of their guilt? They are people, flesh and blood like you! They are not swine to be slaughtered at your whim!"

"See, Lord Ministers, what is reaped from granting rewards and position to a woman!" Paschal commented with disgust.

Acrida did not even heed the remark.

"Would King Filberte have done this?" she demanded. "Would he not have followed the law and allowed the accused a chance to declare their innocence? -Shall the people of Speyron rue the day that you became king?"

"No one has asked for your opinion!" Grey warned her.

"If you do this, King Christian," she continued, "you are not made of flesh and bone! If you sic your knights on defenseless women and children, to be violated and their lives ruined or ended, thou art a monster! *Anyone* who could commit such horrible deeds is a soulless monster!

"Have you so quickly forgotten those boys at the mews, of not enough years even for hairs to bespeckle their chins? They were fighting to protect your horses from the rebels even before we arrived! Although they might have been killed under one strike of a hoof, the boys still braved those wild horses, caught them, and bridled them so that you might flee to safety!"

Lord Olbert was nodding in agreement.

"These are the ones that will pay the price for *your honor!*" Acrida finished angrily. "But what should I expect? Thou art a king who does not repay loyalty, except with suffering and death!"

Olbert and Dewain's faces were full of alarm. Van Necht cringed. None of the assembly uttered a word, as they awaited the King's response.

Struggling to control his temper, King Christian glared dangerously at the witch who dared to reproach him. Acrida, herself, was so angry that she was shaking; her chest was heaving; and she looked like she would jump on the King at any moment.

"So the King should not pursue the rebels," Paschal said with impatient sarcasm, "because a few, innocent peasants might be hurt?"

"We peasants may be lowborn," Acrida argued, "but we are human beings, same as the King- same as any of you! We have the same needs, the same hopes and dreams as any noble-"

"We are not the same!" King Christian shouted back. "We are leagues apart! You and your kind are the dirt under our fingernails! You are *animals!*"

Acrida was stunned.

"Aye, an animal!" King Christian reiterated, seeing how his words found their mark. "True, a human animal, but a beast all the same, here to serve *our* needs, to be used as *we* see fit as any other ox, horse, or cur is. And, Woman, if you would keep your life, as well as your place at Court- you had better remember it!

"And you may wish my father back to life as you like, but he lives and rules no more. -Little good it would do you to still be under his rule, for he followed the law only when it served his purposes to do so.

"And as for what will befall the villeins this night- it is nothing rare!"

"Aye! Surely they knew what the consequences would be for their rebellion!" Paschal added.

"Every man of arms here has performed all those 'horrible' deeds many times!" the King continued hotly. "-Including our beloved father! It hardly makes us *monsters* to do what is necessary to break the villeins' spirit, so as to insure order! And in the end, it is a *trifle* compared with what I will do, for I will discover who was behind this attack! My palace walls will be adorned with the heads of men, women, and children until I find out the culprits! -Now, get thee out of my sight before I order the guards to begin with *you!*"

Quaking, Acrida hardly breathed. Van Necht immediately had her arm and was moving her towards the door of the cottage. She went with him, scarcely knowing what was happening. As they departed the group, she heard Grey say:

"Sire, if you are determined on this course of action, send me to the palace to oversee the-"

"Paschal, go join Felix and the garrisons at the palace! Find out who was behind this uprising- drunken or not! Use whatever means you deem necessary! And if you find the village as a whole still continues to be uncooperative, take away their provisions and let their hunger convince them to talk!"

Acrida was horrified. Agreeably inside the cottage, she could hear no more of what was being planned.

Van Necht accompanied her inside the dwelling and looked around. At the farthest end of the cottage, the King's cousin and her maid shared the one bed. Van Necht picked up two coverlets and spread one out on the floor near the women. Here, at least no one could drag Acrida out or assault her person without the risk of waking Lady Kaithryn. He put Acrida down on the coverlet and covered her with the other musty, woolen blanket. She turned over onto her side and pulled her knees up as the first tear rolled down her cheek.

The sound of the door shutting after Van Necht left the cottage was the last thing Acrida heard except for the maid's persistent snoring. The King's words had deeply wounded her. Was that truly how all noblemen saw commoners? As animals put on earth for their use and pleasure? As she thought about it, she realized the truth of it. What was a serf but a pig not allowed out of its sty? She had gained nothing by being freed from the land. She was now the King's bitch, dependent on his table scraps and favor- and would be killed -or worse -if she showed her teeth to him.

"My Lady, you must wake and be ready to ride. Your cousin, the King, calls for you."

The maid's idle chatter awakened Acrida. She sat up wearily. The night had passed without further incidence, though her sleep had been fitful at best. The door of the cottage stood ajar, and dawn's dim light was permeating the dwelling. Acrida slowly got to her feet and made her way to the door. Outside, she was greeted by Lord Dewain.

"Good! You are roused," he said.

Acrida said nothing as she sleepily brushed a long, loose, strand of hair out of her face with her hand.

"It has been decided," he told her, "that Grey will go to the palace and survey the damage there. Until word is received that the rebels have thoroughly been routed and the palace is completely secure, the King will accompany Lord Olbert and stay at his castle. He will likely remain there until the leaders of the uprising have been found. I go to my lands for a few days to begin making arrangements for the training of foot soldiers there. I will also escort and install the Lady Kaithryn into a suitable convent in the south."

Acrida nodded as she listened.

"You are welcome to come with us if you like. There is plenty of room at my castle," he told her pleasantly.

"Am I free to go where I please, My Lord?"

"Anywhere, but with the King," Dewain smiled. "He will not suffer either of us to be in his company at present."

"That is just as well," Acrida replied with a yawn, "lest we wished to join the dead sooner rather than later."

Dewain chuckled.

"Still, it is a pity for Olbert," Acrida added. "Must the King go to his castle?"

"Olbert's lands are nearest the palace," Dewain informed her. "But fear not for his life, for if Olbert should fall into King Christian's disfavor, he never remains in it for long."

"It is not the King's disfavor that will kill him, but when his castle is besieged," Acrida replied simply with another yawn.

"Besieged? Of what do you speak?" he asked.

Acrida shrugged with unconcern.

"Lord Olbert and King Christian will be besieged. The castle will fall."

Gasping, Dewain looked at her in alarm.

"Art thou certain?"

"Aye, I have foreseen it."

Dewain gasped again and crossed himself.

"How long have you known this?"

"About a fortnight or so, My Lord."

"And why did you not tell anyone? Why did you not tell the King?"

"Tell the King? What should I care for a king that considers me the equal of his cur, and then not quite? Why should I care for a king that last night unleashed his knights on rebels and loyal subjects alike?"

"Acrida! This is no time for petty disagreements and injured pride! Quickly, tell me what you know! Who will besiege the castle? More peasants? Will the King die? Is there a way to avert this siege?"

"Bearded knights."

Dewain gasped again.

"What are you two talking so heatedly about?" Olbert asked, having walked up behind them with Van Necht and Grey.

"There is a problem, Olbert. Your castle will be besieged."

"What?"

"Aye, Acrida has foreseen it."

"Are you absolutely certain?" Olbert asked.

"Where are your lands, My Lord?" she asked bluntly.

"A few hours ride west of the palace."

"Aye, if the King goes there, there is no doubt," she replied with a shrug of her shoulders.

"My castle will be besieged? For how long?" he asked.

"I know not, My Lord. But you will die in the battle, and your wife and daughter will weep over your body," she told him with an air of indifference.

Lords Olbert and Dewain grew pale.

"And is there no way to avert this?"

"Aye."

"And what is it?"

"Why, the King must not go there, obviously. He must travel eastward instead," she said.

"East? Why east?"

"East? Where in the east?" they were asking.

"I know not."

"This can not be true," Grey said then, "for Herryck's army will surely attack from the east. Methinks thou art still angry with the King, and you speak this falsehood to put him in greater danger for vengeance's sake."

Acrida laughed out loud and shook her head.

"No, My Lords, I speak truly. But whether or not the King heeds my words, I care not, for I can stomach no more of him."

"Of what do you speak?"

The men turned to see that King Christian had now joined them. He was haggard with fatigue, and he had dark circles under his eyes.

"Sire, your- *sibyl* has had a vision," Dewain began amicably. "It seems if you go to Olbert's castle, the castle will be besieged by an army of bearded knights and *will fall.*"

The King looked at Acrida doubtfully.

"Is that so?"

"Aye, so the war shall begin and end," she said coolly.

"Will it be a long battle?" Christian asked sarcastically.

"I know not, Sire. But the burning of the dead will last into the night and beyond."

Christian looked into the bruised face of the witch. She seemed unconcerned about this information, even amused. Clearly she despised him.

The feeling was mutual. The woman had no qualities to recommend her. She was neither comely, nor soft spoken, nor submissive; and she had the tongue of a harpy, not a counselor. The King was equally offended that such boldness, intelligence, and natural eloquence should be found in a villein woman. She was, in a word, everything that a woman should not be, and Christian was sorely tempted to break her neck himself.

"Did I not even yesterday ask you if you had foreseen as much?"

"You asked if I had foreseen a rebellion of your own subjects, and I answered you truthfully."

"Well, I suppose I shall have to use more care in asking you these questions," he answered irritably.

"She has been shown a way that the siege may be averted, Sire," Dewain spoke.

All eyes turned back to Acrida again.

"Well?" Christian asked.

"A brief time of peace will abide in Speyron if you travel east, Sire."

"Travel where in the east?" he asked "Outside our borders? In another country?"

"I know not."

"You will have to do better than 'Ride east, I know not where' if you wish to be rewarded for your services," Christian complained.

"You can not go east, Sire! It would only put you in greater peril, for Herryck will likely invade from the eastern border! We know this from the prophecies," Grey warned.

"Aye, the boy from Rothshire did say that the ruling king would come from the east," Dewain agreed.

"That prophecy *could* refer to Herryck if he invades from the east," Olbert said, "but might it not refer to *anyone* from the east, even King Christian?"

"What is your meaning?"

"He did not say 'the ruling king'; he said the *new* king," Grey corrected them.

"Sire, while it may not be possible to change what has been prophesied," Olbert continued, "perhaps you might attempt to become a part of what has been foreseen by entering into it."

"Weave King Christian into the prophecy?" Dewain asked curiously. "Is that possible?"

The men looked to Acrida for an answer.

"My Lords," she answered, "I know not. I have not the wisdom of Jebedye. All I know is if King Christian goes to his vassal's castle in the west, the castle will fall to bearded knights. If he travels east, peace will abide in Speyron for a little."

The ministers all spoke at once.

"But go where?" Christian asked in exasperation.

"This is unwise!" Grey's voice argued over them all. "There is no haven in the eastern section of the kingdom that will afford the King any real protection! The vassals there have no great love for him, nor did they for his father before him! It is perilous for him to travel east!"

"I can not help that, My Lord," Acrida replied simply with a shrug, and the noblemen continued to argue among themselves. "I have told you all that I know. Do as you will."

19

When the group parted at Wodenfeld and Acrida chose to remain with Van Necht, the King's ministers and guards had all smiled queerly at the warlord, and Christian himself had laughed out loud as he rode away. Van Necht himself had said nothing to them or to her, but had simply mounted his charger slightly perplexed at her choice and pulled the woman up behind him.

It was late afternoon when they arrived back at Van Necht's village, very hungry and weary. Although Van Necht was anxious to return to his own lands, they had ridden no faster than a walk most of the way. On their arrival, the pair stopped at the lord's inn for dinner.

The castellan's wife tended Van Necht's wounded hand, washing it out with wine and bandaging it with a fresh cloth. The castellan gave Acrida a headrail to cover her hair; then, they had all sat down to eat, and the castellan told them the most recent word from the palace.

Already, the report of the uprising against the King and the garrisons' retaking of the palace had made it to Van Necht's lands. Apparently the knights were easily able to retake the palace as they found the gate wide open.

Lord Van Necht said not a word during the entire meal. His face revealed no expression whatsoever. The castellan might as well have been talking about the weather. No sooner had he finished eating did the alderman rise from the table and depart. Acrida had to leave the table still chewing to keep up with him.

Once outside, she saw he had already collected his horse and was in the process of leading it down the road. Alarmed, she ran to catch him. The woman's sudden appearance at his side seemed to equally surprise the nobleman. He stopped, noting her anxiety.

"You can stay here if you like," he told her simply.

It was the first time he had spoken to her all day.

"The rooms are free to *my guests*."

"But- I do not know these people, My Lord."

"The castellan and his family are good and true. You will be treated well."

Acrida looked away from him, disappointed. Although she made no further protest, the frown on her bruised face and the sad look in her blue eyes told him clearly that it was not her preference to stay at the inn. She wanted to remain with him.

Van Necht looked at the woman, mystified. She was like a hungry puppy he had made the mistake of feeding, and now it was going to follow him home.

Glancing at the darkening sky, Van Necht shrugged his shoulders.

"You can stay with me if you prefer."

Relieved, she nodded quickly.

"Thank you, My Lord."

The horse snorted as it walked down the path beside them, out of the village toward the lord's field. It was a while before Acrida summoned the courage to break the silence between them again.

"Are you angry with me, My Lord?"

"Why do you ask that?"

"You have not spoken to me all the day."

"I prefer silence to idle banter."

"So you are not angry with me?"

"Should I be?"

"I thought you were angry with the way I spoke to the King last night."

"I do not care what anyone says to him," he replied coolly, but after a moment of consideration, added, "but you are not a cat, C'sara."

"My Lord?"

"You do not have nine lives. If you had attacked the King's honor as you wished to do, Christian would have slain you where you stood."

Acrida frowned.

"If you are going to be his counselor," he continued, "you will have to be more sensible than that. You must learn to separate yourself from your feelings and not allow them to control you."

"Not allow my feelings to control me?" Acrida fumed. "How do I accomplish that? You know what they were planning for the villagers last night!"

"Aye."

"Is that all you have to say about it?"

"The King's order was a reasonable response to the situation. They are his serfs. He may do what he will with them, just as I may do what I will with mine, -just as your Lord Huntingdon-"

"Huntingdon upholds the laws of the land!"

"It is his prerogative to do so," Van Necht answered calmly. "-And your village is fortunate to have such an alderman."

Acrida was shocked at the words.

"Would you have done the same?" she asked abruptly. "Sent your knights against your own serfs?"

"If *my* serfs rebelled?"

Van Necht paused, thinking it over.

"It is difficult to know what I would do in that situation- for every situation is different. I suppose it would depend on what the circumstances were and how they had come about."

"So you would have at least tried to find out what the cause was before you sent in garrisons of knights to retake your castle?"

"Not necessarily."

"But would you not-? Would not *any* honorable man- any nobleman with a *claim* to honor- not at least try to discover the matter before-"

"Not necessarily."

"But-"

"C'sara," he said, stopping in the road and looking at her directly, "rather than ask me every question possible, just ask the one you want to know."

"What question is that, My Lord?" she asked defensively.

"You obviously want to know if I have burned villages, raped women, and killed innocent men, women, and children in order to bend them to my will."

Acrida's heart skipped a beat.

"Aye, I have- dozens of times," he finished.

Van Necht watched the discolored face of the woman fall; she seemed pained at the information. She swallowed hard and did not look at him. For a moment, he thought she might even cry. But she did not weep.

He walked on then.

After a few minutes, she said in a very controlled voice, "Well, I was wrong to expect any of you to understand, I see. You are incapable of it."

"Understand what?"

"Though you may be accustomed to committing such vicious deeds, My Lord, I see that your station shields you from understanding how the victim is devastated by them.

"You are not a commoner. -I doubt that anyone has ever hurt you or raised their hand against you- simply because they could. You have not had your children dragged out of your house and taken from you. You have not had your loved ones killed in front of your very eyes. You have not had your home burned to the ground for sport and everything that means anything to you taken from you. -You have not been beaten at the King's order-"

Van Necht stopped walking and turned to face her.

"No, I am not a commoner," he replied, locking his brown eyes onto hers. "But just because I have not suffered what you or other villeins have suffered, do not presume that *I* have not suffered also.

"You are not a knight! You can not know what it is to be honor bound to follow the orders of -the unwise, the cruel, or the excessively vengeful. You can not know what it is to be ordered to kill the innocent or to be ordered to show no mercy to the helpless against thine own conscience. Yet, oaths must be kept, and duty and honor must be served. For all you suffer, you villeins should at least be thankful that you are free from the burden of honor, for the cost to maintain it and keep it unsullied is dearer than you can imagine."

Acrida made no reply then, moved by his words and the strain in his voice. Van Necht may have done all those terrible deeds, she considered, but perhaps it was not always his wish to do them. Perhaps the knights who had to follow the King's orders found it as terrible as the victims did.

Her thoughts went back to the knight in the church and the look on his face when the King gave the order to desecrate the altar. Perhaps his expression had been more than astonishment. Perhaps it had been horror.

Van Necht walked on again, and the horse and Acrida followed.

Having walked the rest of the way to his camp in silence, Van Necht's thoughts had strayed back to Acrida once more. She had surprised him again. Of the very few women guests that he had been obliged to house since his castle had burned down, she was the first to refuse to stay at the inn. It was hardly a fair comparison, perhaps, since the guests he had had previously were traveling with their husbands and were already accustomed to the comforts of life. Even then, the ladies had considered the inn's simple amenities of a dry bed and a roof that did not leak barely adequate for their social standings and dignities. Yet, the inn was the best that he was prepared to offer anyone; and she had made it clear to the King that she would not be satisfied with receiving an adequate allowance for her upkeep but instead had demanded the luxuries enjoyed by those above her station.

On the other hand, perhaps what she *truly* desired was not at the inn. Perhaps she wished to get to his bed, Van Necht mused. After all, she could hardly choose to stay alone with him and not expect him to touch her if he wished.

When they arrived at the tent, the hound greeted his master with a wag of his tail. The charger, as soon as it was unsaddled and unbridled, lay down in its corral and immediately began to roll. After feeding and watering it, Van Necht and Acrida wearily went into the tent and prepared for bed with the dog joining them.

Acrida watched the warlord take off his heavy, outer tunic and stretch, all the while wondering what the sleeping arrangements would be now that she was no longer his prisoner.

Van Necht sat down on the furs of his bed and began to unbandage his leg wraps. He could feel her eyes on him as the low sound of thunder rumbled in the distance.

"My Lord, where would you have me lie?"

Van Necht made no other answer than to give her an obvious look. Need she have asked at all?

Although she did not comprehend the look that he gave her, Acrida realized that he was in an even less talkative mood than he had been earlier. She shrugged to herself and simply smoothed out the fur beside his where she usually slept. Sitting down, she began taking off her own leg wraps.

She wondered if she should take off the braes and simply sleep in the tunic she already wore which was abundantly long, or if she would need the braes for added warmth. The braes were quite dirty from all the horse riding. In the end, she opted to remove them, and standing up, she turned her back to the nobleman as she untied the braes and stepped out of them.

Van Necht's pulse quickened at the sight of the woman's bare calves. He watched mutely as Acrida yawned and stretched her lithe body enticingly; then she sat down on the fur beside him again and pulled the fur coverlet up to her waist.

"My Lord, as long as I stay with you, what think you of letting me cook?"

Van Necht blinked, then wondered at the unexpected request, but shrugged indifferently.

Acrida smiled.

"No offense, My Lord, but I miss my own cooking."

She said nothing else, waiting expectantly for a response.

"Very well, you may go to the village and get the supplies you want from Aldric, my steward. He can get you anything you ask for."

Van Necht pulled his linen undertunic over his head then, baring his muscular chest and arms with their various scars; then he lay down on his fur bed and pulled a fur coverlet over himself. As he untied his braes, he watched Acrida remove her veil and begin unbraiding her long, luscious, black hair, and then comb it out with her fingers slowly. In the darkness of the tent, the bruises on her face were hardly noticeable.

Outside the rain began to fall.

After combing out the entire length of her hair, he watched her cross herself, close her eyes, and begin to whisper the Paternoster as she did every night. When she finished, she crossed herself again, yawned, and finally stretched out on her fur beside him, pulling the other fur coverlet over her more.

Acrida closed her eyes, her exhausted body seeming to melt into the fur. She finally felt completely safe. She wondered briefly how long this feeling of security would endure. Then she fell asleep.

Van Necht sat up then. Despite the cooling rain and his bare chest, he was already hot, and his heart was beating fast with anticipation as he watched the peaceful rise and fall of her chest.

Would she resist, he wondered? Surely not, after all he had done for her. Clearly she desired him too, he reasoned. She had not even tried to sleep apart from him. And had she not taken off the braes by her own will? -Even so, she probably *would* make a show of protesting, resisting, or even crying, for maids were inclined to do so for modesty's sake -or so he had heard.

He reached over and plunged the fingers of his bandaged hand into her soft, black hair, caressing the smoothness of it. She did not stir at his touch, but only relaxed deeper into sleep.

What was he waiting for? he wondered. Why was he not already on her, claiming his reward for saving her life?

Removing his hand from her hair, he pulled back her coverlet, peeling it slowly from her chest down to her stomach. Then he faltered, dropping the covering straightway.

Despite his intense desire, his yard had suddenly collapsed.

Van Necht groaned internally as he lay back down. His member had not totally failed him in a very, very long time, but as he felt his soft yard with his hand, he knew that it was happening again.

What was wrong with him? Was he not a man after all?

Perhaps he did not find her as comely as he thought he should, he mused. But since when did that matter? It never mattered on the battlefield- nor in the stews- and the wenches there were no beauties.

At one time, this had been his member's customary response to his loathsome wife. The hated shrew could wither his yard at fifty paces without effort.

But why now? C'sara was nothing like his wife. -Or perhaps she was, he thought again. He remembered once more how she had rebuked and insulted the King in her fury as readily as his wife had him.

Van Necht groaned in frustration. He should *not* be thinking about his wife! Where were all these thoughts coming from? This was no time for thinking! He should be acting!

Van Necht worked to clear his head and stiffen his resolve as he observed the pleasant lines and curves of her body. As time went by, her odd request for a child came to his mind.

Had she asked for a child because no women were bearing children in Speyron now or had it been something more? he wondered. She had said she had had no husband. Had she been trying to get with child anyway? From the moment he had met her, he had thought her chaste, despite her age, but perhaps he had been wrong.-

Regardless, if he had known that she longed for a bastard child, he would have gladly bedded her the first day she arrived!

Acrida muttered something unintelligible in her sleep and rolled over onto her side. Van Necht frowned at the woman's back. He sighed with exasperation and let his yard alone. Despite his manipulations, his member was not cooperating. He rolled over away from her in aggravation and shut his eyes, hoping sleep would come to him as rapidly as it had come to her.

20

The two witches sat chattering together before the fire and cackling in delight at their accomplishment. Van Necht, utterly frustrated, reached for yet another sword with which to kill his hated enemies. As he lifted the weapon, the hags, one, his dead wife, and the other, Acrida, watched him with amused expectation, completely unconcerned with either his wrath or his intent to kill them.

Once again, with all his strength, Van Necht swung the large sword fiercely into the neck of his hag wife, only to have the blade break in two on impact. Once more the two women threw their heads back and laughed heartily at the man's pitiful assault. Van Necht looked around in rage. On the ground around him lay a score of swords, all broken or bent, all proving completely useless in his fight.

Finally, his dead wife stood up and accepted the nobleman's surrender and oath of allegiance which Van Necht did not know he had given. He protested. He denied that he had yielded. He declared he would sooner die than cheapen his honor by swearing allegiance to them. But the crones had only laughed and told him that it was too late. Van Necht flinched, adjusted his member, and went cold with panic when he could not feel it. He looked then, even untied his braes, and to his horror, his yard was indeed gone. There was only a bloody hole where once it had been.

Van Necht awoke in a cold sweat. His heart felt like it was about to pound out of his chest, but the witches and broken swords were gone. Realizing it was only a dream, he took a deep breath and tried to relax. But after a moment, he was checking to make certain all of his parts were accounted for. It was then that he, with some alarm, discovered he was completely entwined with Acrida, for in their sleep they had curled up closely together for extra warmth.

Fighting down the urge to escape the entanglement at all costs, Van Necht forced himself to remain calm. He lay in the darkness of the tent and listened to the birds sing as his heartbeat slowed. It was very early.

Although dawn was still long away and it was quite cold, the promise of more sleep could not tempt Van Necht. The alderman carefully disentangled himself from the sleeping woman and quickly got up, dressed himself in fresh clothes and a heavier, woolen tunic and a mantle and went out of the tent. Outside he built his campfire and prepared to shave as he waited for the daybreak.

Van Necht did not wake Acrida before he left. A little after daybreak, he rode to meet with his steward. Afterward, he attended his manorial court, where he heard and decided the disputes of his peasants and assigned various fines. There he announced that all freemen were to assemble for training in the coming days and that the rest of the manor would have to begin to store provisions and prepare weapons for the upcoming war.

By then, it was noon and the accustomed time for Van Necht to meet with his vassal knights. Van Necht mounted his black charger and rode back into the heart of the village to a small building that was just off the road and out of the way. Although there was no symbol displayed to suggest what the appeal of the place was, the small lean-to shack beside the establishment was already half full of horses. As he dismounted, a boy approached, bowed to him, and led the charger into the makeshift mews.

Van Necht entered the small building and hesitated inside the doorway as his eyes adjusted from the bright light outside to the dimly lit interior of the building. Looking around, he acknowledged the bows and greetings of the occupants. He moved to the right of the door to a table where the freeman who owned the establishment handed him a horn of ale.

"Welcome, My Lord."

Van Necht greeted the barkeep and sampled the ale, observing, as he did, a little man sitting in a chair against the wall near him.

"Greetings, Father," Van Necht spoke politely.

"Pax vobiscum, My Son," the priest replied contentedly, making the sign of the cross in the air with one hand, while the other stroked the unbound hair of the woman whose face was in his lap.

Van Necht turned back toward the main part of the room and looked around again. The stew was nothing more than a large room with six tables with benches, and it was filled with the sounds and smells of drink and swyve. Sparsely clad wenches were sprawled on table tops and others on benches, while their customers bucked and labored over them. The alderman made his way through the loud, candlesmoke-filled room to the far table where two lavishly dressed men and a youth were sitting and drinking with three wenches.

The first man was handsome with dark hair and a charming smile. He wore a tunic of the finest blue cloth with embroidery about the cuffs; the scarlet mantle about his shoulders was clasped with a silver broach. He wore a ruby ring, and his polished sword handle gleamed in the flickering candlelight. His slightly younger, blond companion wore a fine green tunic and mantle with a bronze broach. The entire group stood up and bowed when they saw Van Necht approach their table.

Van Necht greeted his two vassal knights, Sir Albern and Sir Geoffrey.

"My Lord, we have missed you this past fortnight!" Sir Geoffrey said, offering his liege lord his arm in greeting.

"Aye, I have been engaged with the King's business," Van Necht replied simply, as he sat on the bench opposite to his vassals.

"Aye," both knights replied, sitting back down. "Of that we have heard-"

"And about the uprising at the palace!" the youth added with interest.

"Were you at the palace during the uprising, My Lord?" Geoffrey asked, having noticed the lord's bandaged hand.

"I was."

"Is it true that more than a thousand serfs attacked the palace?" Colm asked excitedly.

Van Necht raised his eyebrows and glanced at his two knights.

"-And that the battle raged for so many hours with so many killed that the horses had bodies to step on rather than earth and that the King-"

"Not really," the warlord interrupted.

The two knights chuckled.

"Do you know, My Lord, whether the King even survived?" the boy asked again. "They say no one has seen him since the uprising, though some think he has already returned to his palace and simply chooses not to show himself."

"If the King were dead, we would have already received word," Sir Albern told the lad. "The King most assuredly went to one of his vassals' castles, likely Lord Olbert's, Grey's, or Paschal's."

Although they were curious about what Van Necht would say about the uprising, his knights did not press the warlord for the facts, knowing quite well that he would not divulge anything of importance in such public surroundings. Instead, the group recounted the different stories they had all heard concerning the rebellion as well as the latest rumors on the retaking of the palace.

As he listened, Van Necht looked the wenches over. The first one wore a drab, brown gown that loosely laced up over a low cut undertunic that revealed her still youthful breasts. She had sores on her lips and a scar on her neck, and she badly needed a bath. Youngest of the three, she was perhaps thirty years old, and her oily, red hair hung limp down to her waist. She was already drunk and sloppily hung onto Sir Geoffrey as he stroked her thigh.

The second woman whose breasts were being held and stroked by Sir Albern inside her tunic was also drunk. She was a few years older than the first wench and smelled equally bad. She had the dark skin of a moor and was taller than the other two wenches. Her hair was long and dark, and it curled down its entire length. Her gown, which she was falling out of, was similar to the redhead's, except it was dirtier and patched in more places. She kept pulling the loose garment back over her shoulders, but every time she coughed, it slipped back down her arms.

It was, however, the third woman that Van Necht wanted. She was a large woman with long, thinning gray hair. The skin of her face and arms was wrinkled from age and hardship, but her eyes were wise and sharp. When she smiled, the wide gap between her two front teeth showed. Her worn, ruddy-colored dress was laced tight around her very thick waist, and her very large, weathered breasts that had given suck to several children and countless men, hung free from the confines of her clothes. She was not beautiful. None of them were. But her body, the way it was built, and the way she displayed it, appealed to Van Necht. She always looked soft and inviting to him.

Finally, the knight in the scarlet cloak changed the subject.

"Pray, who is your new woman?" Sir Albern asked with a smile.

Van Necht drained his cup.

"She is not mine," he answered coolly. "I was charged with guarding her while she was the King's prisoner. Yesterday, the King appointed her his adviser."

"Really? From prisoner to adviser-" the knights remarked with interest.

"And a *woman* at that-" the old wench commented.

"How did she accomplish it?" the boy wanted to know.

"How do you think?" the dark-haired wench replied with a crude laugh.

"Truly, give me but one night with the King, and I could get such an appointment," the redheaded wench added.

"If she is his adviser, why does she remain with you and not with the King, My Lord?" Sir Albern asked.

"And why does she not stay at the inn?" the redhead asked.

Ignoring the wench's question, Van Necht answered the knight.

"She is out of favor. Last night she berated him in counsel," he told them.

"Not even one day and she is out of favor?" the lad exclaimed.

"She is nothing like the retinue of flatterers that surround the King," Van Necht continued. "She has more spirit than sense, for she does not hesitate to oppose the King, nor to provoke him. At present, he bears the woman outright ill will, and likewise she- him."

"And she has been given a position at Court?"

"What is her title? Is she the King's Fool or the King's Fury?" Sir Albern asked.

"The King's Shrew?" the boy asked.

Van Necht's eyes rested on the youth momentarily, and then he replied, "The King's Bane."

The group chuckled.

"At present, King Christian will not suffer her company at all, and in truth, it is for the best. For if she had remained in his presence, I suspect she would likely be dead by now."

The wenches raised their eyebrows.

"-But how it happened to fall to me to provide her with hospitality and protection, I am uncertain," he added.

The group chuckled again.

Van Necht's eyes once more fell on the youth being trained at arms by Sir Albern and who, at the moment, was fondling the old wench's great teats.

"Colm, are you finished playing with Manda yet?" Van Necht asked abruptly.

"Aye, Lad, let a grown man have a chance!" the knights were saying.

The youth laughed and removed his hand from the wench's copious breasts.

"To be fair, My Lords, the boy is as *grown* as any woman could hope!" Manda replied, slightly whistling as she spoke.

She slapped the boy on the back good-naturedly as she rose from the bench. Colm beamed at the compliment.

The wench walked around to the far end of the table. She sat on the tabletop and pulled up her long gown, baring her legs to her thighs.

Van Necht stood up and went to the end of the table, but then hesitated. He looked about the chamber, noting the many people around, his cheeks reddening with embarrassment.

"How now, My Lord?" the old wench whistled. "You desire something different, perhaps? And why not? There is neither confession nor penance to be done at the moment.- Thanks be to the Bishop!"

"Let us go to the back," Van Necht replied.

Manda smiled and got off the table, leading the way to the back of the brothel. At the back of the establishment were two small niches that at one time had stalled the freeman's cows. Now they were used specifically for patrons that were willing to pay the extra money for the privacy. Each nook was smaller than a horse stall and was only separated from the main room with a worn curtain.

Manda led Van Necht inside the one that was unoccupied and drew the curtain. It was quite dark inside the stall and cramped; the soiled straw that covered the dirt floor took up all the space.

"What is thy pleasure, My Lord?"

Van Necht took off his plain, woolen mantle and hung it on a peg in the wall.

"The usual," he answered as he began to untie his braes.

The usual? Manda raised her eyebrows. Something was amiss. The warlord was not modest after all, particularly not in front of Albern, Colm, and Geoffrey.

Van Necht could feel Manda's eyes on him, which only made him more nervous. But why was he even anxious? He must have been with her a hundred times if he had been with her once. There had never been a problem before.

Manda stood quietly against the wall, noting the nobleman's serious expression and the blush of his cheeks. She observed his frustration increase as it became apparent that his brae strings had somehow become knotted and he could not get them loosed.

"Here, let me do it," she said, stepping up to the noble Van Necht.

He allowed the woman to approach, and she bent down to get a better look at the knot. As she worked with the string, the nobleman's excitement steadily ebbed just as he had feared it would. He should have cut the laces, he realized. However, after a moment, Manda had the knot undone, and she began stroking and rubbing the nobleman's yard to encourage its increase. Van Necht's body immediately and willingly responded to the woman's expert touch, and it was not long before his shaft was reaching to the sky.

"You can well fly your banner from it now, My Lord!" she whistled, satisfied with the results of her effort.

Van Necht was relieved to hear it. Bare to his knees, Van Necht sank down on the straw and pulled her down with him. Manda lay down on her back and pulled her gown up, baring her pale legs, while Van Necht pushed her knees up and wide apart. He positioned himself and then plunged into her without hesitation, gasping as he did with pleasure.

Manda had to smile. He was as direct as ever. As long as she had known him, the warlord had been this way. He reminded her of a thirsty man desperate for a drink of water.

"I see you have missed me," she commented.

"Aye, I have missed you," Van Necht mumbled over her. "He will have no other wench."

"No, *he* would have any wench, but his master is very picky," Manda answered with a chuckle.

If only that were true, Van Necht thought. Then he returned his concentration to his labor and to the sweet sensations coming from his loins.

It was not long before Van Necht finished and climbed off the woman. He sat beside Manda while he caught his breath, relieved that it had gone smoothly.

"A question, My Lord, about this woman who is *not* staying at the inn, but *is* staying with you.-"

"What about her?"

"Is she a married woman? Or perhaps betrothed?" Manda asked, covering her legs again.

The question surprised Van Necht.

"Of course not. Think you that I hold my honor in so low esteem?"

"Your reputation, My Lord, as an honorable man is known throughout the kingdom. King Solomon himself could leave you alone to safeguard his seven hundred wives and not be disappointed when he returned. That is why I wondered if this woman was married, for I think it curious that your desire should be so great, and yet you come to me rather than reach for the woman that is under your own roof."

At her words, the nobleman's amiable mood instantly changed. Van Necht got to his feet abruptly and pulled his braes back over his hips and retied the strings again, frowning.

"She is not to my fancy!" Van Necht answered gruffly, trying to regain his composure.

Manda observed his reaction with interest and wondered what had happened. She had not seen him this choleric since before his wife had died. -Perhaps the wench would not lay on her back for him without raising a fuss, she mused.

"Likely, I will send her away on the morrow," he added.

"What a pity that would be."

"Howso?"

"How will you learn to love again, My Lord, absent from the company of women?"

"I have had enough of love," he said irritably, reaching for his mantle.

"No, you have had very little of it," she told him. "Your wife, Lord Van Necht, was a fool not to count her fate lucky to have you. And despite everything, you still tried to treat her as honor required. Now that Heaven has blessed you with her death and you are free to find a better match for your hot blood, do not waste your chance, My Lord, with prolonged bitterness."

"Think you that you are my priest now and that you may offer me counsel unbidden?" he asked her testily.

Undaunted, Manda laughed as she got to her feet.

"Aye, My Lord, for you and most of the men of the village are on your knees before *me* much more often than you are before the Father. And he is here just as often as the rest of you."

Van Necht made no reply. He pulled back the curtain, and they went back out into the main room to join the others again.

21

The rain fell steadily as the afternoon approached its end. The riders' moods were low, and the horses' ears lay back against their heads as they carried their burdens through the sloppy mud, the cold, relentless rain, and whipping wind. The six riders bore no insignia or color; each wore a plain, heavy, hooded cloak that was drenched with water. Except for the flagrant presence of the horses, the party could have passed for wandering commoners from any part of Speyron, and due to the close proximity of the eastern border, poor pilgrims or even refugees from neighboring soils as well.

Christian the Fair, King of Speyron, was miserable. He, Olbert, and four of his bodyguards had been slowly riding toward the east for four days, and it had been raining for two and a half. He was soaked; his skin was wrinkled and raw from the rain and the strong winds that blew from two different directions. He kept trying to remember the last time duty had called him out in weather as foul as this; then he cursed his rebellious peasants again and the witch who had convinced him to ride eastward.

The King's mount coughed twice but continued to plod along. Christian already had had to relinquish his own horse because his bodyguards were convinced that he could be identified by his white charger. However, he found he rather liked riding this chestnut palfrey because he did not have to watch it carefully. His stallion was fast, beautiful, spirited, and difficult to manage at times. This gelding just quietly followed the horse in front of it.

Christian scratched his chest with irritation. He was not accustomed to wearing anything but the finest cloths and linens, and the group had had to trade their fine, brightly colored clothes for plain, commoners' clothing in order not to attract attention. The youth found these roughly-woven, woolen clothes made him itch unbearably, and even moreso when they were wet. As if the clothes and the weather were not enough for him to endure, this morning his throat had begun to hurt, and now it was on fire with pain.

Christian groaned. What was he doing? He should be in bed- his own bed! -Actually, *any* bed would be acceptable at present, for he would surely catch his death out here!

He and his men had been trying to evade any rebels that might be pursuing them by avoiding people in general and, thus, the roads that people traveled. The first two nights they had slept out in the open. The third night they had happened upon an abandoned shack with a partial roof. Although it was cold and damp, it was some shelter from the steady rain. Today, however, as they neared the eastern border of Speyron, they had by necessity had to take the road, but there were few travelers on it due to the storm.

Christian's thoughts turned back to Kaith once more. He just hoped that wherever his cousin was, Dewain had the good sense to keep her out of the wet weather. The minister had told him that there were two convents near his lands which had excellent reputations for learning, and there were girls from noble families near to Kaithryn's age at both of them. Since Christian himself had had no preference, he had entrusted Dewain with the choice and the finalization of the details of his cousin's entry into one of them.

The memory of Kaith weeping when he had embraced her and bidden her farewell was still fresh to him. Although he had worn a brave face in front of her, he had felt equally aggrieved to be parting from her, perhaps more so, since he feared he would never see her again. Of all his family and kinsmen with whom he had ever been acquainted, Kaithryn was the one that Christian cherished most.

The King was distracted from his thoughts by his bodyguard who was pointing to some buildings on the road up ahead, the first they had seen in hours. As they rode closer, Christian looked around. The pair of buildings seemed to be nothing more than a large tavern and stables set at a crossroads. But where were they? What vassal held this land? How far was the village?

Still, shelter was shelter, and there was smoke rising from the center of the tavern. He would welcome the opportunity to stop and get out of the rain, to get warm and have a drink, no matter the risk. He made a gesture to the group, and the six rode over without delay, dismounted, and tied their fatigued horses up on the side of the building that blocked the wind.

"Now remember, Your Grace," Olbert said, "stay close to your men and do not take offense at anything you might hear these common folk say and do not reveal your identity no matter what occurs."

Christian scowled at the nobleman. Did Olbert think him a complete simpleton?

They entered the tavern. It, in fact, was actually an inn and was warm, smoky, and bright with a large fire that blazed and crackled in the large hearth in the center of the room and candles that burned at every table. The place was full of all sorts of people. Some seemed to be foreign traders, others- simply travelers caught by the storm. Others were probably freemen from Speyron; still others wore the suspicious look of bandits. The people were all talking, drinking, and laughing at various tables.

The patrons of the inn looked up from their talk to scrutinize the newcomers. They quickly surmised that the six men were not commoners, especially as they caught a glimpse of the swords under their cloaks. However, they simply assumed that they were knights who wished to remain inconspicuous and untrifled with; thus, they all turned back to their drink and their talk of women, children, family and the uprising at King Christian's palace.

The six men made their way through the crowded room to an empty table not far from the fire; they peeled off their wet cloaks and removed their swords discreetly, trying to keep them concealed. The pudgy innkeeper greeted them and brought them all a mug of ale, eyeing them carefully. A comely girl of about fifteen years with curly, auburn hair brought them all bowls and spoons and a large pot of stew and a loaf of bread. Lord Olbert thanked them and pulled out his purse. The innkeeper smiled widely as he took the gold coin. When the six men were left alone again with their food, they spoke.

"This is madness," said one of the bodyguards. Then he lowered his voice to a whisper and added, "We cannot keep riding about aimlessly. We need to stop somewhere. -Get our bearings."

One guard agreed; the next disagreed.

"We need to get out of here," another said. "It cannot be wise to be this close to the border. What if we are seen by one of Herryck's spies? What if *he* should be recognized?"

Christian got to his feet and moved out of earshot of the men, retreating with his food and ale to the large stone ring where the fire burned. It was more than a desire for warmth that moved him. He had endured this futile discussion for the last two days and did not want to hear it again at present; the very same thoughts accompanied him everywhere anyway. It was painfully obvious that none of them knew what to do; even Olbert could offer nothing worthwhile. Every choice seemed as unpromising as the next.

The more the King considered his desperate predicament, the more his stomach hurt. In fact, he was ill with thinking about it. Even now, after a long day of riding through constant rain, he had no stomach for food, but he forced himself to eat anyway, knowing he would need his strength.

Christian's eyes drifted around the tables of people and settled on a pair of twin boys with curly brown hair and freckles who looked about four years old. They were sitting quietly together sharing a bowl of food. Christian smiled as he watched them pick out and eat the bits of meat from the watery stew with their fingers, all the while ignoring an older boy who was instructing them to dip their bread into the bowl to soak up the juice.

"I think-" said one of his knights, and then he lowered his voice, "we should acquire passage to Londinium. -It is the safest place."

"No-" another knight shook his head and whispered, "how many times must I say it? *He* must not leave the kingdom, lest Herryck attacks."

"So what do we do? Just keep riding all winter?" the other knight whispered again.

"Eat your food," a different knight answered.

Olbert was silent as he ate, noting the changed manner of the King. Christian had not even given a second look to the maid who had smiled at him, which was proof enough to the minister that finally the youth understood the gravity of his situation. Although Christian was sufficiently serious-minded now, Olbert was still disappointed. Although it had been days since the uprising had occurred, the youth continued to fail to hearten to the challenge of his situation and, even now, remained morose and melancholy.

Olbert knew that this was the first serious adversity Christian had faced in his young life, though it would certainly not be the last. It was unfortunate that it should coincide with his first real trial as king as well.

The youth seemed so despondent over what had befallen him, however, that Olbert was concerned whether Christian was of strong enough mettle to withstand the strain that accompanied kingship.

The minister sighed and began thinking back on his twenty-five years or so of service to the Crown...

King Filberte had been the youngest of five princes and had not been prepared for rule as his elder brothers had. When his brothers perished in battle a few months before his father died, Filberte was nothing more than an undisciplined youth, a young man more of appetites than wits. Yet he had had the wisdom to surround himself with many sage counselors and had relied on their competent advice. Despite the doubts of some peers, Filberte was able to successfully consolidate his power, and his effectiveness as a ruler was undeniable.

Olbert himself had been lucky enough to come to King Filberte's notice a year or so after taking the throne. After a few years, he was appointed Palace Steward.

In the King's later years, however, Filberte had had no appetite for anything but pleasure, and he had given little thought to the distant future. His lust had only increased after the death of the Queen, and the refinement of the Court was reduced to the wantonness of a common brothel. Drunken, whoring knights, courtiers, and courtesans were to be found everywhere in the palace, engaging in debauchery at all hours of the day and night. Guests of the King were either delighted or utterly appalled at the spectacle. Chaste maidservants had refused to step into the palace, much less work there; and virtuous noblemen, if they visited Court at all, had dared not bring their wives and daughters.

Olbert himself had endured the unseemliness as best he could as well as the almost constant separation from his wife and family. Sometimes, when his longing for decency had overwhelmed him, he had stolen away to his own lands for a few days until a summons from Filberte would arrive, forcing him to return to the palace. Yet his loyalty had been greatly rewarded. Over the years he had become one of Filberte's most trusted advisers, and vast lands and the wealth that came with them had been lavishly bestowed on him and his family.

Although Filberte had sought and acted on his advice more often than any other counselor's, Filberte had refused to heed his warnings about Herryck. For years, the invader's strength had grown as he snatched up the neighboring kingdoms around Speyron one by one. Against the advice of all of his advisers, when Herryck had threatened to invade Taews, King Filberte had resisted making an alliance with them and sending them much needed aid; instead he had insisted that Speyron stay out of the conflict. War was expensive in Filberte's opinion, and unnecessary, particularly since Speyron was neither directly nor immediately threatened.

Five years ago, Olbert, along with the other upright men at Court, had longed for the return of Prince Christian from Gaulia who had recently completed his training at arms and attained his knighthood. It had been a number of years since the Prince's last visit to Speyron. Word had arrived from Gaulia long before that Speyron's own son excelled in the arts of war. Christian was said to be unmatched with a sword and showed promise in the designing of strategies for the battlefield. With the Prince's return home, Olbert had hoped that Filberte from shame alone would put aside his licentious ways and take a renewed interest in his kingdom and perhaps even take a stand against Herryck.

To his disappointment, when the youth finally returned to Speyron, the King did not amend his ways, and Prince Christian, rather than being a noble and virtuous influence, immediately joined his father in the frivolous and sinful amusements at the palace -*at first*.

It was clear that the Prince had become more self-confident in his last few years in Gaulia, for when he returned to Speyron, he no longer actively vied for Filberte's attention or approval. The Heir to the throne was actually quite restrained in his father's presence. He seldom offered an opinion about any business of the Court and even seemed quite bored by it. As the months passed and the uniqueness of his presence diminished, the Court had paid little heed to the subdued Prince who did not share in their humor nor particularly relish their daily amusements. In time, Christian and the Court completely parted company, with the Prince usually to be found out hunting or hawking with his 'bachelor court', the entourage of vassals' sons of similar age who accompanied him everywhere.

Not too long after Christian's return home, a few conservative advisers had recommended marriage for the Prince; but with the many wanton women running about the palace, the youth had been less than enthusiastic at the prospect of limiting his lust to a wife. King Filberte had declared that since his son did not particularly wish it, he did not see the necessity of pursuing the matter at the present time. Olbert had known all along that the King would never agree to the marriage. In truth, Filberte in his age and ill health feared his son and resisted his son's marriage lest his throne prove too much of a temptation for his son and his daughter-in-law's family. Thus, the subject of the Prince's marriage was never broached again.

Olbert remembered the excitement he had felt at Filbert's death and Christian's coronation. Here finally was the opportunity to return Speyron to its former glory and vanquish the kingdom's reputation for weakness, frivolity, and immorality that circulated in foreign courts. Olbert had expected that Christian would bring a new dignity to the throne that the kingdom had not known for some time. He had hoped that Christian's rule would finally bring an end to the Court's daily preoccupation with amusing diversions. He had believed that a young king with vigorous ideas and a desire for winning glory and honor would inspire the other nobles to put aside their petty feuds and unite with much needed patriotism, for King Filberte's indifference to the strife between his vassals had served only to divide his subjects further.

Unfortunately, Christian's love of leisure was as great as his father's had been, and the feasting and merriment had continued. Although skilled in the arts of combat, the young King did not burn with the desire to exercise these skills. Matters of valor or honor simply did not move him. And, like his father, when his vassals arrived to pledge their loyalty to him, rather than inspire them with bold plans for the future- he had simply feasted with them and made a weak request for peace to be established between warring factions. In actuality, Christian had had no real interest in putting an end to the private wars between his vassals, for he believed that as long as they were occupied against each other, they were less of a threat to him. Thus, although Speyron had a new king, Christian's vassals, as well as the majority of the Court, had believed that nothing of substance had changed.

Of course, they were mistaken; Christian and Filberte were very different men, and everyone came to realize this very soon.

Most rulers understand that kingship in itself naturally creates awe in people. Put a commoner and a prince together without the peasant knowing who the man is, and the man will prate on and on without hesitation. Tell the villein that he is in the presence of a prince, and he will be too overcome with nervousness to speak, or if he tries, he will only stammer and blush. In similar circumstances, noblemen prove not much better themselves.

Filberte, like most other rulers, had always taken this into account and had tried to put his Court and his subjects at ease. He had not been quick to take offense at their errors or to laugh at their awkwardness. He had been careful not to ridicule his vassals for their weaknesses, nor for any ideas that he found absurd. He even had had the disarming ability to laugh at himself, which further helped to make others feel comfortable in his presence.

Christian, however, could not have been more dissimilar to his father in these matters, though, when he first arrived home, he blended into the Court so well that the differences were not apparent. When he came to the throne, though, he surprised all when he suddenly revealed another side to his personality. To say that the youth delighted in his preeminence was to understate the truth. He relished the groveling of his subjects, as well as the outright fear of those who served him. But even more unforeseen- and most detrimental for a would-be ruler, King Christian had an unpredictable temper- and when riled could become quite dangerous. Criticism or slights, real or perceived, were not to be endured. Thus, no one dared to make a joke for fear of the youth's displeasure.

There were other changes in store for the Court as well. Instead of leaving the court appointments as they had been, Christian dismissed everyone from their posts. Former courtiers, clerks, and advisers each had to pay a tremendous fee to retain the appointments that they had enjoyed under Filberte. Those who could not afford the fee, most notably the several clerics who had served King Filberte as court advisers and clerks, were made to understand that even their appearance at Court was unwelcome. Then Christian had filled the available positions with the youths that had been his companions since his return from Gaulia, although they were wholly unsuited for the posts.

Even more troubling to the seasoned advisers and the remaining Court was the King's love of cruelty that daily seemed to increase. Like many young men of that age, the King and his companions had a love for blood sports and blood-spilling. As Prince, Christian and the youths of his bachelor court had prowled the countryside seeking prey to kill, brawls to start, and such general mischief. Once he became king and had appointed his two favorite companions, Felix and Paschal, to advisory and very powerful positions in his government, the three youths were wild with their new powers and their ability to inflict pain. No longer did hunting the forests for game gratify their desire for blood-spilling. They hungered for cruel sport with which to amuse themselves, but now nothing was off limits to them.

With the youths' devilish approval, Christian had begun ordering beatings and executions and delighting in them, -the more unexpected and ghastly, the better. Anyone showing signs of weakness, incompetence or disloyalty was in danger, no matter if they were peasants or faithful counselors of noble blood that had served at Court for years. And although no other king in Speyron's history had done it, Christian displayed the heads of those he executed on the palace wall, not so much, Olbert knew, as a warning to his enemies, but as trophies.

Many of Filberte's remaining Court were afraid to be in the young King's presence at all. Thus, the crown had not been long on Christian's head before the courtesans, the foreign dignitaries, as well as the fair-weather friends of King Filberte retreated from the palace in packs. Of the eight royal advisers that had paid dearly to retain their appointments, three of them within the first year were forced to leave Court in ill health, unable to cope with the precariousness of the King's favor. The seasoned ministers found themselves blamed for every minor difficulty that occurred, while their wise advice was looked on with suspicion. Many of the newly appointed youths in time departed from fear also, as well as from the pressure of their positions. Gradually, the palace and kingdom were left to be managed by a few: some loyal and idealistic ministers like himself- and others- the dregs of the ambitious, whom no amount of intimidation or humiliation could scare off. With the untimely death of the previous Royal Exchequer, only five advisers now remained to aid the King in ruling Speyron, and Olbert feared that if he and Dewain left Court, Paschal's untoward and harmful influence on the King would increase unchecked.

There had been, however, a few surprising improvements, the Palace Steward admitted. Christian had been appalled by the insolent attitude and lax behavior of the palace servants when he returned from Gaulia. As one of the first acts of his reign, Christian ordered the servant quarters of the palace to be enlarged in order to draw a better quality of servant to work in the palace. The servants were given their own bath and were well provided for in food and clothing. The King had explained to Olbert that he was willing to grant the servants what they needed and more, but they were to behave respectably at all times. To help in this endeavor, the King encouraged the knights in the palace garrisons and the Palace Watch to marry or to take concubines, but informed them that they were to refrain from dallying with the palace servants.

Also, curiously, although King Christian was a man of lust, he never looked at any of the maidservants, nor any vassal's wife or daughter, but restrained his desires to his own concubines. He had started collecting the girls and housing them in an old wing of the palace even before Filberte had become ill. Olbert suspected the King only selected villein girls because they were no threat to him either in matrimony or in honor. And although it was more sinful, with the way he stole the girls from their families and from the service of his own vassals, than having a castle full of half-naked courtesans and serving wenches running around, it seemed less so because none but a few ever saw these girls since they were confined to their section of the palace.

All of this Olbert had borne with patience, but he was deeply troubled by the disdain in which Christian held the Church and the Faith. Filberte had been far from devout and privately felt the Church put constraints on his authority, yet he had tried to make the Church's influence work to his advantage by publicly respecting the role that it played among his people and by making certain that the Church was well represented at Court. He had entertained the Bishop regularly, and he had sought the advice of his parish priests. Christian, in contrast, had not even attempted to conceal his contempt for the Faith, and he had made every effort to minimize its presence and influence in the kingdom.

Olbert's thoughts were interrupted by the sound of someone clearing his throat. He and the guards turned to see the jolly innkeep standing behind them with a broad, friendly grin on his face.

"'Tis a miserable night. Are you in need of lodging?"

The five men offered no answer at first.

"If you would like a bed for the night, I can offer you what I have left," the innkeeper added pleasantly.

"Go on-" said one of the guards.

"For a small price, I have two beds still available; they are both large enough to sleep two of you easily. And one of you could bundle with our boy."

Hearing the promise of a bed, King Christian returned to the table with his half-eaten plate of food and sat down beside a bodyguard on the bench.

"For how much?" Olbert asked.

"And we have horses, too."

The innkeeper nodded, smiled, and mentioned the price.

"That much?" one of the knights complained.

"For half as much," he said with a smile, "you are welcome to sleep on a bench or on the floor in here among some of the other guests.-"

The men frowned.

"Is there nothing else?"

"I will not charge you anything if you wish to sleep in the barn. It is cold, but dry."

As the knights and the innkeeper haggled over the price of a bed, Olbert frowned and stroked his thinning hair. They could not continue this way. The minister had had only his private purse with him when they fled the palace, and it was growing ever lighter with the food they had had to buy already. Either Christian would have to chance taking refuge with one of his eastern vassals or the group would have to return to the palace and get more money from the treasury, -which hopefully the rebels had not discovered and taken. On the other hand, if he could find a Jew to make him a loan, Olbert might be able to borrow enough to get the King and himself safely into a neighboring kingdom where they might seek a friendly advocate for their cause. Whatever choice they made, it involved great peril, for the King would be forced to reveal himself. Regardless, they would have to make the choice soon.

"Just pay the man!" Christian snapped irritably at the end of the table. "I want to get some sleep!"

"This might not be wise," the guard whispered to the King. "It could be a trap."

"I care not! I want to get out of this cursed rain! I want to sleep where it is warm and dry for a change!"

One of the other customers had opened the door slightly to peer out into the weather. In doing so, he allowed a momentary rush of chilly air into the warm room which caused the patrons that were sitting near the door to shiver and complain.

"The storm is getting worse," he announced.

Olbert ended the haggling over the price abruptly by paying the innkeeper what he originally had asked.

The innkeeper, thrilled with the gold crowns he had received, became gregarious, and in an effort to be more hospitable, he said, "You know what is good on a night like this is some warm, mulled wine. I have some from Grenad. It would go well with the cake my daughter has baked. Shall I bring you some while the youth puts your horses in the stable?"

The group froze as they heard the man's last, few words. There was a stunned silence as they all realized together that King Christian was the youngest one in their group.

Christian himself was appalled. However, he did not have time to make a retort before he was ushered into silence by an intense look from Olbert and the bodyguard's sudden grip on his arm.

Christian's countenance changed from hostile to indignant. They did not actually expect him to suffer this? He was King, not a stable boy! Damn the horses! He was not going to go back out in that weather! And he was not going to share a bed with anyone, particularly the innkeeper's son! Two of the guards would have to sleep in here on a bench!

Christian's air of indignation lessened when he saw the alarm in Olbert's eyes. He answered the minister's look with a quizzical one of his own. Then he understood.

The innkeeper had obviously mistaken the group for knights, and Christian, as the newest to come to that status. If he refused to serve them or if they showed him any differential treatment, the onlookers and the innkeeper who were now all watching the group's confusion, would realize that his rank was higher than theirs, and then they might indeed guess that the blond youth was actually their young, golden-haired King.

Seeing the understanding finally come to him, Olbert said calmly, "Warm wine and cake would be most welcome, Friend. We will save you some, Sir -Tillo. Go tend to the horses now before the storm worsens."

Christian had to bite his tongue to keep from shouting in outrage. He glared at the gray-headed advisor dangerously. How dare they order him around like a common villein! On any other day, he would have cut the minister's throat for such a slight. However, after glancing around at the roomful of people that were staring at him, any one of which might be a potential assassin in disguise, Christian resisted no longer.

He gave Olbert one last intense look of hatred and rose from the bench hostilely. The guards and the adviser all kept their seat uneasily at the table as the King rebelted his sword about his waist, then wrapped himself angrily in his water drenched cloak. After gulping down the last remnants of his ale, Christian haughtily walked toward the door. When he reached it, he pulled his hood back over his head and looked back at the table and his comrades who were all watching him. He pushed open the door, fighting against the wind that was trying to blow it shut again, and went out.

When the door shut behind him, the innkeeper turned to the King's party.

"A sullen fellow. How long has he been graced with his knighthood?"

"Not long," one of the guards answered with raised eyebrows.

The innkeeper shook his head and returned to his other patrons, some of whom were beginning to make their way to the back of the room to a ladder that led up to the second floor of the inn. The guards sighed with relief.

"Will he be well?" one of the knights was asking.

"Should one of us go out and help him?" another asked.

"Let him be," Olbert answered quietly. "If we make an issue out of this, we will be discovered."

It was even colder now that the sun was setting. The fierce, chill wind and blowing rain fought Christian every step of the way to where the horses were. The horses, sopping wet, were huddled close together where they were tied, shivering in their exposure to the foul weather. The King, his fingers already numb, had difficulty loosening the knot from the wet reins. Just then, Christian caught the glimmer of something dark out of the corner of his eye.

Startled, he whipped around, grabbing his sword, while his heart pounded loudly in his ears. The cloaked figure was already beside him. Christian did not move, holding the man at bay with his drawn sword.

"It is not necessary to cut them loose!" the intruder shouted to Christian above the loud wind.

And rather than attacking him, the stranger began untying the next horse's reins. He was nimble fingered and made quick progress. Surprised, Christian resheathed his sword and returned to the knot he had been working on. Christian had just unknotted the first horse's tie, when the stranger handed him the reins of the horse next to him. Christian saw the man's friendly smile which was barely observable through the pouring rain and in the shadow of his hood. The King then led the horses to the stable; he had just put each of them in an empty stall, when the man brought two more horses inside the stable. The King no sooner had those stalled when the stranger was back with the last pair of horses. He led these into their stalls while Christian closed the openings with a rail post.

Christian pulled his soaked hood back from his head and observed his companion again as the horses shook off, sending droplets of water everywhere. He was a young man, about his same age and height.

"Do you work here?" Christian inquired of the stranger.

"No, these are my sleeping accommodations for the night. I saw you out there, and I thought you might want some help," he replied.

"Indeed, I am glad to have it," answered Christian. "Do they not have a stable boy here?"

"I have not seen one. Here, let me help you unsaddle these horses."

The stranger lifted up the saddle flap and undid the girth in one motion, then pulled the saddle from the horse and placed it on the top rail of the stalls. The horse snorted in appreciation and then shook again while Christian tended to the next horse.

After all six horses were unsaddled, unbridled, and watered, the King paused to wipe his long, wet locks out of his face.

"There are some dry coverlets over there on that shelf," the stranger said, as he began distributing armfuls of hay from a haystack to each of the horses.

"I appreciate your help," Christian told him hesitantly and then went over to the shelf, took a coverlet and began to dry his face, head and hair.

The stranger paused and looked at Christian closely. The King hesitated, noticing his scrutinizing gaze.

"Have you been on a pilgrimage recently?" the youth asked suddenly, still studying his face.

"No," Christian answered with a smirk.

"You seem familiar to me," he explained with a disarming smile. "Have we met?"

"I do not think so," the King answered abruptly, looking away, unnerved, his heart beating rapidly again.

"Are you native to this part of Speyron?"

"No," Christian replied quickly, walking back toward the open stable door.

"I am very good with faces," the young man commented as he resumed feeding the horses. "I never forget one, though I have difficulty putting a name with them. -I am certain we have met before."

Christian frowned; hundreds of people had been introduced to him since his coronation. It was folly to hope he would not be recognized by anyone.

"What is your name?" Christian asked then.

"Bennet."

The King searched his memory, but he neither recognized the name nor this fellow, although 'Bennet' was a common enough name. Clearly, there was no way to discover if they knew each other without further questioning which was unwise under the current circumstances.

The mews was suddenly besieged with a sudden roar and pounding. Christian looked outside. The rain was pouring down so hard that he could not even see the inn which was but a few yards away. He sighed.

"This brings back memories," the stranger said.

"Of what?" Christian asked absently, staring out into the downpour.

"The weather-" the young man replied pleasantly while brushing the remnants of the hay off his hands and arms. "I thought it only rained this hard in Gaulia."

"Aye, Gaulia does get a fair amount of rain," Christian agreed.

Out of the corner of his eye, the King watched his companion remove his hooded cloak and hang it on a peg to dry. With his back to Christian, Bennet picked up a coverlet and began to dry off his own short, damp hair. While he was occupied, he did not see how the King's countenance changed when he saw his distinctive tonsure haircut.

"You have journeyed to Gaulia?"

"Aye," Christian replied, observing the young man's tunic and braes curiously. "There I spent my childhood and was trained in arms."

Bennet smiled.

"There did I spend my childhood also. What knight trained thee?"

"Sir Gage-"

"Sir Gage? Surely not the vassal of Lord Reynaud-?" Bennet asked, turning around in surprise.

"Aye, do you know of him?"

"Aye and well. At Reynaud's castle did I spend my childhood!"

"I, also," Christian replied in astonishment.

"That must be how I know you! Now wait, do not tell me-" Bennet responded in delight.

The young man smiled at the coincidence and tried again to place the King's face with the faces and names in his memory.

Christian noted again the youth's pleasant expression, mud-brown hair, dimples and disarming smile, but still did not recognize him.

After a moment of further thought, Bennet's friendly expression suddenly changed into one of genuine alarm. He gasped in horror as all the color drained out of his cheeks. He hesitated, swallowed, and glanced at the open door of the mews, but then abruptly went down on his knees to the dirt floor in fear.

"Forgive my familiarity, Your Grace," Bennet pleaded hastily, with a bowed head. "But it has been so many years that I did not at once recognize-"

"Rise, Bennet," Christian said quickly, worried now that his disguise was ruined, "and tell no one what you have discovered. We travel incognito now because We are so close to the border."

"Of course, Your Grace," Bennet said, getting to his feet with another bow.

"Please, give rest to these formalities as well, for one never knows who is listening or watching."

Bennet nodded hastily, and went over to a roan nag that stood chomping her hay contentedly and patted her neck nervously. The stable was quiet again except for the rain pounding against the roof and walls, the boom of the thunder, the sound of the wind whipping between the buildings, and the persistent cough of one of the horses. Even then, it was an awkward lull.

"In truth, I do not remember a Bennet," Christian finally said, still not convinced that this was not one of the Bishop's well-disguised henchmen.

"I was being trained in arms by Sir Ardo, but I did not complete my training, My Lord K-. I was raised there as you were, and we shared the same tutors."

Christian searched his memories again, thinking back to his early childhood and afternoons of making letters and reading Latin, and the other boys that were there.

"I think I do remember you. -You were the only older boy to come to the lessons. You used to help the dull boys with their reading."

"Aye, that was I," Bennet said with a smile.

"Why did you not complete your training? Were you ill?"

"My father decided against it, though he changed his mind several times before making the decision."

"Changed his mind?"

"Aye," Bennet replied. "One month I was to be knighted; the next, I was to go into the Church. A few months later, word would arrive that I was to be a knight like my brothers and that my father's land was to be equally divided among the four of us; a month or so later, I was destined for the Church again because my sisters were in need of a dowry. Then I was to be knighted again because the neighbor wished me to marry his daughter; then I was for the Church once more because the neighbor settled on my older brother instead. And so it went for years."

"That would have been maddening."

"Aye, it was."

"Who is your father?"

"Lord Eamon."

"And his lands are-?"

"A few days ride southeast of here."

Christian nodded, admitting to himself that he was too *unfamiliar* with his many vassals.

"What finally made your father choose the Church?"

"My mother bore another son."

Christian chuckled, and asked, "So how old were you then?"

"Seventeen. I immediately returned to Speyron where I entered the monastery."

"You could have already been knighted by that age."

Bennet laughed.

"I was much better at letters than I ever was with weapons. It would have taken me a few more years to become adept enough at arms to be knighted."

"When did you abandon it? -the monastic life, I mean-" Christian asked, gesturing to the tunic and braes his companion now wore.

Bennet paused and looked at the King in confusion, and then noticed the clothes he was wearing.

"Oh, no," he replied with a laugh. "My habit was soaked from the rain, and the innkeeper loaned me these clothes until it dries."

"Oh," Christian replied, not quite knowing what to say, "-so you are still a monk?"

"Aye, and I find I am quite suited to the life," he replied.

"I would think it tedious."

Bennet laughed again.

"On the contrary, to those that are called to it, it is never tedious, only peaceful. Even this year, I-"

The monk stopped short and looked away quickly.

"You what?"

"I -entered into the priesthood, -so my responsibilities have increased," he admitted anxiously. "-Speaking of which, it is time for Vespers."

Without another word, the monk turned away from the King, made the sign of the cross, and began to sing.

King Christian looked at his companion with raised eyebrows for a moment. Seeing that the monk was quite serious about singing the office, he leaned against the stable door and turned his attention back outside to the storm.

At least he can carry a tune, Christian thought momentarily before returning his thoughts to his present predicament and the choices available to him. He was in agreement with his guards. None of them could endure much more of this aimless meandering around the eastern countryside without the protection of shelter or friends. The disguises had already proven to be troublesome and wholly inadequate.

Initially, he had thought to provide a haven for himself by utilizing the king's right of visiting his vassals. It would have been simple enough to arrive at the castle of his eastern vassals unannounced and while there, inspect their holdings and determine the extent of their loyalty to him. Indeed, if war was inevitable, he would need stronger ties with these vassals, since he had barely met them at his coronation years ago.

However, Grey, Olbert, and Dewain were adamant that he should not take the risk without at least a garrison of palace knights to accompany him, for they feared that if he unwittingly stayed under the roof of a vassal that had turned, four knights could not adequately protect his throat from being cut in the night. Also, the witch's vision of bearded knights laying siege to a castle had renewed their fears that Herryck's spies were surely watching. If Olbert's castle could be besieged and taken, surely strongholds of lesser vassals would be no match for them. Furthermore, if Herryck did nothing more than cut him off from his knights or reinforcements, Speyron could be lost without a battle.

"My Lord-"

The whispered words and the touch on his arm suddenly jolted the King away from his thoughts back to the moment. His quickened heartbeat slowed as he realized it was only one of his bodyguards. Behind him, Bennet was still singing, but outside, the rain had slacked up somewhat but was still falling steadily.

"Forgive me for startling you, Sire," the guard whispered again. "We feared something had happened."

"I am well."

"Most in the inn are retiring to bed now. The two beds that we have for the night are in a common room on the second floor. -We, of course, await your will."

Christian rubbed his eyes and sighed. He knew what his knight was trying to tell him. There was no privacy to be had in the inn. He could not have a bed to himself without creating suspicion. He would have to share as a young knight would, and even then it might create speculation if he took a bed at all while a more senior knight slept on the floor in the main room.

"Retire to bed," he told him. "I will stay the night out here."

"But Sire, you should not remain unprotected," the guard whispered. "And it is cold out here."

"It may not be as warm as in the inn, but at least I will not be anxious about the several strangers who may be watching me, nor will I have to have Olbert or you for a bedfellow."

The guard frowned. He had been able to walk up on the King directly without the youth even being aware of him. It was unwise to leave him unprotected when the King was so distracted.

"I will remain with you."

"Do not! I want not thy company! -I will be well!" Christian argued.

The knight sighed and glanced at the horses that stood eating their hay, then at the man who stood singing quietly to himself.

"What is he?"

"That is a monk."

"A monk?"

"Aye, his habit is drying somewhere."

"Why is he singing in a mews? Is he mad?"

Christian chuckled.

"I have always thought them so. But to answer thee, he sings in the mews because he would rather not sing in the rain."

"But why sing at all? This is no abbey."

"Because that is what monks do. They are supposed to sing their Office whether they are in a monastery or not."

"And you believe you will be safe with him this night?" the guard asked doubtfully. "What if he finds thee out?"

"He recognized me already."

"Already?!"

"Aye, and he is a brave one," Christian smirked. "Despite my excommunication, he has neither berated me, nor shunned me, though for a moment I thought he was going to flee in fear of his life."

The guard raised his eyebrows.

"And still you will stay in here with him? Is it wise to take such a risk with your life, Sire? What if he tries to murder thee?"

"Then I will have two dead priests to my name. -Fear not. I will be well enough. The most peril I face from him is that his singing may keep me awake this night."

The guard raised his eyebrows again at the King's composure. Although he was still reluctant to go, the guard finally returned to the inn, leaving Christian alone with the monk.

The King shut the door of the mews behind the guard, and the stables became substantially darker. The monk hesitated a moment, but continued to sing.

Christian waited for his eyes to adjust to the darkness before he moved. He went over to the pegs on the wall and peeled off his wet cloak, hanging it up to dry. Then he pulled off his tunics and laid them out to dry. Bare-chested and shivering, he quickly wrapped a coverlet about him. Then he removed his wet boots and concealed the dagger he kept in his right under another coverlet and went over to the large haystack and began to arrange the hay for sleeping. He settled down into his hay bed, covering up with his extra coverlet and then piling extra hay on top of it for added warmth, all the while keeping his dagger at hand should he have need of it.

The King had not lain there long when Bennet finished singing Vespers, crossed himself, and went to a part of the haystack where he had already made himself a bed and sat down. The barn was quiet again except for the thunder booming in the distance and the sound of the persistent rain.

"Do you ever think on your days at Reynaud's?" Bennet asked after a while.

"Aye, often. I was fond of my days in Gaulia and greatly miss it. For more than a year, I resisted returning to Speyron after I had earned my spurs."

"Lord Reynaud's was an *unusual* place," Bennet commented.

Christian smiled.

"Our tutors there were some of the most educated priests on the Continent, and Lord Reynaud and his knights were among the most skilled fighters in Gaulia. Still, what I remember most about the place were the extravagant feasts and revelry there."

"Aye, Reynaud would not be outdone by another nobleman."

"Aye," Bennet agreed, "there was always plenty to eat, plenty of ale, and plenty of wenches there. I have never seen anything like it since."

"They were nothing compared to the feasts my father, Filberte, gave," Christian replied, "though he gave so many during the year that their extravagance was considered quite ordinary."

"Were you at Reynaud's that Christmas when it was so extremely cold and by the fourth night everyone was so drunk that the women were at table unclad?"

Christian chuckled.

"Aye."

Bennet shook his head at the memory with a contorted smile.

"I keep remembering that one woman whose green gown was so loose and revealing that her large breasts were in the pudding, all the while she was hanging on everyone, including the page boys. -What a ghastly memory!"

"Hmph! That was mild. When I returned home with my knighthood, I found that what amazed me in Gaulia was but a trifle compared with the indecencies at my father's palace. Day after day, the Court was drunk and stupid and barely clothed. I could not eat at table without becoming ill."

"Why was that?" Bennet asked.

"Usually because the courtesan near me was being swyved by a kitchen servant."

"At table?" Bennet asked aghast.

"Aye, food and flesh were everywhere."

"And did no one speak out against this indecency? Was not your father offended? Was there no chaplain or priest there to admonish them?"

"My father was among those swyving whomever walked by. As for the priests, the courtesans served them well. The others at table would eventually succumb to the debauchery, or else, they had grown so accustomed to the spectacle that they no longer noticed."

Bennet crossed himself.

Christian smiled over at the monk.

The two did not speak for a moment.

"I suppose you were *glad* to finally leave Reynaud's," Christian said.

Bennet hesitated for a moment before replying.

"I was glad to finally know what my future was to be."

Christian nodded.

"Did your time at Reynaud's help prepare you at all for the Church?"

"I believe it benefited me well, even if the feasts were perhaps freer than I was comfortable with. I know that Sir Ardo's training has served me well in the abbey."

"Really? I did not know there was that much brawling in a monastery," Christian replied with amusement.

Bennet chuckled.

"I mean the self-discipline I learned. The vow of obedience is the most difficult vow for novices and monks to keep."

"I would think it would be chastity."

"In an abbey, if one finds oneself on the verge of breaking one's vow of chastity, the vow of obedience has definitely already been breached."

Christian laughed.

"But I could ask the same question of you," Bennet added. "Was Lord Reynaud's an appropriate start for a future King? Did the experiences you encountered there develop the many skills you would need to rule wisely? Did you leave Gaulia with not only your spurs but with the heightened arts of diplomacy, delegation, negotiation, and compromise for the greater good? Did you not only learn how to wield a sword but how to wield authority without antagonizing those who must abide by it?"

Silent, Christian frowned, his stomach tying in knots.

"Ultimately, will Speyron prosper or suffer, due, indirectly, to your upbringing at Lord Reynaud's?" the monk concluded.

Bennet was not particularly expecting an answer to his rhetoric, but, true to his profession, he enjoyed the contemplation that accompanied asking such questions whether there was discussion or not. The two young men remained in quiet thought for some time.

Finally Bennet asked, "So what is it like at your palace?"

Christian was deep in thought at that moment, intently thinking about Paschal and Dewain's argument over the prophesies and the survival of his line. Somewhere in his head, he registered that Bennet had asked him something.

"What?" he asked.

"What is it like at the palace now?"

"What? -Oh, -um, -reasonable," he answered, still lost in his own thoughts.

"Reasonable?" Bennet repeated, unsuccessfully trying to make sense out of the King's response.

"Do you have great feasts very often?"

"Aye-"

"But not like your father's, I should hope."

"Um- no."

Bennet smiled and waited.

Christian said nothing more, however.

"-Are there plans for a royal marriage yet?" the monk tried again.

"Aye-" Christian responded, catching only a word or two of what the monk asked.

"With whom?"

"What?"

"Whom are you to marry?"

"I do not know. My advisers have not decided."

"I suppose you are impatient for them to make a choice."

"Not particularly. When you are King, your bed is seldom empty," Christian answered casually.

Bennet raised his eyebrows.

"So - you have- a concubine then?" the monk said tentatively, uncertain that he should delve into such personal matters and equally uncertain as to how the King would react to it.

"About a hundred," he shrugged.

"A hundred?" Bennet echoed, trying to comprehend what Christian was saying. "Forgive me, Sire, I misunderstand you. You say you have a hundred-?"

"Concubines."

"A hundred concubines?" Bennet repeated in astonishment.

"Aye, all beautiful and spirited- housed at my palace," Christian mumbled.

"What do you do with all of them?" Bennet asked, amazed.

Suddenly focused on the conversation again, the King chuckled.

"Bennet, you have been in that monastery a very long time!"

The monk laughed.

"To answer thee, they live in luxury at the palace and await my summons."

"So many. That is hard for the mind to fathom. How can you ever remember all of their names?"

"Names? That is the least of my problems! I have a kingdom to rule!"

Bennet raised his eyebrows at this, and the conversation ended abruptly again. The only sounds were once again the wailing of the wind as it whipped about the building mercilessly, the thunder, and the persistently falling rain.

Christian's thoughts once more turned to the desperateness of his circumstances, so he spoke in order to distract himself.

"What brings you here, Bennet?"

The monk smiled.

"I was traveling back to St. Brychan and was caught here by the storm. My father became gravely ill recently, and I have been away a month to be with him and my family. It was good to see my parents and brothers and sisters, but now that my father has recovered, I am ready to get back home."

"You miss the monastery?"

"Aye."

"Why?"

The monk chuckled.

"I miss the other brothers. I miss the camaraderie, the prayers and routine, the work, the joy-"

"What joy?"

"The joy of worshipping God, surrounded by others who feel the same joy I do."

Christian raised his eyebrows doubtfully, but noted the tone of sincere conviction in the voice of the monk. The two did not say more for a long while.

Finally, Bennet decided to hazard the obvious question.

"Your Grace, what brings *you* to an inn in this kind of weather?"

Christian paused and wondered what reply he should make. He was tempted to lie, to tell the monk that he had been out hunting or meeting with spies or visiting his vassals in this part of Speyron. However, Bennet was likely to wonder why he had not simply opted to stay at the castle of one of those vassals. He might question the need for a disguise at all.

Surely the answer was blatant enough. Was it possible that the monk had not heard about the uprising that had driven him out of his own palace?

Finally, Christian decided to give the simplest answer:

"I do not know."

The monk was mute for a long while, thinking about the King's response.

"Forgive my boldness, Sire, but you seem oppressed by some matter. I do not know what your plans are or what business brings you to this part of Speyron, but perhaps you would like to come and make a retreat at my abbey -for a fortnight, perhaps."

Christian stifled a laugh.

"A retreat?" he managed.

"Aye. Often people who find themselves burdened with worldly troubles come to a monastery for a period of reflection and rest. After a week or so of prayer, contemplation, and study, they usually emerge from their retreat, back into their lives, refreshed.

"St. Brychan's is a small community, and the accommodations at the guesthouse may not be as grand as you are accustomed to, but they are better than a mews."

Christian had to smile. What he really needed was diversion-amusements of the simplest kind, for it was this constant reflection on his current situation that was depressing him.

Still, he could not so easily dismiss the monk's offer. Although he had no interest in praying or studying scriptures, he had to admit the thought of staying in one place for a fortnight with his meals prepared and a bed of his own was tempting almost under any circumstances. In fact, this opportunity might provide him with the one thing he needed: a secure place to plan out what he would do next.

"Your invitation is *-appreciated,* Bennet."

22

The seven riders were listless and silent, mesmerized after riding the entire day through the dull, gray landscape of bare trees that speckled the rising mountains, and listening to the sighs and occasional snorts of the horses as the mounts slowly and carefully picked their way through the thick mud on the road. Although the storm had come and gone the night before, the wind and cold had remained.

As the sun began to set, the walls of St. Brychan Monastery's had finally come into view. The countryside outside the stone wall that surrounded the community was empty of people, for after three days of rain, the fields were too sticky with mire and standing water to be worked.

The stone wall had originally been part of a small Romani fortress built in the mountains of eastern Speyron to withstand the raids and rebellions of the barbarian peoples of this land. After the conquerors were forced to withdraw from Speyron and to relinquish most of the Continent they had held, the abandoned fortress had fallen into ruin. A century or so later, the Benedictine Monks had chosen the site for their abbey.

The riders rode past a large, gnarled tree that grew near the monastery entrance and through the wooden gate that stood wide open. As the King and his men sat on their horses and looked about curiously, a small but spry, old monk in a black habit suddenly appeared and welcomed them cordially. The kind expression on the monk's face immediately changed to one of pure delight as he caught sight of one rider among the group. He rushed to the young monk's side and warmly threw out his arms and embraced him even before Bennet could dismount.

"Brother Bennet, you have returned to us at last! You have been sorely missed!"

"Truly, Brother Sedgewyk, it is good to be back!" the auburn-haired monk replied with his dimpled smile.

"How fairs your father?"

"He has made a complete recovery by the grace of God!"

"Thanks be to God!"

Then Bennet gestured toward his companions.

"Brother, where is the Abbot? My companions require an audience with him."

"I believe he is in his office," the little monk answered. Then he turned to the riders who had dismounted their horses and said again, "You are all most surely welcome here."

As a group of villein children ran up and took charge of the horses and hurried them to the stables, the King and his men followed Bennet and the old monk through the maze of workshops, livestock pens, and buildings that were inside the monastery. Then the group walked down a small alcove and around a small courtyard.

On the other side of the courtyard, standing a little away by itself, was a large house; there the group was met at the door by another old monk. This man also greeted Brother Bennet with a warm embrace. Bennet smiled warmly with the attention and made a jest about the return of the prodigal son.

When he and the King and his companions entered the Abbot's house, Brother Sedgewyk departed to return to the gate. The party waited just inside the door of the large dwelling while the second monk went to tell the Abbot of the visitors. When he returned, he led Brother Bennet, King Christian, and Lord Olbert past a small feasting hall and then around a corner to a small office.

Three more monks were inside this chamber. Two, sitting at a table, were writing in large books, while the other, a tall, older man with a receding hairline, sat behind a desk with several documents before him. This man observed the weary, unwashed, unshaven visitors and their plain garments carefully as they entered. Then catching sight of a familiar face, the man smiled, rose, and, abandoning his place behind the desk, greeted Bennet with an embrace and a kiss on the cheek.

"Brother Bennet, you have returned safely to us! Praise God! How fairs your father?"

Bennet reported his father's recovery to the Abbot. Then the young monk turned toward the two visitors and was about to present them when the Abbot spoke.

"Lord Olbert, it has been too long since you have graced our community with a visit."

Olbert smiled and embraced the Abbot.

"I regret it has been as long as it has. The affairs of the kingdom keep me occupied."

Christian rolled his eyes and wiped his running nose on his sleeve. Why was he not surprised? Olbert was probably personally acquainted with every Abbot and parish priest in Speyron.

The Abbot held out his hands then and said a brief prayer blessing the visitors, and then kissed Olbert and Christian on the cheek.

"Go," he instructed the two monks in the office. "Bring some water and cloths."

The monks immediately left their books and went out of the room. Then the Abbot looked at Bennet.

"Brother, you needs be off to the wardrobe now and then to the oratory."

Bennet hesitated, but nodded, and glancing at the King one last time, obediently left. The Abbot closed the door behind him.

Both Christian and Olbert noted how expertly the Abbot had cleared his office. All were silent then as the Abbot and the King scrutinized one another.

"Your Grace," Lord Olbert finally began, "may I present Lord Abbot Hunfred."

"Sire," the Abbot bowed dutifully. "This is an unexpected honor."

"Lord Abbot," King Christian acknowledged stiffly.

"May I present Father Desle, the abbey's senior confessor," Abbot Hunfred said, gesturing to the monk that had brought them to the office.

The confessor also bowed to the youth and to Lord Olbert.

The four men said no more as the King curiously looked about the sparse, tidy office for a minute or two. All was necessity, purposefulness, and frugality. There were no excesses, not even a cushion for the benches. Even the candles were unlit; the monks were keeping their accounts by what remained of the poor light that filtered in through the open window behind the Abbot's desk.

"-What brings Your Grace to our humble house?" Abbot Hunfred asked finally.

"We wish-" Christian answered carelessly while examining the open books on the table in the office, "-to make a retreat at your monastery."

Olbert and the two monks looked at the youth in surprise.

"A retreat?" Hunfred asked. "For what purpose, Your Grace?"

Olbert's heartbeat quickened. Had the King had a change of heart? Was he finally willing not only to bring the interdict to an end but his own excommunication as well? If so, there were more direct methods than starting with a retreat.

King Christian turned to face the Abbot and assumed a pretense of seriousness.

"Lord Abbot, We fear that the weight of the crown and the worldliness of Our anointed duties have diverted Us from the *true path*," Christian explained while successfully suppressing his urge to laugh, though he failed to restrain a small smile. "We require a brief respite from Our manifold responsibilities for -reflection and- *spiritual guidance* -to aid Us in Our amendment."

Although the Abbot's face outwardly showed all concern, inside he bristled at the King's clear irreverence. It was not the youth's words that offended the Abbot as much as the light tone and careless manner he used when he spoke them. This was clearly some joke to the youth.

"I see. And a retreat is the recommendation of the *Royal Chaplain?*"

King Christian was startled by the question, but noted the shrewdness of this Abbot.

"At the moment, the post of Royal Chaplain is vacant," Christian answered coolly.

"Is a retreat the recommendation of your *confessor*, then?" the Abbot asked, undaunted.

Christian smiled. Olbert held his breath.

"We do not have a confessor as the sacrament of penance has been withheld from Us for some time now, as We are certain you well know," he answered with feigned pleasantness.

"I beg your forgiveness, Sire," the Abbot responded with feigned embarrassment. "-Well, perhaps a retreat is the recommendation of one of the *priests at the palace church* then?"

Christian laughed out loud.

"We fear a retreat would hardly be *their* recommendation- if We could *find* even one of them to ask."

Abbot Hunfred frowned at the chuckling youth. Olbert covered his face with his hand. If this was a sincere attempt to reconcile with the Church, the King was going about it all wrong.

"And to save you from inquiring," Christian continued with mirth, "it is not the recommendation of the Bishop nor that of His Holiness, the Pope either. Father Bennet, who We encountered on the road last night, recommended the retreat."

"Ah, Brother Bennet-" the Abbot echoed with a smile. "Well, you must forgive him, Your Grace. He is young, enthusiastic, and quite naive, -and clearly in error."

"How so?"

Hunfred smiled sweetly.

"Your Grace, you have been *excommunicated* which means you have been cut off from the entire body of Christ, including our community. It is forbidden for us to associate with you. Therefore, it is quite impossible for you to make a retreat here or *anywhere*.

"-And even if it were possible, I fear I would still have to disagree with Brother Bennet. From the information I have received, I believe that a retreat of any length would serve you no real purpose."

"Indeed? And why is that?" Christian asked, still keeping his composure, "-*if* it was possible."

"Your Grace, a retreat's duration is usually no longer than a fortnight. Retreaters stay in the retreat quarters and for the most part are on their own. Under normal circumstances, they attend Mass daily together and perhaps study together; otherwise they spend their time in prayer and reflection as they please."

"And you do not believe that would benefit Us?"

"Not in the least. What Your Grace needs is an extended period of moral instruction and a directed study of the scriptures augmented by a daily regiment of discipline," Hunfred explained with a smile, adding gently, "-*if it was only possible.*"

The chamber was immediately silent. Olbert's heart sank as he listened. The terms set by Abbot Hunfred were too strict. Even if the Abbot would allow him in, the King would never agree to these terms, and this chance for him to begin his reconciliation with the Church would be lost.

As inadequate as the King's petition must have sounded to the Abbot, Olbert recognized that Christian had made a huge capitulation to even come here. It was equally astonishing and out of character for him to actually admit to anyone that he had 'strayed from the true path.' Unfortunately, since the Abbot did not know the King personally, he could not see the concessions that Christian was clearly making.

The four men looked at each other- waiting for someone to speak. No one did for a long while.

"Very well," Christian conceded finally with a snort from his running rose and a shrug of his shoulders, "We would abide as you prescribe, *if it was only possible.*"

Olbert, astounded, looked at the youth in disbelief. Could he be in earnest? What had that monk said to him last night?

Abbot Hunfred crossed his arms and continued sternly, "Your Grace, do you even understand what would be required of you?"

"We believe We do. *If it was possible*, when might We begin?"

The abbey's confessor listened in stunned horror.

Olbert was not certain, but he thought the chamber was beginning to wobble and turn.

"You will have to submit completely to my authority and the routine of this order and community. You will be expected to adhere to the schedule I prepare for your spiritual direction exactly: praying and studying scriptures under supervision at an appointed time and then contemplating on what you have studied as you participate in the work of this community- at the appointed time," the Abbot told him irritably. "If you are unwilling to do this, there would be no point in you remaining here for any length of time whatsoever."

Olbert inwardly moaned. The Abbot was too plain-spoken. The King would never agree. The old adviser looked at Christian, waiting for the derisive laugh and boisterous refusal he knew was coming.

"We understand. *-If it were possible*, it would be a relief not to have to make a few decisions for a while."

Olbert moved to the nearby bench and sat down. He could hardly believe what he was hearing. His prayers had finally been answered. Then he frowned as another thought occurred to him.

Confounded, Abbot Hunfred sighed internally. There seemed to be nothing that he could say that would deter the youth. Clearly the lad wanted in the abbey and would agree to any condition to be received.

From all that he had heard about this young man, the Abbot did not believe for a moment that the King was interested in amending his ways. More likely he was preparing a reprisal for the interdict. Was the youth planning to defile the monastery's altars as well? Perhaps the retreat was some ruse the King would use to send his knights against the monks.

There was, however, equal danger in outright denying the King, his vassal lord, Hunfred considered. Although the youth's excommunication obligated him to turn him away, if he did so, the King would likely hold the community in contempt and might even order his knights to level the monastery.

Hunfred glanced then at Lord Olbert, sitting on the bench. Would Olbert, his long time friend and a man known for righteousness and devotion to the Faith, be a part of anything that would endanger the brothers here?

And the King did not particularly look like he was on the attack. He and Olbert were obviously dressed in rags to avoid undue attention. Both were clearly fatigued, but the King seemed particularly pale and was already showing signs of illness. Since the usual hospitality offered to travelers was forbidden to excommunicates, perhaps the King's true intent was nothing more than to secure accommodations after days of traveling through the foul weather. Though why he did not stop at one of his vassal's castles in the area was beyond the Abbot's conjecture.

"One moment, Sire."

The monks and the King looked over to where Olbert sat.

"Your Grace, I wholeheartedly regret that I must object to this proposed retreat. -Yet with your *current circumstances*, I fear it *is* impossible."

Before Christian could object, the adviser continued.

"What if you are recognized, My Liege? As I recall, the retreat quarters are hardly less public than the guesthouse."

"We have the guards-"

"I fear that the few that you have will be more of a detriment to your well-being than a help."

"Why is that?"

"Because the guards will certainly draw attention to you, particularly if they are accompanying you everywhere as you participate in the activities of the abbey."

"But-"

"Even if you are not attacked in your sleep by another retreater, there is the possibility of enemies hearing of your presence here and laying siege to the monastery itself -which will become even more likely the longer you stay."

The Abbot and the confessor both raised their eyebrows at this information. Olbert sighed, and Christian frowned.

"Although I am greatly aggrieved by it, perhaps this is not the most opportune time, Sire, to make a retreat -even if it were possible."

The chamber fell silent as the four men thought to themselves.

Abbot Hunfred had spent a lifetime scrutinizing people. Now as he observed the frown on the King's face, he surmised that concealed beneath the youth's carefree exterior was a sincerely frustrated, young man. In fact, both Olbert and the youth seemed drawn with care. Perhaps the King was in greater need than anyone suspected? And although his talk of reform was most likely insincere, Hunfred hesitated completely turning away an opportunity to minister to anyone in need of repentance. After all, the Lord God was more likely to understand his trying and failing, than his not trying at all.

The Abbot cleared his throat.

"Perhaps it is possible."

The three men looked at him.

"It would be extremely unusual, even if you were not a vitandi," he began, "but, to ensure Your Grace's safety during your retreat, you might be allowed to *appear* as a novice of our order. You would be permitted to live and mingle with us, and at the same time, have the same limited exposure to outsiders as any other brother here. Even the other monks would not know of your true identity. And if somehow they discovered it, I could assure their silence."

The King and Olbert both seemed encouraged. The confessor was pale with horror.

"The goals of your retreat can still easily be accomplished this way, but rather than follow a schedule of instruction and discipline of my design, you would simply heed the directions and guidance of our novice master."

"You are certain We will not be found out? -For no one can know of Our presence here."

"I am certain if you do not give yourself away, Sire, that no one will know. Be assured, Father Desle and I will tell no one."

"Indeed," the confessor muttered wide-eyed, with a shake of his head.

"However," the Abbot warned, "in order not to stand out, by necessity, you will have to be treated like any other novice, and you will have to obey the senior brothers of this community like any other novice.

"Neither may you have servants nor knights to attend you. Like the rest of us, you will have only what you need. Only guests of the abbey and those on retreat are allowed any sort of extravagances."

Christian tried to guess at what those 'extravagances' might be, but only smiled and nodded his head in agreement with the Abbot.

"Above all, you must obey the Rule by which our order lives. And you must, of course, submit to *my* authority at all times -or you will be put out instantly.

"-If this is agreeable to you," Hunfred concluded, "you may take leave of your knights, and I will have one of the brothers show you to the wardrobe."

23

"What have you done, Hunfred?" the old confessor asked after the King and Olbert had left the office.

The Abbot smiled and returned to his chair behind his desk again.

"All of Speyron is without the comforts of the sacraments because of this youth."

"He needs our help."

"His excommunication does not allow us to help him! And the interdict forbids it! If word reaches the Bishop that we have defied his command and taken in this vitandi- and if he learns we are allowing him to participate in the singing of the Hours and other holy rites, which is withheld even from the blameless, he will excommunicate *us* for certain!"

"Then I suggest that we pray we can keep the King concealed."

Father Desle raised his hands in exasperation.

"Of course, under this interdict, our house is essentially excommunicated already-" the confessor admitted.

"I will take full responsibility for taking the King in, for it was my decision," Hunfred answered, looking back at the parchment on his desk again.

"The Bishop will have your head."

"He will try, but I could hardly turn the King away and keep a clear conscience."

"Is that what you will tell the head of our order as well?"

"I shall tell *them*, if they ask, that the teachings and comforts of the Faith have been withheld from the excommunicate King Christian for two years now, and the abstinence has failed to move him towards either improvement or reconciliation. Since the lack of sacraments has failed to impress him, I thought, perhaps, immersion in the Faith might profit him more."

"Is it not scripture: 'Do not give to the dogs what is holy; and do not throw your pearls before swine, lest they trample them under foot and then attack you!'?"

Abbot Hunfred smiled.

"Aye, we may well be repaid in kind for our trouble, yet should we not at least attempt to catch this lost sheep that has wandered to our door and return him to the Shepherd?"

"I am not the one you must convince, Lord Abbot. -But the Bishop will be incensed that you dare defy his will!"

"I would sooner defy a bishop's will than God's."

"Still-"

"Besides, by taking him in, I will have a worthy advocate in the future- the King of Speyron," Hunfred added.

"Aye, you may indeed, *if* he remains King."

24

"Allow me to say, My Lord King, how pleased I am that you are making this retreat. Although there are more usual and direct methods for making peace with the Church, by taking the time to make this retreat and by adhering to the conditions set by Abbot Hunfred, the Bishop no doubt will see this as a genuine and public endorsement of the Faith."

"Olbert, what are you going on about?" Christian asked wearily as he unwound the bandage from the leg of his braes.

"I am saying that Dewain and Grey will be interested to hear what political shrewdness you have exercised by beginning the reconciliation with the Bishop in the guise of a retreat at an abbey."

"Olbert-" Christian began with a shake of his head, "for so many years now you have been my adviser, and you still do not know my mind."

"Sire?"

"Olbert, I have told you repeatedly how I feel about *them* and their *superstitions*. Why do you not heed my words? It has never been my intention, nor is it now, nor will it ever be, to reconcile with the Church. If there is never another Mass celebrated in Speyron until the end of time, our kingdom will only be the better for it."

"But, Sire- I do not rightly understand. You requested their help.- They are defying the Bishop in order to accommodate you!"

Christian shrugged indifferently.

"They are even willing to conceal you among themselves to keep you safe!" the alderman complained bitterly.

"It is the least any vassal should do for their king," Christian answered.

"And you have agreed to devote yourself to prayer, study, and work as they direct-"

"My sole intention was to secure lodging *in one place* for a fortnight somewhere safe from foul weather, rebels, and potentially traitorous vassals. In order to do that, I had to agree to the Abbot's terms," Christian explained simply.

Olbert, pained and saddened, looked away from the youth.

"Lodging.-"

"Aye, and in a week or so, Paschal will have discovered the instigators of the palace rebellion, and I will return to the palace and confront them. Then I will begin making preparations for the war."

Noting his adviser's lack of response, Christian looked up at the old man. The disappointment was very evident on Olbert's weary features, but the King refused to console him or to offer him false hope. He would *never* reconcile with the Church. It was, after all, the old man's blind fidelity to superstition that Christian was fighting.

Olbert swallowed his disappointment as best he could. Regardless of whether or not King Christian ever embraced the Faith, it was still his duty to serve him.

"Very well, Sire. If you are determined to go forward with this deception-"

"Of course-" he muttered as he pulled off his damp, outer tunic.

"I have the Abbot's assurance that you will be safe here. If you are expelled, he will send word to me immediately so that you will not be without protection outside the abbey walls for very long."

King Christian paused and looked at the Royal Steward.

"Expelled? What is your meaning exactly? Are you suggesting that they would have *cause* to *expel* me?" Christian asked indignantly. "Truly, Olbert, do you believe me incapable of poverty, chastity and obedience for a fortnight?"

The King laughed as he stripped off the last of his shirts, exposing his smooth, muscular chest.

"I do not mean to vex you, My Liege," Olbert told him, while handing him a plain, long undertunic. "I am just attempting to prepare you, for a monastic order is founded on discipline, not unlike an army."

"Even so, how difficult can it be? What do monks do aside from pray and copy books?" he asked, noting with disappointment that the woolen undertunic itched only slightly less than the commoner's shirt he had just removed.

Olbert raised his eyebrows.

"I fear you will find it very different from what you expect. Your Grace has enjoyed a great deal of freedom since you became King. You arrange your activities at your whim. Your every comfort and pleasure is sought by those who serve you.

"Here, as a novice, *you* will have to serve. You will be told what to do and when to do it. Nor may you question the orders that you are given. -You will have to have permission to do the simplest of things. And you will absolutely be expected to honor the beliefs and rituals of the monks. In fact," Olbert added, while proffering the King the plain novice's habit, "if you wish to keep your *lodgings*, you will have to continue to convince them of your sincere desire to adhere to their *superstitions*."

Christian looked up at the old man, indignantly.

"You believe me to be undisciplined! You think I can not be obedient to someone else's wishes for a fortnight!"

"No! Of course that is *not* what I believe!"

"Do you think I did as I pleased in Gaulia? I did not! Never did I question Sir Gage's instructions, nor once fail to carry them out!"

"There could be no doubt, Sire!"

"Likewise, I was always obedient to the wishes of my parents while they lived!" Christian responded, snatching the garment from Olbert and pulling the black habit over his head.

Olbert handed him the scapular and cowl next, sighing, "That is certainly true, Sire, but-"

"There is no '*but*'!" Christian interrupted. "Enough! It will be well!"

Lord Olbert sighed deeply and unfolded a piece of parchment. While Christian pulled the knee-length scapular firmly over the habit and removed his braes, the old advisor told him:

"Your noviceship begins tomorrow, so I advise you to try to get some sleep as soon as they show you to the dormitory for the novices."

"That should not be difficult," Christian muttered with a yawn.

He picked up the stockings and shoes provided to him by the wardrobe and went about putting them on.

"The brothers have already eaten, so Abbot Hunfred is having them prepare you a snack; likely it will be little more than bread and cheese. They are also brewing you a medicinal tea for your cold."

Christian shrugged. He could hardly expect more, he supposed.

"Abbot Hunfred informed me that since the interdict put an end to Canonical Hours being observed formally by the brothers, he has ordered the novices, since they are not yet clerics officially, to continue to sing the offices."

Christian looked up at the advisor in disbelief.

"You are in jest. The novices are singing the Hours? And I am-"

"Aye."

"I will never get any rest," he moaned.

"Indeed. Tomorrow, the day begins with Matins which is sung sometime after midnight," Olbert began, glancing at the parchment. "Then I believe the novices are allowed to go back to bed. Then you will be up again a few hours later because Laudes is sung at the break of dawn. Prime is sung the first hour after sunrise. After Prime, there is the chapter meeting where you will be introduced as a new novice to the other monks. The Abbot, by the way, agreed that you would be called by your third name, Tillo. Anyway, it is at this meeting that the Abbot gives each brother his work assignment for the day or the week. After the chapter meeting, the novices meet for an hour or so to study scripture.

"At midmorning, you will sing Terce. After Terce, you will begin your work assignment. Incidentally, if Speyron was not under interdict, the priests in the abbey would begin saying their Masses after Terce."

The King sent his adviser a look of impatience.

"Anyway, at midday, the novices reconvene to sing Sext, which would normally immediately precede the Abbot's High Mass. For now, after Sext, you will be sent back to your labor. At midafternoon, you will be summoned to sing Nones. Afterwards, the brothers break their fast. Remember that strict silence is kept during the meal. After eating, the monks return to the tasks they were assigned for the day.

"Vespers is sung around sunset and is followed by Collation, which is the only time that the monks are allowed to talk and relax. After nightfall, the last office is Compline, and there is absolutely no speaking during the ground silence until Matins again."

"They only eat once? And so late in the day?" Christian asked as he tied the rope belt around his waist.

"Aye, but if you find yourself still hungry after the meal, it may be possible to get a cold snack from the kitchen during Collation."

Christian raised his eyebrows.

"Normally, they would ring the bells for each hour," the Royal Steward continued, "but under the interdict, I am certain they have another way to summon the novices together for the offices."

"They govern every minute of the day. Would that they could regulate the functions of the body as well," the King commented sarcastically.

"Aye, they do," Olbert replied, handing the parchment to the King and pointing to the writing at the bottom.

Christian looked up from the parchment in bewilderment.

"I am certain it is not as complicated as it sounds," the counselor said with a smile. "I am certain you will adjust in no time, though I suggest you *ask* before you do anything."

The King looked over the parchment again and then folded it up thoughtfully. He wiped his nose on the handkerchief he had been given and looked around the sparse chamber.

"Well, Olbert, how do I look?"

The old man smiled a little as he observed the golden locked youth in his black habit, scapular and cowl. The lad, with his angel's face, looked quite gentle- truly a 'wolf in sheep's skin' as scripture said.

"Thou could almost pass for a man of God, Your Grace."

Christian smiled.

"One thing more, Sire. Novices and monks are not allowed to have any property. If you will entrust me with your signet ring, I will give it to Abbot Hunfred for safe keeping."

Christian frowned and retrieved the small purse he had among the commoner's clothes. He opened it and removed the large, gold ring with the royal imprint. Unlike the crown he had received at his coronation, Christian had never been without his signet ring. He fingered it momentarily, questioning for the first time what he was doing and what he was about to give up.

For a moment, Olbert thought that he might change his mind. The melancholy the adviser had witnessed in him for several days was suddenly apparent again. The lad's eyes were sad and dim, and his gaze was far away. In the end, however, Christian simply put the ring back in the purse and handed it to the old adviser with his shed clothes and his sword.

The Steward took the items and smiled at the youth.

"It is only for a fortnight, after all," Christian reminded him quickly, his voice revealing for the first time the very real uncertainty he felt. "-It should take Paschal no longer to find the rebels- if he has not already."

"Indeed," Olbert agreed. "And shall I send word to Lords Paschal and Felix and your other advisers that you are here, My Lord?"

"No! Absolutely not!" Christian answered, horrified.

He would not have them snickering behind his back!

"Tell them and suffer Our wrath, Olbert!"

The adviser raised his hands innocently.

"As you wish, Your Grace."

"We- *I* expect to receive word from you. I want to be kept informed of the progress at the palace and apprised of the latest reports on Herryck."

"Of course, Sire. I will forward any news I receive immediately, and the Abbot will not withhold your correspondence for any reason."

"Are you certain he can be trusted?"

"I have known him for many years, Sire. He is a good man and loyal to Speyron."

Christian nodded.

"When Paschal apprehends the leaders of the rebels, send Us word immediately. Then make arrangements for Our guards to attend Us and escort Us back to the palace, even if it is only a few days time from now."

"Of course, Sire."

Neither man said anything more for a moment.

"If there is nothing else, Sire.-"

"Aye, you have Our leave to go," Christian told him.

He watched anxiously as Olbert bowed low and then moved toward the door.

"Wait!" Christian said. "What of you? You will go to the palace directly?"

"Aye, the knights and I will spend the night in the guesthouse and depart tomorrow. We will return to the palace where your knights will report to Paschal and Felix and I can send you word of the situation. Then I will visit my own lands for a few days and then return again to the palace."

Christian nodded.

"Take care, Sire. I look forward to seeing you in a fortnight," Olbert told him kindly, as he touched the young man's shoulder.

Christian nodded his head and forced himself to smile.

"Aye, in a fortnight. It will be well. You will see."

Olbert smiled, nodded, and opened the door to the little chamber. Two monks were awaiting them in the corridor. One led the minister to the guesthouse, and the other took the new novice inside the cloister.

25

The King of Speyron slammed the door to the novice's darkened dormitory and went directly over to the straw mat on the wood floor that was his bed. It was all Christian could do to keep from ripping it to shreds with his bare hands. Instead, he kicked the mat fiercely against the wall, sending the accompanying coverlet flying through the air as well. He grabbed up the mat then and, roaring with fury, beat the wall with it for several minutes, effectively dusting himself and the air with fragments of straw.

At length, he stopped, exhausted. His energy was spent, but not his anger. Leaning his shoulder against the wall, he tried to catch his breath and calm himself.

What had he been thinking when he agreed to do this? And what perverse amusement that Abbot must be getting from his humiliation! He had thought that when the Abbot made his work assignments, he would have at least assigned him something comparable to his dignity! He had thought it would have been nothing more taxing than the copying of manuscripts for which these monasteries were famous! To his horror, he had been assigned as kitchen help, not only today but for the rest of the week!

And how many times today had he been corrected for the slightest errors- not only by that overly-critical novice master, but by nearly every monk in the place? And he was expected to endure this with 'humility and patience'? No! This was more than any king should be expected to bear! If only he had his sword, he would cut them all to pieces!

After a moment, he picked the straw mat up off the floor, noting that even after its severe beating, it had somehow managed to keep its basic shape. He set it on the floor again and lay down upon it with a groan. What a day it had been! How much wood had he chopped and carried? And how much water had he drawn and carried from the stream?

The King closed his eyes and tried to clear it from his mind. Thankfully, this was only for a fortnight. He could endure anything, he reminded himself, for a fortnight. He had already made it through six services, but still had Compline to go before he could officially retire for the night. Now Collation was under way, and the unusual sounds of laughing and talking could be heard throughout the abbey. Christian rested in the dark, hoping to get a much needed nap before the novice master started beating on that accursed drum again.

Well, at least his cold was better, he thought.

Rather than resting, his mind, however, began to retrace the day's events. At one or so in the morning, he had been awakened out of a sound sleep by the pounding of a drum seemingly in his ear. Slowly becoming conscious, he had somehow found his shoes in the dark chamber and had sleepily followed behind the other novices out into the cold night, around the cloister into the church to the choir stalls where Nocturnes was sung.

The choir stall in the church where the monks sang their offices was only slightly warmer then the outside air and almost as drafty, and the six, yawning novices had had to crowd together for warmth. Even standing upright could not keep Christian from dozing off during the office, where the unenthusiastic singing of the sleepy, young cantor and the sluggish, perfunctory responses of the others in the dimly lit church only served to lull him back to sleep. A little way into the office, the novice master had appeared beside him with a large book and a candle and had begun instructing him on what to sing and when in an effort to make certain he stayed awake. Lauds and Prime went much the same.

Then came the chapter meeting. The novices had gathered in the chapter room with all thirty or so monks. The entire community sat around an enormous, circular table while the Abbot discussed the day's business. Brother Bennet, as cheerful as ever, had been formally welcomed back. Christian himself had just been officially introduced to the other monks as "Tillo" when the novice master humiliated him in front of everyone by informing him that he was to keep his hands as well as the rest of his body covered at all times. Christian had looked around the table and only then noticed that every one of the monks and novices had his hands inside his sleeves or underneath his scapular.

Next, the novice master had informed the community that one of the oblates, a boy of about seven or eight years, had been late to Vespers for the third time last night. Abbot Hunfred had shaken his head and said that this was very serious. To help the boy remember to be on time, the Abbot ordered him to be the first to arrive at every service for the next two days where he would stand at the door and ask everyone's pardon when they entered. Then the child had stood up and dutifully thanked the Abbot for the correction.

The Abbot had then asked if any of the brothers had a fault they wished to confess. When no one said anything, the Abbot made the daily work assignments. To Christian's disgust, he was assigned to help in the kitchen. The meeting ended after a reader read a chapter from the Rule of St. Benedict, during which, once again, Christian had had to struggle to stay awake.

The novice meeting which immediately followed had been equally boring. The other novices had introduced themselves to him, and the novice master had corrected him twice more about his hands and lectured him at length on the modest way to sit. Then while the oblates were given a reading lesson, another novice instructed him on the responses to make during the offices and the refrains to sing. Somehow he had endured it all.

Then they had sung Terce. Afterward, with his stomach empty and rumbling, he had reported to the kitchen. The monk there, a kindly old man, took pity on him and gave him a piece of bread and then sent him out to gather the eggs from the henhouse. The monks had a great many chickens and geese also, and the task had taken longer than the King had expected. Immediately afterward, the monk had sent him to draw water, and then the chopping and gathering of wood had begun.-

Just about the time he had finished, a serf had arrived with three pails of freshly caught fish, and to his consternation, *he* was the one that had to gut them. Christian was not certain which was worse, having to gut the fish or having to smell like them for the many days until the monks gave him a clean set of clothes.

He had just finished cleaning the fish when the pounding of the drum summoned him back to the church choir for Sext. When he returned, he was put to hollowing out day old bread for trenchers, and when he had done that, he had to set them around the tables in the refectory, along with the cups. Next, he was put to washing and chopping leeks and preparing the legumes, but he was interrupted to get more wood and water.

Then the drum had summoned him to Nones. By the time it was over, Christian was so hungry that he could have eaten an entire ox. Thankfully, it was time to sup. Everyone gathered in the refectory, which was set up not unlike the feasting hall at the palace except for one notable difference: the Abbot sat at the head table, and *he* was obliged to sit with the other novices.

To Christian's disappointment, after cooking most of the day, all the monk had prepared was an egg dish, the fish dish, cabbage, and legumes. None of the dishes were seasoned to his liking, but he was so hungry that he ate it all without complaint. Of course, there was bread and cheese, but this was strictly portioned out to each brother with the ale.

The novice master had frowned at him for serving himself so much of the egg dish and had corrected him for pounding his cup on the table when it was empty. He had been corrected again for asking for the vinegar at the table because the monks were required to eat in silence while another monk read out loud some boring drivel written by a dead saint. As he had looked around, he had noticed that when a monk wanted something, he made a gesture with his hand, and the item was immediately passed to him.

After dinner, Christian had gathered up the trenchers so that they could be redistributed to the poor to eat and had delivered them to Brother Bennet whom incidentally was the almoner of the monastery. Then he had returned to the kitchen to wash the cups and platters, kettles and ladles, and spoons and knives that they had used that day. Then he had had to run back to the church for Vespers.

Who would have believed that life in a monastery was so arduous? Or so quiet? Although he had spent most of the day in the kitchen, the monk there had only spoken to him to give him instructions.

Wrinkling his nose at the stench of dried fish guts, the King pulled his cowl over his head and crumpling it up, threw it away from him. Still he smelled fish. He sat up again and started to remove the soiled scapular next.

"You are only allowed to take the cowl off," came a voice from the corner of the room.

Christian looked around quickly, suddenly realizing he was not alone. In the far corner of the dark room, a redheaded youth of about fifteen years lay on his straw mat.

"Is that so?" was Christian's only reply as he took it off anyway.

He began thinking about the aggressive display he had given his mat and wondered if the youth would report him to the novice master.

"I did not realize anyone was in here," Christian said.

"You are never alone here. Someone is always around, looking over your shoulder," the youth replied.

"About the mat-"

The redhead chuckled.

"Never mind about it. Such displays are more or less expected the first few days."

"I cried the first day," came a voice from the other side of the dormitory.

The King looked to the other corner and saw the oblate who had been reprimanded at the chapter meeting lying on a mat.

"You cried the first month," the redhead corrected.

"That too."

The King chuckled.

"So a certain amount of frustration is expected."

"Aye, and perhaps that is why they give us mats to begin with, rather than proper beds- extra sturdy mats for the novices of St. Brychan! I believe they are expecting a great deal of frustration from you, for I tell you truly, that is the toughest looking mat I have ever seen here. It must be terribly uncomfortable to sleep upon."

"Are you going to run away?" the oblate in the other corner asked. "I will go with you."

Christian smiled at the boy.

"Have you run away before?"

"He has run away twice," the other novice reported.

"But they always find you and beat you," the oblate told him.

Christian raised his eyebrows, but lay back down on his mat and shut his eyes.

"I am so tired."

"You will get accustomed to it," the redhead said.

The King lay in the dark, torn between wanting to rest and wanting to talk.

"What are your names again?" he finally asked.

"I am Balfrid. That is Cai," the redheaded novice answered.

"How do you ever get accustomed to all of the quiet?"

"You just do."

"You are suppose to be quiet so that you can hear God speak to you," the oblate explained.

"Have you heard him yet?" Christian asked.

"Not yet."

Christian smiled.

"How do the monks stay so cheerful with as little sleep as they get?"

"Most of them are accustomed to it. The others stay drunk all the time," Balfrid answered.

"Brother Esterwine," Cai added from the corner.

"Aye, he and a few others," Balfrid agreed. "Otherwise, if they become truly exhausted, the monks go to the infirmary and claim they are ill. They are leeched, and while they rest in bed for a few days, they eat meat."

"They had mutton today," Cai added.

"They did not have mutton," Christian contradicted.

"They did so!"

"Aye, they did," Balfrid told him, "but you did not know it because the infirmary has a separate kitchen from ours."

"So how did you know what they had?" Christian asked the young boy.

"Since children are allowed to eat meat, the oblates eat in the infirmary also," the redhead told him.

Christian glanced over at the child who grinned at him. The King sighed and shut his eyes. He could have done with some mutton as well.

"By the way, Tillo, you are supposed to bow every time you come into the presence of the Abbot," Balfrid said.

"Why should I do that?" he asked wearily.

"Because he is the voice of Christ," Cai answered.

"Oo- Listen to you! Why should *you* do that?" the redhead repeated sarcastically. "It matters not if your grandfather was Carolus Magnus! Now *you* are only another novice in St. Brychan abbey!"

"Aye, and the one with the least seniority!" the little boy added.

"Very true. And as Cai said, Tillo, the Abbot holds the place of Christ, so *everyone* bows to him," Balfrid told him bluntly.

Christian groaned and shut his eyes. Now even children were correcting him.

26

"And what is our hope? Anyone? -Quintus?" the novice master asked.

The young oblate glanced up at the novice master

"To hear God say to us 'Well done, good and faithful servant' on the day of Judgement?" he answered timidly.

"Aye, 'tis the hope of us all," Brother Septimus replied with a smile. "But what does the Church say is our hope?"

"We hope to know, love, and serve God in this life and dwell with Him in the next," Balfrid answered.

"Indeed!" the novice master answered with enthusiasm. "Thus…"

King Christian rolled his eyes in boredom and fought to stay awake.

"…every breath you take should be for the love of God, for God's love is what grants us life! When God created the world, it was an outpouring of His almighty, all-encompassing love! And love of God in return is the debt we owe, for He loved us first!

"It is easy to love God, for God is good, and it is easy to love what is good and true. Furthermore, if every motive of your thoughts and actions is love of God, then you will be safe from sin, for sin is contrary to love.- But woe to those who refuse to love God in this world, for they are doomed to hate Him forever in Hell!"

King Christian rolled his eyes again and yawned as he sat against a column in the cloister walk in the bright sunshine. The weather had turned out so warm and pleasant that the novices were having their morning meeting outside. They were not the only ones taking advantage of the fair weather. Tables had been set out on the far side of the cloister walk so that even the scribes that were copying sacred texts might benefit from the sunlight and fresh air.

Although the pervasive silence in the abbey was difficult for the King to become accustomed to, he was beginning to prefer it to the novice master's long-winded orations.

"…as we have been discussing for the last few days, for the benefit of our new member. But it is advantageous to all on occasion to recall the benefits of monastic life," the novice master said, looking around at the sleepy faces of his charges. "Who can remind us of the three aims we hope to achieve by entering monastic life?"

"To store up treasures in Heaven," Cai answered, not looking up.

The novice master sighed.

"Well, there is that. Someone else have an answer? Balfrid?"

"We hope to repent for sins, imitate the example of Christ, and come into union with God through charity."

"Excellent," the novice master smiled. "Selby, remind us all of the three obstacles to union with God."

This sandy-haired novice sat against the cloister wall with his knees up, his cheek resting on his crossed arms.

"Attachment to earthly possessions, pleasures of the flesh and senses, and our own will," he answered with closed eyes.

"And the remedies for these obstacles? Cai?"

"Poverty, chastity, and obedience," the oblate answered again.

"Aye," the novice master replied. "All of which Christ demonstrated in his life on earth. By embracing these remedies, you will atone for sins and acquire virtue as you seek that holy perfection which was God's original plan for mankind at creation.

"The pursuit of perfection itself should be enough to help you persevere against sin. Although 'the gate is narrow and the way is hard that leads to life', with the aid of these walls which separate us from the world and all its temptations, and the support of a community of like-hearted brothers who will sustain you with their prayers and example, as well as with reproofs and corrections whenever necessary, you shall be steadfast on the path that you walk. Through perfect poverty, perfect chastity and perfect obedience all performed with a spirit of perfect love for God and neighbor, you will certainly reach the perfection that assures you union with God…"

Fighting to stay awake, Christian yawned again and shut his eyes as he wondered what was happening at his palace. It had been five days. With any luck, Paschal had probably already discovered the identities of the rebel leaders, and word was already on its way to him. He hoped when the messenger arrived, he would bring a change of clothes for him and his white charger. He wanted to make a triumphant return to his palace. Perhaps, he should send a message ahead to Olbert to arrange some sort of procession and celebration for his arrival.

"…The principle work we do is singing the Divine Office, and it is more important than any other work we do," the novice master told them. "We are the intercessors for our community, our kingdom, even the world. But beyond that, the glorification of God is the principle duty of all of creation, and our songs of praise surely mingle with the songs of the angels in Heaven…"

Christian rolled his eyes again and looked dryly at the other novices. His attention settled on the two, young oblates, both of them of similar age. Cai was tracing his finger between the crevices of the stone walk; the other had fallen asleep. He wondered for a moment who their families were. The two boys were the stillest, quietest children he had ever seen. It was unnatural. He surely did not envy them the life that they would have here.

In fact, Christian's stay at the abbey would have been completely unbearable if not for the camaraderie of Brother Bennet and the welcome diversion of Collation. Although most of Christian's day was spent solely in the company of the novices, every evening during Collation, most of the community gathered in a little hall to mingle, socialize and drink ale around a fire. Some of the monks played the lute or sang, while others played games. If a brother had finished writing a poem or a history, he usually read it at Collation. The hospitaler would be there as well, passing on whatever of interest he had heard from the guests at the guesthouse. Since his third night at the abbey, Christian and Bennet had spent Collation together, playing chess.

The King was looking forward to tomorrow which was Sunday. As Bennet described it, it sounded like an all day 'Collation', as any brothers and novices who were not assigned to essential work were allowed to spend the day as they pleased. Christian, of course, would have to sing the Hours with the other novices, but in between, he would finally have the time to write several letters that he needed to send.

"…And now that the kingdom is under interdict and the Abbot has declared that you novices alone will continue to sing the Divine Office, you must see that the work you are doing is of vital importance. Thus, before you even enter the choir, put away every distracting thought. Raise your hearts to God and prepare yourself to appear before Him. Take care that the bows are all observed, and let them be motivated from deep, reverent feeling, and not from mere custom. When you sing, apply yourself with zeal to the chant! Mind the pitch and inflection of your voice- that it may moreso seek the glory of God! Observe the pronunciation and accent of the syllables with exactness…"

The King's gaze moved to the courtyard to where a few of the monks were spending the morning reading in the sunshine. The reality of monastic life was quite different from his expectations, as Olbert had predicted. Although the interdict had altered the routine of the monks, Christian was easily able to grasp how busy their lives were ordinarily. It was a wonder that they were able to accomplish any of their assigned work with their obligation to sing the Office every three or so hours.

He had already perceived that the interdict had done more than just relieve the clerics from singing the Divine Office and Masses. With their sudden surplus of both time and vitality, some of the monks, much to the Abbot's displeasure, were pouring their energies into pranks. Christian found himself quite amused by both the Abbot's repeated scolding of the pranksters at the chapter meetings and by the shenanigans that he had by chance witnessed.

"...Now, who can tell our new novice why we labor?"

"Because idleness is the enemy of the soul," Cai mumbled.

"Aye, but also because the frailty of our bodies does not allow us to pray every minute of the day. Thus, if we are not resting or praying, we should be working, for work diminishes the passions and averts sin..."

A little away from the novices, one of the older monks sat upon a stone bench in the courtyard with a great book open before him. From where he sat, Christian could see that the man had fallen asleep. As the King watched, two young monks approached the old man stealthily and quietly removed his book and replaced it with a different one. Then, pretending to be happening upon him, they *accidentally* woke the man.

"Brother Sedgewyk-" Christian could just hear the young men say.

The old monk awoke and looked around.

"Father, we did not mean to disturb your rest."

"I was not resting. I am accustomed to closing my eyes while I think on the passages of this marvelous writing."

"Please, tell us what you read."

The monk sat up and took up his book and looked about on the page. Next he turned the book upside down.

Christian smiled.

The old man began reading and then stopped suddenly, saying, "No, that is not it."

Then he read another sentence and shook his head. The brothers looked on quietly, concealing their mouths with their hands.

"Something about the-" the monk began as he perused the page and then thumbed through the large leaves- both backward and forward, clearly unable to find the passage he had been reading.

Finally the monk shut the book and opened it to the first page to see what book was before him.

"This is not my book!" the monk declared in surprise.

Christian smirked.

The two monks immediately began to laugh. Brother Sedgewyk shook his gnarled finger at the brothers who returned his book to him without delay. The three laughed together for a moment; and then the two departed, and Brother Sedgewyk returned to his reading.

"...Here, you are assigned a wide variety of work to perform," the novice master droned on. "Some tasks, no doubt, you will find you have a natural affinity for; some you will not. At such a time, remember that work that you find distasteful is beneficial for your soul because it will help to conquer your will. If you still find such labor difficult to carry out, remember that work is the punishment God imposed on sinful man from the time of Adam and Eve. Do it all cheerfully and obediently exactly as you are instructed, for you are performing it for the glory of God and will be repaid with interest in the life to come..."

King Christian of Speyron sighed and shut his eyes again.

27

"...We hope to be nearer to God through submission and love and through similar acts of charity for our neighbor. Although we are separated from the world, yet we are still a part of it, and it is our duty to look to the welfare of all of mankind..."

Christian walked beside the cart with the three older novices. It had rained hard the night before, but the rain and dark clouds had cleared off by dawn, leaving the road outside the walls of the abbey muddy and spotted with large pools of water. This morning, rather than hold their usual novice meeting in the library, the novice master had thought it appropriate to have his older charges accompany the almoner to the village, while the oblates took reading instruction at the abbey.

"However, when one is enclosed within the walls of a cloister, it is easy to lose sight of the state of the world. Therefore, so that we should not become so self-absorbed that we fail to see the needs of our brethren, we must venture outside the cloister to seek out our fellow man to offer him what help and comfort we are able. The Christ said, 'For I was hungry, and you gave me food, I was thirsty, and you gave me drink, I was a stranger, and you welcomed me, I was naked, and you clothed me, I was sick, and you visited me, I was in prison, and you came to me... Truly, I say to you, as you did it to one of the least of these my brethren, you did it to me.'..."

The cart was laden with baskets of cabbages, bread, eggs, cheeses, salted pork and mutton, and barley as well as coverlets and old habits; and it wobbled down long imbedded tracks in the uneven road. Occasionally, one of the wheels would get stuck where the mud was too deep. Then the novices would push the cart ahead, the novice master talking all the while.

"...As you go out into the world, try to see it from Our Lord's point of view. Do not recoil from the misery afflicting your fellow man, but encourage each other to reach out to him in perfect love..."

The end result was the group's eventual arrival to the edge of the village; the shoes, habits, hands, and legs of the tired, sweaty novices were covered in mud while the novice master and the almoner were all smiles and shine.

"...-And if you do nothing else, contribute to the welfare of souls by being a good example, ever mindful of *whom* you represent..."

At the edge of the village, a group of haggard men standing on the side of the road in dirty, ragged clothes suddenly surrounded the draft horse, bring the cart to a premature stop. At first, the King had thought it a band of thieves, but they were not armed. He waited for the monks to say something- to order them to keep their distance at least, but nothing was said. At once, some of the men reached into the cart and, grabbing bread out of the baskets, bit into it ravenously.

Christian was amazed at the rabbles' audacity, but the other novices seemed neither alarmed nor surprised. After getting their bread, these individuals stepped aside so that the other men who were waiting behind them could get something as well. This bunch stood in a line before the cart quietly and waited for the monks to give them what they would.

The novices began distributing food from the baskets then, and each beggar took as much as he could carry. Bennet climbed down from his seat on the front of the cart and helped a few of the men use their tunics as makeshift pouches so that they would be able to carry more food. The novice master distributed coverlets and a few old habits to any of the men who would take them.

Christian gave a cabbage to each man. When the last man stood before him, he put the cabbage into the man's tunic which the beggar held out firmly with one hand, for he had no other.

"Bless you, Brother," he said.

Christian regarded him in surprise. As he watched the group of men depart, he noticed that most were lame or had a limb missing; some limped along with a crutch while others had mangled arms that hung slack by their sides.

Bennet was beside him then, taking the container of cabbages from him and setting it back into the cart.

"Who were those men?" Christian asked him.

"Soldiers."

"Knights?"

"A few; some were archers, but most were foot soldiers."

"What are they doing here?"

"Begging."

"Why?"

Bennet smiled.

"The majority are freemen who fought in some battle somewhere. But being gravely wounded, perhaps sacrificing a limb in the fight, they were no longer able to work their lord's fields and therefore were unable to pay their lord's rent, so they were brought here. Every monastery supports such a group."

The King listened curiously.

"It is very different from the glorious stories and songs of war that we heard at Reynaud's castle," Bennet concluded.

"Really, Tillo, you surprise me," Balfrid commented dryly. "Have you never wondered what became of men crippled by war?"

Christian glared at the youth, but made no reply. Bennet simply smiled and patted the new novice on the shoulder before climbing back into the cart with the novice master. Christian sat on the back of the cart with the other novices, and the group continued on their way.

Every dog in the village barked at the cart as it slowly made its way down the muddy road past several huts where lively villagers were engaged in the day's activities. Bennet stopped the horse next to a small, pathetic hut that looked as if it was going to collapse at any moment. Christian smiled as some villein children, who were equally covered in mud, raced to the cart, shouting their greetings in excited voices. The children ran up to the novices that they knew and hugged them and began talking rapidly to them.

Climbing down from the cart, Brother Bennet scooped up a child of about five years of age and carried her back to her mother who had stepped into the doorway of the hut. The novices and novice master began unloading the baskets, and then each one took the hand of a child who was waiting impatiently to escort him to the dwelling. Christian carried the baskets of cabbages and eggs in silence, noting the absence of fowl or swine anywhere near this hut.

Bennet greeted the mother and set down the child he carried. He asked after her health and the well being of the children. The woman moved out of the doorway so that the monks could bring the goods inside. A very pale, dark-haired boy of about nine years came out of the hut and stood beside his mother. He was cleaner than the other children, but his clothes were ragged, and he had a bad cough. Bennet bent down and touched the boy's cheek.

"Good day, Ian. How do you fare this day?"

The child only smiled and turned his face into his mother's skirts. Bennet smiled and stood back up.

"He seems better today," his mother said.

"I am glad, but I did bring him some more teas."

The eldest daughter of the woman appeared then. Her plain, woolen gown was stretched tight over her skinny frame. The long sleeves of her tunic were too short for her arms, and her ankles showed beneath the edge of her gown.

"Agnes, you must have grown a foot since I saw you last," Bennet told her.

The girl smiled.

"My, how the children are growing," Bennet commented to the woman again. "We brought some clothes for them."

"Thank you, Brother."

A little girl of about six years of age with black locks and brown eyes walked beside Christian, smiling up at him. Christian smiled back at the dirty face. The King entered the very small, dark hut, noting the bare surroundings. The only light that was in the hut was the sunlight that came in through the open door. There was no bed; in one corner of the room was a large pile of disarrayed straw covered with a pile of coverlets. Christian wondered if this was all they had to keep them warm through the coming winter.

And although the hut only contained a table and two benches, it was not large enough to hold the six children, the woman, and the six monks. Thus, while the novices carried the rest of the baskets of food into the hut and set them upon the table, Bennet, the novice master, and the mother remained outside, digging through the basket of the monks' old habits.

Christian watched as the woman held up one dark habit at a time to the oldest girl, guessing at the fit. The girl, who looked to be almost eleven, seemed healthy. The mother, however, was very thin, and she looked exhausted; her own gown was dirty and worn and patched in several places.

As the group continued to visit with the family, Christian went over to Bennet.

"Do all these children belong to this woman?" he asked quietly.

"Aye."

"How do they all live in this little place?"

"They make do."

"Where is her husband? Has he abandoned her?"

"Aye, in death. He died from an accident two months ago. The middle son has been ill for many days, but he is better today."

Christian observed the happy faces of the children as they hungrily chewed the cheese and bread.

Here was a family on monastic lands that was struggling with poverty and misfortune. Were there families on his own palace lands in similar need? Was anyone feeding those children? If the priests at the palace church knew of such families in need and had been caring for them, was anyone helping them now that the priests were gone?

28

Christian wiped his sweating brow with the sleeve of his habit, then drew another pail of heated water from the large cauldron and poured the water into a wooden tub where a few monks were bathing.

The bath at this Romani fortress had fallen into ruin years ago, so the monks had built their own style of bathhouse. It was simply a chamber that contained three wooden tubs that were each big enough to accommodate four bathers at a time. In the center of the room was a stone oven with a large caldron in its top for heating both the chamber and large amounts of water.

"Good day, Tillo."

Christian laughed once sarcastically and turned slowly to see Bennet standing behind him.

"How nice and warm it is in here!" Bennet exclaimed cheerfully, noting how miserable and sweaty the King looked.

Christian laughed again.

"And it seems you are getting a bath as well- without even being in the tub," he added, gesturing toward the novice's wet sleeves and scapular.

Christian smiled pitifully at his friend while he wiped his sweating face with his shoulder.

"It could be worse," he mumbled. "At least I do not have to scrub them myself."

"Oh, now, that does sound tempting.-"

Christian looked pathetically at the monk.

"You want me to *wash* you?"

"Like they do in the palace," Bennet whispered mischievously.

Christian moaned.

"Actually, I am only joking. It is not my assigned day to bathe. The Lord Abbot sent me to give these to you," he told him pleasantly, while covertly handing the King three scrolls and then turning to greet the brothers in the tubs.

Christian turned his back to the bathers and eagerly examined the seals of the scrolls, recognizing the Royal Steward's seal and the seal of Paschal. It had been more than a week. Surely there was good news by now.

"Here, take a moment to rest from your work and come outside with me," Bennet said. "It looks like they have enough water for the present."

Christian glanced at the bathers again and then nodded.

As he and the monk headed for the door, Bennet deftly scooped up the discarded undertunics, scapulars and habits of the three bathers and carried them outside amid the astonished protests of the brothers. Christian grinned as he followed Bennet to a tall tree which was a little ways from the bathhouse but very near the entrance to the guesthouse. With a devilish smile, Bennet hung the clothing on the low branches of the tree and then leaned against the trunk with his arms crossed.

Christian immediately broke Paschal's seal and unrolled the scroll. Whispering as he read, he sighed in disappointment. Paschal had not yet found out the instigators of the rebellion and could only conclude that it was not yet safe for him to return to the palace.

The letter from Olbert was equally dismal. The Royal Steward had recently returned to the palace, and he complained about the way Paschal was managing the interrogations of the peasants. He claimed that Paschal was terrorizing the people and that the morale of the palace servants was very low.

Christian frowned and opened the last scroll, wondering who else had a complaint to make.

"To His Grace, Christian Oengus Tillo Cuthbert, King of Speyron. Dear Cousin,"

Christian smiled. It was from Kaith.

"My Lord, I pray this letter finds you and that you are in good health and spirits and safe from all harm. After we last parted, Lord Dewain placed me at the convent of St. Clovis, as you desired. It is a nice place really, but the scenery here can not compare with the view from the palace. My maid and I have chambers near the other girls, but ours is larger.

"The nuns are very strict here. They have rules for everything, even eating dinner. And we are required to be quiet almost all of the time. We are not even allowed to talk at meals or even to laugh. The sisters teach us about what types of things a lady may do and what is nice for a lady to say, but mainly what is not nice for a lady to do, say, or think about. I find it very hard to control some of the thoughts that go through my mind. But I am trying to be good and to act the way God wants all nice ladies to act."

Christian smiled as he read this part, muttering to himself that he knew what she was going through.

"There are about ten girls here now. I have made friends with three girls especially. Two of them are sisters from the south of Speyron and older than me. The other is a girl my age named Imengardt who is being sponsored by Lord Dewain. So far, besides learning stories of the life of our Lord and the teachings of the Church, the nuns have been teaching us to spin, weave, sew, and embroidery. We help in the kitchen and are learning how to cook. We also sing songs the nuns teach us. Everyday we read in small groups. I am in the most advanced reading group, though whenever I mention it, the sisters warn me to beware of the sin of pride. Right now my group is reading some of the writings of St. Jerome.

"Although I try very hard to behave and not to sin, I did get into trouble the other day. Since the weather was so nice, I had wanted to take a stroll around the grounds before my lessons. My maid and the other girls were still at table, so I went walking by myself and arrived at the convent stables. There I met the young stableman. He was quite handsome, and I began talking with him about the horses."

Christian raised his eyebrows at this information.

"One of the sisters happened upon us and immediately took me away. I did not even have time to wish him farewell! She took me at once to the Lady Abbess and told her where she had found me.

"Truly, Cousin, I did not know they were looking for me! But the abbess would not hear it. She said that the stableman was there to tend the horses, not to talk with me.

"As punishment for an entire week, I have been confined to the cloister, and I have to sit in the 'sinner' seat at table. Also, I am no longer allowed to go out on the grounds by myself anymore; I have to have either my maid or one of the sisters with me."

Christian smiled and read on.

"Well, Cousin, it will soon be time for bed, so I must end this letter. If the convent mistress approves of it, I will be able to send this letter to you through Lord Dewain as we planned. I love you and miss you very much."

The letter ended with her signature: Lady Kaithryn Genevieve.

Christian rolled the scroll back up with the others and handed them back to Bennet so he could return them to the Abbot's office for safekeeping.

His advisers had been correct; the convent was a good place for Kaith. She sounded happy, and she had made friends there.

The King's thoughts were distracted then by Bennet's laughter. Christian looked around to see the three monks, wearing their stockings and shoes, but with only their cowls to cover their privates, running towards them. The monks, scolding Bennet all the while, grabbed their garments off the tree branches and then dashed toward the cloister, their bare buttocks still glistening with bath water.

At the same time, some women travelers emerged from the guesthouse, and they were rewarded with the intimate view of the brothers as well. Their startled cry and giggles caught the attention of the last monk, who, ever mindful of his duty to greet visitors, stopped long enough to bow and say, "You are most heartily welcome here!" Then he was off racing after the others to the cloister, his long and skinny, naked legs making great strides.

The King and Brother Bennet remained near the tree, laughing heartily until tears came to their eyes.

29

"...In the beginning God created man in his image, but the resemblance was distorted by sin. Thus, God sent his son to take on our nature to once again show us that holiness and perfection that He intended for us.

"The Christ said, 'You, therefore, must be perfect as your heavenly Father is perfect.' The Christ and the life he lived is the perfection for which we should all aspire. He told his disciples: 'This is my commandment, that you love one another as *I have loved you..'...*"

Christian sighed, his eyelids drooping heavily.

"...In First John, the scripture says 'And by this, we may be sure that we know Christ, if we keep his commandments. He who says 'I know him' but disobeys his commandments is a liar, and the truth is not in him; but whoever keeps his word, in him truly love for God is perfected. By this we may be sure that we are in him: he who says he abides in him ought to walk in the same way in which he walked.'..."

With his cheek in his hand, King Christian sat glumly at the table, looking blankly at three pitchers of water, some linen cloth, and three basins as the novice master talked on. Tomorrow would make a fortnight, and he was *still* here. He had been here so long now that he knew instinctively when it was time to head to the choir to sing an Hour as well as the words to every chant he sang. His stomach had become accustomed to only one meal a day, and he could immediately fall into a sound sleep on a hard, straw mat among the other novices and awake refreshed in the middle of the night.

"...Thus, it is Christ that we are to imitate, in this and in all things. As Christ loved the Father and his fellow man, likewise we love the Father and our fellow man..."

Christian had received three letters today. Paschal had sent word that he had not discovered the identities of the rebels, but every honest attempt he made to find them was met with condemnation by Olbert, Grey and Dewain. The two letters from Grey and Dewain both accused Felix and Paschal of mishandling the investigation at the palace. Both men complained that the inquiry was going nowhere and that Paschal was overstepping his authority.

Grey felt that Paschal and Felix were growing too powerful in his absence; he candidly requested Christian to return to the palace to oversee the interrogations personally.

Dewain similarly feared Felix and Paschal's power and their influence with the palace knights. He feared for everyone's safety and strongly recommended Christian stay wherever he was until and unless the King could return to the palace with a large company of knights whose loyalty to him was irrefutable. Dewain ended his letter with notice that he was leaving the palace immediately and returning to his own lands.

The novice master paused in his speech then and signaled for Selby to sit up straight from where he slumped on the tabletop, cradling his head in his arms. He placed the Gospel in front of the young novice to read, pointing to the place on the page.

Selby cleared his throat and began to slowly translate the Latin.

"Jesus, knowing that the Father…"

Christian sighed in frustration and brushed his long, golden hair out of his face with his hand. This was ridiculous. His palace was in chaos, and he was stranded here- listening to scriptures and singing songs, utterly powerless to do anything to help himself.

He was so unsettled that he feared himself on the verge of madness. His entire future depended solely on the loyalty of his advisers, and the communications he had received from them were so contradictory that he was uncertain as to what was actually happening in his kingdom. He was not even certain his position as king was as stable as it had been a month ago. After all, with his recent absence and the palace in continued turmoil, if one of his vassals attempted to seize his throne, it could easily be accomplished with a little support. Bloodshed might not even be necessary.

"…Then he poured water into a basin and began to wash the disciples' feet, and to wipe them with the towel…"

Frowning, Christian covered his eyes with his hand and groaned. He knew where this scripture lesson was certain to be leading.

"…If I then, your Lord and Teacher, have washed your feet, you also ought to wash one another's feet. For I have given you an example, that you also should do as I have done to you."

"That is well, Selby. All of you will recall that the Rule prescribes that when we receive guests, we are to wash their feet. Thus, we shall now practice this important duty with the spirit of charity."

As the novice master instructed the novices to pair up, Christian fought down his irritation at the irrelevant exercise, reminding himself it could be worse. At least he was not expected to wash the feet of the villeins who mucked out the abbey stables -nor the feet of Abbot Hunfred, whom he despised.

Still, Christian was glad his father was not here to witness this. He could almost hear his reproach, not to mention the scorn Filberte surely would have had for any king who was forced to hide for his life among monks!

He sighed again, but refused to be ashamed. He had done what he had had to do. In the same situation, he doubted his father would have been able to pass himself off as a novice; he certainly never would have been able to stick to the schedule, much less the rules. Filberte likely would have gone mad in the quiet, and he would have found the sobriety required, not to mention the obedience, to be unbearable.

"Are you going first, or am I, Tillo?" Cai asked him, interrupting his thoughts.

Christian registered the question and then looked about the chamber. Selby was already kneeling on the floor in front of Balfrid, drying his feet. Quintus was actually standing in the basin while the other novice poured the water over his feet, since he was too small for his feet to reach the pan had he been sitting on the bench.

"Tillo! Were you not listening to Brother Septimus?" Balfrid was suddenly asking him.

Christian sighed briefly, but smiled at Cai. He liked the child best of all of the novices. Washing his feet would be no more taxing to his dignity than washing Kaith's.

"Where should I sit?" he asked the oblate.

Cai pointed to the bench and brought the basin over. He knelt on the floor and worked to take off Christian's large left shoe.

"Not so rough, Cai," the novice master corrected. "Would you handle the feet and shoes of the Christ in such a way?"

"Sorry," Cai muttered.

Amused, Christian smiled as the oblate worked his other foot free of its shoe and stocking.

"Your feet stink," the child complained.

Christian chuckled as the oblate put both of his cumbersome feet in the basin and poured water from the pitcher over them and the surrounding floor. Then the child awkwardly picked up one foot, dried it with the linen cloth and set it down in the puddle on the floor and then did the same to the other foot.

"How was it?" Cai asked.

Christian grinned widely.

"'Twas the best foot wash I have ever had."

Cai beamed at him. Then he sat on the bench while Christian stood up, stretched, and then carefully *squatted down* before the child.

"You have to pour the water back into the pitcher because you are supposed to pour the water over the feet," Cai told him.

Christian nodded good-naturedly and did as he was instructed. Then he took off the boy's shoes and stockings and curiously examined his dirty feet for a moment with raised eyebrows. The novices had just had their bath yesterday, and already the oblate's feet and ankles were filthy.

Cradling the basin in the crook of his arm, he set the boy's feet in it and carefully poured the water over them. Then he set the basin back on the floor and deftly began toweling off the child's dripping feet.

"Well?" he asked Cai.

"'Twas the best I ever had," he said with a broad grin.

Christian smiled again as he put the oblate's stockings and shoes back on him.

30

Looking at the lengthy stone floor before him, Christian sat miserably on the lone bench in the corridor and cursed both the Abbot and Paschal. It should never have come to this! He should have been back at his palace long before now. It had been three weeks! How could the leaders of the rebellion still be unknown? What was Paschal doing? No doubt, he was at his ease, eating the palace delicacies and drinking the best imported wine! He was probably too busy making his way through the royal concubines to even oversee the questioning of the peasants!

Christian moaned as he covered his face with his hands. Why had he left Paschal in charge? Why had he not had the presence of mind to put Van Necht to it? The seasoned warlord would have found the rebels out within the first few days.

And why did he continue to linger here? the King asked himself for the hundredth time. He should be preparing for war! He should be visiting his vassals and consolidating his power, not hiding like a woman from the howls of wolves! If he was fated to have a short reign, so be it! He should accept it and go out and face his foes! At least let him be remembered as courageous and dignified when the end came. He did not want songs sung immortalizing him as the king who was dragged out into the snow and butchered in the monk's dress that he was disguised in. Such a ridiculous song performed by a talented bard could easily become the favorite of the Continent!

Still he delayed; but why? Why was it so difficult for him to walk into the Abbot's office and announce his intention to depart on the morrow? He had ample cause.

The simple explanation was that his pride would not allow him to leave. Christian was determined to frustrate the plans of that pompous Abbot Hunfred, for it had become apparent to him that the Abbot had been trying to accomplish his departure from the moment he had arrived at their gates.

From the very first chapter meeting, he had not only been outraged, but astonished by the lowly work that the Abbot had assigned him. A month ago, if anyone had dared suggest to him that a nobleman, let alone a king, should perform the kind of backbreaking, menial labor that he had been forced to do these past three weeks, Christian was certain he would have ordered them put into the stocks at the very least. But as he needed the shelter that the abbey provided and partially because his own minister thought him undisciplined, Christian had yielded his dignity and done what was asked of him.

Thus, a combat of wills had begun between the Abbot and himself, and so far, they seemed equally matched. Each day Christian somehow had managed to bear the humiliation assigned to him; but the following morning, the Abbot would select another, new and worse indignity with which to try his patience.

Every night before he fell asleep, Christian would try to guess what ignoble task he would be put to on the morrow. Working in the kitchen, chopping wood, drawing the monk's bath water, feeding the swine, airing out the monks' bedding, milking the cows and goats- Christian had endured it all and much more.

But this morning, the Abbot had struck a decisive blow. The King, like a disarmed man with the point of a sword to his throat, found he either had to yield at once and leave the field, or suffer a grievous wound to his royal dignity. With the seemingly innocent instruction to wash a corridor floor, that brazen Abbot had actually demanded that his King serve him on his very hands and knees.

This, at last, was too much to be endured. The last time Christian had been on his knees before anyone had been at his own coronation, and he would sooner die than be on his knees before any man ever again. Thus, he was left with little choice now but to depart from the abbey instantly.

Since the morning's novice meeting, Christian had mentally rehearsed informing the Abbot of his decision to depart. However, with the exception of declaring immediate war on Herryck, he could not think of a single thing to say that would adequately conceal his shame. And after considering it further for a hour, he was no longer certain which was more humiliating: cleaning the floor or tacitly admitting to the Abbot that he was bested. The defeat Christian felt was so great that on the way to sing Terce he had actually come to the corridor to examine the floor.

As the King looked at the *very* long hallway with its floor of plain, uneven stones, he noticed then that he was quite alone. He raised his eyebrows.

If no one happened to be in this vicinity, then no one would be present to see *how* he actually accomplished the labor. Perhaps the Abbot had not bested him after all...

Christian lay on the bench hoping to get a much needed nap before the drum summoned him to Sext. He was to have completed the floor before dinner, and dinner was still several hours away. He smiled, pleased with himself. The most arduous effort he had exerted on the floor had been to carry several pails of water from the nearby stream. After that, he had simply poured water evenly over the entire length of floor and spread the water over the dry stones by swabbing a rag over them with his foot. He doubted anyone would notice the difference.

Suddenly hearing the sound of approaching footsteps, Christian stood up quickly and picked up his rag. Abbot Hunfred slowed his pace as he entered the hallway, scrutinizing first the wet floor and then the

King and his dry habit. Neither man bowed to the other, and neither spoke for a moment.

"Are you ill, Your Grace?" Hunfred asked finally.

"No, Lord Abbot."

"Well, you had better get to work then. You will not be half completed by dinner."

"What?" Christian asked in surprise, wondering if the Abbot had missed the wet floor he was standing on.

"Surely you do not believe you are finished when it is obvious you have hardly begun. You have done nothing more than wet the stone. You have not even attempted to remove the dirt-"

"What?"

"Your Grace, we seek perfection here, and so must you also if you would remain among us. When you are given a task, you must perform it perfectly and exactly as you are instructed-"

"You did not give me any specific instructions on how to clean-"

"Well, I am telling you *now*. And you should get started or you will find yourself finishing this floor during Collation."

That was it! Christian could bear no more! He threw the rag he had been holding angrily to the floor.

"You have ordered me to clean the floor! I have complied! I shall not do it again! If you do not like what I have done, do it yourself!"

"As you will remember, Your Grace," Hunfred said coolly, "the condition for you staying at St. Brychan's was that you agreed to do what you were told at all times. You have the privilege to live among us as one of us, and as such, you must submit to the Rule and my authority at all times. If, however, you are inclined to leave us now, you need only to say the word."

Christian's hands clenched into tight fists as he fought his rising rage, his tongue, and the urge to throw himself on the Abbot and strangle him.

"Shall I send for your clothes?" Hunfred asked the youth plainly.

Struggling to control himself, Christian made no answer, staring straight ahead past the Abbot.

"Very well, I shall be back in a while to see how you progress," he said, turning on his heel and leaving the hall.

Red-faced and hot, Christian cursed and kicked the pail violently, knocking it across the hall and splashing the little water it contained all over himself and the floor.

Why had he not said, 'Aye, bring me my clothes and sword and let me be gone from this cursed place!'? he asked himself. He picked up the rag from the floor and threw it with all his might and fury against the nearby wall. Before this was over, he vowed, he would kill that man and have his head hung on his palace gate! -Better yet, the monastery gate!

With rage pounding through him, the King began to slam his fist against the wall, willing the stone to give way to him. After about the sixth blow, his fury was lessening, and pain began to register in his hand. Christian looked at his red fist that was throbbing.

"Owh," he muttered, cradling it in his other hand.

He shook it a little, as if that would ease the pain. It did not.

"Oh, Tillo, what have you done?" came a familiar voice and a laugh.

Christian turned to see the merry Bennet enter the hall, looking at the wet floor. Christian looked again at his sore hand, intermittently squeezing it.

"Forgive me for laughing," the auburn-haired monk continued with some mirth, "but when one has to scrub a floor, one usually does not wet the entire floor to begin with, else you, your habit, and the floor end up equally wet."

King Christian glared at the cheerful monk humorlessly.

"Do not distress; 'twas an innocent mistake," Bennet chuckled, quickly surmising the King's ill-humor.

Christian made a gesture of irritation.

"Nor should you despair over this labor, for every novice at St. Brychan's has had to scrub this floor sooner or later."

Bennet walked passed Christian to a little, wooden cabinet against the far wall; opening it, he removed two large brushes.

"For some reason, Abbot Hunfred never explains to the new novices the correct way to clean this floor before they begin. He seems to want them to be lost at first and to seek guidance. I do not know that it does anything but frustrate the initiates, but he has done it to us all."

The monk watched as Christian again squeezed his palm.

"What is the matter with your hand?"

"Nothing, it will be well in a moment."

The monk nodded and offered Christian a brush.

"No," Christian answered.

Bennet smiled at him, surprised.

"Tsk, tsk, tsk! Such a show of obstinacy, Tillo! I will have to tell the novice master that he neglects his novices by not lecturing on the virtues of obedience."

"I can not."

"Are you unwell? If you are unwell, you should go to the infirmary."

"You do not rightly understand," Christian told him testily. "*I* can not."

The monk raised his eyebrows as he considered the cause of the refusal. As he looked at the floor again and then back at the King who now leaned against the wall resolutely with his arms crossed, Bennet wondered what he should say.

"It must be- greatly humbling to be asked to do such work," Bennet finally said quietly with a sympathetic tone. "I found it so when I came here, and I am not equal to your birth. For we monks, this sort of work has its rewards. Perhaps it will hold some benefit for you as well- if nothing more than to give you an understanding of the labor, as well as the patience required, of those who serve you in such a way as this."

Christian refused to be moved by his words. He made no reply as he stared at the far wall.

"Come, I will help you," Bennet told him, his very eyes encouraging him to take the brush he offered again.

"I said, 'No,'" he answered, his ire rising a notch.

"Then I will do it for you," Bennet said simply, setting one of the brushes on the bench.

Surprised and aghast, King Christian watched the monk turn and go to the corner of the corridor, get to his knees on the wet floor, and begin scrubbing the stones.

If anyone else at the monastery had offered to do this, Christian would have thought this compromise agreeable. It was the least anyone could do for their king. But for some reason, he felt it wholly unacceptable for Bennet to do it.

Christian took a deep breath and suppressed his desire to scream in frustration. What was worse now? Toiling on his own hands and knees for the amusement of the Abbot, admitting defeat to the amusement of the Abbot, or forcing Bennet, his only true friend here, to do this ignoble work for him? It was no contest.

"You will not do this, Bennet," he said, picking up the brush from the bench and going over to the monk.

"'Tis not so bad. This floor and I are old acquaintances."

"I alone was given this labor, and I am not so slothful as to expect you to do your work and mine as well."

"Do not trouble about it."

"I will not *permit* it," Christian told him firmly, getting to his knees beside the monk and beginning to scrub the stone. "Leave me."

"I am determined to do this," Bennet smiled. "But if you like, I will allow you to help me."

Christian sighed in irritation, but did not argue further.

The young monk chuckled then.

"I remember well the first time I was assigned this floor and thought myself nearly finished with it. The Lord Abbot came and reprimanded me heartily and bade me to do it again properly. I was very disheartened. An old monk, Father Ignacious, who is dead now, came and told me about the brushes. We spent more than two good hours on our knees, with him encouraging me the entire time. He was truly a holy man. -Here, Tillo, do it like this."

Christian watched as Bennet scrubbed the stone in a circular motion. The King began to imitate the monk. After scrubbing the area for four or five revolutions, Bennet moved a little beside it. After a little while, he leaned back and observed the King.

"Smaller circles, Tillo, and do not rush."

Christian made his circle smaller.

"Form each circle like it was all that mattered, like it was the only thing you had to do for today, for you are doing it for the glory of God. Only when you are absolutely positive it needs no more attention and that all the dirt has been loosed and removed that can be, then move on to the next area, and begin again. Switch hands when you become tired."

Bennet returned to scrubbing beside him.

"The repetitiveness promotes contemplation, you see. As you focus on each small area, clear your mind. Think on God or the Christ, or you can think on the psalms that you sang today. What was it this morning? 'Levavi oculos meos in montes unde veniet auxilium mihi, auxilium meum a Domino qui fecit caelum et terram.' 'I lifted my eyes up to the hills, from whence does my help come? My help is from the Lord who made heaven and earth.'"

Christian nodded and simply tried to concentrate on the work he was doing. After a few more minutes, he felt he was making progress.

With the two, young men scrubbing, by the time the novices were summoned to Sext, one-third of the floor was completed. After stretching his aching back and shoulders, Christian departed for the church choir while Bennet took a much needed rest. After Sext, the two returned to the floor again.

"Bennet, how many times have you scrubbed this floor?"

The young monk chuckled.

"I am not certain anymore. Perhaps two hundred times?"

Christian raised his eyebrows and shook his head. They fell into silence again as they toiled side by side.

A little before Nones, they finished the floor. The two young men wearily got to their feet, the entire, front, bottom half of their habits and scapulars soaking wet as well as their sleeves. Christian's knees and shins were raw and itching as well. Tired and sore, the pair made their way to the bench and sat down. As they rested there, they were greeted by a fat monk of about two score years of age.

"Well, I see that our new novice has fallen under your influence, Brother Bennet." Then he said to Christian, "I hope you are not his twin and will not join Brother Bennet in bedeviling us as he so loves to do."

Bennet laughed.

"Last night I had not entered my cell but a few minutes after returning from Collation when I heard an excited exclamation coming from Brother Lubin's cell. I went in immediately to discover what the commotion was which caused him to break the ground silence. When I saw his predicament, I was stricken with such irrepressible laughter that I had to hide myself in my cell lest my own outburst be discovered, but I knew immediately you, Brother Bennet, must be behind it."

Christian looked at his friend questioningly, while Bennet snickered wickedly at the success of his prank. The fat monk laughed also, but seeing that Christian required more explanation, he began to explain.

"Since you are but a novice to the order, you may not be aware of the annual trial that Brother Lubin undergoes. In order to prove his steadfastness and his ability to resist the temptations of the flesh, Brother Lubin challenges his resolve by having a young, beautiful woman be his bedfellow for a week. For the last six nights, Brother Lubin has withstood temptation admirably as he has for all the years he has put himself to the test."

The King raised his eyebrows. He had not known that women were allowed inside the cloister for any reason. -But why would any man wish to torture himself in such a way? he wondered. And what a squandered opportunity!

"Believe me, Brother," the monk said to Christian with a nod and a smile, "this was surely not an easy feat, for Brother Lubin was sharing his bed with a comely, healthy, young virgin with firm, round- well, you know," the monk smiled, gesturing with his hands. "-I am doubtful that I could have made it through even one night without questioning my vows, much less breaking them," he smirked. "But, anyway, last night, when Brother Lubin returned from Collation for one last night of temptation, he discovered that the young beauty had been *replaced*."

At this, the two monks began wildly snickering. Christian smiled.

"Rather than the comely, young maid," the fat monk managed, quite breathless, "there stood in his cell- How might one say it? -A copious woman of advanced age and experience."

Bennet and the monk laughed heartily.

"-With wrinkled skin, long thin, gray hair, and sagging breasts, she welcomed our brother wearing only an undertunic and a toothless smile."

Christian snorted and laughed too.

"When I arrived, she was asking the brother whether he was ready to retire."

The monk paused to catch his breath as he laughed, wiping away the tears from his eyes.

"In truth," he continued, "I do not know who I pitied more: the old woman for being immediately covered in a coverlet and put out of the cell and ushered quickly to the guesthouse by the monk, or Brother Lubin as he realized that -his stomach was weaker than his piety!"

The three men howled with laughter.

"Whatever made you think of this?" the monk asked Bennet.

"I was only trying to be charitable to our brother and to keep the trial sincere," Bennet replied. "To me, it seemed an unfair test of his steadfastness for Brother Lubin to only bundle with fetching, young maids."

The men continued to laugh until the monk excused himself and left.

Christian turned back to his friend then and smiled.

"So, Brother Bennet, what became of the virgin? You can tell me."

"I took her to the guesthouse."

"And did you test your *steadfastness*?"

Bennet smiled and rolled his eyes.

"No, of course not."

Christian shook his head and muttered, "I do not believe you learned anything at Lord Reynaud's."

Bennet laughed again, and the two waited there on the bench for Nones or the Abbot to come and check the floor, whichever was first.

31

"Father Confessor, am I disturbing you?"

The senior confessor who had been staring out of the small window in his cell turned his eyes to the young man in his doorway. He smiled and rose from his chair.

"Not at all. Come in, come in, Brother."

Bennet walked into the small room and hesitated, and then shut the door behind him.

"Do you have something you wish to confess?" Father Desle asked with a mischievous smile.

Bennet smiled and shook his head.

"No, Father."

"I could not officially accommodate you anyway with the interdict, but I wondered if you had come to confess the most recent mischief with Brother Lubin. -I knew it must have been you behind it."

Then the old monk threw his head back and laughed out loud. Bennet only smiled.

As the young monk did not join in the laughter and seemed slightly troubled, the senior priest quickly put on a serious face.

"Here, sit down," he said, motioning toward the other empty chair; then he sat down again himself.

As the young priest complied, the smile fell from his face completely, and a pensive look replaced it.

"Does something trouble you, Brother?"

"Aye, Father, for the last few days. Yesterday, I decided I must speak to someone about it."

Bennet paused then and wondered where he should begin.

"Yesterday, I discovered the new novice, Tillo, overwhelmed and quite despondent over the labor he had been assigned."

"Washing the corridor floor?"

"Aye."

The confessor nodded.

"Apparently the Abbot was going to make him repeat it until he did it correctly -as he has done with all new novices."

The old confessor watched as the young man hesitated and pressed his lips together momentarily.

"You have met the new novice?" Bennet asked.

The priest assented.

"You know who *he* is?"

"I do."

The old confessor's face revealed nothing, so Bennet continued.

"-I helped him scrub the floor with the brushes, as I had been similarly helped myself by Brother Ignacious. When the Abbot came to check the floor and saw me waiting with the King, he knew I had helped him, -but I had not tried to conceal the truth from him."

"Umm-hmm."

"However, when he saw me there, the Abbot's countenance changed immediately. After he sent the King on his way, he asked me why I was not at my own work. When I told him I had already completed it, he seemed irritated and left. -This is not the first time of late the Abbot has seemed displeased with me. In fact, on several occasions when he has found me in the company of the King, he has frowned and glared."

"Umm-hmm."

"At first, I simply thought the Lord Abbot to be in an ill-temper. But now, Father, I fear that he is truly angry with me, perhaps for inviting the King here."

"Hmm-"

"But even so," Bennet continued, "I can not understand why the Abbot is assigning the King such rigorous work when his noviceship is most certainly feigned."

Father Desle raised his eyebrows and shifted in this chair.

"Father Confessor, I know it is not my place to question the intentions of the Abbot-" Bennet added quickly, "but we have the singular opportunity now to show the King a glimpse of God's Kingdom on earth. How will we be able to do this if the Abbot drives him away from St. Brychan's through excessive strictness and demands which the King obviously finds burdensome to his dignity?"

Father Desle raised his eyebrows again.

"Now I have begun to fear that the Abbot is not only angry that I invited the King here, but because I encourage and help him, he believes I have sided with the King."

"It sounds as if you have," the old confessor responded.

"That has not been my intention, Father. I hope that I have shown the same concern for the King as I would for any other soul in need of repentance -or for any other novice for that matter. I have offered the King my friendship in the hope that my example, along with the charitable example of our brethren, would recall to his mind the duty he holds to God and to his fellow man."

"An example? He has certainly had that. Have you seen any change in him yet?"

"I believe so. He seems concerned-"

"Has he repented?" Father Desle interrupted. "Has he rent his clothing and washed his face with tears of agony for the atrocities that he has committed? Has he experienced one moment of remorse for what he has done -or acknowledged to you or to anyone that he has sinned against God and neighbor?"

Brother Bennet frowned, but made no reply.

"I think not, and this is the cause," the confessor continued. "When he willfully turned away from God and embraced sin, God hardened the King's heart against Him further. Sin has been the King's constant companion for so long now that he can not acknowledge the wrongfulness of his deeds even to himself."

Bennet swallowed painfully.

"That is why it will take much more than a few days of charitable examples to turn the heart of King Christian- *if* it can be done at all," Desle explained. "Believe me, My Son, you cannot trust your own judgment on this matter. You must trust that the Abbot who is wise and more experienced than you knows what he is doing.

"-Nor do I believe that the Abbot is angry with you for inviting the King here, for ultimately it was the Abbot's decision to admit him. However, he may feel that when you help the King with the work that has been assigned him, you are interfering with his plans for the King's amendment."

Brother Bennet sighed.

"The Abbot's treatment of the King may seem harsh and excessively demanding to you and perhaps to the King, but do you believe that God will be easier on him on the terrible Day of Judgment? The King's very soul is in the gravest of danger, and the man does not even see the peril he faces! -For as long as he refuses to admit that he has sinned- he can neither confess, nor repent and ask forgiveness. Thus, he rejects God's saving grace -and assures his own eternal damnation!"

Bennet frowned.

"Tell me," Desle asked after a moment, "did you really *help* him scrub the floor or did you do it for him?"

The young priest shifted uneasily in the chair.

"We scrubbed the floor side by side, Father, but initially he refused to do the task at all. As you guessed, I offered to do it for him and would have, but he would not allow it."

Desle raised his eyebrows.

"I am impressed that you were able to coax him to even do part of the floor."

"Aye."

"But you know *he* must do it all, My Son."

Bennet looked at the old confessor.

"'Each man must bear his own load,' as scripture says," Desle continued. "The King must amend his own life and 'work out his own salvation with fear and trembling,' *as must we all.* You can not do any of it for him, no matter how much you want to. None of us can. Our prayer is that *he* will want to amend his life and that he will do what is necessary to rescue his soul before it is too late."

"I know, Father."

"Furthermore, My Son, if we interfere with a sinner's amendment, even though in our own ignorance we think it charity to do so, and his amendment is never accomplished, do we not bear some guilt in keeping him bound to his sin and aiding in his damnation?"

The young priest looked miserably at the floor.

"Each one of us who knows his true identity has a duty to be striving for the King's correction- as we hope others would strive for our own correction if our sins threatened to overcome us. Therefore, from now on, when the Abbot gives him a task, do not aid the King. Let him seek his help from God.

"As for the King leaving St. Brychan's, ultimately that is his choice. We can only pray that if he does remain here, God will use our community in some way to help the King achieve his amendment that much sooner."

Bennet sighed.

"But do not dishearten, Brother, for the King may have a stronger spirit than you think, for he has been here three weeks, when he only planned to stay a fortnight."

Bennet nodded his head slowly in silence. Neither said more for a moment.

"So you believe that as long as I do not help the King with his work, the Abbot will no longer find fault with me?"

The senior confessor smiled for a moment before he answered.

"I think what you mistake as the Abbot's displeasure may be his unease with the friendship that you and the King have obviously developed."

"Why should he feel concern?"

"Perhaps he feels the King is a distraction to you and your vocation," Father Desle shrugged. "Perhaps he is concerned with the influence he holds over you."

"Influence?"

"Aye," the old man answered, pausing as he carefully chose the words he would speak next.

"Brother Bennet, most of us struggle to obtain the spirit of love and trust in our fellow man that comes so naturally to you. You bear so much love in your heart that it is natural and easy for you to hope and believe the best about everyone. Cruelty and evil are so foreign to your gentle soul that you believe it must be equally foreign to every man. *It is not.*

"Please, My Son, exercise caution, especially around the King. Do not trust his present congeniality. King Christian is a man who has proven himself again and again to be dangerous and twofold cruel. -I half expect that when he does leave us, at his first opportunity he will order his knights to lay waste to our community."

Bennet crossed himself, his face, pale with horror.

"You believe he would order our execution when we have sheltered and fed him and even allowed him to live among us?!"

"Aye," the old priest reiterated, "or perhaps he will show a rare mercy and only exile us after seizing our lands. -But there is always great risk in associating with a vitandi, which is why it is forbidden."

"Methinks you regard him too severely, Father."

"Do you?" Desle asked. "Are we not talking about the man who desecrated the very Body of our Lord and Savior? Is this not the man who ordered his knights to use one of our sisters to defile the altar at his own palace church? Is he not the same man who murdered a priest two years ago and still has failed to repent for it?"

Bennet sat in misery.

"Even now," he continued, "is this man's very presence not threatening to divide our house by tempting you to question the Abbot, to whom you have promised obedience?"

Bennet swallowed painfully.

"St. Paul writes," the confessor added, "that we are not even permitted to eat with members of the Faith who are immoral, or idolaters, drunkards, robbers, or revilers. We are to drive them out from among us! -And for good reason!"

Desle stopped then and looked compassionately at the youth's sad brown eyes and downcast expression.

"I am sorry, Bennet. My words must cut like daggers, I know. It grieves me to cause you pain, yet you have sought my counsel, and I beg you to *heed* it. -You must not let the kiss of friendship bring your downfall. I will not tell you to avoid the King, My Son, but give your friendship, if you must, sparingly to him. Do not be tempted to break your vows on his account. And do not allow your heart to question the Abbot's design for the King, for even to question him in your heart may lead you later to be tempted to disobey him."

32

After the blessing, the hall of monks sat down in unison at the long tables in the refectory and began to eat their dinner, and the reader cleared his throat and began reading.

"But do not think that the perverse, even though they enter the walls of a church, shall enter into the Kingdom of Heaven; for in the time appointed for them they shall be separated, if they amend not..."

Christian sat in his place in a cheerful mood. Earlier that day, he and Bennet had taken the trenchers to the poor who had gathered at the gate of the monastery. After seeing the gratitude of the wretched creatures, he had felt light-hearted the entire day. Even the indignity of washing the laundry had not affected his pleasant mood.

"...For you are not unaware that many who have the name of Christians do commit all these evil things that I have briefly mentioned. Neither are you unaware that men whom you know to be called

Christians sometimes commit perhaps even graver offenses. But if you have come here with the idea that you may do such things, as it were with an easy conscience, you are much mistaken, nor will the name of Christ avail you when He begins to judge with utmost severity, who before deigned…"

During the meal, as always, the King ignored the reading which today was from St. Augustine's First Catechetical Instruction. As he hungrily ate his food, he looked to the head table at the Abbot. Their eyes met, and Christian smiled as warmly as he could, hoping to unnerve the man. Abbot Hunfred only smiled sweetly back and continued to eat. The King's eyes drifted in the other direction next, observing the monks one by one he had become acquainted with as they ate their food in silence.

"…For all, then, who persist in such works, the end is damnation. When, therefore, you see many not only doing these things, but also approving them and persuading others to do them, put your trust in the law of God, and do not follow those that transgress it. For not according to their way of thinking, but according to His truth will you be judged…"

As the King chewed a mouthful of cabbage, he considered again how fond he had become of Bennet. He found him to be intelligent and amiable with a kind, very generous nature, not to mention humorous and unpredictable. And unlike Paschal and Felix and the rest of the Court, Bennet was not bent upon flattering him. Altogether, it was a refreshing change.

He had even begun entertaining the idea of taking Bennet with him when he left the abbey, although he knew well that the monk would never fit in at the palace, even if he was willing to leave the monastery. Bennet was an innocent, after all. Likely the monk would endure no more than a few days at the palace before he would be so offended that he would leave.

Biting into the bread, Christian looked down to the end of the table at his friend. Bennet was barely picking at his trencher of food. He was chewing slowly as his hand supported and squeezed his forehead.

The reader cleared his throat, took a swallow of drink, and then began the next section: "Associate with the good…"

Christian turned his attention back to the food on his trencher, the sound of the rain hitting the roof, and the distant thunder. The worst of the storm would surely come later tonight. He took a swallow of ale and ate more of the sweet egg dish, wondering then what the Abbot would assign him to do tomorrow.

"…For of God you are sure, because He changes not; but of man, no one can be prudently sure. But if we ought to love those who are not yet just, that they may become so, how much more ardently ought they be loved who are so already? But it is one thing to love man, another to put your trust in man; and so great is the difference that God commands the former but forbids the latter…"

All of the brothers looked up from their eating, and the reader momentarily stopped reading as Bennet left the table abruptly and hurried out of the refectory. The brothers glanced at each other, but no one spoke. The reader then returned to reading, and the hall of monks resumed eating.

"…Now if a man suffers anything for the name of Christ and for the hope of eternal life, and endures it steadfastly, a greater reward shall be given him; but if he yields to the devil, with him shall he be condemned…"

After dinner, Christian went back to the laundry and then to Vespers with some reluctance, for he wanted to find Bennet whom he feared was unwell. At the beginning of Collation, the full force of the storm arrived. The King went directly to the hall where the monks usually gathered, but Bennet was not there. Immediately, he departed for the monk's cell. As he walked hastily around the cloister, the wind howled through the open courtyard, and the rain beat down loudly.

Arriving at Bennet's cell, he tapped lightly. The door slid open a little, and peering in, he saw that it was empty.

Where could he be? Christian wondered.

He went to the end of the walk and climbed the stairs. The library was on the second floor, and some of the brothers met there to talk during Collation sometimes. Christian found six or so monks there, laughing together.

"Pardon me, Brothers," Christian began.

They looked over at him and smiled.

"Have you seen Brother Bennet? I wanted to see if he was well."

"We have not seen him since dinner, Brother. Have you checked his cell?"

"I have, I have," he muttered, turning to go out.

"Have you inquired in the infirmary?"

Christian hurried to the infirmary at the monk's suggestion and was soaked in the process, but Bennet was not there either. From there, he returned to the kitchen and the refectory again, but did not find him. He even checked the guesthouse.

After half of an hour of looking, Christian was very wet, cold and bewildered. Perhaps Bennet was off playing a prank somewhere, he thought. He had looked almost everywhere. The only place he had not looked was in the church.

Christian decided it was worth a try. With the repeated flashes of lightning above him turning the night sky to momentary day, he rushed up the stone steps and, fighting against the wind that almost would not allow him entry, he opened the huge, wooden door and entered the church. After shutting the door behind him, Christian stood shivering inside the silent, empty nave, his nose filling with the smells of dust and burning torches. He wiped his wet face with his sleeve and scanned the dim church that was only illuminated by a few, sparse, flickering torches.

Christian took a half step forward and stopped. Rolling his eyes, he bowed a short bow toward the rood and sloppily crossed himself, just in case any monk was watching him that he was not aware of. Then, looking around, he walked toward the rood screen at the front of the church. On the left wall of the nave, the monks had begun a series of paintings depicting the life of Christ. Opposite, on the right side, in small alcoves, were the devotional chapels, each with a small altar and at least one bench. In two of these chapels were the shrines of long dead men.

Christian saw no one but continued to walk toward the front of the church, his eyes returning to the ornately carved rood screen before him that separated the nave from the choir. The rood, the large crucifix above the narrow opening of the screen, was hidden from view by a long, black cloth that completely covered it. The monks usually only covered the crucifix during the season of Lent, but the Abbot had considered it a necessary measure to properly observe the interdict, or so Cai had told him.

Standing with his nose to the screen, Christian looked through the lattice to the choir stalls and the bare altar beyond, but saw no signs of Bennet. He sighed and turned and glanced to the right at the statue of the Madonna and Child which stood at the front of the nave, near the entrance to the Lady Chapel. It was a huge, marble sculpture of a draped

Madonna, holding her holy babe effortlessly in one arm and reaching out to the world with the other. To Christian's surprise, here, kneeling just inside the chapel in the shadows near the foot of the icon, was an unhooded monk who was keeping track of the prayers he was saying on a long, knotted cord.

"Bennet, here you are!" Christian exclaimed, quite elated, but then he chastised himself for disturbing his friend while he was praying.

The monk did not turn to him, but only set the cord in his lap.

As it seemed that he had finished his prayers for the moment, Christian approached him with a smile.

"I feared at dinner you might have fallen ill."

As he neared the kneeling monk, he was astonished to see Bennet's face was wet with tears.

"You are unwell-"

"No, Your Grace, I am well," the monk replied, still not looking at him.

"What grieves thee then?" he asked, feeling that Bennet addressing him by his title was definitely an ominous sign.

There was a long silence. Christian had a strange feeling that whatever the matter was, it had something to do with him. Was Bennet in trouble with the Abbot -or the Bishop, on account of him?

Bennet sighed, but at last spoke.

"Your Grace, why do you not believe in God?"

The question caught Christian off guard, but he smiled curiously.

"What causes you to ask?"

"Is there another explanation?"

"An explanation for what?"

Bennet closed his eyes and rubbed his throbbing forehead with both hands.

"An explanation of why you interrupted the Mass- and *desecrated the Blessed Sacrament-* and altar- in your palace church," he said solemnly.

Christian's heart skipped a beat in surprise, but he gave no immediate reply.

Bennet sighed again with irritation and turned to face the King.

"Have you nothing to say about it? Did you not know that that church can never be used as a place of worship again unless it is consecrated again by the Bishop?"

King Christian frowned and quickly looked away from his friend. There was an uncomfortable silence as the monk observed his expression.

"I see that you did know it," Bennet answered for him. "But why? Why would you do that?"

"I am king," Christian answered coolly. "If I had a reason, I need not explain it to you."

"What of your knights? -You know you put their souls in jeopardy when you order them to perform such immoral acts! -And the peril to your own soul is equal to theirs, for when you order others to perform acts of evil, it is the same had you carried them out yourself."

"I have never ordered any of my knights to do anything I was not prepared to do myself," Christian answered calmly, glowering at the altar just visible through the rood screen.

Bennet looked at him in surprise.

Seeing the astonishment on his friend's face from the corner of his eye, Christian turned back to him, adding smugly, "If you must know, I was intending to swyve the wench on the altar myself that night, but I was pressed for time."

Bennet crossed himself, aghast, hardly believing what he was hearing.

"Do you boast of your sin so proudly? Have you no fear of God? Have you no shame?"

"I suppose I do not. -Besides, I thought the sacrifice of the Christ on the cross freed us from our sins."

Bennet glared angrily at the youth.

"*You* know well Christ's sacrifice atoned for all sin, and the gift of forgiveness is given to any penitent who asks to receive it; but that does not give us the *liberty* to break God's commandments deliberately!"

Christian smirked.

"The People of God are called to live holy, blameless lives!" Bennet fumed. "God will still hold us accountable for our unconfessed, sinful choices and deeds! -When we sin, we must *repent*, truly, before God will forgive us!" he added testily.

Christian smirked again.

"Sinfulness can destroy anyone of the Faith!" Bennet argued. "-The jaws of Hell will snatch any whose sinful flesh overcomes them! Thus, we of the Faith are an even more desired prey for the Devil 'who prowls around like a roaring lion, seeking someone to devour!'"

Amused, Christian smiled and shrugged his shoulders indifferently. Bennet marveled at him.

"-Is this the way you believe a king is supposed to behave?!" Bennet demanded in outrage. "Did Sir Gage and Lord Reynaud teach you nothing of honor or decency?"

Christian frowned.

"It has nothing to do with them," he replied coolly.

"I see, you believe that this is the way you are *entitled* to act. You believe that your position places you above reproach and above righteous conduct.- You could not be more mistaken. You have been granted authority over these lands and people by God- and you must answer to Him for every decision you make with that authority."

Taking a deep breath to remain calm, Christian answered his friend carefully.

"Bennet, I perceive you are troubled by some matter, and you do not know what you speak."

"Clearly, you do not understand the weight of the responsibility that accompanies kingship!" Bennet replied. "The justice of the land rests on your shoulders! Will you condone these same acts when they are committed by your subjects on their own?"

Christian sighed. This was not what he had intended.

"A king's duty is very similar to a father's duty-" the monk began.

"Bennet," Christian interrupted, "I have been searching for you for half of Collation because I feared you were ill, not so you could lecture me-"

"A father must protect, raise, and provide for his children," the priest continued, undaunted. "If the father is negligent in his duty, his children will be spoiled. -A father must be ever vigilant to potential dangers to his sons, from outside the family as well as from the behavior of the father himself. -For the children only know what they see. And if the father's behavior be low or villainous, then his sons, in witnessing such sinful acts committed by their father, will come to believe such acts are acceptable for all. Thus, they will violate the laws of the land as well as the laws of God."

Frowning, Christian crossed his arms and stared stonily ahead.

"These same children will cry out against their father on the dreaded Day of Judgment because their acts will be judged against a higher standard than they were ever prepared for on earth, but to no avail, for they all will be punished accordingly. The father will be judged even more severely for leading his children and everyone else he influenced astray- *and for every generation afterward that continues to stray.*"

"Are you finished?" Christian asked irritably.

"No, I am not."

"Well and good," the King told him irritably, ignoring his reply. "You should retire for the evening. Perhaps tomorrow we will meet under better circumstances."

"What will be different tomorrow?" Bennet demanded. "You will still deny the existence of God! You will still disregard His commandments! Your soul is in eternal peril! -As are all the souls of those who aid or obey your evil orders! There is nothing more serious or immediate!"

"Good evening then," Christian said and turned to leave.

He was determined to go while he could still control his temper.

"Why will you not listen? Why will not even the warning of eternal damnation in Hell move you?"

The King stopped and turned around to face the monk.

"Why should it? I have never believed in the firepit of Hell," Christian told him plainly. "When you die, you are no more. But *if* there was a life after this one and I could choose the destiny for my 'eternal' soul, I would choose Elysium, not your Heaven."

The young priest stared at him in amazement as a tumultuous crack of lightning outside filled their ears.

"You would put your hope in a *pagan* religion?"

King Christian shrugged his shoulders.

"One religion is much like another. They are all born of myths and comforting lies."

"Myths and lies! Did not Father Armond teach you the same catechism he taught all the other youths in Lord Reynaud's house?"

"Aye, he taught it, and I learned it; but the tales have always been too fantastic to believe."

"Too fantastic?" Bennet echoed.

"Aye! Resurrection of the dead! A god being born from a virgin and living as a man! -A god who walks on water and lets himself be killed to save mankind! A god who is fully human- and a human who is fully god?! -A god who is one and yet in three persons!

"It is all no more than the wishful imaginings of some confused and desperate men who lived long ago! I live now! Where is your god now?! If he exists, why does he not show himself now?!"

"God is everywhere! And He does show Himself, if you would only open your eyes and see His work! -All of creation attests to His Glory!"

"Ha! Nature!" Christian scoffed.

"We also have the accounts of the miracles of the saints which witness to the power and presence of God as well!"

"Why should I give credence to tales of supposed miracles from years past that are recounted every year on predetermined feast days? These accounts are likely no more than legends, sprung from fancy -or local pagan folklore, which for convenience have been added into the legacy of the Faith. I require more! I require present day miracles with witnesses here and now that may be examined!"

Bennet shook his head.

"You must rely on your faith-"

"Why must I?" Christian interrupted. "If your god is so powerful, why does he not show himself to all in each generation? Why does he rely on a few, peculiar individuals to bear imperfect testimony of his will? Why does he not simply make his presence plain and unquestionable?"

"Because He desires us to choose to believe on our own! -As you know quite well! For this purpose, man was given free choice: that each one of us might choose to acknowledge and worship Him by our own free will. It has been that way from the beginning!"

Christian shook his head in disagreement.

"Why can *you* not see the truth, Bennet? The reason your god does not reveal himself to all men is not because he *will* not, but because he *can* not! For he does not exist, and wishing can not make it so!"

"He-"

"The Romani long ago believed in many, many gods: Cupido, Iuppiter, Iuno, Mars, Diana, Apollo, Vesta, et cetera. For many years, Roma prospered, built, and conquered the empire by sacrificing to these gods. Then, the Romani embraced the Faith, the 'true religion', but Roma still fell- and to pagans! What does this prove except that there is no god at all, or if there is, he holds no loyalty to his faithful followers?"

Bennet blinked at Christian in silent horror, but only for a moment.

"The Romani fell into sin," he argued desperately, "and God *allowed* them to be conquered by their enemies!"

Christian shrugged.

"If there was a god, would he allow me to defile what is sacred to him without reprisal?"

"No reprisal?!" Bennet answered, astounded. "Did your own subjects not run you out of your palace? Is your kingdom not under interdict? Are you not in hiding for your very life here in this monastery? Has the Bishop not prayed that you will be cut off from the community of God in Heaven as you are on earth?-"

Christian only smiled, attempting to resist his rising temper.

"You believe my present misfortunes are your god's vengeance upon me? If that is so, why did you interfere with *his* designs for retribution? Why did you offer me refuge here?"

Bennet swallowed.

"I- I had thought that perhaps you were ready to abandon your evil ways and repent-"

Christian laughed once and shook his head.

"Repent? For what should I repent? I have done nothing but be true to myself and my desires!"

Bennet stared at him in disbelief.

"You still do not rightly understand!" Christian explained cheerfully. "This is who I am! -I have no need for your religion's beliefs or its 'salvation'!"

Brother Bennet crossed himself again, utterly dumbfounded at what he was hearing. It was like trying to argue sense with a stone wall.

"This is *not* who God wants you to be-" Bennet muttered, bewildered.

The two were silent for a moment, each lost in thought. Finally the King spoke.

"Have you ever heard why my parents named me 'Christian'?"

The monk shook his head while the thunder boomed outside the church.

"I bear the name because my superstitious parents feared the influence of your religion and those who proclaimed it," the King explained with clear annoyance. "My parents hoped if I bore the name, I too would not only have that influence but control over the god as well.

"I, however, have always scorned my parents for their petty superstition and have despised Christians, Jews, and other god-fearing people alike. But I think you Christians are especially pathetic and superstitious, with your eating of bread and sipping of wine while pretending it is the fallen body of your god. I do not know what is more pitiable: your veneration of bones and 'holy' objects, or your supplications to the dead for prayers.

"-And you monks are the most pathetic of all, for you have unmanned yourselves. You have given up your independence and all the pleasures and comforts a man can enjoy in life- in order to grovel, and work, and wash floors like a woman- while you sing songs- to nothing!"

Wounded and stunned, new tears streamed down the young monk's face.

"-If the Faith is truly meaningless to you," Bennet asked through his tears, "why did you try to steal the holy relics of St. John of Veracis?"

"Steal them?" Christian snorted and laughed. "Is that what they told you? I was not trying to steal them!

"My knights and I had been drinking in the castle of my alderman. And having consumed much wine, we went to relieve ourselves. In going out into the darkness, I came upon a sleeping group of travelers that was taking the remains of a *supposed* saint to a monastery in the west of Speyron. I decided, as a prank," he laughed, "to *rebaptize* the little that remained of him.

"It was easily accomplished for their watchman had fallen asleep also. Unfortunately, one of the priests accompanying the relics was roused from his slumber by our drunken babble. He discovered me and made great protest at my sacrilegious offering. -The man actually had the audacity to lay hands on *me* and yank me away from the bones! A fight ensued immediately, and although my knights and I had beaten the man well enough for his boldness, I still strangled him for sheer spite!"

Bennet's heart skipped a beat, and he turned away, horrified. What had ever made him think well of this youth?

Noting how the monk shrank from him, Christian knew that his hurtful words had found their mark. And seeing the accompanying grief on the face of his friend, he was sorry and wished the truth back into his mouth. He was leagues away from his initial intentions when he had sought out Bennet just a few minutes earlier.

Christian frowned and looked at the rood screen in front of him and then back at Bennet, wondering what he could say to make amends.

"Now that you know the truth about *that*, you must forgive me," he finally said.

Bennet was silent and sad, but no longer wept.

"After all, that is what priests do," the King added cheerily.

There was another long, uncomfortable silence. Finally Bennet spoke.

"Do you admit that you did wrong?"

Christian smirked and shrugged his shoulders, muttering that he was no more wrong than the priest had been for daring to touch his king.

Bennet frowned and shut his eyes.

"I can not."

"What do you mean?"

"Officially, I can not absolve you because you are an excommunicate, and we are under interdict; but more importantly, I can not forgive you *because you are not sorry,*" Bennet told him matter-of-factly, picking up his prayer cord again. "You do not care that your deeds are wicked. You feel you are free to toy with and murder your own subjects because you consider us beneath you, only on this earth to serve your needs. You see no harm in defiling the Body of our Lord or the most holy place in a house of God, no matter the needs of the true faithful, because you do not believe anything bigger than yourself exists.

"You can not acknowledge that God exists because to do so is to acknowledge that ultimately you are not in control and that lack of power frightens you. I can not forgive you, but I do pity you for your pride, ignorance, self-centeredness, and fear, and all it has cost you -*and all that it will cost you.*"

"You? Pity me?" Christian laughed, but not long.

He was angry now.

"Aye," Bennet answered. "And I pity Speyron for having such a ruler as you-"

"Enough-" Christian warned, his fists clenching tightly. "You are too bold."

"-for you believe the only purpose for life on the earth is to provide *you* with amusement. Clearly, you can not care about anyone or anything except yourself. What greater misfortune can befall our wretched kingdom now that you are our king? 'Woe to you, O land, when your king is a child, and your princes feast in the morning!'-"

Christian's mind shut off at that moment as the blow of his fist shut out the young man's words. The next thing he knew his heart was pounding, his right hand hurt, and Bennet was lying on the stone floor. Shock at his deed brought him back to the moment.

Immediately, he was down beside Bennet, trying to help his friend up, saying, "I am sorry. I do not want to fight with you."

The monk got up by himself, however, and would not accept the King's help.

"I am sorry," Christian said again. "Please, forgive me."

"I forgive you for the blow, Your Grace, but with my dying breath I will tell you the *beast* that you are," Bennet said, checking his bleeding lips.

Christian bristled at the comment. It took all his self-control to resist the urge to soundly thrash the insolent monk.

"It is not wise to try my patience further this night. I will see you tomorrow," Christian managed to say and at once started for the door.

Bennet watched him go in disgust.

"'Dixit insipiens in corde suo: non est Deus. Corrupti sunt et abominabiles facti sunt in studiis suis non est qui faciat bonum non est usque ad unum,'" he mumbled to himself, shaking his head, while retrieving the prayer cord he had dropped.

Christian stopped short and whirled around sharply to face the monk.

"'The fool says in his heart, "There is no God." They are corrupt, they do abominable deeds, there is none that does good!'" Christian translated hotly. "You dare call *me*, your King, a fool?!" he demanded angrily. "-I have killed men for *less cause!*"

"Why do you delay, Sire? Need you a cord?" Bennet replied coolly, offering him his knotted string.

Christian glared at the monk and his audacity. Fighting his growing rage, he turned again toward the doors of the church, the thunder booming in the distance.

"Remember, Your Grace," Bennet called after him casually, "a king reigns because he is God's representative on earth, set down to protect the people and to keep order. If God does not exist, then a king is just a man, representing nothing, protected by nothing. Every peasant knows this. Wise kings have always believed in God."

Christian stopped and turned back to the monk, seething.

"Tell me truly, Bennet, who are you praying for here? Do you pray to save my doomed soul or your own for bringing a vitandi among innocents?"

"Both," he admitted quietly, "for I see now that I should have fled you the moment I knew you at the tavern, and I should have *never* invited you here."

"Why? Do you fear I could corrupt the brothers? If the faith of you monks is so easily injured by simple argument, I suppose you belong locked up behind these walls where the world and its harsh truths cannot intrude!"

With that, King Christian turned on his heel and left the monk in the darkened church.

33

It was colder this morning in the library, more so than even yesterday. Since the storm a few nights ago, every day had been dismal and sunless and only promised more, cold rain. The King of Speyron, however, felt the fresh chill in the air more than anyone else at the abbey.

Bennet had avoided him the day after their conversation in the church. Christian had been initially surprised, for in his entire life, no one had ever purposefully avoided him. In fact, people had always vied for his company and attention, no matter if they personally disagreed with him over some matter or not.

The following day, Bennet still had refused to socialize with him. In fact, the monk would not even look at him. The King, however, found himself more amused than vexed by his friend's childish behavior. Clearly Bennet was still angry, but Christian was certain that in time he would return to his side. After all, the monk would be a fool to risk ending such an advantageous friendship over a silly quarrel.

On the third day when Bennet still shunned him at Collation, Christian had been quite galled. He decided that Bennet was a very proud fellow. The monk actually seemed to be expecting his king to seek him out- and perhaps to even apologize in order to save their friendship. The idea was outrageous to Christian, and he was determined more than ever not to seek him out to try to resolve the situation. Although he was in the same hall as the monk, the King refused to see him. But as the dull, uneventful evening dragged on, he found himself sorely missing Bennet's lively fellowship and wishing heartily for it back again.

Yesterday had been no better. He had worked in the bakery, and although Bennet had come to get a count of loaves that could be taken to the villagers, the monk had once again refused to even acknowledge his presence.

Now as Christian sat around the table with the other novices in the cold library, he wondered again why Bennet was allowing a simple difference in point of view to end their friendship. True, he had said some things that were difficult for the monk to hear; but so had Bennet. -And Bennet had wanted the truth. Should he feel guilty now because the monk happened to be oversensitive?

"Very well, I believe we have all had adequate time to reflect on this," the novice master said then.

The novices all shuffled in their seats.

"Who would like to share first this morning?"

Balfrid immediately volunteered.

"I was thinking that it means that God is our protector- like a shepherd is. A shepherd is not afraid of a wolf, but stays with his flock, guarding it from wolves. Thus, the Lord protects us in a similar way from harm."

Brother Septimus nodded and called upon Selby to share his thoughts.

"A shepherd moves his flock to another field to graze after they have eaten down the field they were on before. Perhaps it means that God will provide food for us just as the shepherd provides fresh grazing for his flock."

"Aye, very good."

The novice master looked around at the other four novices. None of them were looking at him.

"Tillo-"

Christian looked at the novice master.

"What have you to add?"

"Nothing-" he said with an indifferent shrug, crossing his arms underneath his scapular. "I was thinking what they already said."

Brother Septimus frowned.

"Surely, there is something more you can add. 'The Lord is my shepherd' is a fertile verse for contemplation."

Then the monk was silent, waiting expectantly for an answer.

Christian sighed irritably and shrugged.

"If *god* is our shepherd-" Christian began apathetically, "then I suppose that makes us- *sheep*."

"That is obvious!" Balfrid complained impatiently. "The verse is about what God does for us, so clearly it is implied that we would be the shepherd's flock!"

Christian only shrugged in reply.

The novice master did not comment, but only looked at his new novice, slightly perplexed. His face continued to hold an expression of bewilderment even as the fourth young initiate shared his thoughts. Hesitantly, the monk instructed the novices to contemplate the same passage again.

34

The gusty, late autumn wind blew cold against Lord Van Necht as he arrived back home just at nightfall. He quietly dismounted his black charger, led it inside the corral, and with a smooth motion, removed the saddle and the horse's bridle. The horse snorted and went directly over to the water, hay, and grain that had been set out for it. After shutting the opening of the pen, Van Necht turned wearily toward his own campfire and the woman who awaited him there.

Wrapped in a coverlet, Acrida sat before the fire in nervous anticipation, trying desperately to appear to be calm. Her excitement had been building since the afternoon. She had anxiously watched the road the entire time that she had prepared dinner, worrying that he would arrive before it was ready, worrying too that he would not like what she had prepared. Finally, all was ready, and she had watched the road even more. Then it had grown dark, and it seemed he would never come.

At last, she had heard the slow, methodical crunching sounds of hooves on icy mud that could only be Van Necht's stallion approaching. Acrida had hardly breathed. At once her eyes had fallen on his familiar figure, and she had been filled with immense, unexplainable joy. Her heart had leapt in delight and then pounded wildly with gladness, as if it were trying to escape the prison of her chest and fly to him on its own.

She had taken a deep breath and reprimanded herself and attempted to regain her composure by not looking at him, for in seeing him, she always began to smile for no cause. Though she had to drag her eyes away from the warlord like small children from their sport, she had managed to force herself to stare deeply into the dancing yellow flames of the fire.

In truth, Acrida could not explain her recent happiness. She had been away from her family for more than three months now. For the most part, she stayed alone in a solitary tent in a field away from all other people. Her main fellowship was with a man whom neither enjoyed conversation nor the company of women in general and whom was absent most of the day. She did not know why she was not mad with loneliness. Yet, she had grown accustomed to the quiet as well as to Van Necht's moods and eccentricities.

Some time ago, within the certainty of their daily routine, the desires of Acrida's youth, desires she had long ago given up on, had returned to her, and she had begun to yearn for a family and children of her own. She had supposed it was because all of the people of Van Necht's village were cordial and kind to her, and aside from missing her aunt and uncle, she was content here. It was a stark change from the village of Brackenbach. The people of her own village had ignored her; and none of the men had ever acknowledged her presence. And if anyone had said more than a word or two to her, it had only been out of necessity.

As the days had passed here, Acrida had caught herself daydreaming about Van Necht and what it would be like to be his love.- At first, she had laughed at the idea. A noble alderman like Van Necht would never desire her! She was no beauty. -Nor did she possess the soft tongue that his kind preferred. Besides, he could never take her as wife anyway, for her birth was too low.

Even as she resolved not to think about him any more, she still had wondered what had prompted her sudden wistfulness. Van Necht had never said anything that suggested that he favored her. He was simply kind to all those of lower station as his honor demanded.

Yet, despite their absurdity, the dreams had not faded, and Acrida realized that, although she might try to deny it, she was wishing for his affections. She longed for him to see her as something other than a woman under his protection. Indeed, she wanted his attention just as much as some women of his village obviously wanted it.

At first, she had thought it remarkable that Van Necht was unaware of how certain married women in his village shamelessly flirted with him. Then she had realized that his honor and virtuous nature would not allow him to see it. Besides that, he was completely preoccupied with his preparations for war. She doubted he thought about women at all, although she knew some time in the future he would surely remarry.

A low sigh of fatigue escaped his lips as Van Necht walked up to the brightly burning fire where the aroma of smoke and cooked meat scented the air. Instantly, her eyes, disobeying her, sought their desire, and she immediately smiled at him. In fact, she could not stop smiling. Although she feared that he would surely notice, despite her best attempts, she could not suppress her joy. In the end, she covered her mouth with her hand.

While she fought to control herself, Van Necht put his saddle down and sat before the fire and stretched. Then he loosened his fur mantle and stretched his hands out toward the heat. His eyes were on Acrida momentarily then, observing once again the lines of her face and neck which were softened by the flickering light of the flames.

The warlord knew well every line and curve of her face and her every gesture, for he watched her often when she was unaware. He knew the fragrance and soft, smoothness of her black hair when it was uncovered and unbound. He knew the sound of her voice and by her tone, what mood she was in. He was, in fact, so familiar with her that Van Necht often saw her in his mind when she was not present. Of late, it was getting difficult to concentrate on anything else, for thoughts of her were always drifting through his mind. Refusing to give in to his desire to admire her, the warlord looked at what she was cooking.

"It smells good," he said, peering into the kettle of stewing cabbage, beets, and onions that sat to the side in the coals.

"Will you eat now, My Lord? 'Tis ready."

Van Necht readily agreed, and Acrida carefully slid the rabbit she had roasted for him from the spit onto a trencher. She poured the entire contents of the kettle over the hare and served it with a portion of bread.

Van Necht wiped his hands on his mantle and took the proffered food. She rose and brought him some mead to drink as he took out his knife and cut off a small piece of steaming rabbit and blew on it.

"Are you going to eat?"

"I ate earlier," she lied, for she had no appetite for food lately.

"Ah-" Van Necht nodded approvingly as he chewed, "'tis well seasoned."

Acrida beamed at the compliment.

"Thank you, My Lord."

She watched with delight as he ate the food she had prepared.

Van Necht licked his fingers, agreeably. He scooped some cabbage and meat onto the bread and devoured it hungrily. They were silent as he ate, and Acrida's stomach began to flutter as she wondered what to say.

"So, how was it today?"

"Slow."

Acrida had to smile. This was usually his response to any of her inquiries about the training of the commoners that he and Sir Albern daily attended to.

"No, I admit," Van Necht added after a moment, "they are showing some improvement, in particular, the archers. As long as they do not get within five leagues of an army, I believe, they will do well."

Acrida smiled.

"But-" he added as he chewed, "I am growing concerned about the foot soldiers. I had hoped that they would show at least some improvement by now, but they have not."

As he spoke, he noticed Acrida's blue eyes locked on his own, her full attention on his every word, which made him a little nervous.

"Just- just the sight- of - of a man running at them with a stick- is enough to scatter them."

Van Necht turned his attention to the fire, finding it easier to address the yellow, leaping flames.

"Perhaps they will improve soon."

"Aye, perhaps," he agreed, but added, "-yet all Sir Albern and I can do is train them to use arms. A man must find his own courage."

"I suppose your task is near impossible then," Acrida replied. "How can anyone hope we commoners will act like anything other than sheep when that is all we have ever been allowed to be?"

Acrida stopped, horrified, realizing once again too late what she had said. However, Van Necht never disciplined her for speaking her mind. She felt she could say anything in front of him, at least when they were alone. She glanced at him, hoping her comment had not ruined his good spirits.

But the alderman was only smiling at her.

"Perhaps we are wasting our time. Let us arm the women of Speyron instead. Methinks Herryck would avoid invasion altogether."

Acrida smiled and looked away as Van Necht chuckled and drank his mead.

"Are they using weapons yet?"

"Aye, though because we still do not have enough for everyone to train with, they must share what swords we have and take turns. The smiths are making swords and lances as fast as they can and are constantly calling for more iron and supplies."

Van Necht bit into the thigh of the rabbit and part of an onion.

"So, what did you do today?" he asked after a while.

Acrida smiled and looked into the fire while she relayed how she had set the rabbit traps that morning, washed clothes, and then went to visit Mae and her children in the village for a while.

Having finished his dinner, Van Necht licked his fingers again and then leaned back on one elbow and listened to her talk. He smiled, observing the happiness so evident on her face and in her eyes, particularly when she spoke of chasing the children around Aldric's home, pretending to be a bear. She would make a fine mother, he caught himself thinking.

They talked for a while longer, but Van Necht was too tired from the day's training to stay up late into the night. He retired into the tent, leaving Acrida to put out the fire.

Saving out a few coals to start the morning's fire, Acrida doused the rest with dirt, and making sure it was out, sat beside the dying embers for a while as she uncovered her hair and began unbraiding it. The dog went over to Van Necht's place and gobbled the scraps of the hare and then ate the tough, old bread of the trencher in two chomps.

After her eyes adjusted to the darkness, Acrida got up and entered the tent. Van Necht was already on his side of the skins. She took off the coverlet she had used for a cloak and, turning her back to him, unlaced her gown and stepped out of it. She folded it up neatly; then, shivering, she hugged her undertunic she wore closer around her and hurried over to the skins. She lay down on her side and pulled the fur coverlet up to her chin. She crossed herself and then recited the Paternoster quickly. When she finished and had crossed herself again, Van Necht, still awake and lying on his back, reached out for her. He pulled her further into the bed and into his arms and hugged her to him snugly.

Resting her head against his chest, she smiled. She felt so safe and content in his arms. These nights were the happiest times she had ever known in her entire life. Through all the sorrow she had experienced, this moment each night when Van Necht pulled her into his arms and held her made her entire life worthwhile.

As Van Necht held her in his arms, he tried to be satisfied with simply having a bed warmed by an agreeable woman. Ignoring his desire, he forced himself to think about the morrow's training again. Admittedly, his own urges would have been impossible to control these many nights if she had shown any inclination toward him at all. As it was, her lack of interest was almost *sister-like*.

Was that how she saw him, as a brother? Van Necht mused.

He rolled on his side and pulled Acrida even closer, her back to his chest. He pushed his knee between her legs and pulled the fur coverlets more securely around them. As he lay waiting for sleep to come, he stroked her thick, unbound hair softly. He wondered briefly if she was even aware of the liberties he took with her. Certainly, this was no way to treat a maid- and certainly not a *sister*.

Van Necht snuggled a little more against her warm, supple body, and slipping his arm about her waist and, taking her hand, meshed his fingers with hers. As her chest rose and fell in even breaths, Van Necht wondered again as he often did, how many more nights they would share before the war came and parted them. His mind drifted back briefly then to the daily concerns of invading armies and unprepared troops before surrendering to sleep.

35

As was their custom, Sir Albern and the youth Colm arrived to collect Lord Van Necht just after daybreak. When they arrived, Van Necht was saddling his excited, smoke-breathing charger that was snorting and tossing its head anxiously in the chill air. Shortly, the alderman was mounted and joining them, and the three were headed at a walk down the road.

"Good day, Van Necht," Sir Albern greeted his liege lord with a cheery smile as he waved a gloved hand good-naturedly at the woman who was adding wood to the fire outside of Van Necht's tent.

"Good day, Albern. -Colm."

As they rode along the road, the youth turned his attention back to the thick clouds above them. Despite the sun's ascent, the sky was resisting giving up its dark cloak, making the early winter landscape surrounding them barely visible in the low light. The colors of autumn were gone now. The fields were gray and barren, and the trees stood naked, their leaves lying beneath them.

"Methinks these dark clouds forebode ill, My Lords."

"I suspect it will snow today," Sir Albern commented while pulling his heavy and expensive, scarlet cloak more securely about him.

"I do not like being out in such weather," the lad commented. "'Tis a day to be spent beside a fire."

"'Tis likely that some of the men will feel similarly and will not come for training."

"What say you?" Van Necht asked, just then aware that his companions were speaking.

"The lad and I were saying it looks like it may snow."

"Aye, 'tis very likely," Van Necht agreed pleasantly with a yawn, hardly giving the heavy, gray clouds that loomed above them a second look. "It will be good practice for the men. After all, we must be ready to fight in any kind of weather."

"It is likely that many will not come for training today."

"Aye, 'tis possible," Van Necht assented.

Albern raised his eyebrows at the gentle reply of his usually irritable friend. As of late, the nobleman had been in such good spirits that he had not had a cross word for anyone or anything.

"If it does snow, are we still going tonight? To the tavern?" Colm suddenly asked.

"Aye," Van Necht replied.

Colm smiled and urged his gelding into a trot. In a moment, he was far ahead of Albern and Van Necht who continued to walk their horses side by side down the road.

Sir Albern glanced suspiciously at the nobleman wrapped in his fur cloak. The warlord even seemed unaware of the biting, chill wind that changed directions every few moments.

"So- how fairs it with Acrida?" the knight asked casually.

The question caught Van Necht off guard. He looked over at his vassal.

"I have no complaints," he shrugged.

The knight nodded.

"Have you two-?"

Van Necht faltered, but then answered quickly, "Of course! What do you think?"

The knight smiled, but shrugged innocently.

"Do you even have to ask?" Van Necht asked defensively. "Why do you think I let her stay with me?"

Sir Albern managed to suppress a chuckle, but continued to smile at the flustered alderman.

"And-?" the knight prompted.

"And what?"

"And how was it?"

"Nothing special," Van Necht managed hastily with a slight shrug of his shoulders.

Sir Albern raised his eyebrows.

"That disappointing, eh?"

The alderman stopped his horse testily.

"If you must know, it was fine," Van Necht answered with annoyance. "-About as good as I could have anywhere."

"Is that so?" Albern grinned. "Then why, My Lord, are you going drinking and wenching with us tonight if you can have 'just as good' without leaving home?"

Van Necht moved his horse forward again indignantly.

"It- takes several to satisfy my appetite."

This time the knight not only laughed- but howled.

Van Necht glared at his vassal. He could see he was found out. But since Sir Albern had long been his confidant, he knew whatever he told the knight would be kept private.

"Very well, I confess it. I have not touched her."

"I knew it!" Albern laughed. "But tell me, why the devil not?"

Van Necht scowled at the handsome knight in his expensive garments who had never lacked for female companionship.

"Lots of reasons-"

"Such as?"

"She is no tavern wench. She may be lowborn, but she is chaste."

"So?"

Van Necht sighed with irritation.

"What do you care whom I bed anyway?"

"I am concerned about you."

"Me? Why?"

"It is not natural for two people, or for any two creatures for that matter, of the opposite sex to live in such close proximity and not-"

"Perhaps in your domain, Albern. I, however, do not have to bed every woman I meet."

"You have certainly proven that, My Lord."

Van Necht sent his vassal a warning look.

"I am not even certain that I fancy her," he said testily. "-I am only permitting her to stay with me out of convenience. -'Tis agreeable to return home from training the troops to find my clothes washed and my dinner prepared."

Sir Albern looked at Van Necht doubtfully for a moment and then laughed out loud.

"Your cool exterior can not deceive me, My Lord! It is not for lack of a servant that you permit Acrida to stay with you, but because you *do* fancy her! Though, how you have been able to deny your natural instincts night after night, I do not know, but it is not healthy to repress your humors in that way!"

Van Necht rolled his eyes.

"Honestly, I am concerned," he continued. "Remember how melancholy you were with your wife-"

"'Twas a completely different situation!" Van Necht snapped. "'Twas not the lack of swyve that put me in that ill-humor, I assure you, but the shrew herself!"

"I am not denying what you suffered, My Lord. But must you continue to keep at sword's length every decent woman you encounter?"

"I am not! She is a *maid*! I doubt she has ever known a moment of lust!"

Albern laughed again.

"Thou art naive, My Lord!"

Frowning, Van Necht said no more, turning his attention to the road ahead. And seeing the warlord's expression change to one of resolute obstinacy accompanied by a touchy reticence, the vassal knight gave in.

"It is not so difficult to overcome a virgin's natural reluctance, My Lord, *if* the lass's chastity is what gives thee pause. Simply choose an opportune moment and speak soft words to her.

"Tell her that she is the most beautiful, gentle creature thou hast ever known, and the stars in the heavens pale in comparison to the light in her eyes. Or tell her that thine only happiness is when thou art near her. Or say that thou art a man of few words, but that she has such a grip on thy heart that thou wouldst gladly lay down thy life for hers in a moment. Any of it, I am certain, will suffice to get you in her lap."

Albern's courtly words, and the ease with which he spoke them, irked the warlord.

"Such gentle speech is not my way."

"The heart of a woman is won or lost with words, My Lord. It is said that God made them so -lest men forget how to pray."

"And you, I presume, would not hesitate to start a maid down that path- to be passed from bed to bed."

"You know well, My Lord, sooner or later it is the fate of every woman of the King's Court who hath no husband."

Van Necht frowned and did not say anything for a long time. Sir Albern looked over at his friend repeatedly as the horses plodded along, wondering what the true cause of the warlord's hesitation was.

"What truly grieves thee, My Lord?" he finally asked. "Ever since thy wife's death, thou hast looked coldly upon every woman who even dared to smile at thee. After all of these years, you continue to avoid a woman's company and the intimacy that such an alliance would-"

"Aye!" Van Necht interrupted hotly. "And for good reason, for nothing can undo a man as surely as a woman! As I have told you so oft before, the man is lost who allows a woman to get the upper hand! Above all else, never, never allow a woman to see your frailties, for she will certainly use them against you!"

"But not all women have the temperament of your former wife! Try to remember that. Methinks, it will be different with Acrida. You will see," the knight stated with some confidence.

"Why would it be different? If I bed her, she will surely hate me, and I-"

"Hate you? For what cause?"

"I know not! -It matters not! -'Twould be more than I could bear."

"But what cause could she have?"

"I know not!" Van Necht gestured in irritation. "-Perhaps she will blame me for stealing the only dowry which she might offer a husband."

Albern shrugged.

"Even so, My Lord, such a cause is easily remedied. Simply compensate her for the loss in silver. Methinks any peasant would consider it a more than fair exchange."

Van Necht frowned in frustration.

"Thou art not listening! I can not take her to my bed! All the silver in the kingdom could not tempt *me* to take the chance!"

"Why not?" Albern asked, bewildered.

"I dare not," Van Necht argued, "for I know I can not bear *her* hate, nor for her to question my honor."

Sir Albern looked at his friend in confusion.

"Believe you truly that she would hate you simply for taking what all men demand?"

"Aye!"

"You *are* in earnest!" the knight declared in disbelief.

Sir Albern made a gesture of exasperation.

"She is a free woman, no man's wife or concubine, and you may have her if you wish! You know this, as does she. If you take her to your bed, maid or no, that is no valid cause to hate you, nor does it touch upon honor."

"Did I say she would have *valid cause* to hate me? A woman needs no cause at all!" Van Necht answered angrily. "They seek any excuse to spit their venom at you!"

The vassal sighed.

"Thou art quite mad, My Lord. And I see thy wife's words haunt thee still, so let mine ring louder in thine ears: Thou art a good man and have acted honorably in *all* matters since I have known thee. Thou art well loved in these lands and for good reason. Thou hast done *nothing* for which you should be ashamed."

The two men frowned, observing the cold, colorless landscape in silence.

"It is not well that you should love her and fear to touch her, My Lord," Albern commented at last with a shake of his head.

Van Necht looked back at him sharply, shocked at the accusation.

"I do not love her!"

"No?"

"No, I say!"

"Thou art clearly mad, My Lord," the knight smiled, "-if not with love, than with lust! I advise you to take the lass to thy bed at once so that you might gain your wits again!"

Van Necht glared at his vassal.

"In truth, My Lord, I do not believe it is her hate that you fear," Sir Albern said after a moment. "Methinks you are afraid that if you reveal your true feelings to her, she will not return them in kind."

Van Necht frowned again. He was weary with talking.

"But for this, I can offer hope," Albern continued. "As you know, I am a fairly good discerner of women, and it is obvious that the lass is quite fond of you."

Van Necht glanced at his vassal. Sir Albern's good looks and cheery disposition had won him a wide sampling of women, and not just maidservants and wenches. He had won more than the admiration of some noble ladies. The knight certainly understood women better than he ever had.

"In fact, methinks she may even love you," Albern continued.

"How do you fathom?"

"Because she does not give me a second look," he answered with an uproarious laugh.

Van Necht had to smile despite himself.

"Seriously, My Lord, I have seen how she looks at you, and how her countenance lights up when you are near her."

Van Necht shook his head.

"Perhaps she likes my company, and that is all. Perhaps she is simply grateful for the charity I have bestowed on her. -If you spent any time with her at all, you would see how truly innocent she is." Then Van Necht quickly added, "-Not that I want you to spend any time with her whatsoever."

Sir Albern smiled.

"Fear not, My Lord. I will keep my distance. -I have no time for her anyway, even if I had the inclination.

"But in all seriousness, take my advice: Make haste and be bold. Speak gentle words to stoke the fire of her heart and then harden thy mettle for the lass," the knight advised with a sly grin and a crude gesture.

Van Necht smiled, rolling his eyes.

"I think you and she would be good together," Albern encouraged.

"Are you yet prepared to take any such instruction yourself?" Van Necht asked.

"Pertaining to what, My Lord?"

"I mean taking a wife and getting sons of your own and not pining after that married woman anymore."

The knight chuckled.

"There are some women who are so perfect that it is impossible to forsake them, no matter if they belong to another man or not."

"*Thou* art the one struck with madness. There is no such *perfect* animal in Heaven or on earth, and particularly no woman," Lord Van Necht replied with disgust.

The alderman shook his head. This affair would no doubt prove the death of his friend.

"Never fear, My Lord. I have recently resolved that after the war, I will marry whomever will have me- with your blessings, of course, for progeny sake."

"Is that so? Well and good. I will hold you to that."

The men assembled for training could be seen in the distance, and the two spurred their horses down the road.

36

The day had been clear and cold, but bright. Lord Van Necht had left the training of the men to Sirs Albern and Geoffrey while he traveled to the neighboring manor to talk with the lord about weapons and supplies and other preparations for the coming war; and he had invited Acrida to go with him. Having finished his business there, he took the longer way back home, meandering through the countryside of his lands.

With Acrida sitting behind him on the back of his charger, Van Necht guided the horse up an overgrown trail that led up to a high plateau. Once to the summit, he dismounted and then helped her off the horse.

Despite the gray, mid-afternoon clouds that had begun to gather, the view was magnificent.

"This is all my land," Van Necht told her, gesturing into the open around them.

Wearing a pair of his tunics for warmth over her gown, Acrida scanned the expanse. She could see a vast area from where she stood. To her right was the little village and north of it was the field where the men were being trained. To her left, off by itself, was the small white spot which she realized must be Van Necht's tent. Near it, the forest began. The stream that ran beside his camp stretched out steadily from one end of his lands to the other.

"It is breathtaking, My Lord! How lovely it must be in spring and summer!"

Van Necht walked a few steps farther to the east and pointed, saying, "That is where the castle was."

Acrida walked to him and looked in the same direction. She saw the raised earth of the moat- all that remained of the former structure. From the sheer size of it, she could tell that the castle had been quite large. She admired again the surrounding view, the village, and all the neatly divided fields speckled with grazing cattle.

"It is beautiful and so peaceful here," she smiled.

"Aye, beautiful beyond belief," he agreed.

She looked over at Van Necht only to see that he was not looking at the view at all, but at her. Her heart skipped a beat, and she looked back at the view quickly.

Van Necht abruptly went over to his horse and retrieved the goatskin of mead. He opened it and gulped down several mouthfuls; it tasted good to his dry mouth.

"Thirsty?"

"Aye," she replied, leaving the view and returning to the horse to accept the drink.

Van Necht sat on a nearby boulder and watched as she drank a few swallows. Then she wiped her mouth with her hand and chased after the one stray drop of liquid that had rolled down her chin and neck.

What was he doing? he wondered. He had convinced himself that C'sara's company was harmless and that it was convenient to come home from working with the men and know that his supper was already prepared. But he had come to these conclusions when she was starved and still black and blue from the beatings at the palace.

She was completely recovered now. There was a good bit of flesh on her, and her face was without a blemish. Van Necht now thought she might be the most dangerous woman in the entire kingdom for him to be acquainted with. It made no difference what she wore now, her gown or his tunic and braes that were too big for her, he still found her appealing. The very sight of her made him happy, and to hear her voice was the only sound his ear craved. Her smile melted his insides. He could hardly concentrate on anything for thinking of her.

Albern had been correct: he was overcome with lust for her. And his desire was only growing more intense. To be away from her was agony; and to be near her also. Albern's words came into his mind again, and Van Necht had to agree with him. It was not natural to suppress his urges as he had been doing. It would lead to madness- or worse. He should either send her away immediately or not wait a moment more to take her to his bed.

"My Lord?"

Van Necht looked up into her soft eyes, which he noticed were more blue-gray today. He accepted the goatskin and took another drink.

"Do you think you will ever rebuild your castle?"

Van Necht shrugged.

"Perhaps in time I will have cause. I am perfectly content in my tent for now."

"Aye," she smiled, "'tis a cozy place. I have grown quite accustomed to it."

"It is strange how accustomed we become to temporary things," he mumbled, forcing himself to look away from her.

He stood up and put the goatskin back on the horse. Still feeling her eyes on him, he walked past her, back over to the edge of the plateau. Crossing his arms, he looked back out at the sky and observed it was growing quite dark to the northeast.

What was he doing? he wondered again. Why had he even brought her up here? For that matter, why had he even taken her with him today? It was bordering on ridiculous.

Somehow, she had succeeded in dividing him, he realized. For the first time Van Necht could remember, his almighty will was struggling to keep control. The warlord admonished himself again. Before she arrived, he had had enough self-restraint to live with a score of women and maintain his indifference. Now he found himself simpering like a lovesick youth. How had she done it? -Perhaps she was a witch.

However she had accomplished it, Van Necht was more determined than ever to resist her power. In the end, his *will* would triumph over her charms as well as the weakness of his body. He might be mad with lust, but he was still in control.

The alderman's heart quickened as he noticed that she was standing beside him again. Quietly, with a mysterious smile, she reached her hands out and softly began to remove a twig that was tangled in his brown locks.

Van Necht immediately felt the pull between them grow stronger, and he began to quake despite himself. The gentle touch of her fingers in his hair was more than he could bear. With his heart pounding in his ears, he grabbed hold of her wrists and held them tightly as if to ward off an attack. His gaze locked on her questioning eyes.

"Owh! My Lord-"

Without thinking, he silenced her complaint of pain with a swift, brief kiss.

Acrida, whose heart was now beating as fast as a fleeing hind, stood amazed.

Van Necht released her wrists. Reaching out, he cupped his right hand under her jaw while his other hand encircled her waist. Despite his better judgment, he kissed her once more, tenderly this time, allowing his lips to lightly brush hers as they might. Feeling her suddenly go limp, he broke off the kiss immediately and gathered her securely into his arms so that she did not fall.

Ignoring the arguments in his mind that pleaded for restraint, Van Necht was kissing her again, passionately this time, pulling her soft body firmly to his until he held her full against his chest, all the while bearing her entire weight in his powerful arms. He stopped kissing her as abruptly as he had started. His blood was up, and his body was ready for a full assault. He glanced momentarily at their surroundings and the lay of the ground behind them, choosing a spot.

Only then did he look at Acrida. Her smile was gone. Her eyes, which had been bright but a moment ago, were dazed; her pink cheeks and lips were pale. She stared up at him with the blankest of looks, scarcely seeming to breathe.

Van Necht's stand deserted him immediately.

37

Acrida sighed as she rolled over in the bed. The rain was beating the roof relentlessly outside and was only drowned out by the boom of thunder and the loud cracks of lightning. She guessed that it was about midnight, but there was no use in trying to go back to sleep. She had tossed and turned ever since she had retired to bed at the inn, for she was accustomed to sleeping on a fur on the ground with Van Necht, not in a soft, lumpy bed by herself.

She and Van Necht would have made it back to camp a little after dark if it had not begun to storm and the horse had not come up lame. By the time they had reached the village, Lord Van Necht was in a frightful ill-humor. He spoke not a word, nor would he sup with the friendly castellan and his family, but immediately retired to his chamber at the inn after giving instructions about the horse.

Acrida also could not understand why he had gotten them separate chambers at the inn, as the entire village already knew they stayed together. Admittedly, there were ample rooms available since they were the only ones staying there. She supposed it was not befitting to a noblemen's prestige to share a bedchamber when he could afford his own.

Her thoughts were immediately back on the plateau again with the memory of the lord grabbing her and kissing her. She could still feel his lips on her mouth and his strong arms around her.

The first kiss had startled her. She could not have been more surprised. The second had taken her very breath away. The third had frightened her.

What was more, she could not recall anything that happened immediately afterward. The first thing she knew, they were back in the village, the horse was limping, and it was pouring down rain. From the first kiss on the plateau and for several hours afterward she had actually been stupid with amazement. She had kept thinking: This was not Van Necht; he could never love her. He was highborn; she was not. It was impossible.

Yet he had kissed her, and Acrida could not rest for thinking of it. She kept reliving those minutes over and over again. Once again, Van Necht had hold of her wrists and was kissing her, and then he was all over her. Without a doubt, he would have dispatched her maidenhood right there. It was a wonder that he stopped when he did, for there was no way she could have escaped him.

She could not understand it. She had lived with the man for over three months. If his intentions were to bed her, he had had ample opportunity long before now.

She reprimanded herself for even thinking it. This was Van Necht she was talking about- noble and virtuous to a fault- not the village rake. He had never given her cause to distrust him. -He had simply not been himself this afternoon.

Surely, he must have been possessed by some errant spirit. -She had heard of such things. No doubt, when it suddenly left him, it took his memory of the incident with it. And if she were ever to mention it to him, he would certainly deny it had ever happened.

On the other hand, perhaps it was not a spirit.- She remembered back to her first conversations with Mae. For a man with a reputation for despising women in general, Acrida had to admit that Van Necht did not seem to hate her company. Perhaps he had had a change of heart. Was it really so unlikely? Perhaps he did love her and had only recently come to realize it as she herself had. Perhaps if it had not started raining when it did, he would have told her so. Who knows what else he might have told her? After all, had he not taken her up to the plateau to show her his lands? Perhaps he intended to go before the King and request that she be his wife. Of course, King Christian would never agree to a match between a noble lord and one who had been born a serf, but perhaps Van Necht would have petitioned regardless for honor's sake.

Smiling at the thought, Acrida stared at the dark ceiling and listened to the sound of the persistent, droplets of water as they leaked through the roof and fell into a pot on the floor. The roof at home had always leaked; when it rained, their hut had had so many vessels set about to catch the rainwater that it was difficult to walk without tripping. Was it raining in Brackenbach now? If it was raining at Brackenbach, no doubt her aunt had all the pots out as usual.

She wondered then if her aunt and uncle had received word yet that they were freed from the land. She doubted that they would leave Brackenbach anyway. Her uncle would not see the sense in abandoning a perfectly good house. In fact, Acrida could just envision him complaining to her aunt about his new freeman's status and the burdens that came with it.

She missed them. They would be butchering the hog soon and choosing the pullets to take to Huntingdon's steward for Christmas. She would miss the feasts at the castle with the singing and dancing. Huntingdon hosted it every Christmas whether he was present or not. She wondered if Van Necht had similar Christmas feasts for his villagers.

Her lips could feel his lips again, and her breasts were being pressed into his firm chest. She could scarcely breathe, he held her so tightly.

Perchance he had gotten her a separate room to test her. Perhaps he was waiting to see if she would come to him- risking what she may when she did. Acrida's heart skipped a beat at the thought, and then it beat wildly.

She was on her feet in an instant, wrapping her coverlet around the undertunic she wore. She opened the door of her small chamber and looked down the corridor. Seeing a dim glow of light at the far end, she knew the fire in the hearth in the central room was still burning. Perhaps he was waiting by the fire for her. She walked quietly down the corridor barefoot.

As Acrida made her way toward Van Necht's chamber, which was nearest the central room, she could barely make out voices and a laugh. She wondered what other guests had arrived and why they had not retired. Perhaps it was the castellan or one of his family, who kept awake by the storm, decided to sit in front of the cheerful fire.

She continued forward and then paused, her heart beating doubly fast, her palms perspiring. The door to Van Necht's lighted chamber stood ajar, clearly awaiting her. Acrida smoothed her black, loose hair once and pulled the coverlet more securely around herself. Taking a deep breath for courage, she stepped into the doorway.

To her horror, the voices had not been coming from the central room, but the lord's bedchamber. Van Necht's room was alight with candles. Sitting on the foot of the bed with her back to the door was a woman with long, unbound, red hair. She was completely unclothed and was chattering away as she poured wine into a goblet. Facing the door, in the middle of the bed, on all fours like an animal, was a naked, dark-haired woman who was laughing and breathing heavily. Behind her on his knees was Van Necht, his bare, muscular body glistening with sweat. His strong hands held the wench's hips still while his pelvis pounded against the woman's upturned, fleshy rump.

Acrida could not breathe, not believing what she saw. Just then, Lord Van Necht looked up at the door and saw her standing there. Without missing a stoke, he regarded her for a long moment with cool indifference. Then he turned his gaze back to the woman before him.

The smiles and eyes of both whores were on Acrida now as well.

"Methinks she wants to join us, My Lord," the redhead laughed.

The brunette laughed again, and Acrida immediately ran back to her chamber, slamming the door. Back in her own bed, her tears kept pace with the rain.

38

Van Necht yawned and stretched his back and shoulders. He had been out before dawn to check on his horse, but it was still limping. He would have to stop by Aldric's on the way back to camp to get another one, but hopefully he would be out to the men in little more than an hour.

A door closed down the hall then, as Acrida emerged from her chamber modestly dressed in the same several layers of clothes she had worn the day before with her headrail covering her braided hair. There were dark circles around her eyes, and she looked pale and exhausted. Glancing at her, Van Necht realized she had gotten less sleep than he had, and he had not had much.

Acrida did not look at him. Van Necht did not bother to speak to her, but simply turned and walked out of the inn. He had nothing to say anyway and certainly nothing to feel guilty about.

The two tolerated each other's presence as they walked along the empty, muddy road of the village in the gray gloom of early morning. It was much colder than it had been the day before, and Acrida was hugging the two tunics she wore over her gown closer to her, her cold hands up inside the sleeves. As they walked passed one of the village taverns, the pair did not go unnoticed by three men who were urinating against the side of the building.

As they continued along the road, each absorbed in their own thoughts, Acrida held up her skirt slightly as she maneuvered around the standing pools of rainwater and filth. Her entire concentration was centered on keeping her balance because the mud was so deep in some places that her entire foot would disappear inside the muck, -and she was in no mood to ask Van Necht for help of any sort today.

"A man and his horse," came an overly loud voice from behind them.

Startled, Acrida looked around and saw the three men for the first time. As there was no one else yet on the road, she knew that the comment was meant for Van Necht and her.

"No, no, a horse is more comely."

"Well, it is obviously some sort of mount."

This remark was accompanied by snickers. Acrida cringed but did not look back. As the men's comments became more distinct to her ears rather than muted from a distance, she quickly surmised that the men were following them. She looked over at Van Necht who did not seem to be particularly concerned.

"Ignore them," he said dryly.

From the corner of her eye, Acrida saw a blur of movement. The men were beside her now. By their shabby dress, they were definitely commoners- possibly runaway slaves or serfs. She moved a little closer to Van Necht and simply walked through the puddles rather than try to avoid them.

"'Tis well trained. See how it walks beside him even without a lead rope."

"You think he rides it often?" another one asked.

"Every chance he gets!"

"I wonder if it has a smooth gait or if it bucks."

One man snickered.

"Depends if it is a mare or a stallion."

"Which is it?" another asked and then laughed.

This one was directly behind Acrida now, taunting her. Even from there, she could smell him. She, intensely afraid, glanced sideways at Van Necht, who only wore a look of boredom on his face.

Finally, one of the men ran forward, stomped in a puddle, splashing Van Necht and Acrida, and then stood directly in front of them, blocking their way with a grin.

Frowning, Van Necht stopped. He had no patience for this today. The knave in front of him was a tall, skinny sort of fellow with yellow, crooked teeth and a scraggly, dark beard on a protruding chin. His dark, unkempt hair hung limply to his shoulders.

Van Necht stared at him, daring him to make a move. But the man only scowled back at him challengingly.

"What say you?" he asked Van Necht with a smirk. "Is that a stallion or a mare?"

"Aye, and does it take the bit well?" another man leered as he joined the first. "Perhaps we might take a ride too."

He was a young, shorter man; his breath was foul, and his face was unshaven and covered in red pustules and pimples. His ears had been cut off.

"Aye," the third agreed, grinning widely as he joined the others.

This man was of average height and build; he had a few teeth missing in front, and his nose had obviously been broken before. He had a few days growth of beard on his face as well, and there was a brand of some sort on his left cheek. He smelled so offensive that Acrida had to hold her breath.

"What grieves thee?" Van Necht asked them. "Were your parents brother and sister?"

"What did you say?" the skinny one asked.

"I said: Are you ready to die?" Van Necht answered coldly.

The man, seeing the unflinching, penetrating look in his eyes, swallowed. He glanced momentarily at his comrades, and to Acrida's surprise, he stepped aside to let them pass.

The other two men, however, refused to back off as their tall companion had. Taking Acrida's elbow, Van Necht maneuvered her around them, continuing down the road.

They had taken but a few steps when Acrida was suddenly wrenched away from his grasp. She screamed as her two captors dragged her away and then screamed again.

"I do not feel any bullocks! It must be a mare or a gelding!" the one with the brand joked.

The shorter man laughed while Acrida kicked out at them.

A fourth, clearly drunken man had appeared now and, with a smile and raised hands, stood between Van Necht and the men that had Acrida, delaying his pursuit.

"Patience, Friend, we are not going to damage her. My friends just want-."

In an instant, Van Necht grabbed the man's nearest outstretched hand and broke the elbow in a quick motion. Ignoring his startled cry of pain, the warlord kicked the man's feet out from under him, plunging the hapless man face first to the muddy ground. Placing his foot on his neck, the warlord bent down and took hold of a fist full of hair on the crown of the man's head. With a fierce motion, he yanked the head up, snapping his neck. Then Van Necht was again moving toward the others.

"Let me go, You Bastard!" Acrida screamed and kicked angrily, her stomach turning at the overpowering stench of drink and body odor.

While the branded one held her arms behind her, the one with no ears picked up a stick and lifted up the hem of her gown, bending down to see under it. Acrida fought and screamed with outrage. Then the man laughed.

"She is wearing braes under this gown!"

"I told you it was a gelding!" the other one laughed.

At this point, Acrida managed to stomp on her captor's foot. Off balance, he momentarily relaxed his grip, and Acrida wrenched away from him, only to be caught again by the one with no ears.

The branded one pulled a knife out of his boot and grinned his missing tooth grin at her. Acrida screamed at the sight of the blade.

Immediately, Van Necht was behind him. He grabbed the man's arm, forcing the man's wrist backward. The branded man screamed in pain, dropping the knife, his eyes wide as he registered the attack from behind. The scream was cut short as the warlord's powerful hand caught his throat and then pulled the rogue around to face him. As the alderman crushed his windpipe with one hand, the man, gasping for breath, clawed at Van Necht's hand and wrist wildly, all the while silently pleading into the lord's unforgiving eyes for mercy. Van Necht's face revealed no emotion as he finished squeezing the life out of his hapless victim and then dropped him to the ground.

Stunned, both Acrida and her earless captor stared at the body of the branded man that had so quickly fallen.

Realizing then the grave error that he had made, the man's heart pounded faster in alarm as the warlord squatted down to pick up the fallen knife. Still clutching his prize to the side of him, almost as a shield, the knave in sheer, fearful desperation kicked out at Van Necht's head. The warlord blocked the kick with his hands and twisted the attacker's foot away from him, then picked up the knife. Unbalanced and slipping in the mud, the assailant lost his grasp of Acrida and fell. In the instant that he swayed, Van Necht grabbed him by his shirt and cut his throat from left to right. Acrida felt the warm spray hit her as the man dropped to her feet. Slumped on the ground, he gurgled and clutched his bleeding neck frantically, his eyes large at his predicament.

"Are you hurt?" Van Necht asked.

Barely hearing his inquiry, Acrida stared at the limp body near her, the brand on this man's cheek facing the sky, the air about him scented with the odor of dung. His neck was already bruised blue and black where the warlord had clutched it, and pink froth was slowly draining out of his mouth.

Then her attention was drawn again to the fruitless flailing of the other assailant, the surprise still evident in his eyes as he struggled to breathe through the blood. His life spurted out of him like the water in one of the palace fountains and then pooled about him in a lake of blood. Acrida could see nothing but red as another wave of heat overtook her, and then there was nothing.

Van Necht frowned as he observed Acrida lying in an unconscious heap beside the men. This was going to delay him further. He squatted down beside her, sticking the knife in the thick mud. After a momentary search, he was certain she had only swooned and that she was not actually injured.

Then Van Necht himself yelled in surprise and fell forward. With a great yank, the skinny man, who the warlord had stared down earlier, removed the dagger that he had imbedded into the nobleman's shoulder. Van Necht answered with another acknowledgment of pain, but then he was abruptly on his feet again ready to face this last enemy. The knave, however, was already at a dead run in the opposite direction.

Van Necht snatched the knife out of the mud again and flung it with all his might toward the rogue. Although he had aimed for his back, the knife landed in the man's left buttock. With a startled cry, the skinny man fell down. Glancing back at Van Necht, he, wincing, hastily pulled the dagger out of his cheek. Then he was up and limping away like a wounded cur.

Gritting his teeth in pain, Van Necht peered over his own hurt shoulder but could see nothing specific. He turned back to Acrida. She was coming around then, and with his good arm, he pulled her to her feet by her tunic. She looked at the nobleman, dazed. Then she looked back up the road and saw the fourth man who had distracted Van Necht in a crumpled heap. Her eyes moved back to Van Necht again who was himself covered in blood; she staggered a few steps, feeling hot and quite dizzy again.

Van Necht maneuvered her carefully away from the bodies with a firm grip. It was at this point that she noticed the grimace of pain on his face and the growing, dark crimson spot at the top of his torn tunic.

"God's eyes!" she cried.

Van Necht's shoulder was bleeding heavily and had already soaked the area around the ripped edges of the fabric. She quickly looked behind him and saw that there was much more blood on his back at the shoulder. Acrida fought to control her immediately queasy stomach.

"My Lord, you are injured!"

Even as she said the words, she felt herself fall, but Van Necht's good arm grabbed her around her waist, holding her up.

"None of that now, C'sara. I need you to stay on your feet. I do not want to carry you right now."

The blood was again draining out of her face.

"Just look down the road and do not think on it. Take off your tunics to cool yourself. We are well. We are both still breathing," he told her, pushing her forward down the road.

"You need help, My Lord. Should we not go back to the inn?" she asked, pulling the tunics over her head quickly.

"No, we will go to Aldric's."

She nodded, worrying, but hurriedly walked beside him, keeping her eyes on the road directly ahead of her.

When the two arrived the short distance to the steward's house who lived just beyond the edge of the village, blood had completely soaked through a large area of Van Necht's shirts, even through the outer one. Acrida beat on the door frantically.

"Open! Open!"

"Coming, coming- A little patience!"

A bright-eyed Mae opened the door of the house. She greeted them with a smile and a curtsy to the alderman. Immediately, however, upon seeing the anguish on their faces and them both soiled with spattered blood and mud, she urged them inside.

"Come in! Aldric, come quick!"

As the two walked past her, she saw in the dim light Van Necht's blood-soaked shirt.

"God's wounds! What happened?" she asked.

Upon seeing the blood, Aldric immediately moved Van Necht to a bench at the table.

"We were attacked," Acrida told them.

"Attacked? By whom? How many?"

"Four men," answered Van Necht calmly. "And do not be anxious; it is not serious."

"You have not seen this wound, My Lord," Mae replied.

She pulled the bloody, torn tunics over Van Necht's head, revealing his scarred, muscular shoulder, neck and back dyed red with blood and the gaping wound that continued to seep out blood. Acrida glanced at the hole and the scarlet fluid escaping it and again felt a bit lightheaded. She looked away and steadied herself with the table.

Mae glanced at Acrida with raised eyebrows and then back at the wound. Placing a cloth over the wound, she applied even pressure.

"It is deep," Mae told them.

Van Necht winced slightly under the pressure, but sat still.

"Did you recognize any of them, My Lord?" Aldric asked.

"They were not from here. They were villeins full of drink. Two of them bore the marks of criminals," Van Necht added.

"In which direction did they flee? I will send the sheriff to search for them."

"I killed three of them and wounded a fourth. He should not be difficult to find. He is a tall, gangly fellow with a hole in his ass."

The steward raised his eyebrows.

"He was fleeing southward out of the village."

"We will find him, My Lord," Aldric told him while dispatching one of his sons to find the sheriff.

"Were they trying to rob you?" Mae asked, continuing to apply pressure to the wound.

"No, just looking for trouble," Van Necht answered, glancing then over at Acrida.

She was staring at the wall, her face still blank with shock.

"If I may speak boldly, My Lord. With all the riffraff passing through as well as the new men coming in to be trained, it might be prudent for you to wear garments befitting your birth or at least a mantle, to let them know who *you* are- for their protection as well as your own," Mae told him.

Van Necht made no reply.

"My Lord, what would you have us do with the bodies?" Aldric asked.

"Take them to the crossroads. Let the corpses- and the birds that feast upon them- serve as a warning to those who would come here seeking mischief."

"Very good, My Lord."

The steward then took the opportunity to tell Van Necht about the results of the harvest, the latest count of new calves, and the progress being made on the repairs to the mill and other such business.

Acrida did not even hear the conversation, for in her mind she was once again seeing Van Necht kill her two attackers with very little effort, and the one with only his bare hand.

After the wound had finally stopped bleeding, Mae poured some wine into the wound. He moved slightly at the discomfort, but made no other acknowledgment of pain.

Mae sopped up the wine after a minute or so and sent her daughter for two of her father's shirts. She washed the skin on the alderman's back with a damp rag. Then she took some more cloth that had been torn into a very long strip and wrapped Van Necht's shoulder and upper chest. She tucked the ends of the cloth under the layers of the bandage and then carefully dressed the alderman in the shirts. The tunics were snug, being too small for Van Necht, but would suffice until he reached home. The last thing she did, refusing to allow the warlord to leave without it, was to fashion a sling for his left arm.

"My arm is uninjured, and the sling will surely slow me down."

"If you continue to use your arm, you will make the wound bleed again," Mae replied. "Do you want something for the pain?"

"No," he said, getting to his feet. "You have my thanks."

"You are most welcome, My Lord," she answered, curtsying to the nobleman.

"Will you not eat something before you go, My Lord?"

"No, I am anxious to see to the training of the men."

"'Twould be best to leave the training to Sir Albern, and for you to rest that shoulder," Mae said.

"Shall I get a cart to deliver you home?" Aldric asked.

Van Necht declined the cart, but explained the need for a horse since his charger was lame and likely needed to be reshod. Aldric nodded and sent his second son to catch a horse for Van Necht. He promised to deliver the lord's black charger to him when it was sound.

When the spare horse was saddled and bridled, Aldric helped Acrida onto the bay gelding, and then Lord Van Necht climbed up behind her. As the two rode off, Aldric shook his head.

"Stubborn as always."

39

The sun was a welcome break from the snow and sleet that we had had last night and the entire day before. I knelt by the side of the stream in the mid-afternoon sunshine and scrubbed the wet material, working to get the blood out of my braes. Strange that my flow which used to come to me but twice a year at most, had for the second time come while I resided with Van Necht. I wondered if my body was finally submitting to, as my aunt would say, the power of the moon.

Whatever the cause, I had been careful to conceal it from Van Necht, lest, with his loathing for women, he might find more fault with me.

It had been a difficult few days since the attack on the road. Daily I experienced moments of elation when I would catch myself thinking about his kiss on the plateau. Just as soon, I would be overwhelmed with disgust and the shock of seeing him naked and swyving the whores. And then I would be back in the hands of those vile men again, terrified and angry, and to both my horror and relief, I would watch Van Necht kill the wretches without mercy or hesitation with his bare hands.

Although I still loved him, I could not deny my new misgivings about him. Nor could I understand how I could have such different and conflicting feelings for the same man. Even more surprising to me was how little I really knew about him even after living with him all this time. How had I overlooked that killing and wenching would be natural to him- as it was to the King? Would it not be natural to any warlord? Still more worrisome was that I was now a part of this world.

I longed to talk about it with someone- my aunt or even the village priest back home; here there was Mae, but I was uneasy revealing such personal matters to her.

With my feelings in a jumble, I had been greatly nervous after the attack, wondering what would happen when Van Necht returned from the day's training. Would he want me? If so, he would surely take me. Would he hurt me greatly?

And if he did desire me, would I have the control to hesitate as a modest maid should, or would I follow my heart and surrender my chastity to him with abandon? Would he take me as he had that wench- in a position that was forbidden by the Church?

Or would things continue the way they always had?

How was it that I could long so much for *change* and be so afraid of it at the same time?

To my great relief and disappointment, nothing happened. Van Necht came in that evening, and after briefly informing me that his knights with the sheriff had apprehended the last attacker -and that the knave had now joined the others at the crossroads, the lord ate his dinner without another word and then retired to bed. By the time I had the fire out and went into the tent, he bade me to make a bed a little away from his, saying only that he preferred that I did not roll over and hit his shoulder during the night. The next morning, he was up and gone at dawn as usual.

The following days I continued to be anxious around him. I did not know what to say. He was not inclined to conversation either, but was especially irritable; and he hardly looked at me, as if he sensed my renewed fear of him.

When he did speak, he snapped at me. That was when I sensed a new coldness in him. I could not grasp why I was out of his favor. Perhaps it was simply as Mae had said, that he simply could not abide the company of women in general- and that included me. Although hurt, I tried to work through my confusion by staying busy, spending my days much as I had before.

At least the lord's injury had not been serious. It now being the fourth day after the attack, I had stopped thinking about it, as it had not slowed him down at all.

Leaving the bank of the stream with my wet laundry, I climbed the hill to camp and noticed two riders approaching in the distance at a slow walk. Thinking little of it, I set out the clothes to dry near the fire, then returned to my preparations for supper. In a little while, they were closer, and I was able to recognize the horses and riders. It was early for Sir Albern and Van Necht to come in, but perhaps they had other business to attend to this day.

I put another stick of wood on the fire to urge the cooking of the mutton I was preparing and went to the horses to greet them. I curtsied to the knight in his scarlet mantle who was nearer to me.

He paid me little heed but immediately swung down from his horse and attended to Van Necht who coughed and sloppily dismounted, holding his upper arm. The afternoon sun shone in my eyes, so I did not get a good look at him, but now that he was on the ground, I saw that he was in considerable pain.

I asked, quite worried now, if he did not want to lie down in the tent, although there was no need, for the knight was taking him straight there. Seeing how very weak Van Necht was and the way he leaned heavily on his vassal, I knew immediately that the wound must have reopened. I entered the tent after the two men, watching as Sir Albern helped him to take off his fur cloak, remove the sling and then the shirts he wore underneath it; all the while, the lord shivered and cursed.

To my surprise, the bandage was dry, although soiled with dirt and sweat. The skin near the bandage was pink and bulging around the snug edge of the wrappings. I lightly touched the injured shoulder, and Van Necht flinched.

"Did Mae wrap the bandage too tightly?" I asked.

Neither replied as the knight began to unbandage Van Necht. With the bandage off, the lord began to shiver anew. Sir Albern and I looked at the rosy-colored shoulder. The wound had repaired itself neatly.

"The shoulder is healed," he told Van Necht.

Albern helped him put on the shirts again. I saw that Van Necht could hardly move his left arm at all.

"It really aches," he winced, squeezing his upper arm.

"I think you are exhausted," the knight was saying. "You have been pushing yourself too hard. You need rest. In a few days, you will be better."

"Are you hungry, My Lord?" I asked.

"I hurt. C'sara, over there-" Van Necht gestured to a crate in the corner of the tent. "There is some wine. Bring it."

I went to the corner of the tent where he directed and dug through a basket until I found a small cask. I brought it to him with a horn cup and a spigot. The knight inserted the spigot and filled his lord's cup, handing it to Van Necht. The alderman gulped it down rapidly.

"Have you eaten, My Lord?" I inquired again.

"I am not hungry," he replied, as he grabbed at a coverlet that was nearby, wrapping it around him.

"Geoffrey and I will train the troops. Do not fret about them. Just rest," Albern said, refilling the horn.

Van Necht coughed on his fist, nodding his head at Albern's words.

"Aye," Van Necht agreed. "I am not well. I will entrust the training to you, but I require a daily report."

"You shall have it, My Lord."

Van Necht nodded and then began to gulp down the wine, and then held out the horn again for the knight to refill. After replenishing the cup, the knight bowed, and I followed him outside of the tent.

"What happened?" I asked.

"Nothing to be concerned about. He has been pushing himself too hard in this vile weather when he should have been resting where it was warm and dry. Knife wounds are painful enough as it is, but now he is ill and exhausted also.

"-I will come by every night to see if he needs anything; or you can send for me through Aldric if necessary. Tomorrow, I will send him a hogshead of strong ale; he will want it."

I nodded.

Sir Albern smiled at me then and commented that the mutton smelled good. I smiled and watched him mount his horse and leave. I walked over to Van Necht's waiting horse and unsaddled it. Then I led it to the corral and removed the bridle. The bay snorted and walked over to its favorite spot, lay down, and immediately rolled.

Returning to the tent, I found Van Necht on his fur bed struggling to find a way to lie down comfortably. Finally, he opted to sleep on his good side. I carefully covered him with a fur and wondered at his ability to withstand pain. Then I remembered the long, twisted scar on his low back. He had been wounded in the past; perhaps he was accustomed to this.

That night, the two of us slept peacefully for a few hours, but then it started. I was first awakened when Van Necht started tossing about uncomfortably and grumbling. I noticed, still half asleep myself, that he was refilling his cup and gulping down the wine with some urgency. For a man who seldom drank wine, he had consumed a great amount this night.

Besides his battle to find a comfortable position to sleep in, he was having an all out war with the blankets. He kept throwing the fur coverlet off of him. Then he would lie still for a while. I would just be drifting back to sleep when he would grab the coverlet and pull it all the way under his chin, shivering. After a while, he would kick it off again. Although I found this maddening, I said nothing, simply thankful that my bed and coverlets were separate from his. After this had gone on back and forth for half the night, I rolled over to face him.

"Are you cold, My Lord?" I asked, seeing the frustration in his face.

"Aye, but in a minute, I shall be hot."

I frowned and reached out my hand to his arm, but he shook off my touch as he struggled with the fur coverlet. Still, I noticed that his skin was very warm, even as he shivered beside me. He pulled his knees up then and huddled for warmth.

Finally he dozed off under the coverlet, and I was able to get some sleep too. When next I was awakened, it was still dark, and I guessed it was about an hour or so before dawn. I looked around to Van Necht then and wondered what had awakened me. He was still sleeping on his good side, but his bed had crept closer to mine.

I could not help the smile of affection on my lips, nor resist touching his face, rough with his whisker stubble. My smile was gone, however, when my fingers registered the heat from his cheek. I quickly put my palm to his forehead and was astonished by its crisp warmth. It was much hotter than his cheek had been.

Why was he so fevered? Perhaps he was ill from all the cold weather and sleet we had had lately.

He coughed and moaned then. I tucked the fur around him more and reached for the second coverlet. Dropping it over him, I lay down again and watched him.

"I want to tell you," he muttered, "your beauty is unmatched."

Noticing that his eyes were closed, I smiled at him curiously. I had never heard him speak in his sleep. However, his breath did smell heavily of wine. Likely, he was drunk.

"I love you. Do you hear me? I love you."

My heart skipped a beat and then raced in joy. Had the drink given him leave to say the words, finally, that I so longed to hear? Did I dare wake him and declare my love right then? Or should I pretend I had never heard the words and wait for him to tell me when he was sober and ready?

I should wait. This was not the time, I knew. He would be embarrassed if I woke him and confronted him in this way. -And he needed the rest anyway.

"My Love, say but you love me a little-"

But how could I wait?! My heart was overflowing already! I had to tell him now!

I could not stop smiling, the tears of joy filling my eyes.

"My Lord, I love you as well-"

"-I would do anything for your happiness," he interrupted. "Anything."

This was the happiest moment of my life! I smiled and stroked his brown hair, my heart almost bursting with joy.

"Say the word, and I will do it for you, G'hilde."

I blinked at him, not understanding.

"Nothing is too great to ask of me, My Lady. Only reward me with your kindness."

Slowly, the smile drifted from my face. My heart sank, and all my joy fled as suddenly as it had come. These words were not addressed to me and obviously were not intended for my ears.

314

"Everything I have done has been for your honor and your pleasure, My Lady. I only wish your happiness and hope that you will love me but a little."

Filled with shame and disappointment, I turned away from him as bitter tears rolled down my cheeks. He loved some other woman, obviously one of his own station.

"...for you alone, My Lady G'hil-..."

He had never mentioned any woman other than Mae in my presence, but it had become painfully clear over the past few days that there were many things about him that I did not know. No doubt, he intended to marry this lady and was only waiting for the King's approval to proceed with the betrothal.

"Our child will be..."

As he began mumbling faintly about children and family, I went pale and numb at the intimate nature of the words that I could distinguish. He had been to her bed already!

They were secretly betrothed! I realized in horror. Perhaps even secretly married!

I wiped my wet cheeks and nose on my sleeve as I wept. Surely not married, I conceded. Surely only betrothed. Marriage without the King's consent would be too bold, although the scandal would be great either way, and the King's wrath would be upon them.

Had he kept this betrothal from everyone? Surely Aldric and Mae knew his plans. How could his steward not know? Likely they did know, and he had sworn them to secrecy.

But what of his kiss on the plateau? What could it have meant? As I thought back on Lord Huntingdon and his servant, and the King with all his concubines, I swallowed my tears angrily as I accepted the truth. What cared these highborn noblemen about the feelings of lowborn women? We were fodder for their lust, to be bedded as long as they cared to have us. And surely to Van Necht, it was only a matter of convenience to make me his wench, for it would spare him a ride to the village whores.

And why should Van Necht care for me at all? I chided myself. I knew what I was, and so did he.

Stumbling to my feet, I put on my gown and wrapped myself in a fur. I went outside with the hound, glad to get away from him even in the cold air. I rebuilt the fire, throwing some leaves on the coals. With one little flame developing and eating the leaf, I wiped my face and worked to restore the blaze, then sat in the dark, hurting. My whole insides felt like they had been torn asunder and were lying at my feet.

Oh, what a fool I had been! Why had I allowed myself to even hope? He was of noble blood and would of course remarry a noblewoman equal to his birth. What possible *respectable* future could we have actually had?

I cried in the darkness, grateful that he had not waked and heard me declare my pitiful feelings. I was thankful, too, that no one else had witnessed my foolishness. There was no one to ridicule me for loving a highborn man who did not love me, nor to laugh at my dreams or the way I had deceived myself.

I cried until I was cold and exhausted with grief.

After my tears finally stopped, I sat for a long while in the silent night, numb. Now that I knew the truth, how could I face seeing him? It was impossible that I could stay here any longer with him- not now, not now. I was already the King's dog; I would not be Van Necht's sheep.

I cradled my aching head in my hand. I had been here too long already, I thought as I wiped my eyes and my stinging, wet cheeks with my sleeve. I would go- and soon. -Perhaps later today, when Van Necht was sober and he could get Mae to come and tend him.

Determined now, I rose to go back inside the tent. I heard him moan then, and I knew I should check on him. It was the duty of those of the Faith, after all, and, I admitted, he would have done the same for me.

Retrieving the water bucket, I entered the tent again and, picking up one of his shirts that I had washed a few days before, I sat down beside him. I dampened the cloth with the water which had a few shards of ice forming on the surface and wiped his face with it.

"Will you have some water, My Lord?" I asked. "You have had enough of spirits, methinks."

He drank the whole cup that I held to his lips, and then he fought to free himself of the fur coverlet. I wiped his hands with the cold water, and this seemed to help cool him.

He seemed to rest easier with my administrations, so I continued to sit beside him, helping him to cover up or uncover as he wished. Since his periods of shivering lasted longer, I finally put a lighter coverlet on top of him, then the fur on top of that, keeping his hands in the open. Finally, completely exhausted, he fell asleep again.

40

When I awoke, it was drizzling steadily outside. From the dim light in the tent, I knew it must be late morning. Van Necht lay shivering under the light blanket. The fur coverlet was halfway strewn over his hips and legs, but not his feet, and his breathing was louder than it had been earlier.

I looked with pity at his pale face and the expression of exhaustion on it even in sleep; his lips were even chapped. The wet cloth I had had on his forehead was lying on the fur pallet beneath him. I picked it up and wet it and placed it back on his forehead. His skin was burning with heat, and at the touch of the cool, wet cloth, he awoke.

"How many are there?" he asked, rising half way up off his bed.

"What?"

"How many?! How many are there?!"

He dropped his head again and shut his eyes, the question seeming to take all the energy out of him.

I looked at him in confusion. After all of this time, could he still be drunk? He began to shiver then, his teeth actually chattering now.

"You are cold?"

"Aye, cold-" he repeated or agreed, I was not sure which.

I pulled the fur coverlet over the thin blanket, and this seemed to help him.

My own stomach, now that I was awake, began to ache from hunger, so I got up and went into the other part of the tent and retrieved the bread left over from the morning before that I had stored in a basket.

I bit into the bread and chewed a large mouthful as I looked outside the tent flap and observed the dismal weather. It would be midday soon, but the sky was dark from the winter rain clouds that threatened overhead. Still, it would take more than bread to get the nobleman's strength back, so I braided my hair and put on my headrail and wrapped up in a coverlet and went out into the drizzling rain. While my breath made smoke in the chill air, I revived the coals of the fire and then went to the stream for fresh water. I would make soup with the uneaten mutton from the night before. Once everything was simmering in the pot, I entered the tent again wet and cold.

Van Necht was groaning in pain and turning over, trying to get comfortable again, but obviously he was suffering in every position he tried.

"You should lie still," I advised him while gathering up the empty horn cup and the wine cask that had been cast aside during the night.

"I hurt," he moaned.

"I know," I told him gently. "Do you want some more wine, My Lord?"

He assented, and I helped him to sit up. Then I filled the horn and handed it to him. He gulped down some of the drink, then started coughing. Finally, he stopped and wiped his mouth.

"Does your shoulder still hurt?"

"Aye, but my side hurts more."

His thumb gestured to the middle of his back on his good side.

"I must have slept on it wrong," he muttered, handing me the horn again, while he attempted to stand. "I must go prepare for the battle."

I looked at him quite startled as he struggled for his balance.

"No, you are staying here. Sir Albern is tending to the men, remember?"

I pushed him back to a sitting position.

"Oh, very good. He is an excellent knight," he muttered, lying wearily back down on his fur again.

I stared at him, perplexed; he was clearly not himself. I watched him for a while until I was satisfied that he was not going to try to get up again, then I went outside to check on the fire and the soup. The fire was burning well, despite the weather, but the broth was not yet warm. I entered the tent once again to find him tossing and turning to get comfortable, all the while shivering with an occasional cough.

When he finally lay still on his good side once more, I went to cover him again. As I pulled the coverlet up, I noticed his red and swollen shoulder through the large neck of the tunic. The wound itself, however, had healed and scarred neatly. I put my hand tenderly to the swollen flesh, and it felt extremely warm- even hot. At my light touch, the alderman moaned. I felt his neck then which was also very warm, but not so much as the shoulder.

I wondered what I should do. I simply had not been around anyone who had ailed like this before. Coughs and sneezes I knew; severe fevers, I did not. Should I get help from Mae? Sir Albern?

I again went outside, trying to think. I sat in front of the fire, warming myself, ignoring the misting rain, while my breath made smoke in the cold. I could hear Van Necht cough and groan inside the tent.

How serious was this? I wondered. He had only been unwell a few days. Likely, he would be completely recovered in a few more. I should not worry, I told myself. Yet, I was still concerned, for even I knew a mild illness could turn grave suddenly.

What would my aunt do? I wondered. I simply had no idea. Whenever she was summoned to a house struck by illness, she had taken her healing herbs and left me with my uncle.

I sat in the drizzle until the soup was ready. I put some in a bowl and carried it inside the tent.

"You must sit up and eat, My Lord."

Once the alderman was sitting up, he immediately began to cough, this time repeatedly and hard. Finally, after a long time, he stopped coughing and took the bowl from me. He seemed quite weak as I looked at him. His weary eyes had dark rings about them from his restless night.

"I am so tired," he commented.

He took a sip of the broth. He bit into the meat, but chewed it without appetite. He took another sip of the broth and then set down the bowl.

"I am too dizzy to sit up."

"You must eat."

He lowered himself back down and rested his head on the skins.

"I am not hungry."

"Have some water then," I offered.

He refused it. He said he would have some when he woke. I watched him pull up the covers as he closed his eyes and rested, only to be suddenly jerked by a fit of coughing.

I knew I should make him eat. He would be slow to recover without his strength, yet I could hardly force the nobleman. I picked up his bowl and went through the curtain to the other side of the tent to eat my own food, leaving him to rest.

The afternoon passed this way; I stayed on the other side of the curtain while he slept and by his side when he stirred to try to get him to eat or drink, which he did very little. I watched with growing concern as he unsuccessfully tried again and again to get comfortable, so he could sleep more.

I awoke abruptly and realized I must have dozed off. Peering out the tent door, I saw the sun was beginning to set. As I roused myself, I heard a low sound- a sound I had not heard in a very long time- and it caused the hairs on the back of my neck to stand on end.

I froze, and in alarm I looked at the curtain wall where it had come from. I must have heard wrong, I told myself; this could not be that serious! He was simply hurting and feverish. He would be well soon. I was tired, and my fatigue and worry were making me imagine the worst. With dread, I held my breath and listened intently.

Again I heard it, very faintly. My heart raced, and I at once entered his curtained side. I knelt down beside him, his low wheezing turning my blood to ice. I bent my head over his back then and listened. I heard what I feared I would, a gurgling sound that sputtered whenever he inhaled and exhaled.

My heart pounded wildly in my chest. I had good cause to be frightened, for I was well acquainted with this. My aunt had cared for many people one winter that had had this wheezing and chest gurgle, and most of them had died. So many in our village were sick at that time that she had been forced to let me help tend them. Although I had been quite young at the time, I remembered that we had ever so often turned the sick on their side and slapped them on the back and commanded them to cough. I hated to wake Van Necht since he was finally sleeping peacefully, but yet I knew that sound!

"Wake, My Lord."

"What-?"

"Wake!"

He sort of moved in a groggy manner, and I pushed him over to his injured side. He complained immediately, but I held him there and slapped him firmly on the back, which caused him to shriek and curse.

"Cough!"

He was coughing without my command. I hated to hurt him, but I continued to beat him.

When he had stopped coughing, I let him roll back over to his uninjured side. He lay there moaning with new pain.

"Forgive me," I told him softly, peering into his brown eyes.

"Who are you?"

I looked at him incredulously.

"Do you not know me, My Lord?"

He looked at me for a moment and then shut his eyes and turned his head away, too tired and weak to care who I was.

I staggered to my feet then as I struggled to grasp the present situation. Van Necht was gravely ill, and he might very well die if he did not receive some help from someone who knew how to tend him.

Trying not to allow my fears to overwhelm me, I quickly wrapped myself in one of the furs. Outside, the drizzling had stopped, but the air was rapidly becoming frigid as I left the camp. I started on a fast walk through the field that instantly became a run as panic seized me.

It was growing dark, and I had not even thought to get a torch for light. Nor was there time to go back for it. I had to make haste to Aldric's house. The steward must send for a physician immediately.

I had not gotten far through the field when a call drew my attention. I looked around, and there was a cart approaching on the road. The driver called me again.

"Acrida?!"

I ran straight for them, knowing the voice of Aldric.

"Oh, Aldric! Mae! I am so glad you are here! I was just coming for you!"

They smiled, and Aldric jumped down to help me into the cart.

"We were coming to visit the lord. We heard he was not feeling well yesterday."

"Nor today," I answered rapidly. "Aldric, is there a physician in the village?"

"No, but there is a physician in Leeds. Is Lord Van Necht that unwell?"

"Aye, he is feverish and does not know me. And I fear he has the breathing sickness."

"The breathing sickness? Are you certain?" Mae and Aldric were both asking.

"Aye, I know he does."

I told them of my efforts to tend him and my inability to get him to eat and drink anything substantial.

"I am certain you have tended him as well as anyone else could have. He is a stubborn man," Mae told her.

Aldric agreed.

The cart arrived at the camp, and we three climbed out of it and entered the darkened tent. Mae knelt down to the fur pallet and looked at Van Necht who continued to toss about, shiver, and argue with no one.

"I tell you that horse is lame," he was mumbling. "Horses can not pretend to limp. They are not men trying to shirk their duty."

Mae smiled with raised eyebrows. She put her hand to his forehead.

"His fever makes him talk out of his head. He is wheezing a bit, but I do not think it is as grave as the breathing sickness."

"You are certain?" I asked skeptically.

"In a few days he should be himself again," she said with a nod.

"Still, he is quite unwell- more so than even this morning. Is there nothing we should do?" I asked.

"Methinks there is nothing to be done that you are not already doing. -Just pray and wait. But if you are truly concerned, I can come tomorrow and put leeches to him. The physician would do no more."

I was surprised by her coolness. Her features showed no signs of real feeling.

My face must have revealed the apprehension that I felt.

"Be calm, Acrida," Mae said. "Try to get some sleep yourself. You are exhausted with tending him. Lord Van Necht is a strong man; and he has survived worse than a fever over the years. I am certain he will improve in a few days."

I looked at her, amazed. Was this all of her advice? Was there no better healer to be found in such a large village?

"And if he does not?" I asked.

She gave me a pitiful look I suppose was meant to be comforting.

"Then it is God's will, and we must accept it," she answered, crossing herself.

I looked at her and wondered how I had ever liked her or enjoyed her company. At once, I wished them to leave.

"Still, there is no harm in sending for the physician, I suppose," Aldric added, guiding his wife out of the tent. "Whether he will be free to come at once, I know not."

Once outside, Aldric went to the cart and unloaded a large basket of food they had brought with them, including fresh baked bread. Then he unloaded a large cask.

"This is the hogshead of ale that Sir Albern requested we bring Lord Van Necht," the steward said. "Acrida, do you want me to send some women to help you tend him?"

I bristled at the very thought of the other village women fawning over Van Necht or making light of what he mumbled in his feverish state.

"That is not necessary," I answered.

"Are you certain?"

"Aye."

Aldric nodded and climbed into the cart after his wife.

"Very well, if you need anything, let me know at once," he added as he urged the horse into a walk.

I watched wretchedly as they drove off back toward their home in the village. I was so stunned by the outcome of this visit and the hopelessness of Van Necht's situation that I sat down by the fire and wept hard and loud for I do not know how long.

Surrounded by darkness, I had almost cried myself out when I heard something. I looked up, and there was Sir Albern standing over me. I was immediately embraced, and I wept anew into his thick, scarlet cloak.

"My Dear Acrida, what ever is the matter? Has Van Necht bullied you all the day? He can get in such a foul temper when he has nothing to occupy him."

For the first time in several days, I felt safe. I wanted to cry all night in the knight's strong arms, but I had not the leisure.

"Sir Albern, Lord Van Necht is going to die."

"What?" he pulled me back away from him so that he could look into my face.

"He, I am certain, has the breathing sickness. Mae does not believe it, but I know he does. She says there is nothing to be done for him, and it is pointless to send for the physician in Leeds because he would only leech him and she could do that as well herself.

"Is there no other healer in the village or even on the neighbor's lands?"

"No," Albern answered.

"What of the castellan's wife?"

"She hath no special skills either. Mae at least has leeches. Other than that, the nearest is the physician in Leeds. But let me have a look at him," the knight said calmly.

I took a small piece of wood from the fire that was aflame, and we entered the dark tent. We knelt before Van Necht, and the knight saw how ashen the nobleman had become. He felt of Van Necht's forehead as well and then listened to his chest.

As he sat up, the torch light revealed the dread that graced the knight's face.

"I fear it is so. He may die without a healer. I shall ride to Leeds this night and get the physician."

"Will he do anything besides leech him?"

"I know not, Acrida. But he will surely bleed him."

"Then do not go," I told him miserably.

The knight looked at me, surprised.

"Do not go for the physician?"

I shook my head as another tear rolled down my face.

"If bleeding will save him, then surely Mae's leeches will work as well as anyone's. But if more is required to save him, then we must have more."

"What?"

"My aunt is a healer. You must go and bring her here."

"What?!"

"She is the only one I know of who might have the skill to save him, besides God himself -unless you know of someone."

Sir Albern admitted that he did not.

"Where is your aunt?"

"On Lord Huntingdon's lesser lands, in the village of Brackenbach."

"Lord Huntingdon's lands! This is madness! It is a full day's hard riding from here. It would take me two days to get her here at least. Van Necht may well be dead and buried before she arrives!"

"Aye! That may be so," I answered through my tears, "or he may live that long and still die after she treats him. Yet, I know of no one else. She is my only hope."

I wiped my wet face on my sleeve. Weighing his choices, Sir Albern looked at Van Necht, then at me, then at his liege lord again who was wheezing and shivering under the furs.

He abruptly turned back to me and with absolute seriousness, asked, "Acrida, do you love him?"

"Aye!" I cried, without even thinking. "More than life! More than sense-" I admitted wretchedly through fresh tears.

The knight was embracing me again and did so for a long moment.

"Very well, I will leave at once," he said, finally releasing me. "What is your aunt's name?"

"Deidre, married to Roe. Ask anyone in the village, they can direct you. -Tell her that 'Cinsara' sends you."

"Get me the bridle for that bay."

Going through the curtain that divided the tent, I retrieved the bridle and saddle and gave them to the knight. I gathered the goatskins and filled them with mead. While the knight caught the horse, I went through the basket of food that Aldric had left and packed some in a sack for Sir Albern to take with him.

Albern approached me then, leading the saddled horse, and I gave him the provisions.

"I will not fail him or you," he said, mounting his own horse.

Then he set spurs to his steed and trotted off down the road, leading the bay beside him and leaving me to my fears and my hope.

That night what little rest I had was when Van Necht himself managed to doze off. Whenever he was awake, I turned him over on his injured side and beat his back to encourage him to cough. Despite my intentions, it seemed to accomplish little except to increase his pain. He continued to wheeze, but by first light, his breathing had worsened. Every breath was accompanied by the gurgling sound in his chest, which I could hear distinctly no matter where I was in the tent.

After dawn, I could not get him to take any water or broth at all. He simply would not or could not swallow it. His body was racked with almost constant shivering and a nagging cough that clearly hurt him. His skin remained hot to the touch and very dry. I kept a cold, wet cloth on his forehead and continued to wipe off his arms with cold water which he now seemed unaware of. He continued to rant, issuing orders to his men and taking orders from his superior. One time, I was too close to him, and he grabbed me and told me to get my sword and get to my horse.

Mae came later that morning, bringing the leeches and more food. She told me Aldric had sent for the physician that morning, and we could expect him at the earliest by dark. While she bled Van Necht, I waited on the other side of the curtain wall, for the very sight of the leeches getting their drink made my skin crawl. Afterward, she sat with me for a while and told me the village gossip. I was too tired to really listen and was glad when she finally left.

After noon, the village priest arrived, for he had heard that Van Necht was ill. He came in and looked at Van Necht, and he and I prayed a simple prayer together over him. The priest said he was sorry that he could not administer the sacrament of Extreme Unction, for the interdict forbade it. After he left, I was more melancholy than before he came.

I worried all the rest of the day as I listened to his ragged breathing. As his condition continued to worsen, I tried to think of anything I could do to help him. I vaguely seemed to remember my aunt talking about how steam could help the sick breathe easier. I grew frustrated with myself then for not paying closer attention to what she had tried to tell me in the past.

As it was growing colder outside, I decided to build a small fire near the center of the tent. Parting the opening in the curtain as wide as possible, I set the kettle on the fire and began to boil water, hoping both to warm him and that the steam would help him to breathe. It seemed to help me.

Finally, I prayed. I prayed I could keep him alive until my aunt arrived. I prayed that the horses would not go lame and that Sir Albern would neither get tired, nor hurt, nor would simply give up.

41

Sir Albern stopped his horse and blew on his chilled fingers while he looked around. It was just after noon, and he seemed to be in the middle of nowhere. What was he doing? he wondered. It was madness to ride all night to fetch some peasant healer to save a man that would most likely die before he returned. Well, perhaps he was mad, he considered as he clicked the bay into a walk and pulled his own horse beside him.

He thought back on his life with Van Necht, his liege lord and best friend. They had been through a number of predicaments together and had saved each other's life a number of times. Similar in age, they had met as young men when Van Necht had inherited his father's lands, and all of the knights had come to swear their fealty to him. They had fought side by side in battles, drank and wenched side by side in stews. They had been inseparable.

The knight did not regret the ride south in the dead of winter night, foregoing his sleep. He knew Van Necht would have done it for him without hesitation. He feared, however, that the peasant woman he sought would be unable to help. It would be heartbreaking to ride for two days only to have his best friend die anyway. Perhaps he had died already. But, the knight admitted, a two day desperate ride across country was far easier to perform than that of simply watching his friend weaken hour by hour.

He urged the horses into a trot. Gradually he approached a village and spied a man walking along the road.

"Good day!" Albern called.

The farmer stopped, waiting on the horses to near him. Then he bowed to the knight.

"Good day, Sir Knight. How may I serve you?"

"I am looking for the village of Brackenbach."

"Well, and you have found it."

Sir Albern was relieved to hear it. He had been crisscrossing the countryside for most of the morning. It had been quite a challenging hunt; of the people that the knight had encountered, few had ever heard of the village and even less had ever been to it or knew exactly where it was.

"Do you know the people here?" Sir Albern asked, peering at the huts up ahead.

"I should hope so, Sir Knight, for I was born here and have lived my whole life in this village. Likely, I will die here too, if I am not killed in this war that is coming."

Sir Albern smiled at the chatty peasant. From what he could see, the *village* contained nothing more than a small cluster of huts. None of them was large enough to even be a public house.

"Then, perhaps you can tell me where I can find a woman called Deidre."

"Deidre? Aye, she lives in the cottage on the far edge of the village, just off the path."

The man made a gesture with his right hand in the right direction. Sir Albern thanked the man who bowed low to him again, and then he trotted the horses in the direction of the village.

Sir Albern walked the horses past the line of village huts and on down the narrow path to where one lone cottage stood by itself near the edge of a wood. As he looked at the crude hut and the chickens that were scratching in the mud in front of it, Albern blew on his fingers again and tried to wiggle his toes, for he could not feel anything below his knees. Although he did not see anyone, someone had to be near, for around the side of the house, a kettle was set over a hot fire.

After slowly dismounting the bay, the knight leaned wearily against the horse, for his legs were weak from riding so long without a break. His buttocks were also numb, and he was more than a little dizzy. He regained his balance just as an elderly man came out of the hut, eyeing him warily. Sir Albern noted the villein's unfriendly manner, for he kept his distance, neither bowing nor speaking.

"Good day," Sir Albern said.

The gray-haired man made an awkward gesture with his body that was probably meant as a bow. Albern realized this man, and likely the village itself, had not seen many strangers and probably even less of the nobility. From what he had heard, Lord Huntingdon had a great expanse of lands, and his main castle and village was more than forty leagues from here. In all probability, this tiny village at one time had belonged to some minor lord whose lands were later combined with Huntingdon's through marriage.

"I am looking for a woman named Deidre. Does she live here?"

"And what would you be wanting with her?" the peasant answered abruptly. "She has done nothing to the likes of you."

The knight was surprised by the man's aggressive demeanor. The gray hair gave the old man a mild appearance, yet Albern watched slightly alarmed as the villein took up a rusted sickle that was leaning against the side of the hut with his earth-blackened hand.

"I am Sir Albern, and I mean her no harm. I have been sent to retrieve her-"

"I will tell you this," the old man interrupted, shaking the sickle at the ruby-ringed, scarlet-caped nobleman. "I will be dead on the ground before I will let any knights near her."

Sir Albern was so astonished by the peasant's audacity and so weary from his journey, that he was not even offended. In fact, he smiled at the thought that he might actually have to fend off the attack of an old man after such a long ride. The more he thought about it, the funnier he found it. He began to chuckle and then to laugh without restraint. In that moment of senseless abandon, Sir Albern's legs went out, and he hit the ground still laughing stupidly, holding his sides.

The old peasant was equally surprised by the knight's response to his threat, but seeing the young man fall to the ground without apparent cause frightened him even more.

"Deidre!" he called into the house. "Come quickly! Help me with this knight before someone accuses me of putting the evil eye on him!"

There was a scuttling sound, as an old, pudgy woman emerged from the hut. She at once went over and squatted down beside Sir Albern.

"What happened?" she asked as she examined the giggling knight.

"I know not. One minute I am giving him a warning, and the next, he collapses!"

"Well, that is using your head, Man! How long do you think you will live if you threaten every nobleman you meet? Here, help me get him to the fire."

Still chuckling, Sir Albern let the peasants help him to his feet. Leaning on the woman, he was taken to a bench beside the fire.

Once there, the old woman took a moment to look him over again.

"Methinks he is well enough, Roe. -Just exhausted and half frozen."

"You are Deidre?" Albern managed.

The old woman had a kindly face, weathered and wrinkled from the sun, soft blue eyes, and she wore a crystal about her neck.

"Aye, I am Deidre. You must forgive my husband. Roe is wary of strangers, -knights especially."

Sir Albern smiled and glanced at the old man again, who continued to regard him suspiciously. The woman went into the hut momentarily, then returned with a cup, a pitcher, and a rag. She handed the knight the wooden cup and poured him some ale.

Although the ale was weak, Sir Albern, who had not thought he was thirsty, gulped it down. Deidre watched him for a moment and then glanced at the horses and the dried sweat on their coats.

"Roe, tend to his horses."

Without another word, her husband left the fire and went to do as he was bidden. Sir Albern looked back at the woman, impressed by her confident demeanor.

"From the looks of it, Sir Knight, you have been riding hard all the day. What is your purpose?"

To the point, too, Sir Albern thought. The woman handed the rag and a bucket of water to the knight, and he wiped his face with the cold water.

"I have been riding all night and day, as you say, sent to retrieve you-"

"Who calls for me?"

"Cinsara."

The woman's expression changed to one of surprise, and she crossed herself immediately.

"What is it?" Albern asked, startled by her reaction.

"*This* that called for me, Sir Knight," she said warily, "was it spirit or flesh?"

"What? -Flesh, of course!"

"She lives then."

"Of course, Woman! Did you think otherwise?"

"Aye, in truth, we thought her dead! For more than three months ago the King and his knights ransacked our village and took our child along with some of the other village girls. We thought they were taken to the palace, which is said now to wreak of death since the knights took it from the rebels. But no one knows what actually befell any of our girls- or if they even live, for there has been no word."

"I see, then," Albern began carefully, "that I am the bearer of glad tidings, for Acrida is alive and well. However, I know nothing of the other daughters from your village.

"I am Sir Albern, vassal to Lord Van Necht, and I was not among the knights that took Acrida from you. I do not know all of the details, for I was not present when she was brought before the King, but I have *heard* that he gathered all the supposed seers in the kingdom in order to question them. Nor do I know why the King spared her life when, I am told, he ordered the death of all the others."

The knight paused when he saw the look of horror on Deidre's face. He realized that he was telling this poorly.

"Fear not, for the worst is over. Acrida survived and was sent to my alderman and friend, Van Necht. He is a man of arms and sometimes is asked to guard special prisoners."

These new words failed to comfort the old woman, who sat down on the bench with the same look of dread on her face. Sir Albern licked his lips and continued.

"Lord Van Necht is a good man and has treated her kindly, never fear."

The woman looked skeptical, but said nothing.

"Anyway, the King was inclined to make Acrida one of his advisers."

Deidre screwed up her eyebrows and smiled.

"An adviser to the King? Acrida?"

"Aye."

"*Our* Acrida?"

"Aye."

She laughed once.

"So where is she? With the King?"

"No."

"The word is that no one knows where the King is either-" Deidre added with a shrug. "Is Acrida at the palace then?"

"No, she still remains under Lord Van Necht's protection until the King calls for her."

Deidre looked at the knight doubtfully.

"So, my daughter is still this alderman's prisoner?"

"No-"

"She lives among his household?"

Albern hesitated.

"Lord Van Necht does not keep a household, but she does stay with him."

"As his servant?"

"No, his *guest*-"

The old woman raised her eyebrows.

"You mean his wench-"

"That is not for me to say."

Deidre frowned, but did not pursue it.

"So how does this bring you here?"

"As I have said, Acrida sent me to bring you at once. Lord Van Necht lies on his death bed, and she believes you may have the skill to save him. She was adamant that you come. She said you are her- I mean, *our* only hope."

Silent, the woman seemed to look straight through him. Sir Albern wondered if she was believing any of this.

"So this nobleman is ill," she said finally. "If he dies, Acrida shall pay with her life, I suppose."

Sir Albern looked at Deidre in confusion.

"No, Woman, not with her life, -with her heart."

Deidre raised her eyebrows skeptically. How much of this was true? She could believe that Acrida was alive and had sent for her, for hardly anyone knew Acrida's baptismal name. That Acrida was the King's adviser now was wholly unbelievable, yet who would make up such a story? And Deidre had to admit, however, that if anything could be won with argument, her niece could do it.

She gave little heed to the last part of the knight's tale though. That Acrida feared this alderman's death was clear, but for what reasons? Perhaps she had poisoned him herself to escape him, and being caught, would be accused of murder if he died.

Sir Albern sighed and looked at the flames that licked the cauldron. He had not foreseen this delay. He had hoped to be on the road again already.

"I will come," she said at last, "but you must tell me specifically what ails this man."

The knight, relieved, stood up. Deidre grabbed his arm, and he sat back down obediently.

"First, we eat. Here, drink some more ale," she said, refilling his cup.

Sir Albern did not argue; he picked up the cup and drank it. Deidre rose from the bench and went back inside the hut. She returned in a moment with a basket of eggs, cabbage, onions and a loaf of very dark bread.

Albern watched as the old woman removed the outer leaves of cabbage that had turned dark and tossed it to the chickens, which immediately fell upon it. She put the rest of the cabbage into the boiling water. She threw the skins and outer layer of the onions to the chickens also and then added the onions to the pot as well. Deidre sat down on the bench again and, with a knife, sawed the hard loaf into three, large, very thick slices of bread.

"Now, tell me what ails this man, so I will have some idea what I will find when I get there."

"Well, I am not certain what ails him-" Albern replied, noticing then that the hut and yard were encircled by a row of stones. "All I know is that he has been really tired and coughing for several days. I thought he had become ill from being out in the wet weather. He felt so poorly two days ago that I had to take him home early from training the men. He was in much pain."

"Pain? Where?" she asked as she began to hollow out the center of a slice of bread that would be used as a trencher, throwing the scraps to the waiting chickens.

"-On his back near the left shoulder. He was stabbed in the shoulder a week ago in a fight in his village. Yesterday evening, I went to see how he faired. He was feverish and had been so most of the day; his breathing also has a raspy sound to it. Acrida thinks he has the breathing sickness."

Deidre raised her eyebrows.

"Well, that will certainly bring an end to him," she said frankly.

The distressed look on the young knight's face was enough to make Deidre regret her words.

"Forgive me, Sir Knight. I forget myself. Tell me, how is the wound from the fight?"

"It is healed. His steward's wife bandaged it up for him."

"Well, I knew Acrida had not done it," she mumbled. "That girl has no stomach for blood."

"-I feared at first that the wound had reopened as Van Necht had refused to lessen his activity but instead continued to train the men," the knight continued.

"Did he not rest at all after he was injured?"

The knight smiled.

"No, he is stubborn that way."

Deidre sighed and shook her head.

"What kind of wound was it? A slicing, glancing blow? A scrape?"

"No, it was a thrusting blow- made by a dagger," Sir Albern replied, demonstrating with his fist.

She nodded as he described. She took the knife and stabbed a slab of old bread, almost all the way through. She held up the knife with the impaled bread at the top.

"Is this what happened?"

Albern nodded and finished his ale, watching as Deidre frowned.

"What is the matter?"

"This type of wound," she said, as she removed the knife and held up the bread to show him the hole that was left, "can not heal in a few days."

He looked at her, not understanding her meaning, except that she was concerned. Then the old woman returned to crafting the trenchers again.

When the trenchers were finished, Deidre cracked nine eggs and dropped the yolks into the boiling water. When they had cooked a few minutes, she ladled the eggs onto the trenchers with the onions and cabbage. She set them in the basket and called her husband and then went back into the hut with the knight following her.

It took a moment for Sir Albern's eyes to adjust to the dark of the small hut, which was lit by one sole candle in the middle of a table. He wrinkled his nose at the stench, for the interior of the peasant's home smelled like a dung heap. He watched as Deidre set the trenches around the table and put the cat which had jumped upon it back onto the floor. Then she set out a loaf of fresh bread, and two more cups and, taking the pitcher from the knight, filled the cups with ale. Deidre gestured to the guest to sit down at the table and then retrieved an additional candle from a shelf. She lit it from the first and, making an odd gesture with her hand, set it before the knight. Sir Albern could just make out the sweet fragrance of lavender. Roe entered the hut and sat at the table on the bench beside his wife. He looked warily at his guest, clearly unsure as to how to treat him.

He was hungrier than he thought he was, Sir Albern realized as he rubbed his weary eyelids. He ate his poached eggs, cabbage and onions quickly and the fresh barley bread the woman served with it with honey. He drained his cup of ale and had another.

Albern awoke with a start. At first he panicked, not recognizing anything, and then he slowly remembered where he was. He looked at his surroundings. He was stretched out on a low bed, and a warm, black cat was curled up asleep at his chest. Hearing a clucking sound, the knight looked up above his head, only to come eye to eye with an inquisitive, old hen that was roosting just above him on the table top.

Sir Albern raised himself on one elbow. Neither Deidre nor Roe were in the hut that seemed to sway slightly as the wind whistled by. Both the candles still burned on the table, illuminating the interior of the hut with soothing flickers. A large hog lay on the floor beside his bed, and chickens roosted throughout the hut in whatever space they could find.

In one corner of the hut were shelves set into the wall which held candles, leather pouches, crystals and stones, a large mortar and pestle, and several small crocks with pictures drawn on them. Above these shelves, leaves and flowers and other parts of plants hung suspended in midair from twine that dangled from the ceiling of the hut. Mushrooms, too, though quite deadly, were among the items.

Sir Albern glanced at the candlelit walls of the hut. Etched into the mud walls were strange designs and shapes that he did not recognize. The hair on the back of the knight's neck stood on end as he realized these were *the ancient symbols of magic*. Though he had not noticed them earlier, the runes were on every wall, and there were more around the door frame. They were in each of the four corners of the hut as well with a crystal that had been imbedded into the corner walls. There was also a large drawing of a snake curled around a nest of eggs on the wall right above the bed where he lay.

As he looked about, a cold shiver ran up Albern's body. For the first time in a long time, he felt raw fear. Quickly, he checked his body; he still had all of his parts, and they seemed to be sound. As he moved, he noticed something on the back of his left hand. He gasped, and as his heart pounded in his chest, he examined the rune that had been painted onto his skin.

The knight immediately crossed himself and said an Ave Maria. Then he took a deep breath to try to calm himself as the black cat beside him observed him with its perfectly round, yellow eyes.

How long had he been asleep? the knight wondered. Days? Weeks? Years? He quickly tried to get his wits about him. The last thing he remembered was eating at the table. He did not, however, remember lying down! Furthermore, he had wanted to leave immediately after eating, for it was a long ride home. There was no way they could have coaxed him to rest!

He sat up. Whatever spell the witch had used on him, at least it had not frozen him. He stood up, disturbing the cat, chickens, and hog, and opened the door. It was dark outside, and the moon and stars were out. The knight moaned and shut the door. He had to get out of here and get back to Van Necht. The knight's heart sank then. Van Necht was probably long dead by now.

The door opened suddenly, and the witch walked in, her sudden appearance alarming the knight.

"Good. You are astir. The moon is up. We can go now."

It took no urging to get the knight out of the house.

Outside, the horses were ready: groomed and snorting, bridled and saddled. Roe was tying a sack to the bay's saddle.

"How long have I been asleep?" the knight demanded.

"A few hours."

"What did you do to me?"

"Nothing. You fell asleep," Deidre replied indifferently.

"Impossible!"

"You were exhausted."

"I do not believe it! You must have put a spell on me! You put something in the ale!"

"'Twould have been a waste of a good potion," she answered dryly.

"Then what is this mark upon me?!" Albern exclaimed, displaying the design on his hand. "Do you deny it is a symbol used by witches?"

Deidre smiled.

"I do not deny it. It is to strengthen your vitality, as will this," she replied coolly, handing the knight a cup. "Drink all of it. It will keep you wakeful."

Sir Albern, his heart beating in his ears, hesitated as he sniffed the brew warily.

"Fear not, Sir Knight. You and Acrida have asked for my help in saving this alderman, and I am willing; but we must get there first."

She spoke truly, and he had squandered enough time, Albern admitted. Despite his doubts and the uproar in his conscience, the knight quickly drained the cup of the bitter drink and then looked into the night sky, trying to guess how many hours it would be until dawn.

"This is not well. We should have left immediately!"

"Perhaps, but you were tired, and so were the horses. They needed to be rested and looked after."

"Did you give them a potion to increase their vitality also?"

"Hay and grain," Roe replied.

Sir Albern sighed impatiently as he checked his horse's girth.

"That is everything," Roe was saying as he finished tying the last sack to the saddle.

The knight went over then and helped Deidre onto the bay. Once atop, she patted the horse's neck. Then she leaned down and kissed her husband on the lips.

"Farewell, Roe. I shall be back as soon as I am able."

Roe frowned.

"Come back to me, Deidre."

The knight mounted his horse and turned toward the path, and the bay followed. Roe watched as the two horses trotted away through the village northward into the night and wondered if he would ever see any of his family again.

42

Acrida jerked and gasped, then blinked slowly. She was still lying beside Van Necht and realized she must have dozed off again. She sat up and looked at the alderman. He was pale and lay very still, and she could not tell if he was breathing now, but an hour ago he had been. She pulled back his coverlet and stared at his stomach, holding her breath to keep her gaze steady. She perceived, more than saw, movement in his stomach- a slight rise and fall motion.

She covered him again and glanced over at the fire; the wood had burned up, and the water had cooled once more. She would have to go gather more kindling.

She would go in a minute, she promised, as she allowed herself to sink down beside Van Necht once more. She just needed a minute to summon her strength.

She had had little sleep the last two days as she struggled to keep him alive; she was weak now with weariness and despair.

She had kept the small fire burning and the water boiling in the tent in an effort to try to keep Van Necht warm, who in his own exhaustion, had even stopped shivering. Despite his pitiful protests, at intervals she had continued to turn him and beat his back to force him to cough. She had stopped yesterday afternoon, however, because he had had no strength left to cough or even to groan from the pain of her blows. She had, however, continued to turn him over occasionally for brief periods.

She had also given up trying to give him water or broth. Any she had put in his mouth had simply run back out. Every breath he took was pure agony for him and was accompanied by the telltale gurgling sound in his chest.

Her only other activity yesterday had been to search for the source of the rank odor in the tent. She had thought a field mouse had gotten in the tent and died, but she could not locate the carcass to remove it.

The smell made her nauseous, but she had finally come to the conclusion that it must be directly under Van Necht's bed of skins, and it was simply not worth the pain it would cause the man to get him up to go through them.

Aldric's son had arrived yesterday just after noon to bring word that the physician in Leeds was occupied, but would come in a few days when he was able if they still required him. He had asked if his mother should come in the morning to leech him again, but Acrida had told him there was no need.

Acrida guessed it was now an hour or so before dawn. Where could Sir Albern be? she wondered. He had left two nights ago, and she was losing hope that her aunt would make it in time. Yesterday evening as night drew near, she had watched and tended Van Necht constantly. She had not even left him long enough to cook herself something to eat. It mattered not anyway. Anxiety and grief had taken her appetite, for she had thought he was going to die then. She had been certain of it, in fact, because he had started breathing in such a strange manner.

The alderman had taken a slow breath at first, then a few moments had passed, and he had taken another slow breath, and then a second or two passed, and he took another, and then another right on top of that one; and then a short breath immediately followed, then another short breath, then another, and another, adding to the series until he was practically panting. Then his breathing would suddenly stop.

After a moment, he would take a very slow breath again, a few moments would pass, until the next slow breath, and then the whole chain would repeat itself. This breathing went on for several hours, all the while Van Necht was awake, too sick now to sleep at all. Although his skin was very dry and hot to the touch, he still seemed somehow to be cold. Thus, she had buried him under the furs and coverlets and had climbed in bed beside him, holding him gently, hoping her body could aid the coverlets in warming him.

Thus, he had spent the night in her arms. She had kept herself awake by saying her prayers repeatedly to God and the Christ, and by saying her intercessory prayers to the Blessed Virgin for prayers for help.

Acrida remembered the dream that had awakened her. It had been night, and a gray horse, pale as new fallen snow, had come to the tent. Without a doubt, she knew it had come to take Van Necht away. All through the dream she had tried to run it off. She had yelled at it, run at it, thrown rocks at it, even sicked the dog after it. The gray had backed off a few feet, even trotted around the field before her, but it had always returned to the tent, undaunted.

Then she had turned around, and there stood Van Necht, healthy, strong, and handsome, coming out of the tent flap into the open air. Her joy and relief at seeing him well had turned to terror as he proceeded directly toward the waiting horse. He obviously intended to ride it.

She had repeatedly shouted at him to keep away, but he had not heard her. Quickly getting between him and the gray, she had shoved him backward, back inside the tent, and then she had turned around and thrown another stone at the horse. When she had glanced behind her, Van Necht was once again coming through the tent flap. Once again she had shoved him back inside, and this time she had jumped on him fully and wrestled with him. He had fought to get loose and to his feet, all the while looking through her as if she was spirit. Finally, she had grabbed a rock, which for some reason was beside them in the tent, and had started smashing it against his head.

Then he had been lying in his bed again, clutching the coverlets and talking wildly. She had breathed a sigh of relief, but it was only to last for a moment. Suddenly, overcome by a sense of dread, her heart had pounded wildly as the tent walls began to quake violently, and with a great noise, they collapsed altogether. The large, ashen hooves and ankles of the gray horse had been beside her then. She looked up into the huge, pale muzzle that was sniffing her and Van Necht in the ruins of the tent. Then she had awakened.

Trying to forget the horrifying image in her mind, Acrida wondered mildly, while sinking deeper into the fur bed, if Sir Albern had perhaps gotten lost, had not found the village, or had simply been killed by a bandit or from a fall from his horse.

She had to get up! she sternly told herself, but her eyelids were heavy on her eyes, so heavy she had not the strength to open them. She wanted to let herself go and ease into the peaceful silence.

No- she had to get up, had to get more kindling!

Her lids were tight over her eyes now, and her own breathing was becoming even. The dream world was pulling her back again.

Acrida could just barely hear the dull sound of huff beats and a low barking noise. She saw before her then a whole herd of stags trotting up to the tent. Van Necht's hound was barking at them. The stags were talking, though she could not make out what they were saying. Then one in the crowd was calling her. 'Acrida!' it called. She moaned an answer in her sleep back to them. The stags continued to call for her, but they could not hear her answer them.

"Acrida!"

Fighting hard, Acrida managed to open her eyes slightly.

"Acrida!"

She could still hear the voices.

"Acrida!"

She was immediately awake. The voices were real! She staggered to her feet and stumbled out of the tent. She could hear the voices, but could not see the faces in the darkness.

"What do you mean he has no castle?"

Acrida smiled as she recognized the voice.

"No servants either? Just what kind of nobleman is this Lord Van Necht?"

"Mainly a man of war, presently without a castle, household, or servants," was the reply.

"Deidre!" Acrida called, immediately surprised how soft and weak her own voice sounded to her.

"Acrida! My Dear Girl!"

There was a thud, and the sound of rustling skirts through the tall weeds. Suddenly Acrida found herself heartily embraced. Smelling the old familiar smell of her aunt, the strange mixture of herbs and other scents, Acrida, in Deidre's comforting embrace, immediately began to weep.

"There, there, Child," the old woman mumbled, holding her to her soft body.

"Are we in time? Does he still live?" Albern called.

"Aye," Acrida answered wearily.

Sir Albern immediately dismounted and went to the fire outside the tent and worked to restore a flame from the few remaining coals.

"Acrida, I feared I would never see you again!"

"As did I!" Acrida cried. "How I have missed you and Roe!"

Once he had it burning, Albern added more wood and lit the end of a small, thick stick. Holding it as a torch, he approached the women and the tent. As Sir Albern neared them with the light, he gasped.

"Acrida, you are so pale, like- like one of the dead."

Deidre immediately pushed Acrida to arms' length and looked at her. She was very pale; her hair was partially braided, but uncovered.

Her face looked like little more than a slipcover for a skull, and her tired eyes were surrounded by dark circles.

Deidre put her hand to Acrida's forehead. Although, she was warm, she had no fever.

"You have almost made yourself ill tending this man, Acrida. Was there no one to help you?"

Then seeing the tent before her, Deidre's eyebrow's knitted together. Obviously there was not.

"You must rest," the old woman told her.

"No, never mind about me!" Acrida answered quickly.

She turned around and opened the tent flap.

"I am so glad you are here, Deidre. I know you can help him."

Sir Albern and Deidre followed the phantom into the tent with the torch. They wrinkled their noses at the rank odor of decay.

"I know. I know," Acrida replied, seeing their faces, "I think a rat or something must have died in-"

"No rat!" Deidre muttered, knowingly.

Albern led them around the dying fire in the center of the tent to where Van Necht lay on the furs upon the ground.

"Is he so poor that he can not even afford a proper bed?" Deidre complained.

Albern knelt down beside the lord with the torch.

"By the Saints!" he exclaimed.

Deidre looked down at the man, buried in furs, with his partially open eyes, his blank stare, miserable expression and his cracked, gaping lips. His skin was ashen as snow, and his breathing was not even visible. A few flies crawled on his eyes and inside his nostrils and lips.

"All this way," Deidre muttered with a shake of her head, "to help you bury him."

A cry escaped Acrida's lips, and the old woman looked up startled.

"No! No, no!" Acrida cried distractedly, her hands in fists, as fresh tears ran down her face.

Deidre looked at her in surprise. Only in seeing the agony in her niece's face did she finally understand what the knight had been trying to tell her. Whoever this man was, Acrida clearly cared for him.

"Is there nothing you can do?" Albern asked mournfully.

Witnessing their distress, Deidre regretted her bluntness. As Acrida and Albern grieved over the man, the old woman took a deep breath and spoke calmly.

"In truth, methinks he shall die. But for you, I will try to fight off death even if it is only for a few hours or so."

Acrida wiped her eyes and thanked her.

"Sir Knight, after riding all the night, I had hoped to send you home, but I need you here."

Albern rose to his feet, his own tears coursing down his face.

"I am at thy command," he managed to say.

Deidre made her way over to the body of Lord Van Necht and put her hand to his forehead, then moved it down to his neck, under his jaw and held it there. Then she pulled back the coverlets and furs and put her ear to his chest, listening carefully.

"I was on my way to get more firewood so to boil some more water to help him breathe-" Acrida said.

"Never mind that now, Child," she told her as she began to uncover the alderman.

The old woman peeled off the furs and then the thin coverlets. She handed the coverlets to Sir Albern.

"There must be water near here?"

"Aye, a stream,"

"Wet these in the coldest part and bring them back. -Be careful not to fall in," she added.

The knight took the coverlets and the burning stick and went out leaving them in darkness again.

"We need light. Hath the lord any candles?"

"Candles? No-"

"Why am I not surprised? I brought a few with me. Luckily, the sun will be up soon."

The two women exited the tent and went over to the horses, and Deidre untied the sacks from the saddles, handing one to Acrida. Returning to the tent, they passed the fire, and Deidre threw a few more sticks of wood on it, causing the flames to leap higher into the darkness.

Acrida picked up a small, burning stick and lit the small candle that Deidre had dug out of one of the sacks. They entered the tent again, and the old woman looked again at the lord and his fur skin bed on the ground.

"Acrida, I am surprised at you! When he first became ill, why did you not raise his bed? You know the spirits of the dead come up from the ground and try to take the sick to their own world."

342

"I did not think of it."

"Never mind. Go and gather wood, rocks, stacks of straw, anything large, and bring it. We must raise his bed."

Giving the candle to her aunt, Acrida went out of the tent.

Deidre set the candle down on a crate out of the way and picked up the kettle of water from the cold fire. She carried it outside the tent and set it on the brightly burning, crackling fire with its brilliant, yellow, dancing flames. Then she returned to the tent and removed the remaining sticks and dying coals; she took them outside and added them to the fire, mumbling her incantation all the while.

Next, picking up the ends of Van Necht's fur bed, she pulled and tugged on it until it was away from the wall, moving it near the middle of the tent. She went outside again and took a long, thick stick from the fire and doused the flame on the end of it. Re-entering the tent again and starting at the door, she dug the stick into the ground and dragged it toward her, plowing in effect a little furrow of dirt. She continued backward around the tent until she had drawn a large circle inside that encompassed the lord and a few items that were in the center of the tent. Inside this circle, she inscribed beside Van Necht three, smaller circles that joined end to end like a chain. Then she intersected all three circles with one line.

When Sir Albern returned with the wet coverlets, halfway wrung out, but still dripping with cold water, he found Deidre in the dimly lit tent kneeling beside Van Necht, painting something on his forehead with a feather while she mumbled to herself.

"Unsaddle the horses and then help Acrida gather wood or straw or rocks even. We must raise his bed," the witch instructed without stopping what she was doing.

Without asking anything, the knight set the coverlets down and went back out into the early morning darkness.

After allowing a moment for the design to dry, Deidre took the remaining fur off of Van Necht. Then she quickly stripped him of his tunics and braes. The lord lay unconscious as the old woman spread one of the wet coverlets directly on his naked body. She frowned, noticing this did not cause him to stir at all. She rolled the lord over onto his stomach then and covered him with the other wet coverlet.

She examined his red, swollen shoulder then. Touching the hot skin around the wound, her fingers pressed into soft mush. As the knight had said, the wound had sealed already. She rolled the alderman onto his back again.

Acrida appeared at the tent flap again, her arms full of wood, and Deidre instructed her to make a large even pile inside the circle, near the healing symbol she had drawn. Acrida did as she was instructed.

"Acrida, I need clean strips."

"There is a tunic over there that I washed a few days ago."

"Wash more later today," Deidre told her, finding the tunic folded up.

The knight entered the tent then with the saddles and bridles. The hair on the back of his neck stood on end when he saw the five pointed star in a circle that Deidre had drawn on Van Necht's forehead. He put down the tack and turned to go outside to gather a load of wood, although part of him wanted to stay and watch what the old witch would do next. He had to admit that he was both frightened and fascinated by her ministrations and instructions. As he left, he was careful not to step into the three circles drawn in the dirt, although he did not know whether it would have mattered or not.

Acrida followed Deidre out of the tent and watched as she tore the shirt into strips and threw them into the kettle of water which was now boiling.

"Watch, Girl. We are calling on the power of the fire and the water now to help us," she told her. "-You may someday need to know this when I am not here to help you."

Seemingly mesmerized by the light of the flames, Deidre then began her incantations to summon the spirits of the fire, air and water.

After a few minutes, Albern arrived with several large logs. He entered the tent, and Acrida and Deidre followed. He carefully stacked the wood as Deidre directed him until the pile was more than two feet high.

"That will do," she told him.

She put the two furs on the pile of wood and secured them.

"Help me move him."

Taking hold of the ends of the wet coverlet beneath Van Necht, she, Acrida, and Albern transferred the nobleman to the pile of wood and tucked the wet coverlet around him that had already grown warm against his skin.

"Acrida, empty that crate and bring it here with the candle," Deidre instructed.

Deidre set the empty crate on its end near Van Necht's head and placed the candle on it. Then she took another candle from her pouch, a large black one, and set it near the center on the crate. Taking the feather and the paint she had used on Van Necht's forehead, she drew on the crate the image of a snake on a tree branch to the right of the candle and a snake among eggs on the left of it. In front of the candle she drew another five pointed star and drew a circle around it.

"Now, both of you come with me," she said, putting the feather and paint back in the pouches. "Acrida, bring some soap. -He does have soap, does he not?"

"Aye," Acrida answered with a small smile, retrieving the soap.

Deidre picked up the last woolen coverlet that had yet to be used, and they all went down to the stream followed by the hound that wagged its tail at all the activity. The sky was growing lighter as they walked. Once at the stream, Deidre spoke calmly as she immersed the coverlet into the icy water.

"Be brave, Sir Knight. Summon all your courage. For against your fear you must fight your hardest battle. And for you, My Dear, summon all your courage also. Your fear will help to bury this man."

In a voice that seemed different than her usual speaking voice, Deidre continued her instruction. To Albern and Acrida, it seemed as though the old woman's spirit alone was commanding them.

"Now, do as I do. Wash quickly. This is to show that our intentions, whether for harm or good, are pure ones, not muddied with misunderstanding or crossed reasoning."

The old woman immediately began to chant as she, taking the soap from Acrida, knelt by the stream and washed her hands.

The water from the stream seemed warm to their numb hands. Acrida took the soap from Deidre and worked her hands into a lather, but Albern froze.

"Must I?" the knight interrupted.

Deidre stopped and looked at the young man.

"Wash?"

"Be so *involved*?"

He hated to say it, but his conscience was rebelling against any direct participation in a pagan ritual- for any reason.

"Would you have him die?"

"I would lay down my life for him at a moment's notice, but I would not damn his immortal soul to Hell, nor mine."

"As you wish, Sir Knight," Deidre answered, rinsing her hands in the cold water. "Bring the coverlet."

Albern pulled up the cold, wet blanket from the stream, now heavy with its liquid burden.

"Do not dry your hands, Acrida. The heat from the fire will do that."

While Deidre chanted, they walked back to the camp with wet, freezing hands to the fire that blazed. The women held their palms toward the heat until their hands were dry and warm. The three entered the tent solemnly, and then the women knelt by the bed. Deidre lit the black candle in the center of the crate from the first candle; then she snuffed out the first candle and put it back in her pouch.

"Sir Knight, thy love for thy lord and friend is strong. Give me thy ring."

Albern immediately took off his ruby ring and gave it to the woman.

"It will render him some of your strength," she explained.

Deidre placed the ring in her right palm and waved her left hand over it, mumbling a few words. Then, holding the ring between her thumb and forefinger as she chanted, she passed the ring through the flame of the candle three times, and then she placed it inside the pentacle drawn on Van Necht's forehead. Taking a knife from her pouch, Deidre cut a lock of the lord's hair and entwined it in the ring; then she put the ring inside the pentacle on the crate. She pointed the knife at the ring there and chanted a few more words.

"Take that top coverlet off of him, turn him over, and put the wet one on him," Deidre ordered.

As Acrida and Albern complied with her instructions, Deidre held the blade in the flame of the candle, mumbling another incantation at the same time.

"We are drawing on the power of the earth which gave us the material for this knife, the power of the fire, and of the air to drive out the evil thing in this man which has invaded him and would kill him," the old woman explained.

Then taking the blade away from the flame, she pulled the wet coverlet away from Van Necht's shoulder, halfway baring his back. Without further hesitation, Deidre cut open the scar on the red, swollen shoulder. It was not a very deep cut, but, at once, the stench, freed from its imprisonment, filled the tent, accompanied by yellow pus that shot through the air and onto the three of them. Acrida, who was choking at the odor, immediately began to wretch at the pus, but since she had eaten nothing, there was nothing for her to vomit out. The knight's stomach also twisted. Deidre, however, was seasoned to dying things and only wiped the vile matter from her face. The flies, attracted by the ghastly odor, immediately landed on the wound.

More of the thick, yellow matter poured from the wound and steadily drained down Van Necht's neck, back, and arm. Deidre reached down to the floor and picked up one of the tunics she had taken off the alderman. She wiped up the pus and, setting it near the wound, let it catch the fluid as it drained out. Deidre looked then at Acrida, who had turned away, her stomach still heaving fruitlessly.

"Acrida, get some water from the kettle that is boiling outside and put it in a bowl with some salt. A handful is too much. Bring it here."

Covering her nose and mouth, Acrida gladly got up and rushed to get the water.

The knight watched Deidre press the flesh around the wound to help push the infection out. Acrida entered the tent again after a minute carrying a bowl of steaming water inside the tent; she mixed some salt with it and handed it to Deidre.

"This will have to cool before we use it."

The three sat down then, a little away from Van Necht for a while, watching as the sun rose through the door of the tent. Acrida leaned her head against her aunt's shoulder, her fatigue catching up with her again.

"Was she wrong? Does he not have the breathing sickness?" Albern asked after a few minutes.

"Aye, he has it!" Deidre answered. "-And the steam was a good way to treat it, Acrida. It helped to keep him alive until our arrival. However, he ails also from the knife wound. Both, in fact, are killing him. -Now help me roll him over. We need to lean him up."

After removing the damp coverlet that was growing warmer every minute around his body, they rolled him over onto his back again, and covered him again. Deidre took one of the saddles from the floor and put it behind the lord's back, propping him up against it. She leaned over Van Necht again and examined the shoulder wound. With the rag, she wiped up more of the pus that had oozed out. Ignoring the crawling flies that were invading it, she took the bowl of water that had cooled, said a few words over it, and poured some of the warm water into the wound until it overflowed. Then she set the bowl down, and smiled at the knight who was watching the procedure with interest.

"The power of the fire, air, and water- in the form of the bubbling water, and the power of the earth- in the form of the salt, combine to cleanse and cure the wound."

Sir Albern nodded.

Deidre soaked up the water with the cloth as it exited the wound and continued to try to encourage more of the discolored water and pus out of it by pressing on the mushy skin around the opening. Still no blood came out of the wound. Deidre sat back down again and wiped her hands and the knife on the nobleman's other discarded tunic that lay near.

"This is all we shall do for now. Acrida, I want you to go to sleep. You will be no help to me if you are weak and tired. -You also, Sir Knight."

Albern and Acrida did not argue. They stood up to find a place to lay down inside the rearranged tent.

"Be sure to stay within the circle," Deidre added.

Acrida was about to stretch out on the floor on the far side of the circle opposite the tent door when Sir Albern stopped her. He quickly removed his cloak and spread it on the ground. Acrida smiled appreciatively and lay down on it; the knight lay next to Acrida for warmth since all the furs were already on Van Necht's bed. Remembering her own woolen cloak, the old woman took it off and covered them with it. It was not long before they were both asleep.

Deidre rubbed her tired eyes and observed the afflicted alderman once more. This was certainly not what she had expected to find, she admitted.

Deidre went over to the side of the tent where the warlord seemed to keep his supplies. She found several crates and small containers. In one crate was some cabbage and onions. In another, all sorts of knives and oils and ropes. Eventually, she found a bowl and a large platter and a smaller platter. She took these outside into the morning light. Going to the fire, the old woman stoked the blaze and added more wood to the coals that were just to the right of the hot kettle.

Finding a variety of clean kettles, ladles, and crocks stacked near the fire, Deidre choose a medium size crock. Transferring a small portion of the already hot water into it, she put the smaller kettle beside the larger one over the brightly glowing coals. Deidre sat then before the fire and began to dig through her pouches again. Finding what she wanted, she threw a large, brown tree root and some garlic cloves into the small crock and covered it with a lid. She said a few words over the mixture and made a gesture with her hand; then she waited.

The air around the fire gradually became scented with the pungent odor of the root and garlic. After some time had past, Deidre lifted the lid to inspect the contents. Satisfied, she removed the crock from the heat.

Deidre stirred the water in the larger cauldron that continued to bubble and swirled the strips of cloth that swam around it. Deidre mumbled a few words over it and then fished out two long strips of cloth and a shorter one with the ladle. She carefully tangled them onto the larger platter she had taken from the tent. She filled an additional, small bowl with water from the kettle also. She carefully removed the cooked root from the crock and placed it on the smaller platter. Then she carefully carried the items back into the tent into the inner circle.

She put the platters and the bowl on the ground and then went over and emptied two of the large crates. She set one of the crates on its end as a table near her makeshift altar and set the platters and bowl upon it.

The cloth in the platters had already cooled in the chilly, winter air. Deidre wrung one of the two long strips of cloth over Van Necht's damp coverlet. Next, she shooed the mass of flies that were crawling in and out of the wound, but even her presence did little to divert them from the treasure they had discovered; and the flies were soon back again. Dipping one of the cloths in the remaining salt water, Deidre bathed the shoulder gently, cleaning the remaining pus from the skin. Afterward, she threw the rag outside the tent and the circle she had drawn.

She placed the blade of her knife back into the flame of the candle, chanting briefly. When it was hot, she cut the soft, grayish root into slices. Shooing the flies one last time, she covered the wound with one piece of the mushy root. The softened root stuck securely over the wound, effectively sealing it.

After placing the rest of the root into a leather pouch, Deidre then carefully removed the saddle from behind the lord's back. She picked up the braes she had taken off him earlier and his discarded pillow and stuffed them directly under the coverlet beneath him and then leaned him against them so that his head and his chest tilted slightly higher than the rest of him. She removed the top coverlet that was almost dry. Then she moved the other crate she had emptied beside the bed.

349

Deidre sat on this crate, and, taking the second cloth from the platter, carefully folded it and placed it on his forehead. She squeezed out the remaining, shorter, wet cloth over his dry neck and chest. Then she dabbed the wet cloth on his dry, cracked lips. She opened his mouth. She frowned when she saw that his tongue was also chapped.

"Hoc es poc us," she muttered, shaking her head, as she made the sign of the cross over his lips, heart, and stomach.

Turning his head to the side, she dipped the edge of the cloth in the small bowl of water she had brought from outside and put it in his mouth, letting the cooled drops of water absorb. She alternated doing this and wiping down Van Necht's face with the other end of the wet cloth.

As she waited for the water to soak in, she noted that the sharpness of his jaw and cheekbones made his face appear very serious, but also handsome. He did not have the good looks of the young knight, but he was far from plain. Certainly, she was not seeing him at his best, she had to admit. Sitting back on her crate, she examined his naked body, admiring his large muscular chest and thick arms. His hands were plump with brawn as were his thick thighs and calves. Truly, he was a well-formed man, a pillar of strength, cut down by fever. His yard was of good length as well, she noted. In fact, his body was far more appealing than any man Deidre had seen naked in a long time.-

Deidre dipped the rag into the bowl of water again and put the end of the cloth back into the nobleman's mouth. Then, picking up the two, damp coverlets, she left the tent and walked off to the stream again.

43

A little before noon, Deidre woke the knight to take over. He got up immediately, ready to do as she bid. She showed him how to bathe Van Necht's face with the wet cloth and how to put drops of water into his mouth as she had been doing for the last five or so hours. Albern was happy to see that Van Necht was no longer unresponsive, but was moving a bit with each cold, wet application of the cloth. He was also relieved that the wound did not smell near as rank as it had earlier, but for some reason smelled of garlic and some other odor he did not recognize.

With the knight's help, Deidre leaned Van Necht up and propped him against the saddle again. She shooed the flies off the poultice that were searching for a way inside the wound.

"What is that?" Sir Albern asked, referring to the dark, oozing mush that covered the wound.

"Tree root," she replied as she removed the discolored pulp and threw it out of the circle, out the open tent door.

The root landed on the ground in the sun where a swarm of flies immediately buzzed about it loudly until the lord's hound appeared and carried it away.

Deidre had already retrieved another skinny, boiled strip of cloth from outside and had seasoned it with salt water until it was cool. After she squeezed the water out, she then carefully folded the cloth in a crinkled manner. She shooed the flies away that were crawling inside the deep wound, then stuffed the cloth into it. Van Necht reacted weakly, trying to move the shoulder away from the pressure. Sir Albern even winced as he watched the witch stuff the cloth deep into the wound with her fingers, forcing it to take all the cloth inside. With the added pressure, more yellowish liquid spewed from the wound. Deidre mopped up the pus with a rag and then opened her leather pouch and removed another slice of root. Wrinkling his nose at the pungent garlic odor, Sir Albern watched as she mashed the gray root over the entire opening of the shoulder.

"Are you certain this will help?"

Deidre shrugged her shoulders as she threw the soiled rag outside the circle into the daylight.

"If it does not, nothing will."

They removed the saddle from behind Van Necht again and rolled him onto his side, propping him up so that his head and chest were slightly higher than the rest of his body, and recovering him with the wet coverlets. She dipped the end of the short cloth into the plain water again and put it back into Van Necht's mouth.

"Make sure to give him water in this way constantly. Also, when his coverlets grows warm, take them down to the stream and drench them again with cold water."

"What does that do?"

"Hopefully, it will drive out the evil spirit that has taken over his body. You see, the evil thing inside him is cold. -That is why he shivered and fought to stay warm when in truth his skin was burning with heat.

Thus, we do two things: We help cool the lord who is himself quite hot, and we increase the discomfort of the evil spirit. Hopefully, the evil spirit will grow so cold and uncomfortable that it will leave him."

"I see."

"Also, every hour or even half hour, you must turn him. This changing of positions will make the spirit uncomfortable also. Even turn him onto the side of his hurt shoulder. It will be well."

The knight nodded. Deidre stood up then and moved to where Acrida slept, preparing to curl up with her as Albern had.

"Wake me if anything changes, his breathing, anything," Deidre told him, lying down and spreading the woolen cloak over Acrida and herself.

"Is there anything else I can- or should do?"

Without looking up, Deidre put her arm around Acrida and answered, "You can pray."

Albern nodded and picked up the cloth and began to drip water into the side of his best friend's mouth as the old woman had instructed and began to whisper a whole series of Paternosters.

44

Deidre awoke against the pressure on her shoulder. She slowly pushed herself to a sitting position and blinked into the blinding light of the late afternoon sun.

"Is he dead?" she asked flatly.

"No, come see," the knight whispered, trying not to wake up Acrida who slept soundly still.

Deidre carefully got to her feet and peered at Van Necht in the warm light. Small droplets of water covered his skin. The old witch held her hand to his forehead, nodded, and then turned and stretched.

"The fever is quit. It is good."

She looked outside at the position of the sun; it would set in an hour or so. There were things that had to be done before the night was upon them again.

"Get some rest, Sir Knight. I will take a turn with him."

Sir Albern made a protest that he could continue for a few more hours, but Deidre told him that it might be a long night, and they would have to take turns sleeping. The knight got up from his seat then and returned to the warm place Deidre had just left beside Acrida.

Acrida's hunger pangs woke her. She sat up slowly, finding the knight sound asleep beside her. She rose groggily to her feet and went outside the tent; she found her aunt sitting in front of the fire roasting some meat and Van Necht's hound stretched out beside her gnawing on a huge bone.

"Ah, you are astir. Good. I was about to wake you."

"I am so hungry," Acrida complained, glancing at the raw meat on the spit.

"I just put it over the fire. Here, eat some bread."

Acrida, after hugging her aunt again, ate the piece of bread she offered, and then gathered all the soiled, stray cloths and clothes and the soap. She noticed as she headed for the stream with the laundry that her aunt had enlarged the circle. A furrow now encompassed the entire tent and the campfire.

She returned from the stream with the clean laundry as the sun set beneath the distant horizon, coloring the sky in a brilliant red-orange. Her mouth watered at the smell of the cooking meat.

"Put the laundry in the caldron."

"All of it?"

"Aye."

Acrida put the freshly wrung out cloths and garments into the kettle which Deidre had refilled with water and had set upon the fire again beside the spit. She then sat down on the other side of her aunt, taking the horn of ale she offered her.

"Where did you get the beef?"

"The steward was here. Patrik is his name?"

"Aldric-"

"Aye, that was it. He brought the meat and some cheese and some bread. He said he usually brought the lord his '*share*'. I tell thee, Acrida, this is the oddest nobleman I have ever heard tell of. He allows his head man to dole him out 'supplies', when in truth every bit of it he himself owns. I suspect that steward thinks himself the liege lord and the nobleman his vassal."

"I know not, Deidre," Acrida answered wearily. "I was told that Lord Van Necht is away from his lands so much that he has not the time to look after his affairs, so the day to day concerns are entrusted to the steward."

"So why does he not get a wife to handle such affairs as every other warlord hath?"

Acrida did not reply, but sat miserably silent.

"-Though one must wonder what noblewoman would have such a man who hath no real roof over his head, nor a servant to attend him," Deidre continued, unmindful of her niece's reticence.

"Drink, Acrida. You look thirsty. And eat more bread. You need your strength," she told her matter-of-factly. "-And I told that steward that we needed a chicken, for it simply makes better broth for the sick."

Acrida sipped the ale which she noted was quite strong while she gathered her courage to ask what she had to know.

"How fares he truly?"

"Better," Deidre nodded. "His fever quit a few hours ago. Now it simply comes and goes."

Acrida took a deep breath of relief.

"Come. Before the light is completely gone, we must get more water for tonight," Deidre told her, rising to her feet.

Acrida drank all the ale in the horn, then picked up two buckets, with Deidre carrying the goatskins and a small crock. While they walked to the stream with the hound, Deidre began her inquires about what had happened after she was taken from the village.

Acrida told her the long story involving the King, but omitted the particulars regarding her relations with Van Necht. She felt relieved to be able to tell someone what had happened and how frightened she had been and what she really thought about all these new people who were in her life.

When they returned with their containers full, the women sat down beside each other before the fire and served themselves part of the roast that was ready. Acrida ate the meat voraciously.

"Had you received no word of me?" Acrida asked, licking her fingers.

"None, nor any about the other girls."

"They live- or they *did* before the uprising at the palace. They were for the King's bed. He keeps concubines for his and some of his vassals' amusement."

"I will tell their families."

"But tell me, Deidre, have you received no word, even from Huntingdon, that we have been freed from the land?"

"Freed from the land?!" she asked, looking up from her food.

"Aye, it was a condition that if I gave counsel to the King, my family and I would be freemen."

"Freemen-" the old woman mused with raised eyebrows, while sopping up some of the juice from the meat with a bit of bread. "-I am not certain that is something that Lord Huntingdon would hasten to tell his own serfs."

Acrida smiled, feeding her scraps and trencher to the hound.

"'Tis possible that the advisers forgot to send word to Huntingdon since the matter was arranged the very day of the uprising at the palace. But, regardless, we are freemen now."

"Hmm," Deidre smiled. "What will Roe think of that?"

The women smiled.

"-So, this Lord Van Necht was not forcing you to stay with him."

"No," Acrida answered quickly and then looked away guiltily. "When I was made adviser, I was no longer his prisoner. I could have stayed anywhere as long as the King and the Court knew where to locate me. I suppose I should have returned to Brackenbach-"

Deidre smiled as Acrida spoke these words. She knew well there was little to draw her niece back to the village. She bit into a hunk of cheese and threw the dog the rest of her scraps.

"Methinks for a while it did not occur to me to return. That night at the palace, when the rebels attacked, I was standing in the dark in the midst of the fighting, terrified, watching as each of the nobles mounted his horse and fled. It was total chaos. I did not know what to do or where to go. I knew the rebels were out for the King. I did not know if they would actually hurt any of the palace servants or not. But I suppose I was in grave danger by being there at all, for late into the night, the King's garrisons retook the palace. Likely the knights attacked anyone they found, whether they were armed rebels or loyal palace servants."

"Aye," Deidre agreed.

She looked at her aunt's wrinkled face and soft, appealing eyes.

"But I never had to face that, Deidre. Before I knew what was happening, Lord Van Necht had somehow found me and pulled me on his horse."

The old woman smiled, impressed.

"We met later with the King at a small camp, and the next day Van Necht was coming back here to his lands. It seemed so natural for me to go with him, for I had already been with him for more than a fortnight. I suppose I should have requested for someone, even him, to return me to Brackenbach, since none of them offered. It just did not occur to me to ask.

"I am sorry," she added with a voice burdened with regret.

Deidre hugged Acrida to her and brushed her gnarled fingers through the young woman's uncovered, disheveled, black hair, murmuring, "It matters not, Child. -And this nobleman sounds quite valiant, coming to your rescue like that."

"Aye, he is valiant," she agreed sadly, "and that is not the only time. He came to be injured- fighting with some men who assailed us on the road and meant me harm."

Her expression became distraught as she remembered the incident, almost on the verge of tears.

"What troubles thee?"

"Deidre, he killed those men without hesitation -without even a weapon -with his bare hands."

The old woman watched as her niece's countenance changed from distraught to agonized at the memory.

"He is such a good man, so honorable, with such compassion for people," Acrida continued on, her words meant to assure herself more than anyone else. "Then, in an instant, he became deadly."

"He is a man of war, Acrida."

"Aye, I know, and when the King first sent me here, I was terrified of Van Necht. -The King is evil, and I did not know why he sent me to this lord except that he intended evil for me.

"-Nor did I know what Van Necht was planning for me, although it was never what I guessed. Above all, I tried not to anger him, lest he hurt me, for I knew he would not hesitate. -I never expected mercy or kindness from him- and that is what I received.

"-In truth, I *never* know what to expect from him!" she wept. "If I expect one thing, I find something else! Here, I expected him to recover from his injury, -only to find him dying!"

Acrida made a fist in frustration as tears streamed down her cheeks.

"God's eyes, I am *tired* of being *surprised!* I just want this all to end!"

Deidre sighed and hugged Acrida to her.

"Torture of the heart, Child, is a part of love," Deidre said simply.

"Oh, no, Deidre, I am *not* in love with him!"

"Are you not?" she asked. "Well, *I* would be if I were you. I wonder how you are able to avoid it?"

Her aunt did not know the half of it, yet she already knew everything somehow, Acrida realized miserably.

"After all, he is a handsome man," Deidre continued, "and if he has treated you kindly, that is a rare thing considering that he is highborn and a man of war. And he has risked his life more than once to protect yours- and you being a commoner. By the Blood of the Saints, Acrida, *I* would be mad with love for him."

The young woman's brave demeanor fell, and she began to weep unchecked at her aunt's words. Acrida thought she was near madness already with the mixture of love and hate and other emotions that she felt for Van Necht. She hated him for being born too high to marry her- and for loving some other woman, but more than anything else, she hated him for threatening to abandon her now in death.

And she hated herself for loving him.

Deidre held her niece close to her and rocked her as in times of old while Acrida's sobbing shook her body.

"Poor Child, how I hoped that love would come for you, and now that it has finally found you, Death is threatening to ruin all of your newfound joy."

"We are not lovers, Deidre."

"'Tis a pity," she mumbled softly.

"I am the one. *I* love him. -He already has a woman he loves, -one equal to his birth," Acrida cried miserably. "He has been kind to me, and that is all.

"-And all this I did not know until he became ill, when he began declaring his love to his lady in his sleep!" she complained bitterly. "All this time he has kept the truth from me!"

Her aunt sighed.

"Who is she?"

"I know not. -Hilta or something. He was mumbling, and I did not hear him well."

"Hmm-. I suppose a warlord as gallant as he would have a lady, castle or no," Deidre admitted with a sympathetic frown.

"It kills me to love him, Deidre!" Acrida sobbed miserably. "'Tis as if my heart has been rent to shreds! -All these months I have stayed with him, and as absurd as it was, allowed myself to hope- to believe that he might desire me, when, in truth, he has only taken pity on me for my situation!"

Deidre sighed and smoothed Acrida's black hair as the fire popped and hissed before them.

Acrida wept for a long while in the matron's arms until she had no more tears to shed; then she stared numbly into the jumping flames of the fire. Yet, there was more she had to know.

"Will he recover?"

Deidre took a deep breath.

"I will not give you false hope, My Dear. In truth, I can not tell yet. When I arrived early this morning, I would have wagered that he would not have lived to mid day. Yet, it is twilight now, and still he breathes. He shows promising signs of improvement now, but it will take much more before he is out of danger. At any time, his condition could worsen."

"Yet there is a chance that he may recover?"

"Aye."

"Then I know what I must do. -I must go."

"What?!" Deidre asked incredulously.

"I can not stay here, Deidre! I can not bear to see him buried! It would kill me! And yet if he lives, I can not bear to face him- not after everything that has happened -not now that I know about *her*!"

"But, Acrida-"

"Deidre, please, understand! I am completely within his power when he is near! I can not think clearly! I can not even eat! If I am here when he recovers, I will never be able to leave! I will make a fool of myself until he sends me away of his own accord!

"-Even worse, perhaps he will be so amused by my feelings that he will make me his wench, to warm his bed until he can be reunited with the lady he truly loves. Either way, the shame would be more than I could bear! 'Tis better that I go now!"

One stray tear ran down her cheek and fell to the ground.

"Acrida, surely this is unwise.-"

"With you here, he has the best of care. You have never needed my help- never wanted it! I have always been in your way! My presence is surely not needed now!"

"But Acrida, you will surely regret it! How can you leave, not knowing what his fate will be? You will be miserable not knowing his condition, constantly wondering if he is quick or dead."

"Aye, I shall be troubled, but I shall know that you were here and did as you were able no matter what the outcome."

Deidre said nothing, shaking her head.

"It will be enough for me! Believe me, Deidre, it is for the best! I will ask Sir Albern to deliver me to one of the other advisor's castles in a day or so, whenever you think you can spare us."

"Will you not even consider returning to Brackenbach?"

Acrida shook her head.

"Now that I have been appointed as a counselor, it is important that I stay visible, lest I lose my position and all I have suffered for."

The old woman sighed and rose to her feet. There was no point in arguing further with Acrida. The girl had made up her mind.

Deidre went back inside the tent and checked on Van Necht. Acrida watched from a distance as her aunt changed the poultice and stuffed a fresh cloth inside the wound. She noticed that the black candle on the altar had burned itself out and now a white candle burned in its stead. After her aunt had finished tending to the wound, Deidre woke the knight. She sent him home with her thanks and the assurance that she and Acrida could care for the lord by themselves through the night.

Sir Albern would not stay to eat by the fire, but taking some food with him, he immediately headed for his home which he had not seen in several days.

45

The next evening at dusk, Sir Albern rode into the little camp to check on his lord's progress. Van Necht looked much better and less parched; and he occasionally spoke, though only in a confused manner. His skin was cooler to the touch, but he was coughing again. Deidre told the knight that that was good, especially now that he had started coughing up the brownish, green mucus that was in his lungs.

The knight watched as the old witch removed the darkened root pulp from the wound. He grimaced when he saw the white maggots that were wiggling and twisting inside the wound.

"What evil witchery is this? He lives, yet the worms already feed on him!"

Deidre smiled.

"Be not afraid, Sir Knight. The worms are feeding on what is dead in this man's body."

"Will they not kill him?"

"'Tis the least of his troubles."

Still unsure, the knight watched as she removed the soiled cloth from the wound, taking out many of the grubs with it. She took a fresh cloth next, folded it as she had before, dipped it in honey, and then restuffed the wound, ignoring her patient's groan of pain. Once again, she pressed a fresh slice of tree root to the wound. Albern smiled as Van Necht groaned and muttered something angrily as Deidre rolled him over onto his injured shoulder.

"So where is Acrida?"

"Gone."

"To the village?"

"No, Lord Dewain's castle."

"You mean, she left?" Albern asked, quite stunned. "Why? Why now?"

Deidre shrugged as she pulled a coverlet over Van Necht, who was mumbling something about the quality of swords.

"Who can understand why the young do anything?"

"This is madness! You did not allow her to walk off alone, did you?"

Deidre raised her eyebrows.

"Acrida is a grown woman and does as she pleases, if you have not noticed," she answered. "It is pointless to argue with her."

Then seeing the genuine concern in the knight's eyes, she added, "She said some men rode through the village this afternoon whom she knew; she said she was going with them."

Deidre turned away from him and went back outside.

"Some noblemen?" Albern asked, following at her heels.

The old woman bent over the crackling fire, checking on the smaller crock that was boiling. She removed it from the fire and put a cloth pouch into the hot water, allowing it to steep.

"I think she said it was Lord Dewain himself. She said she knew the men from Court."

To her surprise, the knight began swearing under his breath. She sat down then beside the fire and warmed herself, wondering why this new development vexed the knight so.

Sir Albern sat down near her, but got up again after noticing the barrel of ale that remained off by itself. Looking amongst the supplies in the crate nearby, the knight found two horn cups.

"You need not worry, Sir Knight. Acrida will fair well; she was born under a lucky star. -Besides, I am capable of tending the lord alone now since his condition has improved. Methinks he may recover after all," she told him while she sorted through a nearby basket of food that Aldric had brought.

Finding and freeing a loaf of bread, she broke it into two parts and offered the knight half.

"I am not so sure-" Sir Albern said ominously, taking the bread.

"Art thou blind?" she interrupted, annoyed that the knight had so little faith in her healing powers after all this. "He is almost free from fever, and he is far more lively than when we arrived."

"That is not what I meant," he said. "Truly Van Necht is much improved. I just can not believe that Acrida departed now, right before she was able to see him recovered."

"Why is that? Did you think she was expecting thanks for tending him?"

Sir Albern filled one horn and then the other with the cool ale.

"No," he answered, handing her a horn. "I suppose I thought -with the way she felt about him that-"

"Acrida is a very proud girl. She did not wish to stay and risk having her feelings scorned or misused by the lord."

"Scorned?! -Why would she think that?"

Deidre observed the knight's passionate reaction curiously as she cut herself a hunk of cheese.

"Lord Van Necht is mad with love for your niece! He loves her so well that he-"

Albern stopped short suddenly, remembering his confidence.

"-I should have told you from the start," he finished simply.

Deidre smiled.

"Clearly it is Van Necht's feelings that are slighted here, not Acrida's, for he has shown her every kindness and gallantry, which he has not bestowed on *any* woman in several years!

"-Your niece well deceived me for I thought she loved him. -In truth, she declared to me that she did! But if she truly loved him, then she surely would not have abandoned him particularly when he is not fully out of danger."

Disgusted, Albern shook his head with a frown and sucked down half of his ale. He bit into the bread and sat down before the fire and stared into the flames.

Deidre chuckled.

"You are not deceived, Sir Knight. Acrida does love him well. She admitted it to me herself, -and it could be her only motivation for all she has done."

"Then why did she leave?"

"She is heartbroken."

"But why?"

Deidre smiled and made a gesture with her hands.

"It is different for serfs, Sir Knight, -at least, the serfs on Huntingdon's lands, for we have always been allowed to marry for love. Acrida has been hoping for love and marriage her entire life."

"She is heartbroken because Van Necht can not marry her?"

"Acrida is no fool. She surely knows *that* would be impossible."

"Then what?"

"She was aggrieved to discover he loves a lady already."

"What?! What lady?!" Albern demanded vehemently. "Van Necht has no lady! He will not even approach a lady! -For he is determined to never remarry as far as he can prevent it!"

"Acrida said that when he was talking in his sleep, he revealed his secret love of the lady," Deidre told him calmly.

"Impossible! Surely it was only a dream!" Albern declared fervently. "If Van Necht cared for any woman, lady or common, *I* would surely know, for I am his best friend and confidant!"

Deidre raised her eyebrows and drank her ale.

"-But *if* he was courting a lady, Van Necht would never do so in secret! His honor would not permit it! It is absurd!"

The old matron put the cheese on the bread and bit into them.

"Another woman?!" Albern continued to complain in exasperation. "How could she even believe it? I have known Van Necht for the better part of ten years. I have never known him to be happier or to be in better spirits; and Acrida does not know that she herself is the cause?"

Listening to the knight in amusement, Deidre smiled and cut another hunk of the cheese. Albern finished his cup of ale and refilled it, and took the piece of cheese she offered him, chewing slowly.

"Then again, I am uncertain that Van Necht ever told her how he felt. He leans toward silence. He believes actions are more important than words- though I have tried to tell him scores of times that women need to hear the words."

Deidre chuckled.

"Did she tell you what he said exactly? Did he say a name?"

"She said she could not hear him clearly. I think she told me it was -Halto?"

"Halto?" the knight questioned, trying to place the name.

"Hilde!" he moaned. "Gunhilde! Lady Gunhilde was Van Necht's wife. She died in childbirth years ago!"

Deidre snickered at this information and then began to cackle. What needless difficulties the young created for themselves! Then she forced herself to stop laughing when she saw the irritated look on the knight's face.

"Forgive me, Sir Knight. I was laughing at my niece, truly. So the lady died in labor, eh?"

"Aye, and took the baby with her."

"A pity."

"Aye, Van Necht went quite mad. -That was when he burned down his castle."

Now it was Deidre's turn to be astonished.

"Mean you that he burned it down himself? On purpose?"

"Aye."

She raised her eyebrows.

"-He must have loved her immensely."

"Actually," Albern replied as he drained his second cup, "he hated her intensely. He claimed he was giving her a head start to Hell."

Deidre raised her eyebrows again at this information.

"She- her body, -was in the-"

"Aye."

"Hmm-. So, why did he hate her so?"

"Gunhilde had made every day of his married life a misery."

Deidre sliced another hunk of cheese and handed the knight a large chunk.

"Van Necht was raised and trained in arms in Grenad. His parents had arranged for his older sister to marry into a noble household in the same kingdom. The match was apparently very successful, and his parents proposed a match for Van Necht with one of their daughters. Rather than return home after earning his spurs, Van Necht immediately went to war for Grenad against Herryck and won much acclaim and many honors on the field.

"After five years, but the year before Grenad fell to Herryck, his father died, and Van Necht at the behest of his mother returned home and assumed his responsibilities here. The family he had been pledged to sent word that one of their older daughters, Gunhilde, was recently widowed, and they betrothed her to Van Necht. She might have been a year or two older than him, but the lady's previous husband had once been a distinguished scholar in Carolus Magnus' Court itself."

"Impressive."

"Aye. Evidently, the old man had taken great pleasure in spoiling his young bride and had granted her every whim. Needless to say, a much earthier marriage to a young man of arms who cared little for learning or Court -with its people, intrigues, and new fashions did not enthrall the lady.

"Methinks Gunhilde despised Van Necht from the beginning for his lack of ambition and learning. I do not believe that they ever met before their marriage feast, but the food was not even cold upon the table before her complaining began, although initially with her speaking Grenadish, only Van Necht could understand what she was saying. Gunhilde made it clear to him that she hated Speyron. She hated Van Necht's lands. She despised the quaintness and vulgarity of Filberte's Court.

"From their first day together, the village was loud with gossip about them. The servants said she did not own a civil tongue, and she pecked at her husband day and night. There was even a rumor that she shut him out of his own bedchamber, though I do not know if it is true. -But once she learned Speyronese, she made her dissatisfaction known to everyone. Whenever I was present, she ridiculed Van Necht; she insulted his friends, his pursuits, his subjects and vassals, -anything he prized.

"For a while, or at least for the months while his mother lived, he attempted to placate Gunhilde, to win her with sweetness and patience and compliments. This accomplished nothing. As the months went by, she only became bolder. She would abuse him in public no matter who was present. Once, she even belittled him in front of King Filberte himself."

"And he endured it? Why did he not beat her?"

Albern shrugged.

"He claimed in the household where he was trained, he was taught not to take advantage of those weaker than himself. At the time, he thought it beneath his honor to strike a woman."

"Where was this?" Deidre asked incredulously.

Albern smiled, but continued his story.

"In all fairness, I think at first he was as astonished as anyone at his wife's ill-humor. For more than six months, he tried very hard to love her and did everything to please her. He bought her jewelry and gowns, took her to Court, and bought expensive furnishings for the castle. Anything she wanted, he gave her.

"She just complained more: He had poor taste; Court was boring or offensive; or it was just not the way she wanted it. There was no pleasing her," Sir Albern explained with a wave of his hand.

"After his mother died, he finally stopped trying. He began spending more time away from home on my fief. -And he volunteered for battle and engaged in any pursuit that required him to be away."

Deidre shook her head in disgust.

"You can not imagine the half of it," he continued. "After a year, she was no better. Then Van Necht thought perhaps Gunhilde might be different if she had a child to care for- or that is what people told him anyway. And the longer he thought about it, the more he wanted children."

The knight drank the rest of his ale and poured himself another cup.

"I thought it a poor idea, for there was no way for him to get Gunhilde with child without being in her presence. I told him he should forget the shrew, abandon her to his castle if he must, and get his sons through the mistress of his choice. There were ample, willing women to select from, believe me."

Deidre smiled.

"He would not hear it. His children would be legitimate. -And he would not shame his wife by having bastards with someone else while she had no children at all.-"

Deidre raised her eyebrows incredulously.

"Gunhilde was not enthused either, but she took the opportunity to demand more from Van Necht. If she were to have a child, then they were going to have to live in a better, larger castle, and they would need more servants to wait upon them. Once more, he agreed.

"I can not imagine what those nights with Gunhilde must have been like for him. I know the servants were threatened with death if they spoke of it. It was then that I saw the real alteration in his temperament. He was clearly wretched, and he became distant toward everyone.

"In the months that followed, the entire household changed as well. No one spoke anymore: neither Van Necht, nor his wife, nor the servants. Invited guests to the castle were unusual, and visitors that happened by felt uneasy there. Gunhilde herself stopped going out of the castle, and when she did, she was silent.

"I will never forget one, rare day when we were all out together looking over the livestock. His steward, Aldric, was showing Van Necht and his wife a stallion that seemed to be fertile but had to be manually 'helped' with each breeding. All Gunhilde did was begin to laugh, and immediately she was on the ground with a bleeding lip, with Van Necht standing over her fiercely, just daring her to say something. -I thought he would surely kill her right then."

Deidre raised her eyebrows.

"About two years later, Gunhilde informed Van Necht that his endeavors were finally going to be rewarded. True to his word, the craftsmen were employed immediately to add on to his castle. Additional maidservants entered the household. Van Necht seemed happier.

"On the day of delivery, Van Necht's other vassal knights and I were all feasting and drinking with him, waiting on the news of the child's arrival. Late, late into the night, the midwife came down from the bedchamber with a dreadful look on her face. She told Van Necht that Gunhilde was bleeding terribly and that the baby would not come. He went to the bedside of his dying wife, heartbroken and disappointed.

"Even the pangs of death could not thaw that shrew's heart of ice. With her last breath, she cursed Van Necht with all the hatred she could muster; then she died."

Deidre listened in disbelief.

"We were all horrified; Van Necht himself was speechless," Albern continued.

"After a while, he ordered everyone out of the castle, even his servants. We all were outside, wondering at his humor, when we saw the smoke and flames. Van Necht walked out of the door soon after and told us to leave the fire be.

"After that, he set up his war tent in this field and would not have anything to do with any woman. He refused to have any servants. Over the years, he has softened very little. We go drinking and wenching at the village stew, and Van Necht will tolerate the wenches' company for perhaps an hour or so, as long as they do not become too pushy.

"But your niece- and the bond they have developed- is uncommon, else Van Necht certainly would not have allowed her to stay with him as long as he has. -The few months they have shared together have done more to heal him than any poultice the best of healers could have made. -And now she is gone!"

Deidre smiled again.

"Sir Knight, do not vex yourself. 'Tis the nature of lovers. By name and form, lovers are quite mad."

There was doubt on Albern's face, and Deidre marked it well.

"You doubt they will reconcile?"

The knight sighed and ran his hand over his hair.

"Life, as you know, is brief. Wars make widows. Who is to say that there will be a tomorrow for Lord Van Necht or myself or you?"

Deidre nodded as she observed the knight's discouraged face, the slump of his shoulders and the knit of his eyebrows.

"I see you have loved and lost. Did you lose her to death or to another man?"

Sir Albern did not look at the old woman, but picked up a stick and poked at the burning logs in the fire.

"My love was married before I met her," he smiled.

"A pity."

"It makes me *aware* of how lucky Van Necht is to have love and joy within his grasp, and it makes me angry to see how he does not snatch it up before it is gone."

"You have a rare gift, in one so young, to know what is most precious in life. Others, if they ever discover this truth, will not know it until they are much older and most opportunities are past."

Albern sat in silence, brooding now.

"This woman, do you ever see her?"

"Very rarely now. A few years ago, her husband used to bring her to Court. Then they stopped coming."

"I am sorry."

Albern shook his head.

"It is as she wished. She asked me to stay away."

"-Because she loves you," Deidre finished.

The wise, old woman surmised that theirs was not an unconsummated love. It must have been agony for both of them to see each other and not be able to touch or speak without arousing the justified suspicions of the husband.

The two sat in silence for a while and finished their bread and cheese. Then Deidre got up and took the steeping cloth out of the cooled water in the small crock. She retrieved another horn cup from the crate and filled it with the brew.

"What is that?"

"Just some herbs to strengthen his condition."

Albern rose to his feet and followed the woman into the tent. She set the drink on the crate beside the bed and rolled him onto his back and leaned him forward, putting the saddle behind him again to prop his head and chest up. The movement woke him from dozing. She put the cup to his lips and poured a bit into his mouth.

Van Necht uttered a complaint and made a face, but swallowed the liquid.

"Hand me that honey," Deidre instructed the knight.

Albern handed her the crock which was nearby and watched as the old woman added a dab to the brew and stirred it with her finger. Then she poured a little more into the nobleman's mouth, who still grimaced, but swallowed.

46

Lord Van Necht, hearing the voices around him but unable to focus on any particular word, slowly roused himself. Feeling a cool, wetness on his forehead that was quite soothing and turning his face to it, he, with some effort, opened his eyes. He could just perceive a warm, bright light and some blurred forms that accompanied the voices. He blinked slowly as his eyes began to distinguish his surroundings.

"Look! He is waking!" came a familiar voice.

Van Necht felt the wetness wipe his face again.

"My Lord, Van Necht? Can you hear me?"

Van Necht's mind registered the question slowly.

"Of course, I can. Am I deaf now?" he mumbled slowly.

Van Necht blinked again and looked around slowly. The light was the late afternoon sun filtering in through the wide open tent door. He was lying on his back in the very center of his tent on something incredibly hard and uncomfortable. What had happened?

He rolled his head to the side and looked up at the person who was still talking, fast and excitedly above him. Sir Albern smiled at him with a grin that showed all his teeth.

"Albern," Van Necht mumbled. "What are you doing here? Why are you not training the men?"

"The men are well, My Lord. I just left them in Sir Geoffrey's care a little while ago."

Van Necht tried to sit up then, but was too weak to do so; immediately pain shot through his body.

"God's eyes, I feel wretched," he muttered, and then he was overcome by a violent fit of coughing.

Albern helped him to roll to one side, and then he beat firmly on his back as the alderman coughed.

"Owh! That hurts!" Van Necht managed to complain between breaths. "Stop that before I break your cursed arm!"

Albern was so happy that he let him have his own way. Van Necht continued to cough for another long minute. When he finally stopped, he rolled onto his back slowly again, while trying to catch his breath, and watched as the knight who was talking wildly, embraced someone.

"C'sara?"

"You did it! You did it! Thank God and the Saints, you did it!" the knight was saying excitedly.

"Did what?" Van Necht was asking.

"*We* did it," the other one answered, coming over to the alderman.

Van Necht peered at an old, heavy set villein woman standing over him. As he examined her shape, her face with its wrinkles, and the gray wisps of hair that escaped her woolen headrail, he was quite sure he did not know her. He continued to look at her, wondering who she was, why Albern was so happy, and why C'sara had not appeared yet.

"I tell you," the knight said gaily, holding the woman in his arms, "if you were not an old, married woman, I would take you out of here and make you mine forever!"

Van Necht observed in bewilderment as his vassal gave the old woman an honest kiss on the lips.

The old woman laughed while patting the knight on the back and replied, "I am not that old, Sir Knight."

Albern laughed and kissed her again.

Letting the woman go, he returned to Van Necht's side.

"You had me frightened out of my wits, My Lord! When you get stronger and back to your old self, I am going to pound you senseless!"

To Van Necht's surprise, the knight hugged his neck and gave him a kiss on the cheek as well.

"What devil has gotten into you?!" Van Necht demanded.

He did not know what had happened, but it was clear that Albern had become a raving lunatic.

"I am well, My Lord! I am better than well! But *you* have been so very ill for more than a senight now that we thought for sure you would die! In fact, we were pondering whether to start digging your grave or to just fill your tent with kindling wood! As you can see, we opted for the latter," the knight added with a gesture to Van Necht's bed.

Van Necht stared at him incredulously, but looking down, realized that he lay a few feet above the ground on a stack of wood. He looked back at his friend in astonishment.

"Have I been that ill?"

"By the angels in Heaven, aye!" laughed the knight in relief. "And this woman- this *wonderful* woman- saved your life!"

"I am still amazed that he lived," she commented dryly.

"Do I know you?"

"This is Deidre. She is Acrida's aunt. I had to go all the way to Huntingdon's lands to retrieve her! We have been tending you night and day, but mainly it has been Deidre."

Van Necht looked again at the old woman, not sure of what to say or think about meeting C'sara's kinswoman under these conditions. This was all happening rather quickly.

"Get him to drink some more of this brew while he is awake," Deidre instructed Albern as if Van Necht was not even present.

She handed the knight the cup. Albern obediently sat back down on the crate beside Van Necht and helped him to lean up. He put the cup to his lips.

After one taste, Van Necht pushed the cup away.

"Ugh! Disgusting! What is this foul liquid?"

"'Tis an herbal brew to make you stronger with some honey to sweeten it," Albern told him, urging him to drink some more.

"I do not want it," Van Necht said.

"Oh, now it starts!" Deidre commented with a wave of her arms. "'Twas much better when he was senseless."

She walked back over to the bed and said in a voice that was not to be crossed:

"Listen well, My Lord! I have tended thee for more days and nights than I cared to. Somehow thou hast lived, but I will not have all my work come to nothing so near the end, so thou shalt drink this potion until I say otherwise. Hear me?"

Van Necht was stunned at her audacity. Then he remembered that this was C'sara's aunt, and obviously she had learned her sharp tongue from someone. He sighed and decided not to argue. He held his breath and drained the entire cup that the knight offered him.

Satisfied, Deidre turned away.

Having finished the cup, the knight gave him a horn of plain water to help remove the unpleasant taste from his mouth. Van Necht found himself to be quite thirsty and gulped down the water rapidly. The knight refilled the horn immediately.

"Where is C'sara?" he asked, drinking more of the water.

"She is not here," Albern told him calmly.

"Where is she?"

"She went to Lord Dewain's castle. -Likely about some sort of business for the King," Albern said casually.

"Oh," Van Necht replied, tremendously disappointed. "-But I suppose that is part of the position she holds- at the King's beck and call like the rest of us."

"Aye," Albern agreed.

Van Necht was silent, wishing she was here. But something very important must have arisen to force her to leave him when he was so ill, he thought.

"Did she say anything before she left?" he asked.

"I was not here when she was collected, My Lord," the knight replied.

Van Necht nodded slowly and lowered his head back down on the furs. Albern tucked the coverlet around him again and turned and gave Deidre a knowing look.

47

After a long fit of coughing, Van Necht sat on the side of his bed and inhaled slowly, a coverlet draped about his shoulders. The room was spinning very slowly, and he was still very weak, but he was much improved. He had been able to sit up for short periods for the past few days. It was easier for him to breathe today in particular, between coughing up mucus. His whole body ached though from the hard bed and from the coughing.

As he sat feeling both ridiculous and helpless in his idleness, Van Necht rolled his arm around slowly, stretching his recovering shoulder. He was rewarded with both a sharp pain and a dull ache. The old woman entered the tent then with a bowl of food and a spoon and handed it to him.

Van Necht looked at it: bits of chicken and bread pressed into mush, mixed with broth. He looked back at Deidre who was sitting down on a crate with her own trencher. She was eating leeks and cabbage, half of a roasted chicken that dripped with greasy juices, and half of a loaf of bread with cheese. Van Necht looked back again at his own bowl of wet mush.

"What is the matter?" she asked, biting into the chicken breast.

Van Necht glared at her.

"Needest thou ask?"

She raised her eyebrows and wiped her mouth with her sleeve.

"You should not complain, My Lord. You were lucky to get solid food at all today."

"Luck, was it? Tell me this, Woman: How do you expect me to gain my strength on nothing more than water and broth? Do they not have ale in whatever part of Hell you come from?"

"Aye, we have it," she smiled. "We have lots of things- including the sense that God gave us. If I give you the food you desire too soon, likely, your stomach, not tolerating it, would throw it back up, making you weaker than you already are. Then where would we be?"

Van Necht glared at her. Deidre, feeling his gaze on her, continued to eat her dinner with unconcern.

Frowning, the alderman picked up the wooden spoon and scooped up the mush and tasted it. Actually, it did not taste near as repulsive as it looked. He swallowed a mouthful and then drank some of the water from a ladle that the witch kept in a bucket beside his bed.

"Will I have whole food tomorrow?" Van Necht asked.

"Perhaps."

"Perhaps! God's Wood, Woman! There is nothing wrong with my teeth!"

"Do *not* take that tone with me, My Lord! 'Tis no fault of mine that you were wounded, nor that you became ill!"

Van Necht glared at her again, hardly believing that this woman was related to his sweet C'sara. He wished she were here. She would never treat him this way, nor allow her aunt to.

His mind drifted back to thoughts of Acrida then as it did a hundred times a day. He wondered what she was doing and where she was. How he missed her! He found that her very absence created a physical ache within his chest.

"I hate this bed," Van Necht began again. "It is impossible to lie in any comfortable position, nor to get any real rest upon it."

Deidre rolled her eyes at the man's tireless complaining. It was all he had done since he had improved enough to speak.

"Is it my fault, My Lord, that you have no bed? Surely it would not be a terrible strain on your subjects to have a carpenter build you a proper bed. -Ah, but why have a bed when you have no real roof to house it under? And why have a house when you have no servants to keep it for you?"

"Witch, why dost thou bark at me? Is your purpose to know why I have no fine house and servants? Hark, I shall tell thee! What care I for a fine house with servants when I am never here to enjoy it? When am I ever here at my own lands?"

"Well, you seem to be here now."

Van Necht's temper flared.

"Always at the King's bidding, am I!" he answered through grit teeth. "Or on some battlefield far away, my duty will lead me!"

"Oh, forgive me, My Lord. I thought being lord of these lands and of these people was also your duty."

Van Necht glared at her dangerously.

"Have I injured these people?" he asked hotly.

Deidre raised her eyebrows.

"Your subjects do not seem to have suffered, My Lord. It is clear to me and to all that you are a man of war who puts his duty to his king before his own desires. So answer me this-"

Van Necht swallowed the mush and scooped up another mouthful, consuming it slowly.

"Who are you at war with?"

"What?" Van Necht asked. "Speyron is preparing for war with Herryck, do you not know? The fighting will begin in the spring most likely."

"That may be so, My Lord, but you are at war already. You have given up your possessions and separated yourself from any who love you."

Van Necht looked at her in confusion.

"You do not live the life of a man who has hopes and desires for the future," she explained, "but as one who is mortally wounded already and is only awaiting the final blow. -Perhaps this is your wish. -Perhaps that is why it was so difficult to pull thee back from the grip of death."

These words further irritated Van Necht, who was completely not expecting them.

"That is absurd!"

"In fact, finding none to fight, you seem to have declared thyself thine own enemy, My Lord."

"Wh-"

"Your vassal Sir Albern loves you well. He speaks highly of you, -as does Acrida. They both say that you are a man of the highest integrity, a good man, -a man they would gladly suffer for. Yet you do not live like *you* believe you are a good man, worthy of a long life and happiness. To me, you seem like a man who thinks himself either a villain -or accursed."

"'Tis not so!"

"There is a remedy for it," she continued undeterred. "-If, by your actions, you have injured your own honor, you will have to take some time and negotiate a peace with yourself. You must accept what you have done and forgive it and resolve not to do it again."

"I have *never*-"

"Go to your confessor when the interdict is relaxed."

"I have done nothing to sully my honor!" he answered hotly.

Deidre shrugged.

"Then perhaps you are in this condition because someone has cursed you, and you gave power to the words by believing it."

Van Necht stared at her, bewildered.

"Assaults of this nature are like poison, My Lord. They are hardly detectable, yet they can cripple or even kill you simply by poisoning your thoughts and wounding your spirit. Yet, they are even more sinister than poison, for they turn you against yourself, and no enemy's attack can equal the damage we can do to ourselves."

"I-"

"-The Devil, too, uses such means to attack us," she continued. "Regardless, if someone attacks you with words and accuses you falsely, My Lord, shut her mouth or flee, but you must not believe what she says! Once you have believed it, 'tis difficult to root out the doubt and criticism that remain."

"I-"

"And yet, if this is what has already happened, there is only one thing you can do: You must tirelessly defend thyself against your own doubts and any self-berating thoughts for as long as they continue to plague you. Be assured, you are lost and will have no good future if you continue to belittle and condemn yourself where you are innocent."

The old witch resumed eating her dinner again quietly, leaving the warlord wondering at her words.

48

"Wilt thou be still!"

Lord Van Necht set his jaw to control himself and his temper, as he sat obediently still on the crate. The witch was changing the dressing on his shoulder and was working a strip of cloth into the wound.

"Owh! Woman, be careful!" Van Necht growled at her, reacting from the intense pain from the wound that was being forced open again.

Van Necht winced again, cursing.

"Enough! Stop, I say! Let it alone!"

"Quit thy whining!" Deidre answered, hurrying to finish.

"Am I not lord here, Woman? I command thee to take that devil magic out of my shoulder now and let it heal the way that God intended it!"

Deidre, with equal irritability, took the nobleman unceremoniously by the ear and yanked him backward toward her.

"Let go of me!"

"Hear me, My Lord. I have saved your life by this potion, and I will continue to use it on you until methinks you are completely cured. When *I* say, not you! -You would be wise not to cross me!"

Eyeing the determination in her face and the crystal amulet the witch wore about her neck, Van Necht, with impressive self-control, forced himself to be still and to endure the humiliation as well as the pain of his shoulder.

With the man's compliance, the witch finished her administrations. She finished by bandaging the entire shoulder with a long strip of cloth; then she carefully helped him get his arm into the sleeves of his layered tunics. Van Necht stood up slowly and made his way to the flap of the tent into the crisp, cold air. Deidre followed him and placed his fur mantle over his shoulders.

"I am brewing you another drink."

Van Necht groaned.

Deidre ignored him and went to the cooling crock that was near the fire. Removing the sachet of cloth, she poured the brew into a cup and handed it to Van Necht. He took it and smelled it, wrinkling his nose.

"What is it?"

"Vervain and Angelica- 'Twill help your cough."

"Angelica? Is not that suppose to ward off witches?"

"Aye, like catmint wards off cats."

Van Necht raised his eyebrows. Then he held his breath and gulped the warm liquid down. He drank the entire contents, then was overcome by a fit of coughing that continued until his lungs were rewarded with the dispersal of some brown phlegm.

Van Necht caught his breath and sat down near the fire, the coughing already making him weak. He sniffed the air then, his nose scrunching at his own stale body odor.

"I want a bath."

"Indeed," she agreed, adding more wood to the fire. "I will heat some water for you."

"I prefer to bathe in the stream."

"Why does it not surprise me," she muttered, "that you would prefer to wallow in a stream like a dog than to take a proper bath like a civilized man?"

He glared at her.

"I have no tub, and I am no villein child," he answered testily, "to be washed with a rag and a pan of warm water by an old woman."

"At present, 'tis your only choice, My Lord."

Van Necht sighed.

"Do not bother with the water then."

Deidre shrugged.

He watched as she sat before the fire and began looking through several leather pouches. His thoughts, as they did whenever there was an idle moment, turned immediately to Acrida again. He frowned.

At last, not able to withstand any more silence, he said, "Tell me about C'sara."

Deidre looked up from what she was doing and regarded the alderman. Although he had made the request casually, his eyes revealed a keen interest in the subject.

"What do you wish to know?"

"How did you come to raise her?"

"Her mother drowned in the lake near our village," was her matter-of-fact reply.

"And her father?"

"He died of a fever shortly after her birth."

"How did her mother drown? Was she a poor swimmer?"

Deidre laughed once and then frowned.

"She could not swim at all, My Lord."

"Then what was she doing in the lake? Did she fall in?"

"Aye, or was pushed.-"

"Pushed? Was there no inquiry into the matter? Were there no witnesses? Was there no one near to fish her out?"

"At the time, she was fleeing the villagers and the alderman's sheriff who had come to arrest her. Her pursuers were hesitant to jump into the lake after her."

"Why was that?"

"They thought her a witch."

Van Necht smiled at the irony of this statement.

"Was she?"

"No," Deidre replied.

"Then why did they think that-"

"Truly, they did not know what to think, My Lord," she explained simply, "for they thought they had caught her trying to make a sacrifice to the Goddess for a good harvest."

"Are you in earnest?"

"Aye," Deidre sighed, wrapping her cloak closer around her.

"Was she?" Van Necht prodded with interest, as he leaned over and put another stick on the fire.

"Oh, no, my sister was devoted to the Faith. She never in her life worshipped the Goddess."

"Then what was she trying to do?"

"I know not. Change the nature of life?" Deidre shrugged. "She was quite mad at the time."

"Mad?"

"Aye."

"What caused her to go mad?"

"-I know not," Deidre replied, shaking her head. "Why does anyone go mad? Hardship. Loss. Pain. -I just know she truly believed she was doing the best for her child."

Van Necht looked at her, bewildered.

"My sister was melancholy after Acrida's birth, then her husband died. Then there was a drought on the lands, and after the village harvested Huntingdon's share of the crops, there was not much left for the village. We were hungry that year, but we lived," Deidre shrugged.

Van Necht looked at the old woman with expectation.

"We do not receive much outside news in our little village, nor many visitors, particularly when Huntingdon is on his other lands. But that spring, a sermonizer happened through our village and stopped to preach.

"He spoke of the evil of the times, the wickedness of King Filberte and his Court, the sinfulness of the Bishop, and he said that all of the kingdom's problems were punishment from God for sins. He said that the drought we had had was nothing compared to the chastisement that was in store for our kingdom if everyone did not repent. God would destroy Speyron and remove the memory of it from those left on the earth. He could not say for certain whether the kingdom would be undone by poor weather, famine, plague, or war. He seemed to think all were likely. And he talked about a monk in an abbey somewhere that had prophesied that a time would come when Speyron would be overrun with barren women."

"Truly? That was prophesied?"

"Aye, though at the time, I scoffed at the idea. Needless to say," she continued, "he frightened many villagers with his talk. The parish priest was busy the entire week hearing confessions.

"My sister was deeply stirred by the sermon. It was all she spoke about. Then she began to say that the barren women foretold of were the ones truly blessed, for they would not have to fear for their children living in this unpredictable and evil world."

Van Necht raised his eyebrows.

"I remember her day by day silently watching her sweet, happy, beautiful child playing in the dirt in front of her hut. But I never suspected what my sister was planning. -Acrida was likely about two years old at the time.

"On that terrible day, I was out gathering plants in the meadow, and one of my neighbors came running to me. 'Come quick, come quick, your sister is killing her child!' she told me."

Van Necht, aghast, stared at the old woman.

"She tried to sacrifice C'sara?!"

Deidre held her hand up toward the lord to calm him.

"That was what she told me, but it was not the truth. My sister loved Acrida with her whole being. It was not her death that was her aim.

"When I arrived at her hut, the sheriff and most of the village were standing outside the door, shouting for entrance. You could hear Acrida wailing in distress. My sister had barricaded the door, but the sheriff and his men eventually broke in. What they saw frightened them.

"The sheriff brought my sister outside before all the villagers and began to question her. She was covered in blood, still clutching her large knife, with the blankest look on her face. She seemed stunned that they had interrupted her. I suppose her Heaven-bent mind did not grasp the harm she had inflicted on her child- or herself.

"'Why have you killed your own child?' asked they. 'Did you drink her blood?' 'Did you do this for the Goddess?' asked they."

Deidre shook her head, disgusted.

"They spoke of Acrida as if she were already dead, but I could still hear her crying. I could not yet get into the hut, but I watched as men and women emerged from it, crossing themselves in distress and weeping.

"When I finally managed to get into the house, I was amazed. It was a mess. There was blood everywhere. Acrida was crying, and her abdomen was sliced open."

"She *gutted* C'sara?"

"Aye, well, no, she did not. I think she meant to cut out her womb. Truly, I am not certain what she thought she was doing; for if you wanted to cut it out, the parts are too small on an infant."

Van Necht stared at her, horrified.

"Perhaps she had tried one thing and then decided to try another," Deidre added. "Perhaps after she saw her child screaming and bleeding, she suddenly did not have the heart to complete what she had planned."

Deidre shook her head at the memory.

"I did not stay to watch what befell my sister, for Acrida needed immediate help. I grabbed her up and took her home and tended her; and she improved, of course. -The wound was not as bad as it looked. What my sister had done, and perhaps it was an afterthought, -but perhaps not, was burn the region, perhaps hoping to make her barren through heat."

Van Necht winced.

"Methinks she must have used the knife, heated red hot. -Anyway, I was told by a neighbor later that when my sister at last had tried to explain herself, she had rambled about barrenness and about blessing. No one understood what she meant, but *I* knew."

Deidre shook her head again.

"Thus, since she was covered in blood and talking out of her head, they concluded she had been offering Acrida to the Devil or the Goddess to assure a good harvest.

"Of course, this could not have been further from the truth, as I explained before, but with all the villagers now decrying her as a witch at the top of their lungs, she became so frightened that when she managed to get free of the sheriff's men, she ran."

Van Necht listened, absorbed in the story.

"With the whole village raising the hue and cry against her and giving chase, she ran to hide among the trees and brush that grew along an overhang at the lake. The men cornered her there, and while trying to arrest her, she fell in the lake and there drowned. The whole incident was senseless really."

Deidre was silent then.

"And Acrida has lived with you ever since then?"

"Aye, with me and my husband, Roe."

There was another silence.

"So, Acrida truly cannot have children then," Van Necht said.

Deidre looked at him curiously and smiled.

"'Tis possible that my nitwit sister was successful, but we will not know for certain until Acrida snares the interest of a man."

"Has there truly been no one?"

Deidre shook her head.

"Even though this happened in her infancy? Methinks over time the village would have forgotten."

Deidre snorted.

"Such tales have a life of their own, My Lord. No amount of time will ever fade it. As the years pass, the story grows even more fantastic. I think the latest version said my sister changed into a bird and flew out over the lake to escape the men pursuing her until, due to her weakened state, the spell broke; and she fell into the water and drowned."

"But why punish C'sara for the deed of her mother?"

"Oh, they are not punishing her, My Lord. The entire village fears her due to her unexpected recovery as well as for her mother's bad end. Everyone knows the story; and all have shunned Acrida's company-especially her peers. Some, no doubt, believe her to be a witch, but others think her possessed by a nether world being. Thus, whenever there is a poor harvest or someone's hog or chicken dies, the villagers never fail to point at Acrida."

Then Deidre shrugged again.

"Of course, my niece's sharp tongue is more than most men would abide as it is."

Van Necht smiled slightly.

"Tell me, My Lord, how did you come to think that Acrida could not bear children?"

"I was only curious because C'sara believes she can not. She actually requested first, in return for her counsel, that the King should repay her with a baby- from a foreign country."

"What?!" Deidre asked with a startled laugh of disbelief. She shook her head, muttering, "I wonder if it ever occurred to that girl to try to get a babe in the usual way before getting the King involved."

"So, why does she not share your knowledge of healing?" Van Necht asked.

"Although we have been serfs on the lands for generations, our neighbors' misgivings have been so strong about Acrida that Roe and I feared for her life, especially as the story was known not only to our village, but all over Huntingdon's lands and possibly, for all we knew, all over Speyron. We had hoped to avert any future charges of witchcraft or devil worship which would surely follow her by taking her daily to see Mass and by not involving her in my practice of the healing arts. To a point we were successful, but then she started to be troubled by strange dreams and nightmares."

"I know about those," Van Necht muttered.

"Aye, I suppose you would," she smiled. "Roe was very concerned about them, for although it comes to her quite innocently, he feared the villagers, when they learned of her foretelling, would accuse Acrida of summoning evil spirits for the information -or of simply bringing about the events that she foresaw through the dark craft."

The conversation abruptly ended then as the wiry, little parish priest approached the fire and bowed to the alderman. Van Necht had been so involved in the tale that he had not noticed the man's approach.

"Good day, My Lord. It is good to see you up and so much improved! I have been praying for your recovery since I heard you were unwell; and I thought today you might welcome a visit."

He warmed himself before the fire and immediately began talking.

49

The sounds of music, idle chatter and laughter filled the small and very warm, smoky hall. While two monks strummed a tune on their lutes, a large group stood about the brightly burning fire, drinking horns of mulled wine as they exchanged the latest gossip.

The cheerful air of Collation, however, could not penetrate the persistent melancholy that lately overwhelmed the King of Speyron. Christian sat brooding in the darkest corner of the chamber, absently observing the brothers at the distant table amusing themselves at various games. After watching Bennet make a move on the chess board and then laugh heartily at some joke made by his opponent, the King moved his eyes away and sighed regretfully.

Long ago, Sir Gage had taught him that some sort of loss accompanied every important decision a man made; it was unavoidable. Over the years, Christian had found that what was true for a knight or nobleman was doubly true for a king. And although he had learned to expect and even anticipate casualties of loyalty, high esteem, and, of course, good men in battle, the loss was still bitterly painful to endure. -Bennet's friendship was one such casualty.

A fortnight after their quarrel, Bennet still had not wavered in his determination to forsake him. Thus, surrendering to his frustration, Christian at last had resolved to depart from the monastery. However, the very hour he drafted the letter to Olbert instructing him to send his bodyguards to retrieve him, the snow had begun to fall. The messenger from the abbey had not been gone three hours when he had returned, reporting that the snow was coming down heavily and was already so deep that the road could not be safely traveled.

Hence, Christian had been forced to continue here. Melancholy had settled upon him almost immediately. He grew lonely; and he began to intensely yearn for home: He ardently missed not only Kaith, Paschal and Felix, but even his bodyguards, his cook, his favorite minstrels, and all the rest of his servants, and especially Cedd, his valet. He even longed for the tedious company of Grey, Olbert and Dewain. There was nothing at St. Brychan's but silence and work, and Christian now found it even more difficult to endure than at first. Even Collation had lost its savor: The King found himself surrounded by people he had nothing in common with- and their simple amusements, neither new, nor diverting. The only relief from the boredom and isolation came to him in sleep, and lately his depression had allowed him very little.

He had been at St. Brychan's for two and a half months now, and it had been more than five weeks since he had received any correspondence from his ministers. Everyday he hoped a messenger would arrive or that the weather and roads would clear enough to send a rider to the palace with his dispatches. However, over the past ten days, the snow had been even heavier at the abbey, thus further disappointing his hopes.

As the talk around him became more distinct, the youth rose from his chair and withdrew to the nearby window, out of earshot, and opened the shutter. The cold air was brisk and refreshed his hot face. As he watched the thick snow fall peacefully to the ground, he could still hear bits of the monks' conversations. He immediately turned his thoughts to Kaith and tried to think about her. Was it snowing where she was?

These past weeks, the King had been so hungry for news from the outside that he had forsaken his common sense and had begun to turn his ear to the guestmaster, for the monk reported the latest rumors brought in by the abbey guests. Although the gossip was less than credible and served only to feed his fears and despondency, he had hung on every word. Lately, however, the rumors had caused him so much unease that for self-preservation alone he would not allow himself to hear anymore.

It was actually from this gossip that Christian had discovered that he was not greatly admired as a king. Although the facts of the events discussed were usually inaccurate- even outrageous, the accompanying low opinions and criticisms allowed no misinterpretation of how he was perceived. At first, he had been surprised, even angered, that his own people spoke as carelessly of him as they did. Then as the guestmaster retold what a pilgrim from New Herrycksland said or what a pilgrim from Londinium said, it became apparent to Christian that he was not highly respected *anywhere*; and this revelation hurt him deeply.

The first rumor he had heard was that he had been gravely wounded during the revolt at his palace and even now lay near death there. The variations to this tale were that he was gravely ill or horribly disfigured; either way, since the uprising, he refused to show himself to anyone, but kept solely to his private chambers. Therefore, some had begun to refer to him as 'Christian the Absent'.

There had also been several accounts about how many had died in the retaking of the palace: numbers ranged from a hundred to thousands. Supposedly the palace wall was covered with the heads of rebels and suspected traitors, and the sight of them was enough to scare the Devil himself away.

Persistent talk had also circulated about recent changes at his palace. Traveler after traveler verified it was no longer the great market place it had been a few months ago. Few merchants gathered there now to trade for fear of the Palace Watch. There were tales of palace knights brutalizing vendors and regarding potential customers with suspicion. The few traders that did dare to gather were unscrupulous knaves who bribed the Watch so that they could continue to sell the sacramental host to the desperate peasants.

Pilgrims from Multimbria said that the reason why Speyron's women were barren was because King Christian had raped a witch who in turn had cursed him and the kingdom with an evil spell. Pilgrims from Gaulia said that the witch, disguising herself as a comely maidservant, had seduced him the night after his coronation and the encounter had shriveled up his yard; and his impotence had affected all of Speyron. In both kingdoms, they called him 'Christian the Lacking'.

The King found other rumors even more troubling. Some believed he was already dead and that the nobles would soon gather to choose a new king which was why Lord Paschal continued to give great displays of power at the palace. Other rumors claimed that Paschal had already declared himself king and was only awaiting the relaxing of the interdict to be crowned.

Looking out into the snow, Christian ran his hand through his golden hair as his thoughts turned back to the disconcerting events of that day. The Abbot had again assigned him to work in the infirmary at the abbey.

Of all the work he had been directed to do since he took refuge at St. Brychan's, he found his duties at the infirmary to be the most humbling. In a small building away from the cloister, the monks cared for the weak and ill among their own as well as any who came to their gate in need. Since the snow began, there seldom had been an empty bed, and they were filled as quickly as they were vacated.

The first time the Abbot had assigned him to help in the infirmary, Christian had gone to his office immediately and protested. He had adamantly refused to tend the sick or even to be in their presence. He had reminded the Abbot that he was *king* and that, royal dignity aside, if he were to become ill and die, what would become of the kingdom? After listening to his angry tirade, Hunfred had simply shrugged his shoulders indifferently and answered that the abbey was required to care for the sick, but it was not required to shelter *him*. Then the Abbot had told him to leave St. Brychan's at once.

Stunned, Christian had found himself outside the Abbot's quarters, wondering where he would go. With the snow as heavy as it was, at best he would only make it to the abbey's village. There was not even a tavern in the village; he would have to be taken in by a family, and from what he understood, the villagers were equally ill there. He had realized quickly that he could be stranded in the abbey or he could be stranded in the village, but he was bound to be in the company of the sick in both places. At least here he was assured food and a dry, warm place to sleep.

Therefore, he had sent word to the Abbot that he was on his way to the infirmary. With great anxiety, he had tended sneezing, coughing patients and emptied pails of vomit and dysentery, but he had performed all that was asked of him. Since then, the Abbot had assigned him several times to work there, and although Christian disliked it, in time, the chores had become routine.

When he first arrived in the mornings, he was usually put to changing bed linens. Afterwards, he administered cloth baths and sometimes shaved the patients. Once the patients were in order, he would help distribute medicinal teas, food and ale to the patients. While the patients cheerfully ate their roasted meat, Christian's mouth would water at the tasty aroma and his stomach grumble as he went without. Most of the patients could feed themselves, but others were so weak that they had to be fed broth one spoonful at a time; and even that little bit was sometimes too much for their weak stomachs.

Otherwise, there was the regular tidying up and the changing of the rushes on the floor to be done, along with helping weak patients to the latrines or to a bucket if they could not make it to the latrines, and, of course, cleaning up any messes that occurred.

After this was all done, if there was nothing else that the master of the infirmary could find for him to do, Christian was encouraged to sit and talk with the patients for their comfort and encouragement. Initially, he had resisted, telling the monk that he did not have anything to say to them. The brother had only smiled and told him not to worry, for the patients would do all the talking. The monk had been correct; as the patients usually slept two to a bed in the crowded, one-room infirmary, the discussions between patients could get quite lively on any given topic, and Christian was lucky to get a word in at all.

The villeins usually talked about their families and the latest happenings in the village; they often talked about the weather or the interdict and how they missed the ringing of the monastery bells. Frequently, they had spirited arguments on how to increase crop production.

The ailing guests from the guesthouse informed Christian of the latest fashions in other kingdoms and often told tales of bandits and dishonest tavernkeepers they had encountered on their pilgrimage. They all had opinions on the architecture of the new cathedrals that were being constructed along their route. Two, old knights who were on pilgrimage recalled the details of battles they had fought in years ago; they also speculated about the upcoming war with Herryck.

The sick monks, whose infirmary section was separated from the other patients by a curtain, talked less, but often they would relate stories about the monastery or of monks long dead. Some would specifically ask him how he was adjusting to his noviceship. Christian was careful how he gave answer, but he usually told them simply that it was proving to be different than what he had expected, which was usually enough to get the monks reminiscing about their own early days in the abbey.

Talking with the patients at the infirmary had both lessened and aggravated Christian's melancholy. On the one hand, the interaction did distract him from his present woes, and any distraction, however brief, aided in lifting his spirits. However, as he began to know and develop a fondness for the patients he tended, he was unable to regard them with his usual detachment. As a result, when some of them eventually died, Christian had suffered immensely; and of late, many had died.

Today had been particularly difficult for him. One of the ill who had come last week was a young villein from the village; his three, young daughters had come with him to the infirmary and shared a mat and a coverlet on the floor beside their father's bed. The man was recently a widower, and illness was so prevalent in the village now that no one there was available to care for him or his children. But even in the infirmary, as the days passed, the man's condition had continued to worsen.

This morning after the novice meeting and Terce, Christian had arrived at the infirmary, glad to be finally free from hearing any more about the seven cardinal sins. He had greeted the now familiar patients, and he had noticed that this peasant was ashen and motionless and that the master of the infirmary was trying to get the man to pray with him, even in his weakened state.

Christian had begun the day's chores, leaving them intermittently to sing the Hours when he was summoned by the drum. When he had returned from Sext, the monks had informed him that because they were shorthanded, they needed him to help Brother Esterwine with the dead.

After hitching up a horse to a cart, he and Brother Esterwine had loaded the corpses that were wrapped securely in their sheets onto the cart. Christian was saddened to see the three, little girls weeping over the last of the bodies.

He and Brother Esterwine had driven slowly away from the infirmary through the snow with their load of dead, and the girls had followed on foot, crying all the way. At the monastery gate, the monk had stopped the horse.

"You children need to be off to the village now," Brother Esterwine had told them abruptly.

The girls, the oldest no older than nine years, had just looked at him blankly. The monk had tied his handkerchief over his nose and then urged the horse into a walk again. Rather than depart, the children had continued to follow the cart, weeping.

He and Esterwine had driven around the outside of the abbey wall, down a small trail that led to the extremity of the monastic grounds, while the children followed behind them all the way. As they had neared the edge of a wood where the monks had taken the dead since the interdict began, Christian had covered his nose with his hand and had thought he would be ill, for the air was thick with the telltale aroma of decay.

At the sight of the approaching cart, a black cloud of vultures, disturbed from their meal, had taken to the sky, but the wolves had only backed away a few steps, boldly holding their ground as the intruders neared. Horrified and sickened, Christian had observed the repulsive sight. Bodies, which at one time had been carefully wrapped in sheets, had been dismembered and scattered by predators. Partially eaten remains, soiled cloth, and bones were strewn about over the open, snow-covered ground.

Esterwine had stopped the horse, climbed down from the cart, and, without pausing, summoned the novice. Together, they had unloaded the new dead from the cart, setting them out one beside the next while the children cried distractedly and looked about in bewilderment. As soon as the last body had been unloaded, Esterwine had immediately climbed back onto the cart.

"You are going to leave him here?!" the children had asked in outrage.

"Will you not even bury him? Or say a prayer over him?" they had wanted to know, the youngest tugging on Christian's sleeve.

While Brother Esterwine had impatiently attempted to explain in brief about the interdict to the children and the necessity of following the rules, Christian had looked again at the miserable view of the discarded corpses in the ruined snow about him and at the vultures that were waiting in the nearby barren, icy trees for the group to abandon the new offerings. The wolves, which were fatter than any he could remember seeing in the past, had already returned to eating the entrails of a woman greedily. He had turned away then, shaken, as he recognized the woman as the lady from Bonaqua whom had told him just a few days ago all about her pilgrimage to Roma.

"There is nothing more we can do for him!" Esterwine had at last declared to the children with exasperation.

Christian had stood with his arms crossed, trying to be patient while the monk argued with the oldest daughter. The youngest girl had found her father's body already and was kneeling at his head, wailing in grief.

"We must return to the abbey now before it becomes any later!" the monk had told the girls for the third time irritably while gesturing to Christian to get in the cart.

Esterwine had seemed as indifferent to the children as he had been to the dead and equally willing to leave both in this place.

Overcome with irritation at the monk, Christian had gone over to the girl among the bodies and picked up the weeping child. She was already quite cold. After putting her in the cart, he had loaded up her two distraught siblings despite their arguments. They had all sat, miserable and shivering in the cart as the scowling monk drove them back to the abbey.

Once at the abbey gates, Brother Esterwine had stopped the horse again. He had ordered the children out of the cart and once again bid them to be on their way back to the village. This time, the girls had complied.

As he watched the three, orphaned children walking away wretchedly in the snow, Christian's heart had ached.

"What will become of them?" he had asked the monk.

Esterwine had shrugged as he took up the reins.

"Someone in the village will likely take them in."

Who would take them in? Christian had wondered. With so many of the villagers ill, would they not be wary of children who had just lost both of their parents? The girls were already cold and miserable. Would they make it back to the village on their own in this weather with their health? Would they find a warm place to sleep for the night and food in their bellies, or would they be cold, hungry and alone in their grief? In the morning, would the wolves be discovered feeding on their half-frozen bodies beside the road?

"Wait," he had said, climbing out of the cart.

"Tillo, 'tis cold out here," Esterwine had said. "-And you will be late to Nones!"

"Go ahead, Brother. I will be there directly."

Esterwine had needed no further urging and had left him where he stood. Christian had hurried after the children and called them back to him. He had picked up the youngest girl and had taken the middle sister's hand and had walked the three directly to the guesthouse.

Explaining the situation, he had turned them over to the guestmaster who had assured him that there was plenty of room in the guesthouse for the children for the night. He had promised to feed them a hot meal and to send word to the almoner of their need for a new family.

As the King thought about the children again, and seeing the guestmaster not far from him, he thought he should inquire after the girls once more. He went over to the hospitaler who was talking to two monks.

"Is it true about the new name for the King?" the younger monk was asking.

"Which one?"

"The Bloody?"

Christian froze in his tracks.

"Aye," the guestmaster answered.

"How came he to be called that?"

"Since the retaking of the palace, they say the King orders a child put to death every day until the conspirators are found, and the innocent blood is collected so that the dying King might wash in it."

Aghast, Christian's hair stood on end.

The two monks crossed themselves and shook their heads, asking, "Whatever for?"

"I know not. Perhaps it is a charm he believes will cure him of his fatal wound or will remove his disfigurement, or perhaps he hopes it will return fertility to the kingdom. -Or perhaps he is simply mad."

"What a monster we have for a king!" the first monk added.

"They have been singing of it," the guestmaster added.

"What? There is a song?"

"How does it go?"

"Let me see if I can remember:

> Hie, my children and conceal yourself well-
> The Devil's men come to take you to Hell-
> If they find nothing to quell the King's wrath
> They will slit your throat to fill up his bath-

Or something like that."

Christian winced at the lyrics and quickly departed the hall, preferring the silent company of the snow.

50

"Scripture tells us story after story about relationship. The Christ himself tells parable after parable about relationship. God is your king; you are his subject. The Christ is your lord; you are his vassal. God is your master; you are his servant. God is your father; you are his son. The Christ is the bridegroom; the Church is his bride.

"Duty, obedience, and loyalty are owed to *all* in authority and especially to God and the Christ…"

Christian rolled his eyes and yawned. He looked at the other novices who were sprawled in various positions around the table; except for Balfrid, they seemed as bored as he, and Cai and Quintus were both already asleep. How many times had they heard these same lectures? he wondered.

"…Thus, be ever mindful of your relationship with the Christ and your duties to him. It is your relationship with the Christ alone that will save you from the fires of Hell, not your individual merit. Your fidelity and obedience to God and faith in God's grace and Christ's atoning sacrifice is…"

Christian scowled in irritation, shifted on the bench, and glanced at Balfrid. The youth was hanging on every word.

"…As long as there is relationship, there is hope, but like any vassal, we must be loyal and submissive to our lord, ever faithful, even unto death, as Christ was, so that God may reward us with the crown of life. For as it says in the book of John, 'He who believes in the Son has eternal life; he who does not obey the Son shall not see life, but the wrath of God rests upon him.'"

The novices' bath day was tomorrow, Christian reminded himself. It was the one thing he was looking forward to. He yearned for a long, unhurried soak in the hot bath at the palace, while minstrels played a soothing tune. However, he would be satisfied with a shorter bath in a tub among the other novices as long as the water was reasonably warm and there was soap.

"…Alas to the souls that are lost because they break faith with the Christ! Some break faith through falling into sin and failing to repent. Others break faith through their own free choice. In like way, a vassal may throw down his glove and break faith with his earthly lord by his own free choice, or he may break faith with his vassal lord by being disobedient to his will. But in so doing, he will suffer the grave consequences of his disloyalty.

"If a vassal breaks faith with the King of Speyron, King Christian may take up arms against him, seize the lands he has bestowed upon him, and banish him from the kingdom. Is it so different with the King of Heaven?"

Christian sniffed. Such a vassal should count himself lucky if that was all that I did to him, he thought to himself.

The novice master smiled then, pausing for a moment to look at each of the youths.

"I hope that none of us will *choose* to break faith with the Christ and turn our backs on his offer of salvation, yet God loves us so much that He allows us to make that choice. He even allows us to choose to make ourselves lord of our own lives. -Yet it is by freely surrendering our will and life to God and the Christ that we gain eternal life."

Christian rolled his eyes and thought briefly of how he could spend his free time today. As it was Sunday and the novices had not been assigned to any essential work today, he could do as he liked between the singing of the Hours. Of course, he could not go riding or hunting or hawking or wenching or drinking. Of the permitted activities, there was nothing that he was particularly in the mood to do. Truly, he might as well go back to the dormitory and go back to sleep.

"On the other hand, as a disciple of Christ, when we do sin and are disobedient to the will of God and Christ, *if we refuse or fail to repent and amend*, we are in effect throwing down our glove and breaking faith with the Christ. The Christ no longer is our lord, but our own will is! The pleasures of the flesh and the delights of this world become our lord!"

"But, Brother Septimus, what if we cannot amend?" Balfrid asked then. "What if by the weakness of our own flesh, we fall into the same sin again? Or what if, by its nature, the sin is easily repeatable- like the sin of anger?"

"Balfrid, it can be difficult to turn from *any* sin, but we must at least make an *honest attempt* not to do again what God hates; and that may mean distancing ourselves from temptations that we know may lead to that sin. -And if we sincerely try, but still repeat the sin, we must trust that God will surely take our earnest attempts to amend into account.

"Salvation is a life long journey, My Son. God is patient. He knows that what we try and fail to do for Him today, perhaps, if we continue to try, we may be able to accomplish for Him tomorrow.-"

Christian yawned again and wondered what they were eating today. It mattered not. One meal was much like the next here. For certain there would be bread, cabbage, and an egg dish. It mattered not anyway; he had had little appetite of late.

"...Thus, a servant of God must keep the commandments and be ever vigilant against sin. Beware the works and temptations of the flesh: fornication, impurity, licentiousness, idolatry, sorcery, malice, strife, jealousy, anger, selfishness, dissension, party spirit, envy, drunkenness, carousing, and the rest. St. Paul tells us that those who do such things shall not inherit the Kingdom of God, and those who truly belong to Christ have crucified their flesh with its desires.

"Therefore, be ever faithful to your Lord Christ and do as he commands: Fill your heart with love for God and love your fellow man as Christ himself loves you. Banish from your mind any stray thoughts to the contrary and keep a prayer for aid on your lips so that you may seek help if you should find yourself suddenly overwhelmed by temptation."

Christian repressed a cynical laugh then as he sat in the cold library, his cold hands tucked under his arms. What could any of these novices know about temptation or sin? They had had little opportunity to do anything!

"...Remember in the Gospel of Mark, when the Pharisees approached Our Lord and asked why he allowed his disciples to eat with defiled hands..."

Vexed, Christian sighed and rubbed his eyes with his sleeve. Brother Septimus was tedious! For more than a fortnight the novice master had spoken about nothing except sin: physical sin, material sin, original sin, external sin, internal sin, sins of omission and commission, sins of passion and infirmity, ignorance and malice, and of course, mortal and venial sins.

"...Then Christ told them 'there is nothing outside a person that by going in the stomach can defile, but the things that come out are what defile. For it is from the heart that evil intentions come, including fornication, theft, murder, adultery, avarice, wickedness, deceit, licentiousness, envy, slander, pride, and folly.'

"Remember, one man's sin does not injure him alone. It touches the entire community, just as one man's virtuous deed does. Thus, be ever vigilant of what you allow into your heart. Beware particularly of the seven cardinal sins: anger, pride, sloth, lust, gluttony, envy, and avarice which are the foundations of other sins, except those caused by the Devil and man himself…"

Christian fought the urge to stand up and offer them some personal stories of sin and excesses. He wanted to tell them about feasts where there was so much meat that even the dogs under the table could not eat all the scraps and where so much drink was consumed in one night that everyone was still drunk for most of the next day. He longed to tell them about fornication in stews with lewd wenches in positions forbidden by the Church. -He wanted to tell them things that he had done that would make the little hair the novice master had left stand on end.

"…For even if a man strives to be righteous, if Lord Christ does not abide in his heart and lead and aid him, he will still fall into sin. For our Lord tells us in the Gospel of John that 'a branch cannot bear fruit by itself, unless it abides in the vine, neither can you, unless you abide in me… I am the vine, you are the branches. He who abides in me, and I in him, will bear much fruit, for apart from me you can do nothing.' We see in the letter to the Ephesians St. Paul reiterate this truth. The apostle does not instruct us to go out and confront the Devil alone, sustained solely by our own meager strength. The result would be failure! Instead, he urges us to 'be strong in the Lord' and to 'put on the whole armor of God, that you may be able to stand against the wiles of the Devil.' With the 'belt of truth', 'the breastplate of righteousness', 'the shield of faith', 'the helmet of salvation', and 'the sword of the Spirit', you will be prepared to withstand and persevere against evil…"

The door to the library opened then, and a small, elderly monk entered. The novice master, upon seeing him, ended his lecture abruptly. He introduced Father Oskitell and turned the meeting over to him.

51

The novice master walked briskly around the covered cloister walk, ignoring the chill wind and the light dusting of snow that blew upon him on his way to the Abbot's quarters. He found the Abbot and Father Desle warming themselves in front of the fire in the Abbot's hall. Abbot Hunfred greeted the novice master pleasantly.

"Brother Septimus, how-"

"Forgive me, Lord Abbot," the old monk immediately began. "I no longer know what to do! I have prayed about it, but my patience has at last failed me!"

The confessor raised his eyebrows in surprise.

"Brother Septimus, I have never seen you so distressed," Hunfred replied. "Tell me, what has brought you to this condition?"

The monk sighed.

"Lord Abbot, I am near distraction!"

"So I see."

"You know I take the teaching of the novices very seriously."

Both Hunfred and Desle knew then what must be coming.

"That new novice, Tillo-" Septimus began with a shake of his head.

"What has he done?"

"Very little!" he replied in exasperation. "He barely sings the Divine Office -even the responses, and he has done nothing except yawn and sigh during the novice meetings and fight off sleep!"

The Abbot and the senior confessor listened intently.

"At first, I did not know where the trouble lay, for I have been able to get little more out of the lad except 'Aye' or 'No' since he came to us. By the sour look on his face, I suspected that the lectures bored him; and since I could not get him to speak, I thought, well, perhaps he knows nothing and is embarrassed. Therefore, I made an effort to explain the teachings in simpler terms, repeating the main points. Then all the novices were yawning with him.

"Next, I thought perhaps the youth is already well versed in the history of our Lord. Perhaps he already understands the meaning of His teachings. So I changed my lectures to suit this taste and, afterwards, had the other novices in utter confusion. Through it all, this new novice only continued to stare off into the distance, his thoughts far from my lecture.

"I confess I did not know what to make of it," the senior monk continued. "My words and teaching have never failed to stir the spirit of a novice before. And I began to fear, Lord Abbot, whether I still possessed the skill necessary to train our order's initiates."

"Brother-" the Abbot began.

"-For how can this lad continue in the vocation he pursues when the teachings of our Lord do not move him? I had thought to come to you tomorrow or the next day with my concerns, but for what happened today."

"What happened today?"

"I had confided my difficulties to Father Oskitell, and this morning, he joined me in the novice meeting to see if anything could help the situation. Upon arriving, he immediately questioned the boys, asking each one to recite any teaching of the Faith or of Our Lord from memory."

The confessor raised his eyebrows.

"The novices at first wanted to recite a Psalm, but Brother Oskitell would not have it. In truth, we felt the Psalms were not a fair assessment of their knowledge since they are sung daily by the novices during the Hours."

"Did Tillo wish to recite a Psalm as well?" Desle asked curiously.

"I know not, Father, for true to his custom, he said not a word, but rolled his eyes about his head in boredom," the little monk complained with a gesture of irritation.

"One by one, the novices began to speak," the novice master continued. "Young Quintus named the seven cardinal sins as well as the cardinal virtues. Selby recited the Magnificat. Cai recited the Beatitudes and very nearly had them correct. After all had recited and Oskitell came to call upon Tillo-"

"He refused-" the Abbot broke in.

"Indeed, he did, Lord Abbot! But Brother Oskitell rebuked him and challenged him. He told the lad that they were novices and still learning, and if he made errors, it was not a disgrace. He said that as the others had tried, so he must also."

Hunfred and Desle listened with interest.

"This young man stood up and recited the Lorica Sancti Patrici perfectly, Lord Abbot. Then when he saw from the faces of the other novices that they did not know what he had said, he smiled an arrogant little smile, and he recited it again, perfectly, *in our native tongue!*"

"He knew The Breastplate of Saint Patrick? And in our language as well?"

"Aye!"

Hunfred and Desle were both impressed.

"Then guess what he did!"

The men looked at him.

"Tell us-"

"He laughed!"

"He laughed?" Hunfred repeated with a frown.

"Aye, Lord Abbot! Obviously this youth has had a great deal of learning and knows well the teachings of the Faith already! I do not know, however, if he laughed to show his contempt for me and my simple lectures or if he was actually mocking that most reverent prayer!"

"Calm yourself, Brother," Father Desle urged.

"My Lord Abbot," Septimus continued hotly, "this novice has the worst case of ascedia I have ever witnessed, and he has only been here three months! I do not know how this lad came to our door or who promotes his vocation, but if he takes his holy vows-"

The novice master was so vexed that words failed him. The Abbot observed the red-faced man with concern. He could not remember the last time he had seen the monk so unsettled.

"Brother," Hunfred said calmly, "I see that you are gravely hurt by the youth's impertinence, but do not question your teaching abilities on his account. You have trained and led our initiates successfully for many years, and I am confident that you will continue to do so for many more.

"I will reprimand Tillo for his insolence, but we all must pray for his amendment. As for your lectures, adapt them to the needs of the other novices. At present, what is said for their benefit should be sufficient for Tillo, no matter what his background, if he has ears to hear it. If ascedia is what ails him, perhaps in time he will recover from it. If not, it will become apparent to him that he does not belong among us, and he will leave of his own accord."

The novice master nodded his head in agreement and seemed appeased. He thanked the Abbot and left with his blessing.

52

The next morning at the chapter meeting, Christian squirmed uncomfortably on the bench as the novice master described his irreverent behavior in detail to every monk at the abbey. The monks, many of whom he worked with on a regular basis, listened with stunned disbelief and horror. The other novices appeared equally self-conscious and would not look in his direction at all.

"This is very, very grave, Tillo," Abbot Hunfred said, "and very disappointing."

Some of the brothers shook their heads in disbelief while others looked upon the novice scornfully.

The King sat pouting with his arms crossed inside his sleeves, staring at the center of the table, refusing to be moved by their disapproval. This was ridiculous, he repeated to himself. *They* were ridiculous.

"In fact, *irreverence* is so grievous a fault that a very serious correction is required," Hunfred continued.

Frowning, Christian braced himself for the forthcoming humiliation. The Abbot would probably make him beg on his hands and knees for bits of food from the other brothers' trenchers at dinner for a fortnight or so. Or perhaps for several days he would be made to lie prostrate on the floor outside the chapter room to beg the forgiveness of every monk who walked in.

"Therefore, beginning tomorrow, you will be excommunicated from the oratory, the table, and all fellowship with this community for six days."

King Christian looked at the Abbot in surprise. Had he heard correctly? Was he to be once again excommunicated?

"This means, Tillo, that you will be forbidden to speak or keep company with anyone. Neither will you attend the Hours with the other novices, nor the novice meetings, nor the chapter meetings, nor will you join us in the refectory for meals. -Your mat will be put in a corner of the novice dormitory.

"Nor shall you be idle in your solitude, but you shall complete a list of chores each day. In the meantime, we shall be praying for your amendment."

Christian nearly laughed out loud at the leniency of the correction. Was this punishment? What exactly was it about excommunication that these clerics found so unpleasant? He had been an excommunicate for more than two years now and as of yet had not found it particularly punitive.

What did he care if they ignored him, after all? And if he did not have to sing the Hours, so much the better; the extra sleep would suit him well. As for the chores, what could Hunfred assign him that he had not already done?

Christian quickly assumed a serious face as he rose and thanked the Abbot for the correction as custom demanded.

The King's light-hearted mood ended later that day when the Abbot gave him the list of chores. The labors of Hercules did not involve so much. The first of each day's tasks was scheduled to begin when the novices rose for Matins, and the last at the beginning of the Ground Silence. He straightway realized he would have no extra sleep and that there would be no time to rest in-between tasks if he was going to finish before the next day's list began. Furthermore, Hunfred informed him that if he did not comply with his punishment fully or if he did not complete each task to the Abbot's satisfaction, he would be put out of the monastery immediately.

King Christian spent most of the following day fuming at the chores and the immense length of the first day's list and at the furious pace he was forced to keep. As he milked the cows, chopped and carried firewood, and plucked chickens, he burned with hate for the novice master who had reported him to the Abbot. He seethed with anger that Oskitell had insisted that he recite something at the meeting. While the regular stable men ate their dinner, he mucked out the stables and berated himself repeatedly for reciting the Lorica Sancti Patrici in their native tongue and revealing his contempt for them all.

Yet as angry as he was, he refused to quit and admit to the Abbot that he was bested. To do so would have been a further disgrace and humiliation. It also would confirm Olbert's suspicions that he was but an undisciplined youth. No, Christian was determined to do all that was required of him. When he did leave St. Brychan's, he promised himself it would be his turn. He would have his revenge then. He would raise the monastery's taxes, and when they could not pay them and they came to beg for mercy, he would shrug his shoulders indifferently and order their lands seized and them put out.

For the most part, Christian did not encounter anyone throughout the day. The Abbot had effectively assured his uninterrupted isolation by arranging the chores so that no one would be in the vicinity when he arrived to work. This was partially accomplished by either the remoteness of some of the activities or the time of day that the chore was scheduled to be done. But any time he did happen upon anyone, monks or villeins, they shunned him as they had been instructed to do by the Abbot.

The novices had long been to bed when he, weary and stinking, returned to the silent dormitory. Blood and feathers were dried to his scapular and sleeves from the chickens he had plucked for the infirmary patients' dinner, and he was covered in a fine layer of dust from sweeping out the granary. He went to his bed like a warrior spent from battle, the day's activities a mere blur through his head as he fell to exhausted sleep.

The second day Christian's anger had dissipated. He grew bored. He was tired of being alone, and he began longing for interaction of some kind. As he scrubbed the great hall floor near the church, he could barely hear the murmuring of the novices as they sang Terce, but around him, there was utter stillness. Only the sound of his breathing and the sound of the brush bristles scratching at the stone floor were his companions. As he labored, his mind wandered aimlessly from one matter to the next, and melancholy began to settle upon him anew.

Gradually, he began to think on Herryck. Spring had seemed an eternity away this past autumn. Now it was only a few months hence. Would Speyron be ready? Would the snows end early this year? Would Herryck come in June or in May? Christian had not instructed his vassals to begin storing arms or food. Would they have the forethought to prepare regardless?

That night Christian was unable to eat from worry, and he failed to rest in his sleep. As tired as he was, he spent most of the night tossing and turning, his stomach knotted with anxiety. He longed for his early days of kingship when he had slept heavily from ignorance and too much food, drink, and pleasure.

On the third day, Christian, exhausted and dispirited, admitted that excommunication at a monastery was completely different than excommunication in the secular world; and the only merciful part of his punishment had been the long list of chores.

Before now, Christian had never truly appreciated how much of his time was spent in the company of other people. As Sir Gage's pupil, he had lived among a throng of knights, youths, and servants at Lord Reynaud's castle. Upon arriving home, he had returned to a large court and had always been in the company of servants and nobles as well as Paschal and Felix and other noble youths. The first time he had ever spent any real time alone had been after he had become king and had moved into his private chambers. But even then, it had only been for a few hours at a time at most, and there had been servants and bodyguards either in the chamber with him or within calling distance. Now, there was no one; truly, he had never been so alone in all of his life.

With nothing and no one to distract him, his mind continued to drift. Gradually his thoughts returned to the dreadful gossip told by the guestmaster and the knowledge that all of Speyron and most of the Continent believed him to be either impotent, dying, or despicable. With his melancholy heavy upon him, Christian tried to concentrate all his attention on his work, but still the same depressing thoughts returned to him. He ached for some pleasant diversion. He longed for company and conversation with, in fact, anyone: monks, villeins, children. But, alas, none was to be had. Any time he came upon anyone, they turned their back to him. Not even a kind look was to be granted him.

Was this what it was like to be dead? he wondered. Silence all around you, the living unable to see or hear you? You, yourself without a voice, doomed to walk about the earth for the rest of time? Or did the dead, at least, interact with each other?

Do not be absurd! his inner voice answered. There is no life for the dead! There is non-existence, as if you had never been born, the oblivion of nothing! The life you have now is all!

This grim thought brought no relief to the youth. Only the knowledge that his isolation would be over in three days brought him comfort, but only a little.

On the fourth day, Christian was drowning in silence. He was so dispirited, he was scarcely able to breathe, for his depression bore down upon him like a great stone set upon his chest. Drained of his energy, even easy tasks were fatiguing to him. It took all of his effort simply to move. The only part of him with any vim were the thoughts that continued to rush with extraordinary speed and clarity through his mind.

Although his mind was alive with activity, Christian had no control over the thoughts that poured through his head. One dismal sentiment replaced another. Angry thoughts lashed out at him and everything around him, filling his head with images that continually illustrated the futility of his situation:

Speyron was going to lose the war. Herryck was going to enslave his entire kingdom.

So be it, the people deserved no better, Christian thought bitterly. They had run him out of his palace, and now he was unable to plan and coordinate the kingdom's defense.

The Church was to blame as well. If they had not put his kingdom under interdict, the vermin peasants would likely not have rebelled. Roma was probably supporting Herryck's invasion as it was, Christian sneered as he picked up pieces of kindling out of the snow and put them on the woodpile.

Herryck was a patient man; he was like a snake that with unblinking eyes waits for the perfect moment to strike its prey. He would likely invade and then avoid battle until the most ideal conditions were in his favor. Fighting could drag on for years as long as Herryck could feed and pay his army.

In the meantime, Herryck would impede the kingdom's harvest and starve them all. Finally, when the people of Speyron were weak from hunger and beaten down, Herryck would have his decisive victory. Anyone left who had the will to fight would be crushed in that battle. Christian himself would then be betrayed and handed over to the enemy and be immediately put to death.

He frowned irritably at the silent, indifferent falling snow, and then his eyes fell upon a black bird that had lighted on a branch near him.

"What do you care?" Christian suddenly demanded, his unused voice sounding strange to him.

The bird cocked its head toward him, then flew away.

Christian angrily slammed the ax into the wood, lodging the blade fast. He raised the ax and wood together then and pounded them fiercely against the tree stump until the kindling cleaved in two pieces.

If, on the other hand, he surrendered quietly and without much fuss, Herryck might possibly spare his life and allow him to remain on the throne as his puppet. The lands that Herryck had conquered were considerable now. He needed and would continue to need faithful vassals to retain it.

Swear allegiance and serve a conquering enemy? The very thought was repulsive to Christian. Yet surrendering sooner rather than later would spare the lives of hundreds of men and perhaps assure the continued life of his cousin and himself.

Christian bristled at the thought. Death for every living thing in Speyron was preferable to such an act of outright cowardice and dishonor on his part! Yet, in the back of his mind, he could hear Grey telling him again that a king must always look to the future. Treaties with hated enemies were components of power as much as vassals, armies, and advantageous marriages.

Setting up the next log, Christian hurled the ax down into it as if it was the head of his foe, and then he pounded the log violently and repeatedly against the stump, roaring with fury.

He hated his life! Why was *he* fated to be king? Why was he fated to be the king who *lost* Speyron? Why should the fate of all of the people in an entire kingdom, whether he knew them or not, or liked them or not, rest on his shoulders alone? Everyone expected too much from him! He had not been prepared to make these kinds of decisions! He was not ready to lead a kingdom to war!

-And the kingdom was not ready to be led. It was pulling itself in all sorts of directions. -And as Olbert had told him so oft before, it was the king's responsibility to unite them.

Christian wiped his sweating forehead with his snow-dusted sleeve.

Unite them? His vassals? -With the way Grey talked, there were only a handful of vassals that were not after his throne. Very well, let them have it, if they think they can do better!

Actually, any of them probably could do better, his inner voice added.

But how was he ever to unite this kingdom? he wondered. He knew what Paschal would say. The hot-blooded youth thought a sword was the answer to everything: 'Make an example of an unfaithful vassal!' he would say. 'Take back his lands, put him and his line to the sword, burn down his home! That is the way to keep treacherous vassals in line!'

-If only it could be that simple.

The King retrieved the final log to be hewn and set it on its end on the stump; then he once again raised the ax.

His father, if he had been any kind of man, would have gone to war with Herryck long ago rather than paying him off year after year. If only Filberte had aligned with Ria, the two countries could have easily defeated Herryck.

'But, no!' thought Christian as he savagely pounded the wood against the stump, 'Filberte was too much of a drunken, lecherous, slothful coward to care about his son or his kingdom's future!'

Christian threw down the ax and began gathering an armful of the firewood to take to the kitchen.

He hated everything! It was all hopeless and Fortuna's cruel trick! His birthright was a future that should have been more promising than anyone else's, but instead it was destined to wither shortly after sprouting! The taste was bitter to him.

Now he was weary with trying and weary with caring and weary with thinking about it! He was weary with waiting for his own demise! He was so utterly frustrated now that if he could have torn the flesh from his body and had an end to it, he would have done so! *Anything* had to be better than this! Even death would be a welcome relief from this endless pondering of his hopeless circumstances and future!

Exhausted and emotionally drained after another sleepless night, Christian looked about the empty refectory that he was to sweep in the predawn darkness of the fifth day and began to weep. He had changed his mind. Excommunication was the worst possible punishment for anyone! The silent isolation was cruel, and it was maddening!

He worked sluggishly the entire day as his mind continued to assault him with endless, disparaging thoughts and scenarios of defeat and ruin:

How could *he* defeat Herryck? He was not clever enough to defeat him! Herryck had been through a lifetime of battles. He knew war; he knew men. He had won entire kingdoms!

What, in contrast, had he himself achieved? He could not even quell a small rebellion at his own palace!

He had been a fool to flee his palace! Herryck would have stayed and fought, if it had happened to him. -Any brave man would have!

And why had he not personally gone out to see the malcontents himself? Why had he sent an inexperienced knight to handle the mob? Likely, if he had seen to it himself, he would not be hiding for his life in a monastery!

And if anything had happened to Kaith, how could he have lived with himself?

And why was he depending upon Paschal to find the rebels? Why was he not at the palace, overseeing the inquiries himself?

The answer was easy: He was slothful and a coward! And he was a fool! He did not deserve to be king!

Christian struggled to think of anything else. With great force of will, he managed to do so, but after a moment, his anxieties and reproachful thoughts immediately returned and began again where they had ended. After wrestling with his thoughts most of the day, he finished his chores long after the novices had retired to bed.

It was long after dark on the sixth day when Christian finished sweeping the floor in the chapter room and wiping down the benches and the great round table. He should have begun his final chore by now, but he had gotten behind earlier when the pigs had escaped their sty, and he had had to spend the better part of an hour chasing them through the snow back into their pen.

He had not taken the time to eat yet today. He was not particularly hungry, but he knew he should eat to keep his strength.

He consulted the list again. There were but two items left, thankfully, and the library would not take long. On his way there, Christian went first to the dark, silent refectory where his meal still awaited him. Beside a faintly burning candle that was now reaching its end, he found a lone trencher of cold food and a quarter liter of tepid ale on an otherwise bare table.

Setting his broom down, he took up his bread and bit into it. As he chewed, he looked around at the long, vacant tables and benches. The monks were at Collation now, and he could hear music, voices and laughter coming from the nearby hall where he was not welcome. Without sitting down, he picked up the vessel of ale and drank swallow after swallow quickly, not bothering to pour it into his cup. Then he picked up the trencher and raked the cold fish stew and cabbage directly into his mouth with a hunk of bread, chewing and swallowing it without appetite. Still eating his last bite of bread, he left the refectory and headed for the library.

As he made his way around the courtyard with his broom, he came upon Brothers Lubin and Swithbert and some of the other monks who were huddled together in the cloister walk, laughing and talking. They, upon seeing him, became abruptly silent and immediately turned their back to him; even little Cai, who was among them, turned away. Christian cringed and hurried past them, on around the cloister walk.

Upon turning the last corner, he stopped short as he suddenly came face to face with the friendly countenance of Bennet. In an instant, the cheerful expression was gone from the monk, and both young men were immediately overcome with embarrassment. From the monk's unsettled expression, Christian knew it especially pained Bennet to see him.

After looking away uncomfortably, the monk stepped aside and turned his back to him. The King winced and hurried on, almost at a run; his former friend's shame of him was more painful for him to bear than a dagger in his heart.

Upon arriving at the library, he entered at once and shut the door behind him, glad to have escaped the scornful gazes of the monks. Turning around, he stopped short again. About ten brothers and Balfrid were looking, quite startled, at him. Apparently they had been involved in an avid discussion just before he had entered.

There was an uneasy minute as they turned their backs to him and whispered among themselves. Christian waited curiously to see if they would break the Abbot's command and acknowledge him long enough to tell him to leave or if they themselves would go.

In the end, they did neither. They simply resumed their discussion as if he was not present.

"...as I was saying, Brother. In that place, there is no love, nor comfort, nor forgiveness, for these are things of *God*. Thus, the soul is left to its bitterness, unable to love, comfort, or forgive even itself because it refused to love, comfort, and forgive others in life.-"

"Aye, by refusing to love and forgive others in life, the soul closes itself off to God's love, mercy and forgiveness and dooms itself to Hell."

Taking up the broom, Christian began to sweep in the far corner of the chamber, all the while listening attentively, for this was the first conversation he had heard in days.

"But what about *fire*?"

"Aye," another brother quickly agreed. "In the parable of the wheat and the weeds, Lord Christ says the angels will gather all causes of sin and the evildoers that have been allowed to live among us and throw them into the *furnace of fire*."

"I disagree. In the parable of the wedding feast, Lord Christ clearly describes Hell as the opposite of Heaven. In Heaven, with all the Saints, the Saved shall feast with God and Christ. The Unsaved shall be-" and the monk was tapping the table with his finger insistently, "turned away, left outside in the dark, outside of all companionship, weeping and gnashing his teeth."

"That can not be all! Apart from being excluded from eternal bliss and the company of God and the Saints, what makes this unbearable?" Balfrid asked.

"Clearly, it is unbearable because of the shame!" the monk answered resolutely. "The soul is tortured with the knowledge that it forfeited its eternal, joyful rewards in Heaven for momentary pleasures on earth!"

"I do not see how that would be particularly unbearable to some godless men," Balfrid answered.

Christian looked sharply over at the novice. However, Balfrid was so completely involved in the discussion that he doubted that the youth had meant the words as a taunt for him.

"There will clearly be pain that the body can feel," another monk answered, "else there would be no point to the bodies of the damned being raised from the dead at the end. For we are taught that our bodies after the General Judgment will join our immortal souls in either reward or punishment."

"Hell is beyond all human comprehension," another monk added. "As Saint Augustine asserts, 'Just as the joys found on earth must pale in comparison to the joys of eternal life in Heaven, likewise no pain or torment on earth man can know can compare to the everlasting torments of the wicked in Hell.'"

"Father Oskitell, what do you think?"

Christian glanced toward the old man curiously.

"In answer to your question, I agree that in this life we can only understand it, like so many other things of God, -imperfectly," the aged monk spoke gently.

The other monks immediately were quiet.

"But I believe that man was made with a hole in his heart," Oskitell continued. "And God created this hole so that each man would seek to fill it with love for God, truth, and goodness. Some men, of course, do not choose to fill this void with these, and laboring in vain, they seek diversion from their emptiness with amusements.

"Thus, when a soul is completely separated from God in Hell, and likewise from God's love, God's mercy, God's understanding, and so forth, the soul is left with its imperfections which it loathes and with this painful feeling of emptiness that nothing can ease."

Christian's stomach tightened.

"Although indescribable and unknowable to us now," the old monk told them slowly, choosing his words with care, "perhaps it may be similar to feelings of inadequacy, loneliness, disconnection, or despair."

At once, a chill ran up Christian's back, and a lump caught in his throat.

"This feeling of complete, permanent, and irrevocable separation from God is so overwhelming," he continued, "that the soul can *never* find peace. In this way the soul suffers for all eternity."

"The consequences of original sin -*magnified*," one of the brothers commented.

There was immediate agreement by some of the brothers and more questions by others around the table, but Christian did not hear any more.

Feelings of inadequacy- loneliness- disconnection- despair-

As Oskitell's explanation continued to echo in his head, Christian felt a wave of heat, and his palms began to perspire. Then his stomach suddenly twisted. Abruptly ill and slightly light-headed, Christian dropped the broom and lunged toward the door, breathing through his mouth in order to control his now heaving stomach.

He made it to the courtyard before he vomited. After his stomach had expelled all his dinner, Christian, cold, faint, and miserable, hurried back to the novice dormitory. He opened the door and found the chamber empty. He shut the door and lay down in the dark on his straw mat in the corner, running his hand through his long hair as he stared into the darkness that surrounded him.

What was the matter with him? his inner voice chastised. He had been taught about the firepit of Hell. What of it? It was a tale told to frighten children and the simple-minded.

But for once Christian found himself uncertain. There was something *familiar* in what that old monk had described and that was what bothered him. He recalled a story he had heard as a young boy before he had even been sent to Gaulia. Some old traveling minstrel had set him on his knee and told him a tale of a banquet where all great warriors feasted after death. Every warrior aspired to be honorable and to perform heroic deeds in life so that they could attend this feast after they died. At this feast, the warriors enjoyed the same pleasures they had had in life. The honor and glory they had earned in life were heaped on them there as well. The food, wine, and entertainment were the kind and the quality that the warriors delighted in and had been accustomed to, and only the greatest warriors of all time were allowed to attend.

Christian had, of course, not known it at the time, but the story had been a teaching of one of the *old religions* about judgment and the afterlife, and the point was that there would be no surprises. In general, these religions taught that you received what you deserved in *this life*.

If you were sick or lame or lonely or poor, et cetera, it was because you deserved to be so. And as you had in life, so would you have forever after death.

A cold shiver ran up the King's spine again.

What troubled Christian now was that the supposed joys awaiting the blessed in 'Heaven' had never impressed him. Perfect knowledge and virtue had never been his heart's desire, nor did he burn with the desire to see, know, love, or dwell with a supreme god. The place was alien to him; obviously, he did not belong there. But this monk's description of the misery of Hell was all *too familiar.-*

He shuttered as the lump in his throat tightened even more at this morbid realization. Christian stared into the darkness as one lone tear rolled down his cheek unbidden: To be doomed to *his present misery-* only worse - *forever.*

Christian remained in the dark helplessly pondering what the monk had said until the pounding of the drum filled his ears and interrupted his thoughts. Collation had ended. He had to get up and finish his work, for the novices were heading to the church to sing Compline and soon would retire to bed.

53

It took a few minutes and every bit of determination he had, but Christian somehow managed to get to his feet. Wiping his face and hugging his habit around him, he walked through the now quiet cloister back to the library. Opening the door, he found it abandoned and dark. He lit a candle from one of the outside torches and then began to set the benches on top of the tables. Then he picked up the broom where it still lay upon the floor and began to sweep again, bending over to get under the tables.

Christian knew that the only reason he had been able to endure this abbey and the many, humiliating tasks he had been forced to perform day after day, was because he was absolutely certain that he could send for his men to retrieve him whenever he wished. He was a stranger in a foreign land, surrounded by alien customs, forced to conceal who he really was, but his exile would not continue much longer, he had told himself every day, several times a day. It would not be much longer before he was rescued from here and from the intense isolation he had felt from the first moment he had arrived. And even if his vassals never came for him, he was still free to leave anytime he wished. He was miserable, it was true, but he was still in control.

Now a new thought troubled him. What if there was a Hell? What if the misery he felt now was just a sample of what was to come? What if he was wrong, as everyone seemed to think he was, and God did exist? Then, surely, he would be damned forever and would end up in a place far worse than this abbey, worse beyond all imaginings. Not only would he burn in a lake of fire, but *he* would torture *himself* with endless self-criticism and reproach. Eventually, he would surely go mad from loneliness and despair, -his soul forever tormented with self-loathing for being responsible for his own demise. And there would be no relief for him there, ever. There would be no one to rescue him. He would suffer that way for the rest of all time as long as there was existence.

Christian shuttered in terror.

'The drivel of a fool! Nothing more than wives' tales and superstition!' the old familiar voice in his head told him again. 'Religion was for the control of the people only! Nothing happened after the body died! Nothing! You can not possibly feel lonely or miserable then- or feel pain! Those are things associated with the living!'

This reasoning failed to console him. Christian stopped sweeping as his tears began to fall again. First, one treasonous tear escaped down his cheek, followed quickly by its comrades until it was an entire mutiny.

Christian's chest shook with heavy sobs of anguish and depression over his situation, which was getting, he admitted, more and more unbearable; and now he feared he was truly going mad.

'It is not madness that is overtaking you', another voice in his head told him. 'It is *the void in your heart!*'

Christian winced at this thought as his melancholy overwhelmed him. The sadness had real weight, and he felt it deep within his gut. He felt himself being pulled down into a raging sea of despair.

His only desire now was to disappear. If only he could stop feeling bad. He wanted to get drunk, go to sleep, do anything, but *stop* feeling sad!

Christian willed himself to stop crying and managed to slow the procession of tears, but that was all.

What was the point of all this? Life was nothing more than uncertainty, struggle, and pain, and then you died.

He remembered again the noblewoman from Bonaqua whom he had gotten to know recently in the infirmary and the hideous sight of her body being eaten by the wolves outside the monastery walls. She had been a good, merry, beautiful person, and she had made the pilgrimage to show devotion to her god, *and this had been her end!* -She had not deserved the indignity of dying, particularly among villeins in a crowded infirmary, and she certainly had not deserved to have her body eaten by beasts of the field!

If there was a god, it was his cruel joke! Christian told himself bitterly. -And he clearly enjoyed tormenting all his poor creatures.

Had there ever been true joy in his life? Christian wondered. Had he ever had one moment free from doubt and suffering? If he had, he could not remember it.

Why did he continue to put himself through this? Why did he continue to struggle against his fate? The seers and his advisers all believed he was doomed. If he was discovered by the wrong element, he would be murdered instantly. Why not just give up and die?

'You can end you pain. Just surrender to your situation!' said one little voice in his head.

'Just go out of the monastery and sleep in the snow. Or go in the village or even the guesthouse and reveal yourself,' it said. 'Could it be so difficult to find a rebel? Or draw on an armed man; allow his blade to find your heart,' it said.

A chorus of voices drowned that one out then:

'That would only hasten you receiving the inevitable torments owed you in the afterlife!'

Christian wept afresh.

54

Solely with sheer determination, Christian fought to control himself. He opened the library door abruptly and went out into the cold. Standing outside, he wiped his wet face and took several deep breaths to calm himself and clear his head of these thoughts. The chill air felt cool to his aching head.

His shivering eventually brought him back to himself. This thinking is madness, he admitted. He was miserable right now, but tomorrow, the six days would be over. He would finish this, and then he would send for his bodyguards and leave this abominable place. He would leave no matter if they came or not, he promised himself.

He glanced about the cloister then and realized it was late. No one was in sight; all was silent except for the wind that howled mournfully about the cloister.

Christian forced himself to concentrate on the last of the tasks. Only the church floor remained, and the novices had probably finished Compline long ago and retired to bed.

He hurried back to the library and finished sweeping. Then he went to retrieve a brush and pail of water for the final chore, determined to complete what was required of him lest he be humiliated before the Abbot again.

When the King arrived with his supplies, he set down the pail of water and looked warily about the cold, dark, and empty church for a long moment. It had the eerie stillness of a tomb. The hair on the back of his neck stood on end as the youth looked at the still, black shroud suspended in the air, hanging above everything like impending death.

Ignoring his feelings of misgivings, Christian started for the front of the church. Then he paused, bowed toward the shrouded rood and crossed himself quickly, knowing that if one more monk caught him being irreverent anywhere, he would be ousted.

As he slowly approached the front of the dimly lit church and the rood screen, he noticed that from a distance the arm of the large statue of the Madonna seemed to point to the mural of the *Doom* painted on the ceiling and walls above the rood. He paused in the nave and examined the details of the painting of the Final Judgment for a moment. The risen Savior was painted in glory at the top center judging the living and the dead. Beneath the Christ, to the left, the joyous souls were being led to Heaven by angels; in stark contrast, the woeful souls of the damned were being marched into Hell by demons on the right. The expressions on the faces of these souls were at once of surprise, horror, and anguish.

Christian swallowed hard and looked away. As he hastened to the first of the small, side chapels, he was further unnerved that the flickering shadows cast by the burning torches seemed to make the entire church and everything in it appear to be on fire.

'These are naught but tricks of the mind,' he told himself, trying hard to disregard his unease.

He set the pail and brushes down in the corner of the first chapel. Getting down on his knees, he took a moment to blow on his hands that were nearly numb with cold. Then, without further hesitation, he plunged his brush into the chill water and began scrubbing the floor in circular motions.

Christian concentrated on the chore and worked quickly, but it was not long before his thoughts returned to torment him.

'As you have in this life, so you will have in the next,' the voice in his head repeated again and again.

Christian gritted his teeth and worked on.

'You might as well give in. You are already doomed. The seers have seen it. Your advisers know it. There is nothing you can do now. There is no hope.'

Christian shook his head to rid himself of these thoughts as new tears, unbidden, began to roll down his face. He was tired, he told himself. He should be tired: It was late, and he had been working since the night before.

'Dying now or later matters little. But die now, and you will not have to endure the shame of seeing your kingdom fall.'

'Aye,' another voice in his head argued, 'but are you in such haste to receive judgment? *Melancholy, loneliness, despair and more are surely yours without end.*'

Christian sighed and moved to his right.

'Fire too. Endless burning fire.'

His heart skipped a beat and then beat violently as out of the corner of his eye he saw a shadowy figure writhing in torment in a lake of fire as a demon struck him from above. Forcing himself to be calm, Christian made himself turn and examine what he had seen.

It was nothing- only flickering shadows cast on the far wall where the beginnings of a mural had been painted of St. Christopher.

Christian took a deep breath as his heartbeat slowed. He turned back around again, and moving the pail closer to him, dipped both hands into the bucket, and sloshed the cold water onto his face, head, and neck. The shock of the icy cold water against his aching features momentarily revived him and cleared his head.

"I do not believe in the lake of fire or Hell!" he reminded himself sternly. "And there is no *next life.*"

Then Christian forced himself to go back to scrubbing the chapel floor.

'As you have in this life, so you will have in the next,' the voice repeated.

I do not deserve this! Christian grumbled to himself. I do not deserve any of it! Not the rebellion, nor the pending war, nor this wretched melancholy that plagues me daily -and certainly not *unending despair and loneliness!* What have I ever done to deserve any-?

Christian froze. He was at that moment scrubbing the floor beside the chapel altar, and he suddenly found himself eye level with the skull and right hand of some saint which was on display beneath it. He stared at the skull with its gaping eye-sockets, scarcely breathing.

A memory of a night long ago suddenly rushed to the King's mind. He watched himself laugh and toss a similar skull back and forth to his companion knights. Then he had tired of the sport and had thrown the skull with the remains of a ribcage to the ground. As he had pissed on the relics, Paschal and Felix had chased each other with the saint's leg bones. Then the priest had appeared, half asleep, and had begun his excited exclamations, grabbing at his arm.

Christian watched as he and his knights beat the monk. Then he was strangling the cleric with the priest's own stole while his companions looked on in astonishment. The King could feel the cloth in his hand again, -could still feel the last struggles of the priest fighting for air. Then the man had slumped and fallen limp and still to the ground, his vacant eyes staring toward the heavens.

Christian shook his head at the memory as he returned to scrubbing the floor fiercely, fighting down his feelings of guilt.

"I am not sorry!" he told himself. "He was too bold! -Daring to lay hands on his king!"

He set his jaw and slopped more water onto the floor.

"I was within my rights!" he suddenly shouted angrily at the skull beside him, the words echoing emptily through the church.

Christian stopped and took a deep breath. This *was* madness. He set his teeth and returned to scrubbing the floor with renewed vigor, all the while hardening his heart against the old memory which continued to haunt him.

After finishing the first, small chapel, Christian picked up his brush and the bucket and went to retrieve more water. When he returned, he avoided the remaining two chapels. He went instead through the gap in the paneled rood screen to the chancel, and setting his pail against the east wall, began working on the floor behind the altar, all the while endeavoring to think of nothing but the task at hand.

In a little while he had finished scrubbing the entire length of the floor. Christian wearily stood up, giving much needed relief to his sore knees and back. Turning around slowly, he paused momentarily and studied the naked, stone altar on the steps before him.

In his mind's eye, he saw a golden chalice, a golden cross, some candles, and a bejeweled book slide off a similar altar table and fall onto the floor with a loud clamor. He saw again the cruets containing the consecrated wine flip over onto the floor, spilling their contents onto the white, linen altar cloth and the floor.

Christian resisted the image, determined not to remember. But the fragments of memory would not leave him. He saw the items fall twice more to the floor before he saw his own hand fiercely shoving them off the altar. Then he saw the hosts and paten hit the wall violently, the wafers strewn everywhere.

Alarmed, Christian blanked his mind. He would not think about it! It was over and done with -behind him! It would serve no purpose to remember! He did not have to explain himself! He was king!

But despite his efforts to restrain the memory, already he could smell the sweet aroma of incense-laden air. His heart beat loud and hard in his ears as he remembered the thrill he had experienced when he had emptied the church of worshipers at only a word. He remembered the pleasure he had felt at baiting the priests and seeing the panic in their eyes.

The altar and its vessels were before him again. Christian swallowed as he remembered observing, for one long moment, the *supposed*, consecrated and most holy Body of the Christ on the shiny, golden plate on the altar, ready to be consumed by the faithful, as the priests barked at him from all sides.

Christian recalled being angry and the voices in the back of his mind urging him on, but not what they had said. He clearly remembered assessing the arrogance and blasphemy of such a brazen act, -then making his decision and assenting to it. He flinched as he watched himself actually reach for the Sacrifice and *touch* the golden plate that held the broken, sacred Body of the Savior -and then *fling* it with all his might and fury against the wall, scattering the host everywhere.

Christian blanked him mind at once, trying to turn his thoughts to Felix, Paschal, Kaith, or his concubines. He would not allow himself to think on this! Nor would he feel guilty! It meant nothing! It had been bits of stale bread and wine, nothing more! *There was no god there or anywhere to offend!* It was all superstition! Nothing more!

Yet, try as he might, his mind would think on nothing else, and Christian then recalled the great amazement of those present around the altar. They had all stared at him, dumbfounded, at his sacrilege. The remaining worshippers had screamed and run for the doors. The clerics had instantly gone to their hands and knees, gathering and devouring the pieces and fragments of the broken hosts as if it was priceless treasure. He had gloated over them as they had scurried about, licking the very stone floor like the vermin that they were, until every bit and crumb of the host and every drop of the wine had been consumed.

Christian squeezed his throbbing head with his hand, trying to block out what came next. He quickly picked up his pail and his brush and moved away from the altar to the choir section, telling himself simply that his inclination for battle had been too strong. While the enemy was reeling from his first strike, he had had to finish them. And the opportunity had been within arm's reach.

Getting to his knees, he began to scrub the floor furiously, trying desperately to clear his head. His mind, however, refused to think on anything else, and with his heart pounding violently in his chest, he watched helplessly as he grabbed the nun and forced her face down onto the altar while taunting the priests and his worried advisers. He could still feel all of their exhilarating fear.

Then he was ripping the veil off of her head again and laughing at her, even as the priests were praying over and over again for God to deliver them from their enemy.

The King frantically fought the images in his head. He would not think anymore of that night! None of them had been innocent! he argued. They had violated the law! At the time, he might have overreacted a little, but he had been within *his rights!*

This time, however, his conscience would not acquiesce. The priests had received his adviser's consent for their Mass, it reminded him. Furthermore, his position would have been better served if he had simply endured the gathering for that one time, even if it had been against his wishes. And although the priests had broken the law by inducting one of his own serfs into holy orders, it would have been enough simply to fine them and to deny them future access to the wench.

For the first time, Christian admitted that he had only been seeking sport; and as he had mistakenly believed that no real diversion was to be had with the prisoners, he had chosen to disrupt the Mass.

He winced in aversion as he watched himself untie his braes and prepare to do what was most vulgar where it was most holy and sacrilegious.

He stopped scrubbing the floor and wondered in horror at himself. What could have compelled him to take it that far? Surely, he must have been drunk.

But Christian knew that was not true. He had known precisely what he was doing the entire time. In truth, he had hoped to provoke the clergy into fighting with him. For if the priests had attacked him, his knights would have killed them without hesitation.

'Where is your god now? Will your king of heaven come down and save you? *I* am your King. This is *my* kingdom. Cry out to me for mercy, and you shall have it.'

Christian flinched as he recalled his taunt. -He had wanted that nun to scream, fight, and beg him for mercy. But even more than that, he had wanted her to renounce her vows and her god. But she had controlled her fear and kept her composure, even after he had left -as his knights had reported it.

Had he really thought that he could break the spirit of a celibate? What one of these monks here at St. Brychan's would not gladly die or endure torture for the Faith? Their suffering served to witness to the truth. What lie or folktale could create such devotion?

Then something he had not thought about in years came to his mind.

'Do no harm to the weak or simple. Defend the innocent and the helpless. It is a point of honor.'

Christian swallowed. Sir Gage and his long forgotten teachings were suddenly vivid in his mind then.

'Do not oppress the poor, nor widows, nor orphans. Serve your vassal lord tirelessly and do not abuse those who must obey you. Be faithful, keep your word, and only speak the truth. These are points of honor.'

'Above all, serve God, defend the Church, and be of good virtue.'

'As a knight, you have been entrusted with training in the skills of combat. Use your skills honorably in the service of others. Do not use your skills for selfish gain. Cherish your honor. -Do not dishonor those who wear the spurs by acting dishonorably.'

For the first time, King Christian paused, aghast at what he had done. He cringed at his own audacity. If his mentors, Lord Reynaud or Sir Gage, both strong supporters of the Faith, had been present in the church that night, they would have decried and challenged him immediately right there. It would have been a point of honor for them to have slain him forthwith. The dishonor Christian had brought on them and on all who knew and served him was tremendous!

Sitting on the floor, the tears began to roll down Christian's cheeks as he realized fully what he had done- *and lost*. He had wanted to hurt the palace priests, but, more than that, he had wanted those religious to recant and, in so doing, to discredit the Faith. But it was *his honor* that had been discredited!

Christian swallowed, understanding then that it was worse than that. In that single hour, he had relinquished any *claim* he had had to honor. He felt nauseous as he acknowledged the total disgrace that he had brought on himself and on those who had raised and trained him.

But even then, the memory of that night would not leave him- not until he had witnessed his orders to his knights. Once again, he saw the look of surprise on the face of two of them, and the wide grin on the third. Christian cried in pain as he realized that not one of them had been honorable enough to even refuse him! Not one of them had thrown down his glove, renounced his vassalage, and challenged him! Not one of them had been willing to fight or die for the sake of honor!

Christian was filled with shame and self-disgust as he recalled more dictums of his youth and training:

'A knight without honor is no better than a villein.'

'A vassal who swears fealty to a dishonorable man puts his own honor in jeopardy.'

Christian howled in tears. Why had he done it? Why had no one stopped him? Why had he not listened to his advisers at the time?

-And how could he avenge his honor when it was he himself that had offended it?

The King was so overcome by self-loathing and guilt that he could hardly breathe. No wonder he was not well-respected by his people! Why should they respect him? He could not even respect himself!

His excommunication and the interdict in particular had effectively released his vassals from their oaths of fealty. Had any abandoned him?

What mean sort of men would freely continue to give their allegiance to a man without honor?

He dropped the brush and wailed in agony at the realization of what he had done. He did not blame the people for despising him, or even rebelling against him. Rebellion was the only honorable action to take!

He howled again as he realized the rebels at his palace had proved more honorable than he or his vassals!

No wonder Bennet scorned him! Bennet had been raised with the same codes of honor as he and by the same honorable men. Surely, he felt the shame and dishonor as sharply as Lord Reynaud did!

He did not blame Bennet for his scorn. He did not want any part of himself either! If he met himself on the road, he would kill himself with impunity! He felt sick. He wanted to tear the skin from his body and throw it to the dogs to eat!

'*A king without honor is no better than a villein,*' the voice in his head reminded him.

Christian sobbed with grief and despair for a long time. Surely he deserved all that he had suffered and more. He deserved to die.

Gradually, his tears slowed, and wearily he picked up his brush again and returned to washing the floor miserably, his tears mixing into the water as he scrubbed.

What was he to do? he wondered. How could he redeem his honor that he himself had tainted?

'*The dishonor you bear in this life you will bear in the next,*' the voice told him.

For a long while, Christian was sorely tempted to hang himself. However, the lingering thought of leaving Kaith to deal with eminent invasion and the many other crisis that bore down upon him at present inflamed his sense of duty. There had to be another way.

Gradually, he decided that although it might be considered weakness by some, and wholly inadequate by others, he might lessen some of his dishonor by making amends to those whom he had wronged. He would make reparations to the priests of his palace church and to the nun and her family. He would even free her from the land and allow her to join a convent if it was still her wish. He would also make an effort to get the interdict relaxed and would ask the Bishop to bless the altar so that the church could be used again.

Why not just build a new church? The old one had formerly been a pagan temple of the Romani after all.

Aye, he would have a little church built in a place of his choosing: somewhere on his lands, but *far* from his palace chambers; and he vowed he would regard it respectfully.

This thought satisfied Christian. Likely, if he followed through on these things, he would recover enough of his self-respect and honor to retain the loyalty of his vassals. He could live with himself.

The King's mood lightened immensely after this decision. He sat up momentarily and stretched his aching muscles. He yawned and looked around. He was so tired now that his vision was blurring. He splashed a little of the cool water upon his face again and looked about the church. After all this time, he was only a third finished with the church floor. He picked up his brush again.

55

Christian walked into the brightly lit and crowded hall. Noise, music, and merriment filled his ears. Around him, revelers at long tables were already enjoying roasted boar and toasting each other with strong wine. His stomach growled, and his mouth watered as he inhaled the delicious aroma of whole hind that was cooking nearby on a spit. His eyes fell hungrily onto the table which was laden with every variety of sweetmeat and bread.

"Hail Caesar!"

Christian looked momentarily toward the very far end of the lengthy hall where a group of men were paying homage to someone at the head table. The King continued then down the length of the lower table and stopped at a vacant place on a bench. Here, the tall, large-muscled guests were listening intently as another reveler recounted the story of a great battle. Although feeling small in their presence, Christian sat down among the men quietly and began to listen to the story. As he examined the face of each man near him, he wondered who they were.

All at once, the warrior stopped his tale, and the group of men glanced at Christian.

"Who are you?" they wanted to know.

Christian's heart thumped hard in his chest.

"Christian, King of Speyron," he answered.

"Who?"

Now more of the revelers were staring at him.

"Christian the Fair, King of Speyron," he told them again.

"Christian who?"

"I have never heard of him-" the warriors were muttering with a shake of their heads.

"Who is he?"

They did not recognize his name! Christian realized. They had never heard of him! His heart beat loudly in his ears as more men far down the hall and even at the head table were on their feet now, demanding to know his name.

"Christian the Fair," he answered hesitantly again, "King of Speyron."

"Christian the Fair," came a booming voice from the head table, "what great and heroic deeds have you accomplished to gain admittance to Elysium?"

Christian swallowed hard as his heart pounded rapidly in his chest. Had he fought and won the war to vanquish Herryck from Speyron's borders, or had he lost? He was afraid to mention it lest they laugh at him and tell him that he had died in his sleep before the first battle ever began. He frantically thought back over the rest of his life, but he could not think of a single great and courageous deed he had ever performed.

The revelers were becoming aggressive, and they demanded an answer; he had to say something quickly, but there was only one thing he could think of.

"I built a little church," he said meekly and then immediately wished he had not mentioned it at all.

To his surprise, the huge, battle-hardened warriors did not laugh, but only looked at him curiously.

"A church?"

"Aye."

"We will see this church!" Caesar himself was saying.

And all the men rose from the tables in expectation. Alarmed, Christian faltered momentarily, but then walked toward the entrance of the hall with the mass of warriors following him, wondering with every step if he would even be able to find the church and what they would do to him if he could not. However, after opening the hall doors, the King was relieved to see it was located just outside.

Christian smiled with pride at the sight. Without doubt, this was *his* church, the church *he* had built. It was much bigger and much more grandiose than he had thought it would be.

The entire mob of warriors followed him outside into the blinding, bright sun of midday, across a few yards of deserted, dusty, parched earth for a closer look.

The exterior of the building was beautiful to behold. It was adorned with decorative molding and reliefs of early saints; the bell tower was quite tall.

"Very impressive!"

Christian beamed with the praise, many compliments, and hard slaps on the back that he received from the warriors. He wondered with excitement what splendor the interior would contain. Would the walls be painted in fleck gold? Would the rood screen be of the finest wood and painted and gilded as well? Would the altar and statues be of marble? Would there be an intricate mosaic floor?

Giddy with anticipation, Christian waited expectantly as a few of the brawny revelers with great effort opened the heavily-carved, massive doors. Then he and the group went inside and looked around.

Christian's heart leaped in his chest again and beat violently. The inside of the beautiful church was dark and in total disrepair. There was no baptismal font. The side chapels were unfinished; the walls were not painted at all. The floor was simply dirt. The rood, the large wooden crucifix that should have hung over the gap in the rood screen, had never been added!

Christian reddened with humiliation as the worthy heroes near him began to grumble. He quickly ventured deeper into the church, wondering what had happened; then he gasped in horror.

The nave itself was full of putrefying corpses: the starved bodies of men, women, and children had been thrown together in piles. The rood screen, the lattice work barrier that separated the nave from the chancel and which symbolized man's inability to reach God on his own, should have been decoratively carved from stone or wood in a way as to allow worshippers to still view the altar. Instead, the screen had been tightly fashioned from spears and swords so that they formed a solid fence. Several, sagging, grotesque heads adorned the top of it. Christian could not even see the sanctuary or the altar from the nave except through the center gap in the screen, and that gap was so narrow that no one could get through it to approach the altar, at least without being gravely injured.

Peeping through the gap, Christian saw in the chancel itself, headless, rotting corpses in the remnants of their vestments. The plain, dusty altar was uncovered; upon it, among the cobwebs, a small, simple box served as the tabernacle for the Reserved Sacrament, but the candle of the sanctuary lamp was not lit, and it looked like it had never been set afire.

And everywhere in the sanctuary, there were rats, rats, rats: eating at the bodies and gnawing at the legs of the weak, wobbly, wooden, unraised altar.

Christian's heart raced as he surveyed the awful sight. His heart skipped again apprehensively as he heard the angry disapproval of the warriors behind him.

Tried as he might, Christian could not turn his eyes away from the horrible view of the rats and the death until a rumbling sound, at first faint but growing ever louder, drew his attention. Around him, the very walls had begun to tremble and shake. He looked about fearfully, wondering if the very foundation was flawed and caving in; but the ground was level and solid, and the trembling was not coming from it. The youth gasped then as he saw a multitude of rats begin to pour out of the walls and bear down upon him.

Christian screamed and fled. Reaching the great doors of the church, he found himself suddenly alone and the doors shut tightly. While the rats fell upon him, he fought them off, falling to the dirt as he did.

The rats were at once gone then. As his heartbeat slowed, it still pounded hard in his chest as he noticed his new surroundings.

As the odor of burning flesh filled his nostrils, Christian tentatively peered up through the darkness. There were flames near him, but, strangely, they gave off no light.

Standing over him was a huge, slimy creature that Christian had never seen before. It stood upright like a man, but yet was not a man, and yet it resembled no animal he had ever seen. Indescribable and yet too hideous to look at, Christian averted his eyes from it as his ears were assaulted by a new and harrowing sound. The hairs stood up on the back of his neck as he slowly looked to his left toward the cries. A little ways from him, two similar creatures were flaying the skin from a nude man with their long claws. Christian shuddered. Never in his life had he ever heard a sound of such utter agony from any living thing. It made his very flesh crawl.

As stark terror overwhelmed his senses, a sharp, cold and mucus-coated talon took him by the back of the neck and dragged him over the rough terrain toward the pair. The creatures left that man and then lifted Christian into the air effortlessly. Christian hung helplessly before the huge monsters, naked, unable to move as they observed him with their beady eyes.

He watched wide-eyed as one of the horrid beasts took a great hook and, without hesitation, impaled his stomach all the way through his back. Christian could hardly breathe from the pain.

"Why are you doing this?" he asked, already knowing the answer.

The beasts did not reply as they tossed him backward into a large lake ablaze with dark flames. Christian shrieked and struggled madly as he sunk under the water. After surfacing, he screamed wildly as he bobbed in the liquid which was scorching his very flesh. His skin burned off his arms, and the meat beneath bled red. He wept and howled from the pain, his eyes smarting from the smoke of the fires, and yet he still feared that he would drown in the burning water.

"Mercy! Pity!" he cried.

As he splashed about in fright, he collided with something hard. Peering through the dark, he gasped. It was clearly someone else, another man perhaps, but any guise of humanness was gone; its eyes, nose, ears, and hair had burned away. It seemed to be suffering and screaming also, as it thrashed in place with its handless stubs, but it made no sound, for it no longer had lips or a tongue.

Christian abruptly moved away from the grotesque thing only to find that he was surrounded in the lake by the faceless, writhing freaks. Panicked and wailing in pain and terror and despair, Christian looked about and saw the two beasts still watching him from the shore. His cries for pity became rants as he observed them turn and *leave him alone* to the darkness and his misery.

Christian awoke screaming and weeping, the images still fresh in his mind. His head throbbed in pain, and his body shook from the sheer pounding of his heart.

It was a few, long moments before Christian knew where he was. He had fallen asleep on the floor in the chancel, he realized, -the floor he was supposed to be washing. He was safe. His skin was still intact; his stomach was unmarred. It had only been a dream.-

Christian shut out that thought. It was no dream! He looked about the abbey church again in all its familiarity and began to weep afresh.

He was doomed. He would receive his just rewards. All of the old religions were in agreement about that. He would deny it no more. Everything was so clear to him. What did he care of his honor- or anything of this world, when faced with the terrors that surely awaited him?

Although he did not believe in any god more than another, Christian knew of only one religion that asserted it could avert the eternal punishment he had justly earned in his life. Only the Lord God, the god of the Faith, would forgive his offenses, even the ones against the god himself, but only if he truly repented and dedicated his life to Him.

But were there even enough days left in his life for him to complete the penance that would be required of him in order to receive forgiveness for what he had done? On the other hand, if he did not try-

Christian went cold as he saw again the visions that remained in his mind.

He was determined. He would repent. He would acknowledge God and serve Him. He would make amends with the Church. He would adhere to the teachings and practices of the Faith and hear Mass regularly and wholeheartedly. He would accept and follow the Savior.

He would have to change drastically, he realized, and remain forever changed. If he returned to living sinfully, he would be lost.

But one problem, one nagging doubt, still remained: Was there truly a god? Was there truly a Hell?

King Christian screamed and wept in renewed frustration, the sound echoing through the church. But the conflict within him was real and would not be denied. Wretched, he continued to sit on the cold floor, weeping, and tearing at his clothes with his fingers.

Why did he doubt? Why did he continue to question and mistrust when he wanted to believe? Why could he not be like everyone else and believe the stories? Why could no one convince him?

His head pounded and ached so painfully, he thought it might burst. He wished he could die. He wished for relief from his pain and doubt.

"Pater de caelis, Deus, miserere mei. Amen.-"

Reciting the prayer he had learned long ago, Christian whispered the words desperately, hoping for help, for anything, in fact.

"Fili, redemptor mundi, Deus, miserere mei. Spiritus Sancte, Deus, miserere mei. Sancta Trinitas, unus Deus, miserere mei. Amen."

Christian recited the entire prayer twice more, crossed himself, and wiped his face on his sleeve, but he felt no better. Looking up into the dimly lit church, his eyes fell on the back of the great statue of the Madonna and Child in the nave.

"Ave, Gratia Plena, Dominus tecum. Sancta Maria, Mater Dei, ora pro nobis peccatoribus. Amen."

Although Christian still remembered all the prayers he had been taught in his childhood as well as the many the novices said daily at the Hours, the words still sounded empty to his ears. Yet he persisted and tried another.

"Ideo precor sanctos Apostolos Petrum, beatum patronum, orare pro me ad Dominum Deum nostrum. Amen."

Christian heard the wind howling outside the church. Otherwise, there was only silence.

This is ludicrous, Christian told himself while wiping his runny nose and face with his sleeve. What exactly had he expected anyway?

The King winced as more tears fell. He had never felt more alone in his entire life. Either there was nothing there or else he was so evil that neither God nor any saint would help him.

If only he knew what the truth was.

He tried again, dropping the Latin altogether.

"God, Father in Heaven, forgive me. -And -I need a sign that you are there. Amen."

Christian crossed himself and frowned, his words sounding ridiculous to his own ears. How could he pray to a god he doubted existed? Would God not be offended?

After a moment, an idea came to him.

"Blessed Thomas the Doubter, pray for me, a fellow doubter," Christian said miserably. "I have done grievous things of which I am ashamed, and I want to make amends, and I want to believe- but I have to know.- If you can hear me, pray to the Lord God on my behalf -that He will send me a sign that He exists. Amen."

The King was silent then in the church's echoing quiet. He forced himself to be patient, his hope struggling feebly against his skepticism. He looked around and waited.

Nothing happened. Nothing changed. All was stillness.

Christian felt utterly empty. In this moment of ultimate need, his hope gave way to real despair.

Bitterly, he picked up his brush again and began to scrub the floor where he had left off, his inner voice ridiculing him for his foolishness. Had he really expected something to happen? How pathetic!

Christian turned his attention to the dirt in the crevices between the stones, which, for the first time that night, was clearly visible. As he scrubbed the cracks with added care, he saw that even the contours of the stone could be distinctly seen. Then he shifted to the side, noticing that his shadow, which was much stronger than before, was shading the area where he was working.

Christian moaned. Was it dawn already? He was not half finished with the floor yet. -If it was dawn, the novices were late, he realized.

He quickly glanced at the small window near the ceiling of the church, but it was still dark.

Christian dipped his brush in the cold water again and moved over a little to begin a new section. He noticed then the strong, sharp, mesh-patterned shadow cast on the floor. Setting down the brush again, he looked up toward the source of the shadow and marveled both at the bright colors and small, decorative details painted on the rood screen that he had never noticed in all his time of singing the Divine Office.

The hairs on the back of his neck and all over his body suddenly stood on end. Christian gasped and scrambled to his feet abruptly. His heart skipped a beat and then beat rapidly as he saw that the entire church was lit brightly now, as if day had come and the sunlight was flooding in the very roof.

Moving quickly to the gap in the screen, Christian's blood turned to ice, and his heart pounded wildly in his chest as he looked around the entire church. He saw clearly the colorful images painted on the walls, the detail in the carvings of the statues, even the design carved on the side of the bare altar.

Christian could scarcely breathe; and still the light increased. It grew so bright that he began squinting, then shielding his eyes with his hand, while he searched vainly for the source of the light which so completely obscured the meager light from the few burning torches.

He shuddered as all his senses suddenly pricked at their surroundings. Chillbumps ran up his entire body as he suddenly felt that, although no one was there, he was no longer *alone*.

As abject fear overtook him, all at once Christian's legs gave out. On his knees and quaking, he was suddenly and slowly pressed backward onto his back onto the floor and held there under the might of a great and invisible force. He could neither move nor see under the radiant, blazing, brilliant light, but lay defenseless under its power in stark terror.

And Christian, King of Speyron, without doubt, knew *Who* was there.

"Mercy! Mercy, Lord Christ!" he wept.

The King's mind was then filled with a booming voice so intense and strong that his senses could barely bear the words it spoke.

"Thy prayers have been heard. Receive thy sight."

Christian gasped, hardly able to draw breath, as fresh goosebumps covered him. His heart, already racing, skipped a beat and then jumped ahead.

And then as suddenly as it all had come, it departed. The light began to fade. The force holding him to the floor was gone, and Christian was slowly able to get up.

Still shaking with fear, King Christian got on his knees, and clasping his hands together, with fresh tears, prayed, "Oh, God, Lord Christ in Heaven, please forgive my disbelief! I promise I will never doubt again, nor disregard my duty to You!"

Then he put his head to the floor and wept in distraction and relief.

The King's whole being was enveloped by warmth then, and his heart was filled with a feeling of peace. His weeping stopped. The pain in his head left him.

After a few minutes, Christian thanked God and the Christ and the Holy Spirit for answering his prayer, and he continued to promise fealty. He also thanked the Virgin Mary and St. Peter and St. Thomas for their prayers.

As his heartbeat and breathing continued to slow, the King sat in the darkened church and wondered what he should do. He did not want to be alone now. He did not want to be quiet. He wanted to scream and dance, ring the church bells, and tell someone- tell everyone! He could not keep this too himself! He had to go out and share the joy he felt!

He was on his feet then with new energy. He hurried toward the church door, stopping to bow and cross himself in the appropriate places. In total elation, he ran through the cloister. He did not know where to go, but he just had to tell someone.

He decided quickly and arrived at a cell door and banged on it furiously. It was quite late. There was a groan from inside the chamber, and some scuffling footsteps. The door was eventually opened by a man wrapped in a coverlet who yawned and sleepily rubbed his eyes.

"Father Confessor!"

The monk was immediately embraced.

"Aye, My Son," he answered, a little off balance, his eyes not quite open. "What has happened? Is there a fire?"

"No, Father."

"Is someone dying?"

"No-"

"Oh, well, come in then. It is cold out here."

Christian entered the cell and said excitedly, "Father, forgive me for waking you, but something wonderful has happened! -And I had to tell someone!"

The old monk, sensing that this might take some time to sort out, took his candle and lit it from one of the burning torches outside his chamber. He entered his cell again and looked around to the young man who had awakened him.

"Tillo?" he asked with some surprise.

"Aye, Father."

"What are you doing up at this hour?"

"Oh, I am washing the church floor."

"At this hour? Whatever for?"

"The Abbot gave me a list."

"Never mind," the confessor said quickly. "What is it that you wish to tell me?"

"Something wonderful! I was in the church, washing the floor and- and-" and suddenly Christian did not know how to explain what had happened.

"And?"

"There was a light! And a voice-" Christian answered joyfully. "-And I was alone!"

The priest looked intently at the youth.

"It said, 'Thy prayers have been heard. Re-'"

"You- were praying?" Father Desle interrupted curiously.

"Uh, aye."

The priest cocked his head to the side and rubbed his chin, and asked, "Was that on your list?"

"No, Father."

The priest raised his eyebrows and gestured for the youth to continue.

"Anyway, I had been praying, and -asking for prayers of help from my patron saints-" Christian admitted with hesitancy, not because he was ashamed, but because it felt very personal.

"Uh- huh."

"And then the church became really bright, so bright, that I was covering my eyes with my hand! And I fell to my knees and onto my back and could not right myself! And then I heard the words: 'Thy prayers have been heard. Receive thy sight.'! And I was so excited that I just had to tell someone! And I came straight here!"

The confessor did not say anything for a moment, absorbing the words and the clear joy in the youth's face. Then he stood up and embraced him.

"I am happy for you, My Son! I am so happy for you. Now, it is very early, and we shall talk more tomorrow. Retire to bed now."

"I cannot! I must finish the church floor first! But I thank thee!"

Overflowing with pure joy, Christian hugged the old man again and then went out of the cell.

"God is wonderful!" he declared.

The confessor stood dumbly at the door of his cell and watched as the King ran back toward the church to finish his work.

"'All the kings of the earth will praise you, O Lord, when they have heard the words of your mouth-'" the old man quoted thoughtfully, as he shut his door, blew out the candle, and returned to his bed.

As he lay back down and waited for sleep to overtake him, he marveled at the mysterious and wondrous ways of the Lord.

56

Sitting at his desk, Abbot Hunfred smoothed his thinning hair idly while he read the illuminated manuscript before him. He looked up and saw that Brother Lubin was once again in the study and was waiting silently to be noticed.

"He is back again, is he?"

"Aye, Lord Abbot, he returned directly after Lauds."

"You may remind him that if he tarries here much longer he will be late for Prime," Hunfred said irritably, turning the page of the book.

"I have so instructed the lad, Lord Abbot, but he persists in waiting to speak with you."

"If this is how he wishes to spend his day of rest-" the Abbot muttered with a shrug.

Hunfred sighed irritably. The King probably wished to complain about their treatment of him or perhaps desired to request less taxing work for the next few days. On the other hand, Hunfred mused, perhaps he was planning to announce his departure.

"Very well, send him in," the Abbot abruptly consented, closing the book and rising from his chair.

The monk bowed and left the room; Hunfred picked up his notes for the Chapter Meeting and began scanning the work assignments for the week. Engrossed in his thoughts, he was only vaguely aware of faint footsteps before his legs were grabbed without warning, and he nearly toppled to the floor. The Abbot seized his desktop for balance and then looked down at the blond petitioner who had hold of his knees and was talking so fast, he could hardly understand him.

"Your Grace?" the Abbot asked quite startled.

"Lord Abbot, I have a most urgent petition."

"Please stand up, Your Grace!" Hunfred said, embarrassed. "I am *not* the Bishop."

But Christian neither moved nor relinquished his grasp of the Abbot's knees.

"What is it? Are you here to tell me you still have not finished the assigned chores of your punishment?" Hunfred asked gruffly.

"No, Lord Abbot, it is all completed."

"Then what-"

"Please, Lord Abbot, I know it is Sunday, but is there a brother or anyone who could be sent out with a message today? I need to send a message of the most urgent nature-"

"The road to the palace," Hunfred interrupted, "was still impassable three days ago."

"-to Bishop Gildas -though I know not where he may be now. I must find out what needs to be done, -what I must do, -to persuade the Bishop to relax the interdict and my excommunication."

Hunfred was mute in astonishment. Had he heard correctly?

"Please, Lord Abbot, not only for me- but out of mercy for our people who suffer without the comfort of the Sacraments. -Please, I cannot bear to be the cause of this, nor for a moment more to pass without making every effort to reunite myself and the people with the Church!"

Totally speechless, Hunfred stared down at the young man for a long moment, scarcely believing his ears. Was this an impostor? Was he even awake? Could he still be in his bed, asleep, and this all a dream?

"Lord Abbot, do not now reveal such a hard heart," a new voice chided.

The Abbot looked up to see the abbey's confessor at the doorway of the office. Hunfred looked back down again and saw that the King was actually weeping, the tears wetting the bottom of his own scapular where the young man clutched it to his face. Only then did he grasp that the youth was interpreting his silence as a refusal of his petition. The sight of his sudden despair further amazed Hunfred.

Father Desle squatted down beside the King and asked, "My Son, have you been up this entire night?"

"Aye," Christian mumbled miserably.

The senior confessor carefully pulled the lad to his feet. The two monks saw that the King was pale and exhausted. There were dark rings around his blue eyes, and he smelled foully, and among other things, distinctly like pig dung.

"Go now and rest, My Son."

"I cannot. I must stay here until the Abbot grants my petition. -And it will soon be time for Prime."

The Abbot, still disconcerted, affirmed quickly, "Aye, never mind about Prime or the other Hours today. Retire to the dormitory and rest. Be assured that we will at once send word to the Bishop of your desire to reconcile."

Relieved, Christian nodded and wiped his wet face on his habit sleeve.

"Thank you, Lord Abbot."

"We will summon you for dinner and inform you of our progress," Hunfred said.

Christian nodded again wearily. The men bowed to each other, and Christian turned and went out of the Abbot's office.

The two men watched him leave, and then the Abbot shut the office door before he spoke.

"What deception is this?"

"No deception, I believe, Lord Abbot, but an answer to all our prayers: The King has finally been awakened out of his long sleep."

"I scarcely recognize him! Has he truly been up the entire night?"

"I believe so. He came to my cell late in the night."

"Why? Was he unwell? I heard that he became suddenly ill during Collation last night, but he did not report to the infirmary."

"I know not. When he arrived at my door, he was in complete elation."

"Elation?"

"Aye, something happened to him when he was cleaning the church floor."

"What?"

"I know not exactly. He said he saw a light and heard a voice. It sounded like he might have been *visited* -perhaps by a saint or an angel."

"An angel or Brother Bennet?" Hunfred asked skeptically.

"Brother Bennet has forsaken him; he neither speaks to the King, nor of him."

Hunfred raised his eyebrows considering this.

"Did he tell you what the voice said?"

"Aye," the old confessor answered, but then hesitated; he disliked divulging such personal revelations.

"Well, what did it say?" Hunfred pressed.

"He said the voice told him that his prayers had been heard and to receive his sight."

"He had been praying?"

The older monk smiled.

"I asked him the very same question. Apparently he had been."

"This is too much to be believed," Hunfred muttered.

The confessor raised his eyebrows.

"Is it?"

Abbot Hunfred stared blankly at the wall, lost in thought. He realized he was as unprepared for this turn of events as he had been for the youth's initial appearance at their gate almost three months ago. In truth, he had never expected this arrogant youth to willingly reconcile with the Church, -and certainly for no reason other than political shrewdness. He had always assumed that the King would leave St. Brychan's at his earliest convenience entirely unchanged.

"And you truly believe his change of heart is sincere?" Hunfred asked.

"I do. And, My Lord, now that his eyes have been opened, methinks he will want to make his confession. Like many sinners who suddenly feel the weight of their sins upon them, he may not be able to bear the guilt for very long without the hope-"

"You think the Bishop's arrival may be too long to wait?"

"I fear it may be so."

"Very well, hear his confession but withhold absolution until the Bishop relaxes the interdict and excommunication."

The confessor nodded and sat down on the bench at the table, but then observed the Abbot's face drawn with care.

"Why do you frown, Hunfred? This is a joyous occasion! The entire host of Heaven is celebrating and so should you be also! Why, if the Bishop arrives in the next fortnight, then all of Speyron may observe Christmas and some of Advent!"

"Have you ever met Bishop Gildas?" Hunfred asked pensively.

"No, I have not had that pleasure."

"Gildas is a faithful servant of the Church, but ambitious. He is a shrewd man particularly when pitted against the opponents of the Faith. Methinks he will find the news of the King's repentance suspicious at best. -I can hardly fathom it now, and I have seen him with my own eyes. The King is so- different."

"So was Paul, Lord Abbot, after his experience."

"Even so, it would be easier to convince the Bishop of King Christian's sincerity if the King's early religious training in Gaulia had not been so thorough. As it is, Gildas will never believe that the King turned away from the Church out of ignorance or that he was led astray by some heretic. He knows the King rejected the Faith on his own, and he certainly will conclude that his reconciliation is in name only, and solely a political tactic."

"As you do?" Desle accused.

"I can not deny it," Hunfred admitted.

"Lord Abbot, the youth is sincere," the confessor told him again. "I know it."

The Abbot nodded and smoothed his thinning hair again.

"Is it necessary that the Bishop be convinced of his contrition?" Desle asked then. "Is the King's desire to reconcile not enough?"

The Abbot sat down behind his desk again.

"Ordinarily it would be. In the past, bishops have relaxed interdicts and excommunications on monarchs after they made gifts of moneys to them or to Roma along with some semblance of obedience to the Church's authority, -though that was secondary. But-"

"But what?"

"The Bishop is in Gaulia now, getting fat on lamb and wine." Hunfred said with a shake of his head. "And unbeknownst to the King, Gildas already sent an answer to the preliminary inquiries of the King's adviser, my friend, Lord Olbert. Gildas made it clear that he would not be moved to relax the interdict without a complete transformation on the part of the King. -He wants not only several conditions met, but a firm commitment of future cooperation and full allegiance with the dictates of the Church."

The Father Confessor listened to the Abbot curiously.

"Methinks," Hunfred continued, "he made this condition with the full knowledge that it was not likely to happen. -It would be difficult for any ruler to keep such a promise and clearly impossible for one who was trying to reconcile in name only."

"Then pray for them both, Lord Abbot, as we all must. Pray that the Bishop will be reasonable in his demands. And pray that the King will have the strength of spirit to walk the coming days in utter humility. For if the King can persevere and the Bishop witnesses his changed and penitent spirit, then the Bishop shall surely be convinced of the King's sincerity and will relax the interdict."

The Abbot nodded and without further hesitation, took out parchment, ink and quill to draft the letter to the Bishop.

57

Christian's palms were already perspiring as he gingerly tapped on the door of the confessor's cell. After a moment, Father Delse opened the door.

"Come in, My Son," he invited warmly.

Christian looked immediately at the floor, unable even to answer the monk's genial greeting as he entered the cell.

As the confessor shut the door behind him, Christian glanced around nervously, his eyes settling momentarily on a wave of purple. The purple stole that hung about the confessor's neck was a cheery and colorful contrast to the monk's black habit and the drab contents of the cell.

Father Desle smiled kindly and seemed to be about to say something, but the King frowned and turned away quickly. Christian knew the confessor was just trying to put him at ease, but he could not even bear to look at him for shame.

In the center of the cell was a chair with a straw mat just before it. Anxiously trying to avoid the priest's friendly gaze, Christian, wiping his damp palms on his habit, went immediately over to the straw mat in the center of the chamber and got on his knees and waited.

Desle came to stand beside him, and Christian crossed himself while the priest made the sign of the cross over him. Then Desle sat in the chair and picked up one end of the stole and laid it over the King's head.

"Confiteor Deo omnipotenti," Christian quickly began, "beatae Mariae- semper Virgini, beato Michaeli Archangelo, beato Ioanni Baptistae, sanctis Apostolis Petro et Paulo, omnibus Sanctis, et tibi pater, quia peccavi nimis cogitatione, verbo, et opere: mea culpa, mea culpa, mea maxima culpa," striking his breast three times as he spoke the last.

"Ideo precor beatam Mariam semper Virginem, beatum Michaelem Archangelum, beatum Ioannem Baptistam, sanctos Apostolos Petrum et Paulum, omnes Sanctos, et te, pater, orare pro me ad Dominum Deum nostrum. Amen."

Then Christian crossed himself again, his heart pounding loudly in his ears in the quiet of the cell.

"Father Confessor: I am King of Speyron. I am an excommunicate," Christian said quickly, swallowing hard to keep back his tears that were already threatening to fall, "-and the land is under interdict through my own fault. I am not married, and it has been more than three and a half years since my last confession."

He paused. Desle waited on the youth to continue.

"I confess that I have not loved God or my neighbor. -I do not want to hide the truth of what I have done or withhold anything. Please, Father, help me make an honest confession."

He took a deep breath.

"I am a wicked man, Father. As king, I am God's anointed servant and representative, and I am a disgrace to Him," Christian winced. "-When I came to the throne, God cursed the people of my kingdom with barrenness, for He saw the darkness in my heart, and He sought to discipline me to encourage me to repent. But I did not heed His discipline. Instead, I refused to care what my kingdom or the people suffered, and I did not repent.

"More than two years ago I was excommunicated for killing a priest. He was trying to protect the holy relics he was taking to another monastery. He discovered my men and I -treating them -irreverently and sacrilegiously. I-"

"What did you do to them?"

Christian frowned and swallowed.

"I tossed the bones back and forth with my knights, and then I threw the relics upon the ground and pissed on them."

Desle raised his eyebrows.

"We were drunk at the time. The priest tried to stop me, and we beat the man. But afterward, by my own will, I strangled him -for sport-" he added as the tears began to flow freely down his face, "and I am *grievously* sorry for it."

"Even after my excommunication, I still did not repent. A few months ago, the kingdom was placed under interdict after I interrupted a Mass in the church at my palace and -*desecrated* -the Holy Sacrament."

Christian could not go on after he spoke these words. He sobbed wretchedly into his hands before the priest for some time. The youth's misery moved Desle to pity.

"-I desecrated the blessed *Body of our Lord* and the altar-" Christian finally continued, still weeping. "I- I put my unworthy hand upon Him- upon His undefiled body that He willingly laid down- laid down for me -for us all, and I- I- cast Him away! I threw Him against the wall!" he wailed in agony.

Desle winced in compassion as the lad cried in remorse.

"-And -and I fully intended to further defile the altar myself by ravaging a novice nun upon it. But my advisers were pressing me to return to the palace, so I- I ordered my men to swyve her on the altar in my place. And they- obeyed my orders."

Father Desle frowned and closed his eyes.

"I deserve to die for what I have done! I deserve damnation!" the youth cried miserably through his tears. "-I have asked myself scores and scores of times why I did it. -I had been drinking, but I was not drunk. -And although I had been angry at the priests at the palace church, they were not to blame for this. -I think, at the time, I thought it sport.

"But, in truth, I hated those priests and what they stood for and what they believed because I could not believe it! As a child, I had tried to believe, but I never could!"

Desle listened silently.

"For years, Father, I have rejected God wholeheartedly- and have encouraged others to do the same!" he sobbed. "I have spurned His priests and prophets. I have scoffed and laughed while laymen have proclaimed Him and His works. I have ignored His holy days and the shrines of the saints. Before I was excommunicated, I loathed to hear Mass and rarely did so. -And I am heartily sorry for it!

"-And that night, -when I discovered those priests had encouraged one of my serfs to be a celibate-" Christian said, frowning and swallowing painfully, "I- well, I wanted to hurt them all! I wanted to strike them such a blow that they would be forced to recant- and finally deny and denounce the Faith!"

The youth was unable to speak, overcome with weeping then.

"God forgive me!" he wailed. "-I confess I have always wanted Speyron separated from the Faith! And since I came to the throne, I have tried to reduce the influence of the Church and its teachings in the kingdom. Although I knew the Faith was important to most of my subjects, because I could not understand why they were devoted to God -whom they could not see, I wanted the entire realm to be free from what I thought were lies and superstition. -And my lack of faith and bad example and the interdict have imperiled all the souls in my kingdom! And I am grievously sorry for it!

"-And although I did not go to the church that night intending to do what I did, on previous occasions I had toyed with the idea of sending my men to burn down the church under the cover of darkness. I regret this also."

Desle sighed.

Christian moaned heavily and wiped his wet face on his sleeve.

"I have also spoken against the Faith and praised pagan gods and religions."

"Have you worshipped pagan deities?"

"No, I have not worshipped any god. -Even here at the monastery, when I sang the Divine Office with the other novices- in my heart, I did not worship God," he admitted as new tears fell from his eyes. "I mocked God in my heart as I sang the Psalms with the novices, and silently I ridiculed the novices as they prayed daily for my repentance and for my return to the Faith and the Church."

The King fell silent then, wincing as he attempted to gain control of his rising emotions. After a minute or so, he continued.

"I have failed to love my neighbor as I love myself."

"How so?"

"In every way, Father. -In more ways than I can either remember or confess."

The King frowned as more tears fell from his eyes.

"I have been most cruel. I have belittled my subjects, had them beaten, and some even killed, for no cause but sport."

"How often?"

"Before I was run out of my palace, several times a week."

"Why did you do this?"

"Because I could. No one could say a word against me."

"Is that the only reason?"

Christian recalled Paschal and Felix's delight in his unexpected orders of violence. He could hardly blame them, though, for the decisions to order beatings and the like had been his.

"Often I sought sport for diversion from the strain of rule. Other times, I worked mischief to win the approval of my friends."

Desle raised his eyebrows at this.

"Before I came here, I had grown to relish more than ever before the torment and mockery of people, particularly those weaker than myself."

Desle frowned.

"Is anyone stronger than their king, My Son?" the confessor asked sternly. "Hunting is sport. Competition at arms is sport. Cruelty to those who can not hope to stand against you is not."

Christian winced.

"I know, Father. -And I was taught better in the noble household that raised me. I have disgraced my noble mentors as I have disgraced God and wounded my own honor, perhaps beyond cure. -I can not fathom how I have so strayed from the life of honor that my mentors live and that they imparted to me."

"What else, My Son?"

"As king, many times I have been unjust to my vassals."

"In what way?"

"On occasion, I have lied to them. I have lied to ambassadors of other kingdoms and sometimes to my own vassals that I would do something that they wanted, when I had no intention of doing it. It was easier to send them away with a lie than to risk a confrontation that the truth would have brought."

"Sire, how can your vassals trust and serve you if they can not trust your word? And how can you rule effectively if you fear speaking your mind to them?"

"I know not, Father."

Desle gestured for Christian to continue.

"I also lied to the Abbot about the true reason I wanted to make a retreat here. It was never my intention to seek spiritual guidance or to amend my ways. I simply wanted a secure place to lodge for a fortnight. -I also lied to him months ago when I told him I had washed the hall floor when I had not."

Desle smiled slightly.

"I have also been unjust in some of the royal appointments that I made," Christian continued.

"How so?"

"The most grievous concerned Lord Van Necht. He is a man who is well-respected among the vassals in the kingdom, a man of integrity, loyalty, and honor. During the last years of my father's reign, he had proven himself dependable and skilled in war and in the leading of men. Yet I did not appoint him as Commander of the Army as he wished, but rather bestowed the honor on my friend Paschal, although he is neither as competent nor as respected as Van Necht. Instead, as a joke, I appointed Van Necht as Queen's Guard-"

"When there is no queen?"

"Rather because he has the reputation for despising the company of women."

"Why did you do this?"

"I thought it sport."

"Sport? To deny an honorable, capable man an appointment he wanted and appoint him to a position he would hate? Why did you do this to him?"

"I did not delight in his company," Christian admitted painfully. "I found him always to be serious and sober. At Court, he never showed any interest in the amusements I enjoyed. Nor did he ever make an attempt to flatter me or to win my favor. However, Paschal and I have been constant companions since I returned from Gaulia."

Christian swallowed.

"I also sent a witch to Van Necht for his bed, -without warning him."

The confessor frowned.

"This was for sport as well?"

"Aye."

"How will you make amends to this vassal for the injustice done him?"

"I know not."

"You must find a way to make restitution to him and to any others you have wronged," Desle told him simply.

Christian was silent as he thought over the events of the last three and a half years. He cringed as the faces of Lord Fenton and his wife confronted him then. Disbelief and grief were permanently etched on their features as they witnessed the unexpected execution of their firstborn, innocent son, upon which all their hopes for the future had rested, for the crimes of his father. After he had ordered Lord Fenton's execution, Christian remembered patting the younger son on the head as a warning to all present. He swallowed at the memory.

"There have been times when, as king, I have had to shed blood to keep order or to protect my position. I know that those acts were justified, but as I look back on them now, I feel some guilt about them. And in a few of the situations, I fear that I acted excessively and brutally when I could have shown mercy."

"How so?"

"Over the summer, a few of my vassals took up arms against me. I waged war and took back their lands. After the castle of the instigator fell, I executed the nobleman as well as his oldest son, although the lad was innocent; and I threatened to kill the younger son as a further warning to the household. I fear-" Christian hesitated as the tears began to fall again, "-it was excessive. I could have simply executed Lord Fenton."

"I see."

Christian closed his eyes. Tears continued to roll down his cheeks as the images of the nobleman's family were replaced by numerous faces of people he could not even name -and the countless suffering he had caused them.

Finally he spoke.

"I am guilty of pride. I do not know how a man can be king and *not* be proud. But I admit I have used my powers as king unjustly -out of pride and anger."

"How many times?"

"Truthfully, I know not."

"How so?"

Christian took a deep breath, remembering the peasants he had killed who had tried to deter him from taking their daughters as concubines.

"-Many times I have ordered the execution of a villein when they cried out for justice against me. At the time, it was easier to execute those who complained rather than to reevaluate my orders. Sometimes I did not kill them, but burned down their homes..."

Father Desle sat numbly with his hand covering his face as he listened to account after account of brutality and the killing of innocents for the sake of injured pride. As the confessor to the monks at the monastery, he had heard very few confessions of murder at all over the years, and never so many from one lad. The details shocked and grieved him.

"...Out of pride and anger, I nearly banished a loyal advisor whose words offended me. Many times I have wanted to kill a sharp-tongued, villein witch who dared to speak boldly to me. -I do not know how many peasants I killed because they resisted my will."

"A score?"

"Aye, perhaps."

Christian winced then as the memory of the seers returned to his mind. How brave and different they had all been- and so amusing! The old, bearded Jebedye was before him again, demanding to be heard. The aged man had been frail, but had spoken with a bold spirit and authority. Christian painfully recalled mocking the stuttering of the mad man as he advised everyone to repent and then laughing at the blond haired boy standing on the chair as he spoke of the future in his grand voice. Then the boy's head was lying beside his body in a pool of blood. Fresh tears streamed down the King's cheeks again.

"-I also executed a group of seers. One was old Jebedye who had been loyal to my family for many years. I struck him down first and - and-hacked his body and put his head on my palace wall because he told me the truth about myself," Christian wept pitifully. "Then I executed the others in revenge for what he had said, and one was a child no older than five years."

Desle shut his eyes, struggling to control his own emotions as the youth grieved before him.

The King remembered the seer-witch again, reproaching and condemning him for ordering the garrisons to retake the palace. He wept as he envisioned his own loyal servants and serfs being put to the sword indiscriminately by garrisons of knights out to avenge his injured pride and tainted honor with blood. How many innocents had died? How many homes had burned? How much suffering had that one order caused? At the time, he had thought the cost was acceptable; now he was unsure.

"I have a violent temper, Father," Christian said weakly. "In truth, I try to resist losing my temper, but once I do lose it, I give myself to the rage willingly and completely. Because of it, I have dealt harshly with many, many people."

"With your servants and Court, too?" Desle asked.

"Aye."

"What causes you to lose your temper?"

Christian shrugged.

"Slights, disappointments, stupid mistakes, bad news-" the youth answered.

"Surprises?"

"Aye, that too. -I also lost my temper one night and struck Brother Bennet when he confronted me about my life," Christian admitted, wincing.

Desle raised his eyebrows.

"If you so easily take offense, Sire, how can you be properly served?" the confessor asked.

Christian shook his head, not understanding.

"How do you think your advisers and servants see you when you lash out at them for the slightest cause?"

Christian shrugged again.

"As a king not to be trifled with, I suppose."

"Truly?" Desle questioned. "If you had to serve such a lord, would you respect him? Would you not wonder if he were mad? Would you not wonder if a man with such an unpredictable humor was able to rule wisely?"

Christian shifted uneasily on his knees.

"If the smallest mistake or disappointment could evoke deadly wrath, would you enjoy serving such a man? Would you not be tempted to flee or not to serve at all? Would you not avoid his displeasure, even by withholding important information he must have?"

Christian made no reply. He had never considered this.

"Life is full of surprises and disappointments, My Son. We all must bear them with patience."

There was a long silence, but then Desle spoke again.

"Does your temper serve you or do you serve it?"

Christian looked up then at the confessor, not understanding the question.

"Many who give themselves to anger believe that it serves a purpose to do so. How does it serve you?"

Christian thought for a moment.

"Aye, I suppose it does serve me. As long as my subjects tremble in my very presence and fear my terrible displeasure, my position as king remains secure. The words of detractors and potential rebels will not inspire many to stand against me for they know what my wrath will bring."

"Are there no better ways to rule? I think, Sire, if you think about it, you will find that fear is a poor servant and gives you no real advantage. As long as there are kings, there will be rebels. And while you must continue in your severity in order to ensure the loyalty of your subjects, you encourage those subjects with that fear to join those who conspire against you. If, however, you inspire the fidelity of your subjects through compassion, agreeableness, fairness, and virtue, your subjects, feeling safe under your protection, will shun any rebels for they have nothing to gain by joining them.

"Moreover, it would be a mistake to believe that anger serves you at all," Desle continued. "Anger is one of the most destructive of sins, and a man who gives himself to it soon finds himself at its service. One moment of anger acted upon destroys relationships and loyalties and all that a man has built. Afterward, he must hurry about rebuilding and making amends to what has been destroyed or injured- where he can- *if he can.*

"A wise master *must* be sensitive to the feelings of those who serve him," Desle reiterated. "For how can you hope to get an honest answer from those you depend upon if they fear their true opinion will meet only your displeasure, ridicule or wrath?"

Christian nodded.

The two were silent as the King thought about this for a moment.

"What else?"

"I am guilty of sloth also. I have paid little heed to the management of the kingdom personally. I have not visited my vassals' holdings. I rely too much on the reports and advice of the palace advisers."

"Are they capable men?"

"Aye, but I would not boast of their trustworthiness. In truth, for too long I have not desired to know the true condition of the kingdom or my vassals' minds."

"'Tis difficult to rule wisely without it."

"Aye," Christian admitted. "And even now, Father, I have been cut off from any word from the palace for nearly two months. Anything could be happening. -And perhaps if I had taken more of an interest in the kingdom, the uprising at the palace might have been avoided."

The confessor nodded.

Christian thought through the remaining seven deadly sins.

"I am guilty of lust-."

The confessor nodded.

"-And fornication."

"With women?"

"Aye."

"How many times have you committed fornication?"

"I know not. Daily almost since I returned from Gaulia before I was run out of the palace. Many times while I was in Gaulia since I was twelve."

"Was it with prostitutes, courtesans, wives, widows, or maids?"

"In Gaulia, they were serving maids and tavern wenches. I know not if they had husbands. When I first returned from Gaulia, there were a few courtesans, but after a few months, I began collecting girls of my own."

"Collecting them?"

"Aye, I have taken the comeliest serfs from my vassals' lands for my bed."

"Serfs?"

"Aye."

"How many?"

"Over a hundred now."

Desle raised his eyebrows.

"A hundred?"

"Aye."

The senior confessor was afraid to ask the next question.

"Do they -live still?"

"Aye," Christian answered, though taken aback by the question. "They are all housed in a wing of the palace, awaiting my beckoning. They have been treated well," he assured him.

"Even so, My Son, thou hast cheated thy vassals of their labor. Were they maids or had they husbands?"

"Some of both."

"Did any have children which you forced them to abandon?"

"I know not," Christian frowned.

"This is very serious," Desle told him sternly. "These women must be returned to your vassals' lands, and your vassals must be compensated. -The husbands or fathers of these women too should receive some compensation for the hardship you have caused them."

"Aye, Father."

Christian thought through the list of deadly sins again.

"I have been envious of my father for the effortless reign that fate awarded him."

Father Desle listened curiously.

"He never faced any hardships or challenges as king, and already I am beset with troubles. Not only has there been an uprising and the interdict, but my advisers do not believe that we can repel the army that will soon attack us. They all believe that my reign is at its end, and it is so unfair, Father, for it has just begun. I resent that a man like my father was granted a long reign and no doubt will be thought well of for the years of peace he maintained through bribing our enemy. If remembered at all, I will be known as *Christian the Lacking,* the king who lost Speyron as soon as possible."

Father Desle raised his eyebrows, but said nothing.

Christian was silent again, thinking hard.

"I can recall no sins of true gluttony. I have eaten large amounts of food at some feasts, but I do not recall anyone, even the serfs, going hungry at the time. Nor can I remember committing the sin of avarice, other than taking the hundred girls as concubines."

The confessor nodded.

Finally Christian could think of nothing more to confess that pertained to the last three and a half years, so then he began to confess all the sins he could remember from the years before, and from his childhood.

After more than an hour, Christian's legs were numb, and his knees ached, but he felt greatly relieved.

"Is there anything more?"

"I can remember no more."

"Very well, My Son. You should be very sorry for these sins, for they are mortal, great, and very grievous. You must make a firm resolution not to do them again."

"I have, Father."

"And you must be certain to fulfill all of your penance and to meet all the conditions the Bishop sets for you, for to die with these sins against your soul will earn you damnation."

Christian nodded, wiping his face with his sleeve.

"You will make restitution where you can to those you have wronged. You will dismiss your concubines and return the hundred women to their rightful lords and families, and you will live chastely until you marry.

"So that your spiritual strength will not be weakened, from this day forward, no longer will you drink to excess, thus making yourself vulnerable to temptation. -Nor will you torment others for your amusement or for anyone else's. Instead, spend your days seeking to strengthen the virtues given by the Holy Spirit and opportunities to do charitable deeds.

"This shall be your penance: From this day forward, except for special ceremonies, you will wear the hair shirt to be mindful that although you are king, you are a sinner as well. You will hear Mass daily, and you will adhere to a discipline of daily prayers. You will go to confession no less than once a month to help you stay accountable and centered on living a virtuous life. For the next three years, you shall eat no meat, neither flesh nor foul, except on holy days or by special permission. Do you understand?"

"Aye."

"Furthermore, as public penance, during the Mass to raise the interdict, and for two public Masses afterward, you will hold the penitent's cross."

Christian nodded obediently.

"Very well. Once the Bishop relaxes the interdict and your excommunication, you will receive absolution. Until then, trust in the mercy of God. Go in peace, My Son."

447

58

Still laden with their heavy cloaks and red-faced from traveling in the cold, the two men huddled around the small fire, soaking in the warmth greedily. As the feeling returned to their fingers, the younger of the two portly men glanced around the Abbot's small hall. His eyes came to rest upon the long, bare table near them, and he noticed curiously that the 'head' table had no side tables at all, for there was no room for them. At best, the Abbot could entertain less than a dozen guests in the modest hall.

"I thought the Abbot's quarters were suppose to be-"

"Extravagant?" the older companion offered.

"Bigger-" he corrected.

"The Abbot's quarters are the best the monastery has to offer. Think then how common and crowded the rest of the amenities must be."

The young man raised his eyebrows, continuing to note the lack of finery, the functional furnishings, and the simple candles in their plain holders, of which, only four were burning. He wondered briefly if the monastery even owned a golden candelabrum. He had heard of extreme communities where the monks not only practiced poverty and chastity in fact, but also temperance and fasting as well.

"Welcome to St. Brychan's!"

The two visitors turned to see two cordial monks enter the hall.

"I am Abbot Hunfred, and this is our senior confessor, Father Desle," Hunfred gestured warmly.

"Abbot Hunfred," the older man bowed quickly, with the younger man following. "I am Julius, and this is Avar. We are secretaries to his Grace, Bishop Gildas."

Hunfred greeted them formally with the kiss of peace and quickly offered a prayer of thanksgiving for their safe arrival.

"How was your journey?" Hunfred inquired then. "We were uncertain of the weather."

"The wind was sharp and bitter, but the sun was an agreeable companion."

Hunfred and Desle nodded amiably.

More of the brothers arrived then; one lit the rest of the candles on the table while another helped the Bishop's men to remove their heavy cloaks. Another monk pulled two chairs out from the table for the secretaries to sit upon, while another pair of monks appeared with bowl, pitcher, and cloth for the customary foot washing.

While the brothers bathed the secretaries' feet, Desle observed the Bishop's men with interest. The secretaries gleamed with splendor, adorned as they were in their expensive, woolen garments dyed deep scarlet, blue and gold. Their fingers were bejeweled with large rings, and both men wore a large, lavish, golden cross about their neck. Indeed, the pair were the only ornaments in the bare, tidy hall, where even the chairs had no cushions. The sheer weight and complexion of the two men attested as much to their wealth as the rich and plentiful foods they were clearly accustomed to eating.

The secretaries smiled appreciably when another brother arrived next with a pitcher and cups. Their smiles diminished, though, when they discovered it was not wine but ale. The younger peered questioningly at the plain cup itself he had been given which was nothing more than an unpainted horn with a jagged rim.

Abbot Hunfred and the confessor took a cup of ale also and, tasting it, approvingly smiled at their guests.

"We brew it ourselves."

The elder secretary tasted it and smiled politely; it was rather flat and had too much gruit for his taste, but he nodded amicably.

"It is pleasing to know that your community still performs such labors yourself," Julius smiled. "-So many of the monasteries have been corrupted by laziness as well as- fineries and luxuries- especially in Gaulia."

"Our hope is to live by the Rule, with God's help," Hunfred answered pleasantly as he and the confessor sat down at the table.

"Well, well, perhaps we should get on to business, Julius, as we must get back on the road," Avar said suddenly.

"Oh, you must not leave today!" Hunfred protested. "We so rarely have visits from our brothers in the Church. At least stay the night with us! We long to hear news. And our guesthouse may be humble, but still it will be more accommodating than an inn on the road!"

Avar sent his older companion a worried look, as he shifted his copious buttocks uncomfortably on his hard chair and wondered if the beds in the place were anything more than sacks stuffed with straw on a dirt floor. And did they eat in the guesthouse more than once a day?

"Your offer of hospitality is very tempting, Lord Abbot, but we are expected in Gaulia on the morrow -for a ceremony, and we must get back on the road at once," Julius replied sweetly.

"That is unfortunate," Abbot Hunfred replied. "The guestmaster will be very disappointed."

Avar breathed a sigh of relief. They would return to spend at least one more night at Lord Norwyn's castle; it was but two hours ride from St. Brychan's. There, the women, wine, and food were plentiful, and the revels went long into the night. They had spent one night there already and had been reluctant to leave their gracious, accommodating host to attend to this chore.

"Now, as to the matter of the King-" Julius said, "we were not a little surprised at your message."

"Aye, there has been no word of the King's whereabouts since the rebellion at the palace some months ago," Avar added. "Though, there has been much talk."

"Was it by message or envoy that the King sent word to you that he wished to reconcile with the Church?" Julius inquired.

"He approached me in person," Hunfred replied simply.

The secretaries were impressed by this information.

"You have seen him. -And, you are certain it was he?"

"Aye, absolutely," Hunfred assured them with a smile.

"And he seemed sincere about wishing reconciliation?"

"Aye."

"Did he look well?" Avar asked curiously.

Hunfred shrugged.

"He seemed tired, but well enough."

"Did he say with whom he was staying?" the other man asked.

"Or where?"

"No, and I did not ask him," Hunfred answered carefully.

Both secretaries nodded again.

"The King asked me to contact the Bishop to inquire of the conditions that must be met for the relaxing of the interdict and his excommunication and to make arrangements for a meeting with the Bishop to complete the matter."

"His Grace, the Bishop, requires one thousand gold coin from the royal treasury."

Hunfred and Desle's hearts skipped a beat at the immense sum.

"One thousand?"

"Aye."

"I will inform the King when he inquires," the Abbot smiled.

It was pointless to argue, after all.

"In addition," Julius continued, "when the news of the sacrilege at the palace church reached him, His Holiness, the Pope, was greatly grieved."

Father Desle raised his eyebrows.

"Word reached Roma about it?"

"Aye, and His Holiness personally drafted a letter to Bishop Gildas in response to it," Avar added.

"Really?"

"Aye, it is the Pope's personal wish that King Christian build a cathedral on his palace grounds and, further, to revoke his father's law and found a religious community there."

Both Hunfred and Desle were stunned for a moment, but the Abbot quickly smiled and nodded, adding enthusiastically, "It is a wonderful idea!"

The secretaries smiled and agreed. Avar even drank the ale from his chipped cup.

"Very well, Lord Abbot, you may expect Bishop Gildas to arrive in ten days."

"Make certain that the King is prompt," Avar added. "The Bishop is a busy man and will feel his dignity affronted if he has to wait for King Christian's arrival."

Father Desle raised his eyebrows at this, but smiled.

"Once the Bishop arrives and finalizes the terms, he will officiate the Mass to relax the interdict and the King's excommunication," Julius continued.

"Very good. All will be ready," answered the Abbot.

"St. Brychan's is rather remote and quaint, but your church is a goodly size and should accommodate us all very well," Avar added.

"How many should we expect to accompany His Grace, the Bishop?" Hunfred asked.

"Likely no more than thirty."

The Abbot and the confessor were nodding.

"Well, if there is nothing more to discuss, we should well be on our way," Julius said, getting to his feet.

Avar agreed and quickly finishing his ale, stood up.

Reluctantly, the monks helped the men with their cloaks and escorted them to the door, fretting repeatedly that the men would not stay the night.

59

𝔄bbot Hunfred perused the tentative agenda again as he walked out of the cloister. The Bishop would be greeted at the gate by a procession, and the monks would sing "Laudes Gildas", extolling the greatness and importance of the Bishop, naming his patron saints, and praising his ancestors and family line. Then he would give a speech of welcome to the Bishop. Bishop Gildas would give his response. Then there would be prayers, the reading of a psalm, and a hymn. Then refreshments would be served in the refectory. Afterward, the Bishop would be given a tour of the monastery. Later, during the feast to celebrate the Bishop's visit, the novices wished to present a short play depicting the life and death of St. Brychan and of the saints whose relics were housed in the monastery.

As he passed the guesthouse, Hunfred noted the villeins were nearly finished clearing the scrap pile left by the carpenters. He smiled approvingly as he looked about the grounds. Everything was on schedule.

The days following the meeting with the Bishop's secretaries had been filled with a whirlwind of activity. Immediately after announcing the Bishop's planned visit to St. Brychan's at the chapter meeting, Hunfred had been besieged with questions and concerns from the brothers.

As expected, the guestmaster had been utterly vexed. He had complained that the guesthouse in its present condition could not accommodate such a large accompanying entourage along with the number of guests they normally housed. At present capacity, it could lodge twenty-five. Nor could an addition be built in less than a fortnight utilizing the skills of the brothers alone. Carpenters, therefore, had been immediately summoned from around the area to build the extra rooms.

The other monks were equally excited by the Bishop's visit. The brothers and villagers had worked tirelessly tidying the premises and making long due repairs to the grounds and buildings. They had cleaned the church, polished the ornaments, and dusted the relics. Brother

Patricus and Brother Lubin had finished painting the mural of St. Christopher and the life of Christ on the wall of the church.

The cellarer had been the most agitated of all, for he alone was told the purpose of the Bishop's visit. He had to make preparations not only for a feast to honor the Bishop, but also the feast to celebrate the end of the interdict which could last for several days, and if the Bishop stayed for many days to celebrate, which he might, the monastery would be sorely tried to feed them all.

The cellarer had thoroughly inspected the stores of grain and provisions the monks had kept for the winter as well as the livestock and had begun to compile a tasty and intricate menu. The cellarer concluded if the Bishop did not stay past a week, there would be enough. However, in the following weeks after the Bishop's visit, the food remaining for the delicacies served at the Christmas feasts would be scant. The cellarer just hoped that by then the brothers' palates would be weary of rich foods and that they would welcome meals of meager simplicity.

The cellarer had further confided to Hunfred that if, on the other hand, the Bishop stayed through the entire twelve days of Christmas, then the monastery would not have enough food, and they would be forced to buy supplies where they could. Thus, Hunfred too had begun to prepare for that contingency.

For the past two days, the monks had fretfully watched the road, fearing that the Bishop would arrive early. He had not come early, however, and tomorrow when he was due to arrive, all would be ready. Everything was in its place and in good repair. The new wing of the guesthouse was large and elaborate enough to rival the amenities of larger monasteries. And even now the brothers were busy at the bakehouse and alehouse baking more bread and brewing additional hogsheads of ale so that there would be an ample supply for everyone when the Bishop arrived.

As the Abbot continued around the monastery grounds, he took the back way to the church and was surprised to find a novice on his hands and knees scrubbing the hallway floor and a monk sitting on a nearby bench, counting prayers by a knotted cord.

"Brother Caedmon?"

The brother immediately stood up and bowed quickly toward the Abbot.

"Brother Caedmon, why is Tillo not in the library at his studies?"

"Forgive me, Lord Abbot, but Tillo has asked me for several days for time away from study for work and contemplation," the monk whispered.

"He asked for work?"

"Aye, Lord Abbot."

Astonished, Hunfred looked again at the King scrubbing the floor on his hands and knees at the far end of the hall.

"As you commanded, Lord Abbot," Brother Caedmon continued at a whisper, "over the past fortnight, daily we have studied scripture and the catechism. Afterward, I questioned him on the creeds and the articles of faith, and every time he made good answer. He has recited his prayers and responses repeatedly, without fault. And I have questioned him repeatedly on the teachings of the early church fathers; to all, he has answered well. Today, after some hours of study, and having nothing new to question him on, I saw no harm in granting his request."

"But why this task, Brother?" Hunfred whispered in response.

"I know not, Lord Abbot. It was Tillo's suggestion."

Hunfred looked at the monk, astonished once more. The King had surprised him again.

A week ago, when he and Father Desle had informed the youth of the conditions put on his reconciliation, King Christian had surprised them both by making no complaint about any of it, not even the immense sum of money that had to be delivered to the Bishop. However, when they told him about the cathedral that he was to build, all the color had drained from his face, as if the specter of death had brushed up against him; nor had he seemed to have heard them when they mentioned the community that was to be started there.

Hunfred observed the King for a long moment, noticing that he was mumbling something as he scrubbed the floor.

"Lord Abbot, shall I stop him and return him to his studies in the library?"

Hunfred shook his head slightly and gestured for quiet as he strained to hear.

"Do you know what he is saying?" he whispered.

"He is reciting 'The Breastplate of St. Patrick'."

Listening carefully, Hunfred could just make out the words as the King began it again:

"'I bind to myself today

The strong virtue of the Invocation of the Trinity:
I believe the Trinity in the Unity
The Creator of the Universe.

"'I bind to myself today
The virtue of the Incarnation of Christ with His Baptism,
The virtue of His crucifixion with His burial,
The virtue of His Resurrection with His Ascension,
The virtue of His coming on the Judgment Day.

"'I bind to myself today
The virtue of the love of seraphim,
In the obedience of angels,
In the hope of resurrection unto reward,
In prayers of Patriarchs,
In predictions of Prophets,
In preaching of Apostles,
In faith of Confessors,
In purity of holy Virgins,
In deeds of righteous men.

"I bind to myself today
The power of Heaven,
The light of the sun,
The brightness of the moon,
The splendour of fire,
The flashing of lightning,
The swiftness of wind,
The depth of sea,
The stability of earth,
The compactness of rocks.

"'I bind to myself today
God's Power to guide me,
God's Might to uphold me,
God's Wisdom to teach me,
God's Eye to watch over me,
God's Ear to hear me,
God's Word to give me speech,

God's Hand to guide me,
God's Way to lie before me,
God's Shield to shelter me,
God's Host to secure me,
Against the snares of demons,
Against the seductions of vices,
Against the lusts of nature,
Against everyone who meditates injury to me,
Whether far or near,
Whether few or with many.

"'I invoke today all these virtues
Against every hostile merciless power
Which may assail my body and my soul,
Against the incantations of false prophets,
Against the black laws of heathenism,
Against the false laws of heresy,
Against the deceits of idolatry,
Against the spells of women, and smiths, and druids,
Against every knowledge that binds the soul of man.

"'Christ, protect me today
Against every poison, against burning,
Against drowning, against death-wound,
That I may receive abundant reward.

"'Christ with me, Christ before me,
Christ behind me, Christ within me,
Christ beneath me, Christ above me,
Christ at my right, Christ at my left,
Christ in the fort,
Christ in the chariot seat,
Christ in the poop,
Christ in the heart of everyone who thinks of me,
Christ in the mouth of everyone who speaks to me,
Christ in every eye that sees me,
Christ in every ear that hears me.

"'I bind to myself today

The strong virtue of an invocation of the Trinity,
I believe the Trinity in the Unity
The Creator of the Universe.'"

Chill bumps covered Abbot Hunfred.

"Amen," he whispered, crossing himself.

He told Caedmon to allow Tillo to continue, and then the Abbot departed, leaving the pair in the hallway.

60

The days passed rapidly for Christian as all of his time for the entire ten days was spent either in private study with Brother Caedmon or singing the Hours with the novices. As the day of the Bishop's visit drew nearer, his anxiety increased as well.

The night before the Bishop's scheduled arrival, he could not sleep at all. He rose from his mat in the novice quarters and went to the church. Kneeling beneath the statue of the Madonna and Child, he prayed to God for strength and courage and a humble heart to meet with the Bishop, and he petitioned the Virgin and his patron saints to pray for him.

As he knelt in the darkness, the memory of his atrocious acts vividly pressed upon his mind again. Weeping afresh for the sins that he had committed, he prayed that his meeting with the Bishop would go as planned so that he might finally receive absolution.

The next day, his anxiety was further heightened by the excitement of the brothers. The monks were nervous, and tempers were on edge. Some of them had actually begun quarreling.

The novice master irritably reported him at the chapter meeting for leaving the novice quarters in the middle of the night, although Brother Septimus grudgingly admitted that when he and the novices arrived at the church for Matins, they had found him already there praying.

Embarrassed, Christian had stood up and apologized, explaining that he could not sleep for anticipation of the Bishop's visit and he had gone to the church to pray in the hopes of not disturbing the other novices. Abbot Hunfred had only smiled and said that in light of the uniqueness of the Bishop's visit, he was willing to overlook the matter this once; he advised, however, that if he or any of the other novices felt they had to leave the novice quarters in the future to pray, they should be certain to ask permission from the novice master first.

After the chapter meeting, Christian had approached the Abbot and asked for some labor in the hopes that he might be distracted from his anxiety, but the Abbot refused to assign him any task lest he become soiled and unpresentable when the Bishop arrived. By nightfall, the entire community was exhausted and disappointed as neither the Bishop nor his messenger had arrived. The monks who kept watch through the night, however, were given instructions to wake the entire community when the Bishop did arrive, no matter what the hour.

The next day, the brothers were even more anxious with anticipation than the day before. Christian himself was so nervous he could not eat.

The following day was the same, and the next, also. Extra monks were assigned to the kitchen and the alehouse again to make more bread and ale as what had previously been prepared had begun to spoil.

On the fourth day, Christian was weary with waiting. When he happened upon Father Desle in the cloister, he confronted the priest.

"Has there been any word?"

"No, My Son."

Seeing his disappointment, the confessor put his hand on Christian's shoulder.

"Fear not. The Bishop will come, if not tonight, then tomorrow."

"And if not tomorrow?"

"Then the next day," the confessor smiled. "Have patience, My Son. Remember, the Season of Advent is the Season of Waiting."

"Aye, and the Season of Faith and Hope," Cai added, joining them.

"Indeed, it is," Desle replied, patting the child on his head.

That night Christian tossed and turned in his bed with new fears, as the unpleasant memory of the non-arrival of his fiancee so many years ago wore him down. He had feared and fretted then, and he was fearing and fretting now.

Had the Bishop become deathly ill in the inclement weather? Had he been attacked by bandits or outlaws on the road? Was he dead? If so, it would delay even longer the ending of the interdict and his excommunication. However, Christian mused, at least *he* would be the one to choose the new bishop.

More days passed, and not a word was received from Bishop Gildas. The days of Christmas came and went, unobserved by the brothers, although they heard that the villagers were celebrating Yule with music, dancing and feasting. For their festivities, the monastery gave the villagers a cart of bread and three hogsheads of ale that had been prepared for the Bishop's visit; it was going to spoil anyway.

Christian was dispirited, miserable and lonely. Every Christmas he could remember had been filled with friends, feasting, music and dancing, and drunkenness.

The brothers were also sad. They had sat morosely in the refectory eating their meals of the usual foods while the reader droned on from the writings of St. Augustine.

Christian thought of Kaith too. Wherever she was, there had been no Christmas feasts for her either. Was she as miserable and lonely as he was? How he longed to see her.

Christian wondered also what was happening at his palace. Had Paschal held grand feasts in his absence, or had everyone returned to their own lands for the winter?

61

Christian had never been truly intimate with his advisers. They knew his mind on certain issues, or what he wanted them to know, but that was all. Now as he sat alone in the library, staring at the quill, ink, and parchment in front of him, he longed for a true confidant. He wished to pick up the quill and empty his heart upon the page and reveal everything he had been through these past few months.

He wanted to tell someone what he had suffered at this monastery and the details of that amazing night when he had heard the voice of God and seen that light. He wanted to confess his present fears, that even with all the efforts he had made, he would still die with his sins on his head, and he would spend eternity alone, being forever tormented in Hell. He wanted to confide that daily he continued to suffer, as now for over a month there still was no word from the Bishop.

But who could he tell?

There was Paschal-.

Christian smiled. No, he would never understand. The youth and he had been cut from the same fabric. His long time companion would see less need for reform than he had when he had first entered these walls. Paschal would not be able to read past the first line about taking refuge at a monastery without declaring him utterly mad.

His other advisers? Grey? Olbert? Dewain?

Christian frowned.

Kaith? How could he write to her? She was all goodness, too innocent and naive and inexperienced in the world to understand youthful indiscretions and knavery or where unchecked sin could lead. Besides, if she learned the truth about him, it would kill her. He did not ever want her to know what kind of man he had been or what kind of cruelty and evil he was capable of.

Truthfully, there was no one that he felt comfortable telling. Christian sighed and glanced at the scripture readings on the table before him. His tutor would be back soon.

The library door suddenly burst open, banging the wall behind it forcefully.

"Tillo!" the two oblates yelled together. "He is here! The Bishop is here! The Abbot has called for everyone to line up!"

Christian's heart skipped a beat and then pounded wildly as he got up from the bench.

"Do you remember the song?" Cai was asking Quintus.

"I do not remember beyond the first verse," he admitted as the pair ran out the door.

Christian left the library immediately. The hue and cry was being raised all over the monastery. The brothers were knocking on doors, and all were putting down their work and running to the main gate. Christian hurried among the rest and stood with the other novices near the end of the line. The choirmaster was handing out a parchment with the words to the Laudes Gildas.

Christian stepped out of line with Cai and looked out the main gate. A long line of horses were approaching slowly at a walk through the snow. Two colorful banners flipped in the mid-morning breeze, one bearing a cross and the other a chirho. A large crowd was following the entourage on foot.

"Cai! Tillo! Return to your place!" Brother Septimus ordered.

Christian and the oblate returned to the line obediently. They huddled with the other novices and shivered in the cold as they waited for the Bishop.

Just as the first of the horses entered the gate, the monks began to sing their song of welcome. The horse and riders paraded in and stopped opposite to the monks. About fifteen knights and ten mounted servants accompanied the Bishop and his secretaries.

The crowd of villagers cheered when the man dressed in a purple, fur-trimmed cope and jewels and with a white, conical mitre atop his head entered the gate and began waving. While a servant held his great horse, this man dismounted and waved and smiled again.

Abbot Hunfred approached him, bowed, and kissed his ring. The Bishop made the sign of the cross over him. Then the men stood smiling while the monks continued singing the Laudes Gildas for several minutes.

After the song, the monks shivered in the cold, their breath smoking the air, as Abbot Hunfred delivered his welcome address. The villagers and monks cheered at the end of it. The Bishop answered with a very short speech of appreciation and bestowed a blessing upon all present, and everyone cheered again. Then the Abbot led them in prayer. After the prayer, the reader stepped forward and opened his book. He was about to read, but the Bishop cleared his throat and gestured toward the monastery. The Abbot smiled and signaled for the reader to close the book. The villagers cheered again as the entire entourage and the monks proceeded toward the guesthouse, stables, and the cloister as the monks sang.

While the knights led their mounts to the stable, the Bishop and his secretaries followed the Abbot to the refectory where a warm fire was burning brightly. The Bishop made his way to it immediately, followed by Julius and Avar.

The cellarer and the brothers assigned to kitchen duty were hustling around madly, setting out cups and ale and warmed mead. They had put out some bread, butter, honey, and some cheese, but they had not yet had time to prepare anything more extravagant.

Abbot Hunfred was neither alarmed nor disappointed; he smiled appreciably at the brothers' efforts.

"Your Grace, here is a copy of the proposed agenda we have drawn up for your visit," Hunfred said amicably, handing a parchment to Avar. "After you have a chance to warm yourself, we would be honored to show you the grounds and church. We have planned a feast in your honor tonight, and tomorrow, after the Mass, we will have the feast to celebrate-"

"Is the King here, Lord Abbot?" Bishop Gildas asked abruptly, ignoring the proposed agenda Avar offered to him.

"Aye, Your Grace. He has-"

The secretaries seemed surprised to hear this, but the Bishop's face revealed nothing.

"I will meet with him immediately then."

Abbot Hunfred bowed.

"Of course, Your Grace. I will send word at once."

The Bishop nodded and turned back to the fire. Abbot Hunfred turned and left.

62

Christian hurried behind the monk who led the way to the Abbot's quarters. As he entered, he saw Abbot Hunfred, Father Desle and two elegantly dressed men waiting in the entry way. Christian bowed to the Abbot, but this time, Hunfred and Desle bowed low and formally to the sovereign.

"Sire," Hunfred said carefully, "if you will follow me."

He led the youth past the Bishop's men down the corridor. Avar and Julius stood speechless as he passed them, stunned by the sight of the excommunicate king in a monk's habit.

When Abbot Hunfred and the King entered the modest office of the Abbot, followed by the confessor and the secretaries, Christian's heart began to pound rapidly as he immediately recognized the man who had crowned him king three and a half years ago. Bishop Gildas was a large, balding, fat man. He wore a long, scarlet tunic, several jeweled rings, and a large, golden cross around his neck. He stood peering out the open window, idly stroking his double chin.

"Sire," Hunfred said, "may I present His Grace, Bishop Gildas."

The Bishop turned and glanced at Christian. His face wore an expression of clear disdain, but his attention settled quickly on the novice's habit the King wore.

Although the Bishop neither acknowledged nor greeted him, Christian dutifully went to his knees before the man and, tenderly taking the Bishop's plump hand, kissed the ring of office.

"Your Grace, We are so grateful that you have come," Christian said joyfully, overcome with relief that the Bishop was here at last and finally he would receive his absolution. "I have fervently prayed for this day-when Speyron and I would be welcomed back into the Faith!"

The Bishop made no reply but instead took back his hand. He crossed his arms and regarded the wall indifferently.

Uneasy at the Bishop's reticence, Christian looked up and saw the Bishop's coldness. The King lowered his gaze quickly and swallowed hard.

Had he misspoken? he wondered. He did not know what to do next, so he remained on his knees, his heart pounding loudly in his ears as he awaited instructions.

Hunfred and Desle observed in alarm. Would the Bishop not even hear him?

Hunfred immediately stepped forward.

"Your Grace, may I present our senior confessor, Father Desle," he said sweetly.

The old confessor came forward and bowed to the Bishop.

"Your Grace, I have observed the King since he arrived here and can affirm his contrition and his sincere desire to reconcile with the Church. He-"

"How long have you observed him, Father? A few days?"

"A little more than four months, Your Grace."

"Four months?!"

"Aye, Your Grace."

"Am I to understand that this man has been *here*- since the interdict began?!"

"He came to our gates some months ago, requesting to make a retreat for a fortnight so that he might receive spiritual guidance for the purpose of his amendment."

This was all the Bishop needed to hear.

"And you took him in?! An excommunicate! And after what *he* has done to our brethren and to our Lord Christ!"

"Your Grace-"

"And you have even allowed him to pose as a novice!" Gildas said angrily, his hands on his wide hips.

"Your Gra-"

"Why was I not informed long ago that he was here?"

"Your Gr-"

"Tell me what compelled you, Hunfred, to not only disregard my edict by sheltering an excommunicate -but to further mock the Faith by allowing *him* to pretend to be one of your novices?!"

"It was out of mercy that the Abbot took Us in, Your Grace!" Christian interrupted quickly, still remaining on his knees. "-And out of *necessity* alone that he allowed Us to appear to be a novice, for We insisted he conceal Our presence here *from everyone.*"

The Bishop glowered back down at the youth in front of him. There was a long silence as Hunfred, Desle, and Christian all wondered what to say next.

Finally, Abbot Hunfred gestured to Father Desle. The confessor cleared his throat and continued:

"Your Grace, since he arrived, King Christian has been led daily in scripture study and the teachings of the Church and has sung the Hours with the other novices."

Horrified, Avar crossed himself, and Julius covered his eyes with his hand. Bishop Gildas frowned as he listened, but said nothing.

"When the King-" Father Desle hesitated momentarily, seeing their reactions, "-felt he was ready to petition you to relax the interdict and raise his excommunication, I heard his confession. He has repented sincerely, but I left his absolution to you -for when you raise his excommunication and relax the interdict."

The Bishop stared hostilely at the confessor. Desle swallowed and glanced at Hunfred, then went on.

"For his penance, I assigned a daily discipline of prayers and hearing Mass, and monthly confession. He shall wear the hair shirt except on special occasions, and for three years, he shall eat no meat, except on holy days or special occasions. For the next three Masses, he will carry the penitent's cross."

"Is that all?" Gildas asked brusquely.

"Aye, Your Grace," Desle answered meekly.

There was another awkward silence until the Abbot spoke.

"Your Grace, perhaps you would care for some refreshment while you speak with the King."

"Aye," Bishop Gildas replied gruffly.

Hunfred bowed and left the chamber. Gildas frowned again, stroked his double chin, and sat down irritably in the chair behind the Abbot's desk. The two secretaries promptly took the seats near the desk, and the confessor sat on the small bench in the corner.

As everyone else was sitting down, Christian slowly got to his feet, noticing when he did that there was no chair remaining for him.

"Well, Sire, we are here at your summons," Gildas finally said with an impatient gesture. "Abbot Hunfred and the confessor have attested to your contrition and your desire to reconcile. What do you have to say for yourself?"

Christian's heart thumped rapidly in his chest.

"All they have said and more, Your Grace. It is Our deepest desire to return to the Church and We regret- *I* admit and regret all my sinful and evil acts."

"And you are prepared to make amends to the Mother Church?"

"Aye, Your Grace."

"Do you promise to uphold the Church and her beliefs from this moment forward?"

"Aye, Your Grace."

"Unfortunately, Sire, it is not as simple as an 'Aye' or 'No'."

Christian's heart skipped a beat and then pounded loud in his ears.

"As a member of the body of followers of Christ, you are as much a *vassal* to the Lord Christ and the Church as any lord or knight that has sworn fealty to you.- Thus, we must ask this question: Once *your* vassal has demonstrated disloyalty by taking up arms against *you*, Sire, how may such a vassal ever be trusted again?"

Christian's blood ran suddenly cold at the question.

"Perhaps- perhaps such a vassal might be given the opportunity to prove his loyalty," Christian answered quickly, his stomach twisting with anxiety, for in truth, he had never given a second chance to anyone who had taken arms against him.

"Hmm- perhaps-" Gildas answered, "but still there is always the danger that if trusted again, he will once again rebel and lead other impressionable vassals astray as well."

"There is that fear, but Christ's command to love and forgive one another demands that we risk this in pious Hope," King Christian replied carefully.

Desle smiled.

"Then how will you go about proving your loyalty?" Gildas asked.

"By humbly submitting myself to all the conditions of restitution set before me by yourself, the Pope, and Father Desle, as well as any by my own conscience. And by performing every act of penance that I have been assigned-"

"And when will the construction of the cathedral begin?"

"Your Grace, as soon as possible, I promise you. As for now, it is necessary for me to defend my kingdom against a foreign invader. But as soon as this war is at an end, I will look to the matter personally."

"Thou art obligated to build the cathedral and fulfill all other conditions whether or not you are at war, and whether or not the war is won or lost, Sire. Failure to fulfill the conditions in an appropriate amount of time or to keep your promises of fidelity to the Church will result in Speyron being placed under interdict again, as if it had never been relaxed."

"I understand, Your Grace."

The office door opened then, and two monks entered with cups, wine and fruit. They served the Bishop, the secretaries, and the confessor. The Bishop tasted the wine and nodded approvingly.

"So you believe yourself reformed and ready to join the company of the faithful again?"

"Aye, Your Grace."

"Do you renounce Satan and all the spiritual forces of wickedness that rebel against God?" the Bishop asked.

"I do, Your Grace."

"Do you renounce the evil powers of this world which corrupt and destroy the creatures of God?"

"Aye, I do."

"Do you renounce all sinful desires that draw you from the love of God?"

"Aye, I do."

"Do you turn to Jesus Christ and accept him as your Savior?"

"Aye, I do."

"Do you put your whole trust in his grace and love?"

"Aye, I do."

"Do you promise to follow and obey him as your Lord?"

"I do."

"Will you continue in resisting evil, and repent whenever you fall into sin?"

"Aye."

"Sire, if you are received back into the community of the faithful, how will your life and example aid the spiritual progress of the faithful?"

"I am aware of the distinct visibility of my life due to my high birth," Christian answered, "and I vow my life and deeds will serve as a good example to aid in the spiritual progress of my brethren."

"In what ways?" Gildas asked, selecting an apple from the tray.

"Of late, I have taken on a discipline of daily prayer. I have reapplied myself to the teachings of the Church and Christ. It is my hope that the influence of these teachings and devotions on my daily life will be obvious to all. I hope with my daily hearing of Mass together with avoidance of sin that I will be able to support others in their faith and discipline as well."

Gildas raised his eyebrows skeptically.

"You have reapplied yourself to the teachings of the Church? Is that so?"

"Aye, your Grace."

"Let us see what you have learned. Explain to me," said the Bishop, as he bit into the apple, "what is the Trinity?"

A little surprised at the question, Christian hesitated before giving answer.

"There is only one God, but in three, distinct, divine persons, sharing one divine nature: the Father, the Son, and the Holy Ghost."

"And how can we believe that three, distinct persons can be one and the same God?"

"It is a mystery that although we may not fully understand it, we must accept it on faith."

Father Desle smiled. Christian took a deep breath.

"What is meant by actual sin?"

"Actual sin is any willful thought, desire, word, act, or omission forbidden by the law of God."

"What does mortal sin do to the soul?" the Bishop asked as he took another bite of the apple, and the juices dripped down his chin.

"Mortal sin deprives the sinner of grace, makes the soul an enemy to God, takes away the merit of all its good actions, deprives it of the right to everlasting happiness in Heaven, and makes it deserving of everlasting punishment in Hell."

Christian exhaled in relief at getting the long answer out correctly.

"What three things are necessary to make a sin mortal?"

"The thought, desire, word, action, or omission must be seriously wrong. The sinner must know that it is seriously wrong, and he must fully consent to it."

"Can we always resist temptation to sin?" Gildas asked.

"Aye, we can always resist temptation because no temptation can force us to sin and because God will always help us if we ask Him."

"What are the chief punishments of Adam which we inherit through original sin?"

"Death, suffering, ignorance and a strong inclination to sin," Christian answered.

"Who is Jesus Christ?"

"Jesus Christ was conceived by the Holy Spirit and born of the Virgin Mary. He was crucified, buried, and on the third day, he rose from the dead. After forty days, he ascended into Heaven. He is the Savior of all mankind, God made man, the Son of God, fully God, fully man, and the second member of the Trinity."

"How did Christ save us?"

"Christ, who lived a life without sin, offered His sufferings and death to God as a fitting sacrifice in satisfaction for the sins of men, -because animal sacrifices were not adequate to atone for sins, and in so doing, he regained for us the right to be children of God and heirs of Heaven."

"What did we learn from his suffering and death?"

"We learned of God's love for man and of the evil of sin, for which God who is all-just, demands great satisfaction."

"What must we do to be saved?"

"We must accept Jesus Christ as our savior, believe what God has revealed, and keep His law."

"What is grace?"

"Grace is a gift from God bestowed on us through the merits of Jesus Christ for our salvation."

"Can we resist the grace of God?"

"Aye, we can resist grace because our will is free and God does not force us to accept His grace."

"Will we meet the Christ?"

"Aye, he will come again on the last day and judge those who live and those who have died who will be raised from their graves."

"On what does success in life depend?"

"Success in life depends on serving God and neighbor, not on collecting riches or honors."

"What is the great commandment?"

"Love God with all your heart, mind, and soul, and your neighbor as yourself."

"What must we do to love God, our neighbor and ourselves?"

"We must keep the commandments of God and of the Church and perform the spiritual and corporal works of mercy."

"How do we know God exists, Sire?"

"The world could not have existed, nor have been so beautiful or orderly, by chance, but only through the benevolence of a wise, eternal, and all powerful God."

"Are all men obliged to practice religion?"

"Aye."

"Why?"

"Because all men are entirely dependent on God and must recognize this dependence by worshipping God."

The minutes went by as the Bishop calmly and without even looking at the King, asked question after question. The minutes made an hour, and beyond, and still the Bishop continued with the questions while the monks who served in the Abbot's house brought more food and drink.

After a time, the door opened, and the confessor exited the office. He found the Abbot standing in the corridor talking to another monk. As the door slowly closed, all in the corridor could hear the Bishop's voice asking, "What does mortal sin do to the soul?" and then the beginning of the King's reply, slowed by fatigue now.

"How-?"

Desle shook his head and frowned at the Abbot.

"At first, I thought it went well. The King has made good answer. However, the Bishop has kept him in there for near two hours now and still continues to question him. He has asked some things repeatedly. This is the third time he has asked about mortal sin. The King has recited his creeds four times and has explained them twice. I am very worried, Lord Abbot."

"Perhaps we can hasten this along," Hunfred said.

He and the old confessor went back into the office. As they entered, the Abbot observed the scene carefully. The Bishop was standing up, looking out of the small window, his back to the King. Christian was answering slowly about the infallibility of the Church; he was clearly exhausted, and although the chamber was chilly, he was wet with perspiration.

"Are all men obliged to practice religion?" came the immediate response to Christian's completion of the last answer.

There was silence. Christian thought and then could not remember what had been asked. He knew he had been asked it several times already. Then he remembered the question. But, by his life, he could not remember the answer. It had just gone out of his head! He wondered again why this was not over by now. Surely he had demonstrated his knowledge of the Faith and his desire to return.

The Bishop turned around then and glared at Christian.

"Must all men practice religion?"

"Aye-"

"Why?" the Bishop demanded.

Christian closed his eyes and took a breath. He could not think. He silently petitioned the Christ and the Virgin for prayers for help.

"Why?" the Bishop asked again.

"Because-" Christian answered, and then hesitated.

The Bishop stood with his hands on his hips and waited.

Christian looked at the wall as he searched his memory frantically, but could not remember the answer.

"Well?" urged the Bishop.

Christian's heart pounded wildly, and the room was beginning to turn very slowly.

"Why must they practice religion?" the Bishop prodded irritably.

"For help- for guidance- for forgiveness-" Christian suddenly found himself answering, with a shake of his head.

Hearing no response nor a new question, he glanced to his inquisitor; he was surprised and alarmed to see the secretaries helping the Bishop with his heavy, purple cope.

"I have heard enough," the Bishop told Hunfred with an irritated gesture as Julius opened the office door.

Christian watched in disbelief as Bishop Gildas walked out of the chamber without even a word to him. Had he made poor answers? His heart pounded in his ears. He knew the last one was wrong, but he had already answered it correctly a few times.

Hunfred and Desle hastily followed the Bishop and his secretaries out of the room, leaving the King alone. Still stunned, Christian moved slowly to sit in a chair. He was tired from standing for so long, and uncertain of what had just occurred.

"Your Grace, did he not answer well?" Hunfred asked outside in the corridor. "Did you not find him honest and truly changed? Surely his demeanor alone is proof of-"

"I am not satisfied," Gildas replied, "by either his answers or his deportment."

The monks listened with disbelief.

"You do not believe that with everything he has just undergone that it is his true desire to return to the Church?" Father Desle asked.

"I do not," the Bishop answered testily. "And allow me, Brothers, to enlighten you concerning the change you believe you have witnessed in this young man. King Christian has many faces and assumes whichever one will achieve his aims."

"Many have the talent of the chameleon, Your Grace, even within the Church," Hunfred answered coolly.

The Bishop regarded the Abbot coldly and then nodding to Julius, turned to go down the corridor.

Father Desle grabbed his sleeve then.

"Your Grace! Please-"

The Bishop turned and glared at the aged monk who had dared to stop his leave with his hand.

"Have mercy on him and our people!" Desle pleaded. "What will it take to satisfy you of the King's sincerity?"

"If I were you, Confessor, I would be less concerned with what the King has brought on himself than what will befall *you*. How do you expect your Order will react when they hear that you have put aside the edicts of the Church as it suited you and sheltered a vitandi inside your community?"

Father Desle removed his hand from the Bishop's arm, and Gildas turned again to leave.

"Whatever their response, I am willing to face it, Your Grace, as it was my decision alone," Abbot Hunfred answered. "However, I believe His Holiness the Pope, *when I send him word of this*, will be very curious to know why you refused the King's petition to relax the interdict when he has agreed to every condition of restitution and penance put upon him and when the souls of an entire kingdom are entirely dependent upon it, and not simply one man's."

The Bishop turned back to the Abbot, angrily. He wondered briefly if this was an idle threat or not.

As if reading his mind, Hunfred continued:

"You leave us no choice but to appeal to the Pope directly, Your Grace, for we are satisfied and completely convinced that the King is sincere."

There was a moment of awkward silence as the men regarded each other.

"Very well," Gildas finally conceded, "since *you* are so convinced and since, as you have said, so many souls are in peril, I will relax the interdict, -but not the King's excommunication! Prepare the Mass-"

"This cruelty is beyond measure!" Father Desle protested. "The King clearly longs for reconciliation with God and the Church. He needs it! What right have you to deny him?"

The Bishop crossed his arms as he answered.

"The writer of the book of Hebrews says that 'if we sin deliberately after receiving the knowledge of the truth, there no longer remains a sacrifice for sins, but a fearful prospect of judgment, and a fury of fire which will consume the adversaries. A man who has violated the law of Moses dies without mercy at the testimony of two or three witnesses.' The writer then asks, 'how much worse the punishment do you think will be deserved by the man who has spurned the Son of God, and profaned the blood of the covenant by which he was sanctified, and outraged the Spirit of grace?'

"King Christian is that man," Gildas continued. "He was diligently raised and educated in the Faith, and then he most willfully rebelled against the Kingdom of God. What can he *ever* do to escape punishment or restore that broken trust?"

"What old rhetoric is this? Thou knowest that the Church is obligated to take back a penitent, no matter what his former crimes!" Desle answered hotly.

"Aye, he has repented," Hunfred agreed, "and the Church must take him back! May God deal with him as He may!"

"Repented, has he? For what has he repented?" Gildas demanded.

"For all his acts, every cruel deed!"

"I hardly think so. King Christian's contempt for us and our beliefs is great. You forget that the King has pissed on the Church just as he pissed on the sacred relics of St. John of Veracis, and he will do so again at his next whim. The King has only come to understand that it is to his *advantage* to reconcile with the Church for the sake of his throne. He cares neither for the Church, nor for any of us, nor for any of you.

If we are too mild with him, soon he will be back to killing priests for sport!"

Father Desle shook his head sadly.

"Thou art blind. The King wades through the drowning waters of remorse even now."

"Think you his conditions too light?" Hunfred asked abruptly. "Pray, burden him more! Charge him to further prove his desire to reconcile, but allow his soul some hope!"

The Bishop was silent for a moment as he considered this.

"What condition has the King agreed to meet for the raising of his excommunication?" the Bishop asked Julius calmly.

"Your Grace, no condition has been set as of yet," the secretary replied.

Laying a hand on the confessor's arm, Hunfred cut in quickly, "Whatever condition would satisfy thee is the condition the King shall meet."

The Bishop nodded.

"Very well, let the King leave immediately from here upon a pilgrimage to Roma, stopping at every church and shrine along the way to say a prayer and an act of contrition for the killing of that priest, and I will be satisfied."

The monks frowned at the words.

"Thou knowest already that he can not go on such a journey now, for an invader waits on good weather alone to invade Speyron's borders."

The Bishop sighed with feigned frustration.

"Very well, if the King can not go on the pilgrimage, let him submit to be flogged in public. Either way, I will be satisfied of his remorse and of his desire to surrender to the authority of the Church; and I will raise his excommunication. He must make his decision soon, though, for I will say the Mass to relax the interdict at the hour."

Stunned, the two monks stared dumbly as the Bishop and his secretaries walked away. The Abbot and confessor turned slowly around and found the King standing behind them, his features pale with horror.

63

Christian numbly emerged from the Abbot's quarters and took several deep breaths of the cold, winter air; then he meandered aimlessly through the cloister and courtyard, ignoring small groups of the Bishop's entourage who were waiting on their instructions. Seeking a solitary place to think, he found himself at the door of the church.

Inside, already the brothers were busy putting out holy objects and candles and preparing the altar for the Mass. One of the priests had already blessed some water and filled the stone, baptismal font at the door of the church. Christian dipped his finger into the holy water, crossed himself, and bowed toward the rood.

It would take ten weeks to reach Roma, he reasoned. Two months if they rode hard from dark to dark. It was mid-January now. If he left immediately, he could potentially be back by the beginning of June, provided no one became sick and they were not attacked by bandits, nor captured and ransomed, nor killed by Muslim raiders...

By that time, Herryck will have had time to tour and divide up Speyron and redecorate the palace.

Utterly vexed, Christian covered his face with his hands and fought down the urge to scream and throw things.

Still, he could not submit to a flogging, particularly in public! The royal dignity could not abide it! What would his father say if he were alive? Would not his enemies think him weak? Would his vassals hold any respect for him? It was out of the question!

He watched as Brother Lubin unfolded and spread the fair linen onto the altar.

Perhaps he could leave Van Necht in charge of his forces, -commission him to defend the kingdom, Christian considered. Perhaps the warlord would be able to hold off Herryck long enough for him to make it to Roma and back. Even so, there were serious risks in leaving any one man in charge of a kingdom, no matter how loyal he was...

His eyes fell on the painting of the Doom then, specifically on the miserable souls being led to Hell. Christian swallowed. He really had no choice but to hazard the pilgrimage despite the many dangers. He did not want to risk a case of the sniffles, much less go into battle with Herryck, while his soul remained in peril.

Christian was so frustrated he wanted to cry. He wanted this to be over! He wanted to be absolved, assured of forgiveness today, not four months from now!

He watched absently as the monks carefully removed the black cloth that covered the rood.

Sighing, Christian bowed to the Christ which the rood represented and glanced at the cross. Curious, he walked toward the screen to get a better look at it. The cross bore a simple painting of the crucified Christ, his arms stretched wide and straight. His face was serene as he looked out into the world, accepting his fate without complaint.

The Christ had been flogged, Christian mused. He had been more than flogged; he had been scourged. The Christ had allowed himself to be publicly humiliated and tortured, and he had been innocent. And then he was crucified naked, an execution considered so heinous and shameful that Romani citizens were never subjected to it.

Who was he, then, to presume to be above a public flogging, when he deserved it? Christian reasoned. Was it the sin of pride that caused him to hesitate or was he simply a coward at heart? If he feared being flogged, how could he ever summon the courage to lead his forces into battle, particularly if they were outnumbered or outmatched?

As he studied the painting on the cross, Christian noticed something peculiar. The painted face of the Christ was more than serene.

The King took a few steps closer. He could just barely see that the slightest smile had been painted on the Christ's face. The Christ was mocking the forces of death and sin. This agony and humiliation was *his triumph- his opportunity* to save the world for all time- and he was willing, even *eager*, to do it.

Christian studied the crucifix for a few more minutes, summoning his courage and praying for more. He knew what he had to do. He bowed respectfully again and hurried out of the church to find the Bishop's secretary.

64

Christian stood against the cloister arch praying anxiously to God for courage as he waited for the Bishop's knights to collect him.

"Your Grace!"

The King turned to see Lord Olbert dressed in his familiar green of office accompanied by three of the Royal Steward's familiar knights. They bowed respectfully.

Overcome with joy, Christian hugged each of them warmly.

"I see you have missed us," Sir Eldwin commented, surprised at the King's show of fondness.

"And the cooking at the palace," young Sir Ecktor added.

Lord Olbert laughed and agreed. The blond king had lost weight and was considerably pale. The adviser wondered then if the youth was fevered, for as cold as it was, the King was visibly sweating.

Christian only smiled and hugged them each again.

"It is so good to see you, Olbert! I did not know that you had arrived!"

"I am delighted to be here and on such a happy occasion," Olbert replied. "We have brought the money you requested."

"We have been here some weeks," Sir Ecktor added.

The King looked at Olbert questioningly.

"Indeed. We arrived about a fortnight ago, thinking we certainly missed the Bishop. But we had not! -And I asked Abbot Hunfred not to inform you my arrival, for he feared the news would distract you from your preparations."

"Thank you," Christian told the four men sincerely. "I am grateful for your service and devotion and your concern."

Although surprised, Lord Olbert and the three knights bowed dutifully.

"Now tell me," Christian said, "What news? I have not received dispatches in months!"

"Aye, I have several for you. Our messengers were unable to get through the pass-" Olbert agreed.

"I can not remember a winter that has been as harsh- and so early in the year!" Sir Eldwin agreed while wrapping his cloak tighter around him.

"Aye, we had similar difficulty here. Luckily, we had no difficulty getting word to the Bishop," Christian told them. "Have you received word of Kaith?"

Olbert smiled.

"Your cousin is well, Sire."

Christian nodded.

"And what news from the palace?"

Sir Eldwin and the other knights quickly frowned and looked away as Lord Olbert smiled again.

"Sire, perhaps after the Mass we might have time to talk at length about-"

"Here are the Bishop's men, My Lords," Sir Ecktor commented as he blew into his hands and stomped his feet to warm himself.

"Aye, after the Mass-" Christian echoed, catching sight of the group of knights approaching, his heart beating wildly in his chest.

"-Did Abbot Hunfred already tell you?" Christian asked Olbert shortly.

"Tell me what, Sire? I have not had an opportunity to speak to him as of yet today."

Before Christian could answer, the Bishop's knights arrived and bowed to the Royal Steward.

"The gold to be paid to the Bishop, Sir Knights, is in our chambers at the guesthouse under guard," Olbert told the leader pleasantly. "Send your men to retrieve it; Sir Ecktor will show you the way."

The leader nodded and instructed four of his knights to follow Olbert's vassal to the guesthouse for the chests. As they hurried away, the knight in command gestured for the King to come with them. Christian's mouth went dry, but he immediately departed the cloister with the knights without a word.

Curious where they were going, Lord Olbert, Sir Eldwin and the remaining knight followed behind the King and the Bishop's men, joining an ever growing crowd of monks, servants, and villeins. The crowd of people walked through the monastery grounds, past the guesthouse, to the main gate and then outside it. Even visitors of the guesthouse hurried out into the cold to meet the mob.

Christian swallowed hard when he saw that the entire village with their many dogs already waited outside the monastery gate. Most had been there since the Bishop and his entourage had arrived. Now it was nearly noon, and the beggars, coming for their bread, had joined them.

Christian was surprised by how many of the villeins he knew or recognized; some he had tended in the infirmary and others he knew from their occasional work inside the monastery. The three, little orphan girls he had sent to the guesthouse weeks ago were among the rest. They looked well, Christian observed, and when they saw him, they smiled and greeted him as he passed.

The great, gathering mass of people mixed together outside the entrance to the monastery and waited curiously to know what was happening. Christian turned and saw Olbert and his six knights standing together among the rest and nearly all the monks of the monastery in one long line.

The Bishop's secretary, standing beside the bare, snow-covered, gnarled tree, unrolled a parchment with his bejeweled hands and called the crowd to silence, his breath fogging the air.

"'A decree of His Grace, Gildas, Bishop of Speyron to the people of Speyron. Let it be known on this, the sixteenth day of January in the year of our Lord Eight Hundred Eighty-three that the interdict on the Kingdom of Speyron is relaxed. His-'"

Cheers of joy from the crowd immediately drowned out the portly secretary. The peasants threw up their hands and hugged each other in celebration, and the monks, equally surprised, praised God joyously. Standing beside the Bishop's knights, Christian smiled as he watched them celebrate.

Julius waited for the mob to quiet down. When it did, he continued to read loudly.

"'His Grace, Christian Oengus Tillo Cuthbert, King of Speyron by the Grace of God, and excommunicate, has repented of his sins and is surrendering to the Church's authority.-'"

Again there was loud rejoicing from the commoners and monks. Julius cleared his throat but continued reading.

"'Thus today, also, the King's excommunication is raised, and he will be welcomed into the fold of Christ. As a condition of the raising of the excommunication upon him, he is presenting himself here publicly to be disciplined.'"

Amid the cheering, the smiles fell from the faces of Lord Olbert and his knights; they stood stunned, not believing their ears.

"What sort of discipline?" Sir Ecktor asked.

"Surely- a token discipline only," Sir Eldwin muttered.

They looked quickly at the King and then back at Julius.

Brother Bennet too stopped hugging Brother Caedmon abruptly and turned back to the secretary, equally astonished. Immediately, he looked to the Abbot and the confessor; both Hunfred and Desle stood solemnly side by side in the cold, their faces etched with gravity.

Julius rolled up the parchment then and nodded for the Bishop's knights to step forward. Two came forward with ropes and bowed to the secretary; then they turned, waiting for the knights who were pushing a cart into the center of the mob.

All the spectators began to talk excitedly among themselves as they wondered what was happening and who was in trouble. Christian swallowed hard at the sight of the last knight who carried a short-handled whip with seven, long, leather strips.

"You must remove-" one of the knights was suddenly telling the King, gesturing at the novice's scapular and cowl.

Christian's heart skipped a beat and then pounded. He nodded and began to disrobe.

Horrified, Lord Olbert and his knights immediately knelt in the snow in homage. Abbot Hunfred, Father Desle, and Bennet quickly went to their knees as well.

The entire crowd of spectators looked questioningly from them to the golden-haired novice undressing and then gasped as one.

"It is the King!" was the astonished whisper repeated through the mass of villeins, monks, guests of the guesthouse, and many from the Bishop's entourage.

The peasants and the beggars crossed themselves in shock and alarm, and all of them obediently went to their knees in the ruined snow and dared not look up at their King. The pilgrims bowed respectfully as well.

Avar swallowed hard as he saw in the corner of his eye the entire, black line of Benedictines go to their knees at once. Only the Bishop's secretaries and knights remained standing before King Christian.

Awkwardly, Gildas' knights knelt with the rest. Last of all, Julius and Avar grudgingly joined them.

Christian, having removed the scapular and cowl, shivered and looked about at the crowd of people on their knees in the snow around him. Touched deeply by his subjects' devotion, he swallowed hard as the tears welled in his eyes. Despite his insensitivity and mistreatment of them, their loyalty had remained constant. He vowed to remember this moment. He would be a new king; he would become worthy of their loyalty.

"Rise," he called to them.

Obediently, the crowd got up and dusted the snow off of themselves.

After the hefty secretaries were helped to their feet, Avar collected the scapular and cowl from the King and gave them to Father Desle; Julius signaled for the knights to proceed. The Bishop's guards approached the youth, but hesitated putting their hands upon him.

Understanding their hesitation, Christian put out his wrists, saying simply, "I willingly submit to your authority."

The knights slipped a noose around each wrist and led him to the cart. Christian stretched out his arms and took hold of the raw, wooden edges of the cart. As they bound his wrists securely to either end of the back of the cart, Christian shivered in the bitter wind as he looked out into the crowd before him. The withered, dirty and drawn faces of old, lame veterans and beggars, along with the concerned faces of villagers and children looked back at him. Thankfully, the monks and Olbert and his knights stood behind him, and he did not have to face them during this ordeal.

One of Gildas' knights put his hand inside the neckline of Christian's habit then, and with a fierce motion, ripped the material down to the waist. He was surprised to find the King wore a hairshirt beneath his habit. He ripped it to the waist as well, revealing then the youth's perfect, unmarred back and shoulders. With only the rope belt holding the tattered habit and shirt about his hips, Christian shivered repeatedly, and his teeth chattered as the winter wind blew against his bare skin.

As the knight with the whip paused to ask the secretary something, Christian shook with cold and began again his petitions to Christ and to his patron Peter and to the Virgin for prayers for courage and aid. The villagers in front of him pulled their cloaks more securely about them as they waited.

Christian said his prayers three times and wished they would hurry up and begin. He wanted this to be done with.

"Lord Christ, be with me," he whispered again. "Ave Gratia Plena, Dominus te-"

Christian shut his eyes as the breath was suddenly knocked out of him and his back was burning with pain. His eyes watered as the second blow landed before he had recovered from the first. Catching his breath, he grit his teeth to keep from screaming as the third blow landed.

Sir Eldwin and Lord Olbert watched in abject horror, realizing after only the first, few lashes that this was not a *token* punishment. The Bishop's knight applied the whip fiercely using all his strength, as one might whip a thief and a knave.

Christian gripped the edge of the cart tightly, pouring all of his concentration on his hands while trying to ignore his back that was on fire with pain. Tears wet his cheeks, but he kept tight hold of his dignity and stifled the urge to cry out. He told himself the pain would soon dull, and shortly it would be finished.

He was wrong on both accounts. After more than a dozen strikes, the leather straps began to draw blood from the raw skin, ripping a shriek from the King's throat. As the blows continued, his weakened skin tore readily, and the seven leather straps, which landed again and again upon the same flesh, antagonized and deepened the gashes already there. Eventually, Christian screamed, wept and writhed with every strike as he gasped for air, unaware of anything except the agony of his back being ripped open.

The villeins in front of Christian winced and flinched in pace with the flogger. The orphaned girls wept pitifully. Young children hid their eyes and clung to their mothers' clothes, crying at the sound of the 'thwacks' of the whip and the miserable wails of the young, blond novice.

Most of the monks turned away from the spectacle also, unable to bear the sight of the youth's pathetic twisting or the blood that now drenched his back and the snow around him. Many prayed; others crossed themselves and looked to the secretaries for its end. Cai and Quintus clung to the novice master and sobbed.

Near the thirtieth blow, Christian's legs gave out. He hung limply from the cart, panting and gasping for air, unaware of anything except pain.

Avar watched the scene impatiently, blowing on his hands. It was cold out here; and it was growing cloudy, and he could no longer feel his toes. It was not going to be much warmer in the church either, but at least it would be out of the wind.

Frowning, the Bishop watched from the monastery's upstairs library window, far out of sight of the people. Instead of gloating over the King's submission, Gildas felt defeated. He had assured Herryck that nothing could compel him to raise Christian's excommunication. How would he adequately explain his failure to him? In truth, he had underestimated this youth, for when he had made the option of flogging a condition, he had never dreamt that he would agree to it.

Christian panted weakly from beneath the cart, and then held his breath as the next blow landed. He gasped and wept with pain and then panted hard again as he awaited the next blow, dimly aware that the ropes, his sole support, were cutting into his wrists and that he had wet himself. The next blow arrived, and he gasped again- and then there was nothing.

The knight hesitated, lowered the whip, and looked at Julius. The secretary gestured to one of the Bishop's servants who hurried to the King's side with a pail. The entire crowd watched numbly as the servant doused the King with cold water, bringing him instantly back to consciousness.

Christian, registering the ache of his back and his cold, wet condition in the bitter wind, shivered and moaned miserably and wondered if it was over. He took a few more breaths before the renewed, bite of the whip against his wet, bloody back answered his question.

The line of monks glared in outrage at the secretaries as the knight resumed the whipping. Julius and Avar ignored them and crossed their arms resolutely.

Olbert and his knights pitifully looked from the King back to the secretaries and back to the King again.

Abbot Hunfred frowned as he counted the blows silently, not taking his eyes from Julius. How much more? -And how many more before he should intervene? A dead king would be of no use to Speyron, after all.

Finally, Julius made a gesture, and the knight lowered the whip and stepped back. Two waiting knights cut the ropes that bound the King's hands. Freed at last, Christian fell into the blood-stained snow and was immediately doused with another pail of water.

Olbert and his knights rushed immediately to him. As they helped him to his feet and then to sit upon the cart, Avar appeared before them and held up his hand before the King.

"Misereatur tui omnipotens Deus, et dimissis peccatis tuis, perducat te at vitam aeternam. Amen," he recited quickly.

"Amen," Olbert, Ecktor, and Eldwin echoed, crossing themselves.

Sir Eldwin wrapped the youth in his own cloak and wiped his face with its edge.

"Indulgentiam, absolutionem, et remissionem peccatorum tuorum tribuat tibi omnipotens et misericors Dominus. Amen."

"Amen," the men around the King echoed, crossing themselves again.

Father Desle was beside them then and gave them a clean linen shirt to put on him. The knights helped him into it, and then put his scapular and cowl on him again to help guard against the cold as Avar administered the final absolution.

"Dominus noster Jesus Christus te absolvat: et ego auctoritate ipsius te absolvo ab omni vinculo excommunicationis, et interdicti, in quantum possum, et to indiges. Deinde ego te absolvo a peccatis tuis, in nomine Patris, et Filii," and making a large sign of the cross over the bloody and exhausted king, "et Spiritus Sancti. Amen."

"Amen," Christian mumbled with the rest, crossing himself weakly.

Avar turned and departed for the church then. Ecktor rewrapped the King in Eldwin's cloak, and the pair carefully helped him to his feet.

Already, the Bishop's men and servants had gone back into the monastery and were preparing to begin the Mass. With a knight supporting him on either side, Christian weakly made his way back inside the monastery walls, the mob of villeins, beggars, and pilgrims following behind him. Outside the church, the Bishop's clerics and the monks were already forming the line for the procession. As the King and his vassals slowly made their way toward the church with the villagers, Brother Lubin approached the King with a long staff with a cross atop it.

"Your Grace," he bowed, "Father Desle instructs that you must carry this penitent's cross to the Mass."

Christian feebly took the staff and leaned upon it for support. The brother bowed again and went to his place among the other monks in the line. The King and his vassals carefully went up the stone steps of the church, following a villein and his goat through the great, wooden doors that were wide open. They paused behind the rest just inside the entrance to wet their fingers in the baptismal font and cross themselves.

Every torch and candle that the church had was burning, filling the air with light and smoke and brightly illuminating the newly completed wall paintings of the life of Christ. Groups of villeins gathered along the entire left wall beneath the murals, studying the paintings one by one.

The nativity was painted near the entrance of the church; next, the baptism by John the Baptist, then the call of the fishermen, the healing of the blind man and the lepers, the feeding of the five thousand, and the raising of Lazarus. Larger still were the paintings of the Last Supper, the Crucifixion, the empty tomb, the risen Christ showing his wounds to his startled disciples, and next to the rood screen, Christ ascending into the clouds. The villeins lingered before these pictures in awe, marveling at the vibrant colors and the details. Some knelt there and prayed.

Christian and his vassals continued slowly toward the front of the church, stopping on the left, in front of the rood screen, a ways from the large statue of the Madonna and Child. The group bowed toward the rood and crossed themselves. Leaning wearily on the staff, Christian looked again at the cross above him at the painted image of the triumphant Christ.

Just outside, singing began, and with it, the villeins left the decorated walls and went to stand before the rood screen, the men on the left of the rood, and the women on the right near the statue of the Madonna and Child.

The people parted more as the procession of clergy and monks entered the church. They came down the center of the nave, singing loudly, and brought with them the sweet aroma of incense.

Christian wearily watched the parade of clergy and black and white vestments pass him: The acolytes led the procession, followed by the incense carrier and the bearer of the processional cross. Next came Cai and Quintus, then the other novices, then the rest of the monks in order of their seniority. The monks who had taken priestly vows wore their white stoles over their black habits. Abbot Hunfred followed the monks, and he, in turn, was followed by Avar and Julius dressed in white albs and stoles, with their maniples wrapped about their left hands. With a maniple draped about his left forearm and the flame-shaped mitre on his head, Bishop Gildas serenely brought up the rear bearing the crook-headed crosier; the edge of his dalmatic was just barely visible under the white chasuble with its golden embroidery.

Each one in the procession paused before the screen and bowed to the Christ which the crucifix above represented before they continued through the gap to the altar. Then the monks smoothly processed to their places in the choir.

Trying to ignore the agony of his back, Christian stared wearily at the screen before him and tried to listen as the opening prayers were sung. The celebrant was hardly audible at all, and even the specifics of what the choir of monks sang was barely discernible in the nave.

"It is time, Sire," Olbert whispered to him.

Christian focused his eyes back to what was happening in the distance at the altar. The Bishop was singing his confiteor.

Christian weakly bowed toward the rood above him; still leaning on Sir Eldwin and supporting himself on the penitent's cross, the two of them went through the gap in the screen, passed the choir, and approached the high altar. Bishop Gildas and Avar and Julius waited for him with clasped hands. When he reached the altar, Christian turned and faced the choir and the people, and leaning upon the staff, recited the confession as loudly as his hoarse voice could manage:

"Confiteor Deo omnipotenti, beatae Mariae semper Virgini, beato Michaeli Archangelo, beato Joanni Baptistae, sanctis Apostolis Petro et Paulo, omnibus Sanctis, et tibi Pater, quia peccavi nimis verbo, et opere: mea culpa, mea culpa, mea maxima culpa," hitting his chest three times as he said this. "Ideo precor beatam Mariam semper Virginem, beatum Michaelem Archangelum, beatum Joannem Baptistam, sanctos Apostolos Petrum et Paulum, omnes Sanctos, et te Pater, orare pro me ad Dominum Deum Nostrum."

The Bishop responded abruptly in a booming voice:

"Misereatur tui omnipotens Deus, et dimissis peccatis tuis, perducat te ad vitam aeternam."

"Amen," the entire choir of monks responded.

Then Gildas stepped forward and put his hands on the King's shoulders and kissed him on the cheek, thus officially welcoming him back into the community of the faithful.

The Bishop returned to the altar then, and the prayers of the Mass continued. As the Bishop censed the altar, King Christian slowly returned to his place outside the rood screen. His eyes returned to the rood above him, where the likeness of the triumphant Christ seemed to regard him with approval.

Bishop Gildas began to liberally sprinkle the choir of monks with holy water, then he came through the gap in the rood screen into the nave and generously sprinkled the worshippers on either side of the center aisle whom crossed themselves quickly in response; then he returned to the chancel and altar.

As the chorus of monks sang the Kyrie and then the Gloria, the King rested heavily on his knights and tried not to fall down.

As the Mass continued with the singing of more prayers, followed by the first reading, most of the congregation watched attentively through the screen with quiet reverence, the children standing by their parents, swaying slightly to the songs being sung. However, some of the villeins and pilgrims went back to the wall paintings and were admiring them again while others talked softly among themselves. Other worshipers entered the side chapels to view the relics on display. The Bishop's knights and servants conversed together in a group at the back of the nave. A few women knelt before the statue of the Madonna and Child and began saying prayers by their prayer cords. A group of dogs growled at each other, threatening to fight even there.

Christian shivered again and looked about him feebly, trying not to think about his pain. He noticed how odd the service seemed without even a few crying infants to oppose and overwhelm the readings, indistinguishable though they were to him in the nave. As his eyes fell on the women near him, he noticed that none were pregnant, although they were well of age.

The loud peal of the church bell brought the King's thoughts back to the Mass. They were preparing to read the gospel and were censing the book. The villeins paused in their personal devotions, and looked toward the altar, said their response with the rest of the congregation and crossed themselves, and then returned to what they had been doing.

After the gospel reading, the Bishop began to speak, but he remained near the altar, directing his homily to the choir of monks. As the villeins in the nave could not hear him, some returned to their conversations and private devotions, while others stood silently watching and waiting.

Christian continued to balance between his knights, wishing he could concentrate more on the Mass. Despite his desire, his pain was too intense for him to even try to follow the liturgy. After a while, the loud bong of the church bell drew his attention back to the altar. The Bishop had elevated the round host for all to see. Again the various people paused again in what they were doing, looked toward the altar, and crossed themselves reverently with the rest of the worshippers. Then the Bishop lowered the host onto the altar again and bowed reverently to it.

Christian crossed himself and watched the Bishop continue to pray over the host at the altar. Then Gildas held the host in the air again and made the sign of the cross repeatedly with it.

Another church bell rang, and the entire congregation began to recite the Paternoster as one; Christian whispered it with them. With anticipation, he watched the Bishop lift the host into the air and then break it in two, signifying the breaking of Christ's body and the breaking with the past. Then Olbert and the knights were exchanging the kiss of peace with him and each other.

After exchanging the peace, the villeins returned to their devotions and the Bishop, his prayers. Inwardly groaning, Christian patiently continued to endure his pain and fatigue, his exhausted gaze affixed on the image of the Christ on the rood above him as he waited to be finally united with his Lord Christ.

His heart skipped a beat and then raced when he saw at last the Bishop and Avar making their way toward the nave and the opening of the rood screen with the golden paten in hand.

The knights helped Christian forward to the gap beneath the crucifix.

"Corpus Domini nostri Jesu Christi custodiat animam tuam in vitam aeternam," the Bishop said while placing the host on the King's tongue.

Christian crossed himself and ate the wafer quickly.

Tears of relief flowed down his face as his knights helped him back to the place beside Lord Olbert in the nave. Bishop Gildas and Avar turned and went back through the gap in the screen to the high altar. The King remained in a daze, muttering a prayer of thanks to God and the Christ and the Holy Spirit again and again as he waited on the Mass to conclude, only dimly aware of the Bishop singing a blessing and the response of the choir of monks.

With the thunderous, joyful tolling of the church bells reverberating through the church, the monks, clerics and the Bishop processed out as they had entered, followed by the faithful.

65

As the church bells continued their exuberant, unrestrained peals, Bennet scanned the throng of commoners that were leaving the church and heading back to the gate. He did not see the King anywhere.

He did catch sight of Brothers Eliud and Caedmon hurrying towards the church with two baskets, however.

"Where are you going?" Bennet asked curiously, seeing that the baskets were laden with food, bread, and wine.

"The Bishop is leaving directly!" Caedmon answered without stopping. "He will not attend the banquet and sent word that his food was to be delivered to the sacristy immediately after the Mass!"

"Hie, Brother, and help the cellarer," Brother Eliud instructed Bennet excitedly, "-for the kitchen is besieged!"

As the brothers hurried past him to the church, Bennet immediately hastened through the crowd toward the kitchen and refectory.

The monk stopped short as he arrived at the cloister. The courtyard was in utter chaos. Unattended horses, some saddled and bridled, some not, meandered idly in the courtyard and inside the cloister walk itself while the Bishop's knights and servants furiously ate and drank where they stood.

Bennet quickly weaved his way around the intruders toward the kitchen. Outside of it, an empty hogshead of ale had been tossed aside indifferently, and the Bishop's men were busily draining two more horn by horn. The knights were inside the kitchen as well, snatching the food from the cooks before it could be served.

"They will not sit at the table, nor even await a blessing upon the food!" one of the monks in the kitchen was complaining.

"What can I do?" Bennet asked.

"Here, take them that old bread!" the cellarer told him pointing to a basket in the corner. "We had saved it to make trenchers for the feast, but they will care not. Take heed, Brother, lest they bite your hand in their haste!"

Bennet smiled as he went to retrieve the basket, passing, as he did, the doorway of the refectory. Inside the dining hall, he saw Julius and Avar sitting alone at the great length of table. They were eating a haunch of pork quietly, seemingly oblivious to the commotion in the courtyard and kitchen.

"Will you eat anything, Sire?" Abbot Hunfred asked.

Christian wearily shook his head. He sat on a bench beside the brightly burning fire in the hall inside the Abbot's quarters.

"Drink this, Your Grace. 'Twill dull your pain," Brother Trumwin said quietly.

Christian took the cup and swallowed the bitter drink quickly.

Lord Olbert and his knights, Abbot Hunfred, and Father Desle stood a little away, watching with concern as the monk tended the King.

Brother Trumwin carefully removed the cloak from the youth, then the cowl and scapular, noticing that every movement the King made was agony for him.

The spectators then winced at the sight. The linen shirt was caked thick and brown with dried blood, and it had adhered to the youth's entire back. They watched as the monk took a knife and cut the shirt apart at the shoulder and side seams. The front dropped to the floor easily. Christian shivered anew.

"Are you ready, Sire?" the monk asked.

Christian took a deep breath.

"Aye."

The monk slowly began pulling the cloth from his skin. Christian gasped, and new tears rolled down his face as the linen took scabs and raw flesh with it. Open-mouthed wounds spewed out fresh, red blood that poured down his back.

As the monk removed the last fragments of the linen from Christian's back, shoulders, and arms, the onlookers recoiled at the sight. The King's perfectly smooth back was gone forever. Where his skin had been, there was now a crimson and black tapestry of deep gashes, cuts, and bruises.

Brother Trumwin pressed clean cloths against the wounds until the bleeding subsided. Then he and Brother Patricus removed the torn habit and hair shirt and carefully bathed the King with warm water. After Trumwin had applied a salve to the gashes and another to the entire back and to the rope cuts at his wrists, they dressed the weak youth in a clean, long, loose-fitting, linen tunic, and helped him to his feet. With his vassals close behind, the two monks took the King into a private guest chamber within the Abbot's quarters and helped him into a large, feather bed dressed with clean sheets and coverlets.

Lying on his stomach, Christian blinked, exhausted, at the tall candle that burned on a small table beside his bed.

"Come, let us allow him some rest," Hunfred said, urging the concerned adviser and knights out of the chamber.

"Sire-"

Christian awoke with a moan, immediately registering pain and the aroma of food. Barely opening his eyes, he saw that the candle had burned three quarters of the way down in the dim chamber. Brother Trumwin was beside the bed with a tray.

"Can you sit up?"

Christian slowly pushed himself up, heeding the emptiness of his stomach more than the pain of his back.

The monk set the tray of food beside the candle at his bedside. Christian reached for the bread, but then stopped. He said a brief blessing and prayer of thanks and crossed himself quickly. Picking up the bread, he bit hungrily into it. He picked up the bowl and tasted the soup. It was salty fish stew, and just the right temperature. He gulped it down quickly, and then bit off another bite of bread. Brother Trumwin poured him a horn of ale and handed it to him.

Christian took the cup. The ale tasted cool and sweet, and he drank it all, surprised at his thirst.

While the monk refilled the cup, the King wiped his mouth on the sleeve of his tunic and then for the first time glanced around the chamber at the nice furnishings within. It was then that he saw that there was something large and black on the rug on the floor.

Christian leaned forward for another look; then he glanced at Brother Trumwin questioningly and then back down at the monk that was lying face down with his arms outstretched.

Embarrassed but curious, Christian cleared his throat.

"Rise, Brother, and be noticed."

To his astonishment, Brother Bennet got up off the floor and bowed low on one knee before him.

"Bennet!" Christian managed, not knowing what to say. "You surprise me."

"-I have come to beg your forgiveness, My Liege," he said without looking up.

"Please, rise, Bennet. You did no wrong to me. You treated me as I deserved, -and We will not hold it against you."

"You will never know how difficult it was for me to shun you, Sire," Bennet replied, on the verge of tears. "-And if my actions added to your distress, I beg you to forgive me, for it was never my desire to cause you pain."

"I know. And I forgave any pain you caused me long ago, Bennet. Now embrace me as a brother," Christian said, as he carefully stood up.

Bennet rose and stepped forward, and the two formally, but carefully, embraced each other.

"Truly, Bennet, I must thank you for saving me, -doubly so, by first befriending me on the road and inviting me here and then by helping me *to see*."

Bennet smiled slightly, but said nothing.

The King sat down on the bed again.

"Are you hungry?" he asked, proffering the bread.

Bennet took the bread and broke off a small piece and ate it. He handed the loaf back to the King.

"How long have you been down there?" Christian asked curiously gesturing to the floor.

"A few hours-" Bennet shrugged.

Christian raised his eyebrows.

"'Tis well that I finally brought your dinner," Brother Trumwin cut in cheerfully, "else Brother Bennet might have been down there for days."

Christian and Bennet both smiled weakly.

Christian noted the monk's sad smile with accompanying dimples. How he had missed even the slightest smile from Bennet, not to mention his fellowship! He did not want to do without either again.

"Bennet, will you sit and visit with me a while -unless you are pressed to go?"

"Of course I will."

The monk brought a chair beside the bed and sat down while the King continued to eat his dinner.

66

"It is an immense honor for you and for this community, but -"

"You must wear the armor of God," the novice master cut in.

Bennet smiled at Brother Septimus, Father Desle and Abbot Hunfred, trying to conceal both the excitement and apprehension he felt.

"Aye, temptation will be everywhere," Hunfred agreed. "Temptations of power, -of influence and wealth, -of the flesh, -of sloth."

"Mind you avoid them at all cost," the novice master finished. "Help the King avoid them as well through counsel and by example."

"The sloth I am not so concerned with," Hunfred said. "You will sing the Mass daily and the Divine Office also, as if you were here."

"You may find them somewhat burdensome without the support of your brethren, but we will be with you in prayer," Brother Septimus said.

Bennet nodded.

"Spur the King to fulfill his penance and the conditions of the relaxation of the interdict," Hunfred told him directly.

"Aye, you are his soul's only advocate there," Desle added. "Amid the quarreling of his vassals and the temptations and politics of the palace, you must keep the King mindful of his soul and of his obligations to God and the Christ and the Church."

"The King has repented *here*, but likely he will be sorely tempted to return to sin as soon as he leaves these walls," Hunfred told him.

"Aye," Brother Septimus agreed. "Remember the parable of the sower: If the truth is not planted in fertile soil, it will soon wither and die. You must do all you are able to keep his soil fertile and tilled and to protect the tender shoots of the sprouting Gospel so that it will continue to grow and flourish in his heart."

Bennet nodded.

"Be firm with him, Bennet," Abbot Hunfred told him. "Do not allow friendship to hinder you in your duty! Admonish him if he falters!"

"But only in private-" Desle added.

"I will do all that you instruct, with God's help," Bennet told them.

Abbot Hunfred frowned. From Bennet's calm, cheerful demeanor, he doubted that the youth had any real understanding of what challenges awaited him.

"We will keep you in our prayers," Hunfred said gruffly.

Desle saw the Abbot's serious expression and smiled. He rose out of his chair and hugged the young monk affectionately.

"This community will sorely miss you. And this parting could not be more painful for me if you were my own son."

"It pains me as well, Father," Bennet replied, trying to smile as a single tear rolled down his face.

Brother Septimus smiled also as he attempted to hold back his gathering emotions.

"Very well," Hunfred said abruptly, holding his hand up. "The Lord bless you and keep you.-"

Bennet went to his knees immediately before the Abbot.

"-The Lord make his face to shine upon you and be gracious to you. The Lord lift up his countenance upon you, and give you peace."

The Abbot and the confessor made the sign of the cross over Bennet as Bennet crossed himself. They pulled him to his feet then, and each man hugged him and kissed him on the cheek.

67

ord Dewain's horse exhaled white fog, and its muscles twitched fitfully in the cold while its master scanned the far distance. It was gray and hazy today, and Dewain could not make out anything but empty road in the distance. Catching a bit of movement, he looked again, but it was only a group of deer crossing the way. He sighed impatiently and glanced at his companions who waited with him beside the road.

The alderman had traveled since before light from his lands in order to meet the King on his return home. Tate and Acrida had accompanied him. They had only just arrived at the palace an hour ago when word came that the King approached. Thus, remounting their horses and joining with Lords Grey, Paschal, and Felix and a number of knights, they had ridden out a short ways from the palace. They all waited now in a line beside the road to pay homage to the King.

Dewain had rejoiced to hear of the King's reconciliation with the Church and of the relaxation of the interdict, yet he still continued to wonder what had finally convinced King Christian of the necessity to do so. Had their counsel been heard after all? Perhaps all the lad needed was some time to consider the wisdom of it.

And where had the King been these past months? Had he traveled to a neighboring kingdom and made alliances on his own?

-Perchance he had taken a wife of the Faith and making peace with the Church was a concession of the union. This would explain why the King was returning to the palace now, after so many months had passed and with the rebels still a potential threat. Most likely he was returning with his bride to rally his vassals' allegiance and to end the rumors of his death and ill-health that had been circulating. It was the wise thing to do, and yet, Dewain was surprised by it. He had not expected Christian to bother to emerge from his safe haven until Herryck at last invaded their borders and forced him to do so.

As Dewain's eyes drifted to the rich, red color of his cloak, he wondered again if he would wear the crimson of Royal Chancellor for much longer. Could he return to the King's favor? Was it futile to even try? No doubt Felix would don the red next. It mattered little that the lad could not read himself. With the right staff, the youth-

Dewain sighed. His thoughts had turned negative again. Over the past months, he had considered the King's criticism of him and found it justified. He did tend to see the dismal side of everything. Even his wife had admitted it to him.

Since his near banishment, he had been training himself to hold his tongue and to think before he spoke, lest he offend the King again. Now he questioned how words or ideas sounded before he spoke them and tried to rephrase any that sounded discouraging or grim. It had been difficult, but what had surprised him was how many bleak thoughts went through his mind which were never spoken.

"There-" one of the knights said, pointing to the distance.

All of the vassals looked. A small group of knights could just be seen in the distance making their way at an unhurried walk down the half-frozen road toward them.

The noblemen's horses snorted and coughed and shifted their weight from one leg to the other as their riders returned to their thoughts.

Lord Grey shivered and rubbed his cold nose with his numbing fingers. Olbert had proved to be far cleverer than he had anticipated. Somehow he had managed to keep the King's location secret even from him. His best spies had not been able to discover him anywhere in Speyron, nor in the neighboring kingdoms.

The Chamberlain had been startled to hear of the end of the interdict, especially as the King had somehow arranged it without *his* help. The reconciliation with the Church was a sound political decision before the coming war, but he doubted that Christian had seen the vital importance of such a move on his own. Clearly some new and powerful rival now had the King's ear, -perhaps even Olbert himself.

However, as much as he wished to, Grey could not totally dismiss the possibility that Christian had matured since his expulsion from the palace. Perhaps the youth finally understood that leaders must sometimes compromise small items in order to achieve more important goals. Grey frowned and noted his yawning horse. The last thing he wanted now was a king that was *ready* to rule; it would ruin everything he had worked for these several years.

Paschal sat upon his horse and bit his nails anxiously as he waited with the rest. One day's notice was hardly enough time to prepare a welcome feast worthy for the return of the King. And he dearly needed to please Christian before he told him that despite his every effort he had failed to learn the identities of the instigators of the palace revolt.

One day's notice of the King's return, however, was all he had received, and not only had Olbert made certain of that, but the Steward had actually sent word that Christian did not wish to celebrate his return with feasting. Paschal knew this was a lie and no doubt a ploy to make him look ill-prepared and inhospitable when Christian arrived.

As the young alderman looked at the vassals around him, he bristled at the sight of Dewain. The adviser had hardly spent more than a fortnight at the palace since the uprising, yet he had been sent word to gather here with the rest of them, as if he had been here working on the King's behalf the entire time. He probably had received more than a day's notice too.

Dewain had brought that peasant witch with him also, as if Christian needed her! If he had had his way, Paschal fumed, she would be out in the fields working with the rest of the villeins!

Paschal spit the bit of nail upon the ground testily. Christian had left *him* in charge! *He* should have been the one to summon the other aldermen and to choose *whom* was summoned. *He* should have been the one to know the whereabouts of the King! As it was, he had been forced to send his correspondence intended for the King to Olbert. Who knew if Christian had actually received all of the dispatches, or for that matter, any of them?

Paschal vowed he would discuss it all with Christian soon, and he would not be satisfied until Olbert was dismissed from Court altogether!

Tate sat on his horse and again counted the score and more of knights that accompanied the noble group. All but four were vassals of Grey. How many more did he have elsewhere, preparing for Herryck's army? And why did he bring so many to the palace when it was already well protected? All of his knights were armed with expensive, foreign-made swords, and their mounts were grain fed and in excellent condition, their sleek, winter hair brushed to a gleam.

In contrast, Dewain's horses, two of which he and Acrida rode, were large bellied on the remnants of autumn grasses; their winter coats were dull and unruly. All of the palace horses, including those of the garrisons as well as those that Felix and Paschal and their two knights rode, were in similar condition.

Acrida patted her horse's neck. She had departed Van Necht's lands after meeting Lord Dewain and a few of his knights by chance when they were passing through the warlord's village. The alderman had been visiting one of his sisters and was then returning to his own lands; Tate was with him. She had asked the Chancellor if she could come to his lands, and he had agreed; there, Dewain and his family had warmly welcomed her into their home.

Although she would have never guessed it, Lord Dewain was a warm and jovial man *away* from Court. He was beloved on his lands, and he kept a merry household. His young wife and children delighted in music and games, and minstrels played and entertained daily. Devoted to the Faith, the family had welcomed several priests and clerks to their castle also who had sought refuge when the interdict began.

While she was there, Dewain had introduced her to unmarried freemen at every opportunity. He also had asked his wife to teach her the ways of 'highborn' women so that she might not look out of place at Court, including how to ride a horse sideways like a proper woman.

But every waking moment, no matter what she did, her thoughts had always returned to Van Necht. Although too embarrassed and ashamed to ask outright for news of him, she was certain he must have recovered, else word would have arrived of his death.

He was likely training the men as before, and her aunt was surely back in Brackenbach by now. Shivering in the bitter wind, she wondered if Van Necht would come to the palace now that the King was here, perhaps to gain the King's consent for his marriage. As shameful as it was, she longed to see him.

The advisers' thoughts were shortly interrupted by the sounds of crunching snow and ice and snorting and blowing horses as the group of ten riders at last arrived. The throng of vassals beside the road dismounted. Standing beside their mounts in the frozen sludge, they all looked with anticipation from the six knights, to the two, dark cloaked and hooded riders, to the alderman's valet, to Lord Olbert wrapped in his heavy green mantle that flitted slightly in the low breeze. They looked back then at the knights and then back to Lord Olbert again, concerned.

"Where is the King?" Dewain called out to Olbert.

In response, one of the cloaked riders pulled back his dark hood, revealing himself to the group.

The crowd of vassals, surprised but relieved to see King Christian's familiar features, went to bended knee immediately.

"Pardon me, Sire," Lord Dewain said quickly, paling as he knelt to the cold ground. "I knew not you still traveled in disguise."

Lord Olbert covered his eyes and sighed, but Christian only smiled. It was good to be home.

"You each do Us great honor by greeting Us here," King Christian told them. "Shall we be on our way?"

As he waited for his vassals to rise and mount their horses again, Christian blew into his cold hands and wondered briefly who had organized this show of homage. He scanned the familiar faces among the group and could not refrain from smiling when he saw Filberte's old Fool, undeterred as usual, among the rest.

The King's eyes then fell on a woman among the group. Her face seemed familiar, but Christian could neither recall who she was nor how he knew her. Her skin was pale and smooth, and her lips were flushed red in the cold air. Together with her blue eyes, her face was not unappealing. She wore a plain, woolen cloak, and a plain, woolen headrail covered her head. -Perhaps she was the wife of one of the knights, he mused.

The King's silent survey of the woman did not go unnoticed.

"Well, he has been a long time in that monastery after all," Sir Ecktor whispered.

The knights around him smiled.

"Sire-"

King Christian turned to Lord Olbert.

"You remember your sibyl, Acrida? -The one who advised you to go east?"

The King looked back at the woman in surprise. The last time he had seen her, her face had been black and blue with bruises. The advisers had cleaned her up considerably, he realized. In fact, aside from her plain clothes and lack of jewelry, she was indistinguishable from any other noblewoman in the kingdom, -except that no *lady* would have looked upon him as boldly as she now did.

Acrida observed the blue-eyed, handsome, young King in silence, her hate boiling up at the sight of him. He looked different. He was pale and thin, but it was still him. And he was staring at her as if this was their first meeting! She immediately chastised herself for not fully appreciating the months she had spent away from him.

Christian continued to marvel at her for a moment. He had taken her from her village and family, nearly had her executed, and then sent her to be the prisoner and amusement of his fiercest vassal. She had not only returned to his palace with her spirit intact, but she, somehow, had managed to get a post from him at Court.

If she was not a witch, she was, no doubt, the luckiest woman Fortuna had ever smiled upon, the King mused, for she managed to benefit from every cruelty served her. Let Herryck's army overrun Speyron- *this* woman would still be here, he wagered.

Perhaps his counselors were wise to befriend her. Perhaps her luck would touch those in close proximity. Had not even he benefited from her vague advice: 'Go east. I know not where'?

Finally, Christian spoke.

"Woman, I have treated you unjustly. I hope you will forgive me."

Everyone raised their eyebrows in wonder. Paschal looked again at the King, certain he had misheard him. Acrida herself was dumbstruck. These words were as unexpected as a blow would have been.

Christian looked toward his palace and then back at her again, and smiled.

"Your advice proved useful by the way."

Acrida's heart leaped and then raced. She stared after him, wondering what to make of this.

Christian urged his horse forward, and it began its slow plod up the hill, the nine riders following him in silence. The advisers and the many knights fell behind them as they made their way to the palace that loomed ahead. As they rode along, they passed between the three garrisons of knights that had lined both sides of the road; still mounted, these men cheered loudly as they recognized the King. Then they turned their horses and joined the back of the line that trailed behind the monarch to the palace.

While his horse ambled up the soggy road, Christian blew on his hands and moved his fingers that were numb with cold. He and his companions had been traveling for days, spending frigid and uncomfortable nights in stables at inns and taverns along the way to keep from attracting attention. Each day they had ridden until dusk and returned to the road just after first light.

Now at early afternoon on the fourth day, they were finally here, and Christian's mood was light. He was excited and happy and relieved finally to be back home. Soon he would be in front of a roaring fire, enjoying a good cup of wine, surrounded by old friends and familiar servants. He was looking forward to a hot soak in the bath. Boisil would prepare him a tasty meal, and he would have a good night's sleep in his own bed!

Christian glanced at the youth who rode beside him. Wait until Bennet saw the Romani baths! It was just one of the many things he wanted to show him, but there would be plenty of time for that after the monk had settled in.

However, as excited as he was to be home, Christian was equally apprehensive as to what he would find here. Before leaving St. Brychan's, Olbert had told him he would find the palace different, but the Steward had been hesitant to elaborate further, telling him it was best that he see it for himself.

Christian had read the dispatches that had failed to reach him the past few months. The majority were from Paschal and Grey. Paschal's frustration at being unable to discover the rebels was very evident; he repeatedly alleged that Grey and Olbert thwarted his every endeavor to ascertain them.

Grey accused Paschal of being more intent on frivolity and feasting than a methodical search for the rebels. He reported that the only time Paschal and Felix put down their cups was to execute a peasant.

Olbert himself sent a letter reporting that the interrogations and executions had not only interfered with the running of the palace, but, together with the casualties from the retaking of the palace, had seriously reduced the number of servants and field workers. Aside from this one letter, the remaining letters from Olbert were simple pleas for him to return immediately to the palace.

Although none of his vassals seemed to be scheming to take his throne, it was clear to Christian all of them had taken liberties in his absence. Paschal, Olbert, and Grey were the three most influential and powerful noblemen in Speyron, and they were very different. In his absence, the rifts between these men had increased. For Christian, it was dangerous for them to align, but *disastrous* if they seriously quarreled, for it was possible that they could divide the entire kingdom. -And if only one of them joined with Herryck, it was finished.

Above all else, Christian knew he could not appear weak or vulnerable to them. As long as he appeared strong, likely they would fall into line as they always had, no matter how much they disliked each other or what sort of changes he instigated; and changes were on the forefront of his agenda.

As the riders neared the palace, villagers, pausing in their labors in the fields outside the walls, lined the road too. Many stood silently as the riders went by, but others paid formal homage on one knee as the aldermen passed; *none* cheered.

"Who gave them permission to stop their work?" Paschal demanded angrily.

"*I* did not," Felix replied, riding beside him.

"This is Olbert's doing!" Paschal grumbled hotly.

Christian heard them, but said nothing as he surveyed the grubby peasants. The villeins looked hungry and tired, and their faces bore grim expressions. Some did not look at the nobles at all, keeping their faces down as the riders passed.

Christian wondered at their listless demeanor. And some of them seemed oddly familiar to him, but he dismissed this thought, as he had never been acquainted with the field workers at his palace.

The large band of nobles continued up the hill into the shadow of the towering palace walls. When they neared the open gate, Christian stopped his horse abruptly, the pleasant expression falling from his face.

The King was actually so stunned, he could not, at first, think. Bennet, too, was shocked speechless, his heart racing; he crossed himself weakly as he took in the ghastly sight before him.

Near the gate, the palace wall was lined with the heads of men, women and even children, both old and young, preserved in tar, and caked with a layer of snow. Each face held the expression of agony, as if the gaze of their eyes were forever affixed on the horrors of the damned.

Christian stared numbly at them, his very blood turning to ice. In some places, there were more than four rows. There were so many that they could have easily peopled an entire village.

If these were not rebels, why were they on the wall? Christian wondered. Were these killed during the retaking of the palace?

"So many more now!" Sir Ecktor commented. "They have been busy while we were away!"

Bennet and Christian turned and glanced at the knight in alarm.

"Look! The one on the end is fresh. 'Tis likely only a few hours old," Ecktor continued, pointing at the bottom row, not seeing their concerned looks. "You can tell as it still drips, and there is no frost upon it."

Bennet's mouth went completely dry. The monk crossed himself again in horror as he examined the head to which the knight was referring.

"*...likely he will be sorely tempted to return to sin as soon as he leaves these walls...*"

Bennet's heart beat loud in his ears as he recalled the words of Abbot Hunfred. Tempted to sin? This was beyond sin! This was an invitation to pure evil!

Bristling at the knight's observations, Acrida's thoughts turned from Van Necht to fresh loathing for the King. She did not look at the heads, herself. They had heard about them at Dewain's, and she had just seen them an hour ago. Besides, her stomach was already beginning to twist simply at the proximity of them.

Instead, she hostilely watched the King while he examined the display of *traitors'* heads on the wall. Unfortunately, from her position in the group, she could not see his expression. She hoped he was pleased by the offering his people had made for his injured honor.

"They might consider tying a few curs at the gate if they wish to keep strangers away," Tate commented. "Of course, curs do bark, fight, and hump each other excessively- and that might give visitors a poor impression of the King."

Acrida, Grey, Olbert, Dewain and a few of the knights smiled.

The King frowned and urged his horse forward leading the crowd of riders inside the palace grounds, completely oblivious to the cheering of the entire Palace Watch that lined both sides of the road just inside the gate.

Once beyond the gate and the cheering had subsided, the garrisons disbanded, and Christian looked around, the hair on the back of his neck standing on end. The silence was remarkable. Aside from the Watch, there was no one on the road inside the palace walls. There were no merchants or traders with their stalls anywhere. There were no villeins, neither the lame, nor old men and women. There were no children. There was hardly a stray dog.

The group of alderman paused and dismounted outside the great columns at the entrance to the palace. Nervous from the King's reticence, they were quiet as well as they waited on the stable hands to collect the horses. King Christian stared perplexed at the young women in the soiled but elegant dresses who arrived suddenly and took charge of the horses.

The King did not tarry but went through the great column entrance into the courtyard. He paused there near the fountain and looked around, bewildered by the deserted enclosure. The advisers stood together mutely and watched as the King assessed the changes.

"My Liege!"

Christian turned to see Paschal and Felix kneeling before him. He smiled at his favorite companions and gestured for them to rise.

"Welcome home!" the youths said, each taking a turn to embrace him.

"Indeed, it is good to be home!" Christian answered genially.

Hearing this, Bennet glanced at him with concern.

The other advisers then crowded in toward the King, wishing him welcome. His bodyguards approached next and bowed formally; Christian pulled them to their feet, embracing and greeting each one warmly.

"You must be hungry after your journey!" Paschal said.

"Indeed, We are."

"Olbert did not give us much warning, but we are preparing a great feast in celebration of your return! It should be ready forthwith," Paschal said.

"We thought We sent word ahead that no special feast was to be held on Our account," Christian said, glancing toward Olbert.

Paschal flushed in surprise and embarrassment.

"Of course, Sire, the feast shall be canceled at once if that is your wish!"

Christian smiled, clearly able to imagine the great labors the cooks in the kitchens were undergoing.

"Of course We will attend if you have gone to much trouble, but Our diet is simple now and-"

"Certainly Boisil can prepare whatever you require," Lord Dewain stated pleasantly.

The horrified looks of Olbert, Paschal and Felix were unmistakable. Dewain faltered and looked questioningly back at them.

"Boisil is no longer the palace cook, Sire," Felix told him directly. "But the new cook is talented and can prepare whatever you like."

He turned and gestured to one of his men to summon the cook.

In the distance, the church bell began to ring.

"My Liege, come. There is a warm fire burning in the audience chamber," Paschal told him. "Let us drink, have music and hear of your journey!"

"Summon the minstrels," Felix ordered a nearby knight.

Christian sighed. A warm fire, a hot bath, some soup, and a good night's rest in his own bed was exactly what he wanted, but clearly his vassals had missed him. They wanted to feast and hear news of where he had been, and he should oblige them.

"Or perhaps Your Grace would care to retire to your chambers and rest after your journey. Perhaps change out of those clothes," Grey smiled, glancing again at the plain, soiled, woolen garb and cloak the King wore. "Or perhaps you would like to bathe before-"

"Aye, a bath and a swyve before dinner would be well on a cold day like today," Paschal agreed, rubbing his cold hands together briskly.

"Delightful suggestion," Tate agreed.

Christian blinked at the youth.

"This is Father Bennet, Our Chaplain," Christian said quickly, gesturing toward the other cloaked figure a few feet away from them who was admiring the fountain.

At this introduction, Bennet pulled back his hood and bowed to the noblemen.

The entire entourage stopped and looked at the young man with the tonsure, and then back at the King, wondering what to make of this.

"You must surely come, Brother," Tate told him cordially. "The baths at the palace have no equal in the kingdom. They were built by the Romani, and the water, ingeniously heated from beneath the floor, is quite hot. -And with choice maidservants to attend you, the only other place to have a more assured *sweat* -is in Roma herself."

Bennet looked questioningly at the old man.

The church bell continued to clang, repeatedly and erratically now, drawing the King's attention. The church at the palace had never had a belltower, nor the large, elaborate bells like at a monastery. The palace church had a simple, medium-sized bell mounted near the doorpost. At the moment, it did not ring with the solemn peals of a summons for Mass or any service. Rather, it sounded as if a child were pulling the rope for amusement.

"Have the priests returned?" Christian asked abruptly, wondering if some of the absent villagers were attending a midday service.

"We have not seen them, Sire."

"If the priests have not returned, then why does the bell ring?" he asked.

Paschal and Felix grinned. Olbert frowned.

Seeing their smiles, Christian's heart beat fast with alarm. Immediately, he went out of the courtyard, back through the column entrance down the road toward the church, the group of vassals following close behind.

As they approached the steps and entrance to the church, Christian's heart skipped a beat and then pounded wildly. The bell was not being rung by a priest, nor by a mischievous child. On the very steps of the church, where numerous blessings, marriages, and vows had been solemnly pronounced and witnessed, a drunken knight with a scantily-dressed wench on his arm was yanking idly on the rope while laughing at some joke.

Catching up to the King, Paschal explained with clear amusement, "As the building was empty, we saw to it that it was put to good use!"

"Aye!" Felix added. "It has far more regular attendance now than when it was a church!"

Pale, Christian was so horrified he could not speak. He turned toward Paschal, and, in doing so, saw the look of outrage on Bennet's face.

Christian frowned and went up the steps and into the church, followed by his bodyguards. Once inside, his hair stood on end as he looked around.

The church was different than it had been that night so many months ago. That night the church had been bright with light and shoulder to shoulder with people.

Now with only a few candles burning, the place was dark and eerie, and it stunk of urine, old ale and swyve. The cross had been pulled from the rood screen, and it lay discarded on the floor near the overturned altar in the small sanctuary. Tables, benches and straw mattresses had been brought into the nave, and at least a score of drunken, naked men and whores were making sweaty use of them.

Overwhelmed with anger, guilt, and pain, Christian shut his eyes at the sight. He turned away, his hands in fists. He was surprised to find Paschal and Felix standing directly behind him, quite pleased with themselves.

"What have you done?!"

Paschal and Felix looked at him, not understanding.

"Have either of you no shame? To make the church- a brothel?!"

"We thought you would be amused," Felix answered, bewildered.

"Amused?!" Christian echoed, the tears of agony streaming down his cheeks. "This is on *my* head!"

The two youths looked at him, confused.

"My head!" he screamed at them. "MY HEAD!!"

Everyone in the stew stopped what they were doing and stared at the enraged youth whom in his fury was now savagely ripping and tearing the clothes he wore with his bare hands.

Suddenly, Christian turned upon the naked men and women near him and shouted at them angrily.

"Have *you* no shame?! Have you no fear of God?! This is a place for holiness and penitence! And you defile it further with your wickedness?!"

He snatched up a bench and threw it violently against the wall, breaking it.

A few of the patrons fled. Startled and amazed, Paschal and Felix took a step backward.

"You Lechers!" Christian screamed, tears pouring down his face. "Do you believe that you may use the church as an alehouse and stew and not invoke His wrath?! Get Out! GET OUT!! The fires of Hell are dark and blistering!!"

Almost as one, the remaining people all grabbed what garments were near and rushed out of the church, terrified. The barkeep overturned a hogshead of ale in his haste to escape.

Astonished, Paschal and Felix marveled at the King, their hearts racing.

Christian fought the urge to strangle the youths right there. He took a few, deep breaths and wiped his wet cheeks with his hand and tried to quell his temper.

"Amused-" Christian echoed angrily after a moment, his hands in fists. "Aye, I am-. *We are -very amused.*"

Felix and Paschal swallowed fearfully as they watched him struggle with rage.

"This is on *my head* and, rightly so, for my past deeds led you to it," he told them after a moment. "But from this day forward, Felix, Paschal, *your* sins will be on *your own heads!*"

Turning then, he went through the gap in the screen to the chancel. He tenderly picked up the flat, wooden cross that lay upon the floor and looked at the simple depiction of the Savior painted upon it. With new tears falling from his eyes, Christian wiped off the soiled painting of the Christ with his sleeve and kissed the pierced feet.

"Forgive me," he whispered.

While a pair of his bodyguards righted the altar, another of his bodyguards put the King's black cloak which had fallen to the floor around Christian's shoulders again.

Frowning, Christian looked about the filthy, cluttered church one last time before leaving; he saw that Paschal and Felix were still regarding him with amazement.

"By nightfall, Paschal, this church will be empty and the doors boarded up as the priests left it -or you will answer for it!"

The youths bowed immediately.

Outside, the drunken couple, the rest of the advisers, Tate, and the Chaplain all heard the shouting and then watched with raised eyebrows as men and women, naked and half-clad, poured out of the building as they were and ran down the frozen street.

A few minutes later, King Christian appeared at the church door, agitated and cradling the rood in his arms. He paused and glared at the drunken knight and the wench still standing on the steps. Panicked, they both bowed quickly to the noblemen and then hurried down the road behind the rest.

His pleasant humor gone, the King returned to the road where the rest of the group waited, followed by his guards and a visibly shaken Felix and Paschal.

All was ruined, Christian realized. He had wanted to come back here and start anew. He had wanted to show Bennet all the wonderful things the palace had to offer and how good of a king he could be; and already it was ruined. Remnants of his old life were everywhere. He realized that if Bennet had had little esteem for him before, during the next few months, it was going to be greatly lessened as he discovered the everyday facts about his old life.

Christian's shame so overwhelmed him that he could not bear to look the Chaplain in the eye. Swallowing, he carefully handed the crucifix to Bennet and then, without a word, turned and began walking back to the palace. Impatiently, he strode through the column entrance, through the courtyard and up the steps through the great, wooden door into the main corridor, his entourage almost running to keep up with him.

After he entered the main corridor, the few maidservants he encountered were all young and comely strangers in fine clothes who curtsied briefly to him and the other aldermen before hurrying along their way. In fact, there was not a single manservant inside the entire palace and no servant at all that he recognized.

Christian, irritated at the changes, stopped short in the corridor. He turned again and abruptly met a knight and a young woman bowing before him.

"This is the cook, Sire," the knight said simply.

Christian looked blankly at the unfamiliar woman in the dirty, elegant gown who smelled of meats.

The woman did not know what to say, as she and the knight observed that the recently returned King was disheveled and enraged, though they knew not the cause.

"Tell the King what you have prepared," Felix, slightly winded, instructed from behind.

"Roasted pork, geese, and beef, My Lord King."

Christian's stomach panged hungrily at the mention of the menu.

"We can eat no meat or foul," he told her simply.

"We have no fish today, My Lord King. But if it please you, I can cook some cabbage and eggs and cheese for you."

"It will please Us well."

The young woman curtsied and went away.

"Royal Steward!"

Olbert was immediately beside the King, bowing.

"Sire?"

"Olbert, what has happened here?"

"My Liege?"

"I mean, why is a kitchen maid in charge of the royal table? Why have we stable maids instead of stable boys? Where are Our accustomed palace servants?"

"My Lord King, those that previously served in the palace you passed already in the fields."

"The fields?"

Christian frowned and wiped his eyes. He recalled to mind again the faces of those on the road. No wonder they had looked familiar.

"Was that Cedd, my valet, that we passed on the road?"

"Aye, Sire."

"Why are they in the fields?" Bennet asked curiously.

Paschal and Felix glared at the cleric indignantly, but did not reply. After a moment, Olbert cleared his throat uncomfortably.

"Because-" Olbert began.

"Give *him* answer, Paschal," Christian interrupted.

"Who?" Paschal asked irritably.

Christian looked at the young nobleman sharply.

"*Our* Royal Chaplain would like to know why Our valet is in the fields."

Grey, Dewain, Paschal and Felix all looked at the King in astonishment. *Never* had they seen Christian show deference to a priest, to the Bishop, perhaps, at his own coronation, but never a priest. Now he was showing regard to this lowly monk.

"Very well, Father," Christian frowned, "the most likely reason why the palace servants are in the fields is because so many of the villagers perished during the retaking of the palace and from the search for the rebels that there are now not enough serfs left to prepare and plant the fields. Are We correct?"

"Aye, Sire," Paschal admitted sourly.

The Chaplain grew pale and crossed himself in horror. There was silence in the chamber.

"Olbert, summon Cedd from the fields to attend Us."

"Immediately, Sire," Olbert bowed.

"Send for Boisil, Our cook, as well."

There was silence. Lord Olbert frowned.

"I regret to inform you, Your Grace-" Olbert began.

The King looked from the Steward to Paschal and Felix.

"He was suspected of conspiring with the rebels," Paschal said flatly.

Christian looked at the youth.

"So he is in the tower? Send for him. We will vouch that he is no traitor. We have known him since Our boyhood."

No one made answer.

"What?" Christian demanded.

"He is not in the tower, Sire."

Christian blinked at this information, his heart beating faster. They had killed Boisil.

"You executed him?" Christian asked Paschal hotly. "On what evidence?"

"We did not execute him. He died *during questioning.*"

Christian went pale, his heart beating wildly. And then another, awful thought occurred to him.

"Is- Is he on the wall?"

Paschal and Felix looked away.

"IS HIS HEAD ON THE WALL?" Christian demanded to know, his hands in tight fists.

"Aye, My Lord, but we did not execute him!" Felix explained hastily. "He was still suspected of helping the rebels, -and he was dead anyway. -We thought to make an example of him -as a warning to the others."

"A warning?"

"-To encourage the villeins to talk," Felix finished.

"Those heads out there-" Christian asked through grit teeth, "are they *all* warnings -to encourage the people to talk?"

Felix swallowed and looked away, clearly afraid to answer. Paschal crossed his arms and frowned. He would not look at the King.

Christian felt suddenly nauseous. He could taste the gall. Aghast, Bennet crossed himself again. Dewain stood amazed. Tate frowned and shook his head. Acrida glared at the youths with hate.

"WELL?"

"Aye!" Paschal answered.

"What have you done, Paschal?!" Christian shouted. "Do you not know that the deaths of these people will be on *my head*, as well as your own?!"

"But-"

"How will I ever do enough penance?!" Christian exclaimed, as fresh tears streamed down his cheeks.

"I have done what you commanded me to do!" the redheaded youth yelled back. "You told me to retake the palace and find the rebels! -Use whatever means I thought necessary! Starve the peasants if they refused to cooperate! Truly, after the retaking of the palace, almost half of the village was dead anyway. The other half has been stubborn in their refusal to talk. We starved them, and then we interrogated them, but they gave no answers! Then we discovered some of the palace servants sneaking them food, Boisil among them, so we starved them as well! But that took time, and we received your dispatch insisting that we make all speed to find the instigators! So we put every tenth villein to death, and still they would not talk! So every few days we measured their children by the sword and-"

"You killed children?! -And when none are being born?!!"

Hugging the crucifix to him, Bennet covered his face, horrified by what he was hearing.

"But Sire!" Paschal complained.

"Enough!!" Christian hollered. "Is there no restraint in you? Did it not occur to you that perhaps the villeins had told you already all that they knew? Was it not possible that they were innocent, and you were too stubborn to admit it?"

Paschal said nothing, crossing his arms again, glaring at the wall.

"Will my hands ever be clean again?!" Christian wailed miserably.

"I did as you ordered!!" Paschal yelled again.

"Did I order you to condemn me to Hell?!" Christian yelled.

He covered his face in frustration. His vassals stood mute in astonishment, and Felix and Paschal exchanged bewildered looks.

Dazed, Christian slowly turned and went into the audience chamber and looked around. It was all the same; the throne was at the far end, the table to the left wall, the stairs up to the landing, the mosaic floor and painted walls.

Ample fires were burning in several small, free-standing hearths, and Christian's vassals poured in after him, moving directly to the fires, whispering among themselves. A few, finely dressed maidservants began helping the men remove their heavy cloaks.

The King did not join them. Almost in a stupor, Christian, wrapping his cloak around him more securely, went over to his throne and sat upon it. He stared at the wall as if he had never before seen the painting.

Still in the corridor, Lord Olbert summoned one of the elegantly dressed serving girls and approached the Chaplain.

"Father, if you will permit me, I shall have the cross taken to your chambers."

Bennet smiled and thanked the Steward; he handed the crucifix to the serving girl, who curtsied and crossed herself before taking it.

Bennet then followed Tate and Acrida into the audience chamber.

"This palace is a marvel to behold," the Chaplain whispered tentatively, uncertain of what the appropriate thing to say was now.

"Indeed," Tate and Acrida agreed.

"I wonder," the monk asked timidly, "is it customary for all palace maidservants to wear such fine clothes or do they wear it for the occasion of the King's return?"

"Indeed not! No palace servant has ever been allowed to dress above his or her station- no matter what the occasion!" Tate replied with mock outrage.

Bennet looked at the old man in confusion.

"But-" Bennet asked, gesturing toward the three, young women in elaborate gowns who were collecting the heavy mantles from the knights and aldermen.

"Oh, you mean these women-" Tate replied. "Father, they are not palace servants by birth, nor is there, I would wager, a maid among them. -But every mount in the King's stable is so adorned with the finest rigging."

Bennet flushed red as he took the old man's meaning.

"These are the concubines?" Acrida cut in. "Truly? I thought Paschal was going to buy slaves."

"Olbert would never have given him the money without the King's explicit command," Tate replied, cheerfully. "Besides, the King's concubines number more than a hundred. Paschal had little need to buy slaves with them here. Likely he needed something to occupy them anyway as the King was away."

Oblivious to the people and conversations near him, Christian's mind jumped between his last memory of speaking to Boisil and images of children being measured by the sword and then beheaded. He could just envision the villeins huddled together, hoping it was not their turn to be questioned. He imagined the look of surprise on Boisil's face when he was accused and taken to be interrogated. He could see the villein mothers screaming, as the knights tore their children from their grasp and took them to be executed.

Christian fought to clear his head. If only he had been here, it would never have happened! He was *not* Christian *the Bloody*! He was *not* the killer of children! He was *not* the killer of innocents! He was-

The memory of Fenton's first son came vividly to his mind. The youth's eyes had been large with panic as his hands felt of his severed throat. His blood had spurted into the air like a fountain, wetting all his family. Christian could hear again the anguished cries of the women as they had rushed to the lad.

Christian resisted the memory, arguing that the lad's execution served as a warning against future rebellion and was therefore necessary. Executing the child of a rebel was justified. It did not make him the killer of innocents. Besides, the lad had been nearly grown.

He paused and frowned then. Had not Paschal used this same logic to people the wall with heads?

Aye, but Paschal had taken it too far. Paschal thought the sword was the answer to everything. If he had been here, he would not have been so rash, Christian told himself.

He stared at the circle in the mosaic floor that depicted the Romulus and Remus twins suckling the she-wolf until gradually it became covered in blood. Christian shut his eyes, but the image remained in his mind. The brutally hacked body of the old seer lay gulping out its flood of scarlet onto the design. The blond seer-child was cowering a few feet away, screaming in terror; the head of the seer had stopped rolling a short distance from him.

Christian remembered regarding the boy for a moment and the mad man too. A few minutes before, he had found them both amusing, innocent, and harmless, but then he had been offended, and his heart had pounded with rage; and he had decided in an instant that they too must pay. The boy had shrieked when he saw the knight raise his sword over him. The single motion had taken off his head and ceased his pathetic crying. His headless body had slumped to the stone floor and twitched fitfully as it added its blood to the scarlet pool on the floor. The mad man had not screamed at all as his life was taken.

Christian recoiled at the memory. How could he deny what he had done or what kind of man he had been? What truly would have been different if he had been here? A few more executions? A few less?

Christian's heart beat loudly in his ears as the tears coursed down his cheeks. He *was* the killer of children and innocents! And as he had done to them, *so he had done to the Christ!*

Gasping for air, he bolted out of the audience hall away from the blood of the seers that accused and haunted him. Weeping in agony in the corridor, he wondered where he could go. He had to flee, but where? Where could he go to escape this prison of his own making?

The crowd of vassals and guards was immediately about him again, pulling at him, confining him.

"Away! Away!" he screamed, fighting their grasp.

"Sire!" a crowd of voices called to him.

"My Lord, what ails thee?"

"The King is unwell!"

"Hurry, Girl, bring some water for the King!"

"Peace, peace, My Lords! Let him alone!"

It was a sea of voices and a blur of faces, overwhelming Christian on all sides. He screamed with all his pain and rage until there was silence.

"Sire? My Lord, do you know me?"

Christian blinked slowly.

"Of course, I know you Olbert," Christian said, looking around, wondering what had just happened.

Christian was in the corridor, and his bodyguards had encircled him. They were holding the crowd of vassals away from him. His Steward was calling to him from the other side of his guard.

"We should send for the royal physician-" Dewain whispered to Olbert, noting the King's ashy complexion.

"Come, Sire. Come to the fire-" Grey urged, gesturing for the King to return to the audience hall.

Christian shook his head, remembering everything then. He could not go back in *there*, his heartbeat quickening again.

"Will you sit, Your Grace?" Dewain asked, gesturing to a nearby bench.

Christian glanced at the bench that was nearby beside the wall in the corridor. He nodded and allowed them to sit him upon it. After a few minutes, his heartbeat slowed more, and he could think clearly.

"Sire, you are unwell. Will you not come to the fire?"

Christian shook his head again, staring off into space.

A concubine appeared beside him then with a cloth and a pan of water. She dipped the cloth in the cool water and offered it to him. Christian observed her momentarily. She was young and fair and slightly familiar, and she glared at him with an intense look of hatred. Christian recoiled under her gaze.

Olbert took the cloth and held it to the King's forehead.

"Will you not retire to your chambers then and rest, Sire?" he asked.

Return to the chambers where he had bedded countless maids and young wives without thought to the consequences? Christian mused.

He shook his head.

"But- Sire," Olbert began, bewildered.

Christian shook his head once more.

"There is no place *here* I can go, for there is no where that I have not already been," Christian muttered, realizing to his horror that everywhere were reminders of what he had done and what he would certainly suffer torment for in Purgatory for a very long time *if* he escaped Hell.

As the advisers, knights, and Chaplain stood around the King wondering at his words and condition, Filberte's old fool called to him from behind the crowd.

"Sire, come. Follow me. I know a place where you may rest," Tate said. "There is a small feasting hall down this way. -Part of the old additions. I do not think you have ever been in there. It has not been used for many years and will need some airing and some light. But, methinks, it will be to your liking."

"Well, if it has a hearth, it may well suit our needs for the moment," Olbert commented, noting the King's hand was quite cold. "Lead the way."

The fool bowed and gestured for the crowd to follow him. He stopped a passing concubine and, smiling sweetly, told her, "Dearheart, bring bread and warm wine for the King."

She smiled at the fool and hurried away.

Tate led them past the audience chamber, beyond the advisers' offices to the far end of the corridor to a long ignored and forgotten, dust-covered door. Taking a torch from the wall, he waited while a pair of knights pushed it open.

He entered the darkened chamber first. The hall was much smaller and plainer than the audience hall and was filled with benches, tables, cobwebs, and a thick layer of dirt. The walls were of undecorated wood and the floor- uncut stone. An old, faded and moth-eaten tapestry of a martyr of the Faith being ripped apart by a wild animal still hung on the walls. There were several, old torches still in their holders along the walls, and Tate and another knight went about lighting them.

The King and the rest of the crowd slowly entered then and looked about the chamber. It was simple and very dirty, but Christian thought it acceptable. He sat down on a nearby bench, oblivious to the distaste felt by the other noblemen.

Soon after, the concubine arrived with three other servants, bearing goblets, bread and wine. After a bit of bread and a sip of warm wine, Christian began to feel better.

"Lord Olbert, the smoke hole will have to be hollowed out again," Tate said, pointing to the ceiling above an old hearth he had found, "but if we had some wood, we could build a fire."

Olbert agreed and sent a pair of knights after the kindling.

"I believe this was thy great grandfather's feasting room, Sire," Lord Olbert offered.

"Aye, and if thou goest through that door," Tate said, pointing to the far wall, "thou will enter the palace that King Godewyn built. Although it has not been used in more than a generation, the chambers may still be in good repair. If I remember correctly, there is even a small devotional chapel where Godewyn used to pray."

"Why were such pleasing chambers abandoned?" Bennet asked.

Tate and Olbert both shrugged and smiled.

68

"It was cold out there, even with that many people huddled together," Acrida said as she and her two companions walked down the palace corridor to the Royal Steward's office.

"The wind was excessively sharp this morning," Dewain agreed.

"-Could have been worse. -Could have been raining," Tate commented.

They all agreed.

"Still, it was-" she paused, searching for the right word.

"Inspiring-" Lord Dewain offered pleasantly. "The King holding the Penitent's Cross, and the entire Court, the village, and most of three garrisons of knights- all in the courtyard, worshipping together at the rising of the sun."

Acrida raised her eyebrows.

"I was going to say 'odd'. Did you not feel the agitation? The commoners looked like they would bolt and run at any moment, and a good many of the knights looked like they were ready to give chase."

"Aye, I saw more than a few sneers among the knights and nobles, but methinks it was not the serfs that received the brunt of their hostility," Tate answered.

Seeing Lord Grey just behind them, Dewain bit his tongue to keep from adding his opinion.

The group arrived at the door of the Steward's office and entered the chamber, followed by a pair of servants bearing food and drink. Paschal and Felix entered the chamber after them, yawning.

Paschal frowned at the palace manservant who offered him a goblet of mead, but grudgingly took it. As his eyes fell upon Filberte's old fool, uninvited as usual, standing in the corner with the witch, he bristled. The redheaded youth grumbled irritably to Felix about it, flung himself into a cushioned chair at the long table, crossed his arms irritably, and scowled.

"...the change in him is remarkable, My Lord," one of the palace maidservants was saying to Olbert who entered the chamber then. "I would never have expected the King to even visit a monastery-"

"Lest to raid it-" Tate finished for her.

Everyone glanced toward Tate and smiled. The maidservant, upon seeing Lords Paschal and Felix immediately became self-conscious and silent. She curtsied briefly to the aldermen and then began collecting their cloaks.

Olbert's knight Sir Ecktor entered the chamber and bowed to his liege lord. Another servant entered and delivered a rolled parchment to Lord Grey, bowed, and then left.

"Olbert, what do we know about this monk?" Grey asked, as he broke the seal on the scroll.

"He is a spy, no doubt," Paschal muttered.

Olbert glanced sharply at the youth, but smiled at Grey.

"Very little, except he is from the monastery."

"He is here to press the Church's interests, of course," Felix added.

"He will try, perhaps, but he will get no where with Christian, I warrant," Paschal said coldly. "All this that you see, -the Royal Chaplain, the fasting, the mandatory Mass at dawn for everyone including the entire Court, it is all for show. Christian is drawing the monk in, nothing more."

Acrida listened carefully, but said nothing.

"He *did* bestow royal favor on that monastery," Dewain argued.

"He can just as easily withdraw royal favor-" Felix spat.

"Aye, when he has no more use for them, he will sack it for certain," Paschal agreed.

Dewain crossed himself in horror.

Olbert frowned at the youths.

"He agreed to all of the Bishop's terms, without argument or negotiation," he told them calmly.

"There is no need to argue terms if you have no intention of fulfilling them," Paschal answered.

"What were the terms?" Grey asked.

"One thousand gold crowns-" Olbert answered.

"One thousand!"

Tate raised his eyebrows at the immense sum.

"Did the treasury have that much?" Dewain asked.

"We melted and stamped for days," Sir Ecktor spoke up from behind them, "but those chalices were hardly used anyway."

Paschal glanced from the knight back to Olbert, noting the seasoned Steward's usual composure.

"So he paid money? That was to be expected," he shrugged.

"He also agreed to build a cathedral and monastery on palace grounds," Olbert continued.

There was a moment of silent surprise.

"And what of it?" Paschal finally replied with a shrug. "Promising is one thing. Doing is another. I wager not one stone of it will ever be laid."

"Aye, ne'er a stone of it," Felix agreed.

"You are wrong," Olbert told them. "He will do it. King Christian has changed. He has seen the evil of his ways and has repented-"

"Ha!" Paschal laughed. "Believe it if you wish, Old Man, but no matter who he orders to Mass, it is still Christian. Whether his present bend toward 'piety' is pretense to gain support from the Church during the war or simply the result of the monks' undue influence upon him, I know he will be back to his old, *meat-eating* self in due time."

"And absent from Mass!" Felix added.

"Aye! In two months time, he will be drinking and wenching most of the night with Felix and me and sleeping till noon. No one will be attending Mass at dawn! The monk will be singing it to a few of the village women, but that is all."

"*If* the monk is still here-" Felix added.

"Aye," Paschal agreed.

Olbert and Dewain frowned again.

"I hope you are wrong, Paschal," the Royal Steward told him. "I hope that after everything the King has suffered, he will not turn his back on God and the Faith again."

"T'would be a pity, indeed," Sir Ecktor commented with a shake of his head, "to undergo flogging and still burn in Hell."

All eyes were on the young knight then.

"What did you say?"

"T'would be a pity for the King to still burn in Hell."

"No-" Paschal said, "the other-"

"The King-. They flogged him."

Everyone stared at the young knight in disbelief.

Paschal suddenly laughed out loud, but then stopped abruptly.

"You lie!" he accused the knight, hotly.

"I do not!" Sir Ecktor responded indignantly.

"Who flogged him?! The monks?!" the others were asking, amazed.

"The Bishop's men-. They bound him to a cart and everything."

"Who told you this?" Felix demanded.

"He is a liar! Christian would never allow-"

"I saw it! We all did! They whipped him in public outside the monastery gate! Fifty lashes just before the Mass! He was in bed more than a day on account of it!"

The servants and counselors all stared at him, aghast. Lord Grey was so stunned he was forced to sit down. All eyes turned to Olbert.

"It is true," Olbert admitted reluctantly, frowning at Ecktor, "but the King did not wish it widely known for obvious reasons."

Horrified, Felix and Paschal stared at the table, the color gone from their faces as they realized the extent to which their king, liege lord, and friend had abased himself -*and them.*

Just then King Christian entered the chamber, followed by his bodyguards, his Chaplain, and a servant bearing the King's heavy mantle. Christian, wearing a purple tunic with gold embroidery over braes of the same color, seemed in good cheer.

Everyone in the entire chamber stood up and bowed to the King. Christian gestured pleasantly for them to relax, and he went and sat in a cushioned chair at the far end of the table. As the advisers and the Chaplain took a seat around the long table near the King, Acrida sat on a cushioned bench in the corner near the door with Tate.

Christian's eyes fell on his former companions.

"How now, Paschal? Felix? What ails thee?" he asked cheerily. "You are both quite pale."

Neither could speak, nor hardly look him in the eye.

"Perhaps it is the early hour. -'Twill teach you to find your bed earlier than an hour before dawn," he joked merrily.

He took a goblet of mead from one servant and a hunk of cheese from the tray of another, smiling at them as he did so.

"We see Our palace servants have returned. Have the *other* reassignments been carried out?"

"Aye, Your Grace," Olbert answered. "All of the servants who previously served in the palace have returned today. They have begun cleaning and making repairs to the old additions. They should have them ready in a few days. Likewise, two of the three garrisons have gone to help prepare and plant the fields."

"Very good. -And your men, Felix?"

The youth cleared his throat and nodded.

"The Palace Watch are removing the heads from the wall as you commanded, Sire, and will reunite them, as best they can, with the bodies so that they may be buried."

"Very good. And what of the other dead? Are their bodies still laying about or-"

"As you may remember, Sire, *you* ordered that the interdict be ignored at the palace," Felix answered.

"Aye, so We did," Christian muttered, with an embarrassed glance toward Bennet.

"All who died from age or infirmity, as well as the Palace Watch and knights who were killed in the uprising and retaking of the palace, were buried in the churchyard as usual," Felix continued. "However, the bodies of the vast majority of rebels who were killed in the uprising and in the retaking of the palace were burned."

Christian nodded.

"Dewain, has there been any word from Bishop Gildas as to when he will come and bless the church altar or when we may expect the arrival of the palace priests?"

"No, Sire."

Christian frowned.

"We can hardly wait on them," he muttered. "Very well, Father Bennet, will you say a Funeral Mass for all of the dead?"

"I will, Sire," Bennet smiled.

"Very good. -Now, Olbert, what of the girls? Have the arrangements been made?"

"They have, Sire."

"Aye," Sir Ecktor cut in. "As you ordered last night, every one that has been to your bed will receive a silver crown, and another for each year they have been at the palace. Their liege lords will receive the same. We depart within the hour- by your leave."

Christian smiled at the verbose knight.

Acrida, Grey, Paschal, Felix and the servants were all startled to hear this. Acrida glanced at Tate, but he seemed not to be surprised at all.

"And they have adequate protection for their journey?" the King asked.

"Aye," Sir Ecktor replied.

"Sire, the women travel under the protection of our most trusted knights," Lord Olbert added. "Dewain and I assure you they will be delivered safely to their lands with their money."

"Aye," Dewain added.

Christian smiled.

"Very good."

"Sir Ecktor, you have my leave to depart," Olbert told him.

The knight bowed and left the chamber.

"Now, what news of Herryck?" Christian asked, sipping his mead.

Grey smiled, shuffled the papers before him, and cleared his throat. He looked at the monk and then back to the King, expectantly.

"Well, Grey? Speak up."

Grey blinked at the King, surprised. Apparently, the youth had no intention of sending the monk away. Was the monk in the King's confidence already?

Coming to the same conclusion, Paschal and Felix were aghast that the King was prepared to discuss such secret matters in front of the monk. Surely Christian realized that he was a spy and that everything he heard would be reported to his superior and circulated around the Continent via the Church hierarchy. What was Christian thinking?

Uncomfortable, Grey cleared his throat again.

"My spies have sent word that Herryck's forces are amassing on the western border of Multimbria near Cadell," he said hesitantly. He cleared his throat again, glanced once more at Bennet, and added, "By last count, they are three thousand strong."

Christian frowned. The Chaplain raised his eyebrows and glanced at the King.

Grey unrolled a map of Speyron and spread it on the table before the King.

"They are here," he pointed. "We have begun storehousing supplies here, here, and here. The most likely entry point is here, at the Frida Valley, once the snow starts melting. This shallow ford on the River Terrill is also a possibility, but unlikely unless Herryck waits very late into spring to invade. There is a good bridge farther north, here, but he could not move his men as fast, and they could not all get across before we were able to head them off. But-"

"Aye, it will be the valley," Paschal agreed.

"Aye, and our scouts are positioned at these points. When Herryck moves, we will know," Grey told them.

"They will come through a wood."

All eyes turned to Acrida then.

"What?"

"I have seen them come through trees, -a wood, I think.'

"Woods? Are you certain?" Dewain asked.

"A forest?"

"Where? Which forest?!" Grey was asking.

"I know not," Acrida said with a shrug.

"You know not?!" Felix and Paschal hounded. "What use are you?!"

"Paschal, Felix, be calm! Acrida, tell us what have you seen-" Dewain said.

She shook her head and said, "I have seen a bearded army come through snow and trees. -Leagues of thick trees. That is all."

Grey shook his head and crossed his arms.

"Just like a witch to prefer woods-" Felix sneered.

"Trees!" Paschal threw up his hands. "You have seen trees! Not the number of the enemy, nor the location of the forest, nor the day or hour of the invasion, but trees!"

Acrida glared at the youth.

"Multimbria is full of trees," Grey was saying, exasperated. "You only saw Multimbria!"

Christian was scanning the map.

"There is a forest at Thorin near the border of Multimbria," Dewain commented.

"Aye, but it is too thick for an army to march through," Olbert said. "They would have to clear it as they went."

"-And to get to it, they would have to cross the Terrill Mountains," Christian added. "It is a natural defense. An army could not make it through those narrow mountain passes quickly -and certainly not with snow on the ground."

"Herryck would be mad to try it!"

"There are many other forests, though," Christian added. "Is there nothing else you can tell us?"

"No, My Lord."

"Then what would you have us do with this information?" Paschal asked sarcastically. "Shall we dispatch scouts needed elsewhere to every forest on the borders of Speyron? Or should we send them to every forest and grove in the entire kingdom?"

"Indeed, what can you do, My Lord, when we will be at war in less than a month?"

Everyone froze at these formidable words. The servants crossed themselves.

"Less than a month?! What can you mean by this?" Felix and Paschal were demanding. "Herryck will not attack in the heart of winter! He never has made war earlier than late spring!"

"How long have you known this?!" Olbert was suddenly demanding. "Why have you not informed us?!"

"My Lord Steward," Acrida answered calmly, "I thought I was in the employ of the King, not your lordships-"

Tate smiled at her nerve.

"What you say is impossible!" Grey argued. "To invade in less than a month, Herryck's army would have to be moving now, right this minute! As of the dispatches this morning, his army continues to amass near Cadell- the same place they have been camped for the past three months."

Acrida shrugged off their hostility.

"Even so, My Lords-"

"She is wrong, Sire!" Grey was saying vehemently. "Herryck will invade through the Frida Valley or the River Terrill!" he pointed. "I stake my life upon it! -And he is months away from invasion!"

Christian sighed and held up his hands.

"Enough! We will think on this matter! -Now, Grey, is there anything more?"

There was a moment of silence as the servants refilled the goblets and tempers cooled.

"At present, we have received word from fifteen of your thirty-seven vassals giving a preliminary count of the men they will be supplying. All of them have at least twenty-five knights with horse who await your summons."

"Lord Manton pledges eighty knights, most notably Sir Horton and Sir Chadde. Lord Abbot Sebastian pledges fifty knights, most notable and experienced, Sir Michele, Sir Phelps, Sir Linford…"

After more than an hour, when the subject of troops had completely become exhausted, silence once again dominated the small chamber.

"Is there any other business to be discussed?"

"Aye, Sire, I have some business which I hope you will find welcome," Lord Grey said.

"Well, let Us hear it, Chamberlain," King Christian smiled. "This talk of war is mirthless and tiring."

"Sire, while you were away and *others* were occupied with searching vainly for hidden rebels-" Grey said, glancing at Paschal disdainfully, "I took it upon myself to attempt to strengthen relations between our realm and other kingdoms. In your absence, I continued to receive ambassadors from Fors regarding King Roderic's missing niece. I hope it will not offend Your Grace to know that I gave them the support they required to search our kingdom for the lady."

Christian only shrugged his shoulders and smiled. He should count himself lucky if that was all Grey had done in his absence.

"And did you find the wayward wench?" Paschal asked with an air of boredom.

"Indeed we did. Right before Christmas."

Gooseflesh pricked Acrida's skin as she listened intently.

"After some inquiries and a great many letters circulated among your vassals throughout the kingdom, I was finally able to send word to King Roderic that indeed his niece might reside within Speyron's borders as they had come to believe.

"Her father, Lord Thurmonde, and her older brother, Leander, arrived a few weeks ago in order to verify the identity of the lady and to convey the girl home. I found them both to be intelligent and agreeable, and also insightful-"

"Where was the lady?" Acrida interrupted.

"She was in the northwe-"

"I fail to see, Grey," Paschal cut in irritably, "why the news that one foreigner has been removed from our borders requires the Council's attention? I-"

Grey glared at the youth testily.

"If I may continue, Your Grace."

Christian nodded and gestured for Paschal to be quiet.

"Lord Thurmonde also brought word from King Roderic regarding our queries for a bride. Dewain had sent dispatches to all the kingdoms on the Continent and beyond. I am pleased to inform you that King Roderic, in a gesture of gratitude for Your Grace's help in finding his niece, proposes a match."

Everyone looked at Grey.

"Did he offer one of his daughters?" Christian asked.

"Actually, no. Roderic was blessed with an abundance of sons. The few daughters he has are married already. -Instead he proposes a match with the Lady Elise, recently recovered."

Silence rebounded in the chamber as everyone stared at Grey and then looked at the King. Suddenly Felix laughed, but then he stopped short, as he noticed that no one else was laughing.

"Are you in earnest?" Olbert finally asked, appalled.

"How old is she?" Dewain asked, alarmed.

Grey hesitated, but continued with complete poise.

"The Lady Elise is still of childbearing age. She is of the royal bloodline, and King Roderic pledges that if Your Grace marries her, and by doing so return her to a reputable state, he will not delay to send the much needed troops that will be necessary to repel Herryck from our lands."

All eyes were on the King as he carefully regarded Grey. Paschal and Felix smiled; and the servants quickly backed away and prepared to dodge flying objects, anticipating the King's insulting tirade which was sure to come for the affront to his royal dignity.

Christian took a deep breath and successfully repressed both the urge to laugh out loud and to shout the stinging retort that was at the tip of his tongue. After a long, awkward silence, he finally remarked with a slight smile, "Indeed, it is an- *interesting* proposal."

The listeners in the room marveled at the sweet reply. Paschal covered his face in dismay and shook his head. Felix frowned.

Lord Olbert, however, could not be silent.

"Lord Grey, am I to understand that you have entertained this proposal seriously?"

"You would have the King make a runaway and an outlaw his queen?" Dewain echoed.

Bennet listened curiously.

"How will this match raise Speyron's respectability in the eyes of other kingdoms?" Olbert asked.

"Or in the eyes of our enemy?" Dewain added.

"It could hardly make it any worse-" Paschal whispered under his breath, rubbing his throbbing head.

Lord Grey shrugged his shoulders slightly.

"After months of sending countless inquires across the Continent regarding potential brides and allies, this was the only response we have received," Grey replied.

"Is this true, Dewain?" Christian asked.

"It is, Sire," he admitted quietly.

Christian frowned but remained silent.

"-And while the lady may have been a fugitive for the last five years, she is from a noble Romani bloodline and a powerful family, and they will provide a hefty dowry if you should settle on the match."

"What of her husband?" Lord Felix asked. "I thought she was already married."

"He died two years ago after a fall from a horse. He had searched unsuccessfully for his wife for some time throughout Fors before the family received reports that she was living within our borders."

"Is this the best to be hoped for?" Olbert was asking again, outraged. "The King is not even to have a virgin for the mother of his children and the heirs to the throne?"

"Come now, My Lord," Tate said. "The King has had his share of virgins."

Acrida smirked, but the others hardly heard the jest.

"Can this woman even be ruled?" Dewain asked. "Did she flee her husband or did he in anger put her out? Does anyone know the particulars?"

Bennet raised his eyebrows again.

"A very good question," Lord Grey admitted. "We will need that information."

"If the King marries her, will she flee again -this time with the kingdom's treasury? Must we guard her night and day? Will we spend our valuable time searching for her?" Lord Olbert continued, on his feet now in exasperation.

Tate smiled, but suppressed the urge to make another jest.

"Excuse me, My Lords," Bennet asked tentatively, "but did the lady object to her first marriage from the beginning?"

Grey professed that he did not have that information.

"And what of her virtue?" Olbert was declaring vehemently. "Who knows what liaisons the lady has submitted to? Without friends or family, her survival would have depended on- debauchery! No! I could never support such an unseemly match! I cannot believe that you offer it seriously for the King's consideration, Grey! The lady, despite her noble birth, will lack the *virtue* necessary to be the mother of princes- or the mother of any family for that matter!"

"As I have already said," Grey answered defensively, "this is the only proposal I am able to present at this time. Unfortunately, due to the King's infamous behavior and reckless dealings with the Church, this is the best match to be had. You should remember, however, that the lady, being foreign born to our nation, should in all likelihood conceive as no Speyron woman can. And as I have already said, such a match would provide our kingdom with the troops we so desperately require. If there is no better choice forthcoming, it is no fault of *mine*."

Lord Grey stopped short, and everyone looked at the King for the sound rebuke that *must* follow now. However, King Christian only sat in his place, holding his head that was beginning to ache.

"My Lord King," Felix said quickly, "the world is full of women. We need not be so desperate as to believe that only this one woman can solve our troubles."

"I concur, Sire," Lord Dewain added.

Olbert sat down again and covered his eyes with his hand. The room grew silent again.

Finally, King Christian looked at Acrida.

"Have you nothing to add on this matter?"

"Me, My Lord?" she replied, surprised to be brought into it at all.

In the silence, her mind had returned disobediently to thoughts of Van Necht again.

"Aye, what think you of this proposed match?"

Paschal stared incredulously at Christian.

Acrida swallowed and shrugged her shoulders slightly.

"I am no expert on marriage or matches.-"

"You have never spoken truer-" Paschal agreed.

Acrida glared at him, but then looked back to the King.

"But this I know, Sire. If you would marry before the war begins, you must choose quickly. I have seen that it will not be long before children will return to Speyron. If it is thy pleasure, thou may take a Speyron woman for wife. She will be as good as any other."

"But-"

"If thou seekest a bride within Speyron's borders," she continued, "perhaps a more suitable girl might be procured. I have met Lord Dewain's two older daughters, and I would think that either of them would be acceptable."

The look of horror on Grey's face did not escape the fool's notice, nor the accompanying looks of confusion and surprise on the faces of Dewain, Paschal, Felix, Olbert and the King. Tate smiled behind his hand. Obviously Acrida was unaware of the noblemen's rival ambitions and the fact that the family that joined with the King through marriage would double in power and influence within the kingdom and the Continent beyond.

"What you fail to see, despite thy powers of sight, is that no benefit would be gained by such a match," Grey informed Acrida condescendingly. "If the King marries a woman of Speyron, he will gain nothing more than a wife, for all his vassals fulfill their requirements for men and arms already. No more are to be had for such a match."

"Is it absolutely necessary to seek help from foreign realms?" she asked.

"It is doubtful that we will be able to repel Herryck on our own when his forces are so great," Dewain told her kindly.

"Hmm, allies are thy goals, and this woman the only means to them," Acrida mused. "Is it possible for you to meet with her, Sire, and find out what virtue and breeding, if any, she has retained? In truth, I do not know how she could have survived as an outlaw without compromising her virtue, but if she perhaps fell under the protection of a righteous and honorable man-"

Felix and Paschal laughed out loud.

"Thou art naive-" Paschal said flatly.

"She is not so far from the truth as you might believe," Grey cut in quickly. "When my knights intercepted Lady Elise, she was living a quiet life on Lord Gumphreu's lands, spinning wool and flax with other village women. Old Gumphreu was not even aware of her presence.

He thought her merely one of his serfs and took no notice of her. She has been in his village for the past three years, working and living there a simple life, -and spurning the advances of any lustful men who approached her."

"Indeed!" Paschal smirked.

"I have found the woman to be meek, genteel and soft spoken, as a noblewoman should be," Grey finished.

"Do you know if this woman longed for a religious life that her family disapproved of?" Bennet suddenly asked.

Lord Grey smiled at the monk.

"I know not, Brother. I only know that though we did not find her in a convent, we did find her among her own sex. Nor do I know how much of the day she spent in prayer, though I am told that she worked humbly and diligently alongside the other women in the village without ever revealing her high birth."

The listeners considered all this in silence.

Finally Christian spoke.

"Has the lady returned to Fors already?"

Grey smiled again.

"No, Sire. They have been guests on my lands all this while as they hoped for an audience with you. I sent word to them yesterday of your return, and I was notified a little while ago that they are here. Will you grant them an audience, Sire?"

"Aye, We will."

69

"**F**ind out where Lord Thurmonde and his children are," Lord Chamberlain Grey, with a satisfied smile, instructed one of the servants.

The servant bowed and left, but returned abruptly.

"They are in the audience hall by the fire," he replied with a short bow.

"Let us proceed to them," Christian said, rising from his chair.

Christian led the way out of the chamber, with Paschal, Felix and Grey right behind him, followed by the Royal Chaplain.

"He certainly is in good spirits this morning," Dewain commented quietly to Olbert as they followed the group out.

"Indeed," Olbert answered with concern.

"Is it true that he slept the night on a table in the old hall?"

"Aye, and he claimed it was softer than the mat he was accustomed to sleeping on at the abbey," Olbert answered.

Dewain smiled.

"You were not surprised by the news that the King is sending away the concubines," Acrida told the fool quietly as they filed out of the chamber behind the others.

"Indeed, I heard last night."

"How did you come to hear it?"

Tate grinned.

"It came up during *pillow talk*."

Acrida smiled at the old man with raised eyebrows.

"'Twas not the only thing that came up, of course," he added flirtatiously.

Acrida snickered and rolled her eyes as they made their way down the palace corridor to the audience hall. After weeks of his fellowship, she had grown accustomed to the fool's wit and company and the boasts of his exploits. She found the old man to be a wise and merry soul, and she liked him well.

Just inside the audience hall, two dark-headed men dressed in long, gold and crimson, velvet tunics talked together. At the sight of the group's approach, the two foreigners smiled and bowed formally and then looked at Lord Grey.

"Sire," Grey spoke in Latin, "may I present Lord Thurmonde of Fors, youngest brother to King Roderic, and his eldest son, Leander."

The two men bowed again to King Christian.

"At last we meet, Your Grace," Lord Thurmonde replied in Latin with a thick, foreign accent. "On behalf of my family and my brother, King Roderic, I thank you for all your efforts to find my lost daughter. You have relieved at last the great distress that has burdened my family for so long."

"We rejoice that your daughter has been found, but no thanks are necessary," Christian answered smoothly in Latin. "We assure you, We did nothing."

The advisers smiled.

"Your Grace is too modest. You appointed your faithful and most capable vassal, Lord Grey, to see to this matter personally, and he has worked tirelessly to see it to a satisfactory end."

Again Christian smiled a very small smile, noting the favorable impression Grey had had on the men.

"You arrived this morning?" Christian asked.

"Perhaps an hour ago."

"Are your accommodations adequate?" Christian asked.

"Aye, very much so. Thank you."

"You and your children are welcome to stay as long as you like."

"We are very appreciative of your gracious hospitality," Thurmonde bowed.

"And the people here in Speyron are quite charming. I easily see why my sister is resistant to leaving," Leander said.

"It is a pity for Speyron to have to surrender such a beauty as the Lady Elise," Grey said.

The foreigners smiled. The four men were silent for a moment.

"We would like to meet your daughter-" Christian said.

"Of course," Lord Thurmonde said with a warm smile.

With a gesture, he and his son led the King and Lord Grey to the far end of the audience hall up the stairs to the landing above.

The great doors leading out to the parapet were ajar, and two women stood near the edge of it, looking out into the distant view; the sound of the whipping wind filled the air. The servant woman closest to the wooden doors, turned and curtsied to the party meekly.

The other woman was so absorbed in her thoughts that she did not even notice the group's approach, but continued looking out over the snow-covered land in the distance.

Christian observed the back of the lady with interest. She was taller than he had expected, but of agreeable height; and she was clearly no child.

"Daughter, King Christian calls for you," Thurmonde said in Latin.

The woman almost jumped at the voice. She turned, startled, to find the group of men behind her.

King Christian caught his breath. The Lady Elise's face was like that of an angel with skin, pure and smooth as fine marble. Her cheekbones were high, and her lips were full. Her head was covered modestly with a linen headrail, and the maroon gown of velvet she wore emphasized her round, ample breasts and slender waist. She was easily the most beautiful woman he had ever seen in his life.

Leander crossed to her, confidently smiling.

"Your Grace, may I present my sister, Elise?"

Christian's heart skipped a beat, and then raced in his chest as her doe-like, brown eyes regarded him. Lowering her eyes from his gaze shyly, and with a most solemn expression on her face, the lady curtsied gracefully to King Christian.

Her beauty so mesmerized the young King that he could neither speak nor tear his eyes from her. He could scarcely breathe.

Lord Grey smiled in satisfaction as he watched; he knew Christian's lust well. If the youth had had any objections to the match, there would be none now.

"My Dear Lady, it is quite cold out here," Lord Grey said. "Shall we go into the fire, Sire?"

Christian could do no more than nod, barely registering the request.

"Aye, Daughter," Thurmonde agreed. "Come inside to the fire."

Leander led his sister off the parapet back through the doors and down the steps to the audience chamber, where the eyes of every man waiting below watched her descend like a heavenly being. Everyone marveled at her beauty.

As Grey followed King Christian down the steps behind the others, he saw the look of surprise and disappointment on the faces of Olbert and Dewain, further heralding his triumph.

"She is beautiful!" Acrida whispered, amazed.

The seer had never seen a more beautiful woman. There were, of course, handsome girls among commoners, but their beauty faded quickly from the strain of bearing and raising children, long days of hard work, and exposure to weather and hardship.

"Indeed, a practical 'Helen'," Tate commented, noting the lady's sad countenance.

"And you remember what trouble *she* caused-" Olbert added with a sigh.

Tate smirked.

"What a merry pair these two will make," the fool complained with a shake of his head. "I pity the minstrel that is bidden to make her smile."

"If he will not marry her," Felix whispered to Paschal, not taking his eyes from her, "*I* will."

Acrida frowned as she gloomily compared the noblewoman's perfect features to her own. How would she ever manage to gain any man's interest with a woman of such flawless beauty commanding their attention?

Leander escorted his sister to a bench near a brightly burning fire in a small hearth. With her back perfectly straight, she sat upon the bench and stared sadly at the elaborately painted wall before her of Proserpina's abduction by the god of the Underworld.

Christian made his way to his bejeweled throne and sat down, not taking his eyes from her.

"The King, I believe, will wish to commence with the marriage at all speed," Lord Grey was whispering to Lord Thurmonde in Latin.

"As will we."

Olbert cleared his throat.

"My Lords," he said shortly in Latin, "before the King makes a decision, he requires some specific information regarding the Lady Elise."

Grey's expression changed from cordial to irritated.

However, Lord Thurmonde only smiled.

"Of course, My Lord, what question may I address?"

Lord Grey and the two men from Fors were suddenly surrounded by the other advisers and the Royal Chaplain.

"Is she in good health?" Felix asked in broken Latin.

"Excellent, would you care to see her teeth?"

"The King would also like to know," Olbert said, taking a step closer, "how she came to be *lost* in the first place. Did her husband turn her out because she displeased him or did she flee of her own accord?"

"Was she caught or suspected in adultery?" Dewain asked.

"Does the Lady hear Mass regularly and make confession at least three times a year?" Bennet asked. "And has she completed her penance for abandoning her first husband?"

"Were there no children produced in the first marriage?" Lord Dewain asked.

"Aye, are you certain she is fertile?" Olbert asked.

Thurmonde and Leander were both overwhelmed by the assault and speed of the questions. They smiled and gestured for them to slow down as they gave an answer to each one.

Grey only smiled as he watched. Let them raise questions. These concerns might serve well to increase the troops that would result from the match.

King Christian only partially listened to his advisers' queries and the Forsians' answers. His eyes continued to drift back to Lady Elise.

As he watched her intently, their eyes momentarily met. She looked away, immediately blushing. Then she suddenly rushed from the chamber without a word, the maidservant following quickly behind her.

Christian smiled at her modesty. Her abrupt flight out of the chamber caught the attention of her father and brother as well as the other advisers.

"Is your sister ill?" Dewain asked with some concern.

"No, no. She is overwhelmed with meeting the King, is all," Lord Leander said pleasantly. "Fear not, I will attend her."

"Aye, we both will," Thurmonde added with a smile.

Lord Grey smiled affably. The two foreigners bowed to the advisers and to the King and then quickly hurried after the lady.

"Dewain-" Christian called.

"Aye, Sire."

"Have the papers drawn up at once."

Dewain looked at the King hesitantly. Successfully resisting the urge to caution him further, he nodded and bowed.

"As you wish, My Liege."

70

Lady Elise rushed into her bedchamber and flung herself on the large, curtained bed, allowing the coverlets to muffle her loud sobs. Her maidservant entered behind her and shut the door. Observing her misery, she wondered what consoling words she could speak.

"Are you hungry, My Lady? Shall I bring you something to eat or some warm, mulled wine?" she asked in native Forsian.

"No."

The maidservant frowned.

"Perhaps it will be different with King Christian, My Lady. Perhaps he will love you so well that-"

"Love? Ha! What does *Christian the Bloody* know of love?" Elise sobbed.

The maid sighed.

"'Then perhaps you can endure him for a time, until you can find the means to escape him. Or perhaps he will be so preoccupied with the war, that he will have no time for a wife.-"

"Is King Christian different from other men? He will surely have me out there in the field with him, engaging the enemy during the day, and me at night. -And if somehow I did manage to escape him, *he* would have the means to discover me again."

The maid frowned; it hurt her to see her lady distraught.

"My daughter has always been modest and shy!" boomed the voice of Lord Thurmonde in thick Latin from the corridor.

Elise moaned.

A moment later, the door swung open, and Elise's father and brother entered the chamber abruptly, followed by Lord Dewain.

"Daughter, is this where you have disappeared to? The King-"

The three men stopped, taken aback to find the woman prostrate with weeping.

"My Lady," Dewain told her in Latin, "you are unwell! I shall send for a physician at once!"

"Unwell? My daughter? Oh, no! Our entire family is of hearty stock! She has not been ill a day in her life! No need for a physician!" Thurmonde declared forcefully as he sat beside her on the bed and coaxed Elise to sit up.

"Are you certain?" Dewain questioned.

"Aye. 'Tis nerves, is all. -The excitement of meeting King Christian," he added, touching his finger to her chin and smiling.

"Aye, all the excitement, surely," her brother added. "She should have some wine to soothe her. Girl, bring my sister some warm, mulled wine," Leander ordered in his native tongue.

The maid curtsied and left the chamber.

Dewain watched curiously as the lady wiped her face with the sleeve of her gown.

"Tell me, Sister, do you not find him handsome?" Lord Leander asked cheerfully with a contagious smile. "They call him 'Christian the Fair' for good cause, I see!"

The three men smiled again and looked at Elise.

She said nothing, but stared at the far wall blankly.

Leander laughed then and said to Dewain, "She is too modest to answer."

Dewain smiled.

"Aye, and the King seems very taken with you as well, Elise, as we knew he would be," said her father, smiling and kissing her on the forehead.

"Aye," Dewain agreed. "The King has ordered the dower drawn up. He wishes to marry in three days time."

Elise winced. Lord Thurmonde jumped to his feet at the news.

"Three days! That is wonderful! King Roderic will be very pleased!"

Leander and Dewain smiled and looked again at Elise who was not smiling, but continued to stare at the wall. There was an awkward silence.

"Perhaps, Lord Dewain, you will give me a moment with my daughter," Thurmonde said pleasantly.

"Of course," Dewain bowed and left the chamber.

The door had barely closed behind him when Lord Thurmonde turned and slapped Elise hard across the ear, receiving an answering shriek from his daughter.

"You will stop this defiance at once, Elise!" he told her angrily in their native tongue. "Do you hear me? You will not shame us again! You will speak and *sweetly* when I or the King or anyone addresses you and *with* a smile upon thy lips! And you *will* marry King Christian, for it is the will of King Roderic and I that you do so!"

Holding her throbbing ear, Elise turned her watery eyes upon her father.

"Have you no pity?" she asked sadly. "T'would be more merciful to strangle me here and now than to give me to King Christian."

Thurmonde scowled at her, fighting the urge to strike her again.

"How did I beget such an unnatural child?" he complained in his native tongue. "You should have had a house full of children by now, like your sisters. God blessed me with a daughter whose beauty is unmatched in the entire kingdom of Fors, and lo, she is cursed with a rebellious spirit and-"

"Father-" Leander interrupted.

Thurmonde glanced at his son, then turned back to his daughter.

"But you speak aright, Elise," Thurmonde continued. "King Christian is not a man who will tolerate rebellion from anyone -and surely not from his wife! You saw those heads on the wall! You have been living in Speyron for years; no doubt, you have heard the tales of him. If he discovers you to be anything other than amenable and loyal, your head will be among the rest!"

Elise cringed.

"Father!"

Lord Thurmonde frowned at his son, who glared at him.

"Let me talk to her," Leander told him.

Thurmonde angrily glanced again at his weeping daughter. Then he stormed out of the chamber. When he had gone, Leander sat down beside his sister on the bed and put his arm around her.

"Elise, you are not thinking," he told her gently. "I know you were unhappy with Lord Viri, but-"

Elise laughed out loud as new tears coursed down her cheeks. She irritably pushed her brother's arm away.

"Unhappy? Aye, you knew how unhappy I was with him, and how mistreated, both from the letters I sent to you and from your one time visit. How many times did I beg you to help me, Leander? But never did you aid me."

"Elise, I was always concerned about his treatment of you, but I could not interfere with another man's wife. -None of the family could."

"Not as long as Viri gave the support you and Father required at the time."

"That is not just, Elise."

"Is it not? Am I not simply a pawn in the game that you and Father and Uncle are playing?"

"A pawn? Perhaps, but make one move more, and the pawn will become a queen! You will have more power and influence than you have ever known, and you will want for nothing!"

"Power and influence? Those are not the things that I desire, and if ever they were, I have learned that they come at too high a cost."

"Elise," Leander said gently, "it will be different when you marry Christian. You will not be alone. I will be here at Court as will Father, Leweson, and Marden. King Christian will not dare to mistreat you as Viri did."

"Not dare?! Do you know nothing of this man? This is Christian the Bold! Christian the Bloody! Christian the Terror! There is nothing this man fears in this world- neither God, nor man, nor beast! The entire kingdom of Speyron fears him and with good cause! *No one* is safe from his whim or his temper! He murders all that dare displease him, be they nobles, holy priests, or children!"

Leander made no reply. Elise swallowed as she beheld her brother's unconcern.

"Now I see how much my own family must despise me to match me to such a monster," she said sadly.

"Sister-"

"It is said that King Christian keeps more than a hundred concubines. What will I ever be to him but the latest of many, and just as easily replaced if I disappoint him? Father speaks truly, Leander: When King Christian finds me displeasing, my head will be on the wall."

"Elise, if we thought your life would be in jeopardy with him, we would not have arranged the match."

"Believe you so, Leander?" she said sorrowfully. "Then you are as naive as I when first I married Viri to what truly rules the hearts of men- and the indifference they are capable of."

Leander sighed and put his arm back around his sister's shoulders.

"Elise, I love thee as much as any brother ever loved a sister. So harken to my words which I speak from love: Put this willfulness behind thee. Truly, the life that you have lived for the past few years and the independence it afforded you- has ended. You must reconcile yourself to it. If King Christian does not take you for wife, our uncle will still match you to whomever he finds with adequate lands in Fors. The honor of our family requires it."

Elise made no reply as more tears of frustration rolled down her pink cheeks and her brother rocked her tenderly in his arms.

71

Elise sat on the bed as the maid combed the woman's long, dark hair soothingly. Her brother had left her to her woes some time ago, and so she sat, barely aware of the maid's labors, as her brute of a husband appeared before her again.

She had met her betrothed in the summer of her fourteenth year. Lord Viri had been a tall, gangly man in his thirties. Some in her household had thought him handsome, but she had never found him so. The thick, black hair that covered most of his body repulsed her, and the very smell of him sickened her. -Worse yet had been the unnerving way he had stared at her.

Her parents had arranged the match when she was twelve and had sent her to him three years later. Her mother had told her that a husband and a home of her own were what every woman wanted, so despite her misgivings, she had looked forward to the marriage and her new life.

Remembering their first night together, Elise knew Viri had been kind to her. He had taken her maidenhood matter-of-factly and then rolled over to sleep. Not many days afterward, however, he began to show his true nature.

Viri had the manners, the interests, and the appetites of a beast. Most of the time, he was occupied either with the management of his lands or hunting with his companion knights. He gave her little attention at all, but when he did, it was for one purpose only.

Elise shuttered at the memory. Viri had known nothing of tenderness. When he touched her, he had been rough, and when he bedded her, he had held her down as if he believed she had had the strength to flee him. Initially, she had tried to tell him that he was hurting her, but that did not deter him. Gradually, she had realized that tears and complaints of pain only encouraged him. Thus, she had learned to lie still under his enormous weight while she endeavored to control her nausea, for he became violent when she vomited on him.

She had told herself repeatedly that it would get better with time, but it never did. In fact, it became worse. Viri began seeking her out when he was angry or frustrated. Whenever she did or said anything wrong, he beat her with all his fury. Then, whenever she spoke, he beat her, until for days she went without speaking, without looking at anything, living in terror every time he came near. Finally, the beatings came with the bedding and the bedding with the beatings until she had thought she would surely die.

A knock on the door interrupted Elise's thoughts.

The door opened, and King Christian, accompanied by a monk and a servant carrying a small chest, entered the chamber. The maid immediately covered her lady's loose hair with a veil.

Christian smiled. He had wondered. Her hair was dark brown, thick and copious, and went to her waist. Already he longed to run his hands through it.

Lady Elise stood up instantly, and she and the maidservant curtsied to him.

Christian looked at her for a long time without saying anything. She was a classic beauty, the kind that sculptors tried to imitate in their statues. She seemed a little sad, but even her somber expression could not mar the perfect harmony of her face.

Elise looked away, her cheeks reddening slightly as she realized that she had captivated the three men, even the monk. It was a common occurrence for her. Men had been staring at her for as long as she could remember.

"We did not mean to disturb your rest, My Lady," King Christian finally began in Latin, almost in a whisper.

Lady Elise did not look at him.

"Our betrothal will be formally announced at tonight's feast. To finalize the dower, We present you with a ring. You may have your choice, but as exquisite as they are, We fear they will seem paltry next to your beauty."

He gestured to the servant who stepped forward and opened the small, wooden chest, revealing a mass of golden, bejeweled rings. The dazzling collection of jewelry drew the momentary attention of the servants and the monk.

The pleasant expression drifted from King Christian's face as he saw that the lady did not even look at the offering. In fact, she seemed to grow paler.

With all the self-control she could muster, Elise fought her gathering tears and managed to hold her composure for a moment more. However, the fear within her continued to swell, for to disappoint King Christian was to forfeit one's life.

"Are you well, My Lady?" he asked.

When she made no reply nor any sign that she had heard him, he glanced at Bennet in concern.

Staring at the wall, Elise frantically wondered what she should do. She was too frightened to answer him for fear she would anger him. Should she prostrate herself and beg for mercy? Was 'mercy' a word King Christian even knew?

"Will you speak, Lady? Or do you intend to be silent our entire married life?" Christian asked, irritated now.

The testy tone of his voice was enough to overwhelm her defenses. Elise fell to her hands and knees at his feet and began to sob loudly.

"Mercy! Mercy, Great King! Have pity and spare me from your wrath!" she wailed miserably in Speyron's own tongue.

Surprised and embarrassed, Christian recoiled as he witnessed her earnest supplication. He moved away abruptly and glanced at the servants.

"Leave us."

The two servants bowed quickly and left the chamber, shutting the door behind them.

When they had gone, Christian looked back at the woman who was crying on the floor.

"What is the meaning of this?" he asked in his own language.

"Have pity upon me, a most wretched woman, and refuse this match that my family proposes!" she wept.

"What?!"

"You do not wish to marry His Grace, the King?" Bennet asked her plainly.

"No!"

"You are withdrawing your consent to the match?" Bennet asked.

"I have never agreed to it! Any that say that I have lies."

"Your father and brother assured Us that you -"

"They lie! I have not consented!"

"Why do you refuse? Why would you even hesitate to consent to our marriage?" Christian demanded to know. "Have you not brought dishonor upon thyself and family by fleeing thy husband? Have you not cheapened thy noble blood by laboring among villeins for food? Have you not made alliances with the most common of persons these last five years in order to survive without home or the help of family or friends?"

Elise did not reply as she cried distractedly upon the floor.

"How dare you frown upon an honorable proposal of marriage to a king!" Christian told her hotly. "You should readily embrace this opportunity to reinstate thy honor and position!"

"I can not deny what you have said, My Lord," Elise wailed. "But I- I have my reasons- which are between myself and God."

"Have you pledged your life to God?" Bennet asked.

This question caught Elise off guard, and her weeping slowed. She looked up at the monk and shook her head.

"No, Brother, the religious life is not my desire."

"Then what mean you?" Christian demanded.

"Have you in secret given your pledge of marriage to-" Bennet began.

"Does another man claim you as his own already?" Christian cut in impatiently.

Elise cringed as the tears rolled down her smooth cheeks.

"Please, do not force me to speak my heart, My Lord."

"Are you with child?"

"No."

"What is the impediment then?"

Elise only wept, not knowing how to answer.

"Are you another man's concubine?" Christian demanded again.

Elise only shook her head in the negative and sobbed, overwhelmed by the men's growing anger.

"What then?" Christian snapped.

He stared at the woman, miffed. What could be the impediment? By all logic, she should want this marriage as much as he. Was she simple? Perhaps the years of hiding from her family had driven her mad.

Elise wept miserably onto the scarlet rug that covered the stone floor. She dared not say anything more, for no matter what she said, he would surely become irate and kill her.

Yet she feared to remain silent. If they married, eventually he would learn the truth of how she had lived these past years, and it would shame him as it had shamed her father. Then, too, he would murder her as her father nearly had done!

But if he did learn the truth now, would it not also deter him? And why should she have to tell him at all? Perhaps all that was needed was time for him to discover it on his own before they married. With this reasoning, Elise's tears slowed.

"Must we marry in three days?" she suddenly asked.

"What?"

"Can we not wait three or four months?" she asked, pushing herself up to a sitting position on the floor.

Christian blinked at the question and then glanced at Bennet, confused. After stopping and considering again what she had said, he took a deep breath and began again as calmly as possible.

"My Lady, if you are not secretly married nor the concubine of another man and likewise not with child, then perhaps this display is simple nervousness. Perhaps it will comfort you to know that I am similarly oppressed by nerves and also wish we could delay our nuptials. But it is impossible."

"One month then?"

"No."

Elise frowned.

"Marriages of state are by nature, necessary evils," Christian continued. "We must both grit our teeth and bare this thing. With this marriage, honor will be restored to both you and your family name, and my kingdom will receive a generous supply of troops in our hour of need. Beyond this, I promise you, I will treat you honorably, and I will try to see that you are comfortable here."

"If troops are your sole aim, My Lord, then take me as wife in name only, and let me live with you as a sister. You will restore my family's honor and get your troops. Or even better, put me away quietly in a few months and take a better wife after your war."

Christian and Bennet stared at her in surprise.

"I can not take a wife in name only," Christian answered. "I require sons to continue the royal line."

"Speak plainly, My Lady," Bennet said gently. "Why art thou resistant to marriage to the King?"

Elise swallowed, her head hurting from weeping.

"-When I fled my husband," she answered quietly, staring at the rug, "I vowed I would never marry again. I will never -*never* pay the debt to a man again."

Christian and Bennet blinked at her and then exchanged glances. Was her objection simply a dislike of swyving? Christian smiled, amused. No woman *liked* swyving. Why would they? It was God's gift to men.

"But do you not desire children?" Bennet asked.

Elise shook her head.

"Thou liest," Christian replied. "There is not a female among man or beast that does not desire children."

"Aye, it would subvert God's holy intentions," Bennet agreed.

Elise frowned and rubbed her aching head. Christian and Bennet were silent again as well as they wondered what to say. Christian sat down on the bed and regarded the beauty whose silent tears still streamed down her face.

After a very awkward silence, Christian said, "As you have been married before, My Lady, I will be direct. As much as I need troops, I need sons. And while- I have heard it said- that women find the marital debt - unpleasant-"

"'*Unpleasant*-'" Elise echoed with a bitter laugh.

"-in time, it is a duty to which they become accustomed."

Elise laughed again and wiped her wet cheeks on her sleeve. He could have no idea just how *repulsive* she found it. Even now, his close proximity made her skin crawl.

But he was a man- she reminded herself, and what did men understand about anything? And what was swyve to a man? It was not an assault and invasion of their bodies. Nor did it devastate their wholeness or wound their spirit.

Exhausted, Elise wondered again what more she dared tell him, what further resistance she could offer to the marriage without endangering her life.

-Her secret would deter him, she knew. He would despise her as her father had. He would surely kill her, but would death not be preferred to ten minutes in his bed?

"My Lady-"

"I have a lover."

Elise was stunned and horrified that she had finally said it.

"You just said you have forsworn the bed of men!" Christian argued.

Elise swallowed carefully as she saw the surprise and irritation on their faces.

"Indeed, I spoke truly, My Lord, for I do not love a man," she answered.

Bennet and Christian looked at her blankly, not understanding her. Elise took a deep breath and prepared herself for the chastisement and curses that were to come.

"Do not pursue this match," she continued, looking at the floor. "Rescue thine own honor, Lord King. For before I left my husband, whose manner was beyond cruel, I defiled myself and our marriage bed with a woman."

Astonished silence reverberated through the chamber. Christian stared at her, and Bennet slowly crossed himself.

"When I left Viri, I forswore men completely," Elise continued with an eerie calmness, as she resigned herself now to death. "For five years, ever since I entered Speyron's borders, I have kept the company of women -only women. I have shared everything with them, *-done* everything with them."

Christian was so amazed that he could not think. Elise was the only woman his ministers had been able to find for him to marry that could provide the troops to defend and save his kingdom. She was already here, and her family was willing, and the papers were drawn up. She could even speak the language. Everything had been arranged for the marriage to proceed, only for him to discover that she was unwilling to wed him.

Bennet was struggling to control his own feelings of surprise and disgust. This beautiful woman, clearly the embodiment of divine love which God held for creation, and who he was lusting after mightily despite his best efforts to control himself, had defiled herself with unnatural acts with her own sex. He prayed silently for patience as he watched the range of expressions that crossed the King's face.

Not looking at either man, she wretchedly awaited the King's wrath and the pronouncement of her death sentence.

At last, Christian spoke.

"My Lady, you know well that *that* is not a legitimate objection to marriage. I am, however, prepared to forgive you of this and all of your past sins, as you will have to forgive mine."

He glanced at Bennet for support and gained it readily.

"Aye, My Lady, thou should have some concern for the state of thy immortal soul. It is essential you confess and renounce your past sin, and amend your life by marrying His Grace, the King. In fact, it is the duty of all of the faithful, especially your family, to impede you of this sin in the future by insisting that you marry."

Elise stared at the pair in horror and shook her head in disbelief, muttering, "Impossible- impossible."

"I do not rightly understand you," Christian replied angrily. "It is not only possible. It is necessary! This marriage is necessary for the state of your soul and for the survival of my kingdom! Our personal feelings do not enter into it. Duty is our master!"

"I will never give consent," Elise answered, angry and defiant now, "no matter what you or my family do to me! Whether you lock me away forever or starve or beat me, I will never-"

"What do you hope to gain by this obstinacy? Think you a woman's lack of consent is of grave importance to a man when her family and king's consent for the match is adamant? 'Tis no concern at all, particularly when much is to be gained," Christian replied. "Thus, protest all you wish, My Lady, for as long as your family and I and King Roderic desire this match, you will still come to my bed!"

Lady Elise sat mute as she listened to the truth of his words, while new tears began to rain down her face.

"Is it your hope that you will be reunited with this other sinful woman that makes you so resistant?" Bennet asked.

There was a moment of silence before she answered.

"No," she admitted sadly. "I hope we are reunited, but, alas, I fear that I will never behold Haether again."

"Then why persist, My Lady?"

"I have made a pledge," she explained simply. "-Given myself, all that I am, to it. -And I will not forsake it for anything."

"Surely, there is no shame in breaking a vow of unholy love," Christian replied.

At this, Elise smiled a little, strained smile through her tears.

"'Tis the only happiness I have ever known, and the most wholesome and filling love I have found," she whispered.

At these words, Bennet was crossing himself again with a frown and a shake of his head. She was a slave to her sin, and she did not wish to be free.

The three were silent again until Elise spoke, her words echoing years of misery.

"Have pity, Lord King, now that you know my secrets. You will never know how greatly I have suffered in my life. Take pity upon me-"

"We will hear no more of this!" Christian told her firmly as he stood up. "Your lack of consent is of no concern! We shall wed in three days- and bed together tonight! The sooner you put this vile woman out of your mind and embrace your duty, the better!"

Elise's countenance crumbled.

"My Lady," the King said with a brief bow of courtesy, ignoring the wretched look on her face.

He opened the door and left the chamber followed by the monk.

The maid rushed back into the chamber and finding the Lady Elise distressed and on the floor, immediately hugged her to comfort her. The woman's crying gradually began to subside as the maid gently held her and soothed her.

So it had been years ago too, Elise remembered. As Viri's wife, she had been lonely, and the servants of his castle were her only companions. One of the maid servants was a woman slightly younger than her husband, named Mersia. She was a kind, gentle, and practical woman who often tended her after Viri had had his fill of her.

Elise could still remember her soft features vividly. She had comforted her and quieted her tears countless times. She had applied ointments to soothe cuts and brought her brews to ease her pain. And after a while, she had found Mersia to be the most beautiful woman she had ever known, and she, herself, drawn strongly to her. In time, she physically needed to be in Mersia's presence. When they were apart, she felt empty and alone.

One time, after one of her husband's tantrums, Mersia had rushed in with consoling words and a damp cloth for her bleeding lip. She had knelt beside the bed and stroked her hair to calm her, as she so often did. It was at that moment that Elise had wished that Mersia would really touch her. She had wished that she would take her into her arms and cradle and rock her, never letting her go.

Elise had looked into her face -and perhaps her eyes had given it away. She had reached up and touched Mersia's face and then kissed her cheek briefly. Mersia had smiled, and to her surprise, the maid had kissed her lips without hesitating.

Thus, it had started. Laying timidly in Mersia's arms, that day and for many days after, she had found the first tenderness and love she had ever known. Mersia had shown her what love was, what it could be, what it was meant to be. It had not been brutal, painful, angry, or scary. At any time, Elise could have stopped, had fear or propriety insisted, but it had never felt like sin, nor had she been afraid. It had all seemed so natural. She had not wanted to stop. She had never wanted it to stop.

Two months later, the beatings from Viri had become so violent that Mersia had feared Elise would not survive more; she had insisted that she flee the household at once. Elise at first had been unwilling to go, but each time it took longer to recover from Viri's rages. Finally, she was willing to leave, and she had wanted Mersia to come with her, but she would not; Mersia had children and a husband of her own that she would not abandon.

Thus, they had waited until Viri left for Court. He was to be away for a month, and when he had gone, Elise, in the care of a freeman, left everyone she knew and fled her husband.

The freeman had taken her directly to the borders and into Speyron. They told anyone they met either that they were on a pilgrimage or that they were going to visit relatives. After a week, the freeman had had to return home or create suspicion himself. Thus she had traveled deeper into Speyron alone, moving steadily away from the border towns. In almost no time, she had run out of money. Her frugality and the wear and tear on her clothes had made it evident that she was not simply traveling to see her cousin in such and such place.

Eventually, she had arrived in a quiet little crossroads where she worked in a tavern serving drinks in exchange for food and a place to sleep. She had not worked there many days when, one night, some of the drunken patrons cornered her. By chance, a small group of women who had also been traveling through the area had stopped there to eat, and they rescued her when no man would.

Once out of danger, the women invited her to join them. They had not cared who she was or where she had come from. These women traveled about the kingdom unescorted, living outside the law, with neither brothers, husbands, nor fathers dictating to them. A few were petty thieves, but most of them were simple laborers.

Although grateful for the rescue, initially she had regarded them as unworthy of her acquaintance. She had thought them lowborn, brazen, and disreputable- these who would become her dearest companions, whom she would come to love as dearly as she had loved Mersia. Elise smiled at the memory. She had accepted their offer to travel with them, planning to depart from them at the first good opportunity. Unexpectedly along the way, she discovered she had more in common with them than she could have guessed.

In their company, she had found herself surprisingly happy. As she began to explore and embrace the truth about herself, she had realized that she had always been drawn to women; from her earliest childhood, it was they she had longed to touch, hold and love. Elise doubted Viri had ever suspected the truth about her, but she believed that he sensed her aversion to him, and that that had helped to fuel his rages.

Wherever the group journeyed, they labored in the fields with the rest of the peasantry for money or a portion of the food when the planting and harvesting seasons came.

After a year or so, most of the group had become weary with wandering. The majority had settled in a rural section of land in the north of the kingdom. There they had worked the fields and spun thread, and weaved cloth during the off months without attracting much notice. They had kept to themselves and had not made any trouble; and the locals had let them be, deciding that the group must be runaway slaves who were attempting to establish their freedom. The villagers accepted them into the community and had made no attempt to discover them to the lord of the manor.

Haether had arrived at the village only about two and a half years ago; and Elise had never met anyone like her. She was a strong, quiet, serious woman, older than she, with snowy, blond hair. She refused to wear gowns or a headrail. She always dressed like a man, and from a distance could easily be mistaken as one. But most of all, Haether was both prudent and brave. She was so much braver than anyone Elise had ever known.

In the beginning, Haether had not shared much about her past. No one knew whom she was fleeing, whether it was a sheriff or a husband. But seeing how she grieved with some inward pain, Elise had been immediately drawn to her. She had shown Haether many kindnesses to earn her trust, until finally, they became confidants.

She and Haether were in the habit of bathing in the warm summer evenings. On one such night, they had retired to a glade and lain naked on the tall grass to dry, talking before going to sleep.

Elise had been surprised how timid Haether had been. She remembered how Haether had trembled when Elise had first leaned over and kissed her on the mouth. That kiss, so unlike anything a man would give, was soft, barely a touch, a simple, fleeting sweep, a question- that did not demand an answer.

She had loved Haether sweetly that night, and they had formed a lasting bond over the days that had followed. Even now Elise could still vividly remember the feel of Haether's hands as they caressed her, the familiar smell of her, and the warm sense of shelter and peace of mind she had experienced when she had slept in her arms.

In the midst of all these memories, fresh tears sprang from Elise's eyes as her thoughts turned from Haether to King Christian and the coming of the night.

72

Elise sat in the cushioned chair near the wall in the dimly lit chamber watching the flickering flame of the candle that set on the small table near her. Her head ached from crying, but she was finished with it. There were no more tears to shed.

Silly, useless tears- that have no power to help anything, she thought. When girls are troubled, they are expected to weep and then to surrender to their misfortune. But when men are troubled, they are expected to confront their trouble and act.

If only she had been born a man- she mused.

Ignoring her pain, she glanced at the small dagger she had been tapping idly on the table's edge. It was the only possession left her from her old life. All the women she had lived with carried one somewhere on their person.

She wiped the blade over the skirt of her gown lovingly. Haether had given her this one. It was small, but sharp and, luckily, easy to conceal, for if her father or brother had known about it, they would not have allowed her even this one keepsake from her past.

The light knock on the door of the chamber startled Elise. With her heart beating rapidly, she quickly hid the knife under the cushion of her chair. It was a servant coming to escort her to the King's bedchamber, she knew, but she had not expected him so soon, for the hour was still early.

The chamber door opened then and, to Elise's surprise and horror, it was not a servant, but King Christian himself that entered, followed by the monk.

With her heart now racing, Elise rose from her chair and, a little off balance, curtsied to the floor to the King.

She wondered again at the presence of the monk and then realized, growing pale, that the King had brought him as a *witness*.

Christian looked at the woman kneeling before him. His eyes moved from her angelic face down her elegant neck to her full breasts. He licked his lips as he imagined again what she must look like naked and what those breasts would feel like heaving against his chest.

Resisting the images running through his mind, he gestured for her to rise. He watched as she sat in her chair again. Even the very way she moved was graceful and alluring.

Her absence from this evening's feast was further proof to him that her objection to their marriage was sincere. And during dinner, while minstrels had played music and Lord Thurmonde had entertained the table with stories, Christian had hardly eaten a bite as he continued to question what kind of queen she would make.

Although he doubted that she would ever be unfaithful with another man, he had wondered if he would ever be able to trust her. Would she flee him when his back was turned as she had her first husband? Or would she, given time, become the bedfellow of every serving wench in the palace? Either way, he would be the jest of the Continent!

In the end, he had decided not to officially announce their betrothal at dinner. Grey and the Forsians had managed to conceal their disappointment.

Christian now silently prayed to the Virgin and St. Peter for prayers for wisdom for this situation as the familiar arguments once again paraded through his head: He needed allies and troops immediately, and he needed a wife who would give him an heir to secure the uncertain future.

Admiring her perfect face again, he knew she was the one. She still did not look at him, he noticed, but at least she was not crying.

Would she ever be happy as his wife? he wondered. Would she ever greet him with anything other than tears, frowns, misery, or silence? Truly, a few months ago, he would not have cared. All of his advisers would have agreed it was irrelevant. What was one woman's unhappiness compared to the security of his throne, after all?

Now, as he looked at the pale, somber beauty before him, he was no longer so certain. Sometimes the quickest and easiest solution was not the best.

Part of him, too, longed to reach out to another lost soul and help her on the path to repentance and righteousness as he had been helped. What troubled Christian, however, was the realization that his own lust was proving stronger than his desire to save either his kingdom or this woman's soul. More than anything, he simply wanted to bed her. In her presence, he could think almost of nothing else, and right now, it was taking all of his self-control to fight the urge to take her.

As Christian stood observing Elise's pallid, sad expression, he faintly knew it would be best if they did not wed, not because he feared she would shame him, for in truth, there was very little she could do that would surpass the shame he had already brought on himself. He wished to let her go, finally, because he did not wish to be the cause of her tears. -And he would be the cause, he knew, if he took her as wife.

It was so easy for him to be self-centered, angry, vengeful, cruel and unjust with those weaker than himself -as easy as it was for Bennet to be good, kind, generous and loving. Christian could not allow himself to go back to the way he had been before. Nervously fingering the exposed edge of the hair shirt at his neckline, he admitted again to himself that he should not keep anything around him that tempted him to sin. And she was nothing if not temptation.

"I have decided, My Lady," Christian said softly, "to honor thy wishes. I will inform your family that the match is out of the question."

Bennet looked at Christian in simple astonishment. Even Lady Elise regarded him in awful surprise. No one said anything at first.

"Thank you, Your Grace," she finally murmured with a smile of utter joy, as a lone tear fell from her lovely brown eyes.

It was the most beautiful smile Christian had ever seen. It made him happy.

"Would it not be wonderful- if you would return me to Haether?" Lady Elise said more to herself than to him, as tears flowed unchecked from her eyes. "How grateful I would be- if thou used thy position to free me from my family's grip- and returned me to the lands where I was discovered."

"Return you to your lover? Oh, no! Look not to me to further aid you in your sin, Lady," Christian was saying with a determined shake of his head. "I will, however, recommend to your family that they permit you to remain a widow. -Perhaps they will put you in a convent."

Christian turned to leave the chamber, a wave of relief passing over him. This had to be the right decision. As he turned, he noticed the frown on Bennet's face, as the monk bowed shortly to the lady.

"Art thou a priest, Brother?" she asked the monk slowly.

Bennet turned back to reply in the affirmative when he saw the lady slump in her chair.

"My Lady?" Bennet asked with concern.

The monk drew near her and placed his hand to her ashen face, which was cold to the touch.

"My Lady, art thou well?"

There was no response, as Elise slowly closed her eyes and fell to the floor, toppling the chair in the process.

"The lady swoons!"

Christian was at her side immediately. Without delay, he began to gather her in his arms to move her to the bed. As he raised her limp body off the floor, Bennet caught sight of something shiny near the fallen chair.

The King quickly put Elise down on the bed, only then noticing that the back of her maroon skirt was soaked and his right arm was covered in warm blood.

"God's eyes! She bleeds!" Christian exclaimed.

"Christian!"

Bennet showed him the dagger he had found on the rug near the blood-drenched seat cushion.

"God's wood! My Lady, what have you done?"

Christian quickly whipped up the skirt of her heavy gown. Her undertunic was soaked dark, watery crimson with her blood, and underneath, her legs were stained red also.

"By the saints!" Bennet exclaimed.

"The saints help us! Where is the wound?"

Ripping up her clothes, the young men bared the unconscious woman to her privates and found a deep gash in her left thigh that spurted out a stream of blood rhythmically. Covering it with a wadded up part of her skirt, the two pressed on the wound, hoping to prohibit the bleeding.

"See what thy sin has brought thee to?!" Bennet muttered angrily. "Methinks thy *soul* will regret thy rashness!"

Bennet hastily removed the rope belt from his habit and tied it tightly around the lady's thigh above the wound, effectively slowing the bloodflow. After a moment, Lady Elise began to come around, moaning weakly as her heart pounded rapidly and her thigh throbbed with pain. Her face was stark and colorless against her brown, disheveled hair.

"Do not die, My Lady," Christian pleaded, as he held her cold, clammy hand. "Was thy fear of me as husband so great that you would damn thy soul? I did not seek thy death! Forgive me, forgive me! I was too bold! And you- too harsh a taskmaster!"

"Lady, I am a priest," Bennet was saying quickly as he turned her face so that he might look into her eyes. "Have pity on your soul and make thy confession."

"Aye, Father, forgive me for I have sinned-" Elise answered.

She was struggling to stay awake, for she longed to sleep now.

"It has been a very long while since my last confession."

"Just repeat after me, My Lady," Bennet began quickly, "I confess to Almighty God-"

"I confess to Almighty God."

"To blessed Mary Ever-Virgin, to blessed Michael the Archangel-" Bennet said while he shook her to try to keep her conscious.

"To blessed Mary Ever-Virgin, to blessed Michael the Archangel-"

"To blessed John the Baptist, to the holy Apostles Peter and Paul and all the Saints that I have sinned-"

"To blessed John-" Elise repeated softly.

Standing up from the bed, Christian watched as the monk shook her again and then bent his ear closer to the woman's lips, for her strength was failing her. Christian leaned against the wall, covered his mouth and wept in grief as he watched.

Why had she done this? Why had she thought him deaf to her objections? He remembered her fearful pleas for mercy and pity again and his cold response. And then he had told her they would bed together this very night.

Even so, was this cause for despair? Why did she fear him so? Why would she prefer to die than to wed him? Why would she choose to die rather than to bear his children?

It was madness! How could a highborn lady prefer the life of a runaway and outlaw to a life of respectability as queen? How could she prefer the sinful, unnatural love of another woman to the love of a man? Did she really have someone else or did she simply not want *him*? Why would she fear less an eternity in Hell than one moment in his bed? What kind of monster was he that women died rather than marry him?

Christian looked at his blood-covered hands and winced. Glancing around the chamber, he saw a pitcher of water set in a basin on the small table. At once, he went over and poured the water over his sleeve into the basin and then vigorously began washing the lady's blood off his hands and arm. As he washed his face, he faltered as he observed the water had become as red as blood.

Christian cringed and immediately slapped the basin and its contents away from him, shattering it against the floor. At the commotion, Bennet glanced over at him, but then turned his attention back to Lady Elise and the completion of the sacrament.

"... et dimissis peccatis tuis, perducat te ad vitam aeternam."

It was finished now. She was dead, and Bennet was making the sign of the cross over her. Christian watched as the monk closed her doe-like eyes, placed her hands together on her chest, and pulled the hem of her skirt down over her shoes, as the body relaxed and fouled itself.

Bennet glanced at his bloodstained hands and sighed, then wiped them on his scapular. Turning, he saw her linen headrail on the rug.

He picked up the lady's veil, shook it out, and draped it as best he could over her hair. He then went over to Christian, observing the remnants of the youth's grief.

He waited silently, watching the King's pained expression change to one of anger and then to sternness. Without a word, Christian opened the chamber and went out into the corridor, followed by the Chaplain. The King's bodyguards were outside the door, and Christian dispatched one to retrieve Lord Olbert.

Lords Grey, Thurmonde, and Leander came down the corridor then in high spirits, laughing and talking in Latin. They stopped when they saw the young King outside the Lady's chamber.

"Your Grace?" Grey asked awkwardly, noting the King's reddened face and his agitated expression. "Art thou well?"

King Christian did not answer.

Thurmonde raised his eyebrows and smiled.

"I hope my daughter has not vexed thee, Your Grace, with her silly coyness," Thurmonde said warmly in Latin.

The three noblemen smiled. Christian took a deep breath, struggling to control his rage. He looked away from them.

"The Lady Elise has not been coy, Lord Thurmonde, but adamant in making her wishes known," he answered in Latin. "There will be no marriage between us."

"What?!"

"Your lady daughter does not wish to marry Us and will not consent to the match."

"Nonsense!" her father smiled. "Only allow me to talk to her again. You have to be firm with her sort, Your Grace. In many ways, she is still like a child and must be handled as such."

He took a step toward the chamber, but Christian crossed his arms and stood his ground, barring the man's entry into the room.

"The time for talk has passed. There will be no marriage."

Lords Olbert and Dewain arrived in the corridor then, followed by Paschal and Felix, Acrida and Tate, and a large group of knights and servants.

"This is some misunderstanding -or simple excitability- that women are prone to," Thurmonde said genially. "My son and I both talked to Elise earlier, and she gave her full consent to the match. We would not have proposed it otherwise."

"Thou art a liar," Christian told him coldly.

Thurmonde and his son turned pale, and King Christian's advisers watched in amazement.

"Felix, gather some of your men and escort Lord Thurmonde and his son to the border," Christian said suddenly. "Wait not for dawn, but go immediately."

"But Your Grace!" Thurmonde and Grey protested.

Felix made a single gesture, and his knights immediately seized the foreigners.

Everyone gasped.

"What is happening?" Acrida whispered, unable to understand the Latin like many of the spectators.

"Methinks the marriage is off," Tate replied.

"But your Grace-"

"And what of my sister?" Leander demanded.

"Lord Olbert," Christian ordered without pausing, "We are entrusting the Lady Elise to you. In the morning, you will send her back to the lands where she was discovered."

Lord Olbert bowed immediately, noting with concern what resembled spattered blood on the King's shirt and wet sleeve.

"What!"

"You dare not deprive me of my daughter! If you will not marry her, then so be it, but she will return with us to Fors!" Thurmonde said angrily in Latin.

"We have only just found her after searching all of these years!" her brother complained.

"While she is in Speyron, she remains under Our protection. And she will be taken to the place she has requested and left with her friends," Christian answered him sternly.

"You can not mean to support her in her renegade behavior! If you return her there, you will be sending her back into the grip of those women who have corrupted her very nature!" Lord Thurmonde shouted, struggling against the knights who held him.

"Your Grace," Lord Grey said coolly, "if you will remember our kingdom's *need* for an *ally*. Perhaps you will reconsider the matter, when you are calmer."

Christian regarded Grey coldly.

"We have made Our decision. It is dangerous to argue further."

Grey frowned, but remained silent.

"Olbert, the lady will require some moneys. See to it," King Christian ordered.

The Royal Steward bowed once more.

Without another word, Christian turned on his heel to leave the corridor.

"Your Grace, have pity! May a brother not even take leave of his sister?" Leander desperately called after him.

Christian stopped short.

"-Allow them to take their leave of the lady, Felix," he instructed in Speyronese.

Then King Christian walked on. All moved aside, bowing as he passed. While the foreigners spoke hotly together in their native tongue, Lord Olbert looked at the young Chaplain curiously, noticing the red spot on the cleric's forehead and his soiled hands and scapular.

"Brother, do you know what the King intends with all of this?" Olbert asked quietly.

"I believe he means to bury the Lady Elise where she wished."

"Bury her?"

"She is dead?"

"He killed her?!"

"Has he killed her already?!!" the growing crowd of spectators was asking.

The corridor was immediately loud with whispering.

"This evening, when His Grace came to speak with her further about her objections to the marriage, we discovered that she had in her desperation already taken upon herself the only means she could think of to avoid it," the monk explained quietly.

"'*Killed*'?" Leander questioningly repeated, catching that Speyronese word. "'Necavit'?? No! Not my sister! Not dead! No!" Leander cried.

Thurmonde cursed in his native language angrily.

Leander ripped free of the knights on either side of him and ran to the chamber door. He hurried into the chamber and fell upon his sister's lifeless body, wailing in agony. The knights hurried in after him while the aldermen and servants huddled inside the doorway and gawked at the scene, crossing themselves.

Gradually, the murmuring crowd dissipated, leaving the foreigners to their grief. Lord Olbert went to the treasury to get the burial money while Felix ordered horses saddled; the servants returned to their chores, and the Royal Chaplain went to sing Compline.

In the light of a single, burning candle and under the guard of a few of the Palace Watch, Lord Thurmonde sat sullenly on a chair inside the bedchamber as his son grieved for Elise. Thurmonde neither shed one tear nor whispered one prayer of mercy for his daughter's soul, but waited bitterly to be escorted from the kingdom of Speyron.

73

The Royal Chaplain entered the quiet, dimly lit feasting hall and glanced around. The servants had thoroughly cleaned the old hall, removed all but two, long tables and a few benches, and put fresh rushes over the floor. The hall, however, remained cheerless and stark, crypt-like, particularly compared to the rest of the palace. The sole decoration on the bare walls continued to be the old tapestry of the martyr of the Faith.

The only light in the hall came from a single, burning hearth at the far end. As Bennet went further inside, he noticed a gray, striped cat in the shadows hunting something among the straw.

The monk's eyes returned to the bright, crackling and popping fire and the lone figure sitting in a chair with his feet propped up on a bench before it. King Christian did not look up at his Chaplain's approach; he was rapt in thought, and the expression on his face was grave.

"Your Grace," Bennet bowed. "I hope I am not disturbing you."

Christian started at the voice.

"Forgive me, Sire. I did not mean to startle you."

"Bennet, I did not hear you come in. Here, sit," Christian offered with a smile, as he hastily began gathering up the pile of parchments and scrolls he had discarded in the empty chair beside him.

Bennet sat down in the cushioned chair, and picked up some parchments that had fallen onto the floor.

"What are these?" Bennet inquired curiously.

"Marriage petitions."

"For you?"

"If only they were," Christian sighed. "These are proposed matches between my vassals or the children of my vassals. They may not wed without my approval. -A few are even proposing marriage with my ward, and she is but a child!"

"It seems that many are wanting to wed," Bennet smiled, looking at the immense stack of papers.

"Aye. Some of these petitions date back to last spring. There were only a few of them then and, like everything else, I delayed in tending to them. Now, there are many more."

"Perhaps they too are trying to prepare for the war."

"Aye," Christian agreed. "And, worse, I do not know half of these families."

Bennet raised his eyebrows.

"That must make the task difficult."

Christian muttered an agreement, but said nothing more.

The two sat in silence for a long while, becoming mesmerized by the dancing flames in the otherwise dark feasting hall.

"How are you liking it here?" Christian suddenly asked.

Bennet smiled.

"I still find the palace overwhelming, but I will grow accustomed to it in time."

"Are your chambers to your liking?"

"Aye, they are generous, Sire, and much more than I need."

"And my great grandfather's chapel? -It is small and plain, but-"

Bennet chuckled.

"It is more than ample for our purposes, Christian. -It is good that we are making use of it again."

Christian nodded, pleased that his Chaplain was so easily satisfied. Bennet could make the best of any situation.

"Do you miss St. Brychan's?"

"Aye," Bennet admitted shyly. "I miss my brethren, and the villagers, and my old duties there. But I know in time, I will grow accustomed to the people here as well."

"Until then, perhaps We can find some pleasant distraction for you. Tomorrow, if the weather permits, we shall go hawking," Christian said pleasantly.

There was silence.

"Hawking?"

"Perhaps not," Christian corrected after seeing the monk's lack of enthusiasm. "Perhaps you would rather visit the villagers and see if they have adequate food, clothing, and shelter."

"Aye, I would indeed," Bennet smiled.

Christian nodded and smiled, settling back comfortably in the chair.

He had chosen Bennet as chaplain because he trusted him and because the monk knew him better than anyone else. He also liked the youth well. He found him insightful, intelligent, and witty; and he admired his integrity and strength of character. With the rifts they had already been through, he knew Bennet was strong enough to stand up to him if he fell into sin. And there was nothing more important to Christian now. There was nothing more important in the days that were ahead of him.

In the flickering light of the flames, Bennet saw the solemn expression return to the King's face. He frowned, wondering again what could be troubling him.

The young priest looked back into the fire and sighed. Bennet had expected their relationship to be different from their time together at St. Brychan's; however, he had thought as Royal Chaplain he would be privy to the King's most private thoughts. Yet, since his appointment, Christian had hardly spoken a word to him that was not of an official capacity; and he was uncertain how to interpret his continued reserve.

"Christian, My King," Bennet began gingerly, "you do not blame yourself for the death of the Lady Elise?"

"No!" he answered, startled by the question. "I offered her an honorable life as a wife and mother and a life of respectability and distinction as queen. She refused it. Neither her family, nor I, nor you could make her see the wisdom of it."

Bennet nodded, and silence returned to the hall.

"Besides, I had decided to refuse the match," Christian suddenly said. "-I was not deaf to her pleas. I saw that she would never have been content as my wife.

"-If she had only been patient, she might have found haven from the marriage bed, perhaps at a convent. And if not, perhaps she could have escaped her family again. Who knows? Perhaps in time she could have even reunited with her lover."

Bennet raised his eyebrows.

"But she was not patient," Christian added, growing angry. "She was instead willful, defiant, and unreasonable! -The least desirable qualities for any woman to have! I would not suffer these qualities in a dog! And I am just grateful I did not take her as wife -only to discover her true nature later!"

Bennet blinked and turned his attention back to the fire, uncertain of what to say. They were both silent for a long while.

"Why do you ask?"

Bennet swallowed and cleared his throat.

"I do not wish to overstep my place, Sire, particularly if it is not thy desire to confide in me- but I have noticed thy solemn expression of late and feared that the lady's death, or perhaps the strain of the coming war, was weighing heavily upon you."

Christian smiled slightly and ran his hand through his golden locks. Clearly, Bennet still did not understand what a king's life was. He did not see that under the guise of smiles, feasting, and acknowledging bows, a king's life was making hard, often unpopular decisions solely to fortify his position against friend and foe alike. The monk could never completely comprehend the *strain* of it.

"You are well within your bounds, Bennet, and in my confidence as well. I have resisted confiding in you as yet, as I wanted to give you time to adjust to the palace and your life here before I began burdening you with secrets that I will not divulge to anyone else."

Bennet was relieved to hear this.

"Then pray tell, My Lord King, what troubles thee?"

Christian sighed.

"'Tis not her death nor the coming war, but the daily strain of kingship itself that encumbers me."

"Howso?"

Christian smirked.

"'Tis too long a song to sing. Suffice it to say-"

The King paused and thought for a moment.

"-Suffice it to say, at present I am vexed by my advisers," Christian continued, lowering his voice and switching to *Gaulian*.

Bennet glanced at him.

"Your advisers?" he asked, also in the language of their youth.

"Aye, I am dependent on my advisers; and that dependence makes them too powerful, for I am at the mercy of their fidelity. If they are shirking their duties or scheming against me, I have no way of discovering it. And I do not know where to begin to either take back control or to perform the duties that my advisers do."

"But do not all kings depend upon advisers? You are only one man. You alone can not perform all the work that they do."

"Aye, but I am *too* dependent on them, for I yielded a great deal of my authority early on. When I first became king, I preferred that my advisers manage the affairs of the kingdom. I was too busy with the pursuit of amusements to take an interest in what my advisers, vassals, or any of my subjects were doing or planning. If they brought me a problem at all, I listened to the reports that they had made, listened to their advice, and usually upheld the decision that they had already made. Rarely did I ever see to anything personally."

"They are capable men and have sworn allegiance to you-"

Christian smiled again.

"Aye, but what is an oath of allegiance to a vassal with ambition?"

Bennet looked at Christian, alarmed.

"To betray an oath is to earn damnation."

Christian smiled and shrugged and looked back into the dancing flames burning in the hearth.

"A king's position is the most precarious of positions. By my blood, I am enthroned, and by my blood *spilt*, I may be deposed."

Bennet's mouth went dry.

"And you believe your advisers will betray you?"

"I have suspicions and nothing more. Last year I began to suspect the veracity of what they told me and also that they were withholding information from me. Now there is this incident with the Lady Elise and the Forsians."

"What do you mean?"

"Lord Grey found her. He must have known how compromised she was, just as her father and brother did, and yet he presented the match anyway."

"Grey?"

"I know not what they promised him in exchange for his support, but I fear it went beyond a simple reward; likely it was lands in Fors. Whatever it was, I fear he made a direct alliance with Roderic."

Bennet looked at him, startled.

"Would he do that? Without your knowledge and consent?"

"Aye, Grey would. -Almost any of my vassals would."

"But how would-"

"If I had married Lady Elise, Roderic would have had members of his court here as well as troops. Much could be done with such leverage."

"Wh-"

"Perhaps, after we defeated Herryck, Roderic and Grey might have united to take Speyron as we celebrated our victory. -Or perhaps during the worst of the battles with Herryck, they, joining forces, might have taken arms against us and crushed us and then moved against Herryck. -Or perhaps they might have revolted against us and aligned with Herryck to defeat us. -Or perhaps as soon as Elise delivered a live child, I would have been suddenly poisoned to death, and either Roderic or Grey would have ruled Speyron 'in proxy' until the child reached the age of majority. There are many possibilities."

Bennet was pale and crossing himself.

"Now with the marriage refused and his niece dead, perhaps Roderic will join with Herryck for retribution's sake."

Bennet was speechless with horror.

"How can you stop your vassals from betraying their allegiance?" he asked after a moment.

"Without putting a few of their heads on the outer walls as a warning to them?" Christian mused. "I am not certain. -But if I do move against a vassal who does not *clearly* seem guilty of treason, I risk further estranging my vassals."

"Further estranging them?"

"Since I came to the throne, I have made many mistakes. Besides depending totally upon my advisers to rule, the most grievous was the estranging of my vassals, -and I accomplished it without even raising their taxes.

"My father was a popular king. He feasted and reveled with his vassals and generously rewarded their loyalty with gifts, visits, appointments and lands. He taxed them lightly and avoided war which vassals always find costly. His Court was a large, extravagant, lascivious mob that he loved and that loved him.

"When I came to the throne, I was not interested in Speyron's noble families! The ones I knew I did not care for. Almost immediately after their oath of allegiance, I disbanded the Court and withdrew from them. Dewain, Grey, and Olbert are the only ones left of the old entourage.

"I neither visited my vassals, nor supported them. In truth, I cared not what they did, or even if they slew each other in petty feuds, as long as they paid their taxes and left me alone. I allowed conflicts between them to escalate, rather than personally intervene and encourage them to put aside their differences. It never occurred to me that I would *need* their support in time. Nor did I foresee that my indifference would fragment the kingdom.

"Fragment, it has, and now it can be easily conquered. Vassals sworn to serve me, now desperate for self-preservation, are making alliances with each other -and possibly with foreigners. And every alliance they make could jeopardize my throne.

"If they withhold the support they owe me, my crown is lost. Yet some of them, no doubt, will remain true to their oaths for honor's sake, no matter what new alliance they make, no matter what cost to their lives and lands. Unfortunately, I just do not know which are the hounds and which are the wolves.

"The only way we will stand against Herryck is if all of my vassals put aside their ambitions and grievances and work together, but I do not know how to unite them."

The two young men sat in silence again.

"I shall pray that God gives you wisdom on how to unite the kingdom," Bennet said after a minute. "And if I may speak plainly, Sire, I believe I know of a way to increase your control of the kingdom."

At that moment, the cat pounced on its prey and snatched it up and then began to consume it.

"Christian, when Hunfred became Abbot some years ago, he ordered an accounting of the lands to be done every other year. He wanted to know exactly how many serfs he had, how many freemen lived on the lands, how many paupers came to get bread at the gate, et cetera. He wanted to know a count of every hen, sow, sheep, and cow on the lands, so that he could plan wisely for the coming winter.

"Perhaps you too could order a similar accounting of your lands. Get a count of your people, serfs, and freedmen. Get a record of your aldermen and their families, the boundaries of their lands, their possessions, the amount of livestock and type of commerce they support, and how many vassal knights they have and how many they house. Discover the marriage ties between their families and the amount of lands and wealth they already control. Surely this information would help you discover whose ambitions lie where and what is to be gained by a particular marriage alliance between families. Such far reaching information would not only help acquaint you with your people, but also would help you make more informed decisions, without having to rely so much upon the opinions of your advisers."

"An interesting idea. But who can I depend upon to take such an accounting? Few of my vassals are able to read and write. And of those that do, can I trust them to be honest?"

"Order it to be done, Sire, and the clerics in every parish to do it."

74

Paschal, Grey, and Olbert gathered around the edict that Dewain handed them, while Felix yawned, sat on the table top, and picked up his cup.

"What does it say?" he asked.

Grey read the declaration with a furrowed brow and frowned.

"Is he serious?" Paschal asked incredulously after a moment.

"He seems to be quite serious," Dewain replied.

"Aye, I have always found Christian to be so. Even as a child he hardly laughed-" Tate answered.

Dewain and Acrida smiled.

"What does it say?" Felix demanded.

"The King commands," Dewain told him, "that every alderman and vassal sworn to him shall give an accounting of their families, including their family lineage, their livestock, and holdings; further, they shall count the vassals sworn to them and their vassal's families and holdings, and everything else on their lands down to the last freeman, serf, and slave, both adult and child, '-to the last coin, vessel, shirt, sword, shield, horse, cow, sow, sheep, hen, and trinket.' The information is to be written down and sent to him within a fortnight."

Felix blinked.

"What? Is he serious?"

"Aye-" Dewain replied. "He has not only ordered the edict sent to every vassal, but to every cleric in every parish in Speyron, instructing them to do the count if the vassal is unable or unwilling. Any that willfully disobey this command will suffer dire consequences."

"This is an odd order for Christian," Felix complained.

"That monk is behind this, I wager," Paschal answered.

"At least it should not take you very long, My Dear," Dewain told Acrida with a smile, "and I will write it down for you."

"I, also?" Acrida asked, surprised.

"Aye."

"Why does he want to know?" she asked.

"Likely, he needs money and will raise our taxes," Dewain answered kindly.

"He will want a counting of everything on his own palace lands as well," Olbert added.

"Aye."

"I shall see to it."

"No need; I believe his Chaplain is seeing to it personally," Dewain told him.

"Ha!" Paschal sneered. "So he has *less* need of *you* as well, Olbert."

The elder adviser frowned but made no reply.

Grey raised his eyebrows and put the edict on the table.

"-Aye, 'tis a marvelous idea!" Paschal declared sarcastically. "We should not only take a count, but we should make two copies, one for Christian and one for Herryck!"

Olbert gave him a tired look.

"Do not speak so."

"Why not? Our kingdom will soon be at war, and rather than try to make an alliance with another kingdom, our King is hearing Mass and brooding over a dead woman! Now he orders us to take inventory of our holdings. Yet, it will be useful to know the amount of our present holdings so that we can see how much is to be *lost!*"

"We do not know that he is not trying to make other alliances," Olbert commented.

Paschal turned to Acrida.

"Even your possessions -what *little* you have. You and your family will go from being serfs to freemen to slaves! Who knows what kingdom you will finally reside in after you are sold a few times!"

Acrida paled.

"Let her be, Paschal," Dewain told him irritably.

"I am only speaking the truth-"

"Perhaps he intends to pay mercenaries," she replied, "with the holdings of young, rash aldermen who are out of favor."

Tate laughed out loud as Paschal glared at her.

"Paschal, now that you have seen the King's edict, you may return to your amusements," Olbert told him.

"Aye, the only sensible thing I have heard today," the redhead replied sourly.

With a nod to Felix, the youths left the chamber.

"Well, there is work to be done," Grey muttered and left the Chancellor's office.

Olbert took his leave as well, leaving Dewain with Acrida and Tate.

"Grey was unusually quiet," Acrida commented.

"No doubt thinking of all the accounting ahead of him," Dewain said. "-That and the King is proving more resourceful than any of us expected."

"The King smells a rat-" Tate surmised, picking up the cup Felix left behind and filling it again with wine.

"Aye," Dewain agreed, "but he is using a different approach to discover it. Paschal is correct. The Chaplain has the King's ear and is definitely behind this counting."

"Aye, but it is even more than that," Tate said, draining the cup. "With this edict, our young, boy-king announces he is finally ready to rule."

75

Olbert looked about the sparse chamber of the King's new study. The chambers King Godewyn had built and occupied had an eastward view, and were plain and smaller than the chambers in the Romani palace. The sole adornment was an uncomplicated painting of a kneeling saint at prayer that had been painted long ago on one of the walls.

Christian seemed to prefer the chambers' simplicity. He would not even suffer a tapestry to be hung on the remaining bare walls for either decoration or warmth. A small hearth, a table, and three cushioned chairs and a tall window with a modest wooden shutter was all that was in this chamber. Not even a rug covered the stone floor.

The King's bedchamber which joined the room was equally plain. There were neither tapestries nor rugs. The King's bed alone had any embellishment to it, for the curtains that hung about its sides were bright purple.

Christian sat at the table near the open window, making notes as he studied the map of the kingdom that was spread out before him. There were stacks of documents around him. Olbert glanced at one parchment that was off by itself. It was a drawing of the current palace and grounds, but it included a plan of a cathedral. The cathedral was actually larger than the palace, and with its current, intended size and prominent location, a large section of the wall that surrounded the palace would have to be moved to accommodate it.

The King looked up then.

"Olbert-. We did not hear you enter."

The Steward bowed briefly and smiled.

"Forgive the intrusion, Sire. There is a matter I wish to discuss with you, but if this is an inopportune time, I will come again."

"'Tis well. We have business with you also."

Christian gestured to an empty chair across from him at the table.

"Are your new chambers to your liking, Your Grace?" Olbert asked, sitting down.

"Very much so," he replied.

He shuffled through the pile of papers near him, and pulled one from the stack.

"This is an accounting of the Royal Seer's possessions submitted by Lord Dewain," he explained to Olbert.

Then he began to read the document.

"'Acrida, whose baptismal name is Cinsara, originally born a serf on Lord Huntingdon's lands to-' et cetera, et cetera- '...recently freed from the lands and given a position as sibyl and counselor to King Christian in the year of our Lord Eight Hundred Eighty-two,' et cetera.

"'She possesses two woolen gowns, one given to her by the wife of Lord Dewain, with a woolen headrail, a woolen cloak, and a comb. The other woolen gown and also a woolen undertunic and another headrail with a pair of worn slippers were given her by the wife of the steward of Lord Van Necht."

Christian looked up at the Royal Steward.

"What is this?"

"Sire?"

"When you had Us appoint her counselor, We seem to recall that We promised her much more than some worn, woolen clothes and a comb. It is a wonder she has not nagged the royal ear night and day about it."

Olbert smiled.

"You *have* given her chambers in the advisor's wing as she wanted?"

"-Um, no, Sire."

Christian looked at him blankly.

"Why not?"

"Well, Your Grace, as you will recall, she was appointed the same day as the uprising, and no arrangements were officially made-"

"Not officially, but as Steward to the King and the Royal Household, We thought *you* would have fulfilled at least some of Our obligations by now. -Did anyone notify Huntingdon that she and her family have been freed from his lands?"

"I am not certain whether Dewain wrote to him or not, My Lord."

Christian frowned.

"Find out."

"Aye, Sire."

"Where has she been staying these past days?"

"Since her return to the palace, she has slept in Dewain's sitting rooms, off his chambers. She has spent a great amount of time at his lands of late and seems quite happy-"

"No, that will not do. She demanded chambers of her own, and *We* agreed that she would have them."

"I shall give her chambers, Sire, but the ones that are available are near Paschal's, and I hesitate to put the two of them near each other.-"

"Give them to her. Move Paschal to my old chambers. That should appease him."

Olbert nodded, not a little surprised.

"Also, order her a livery. She will have gowns, more than *two*, of the richest cloth, made by the best tailor, and headrails and undertunics of fine linen. Get her a trunk to carry them in. Order her a pair of leather boots, at least calf high and a good, heavy cloak. She will have a silver comb beset with jewels. -Does she have a servant?"

Olbert, clearly astonished, shook his head.

"Get her one. She will need a maid to get her in and out of those gowns."

Olbert nodded.

"Anything more, Sire?"

"Aye, get her anything else you feel befits the lofty position of King's Counselor and Seer."

"I will see it is all done, Your Grace," Olbert promised.

"Good," he said, setting aside the parchment and looking back at the map. "Now, Olbert, what business did you wish to discuss?"

Olbert had to think for a moment to remember what it was.

"Aye, I have a recommendation for a wife for Your Grace."

Christian looked up.

"I have been pondering the potential of the match for some time," Olbert continued, "and I believe it is our best option."

"Why did you not bring it to Us before?"

"Grey was set upon his choice. Apparently, he had been working on the alliance with Fors for months. And my recommendation, I fear, you will take exception with."

"What kingdom does she hail from? Do they offer troops?" he asked, looking back at the map.

"She will bring no more troops, I fear, than we already have at our disposal. However, if you do not take her for wife, and another does, I fear we could lose a third of the troops that we command."

Christian looked up at him again.

"I am not understanding you."

"I am speaking of your ward."

Christian blinked in surprise.

"Kaith? Are you mad, Olbert? She is but a child-"

"She will be twelve this spring, Sire."

"She is only eleven years!" he complained, getting up from the table. "She is too young to marry! She is hardly old enough to speak of husbands.- She is not yet of enough years to have a marriage arranged for her!"

"Sire, you know well daughters of royal bloodlines are betrothed very early, some even at birth."

Frowning, Christian crossed his arms and looked out his window at the icy view.

"Sire, I know how fond you are of your ward. And I know you have been reluctant to even consider matches for her. -It was difficult for me to arrange matches for my own daughters. -But Kaithryn is practically twelve, Sire, and, by Church Law, of marital age. As long as she remains your ward, you hold her lands in trust. Moneys, knights, supplies and provisions, and troops from her lands are all at your disposal.

"If by chance, Herryck captured her, he could easily have one of his men marry her and then all of those assets would be at Herryck's disposal, not to mention a legitimate claim to the throne."

Christian continued to frown as he listened to Olbert's reasoning.

"More than a third of the kingdom are lands you hold in trust for the Lady Kaithryn," he told him, pointing to a section on the map. "*She* is your most indispensable vassal. If we were to lose those lands and assets, Speyron would likely fall."

Christian glanced toward the map on the table, covering his mouth with his hand.

"Aside from the lands, there are clear benefits of a marriage alliance with your cousin," Olbert continued in his soothing tone. "Lady Kaithryn's family was always held in high esteem throughout the kingdom, and marriage to her would prove popular with the people. A uniting of your bloodlines would unite Speyron as well. Some, no doubt, would see your marriage as a restoration of your Great Grandfather's reign, from which you are both descended."

Christian made no reply. He slowly turned and looked back out the window at the snow.

"If you do settle upon your cousin," the Steward added, "it would be wise, Sire, to have her crowned -so that if something were to happen- the question of succession would already be settled."

There was a long, uncomfortable silence before Christian finally spoke.

"I think of her as my little sister," he said quietly. "How can I think of her as wife?"

"Perhaps in time you will be able to, My King, for, in truth, your blood is so distant that a dispensation is not even required from the Pope."

76

Lord Olbert sat in the Abbess's office, his hands clasped neatly in his lap, his brilliant green colors of office in striking contrast to the nun's black habit.

The door to the office opened abruptly then, and the Royal Steward smiled as the Lady Kaithryn entered, her long, blond hair hanging loose down her back. The child, a delighted smile on her face, curtsied to the silver-haired, old man who had risen from his chair and bowed to her simultaneously. Then she hugged him.

"Oh, My Lord! I have missed you so much! And everyone at Court!"

"It is fine to see you, Lady Kaithryn, and in good health," the Steward said pleasantly, noting the girl's beaming face. "How much you have grown since I last saw you!"

The young girl laughed.

"Aye, my maid has had to let out my gowns! How fares my cousin?"

"He is well, My Lady."

"Is he back at his palace now?"

"Indeed he is. -Have the sisters treated you well?"

"Aye, My Lord. They keep all of us girls very busy!"

"I am glad to hear it," Olbert answered warmly.

He glanced over at the Abbess whose smile was equally telling. Clearly Lady Kaithryn had endeared herself to the nuns.

He gestured then toward the chair beside his in front of the Abbess's desk. When she had sat down, he pulled his seat a bit nearer and sat down as well.

"Lady Kaithryn, I have very exciting news."

"Tell me!"

The girl's smile, enthusiasm, and happy disposition not only reminded Olbert of his own daughters years ago, but also of Kaithryn's parents whom he had admired immensely.

"Well, My Dear, what think you of marriage?"

"I expect it comes to us all in time, does it not, My Lord?"

"Indeed. And is it your wish to marry when the time comes?"

"Aye, My Lord, I wish one day to call some man husband and to have children and a family of my own."

Olbert smiled and nodded.

"Your cousin has arranged a match for you, My Lady."

Kaithryn's face and eyes lit up with surprise, and she uttered a scream of delight.

"I am going to marry!" she exclaimed. "I can not wait to tell the girls!"

She was on her feet hugging Lord Olbert, and then she hurried around the desk and hugged the Abbess. Olbert and the Abbess smiled at her.

"Do I know him? When shall I meet him? My friend, Berget, is matched, and she has never met her betrothed. This is so exciting! Pray, Lord Olbert, tell me about him!" she said ecstatically, sitting in the chair once more.

The Steward smiled and was about to reply when she interrupted him again.

"No, first, tell me when I shall wed. When I am fourteen years? Felda, another girl here, is to leave next summer to wed, when she is fourteen and no later."

"Well," Olbert replied with a little laugh, "we would not have you wait so long, My Lady."

"When then?" she asked, an eager grin on her face.

"We had thought- next week."

"Next week?" Kaithryn repeated, quite astounded.

The look on the Abbess's face held equal surprise.

Olbert watched as the smile faded from Kaithryn's face.

"Are you well, My Lady?" Olbert asked in a reassuring voice.

"Aye," was Kaithryn's weak reply, the color draining from her features. "Tell me, who is he? Where are his lands? -Is he a lord?"

Olbert patted her pale hand and smiled soothingly at her.

"He is a king, My Lady, and you will be his queen."

"A king? Not even a prince?" she answered numbly. "And I- a queen? -It is such a great honor."

She was silent and frowned at the floor.

After a moment, she swallowed and asked, "Is - is he very old?"

"He is four and twenty, My Lady."

"That is old, but not very old," Kaithryn said, nodding to the floor.

Olbert smiled, but watched as the girl's face became troubled again.

"But to leave next week- and to never see my home again-"

"Well-"

"Is he handsome, or do you know, Lord Olbert?" Kaithryn interrupted again.

Olbert smiled.

"I believe he is, My Lady."

Kaithryn seemed reassured at this, but the sad look on her face remained.

"Even so, My Lord, I will be sorry to leave Speyron and you and my cousin-"

"My Lady, 'tis your cousin who seeks your hand in marriage."

"Christian?! Christian wants *me* to be his queen?" she stammered, her eyes wide with surprise.

The smile of joy on the girl's face was inescapable.

"Aye, My Lady."

"I can scarcely believe it!" she said. "Only in my dreams did I ever hope-"

Olbert smiled.

"But why does he want to marry me, My Lord?" she suddenly asked, her heart fluttering like a bird in her chest. "He could have any woman in the world! Any woman in the world would be lucky and happy to call him husband-"

"Does that include you, My Lady? Would you count yourself lucky and happy to marry him?"

"I fear I would die of joy before the wedding day ever arrived! -But why me?"

"Because," Olbert said with a sincere smile, "he loves you, My Lady."

"Oh-" Kaithryn beamed and blushed and looked at the floor again.

"So, My Lady, what shall I tell him? If you will not have him, I can easily send him word."

"No! Lord Olbert, before when you spoke of me being queen and marrying a man so much older than myself, and so soon, I was unsure. But you only had to speak my dear cousin's name to make it right again. I love Christian more than anyone in the world, and I am only truly happy when I am with him.

"Gladly I will be his wife! It will make me the happiest girl in the world! Oh, Lord Olbert, tell him 'Aye, a hundred fold!'"

The young girl embraced the old adviser then, laughing in delight.

"I am so glad, My Lady," Lord Olbert whispered. "Truly, King Christian is the luckiest man alive to have you for wife."

Lady Kaithryn hurried around the desk and hugged the Abbess again.

"If there is nothing else, I should like to go and give the news to my friends," she said eagerly.

Smiling, Lord Olbert stood up and bowed.

Lady Kaithryn curtsied quickly to him and the Abbess and then ran out the door, yelling excitedly, "Wait until Felda and Berget hear!"

Then she was gone.

77

" Now, Lady Kaithryn, you must tie two or three long coverlets around your shoulders and practice walking around in them," the royal tailor told her.

Kaithryn was smiling radiantly as her hands smoothed the soft, purple, velvet cloth of the gown she was trying on.

"Stand up straight, My Lady."

The girl complied, standing up straight before the long mirror as the tailor on his knees before her continued to mark the hem of the gown.

"'Tis such a beautiful gown. You will look so beautiful, My Lady," her maidservant told her.

"Aye, I wish my cousin were here to see it."

"He will see it when it is finished," another maid replied. "That will be soon enough."

The tailor cleared his throat.

"My Lady, you must practice walking with the coverlets, for your train will be quite heavy and very long. And you will want your posture to be perfect for the coronation."

"I understand," Kaithryn answered.

The royal tailor stood back up and helped the future queen step out of the velvet gown that had only been tacked together temporarily.

"Why can I not practice with the train itself?"

"Even now it is being embroidered by a group of very talented women. I think you will find their work most becoming."

Kaithryn smiled and smoothed her silk undertunic before removing it and putting on her plain linen one again.

"That is all we need at present," the tailor told her.

He gestured toward the woman who waited in her undertunic in the corner.

"Acrida, the King has commissioned us to make your gowns. Do you have a color preference?"

Acrida smiled, but answered in the negative.

"Well, let me see-" he said, motioning to his assistants.

The tailor's assistants approached and held a large piece of green fabric up to her face, studying her complexion. After a moment, they held up a different piece of fabric, as the tailor and Acrida, observing through the mirror, studied the rich blue color of the fabric. Acrida was mesmerized momentarily at the beauty reflected by the mirror and wondered if it was not all a dream.

"To be honest, each color suits your complexion well," one of the assistants commented.

"Aye, but the blue brings out her eyes-"

Everyone in the chamber looked to the door to see who had intruded. The gray-haired fool stood just inside the chamber, assessing the situation with silver goblet in hand.

"What are you doing here? This is a private fitting!" the tailor complained. "Call someone!" the tailor ordered his assistant indignantly.

"I am only here to supervise. Let not my presence disturb thy work, Good Man. Pray, commence with the measurements," Tate replied dryly as he gestured with his cup.

Kaithryn immediately went up to the old man and standing on her tip toes, kissed him on the cheek.

"Uncle, you have found me. I hoped you would not go riding without me."

"No chance of that, Dear Kaith," Tate replied, putting his cup down and grabbing the half-clad girl and spinning her around him. "Do you think the stable boys could be coaxed to give a fool a horse without an accompanying smile from a lovely, noble lady?"

Kaithryn laughed.

"Do you know this man, My Lady?" the tailor inquired hesitantly, his assistant pausing at the door.

"Aye, he is my uncle," she giggled.

"Thine uncle? How extraordinary-" the tailor commented skeptically, noting the man's shabby, drab, common clothes with their several patches.

Seeing how Kaithryn was dancing about with the old man and was paying no heed to the concerns of the clothier, Acrida intervened.

"Never you mind him, Good Tailor. That is Tate, King Filberte's old Fool. He is always to be found where he should not be," Acrida said with her hands on her hips, feigning reproach.

"Aye, you may try to shut him out, but he will only knock upon the door until you let him in!" Kaithryn's maid said.

"Much to a woman's delight and a man's chagrin!" the other maid jested.

The maidservants cackled wickedly. The tailor raised his eyebrows, but took Acrida at her word. His assistant returned to Acrida's side and began gathering her measurements.

"Uncle, did you see my ring?"

"My Dear Child, one would have to blind *not* to see it," he replied.

Kaithryn giggled.

"Aye, I had my choice from a chest of rings, and I picked the one with the biggest stone."

"'Tis a beautiful ruby. Thou hast selected well."

"So has the King-" her maid answered.

"Uncle, I have decided that you should give me away at the wedding, for there is no one else. My father is dead."

"I cannot give you away, My Lady," Tate protested. "No man could who knew your worth. Let the King give you away, for lest he be a fool, he shall take you right back again."

"Then the King must be wise, for he shall take her and never part with her," her maid answered.

"Well, and what color?" the tailor asked Acrida again.

"The blue will be well for the coronation feast," Acrida answered.

"And the other gowns?"

Acrida smiled and shrugged.

"Make one of each color."

"Very good," the tailor nodded, then turned to the girl again. "The next time I will see you will be on your coronation day, My Lady. Until then- practice, practice, practice!"

The tailor and his assistants gathered up their supplies, bowed to Lady Kaithryn, and left the chamber. Acrida's maid put the brown, worn, woolen gown over the counselor's head, but Acrida tied up the front herself, while Kaithryn's maid finished dressing the young lady. Tate went and sat on a bench across from them, picked up his cup again, and watched as the maidservant began to lace up the girl's gown in the back.

"Uncle, do you miss thy position as the King's Fool?" Lady Kaithryn asked.

"Aye, My Lady," Tate replied, "'twas an honest living."

The two serving women both raised their eyebrows and chuckled. Tate smiled at them.

"Were you in the service of my kinsman, King Filberte, for a long time?"

"Aye, his entire reign. I met him when he was prince, long before he came to the throne. He and his companions were always out looking for sport, much to his father's discomfiture. When we first met, he was so impressed by my wit, and his other companions so sorely lacking it, that he bade me to keep him company as well."

"And where did he meet you?"

Tate hesitated and smiled as he searched for an appropriate response, until the lady's serving woman made answer for him.

"I believe it was in the palace village- in a stew-house, was it not, Tate?" she said teasingly.

Acrida raised her eyebrows.

Tate smiled daringly at the woman.

"Indeed, it was. As a youth, Filberte was often to be found at a *stew-house,* sampling the *raw meat.*"

"Raw meat?" Kaithryn gasped. "Are you in earnest? I never would have guessed King Filberte had such a barbaric preference with all the elaborate dishes that are served at the royal table!"

Tate smiled, and the older women snickered.

"So, because he admired your wits, when Filberte became king, he made you his fool," Kaith surmised, moving to stand beside Tate.

"Aye, My Lady."

"Were your wits the only cause?"

Tate smiled again.

"Well, we had interests in common," he admitted.

"Similar interests? Like what?"

He shrugged.

"Hunting- and the like."

Again the women were giggling wickedly.

"Hunting-" Lady Kaithryn echoed, glancing questioningly at the women.

"Aye, we pursued a hind or two together on many occasions."

Again the women were tittering in laughter. Acrida was smiling at the fool with raised eyebrows.

"What is so funny?" Kaithryn asked in annoyance.

When she did not receive an answer from them, she turned her attention back to the old man.

"Why did Christian not appoint you his fool as well? He is fond of hunting as well as hawking."

"Indeed he is!" Tate answered, shrugging his shoulders. "At the time, I suspected that he himself had already filled the position of fool, My Lady."

Acrida snorted and covered her mouth while the servants smiled behind their hands. Kaithryn glanced at them, not seeing the joke.

"I do not understand you rightly," she said. "It seems odd that Christian did not give thought to how you would survive without your position and income. Did no one approach him on your behalf?"

"No, My Lady. But at the time King Christian did not seem to desire a large court about him," Tate answered sweetly, "for he dismissed most of Filberte's courtiers when he came to the throne."

"Hmm-" Lady Kaithryn mused.

The chamber grew quiet then. Tate glanced at Acrida, who was staring off into space.

"I wish Christian were here," Kaith complained. "Why did he go visit his vassals now? If he had waited but a day, I would have been back from the convent and could have gone with him."

"No doubt he knew you would be too busy preparing for the coronation to go with him," her maid told her. "And remember what the sisters told you, My Lady: You must learn to be patient. You will see him in a few days."

Kaithryn nodded, satisfied by this information. She went over to the mirror and began to gather up her long, golden blond hair. She rolled it into a large bun and held it on top of her head, examining herself in the mirror.

"I can hardly believe that I will be married in just a few days. I wonder if it will feel much different."

Tate skewed his lips, raised his eyebrows, and was about to make reply when he was suddenly jabbed in the ribs by the lady's maid and given a stern glance. Obediently, he remained silent with the rest.

"How do I look, Tate?"

"Beautiful, My Lady."

"Do you think my cousin will find me pleasing?"

"Has he not always found you so?"

"Aye, but that is not what I mean.-"

"Your ladyship will make a beautiful bride," the maid told her lovingly.

Lady Kaithryn smiled.

"I hope so, but what I mean to ask is whether you think Christian will find me pleasing as a *wife*?"

"No one can speak for the King, My Lady," Tate began, "but if you were my wife, I would find you pleasing, as I am sure most any man would."

Kaithryn smiled at this and dropping her hair, turned and went over and hugged the old man. She kissed him on the cheek.

"Uncle, if you were my bridegroom, I would cover you with kisses all the time."

Tate laughed.

"You will make a bonnie wife indeed, My Lady!"

The servants laughed.

"But will I make a good *queen*?" she asked turning back to the mirror. "What will I do? How will I spend my days?"

"Your days will be spent on your feet, and your nights on your b-"

"-You will be as busy as any other married woman," her maid cut in, glaring at the old man.

"Busier!" said the other servant.

"Doing what? What does a queen do?"

"You will run the palace, My Lady, and oversee the servants," her maid answered.

"You will entertain guests who come to the palace," the other added.

"You will organize feasts and order the King's wardrobe."

"You will tell the cooks what to cook and the minstrels what to play."

"You will keep the King informed of what is happening at the palace, what gossip you overhear, and such."

"Of course, you will oversee the nursery, when you bear the King's children," the other servant answered.

"Aye," replied the maid, "and you will supervise the education of his vassals' children when they are sent to the palace as pages."

"Is that all?"

"Embroidery," her maid added. "In her spare time, a queen is expected to sew fine embroidery, so that her husband may give it for gifts."

"Embroidery? Indeed, I will have to practice. But is there nothing more?"

"More?" the maid answered in exasperation. "Do you wish for more?"

"No, -but is there nothing more expected of a queen?"

The fool came up behind her and looked into the mirror with her and stroked the girl's long, loose, golden hair.

"Time will tell, My Lady," he told her simply.

Acrida did not hear this idle chit chat. She was far away, once again on the hillside with Van Necht, her breath being whisked away from her as he held her and kissed her again in her memory. She had relived that moment a hundred fold, for, unbidden, his image came to her no matter where she was or what she was doing.

"She is smitten-."

"Has she a secret love? Who is it?" Kaithryn asked with excitement.

"Well, I do not know for certain, but I suspect that it is none other than Lord Van Necht."

At the mention of his name, Acrida was suddenly back to the moment. She blushed with embarrassment as she observed that Tate and Lady Kaithryn were indeed talking about her. Even the maids were smiling at her. Acrida flushed with self-consciousness again.

"Does he ever write to you?" the young lady was asking her excitedly.

"No, My Lady," Acrida answered weakly.

"Do you write to him?"

"Little good that would do," Tate cut in, "for Van Necht can neither read nor write."

"Can he not?"

"No, Lady, nor any of us present, except for you."

Lady Kaithryn looked at them all curiously.

"Well, I suppose you could tell me what you wanted to say, and I could write it down. And Van Necht's cleric could read it to him."

Tate laughed.

The women looked at him.

"I was just thinking how Lord Van Necht might respond to soft words of love being read to him by his parish priest," Tate explained, chuckling again. "It might be more than the warlord could endure!"

The serving women were all laughing out loud, and Acrida cringed internally. She curtsied quickly to the child and hurried for the door to escape.

"Now, now, do not leave us, Acrida!" Tate told her hastily. "We will keep thy secret."

"Aye, we will!" Lady Kaithryn agreed.

Acrida paused and frowned.

"You demean a loyal vassal of the King with such talk, My Lady. The lord has no interest beyond courtesy in one such as me, and he would be much aggrieved to find his honorable name tainted with such gossip."

Then she curtsied again and quickly departed the chamber. Tate raised his eyebrows, regarding her curiously.

78

$\mathfrak{I}$t was dusk when the King of Speyron entered the main gate of St. Benedict's Abbey escorted by his Royal Chaplain and a group of knights and servants. The abbey and church was the largest in Speyron; it was on the main road to Roma, and it regularly housed multitudes of pilgrims year round. Already its guesthouses were filled to capacity with noble families and knights who had arrived a day early for the festivities celebrating the coronation of the queen.

The abbey grounds were teeming with activity as servants scurried about on errands from their noble masters and squires saw to their knights' horses and tack. Groups of knights stood together talking and laughing as they waited for word that the food was ready to be served in the guesthouse hall.

As Christian dismounted his white charger, a monk met him and bowed.

"Welcome to St. Benedict's Abbey, Your Grace."

"Thank you, Brother."

"And you also, Brother," the monk said to Bennet.

Then the monk turned and welcomed the King's escorts and servants.

"Sire, you have arrived at last!" came a familiar voice.

Christian turned to see Lord Olbert approach him and bow.

"We were expecting you earlier," the adviser said.

"We had a late start," Christian replied.

"How was your journey?"

"It proved very instructive. -Is everything prepared for tomorrow?"

"Aye, Sire. All is prepared."

"Did Kaith make her confession?"

"Aye, Sire. She went this morning to the abbey's confessor and then heard Mass."

Christian nodded.

The abbey servants arrived then and took charge of the horses, leading them away to the stables.

"Is Bishop Gildas here?" Christian asked.

"He is, Sire," Olbert smiled. "Do you require an audience with him?"

"No," Christian answered, relieved.

"Is Abbot Hunfred here?" Bennet asked hopefully.

"Alas, no, Brother. He sent word that the new snows make the journey too slow and perilous. He wrote that you and the King remain in their constant prayers, as well as the Lady Kaithryn."

Lords Grey and Paschal approached then and bowed to the King.

"What word?" Christian asked.

Lord Grey handed him a scroll.

"Herryck's forces remain at Cadell and show no signs of preparing to advance," Grey told him. "Furthermore, my spies tell me it looks like it will snow again."

Christian took the parchment, unrolled it, and looked it over.

"You have many invitations to sup, Sire," Olbert told him. "The Abbot of St. Benedict's has invited you and the Chaplain to dine with him and Bishop Gildas at the Abbot's table. Several of your vassals have extended invitations as well. Your cousin also has been asking after you regularly, Sire," Olbert said, "and wishes to know if you will sup with her."

Christian glanced up from the parchment.

"You may send word to the Abbot that We will attend shortly. Send Kaith word that We have arrived and will see her tomorrow. Make Our excuses to the rest."

"As you wish, Your Grace."

"We will, however, see Van Necht now."

"He has not arrived as of yet, Sire. He has sent word, however, that although he is delayed, he brings two hundred spirited souls, among them more than sixty knights, all eager for battle. He will be here by the morrow."

"Well and good," Grey said. "At the moment, there are few more men we can provide him."

"It is an impressive force camped outside the walls," Bennet said.

"The count is nearly six hundred strong, and of that, two hundred twenty are knight and horse, waiting for you to take charge of them. Fifty knights are from this very abbey," Grey reported.

The five men walked toward the abbey guesthouses where they were met by the hospitaler who bowed and greeted the King warmly.

"Sire, I will show you to your chambers," the little monk began.

"Thank you, Brother."

The hospitaler smiled and gestured for the King to follow him.

Christian looked at Grey and Paschal.

"Go be with your families. We will see you both on the morrow."

The two men bowed and left the King.

"Shall I attend you, Sire?" Olbert asked.

"Aye."

The monk led the King, Lord Olbert, the Chaplain, the King's valet and bodyguards and the servants carrying the chests of the King's wardrobe to the most central guesthouse. Entering the building, he took them up the stairs to the chamber that had been prepared. He opened the door and bowed as the King and his entourage entered.

The chamber was impressively large; and it was warm from the heat from the burning hearths on the ground floor. Numerous candles burned in the chamber, giving a soothing feel to the room. There were two large shuttered windows. On one side of the chamber, a large bed with thick, scarlet curtains stood. On the other side was a table and four chairs, a pitcher of wine and several golden goblets.

Cedd removed the heavy cloak from the King's shoulders and shook the snow off of it.

Christian went to the table and picked up one of the bejeweled chalices and examined it with curiosity, then glanced at Bennet who only smiled and shrugged. Then the King poured the wine, offering a drink to the others.

"A health-" Olbert began.

Christian smiled mildly and raised his goblet with the rest.

"To a productive alliance and a swift victory," Olbert said and then tasted the wine.

"Excellent-" he commented.

Bennet nodded in agreement.

Christian, musing silently, did not drink, his face serious as he looked at the dark red of the wine in his goblet. After a long moment, as if finally coming to some decision, he gulped down his entire cup rapidly.

The bodyguards, servants, and Cedd finished their cups and placed them quietly on the table again. Then they withdrew to the corners of the chamber where their presence would not be noticed.

King Christian sat in one of the chairs then and looked into the flickering light of the candles on the table, turning his chalice slowly around and around in his hands, meditatively. Olbert and Bennet took off their cloaks and sat down as well, watching the young king in silence. No one said anything for a long time.

"Lord Steward, did you look into that matter as I requested?" Christian suddenly asked, still looking at the flame.

Olbert did not reply at first; he had been so busy, he wondered exactly which matter Christian was referring to.

"Regarding my cousin-"

Olbert thought for a moment.

"Oh, did I talk to her maid? Aye, I did."

"And?"

"She says Lady Kaithryn knows nothing, of course. There is no point to burdening a child with information she will have no use for until marriage."

"What of the nuns? Would they have told-"

"Absolutely not!"

Christian nodded.

"Though Lady Kaithryn herself did ask me something."

Christian's eyes moved to the Steward's face.

"She said her grandmother told her many years ago that when a couple married, God gave the woman a baby. What your cousin wanted to know was how God decided to give a boy or a girl."

Bennet smiled.

"And what did you tell her?" he asked.

"The truth, Brother. I told her I did not know."

The men smiled.

"You *did* instruct all those around my cousin to continue her ignorance?"

"Aye, Your Grace. But would you not prefer that her maid prepare her- perhaps after the feast- for-"

"No," Christian interrupted. "Leave it to me. -I would not have her apprehensive."

"As you wish."

The three men sat in silence a while longer, and then Lord Olbert took his leave, wishing the King a good night's rest.

After he had departed, Bennet rose from his chair.

"Your Grace, I will take my leave so you may rest before we sup."

"Must you?"

Bennet smiled.

"I will stay if you wish. I simply thought that on the eve of your marriage you might want some time to yourself- for prayer or meditation. And this dinner with the Abbot and Bishop Gildas could last long into the night."

Christian did not reply as his eyes moved from his friend back to the light of the candle, his face marred with weariness and gravity.

"Your Grace, are you well?" Bennet asked hesitantly.

Christian did not reply.

"If I may speak boldly, Christian," Bennet said *in Gaulian* after a moment, choosing his words carefully, *"you* seem *apprehensive* about this marriage."

Christian sighed, frowned, and looked away. He refilled his cup with wine and stared again at the color.

"It is not what I wanted for either of us," he explained at last in Gaulian. "But what must be done, must be done. I have always understood what marriage would be for me and what it had been for my parents and for the vassals of my kingdom who marry to unite their lands. -But understanding it does not make it more *palatable.*"

"Do you not like Lady Kaithryn?"

"I love her well."

"Was there someone else you preferred to marry? One of your concubines, perhaps?"

Christian smirked.

"No."

"What troubles thee then?"

Christian sighed again.

"I have always thought of Kaith as a little sister- to be protected and spoiled. When her parents died, it was easy for me to be her guardian and she- my ward. It seems strange now to call her *wife*."

"I see."

"But that is not all. I wanted better for her. I wanted a man of good character, impeccable honor, and high ideals for her, not just someone of noble blood.

"-I would have never considered a match for her like the one I am making. I would never have betrothed her to a man with an infamous past, to a man with dubious honor, and certainly not in a kingdom threatened with eminent invasion," Christian frowned. "I would have laughed at such a proposal! I would have been offended by it!" he said, clenching his fist.

Bennet raised his eyebrows.

The King opened his fist quickly.

"I do not want to be my cousin's downfall," he continued quietly. "I fear I shall *fail* her."

Bennet smiled sympathetically.

"Christian, you are not the man you once were. Although you must live with the consequences of your wrongful deeds, find comfort in the knowledge that in the future your honor and reputation will be eventually mended through the acts of your changed heart. And although your cousin may marry a man with sullied honor in a time of turmoil, at least she marries a man whom has repented of his past, amended his ways, and returned to the Faith- and whom is truly concerned with her well-being and holds her best interests at heart. Can any woman hope for more when she marries?"

79

"Do you see her, Jenkyn?" Lord Dewain asked.

"Not yet," the lad replied.

Balancing on the top edge of a tall pedestal that bore a statue of a saint, Dewain's eldest son loomed over the slow moving crowd inside the narthex.

"Perhaps she is lost," Dewain's youngest son answered. "Mother, I do not like this tunic. It is too tight."

"You look precious, and you only have to wear it today," Dewain's wife smiled as she stroked the boy's dark, curly hair.

"It did not fit me any better when I wore it," his other brother answered.

"How can Acrida be lost?" their sister asked. "There is only one church at the abbey, and with all of these people coming here, there is nothing more for her to do but to follow the person in front of her."

"Dewaina, mind your tongue," her father warned.

The girl frowned.

Seeing Dewain and Olbert standing near the door of the church, Paschal pushed his way through the throng of people towards them. The redheaded youth wore a tunic and braes of muted gold, with extensive embroidered ivy about the neck and cuffs.

"Olbert, Dewain," Paschal greeted, "I thought that you would have been inside by now."

The noblemen exchanged pleasantries, and Paschal was introduced to Dewain's wife and four children and Olbert's son and daughter-in-law, all dressed in their finest clothes and jewels.

"Where is your wife, Olbert?" Paschal asked. "She did come?"

"Aye, she will be along directly," the Royal Steward smiled pleasantly.

"Everyone else is here," Paschal continued. "Every noble, that is, who could get here on such short notice."

"Have you seen the large gathering of peasants outside, My Lord?" the lad hanging from the statue asked excitedly. "They await the toll of the bells that will signal that Speyron at last has a new queen!"

Paschal snorted.

"I am certain they will be as glad to get a crust of bread from the monks as to hear news of a queen," he replied.

A short, pudgy, young girl in a crimson, velvet gown with similar embroidered ivy at the neck and on the cuff of her sleeves joined the group then. Paschal glanced at the smiling girl.

"My Lords, you remember my wife, Manton, daughter of Lord Manton," he said without enthusiasm.

"Of course," Olbert and Dewain said, bowing courteously to the girl as she curtsied.

The introductions began again for the wife of Paschal.

"What are you doing up there?" Lady Manton asked the youth wearing a deep green tunic with blue sleeves who was hanging from the statue.

"I am looking for Acrida, the King's Seer."

"She is lost," Dewain's youngest son began again.

"How can she be lost?" the daughter answered.

"Enough, Children!" Dewain scolded, while stepping aside to allow other noblemen to pass into the church.

"Indeed, how can a *seer* be lost?" Paschal asked sarcastically.

"Perhaps she is outside where all the other commoners have gathered-" the middle brother offered.

"If only that were true-" Paschal muttered.

Dewain smiled, then purposefully turned to Paschal's wife.

"Lady Manton, you must come to Court. Now that the King is marrying, the Queen will need companions."

"Indeed, I said the same to Paschal-" she answered.

Paschal glared at Dewain and cleared his throat.

"Manton, go in and reserve our place, lest there is no room."

"My father and brothers are there already."

"Then *go* and *join* them. I will be along directly," he told her.

"As you wish, Husband," she frowned.

"Aye, go with her," Olbert instructed his son and daughter-in-law.

The advisers watched Olbert's children and Lady Manton proceed into the church.

"You are a rich man indeed to have such a healthy and *fleshy* wife, Paschal," Olbert said. "Surely, she will bear you hearty children."

Paschal snorted and shook his head.

"She must be eating everything in the castle! I was amazed when I met her yesterday! I think she has near doubled in size since last I visited her!"

"Likely she will grow out of some of it," Olbert answered with a smile. "How old is she now?"

"Sixteen."

"Ah, just a bride," he smiled.

"Hardly that-" Paschal grumbled. "We have been married well over a year."

"There she is!" Jenkyn suddenly exclaimed.

The advisers looked in the direction the lad was pointing.

"We can not see her. What is she doing?" Dewain asked.

"She is looking at the wall."

Paschal sighed and threw up his hands.

Oblivious to the pushing and talking throng around her, Acrida was moving slowly through the narthex. Jenkyn watched as she paused to examine a large, brightly painted carving of St. Martin wearing half of a cloak. Then her attention went back to the painted wall that documented the history of the founding of the abbey.

"Call to her, Jenkyn!" Dewain instructed.

"Acrida! Ac-ri-da!"

Hearing her name, Acrida looked around and saw the boy way above the crowd waving to her with one hand while hanging onto the arm of a wooden statue with the other. She hurried toward him through the mob and found the advisers and Dewain's wife and children. She curtsied to them as Jenkyn leapt down from the statue.

"Acrida! At last, you are here!" Dewain said; then he paused and smiled.

"What took you so long?" the children asked.

"Were you lost?" the youngest son asked.

"Children!"

"My Dear," Dewain's wife said, kissing Acrida on the cheek, "you look lovely! You will surely catch some man's notice this day."

"Indeed," Olbert and Dewain were nodding in agreement.

Paschal stared speechless at the woman. Truly, he would not have known her. Acrida's new gown was of the softest, most expensive velvet and deep blue in color. The tailor had cut it exactly to her form, so that it draped gracefully about her curves, accentuating her breasts, hips and slender waist. Her headrail was of the whitest linen, and her blue eyes shown like gems.

Acrida looked away shyly, the unexpected attention from the group bringing a blush to her cheeks

"Forgive me, My Lords, for making you wait. I was just looking at the paintings and statues and forgot the time."

"Aye, this is your first visit to St. Benedict's. You will have to come see the church again tomorrow. There is so much to see," Olbert said.

"Father, we must hurry, else there will be no place for us!" Dewain's middle son was saying excitedly.

"Indeed, let us go," Dewain said, ushering the group through the nearby doors into the church.

The group just managed to clear the door before they had to stop and wait behind the crowd of people making their way to the baptismal font.

Acrida gasped at the sheer size and brightness of the church. The pale ceiling towered above them. It was so high, it could have been the floor of Heaven. Just below the ceiling was a line of windows that allowed sunlight to pour in. Several, large chandeliers with numerous burning candles hung from the ceiling, providing even more light.

The line of people slowly moved forward until finally the group reached the baptismal font. The font was of beige marble, and the edge had been etched with doves, and a large marble statue of an angel stood above it. They each dipped their finger into the water and crossed themselves. Then they proceeded down the long nave toward the chancel, passing numerous noblemen, knights, and families who were talking in groups.

"The monks are to expand this south side, are they not?" Dewain asked.

"Aye, I believe they are planning to build a few more chapels to house their newly acquired relics," Olbert replied.

"It is remarkable the number that they have already," Jenkyn said.

"Indeed, they have many benefactors who give generously to them," Dewain answered.

"And many visitors," Dewaina said.

"Aye," Jenkyn said, "and the more relics they have, the more visitors, and the more visitors, the more benefactors, and the more benefactors, the more relics-"

"Son-" Dewain chided, gesturing for quiet.

Oblivious to the conversation around her, Acrida was breathless as the view opened up before her. The entire fields of Brackenbach could have fit into the nave. There was a long line of tall pillars down both the left and right sides, beside which private chapel after private chapel had been built, each with an ornately carved tomb, candles, and a wall painted to depict some part of the life of Christ. Some chapels even had a small window of colored glass.

As they proceeded toward the chancel, she marveled at the immense rood screen before them. The top of the wooden screen was intricate lattice; the bottom were panels decorated with paintings of saints and angels; and the entire screen had been gilded with gold leaf.

The group paused beneath the rood and bowed to the Christ which the crucifix represented. With her heart pounding in her chest, Acrida was breathless with awe as she stared up at the life-size, painted, wooden statue of the Savior upon the cross that hung above her. The expression on his face was one of perfect serenity. The four points of the cross had been gilded as well. Under the cross were the smaller, painted statues of the Virgin and Saint John.

"Look, you can just see the organ!" Jenkyn exclaimed, pointing to the loft on top of the rood screen. "I have heard so much about it! It is much bigger and louder than the old one, and it plays quite low pitches. They say it has fifty pipes and several bellows."

"Two monks of this abbey are renowned for their playing. I wonder which will play today," his mother commented.

The group proceeded through the gap in the screen, but Dewain stopped when he realized that Acrida was no longer with them. He turned and went back into the nave. He found her still standing before the rood, her eyes affixed on the likeness of the Savior above her.

"Come on, My Dear," Dewain said.

Acrida looked at him, startled.

He smiled and gestured toward the choir.

"The King's Court is *up here*, so we can see."

He took her by the arm and escorted her through the screen into the chancel. To the left and right were the large choir stalls and directly in front on a raised step was the high altar and upon it, the tabernacle and its lone burning sanctuary lamp.

The altar was white marble, and it was covered with a beautiful, brocaded cloth. Near the tabernacle, a cross, a book, a crown of gold, a small container, and a pair of candelabras were set upon the altar. Beyond the altar on the wall was a large panel, gilded and painted with the enthroned Christ and his saints, including the Virgin and St. Benedict. Golden rays encircled their heads.

With her eyes locked on the burning candle and the golden, dove-shaped tabernacle that held the Real Presence of the Christ in the Reserved Species, Acrida swallowed and faltered in her steps. She did not belong here, she knew, so close to the holiest of sights, so close to God. She was not worthy.

Dewain smiled, and together, they bowed to the Real Presence and crossed themselves, then the Chancellor led the reluctant woman to the left into the choir stall where his two other daughters and Olbert's family waited on them. Lord Grey and his wife, his children and grandchildren were present as well. Felix was already there, as were several other high ranking nobles. Paschal had joined his wife and her parents and brothers and sister.

Acrida stood between Dewain and Jenkyn, her eyes on the intricate wall painting across from them above the other choir stalls of the Archangel Michael, triumphant sword in hand, his foot crushing the head of the beast.

Suddenly trumpets sounded. Acrida looked up and saw that atop the rood screen was a loft where several trumpeters were playing a fanfare. Other musicians were there as well and began to play.

As the music began, the crowd of spectators hushed. When the fanfare ended, the organist began to play.

"The new organ is very impressive!" Dewain called loudly to his son.

Jenkyn turned and nodded in excited agreement and was startled to see Acrida with tears running down her face.

Overwhelmed, Acrida wept. Never before had she heard such beautiful music. It was loud and vibrant, and it filled her very soul as much as it filled the entire cathedral.

The music played for a long while before the acolytes emerged through the gap in the rood screen and proceeded toward the altar; they bowed to the Real Presence and then began lighting the candelabras there. They were followed by the censer bearer who swung a golden censer on a golden chain; next came the bearer of the processional cross. As the sweet smoke of burning incense fragranced the air, Acrida watched the long line of singing choir boys parade past her to the altar where they bowed to the Real Presence and crossed themselves and then lined up on either side of the altar.

"Are all these boys oblates in this monastery?" she asked.

"Many are village children, no doubt," Dewain answered.

After the choir boys, the monks of the abbey appeared, two by two, in their black habits, many with white stoles about their necks. The monks first filled the choir stalls across from the nobles with the excess lining up on each side of the altar just behind the choir boys. Acrida was bewildered by the number of monks. She wondered if there would be room for everyone inside the chancel. Next, Abbots and Abbesses from other monasteries came after the monks; they too crowded in a line in front of the choir stalls. The Abbot of St. Benedict's came then, his brocaded stole decorated with elaborate designs in golden thread.

The hymn ended then, and another hymn began as an oblate emerged from the screen carrying a purple pillow with a ring upon it. He approached the altar and bowed to the Real Presence. Following the boy came the Bishop's two assistants, Julius and Avar, dressed in white albs and stoles, with maniples wrapped loosely around their left wrists. With mitre upon his head, Bishop Gildas appeared then with the crook-headed crosier in hand; he wore a dalmatic and chasuble of gold with red and green embroidery; he approached the altar and bowed to the Real Presence of the Christ, crossing himself. Then he began censing the altar.

Dressed in a gown of brilliant green with copious embroidery, Lord Olbert's wife emerged through the rood screen. She led Lady Kaithryn by the arm toward the altar.

"'Tis quite an honor, Olbert!" Dewain called out. "To have thyne own marriage publicly recognized as the happiest and most blessed union in the kingdom!"

"Indeed, we were quite flattered to be asked," Olbert smiled.

The young Lady Kaithryn, her face beaming with joy, walked smoothly and gracefully beside the elderly matron. Her gown was royal purple, and the gold embroidery on the sleeves and about the neckline were of an angular design. Her long, fine hair hung loose down her back and resembled spun gold. The train of her gown was of purple velvet also, and it trailed the floor for several feet behind her. Acrida gasped when the girl passed her, for the stars in the sky, large and vibrant, had been spectacularly embroidered on it.

The Queen's Royal Guard, dressed in black, followed the women. Acrida would not allow herself to look at Van Necht as he passed. She would use this opportunity to meet suitable freemen, she firmly reminded herself, not to brood after the noble lord like a lovestruck child.

Next, the Royal Chaplain entered the chancel. The monk simply wore the same black habit and white stole that he always wore. He approached the altar, bowed to the Real Presence and crossed himself, and then stood beside Van Necht, behind the matron of honor.

A few paces behind him came Christian, King of Speyron. He wore a purple tunic of Romani style that reached the floor; the gold embroidery on the sleeves and neckline matched the embroidery on Kaithryn's gown. Over his shoulders hung a mantle of the finest white ermine that reached the stone floor. His hands were bejeweled with rings, and his belt was of gold and silver. A silver-handled sword hung at his waist, and a circlet of gold rested evenly over his golden locks. The entire choir section bowed as he passed. When he reached the altar, he bowed to the Real Presence of the Christ and crossed himself, then stood a little away from Bennet, behind the bride, awaiting the end of the Te Deum hymn.

At least half of his vassals were here at the coronation, King Christian surmised. Not only had they brought their knights, but some had brought all of the men of arms they were providing him as he had requested. He wondered again what the latest count was.

Although Grey had complained that there was no need to begin gathering forces for a few more months, and that to do so placed an additional burden on the Royal Treasury, Christian was resolute that any troops that were ready should be brought to the coronation. It was as convenient a time to assemble them as any other, he had told his advisers. Truthfully, however, no matter how many reports Grey showed him of Herryck's inactivity, Christian could not wholly dismiss the warning Acrida had given him more than a fortnight ago that the kingdom would be at war in a few weeks.

As the Bishop began to pray, Christian wiped his sweating palms on his purple tunic, noting again how strange the soft velvet of the tunic felt against his flesh. This, along with the incense and the absence of the pricking of his hair shirts, made him wonder if he was not asleep, and this all a dream. His gaze drifted from the ornate Bishop, who was reading out of a large book, to the altar behind him to the waiting crown and oil until it finally settled upon the golden dove tabernacle with its burning candle.

"Amen."

The matron of honor, leading the bride to the right, slowly began to walk around and behind the King. Christian took a deep breath to calm himself; he smiled as they began to circle him three times.

The tailor certainly knew his craft, he admitted. From the cut of the gown alone, Kaithryn looked at least thirteen years. The nuns also had done well, for his cousin's posture was excellent and she walked and bore herself like a noblewoman.

The third and final time, Kaithryn came to stand beside him on his left. The matron put Kaithryn's small right hand into his, curtsied to the King, bowed to the Real Presence and crossed herself, and moved to stand in front of the Royal Chaplain.

Hand in hand and smiling, Kaithryn and Christian turned around to the spectators behind them. Everyone in the chancel cheered wildly. There was a pause in the cheering then as all watched the bride raise the hem of her gown in order to display her slippered foot. With due ceremony, King Christian stepped on it as custom demanded. The entire Church broke out into cheers. The royal couple laughed and then turned back to the Bishop. At his gesture, together they came forward and stood before the altar.

The Bishop, smiling, made the sign of the cross over the couple and began to read from the book his assistant held again:

"Nubas in Christo obnupta nube caelesti, et refrigerata gratia spiritali, ac protecta ab omni inlicita concupiscentia, pangas foedus cum oculis tuis, ut non videas alienum virum ad concupiscendum eum, et non moecheris in corpore vel corde tuo, et avertas oculos tuos ne videant vanitatem: quatenus in via Domini vivificeris, ut possis dicere cum propheta…"

Christian smiled, noting his cousin's face aglow with joy. As the Bishop droned on, he thought of the many happy times they had spent together over the years. He recalled her laughing with pleasure and excitement when he had taken her to ride with him on his great, white charger and her delight when he had told her stories at bedtime. Many years ago, when he was but a lad and home from Gaulia, they had spent many a merry hour playing seek games in the castle of her parents and throwing food at one another at table- and getting scolded for it. Kaithryn had always been pleasant company. Truly, some of his happiest hours had been spent with her.

-But this was the happiest he had ever seen her by far. As she smiled up at him, Christian realized that it was love- that look on her face, the purest and most potent love he had ever witnessed from anyone. And it was *he* whom she loved, worthy or not, whether he wanted her to or not. He swallowed hard and smiled back weakly.

With her heart pounding in her chest, Acrida's eyes were locked on Van Necht. She had allowed herself one look and now could not turn her eyes away from him. His strength and color were back. His brown hair had been combed neatly, the curls at the end just framing his chiseled face. He wore a tunic and braes of black velvet, the neck and edge of the sleeves embroidered in silver, -such clothes she had never known he even possessed. A heavy, black, fur mantle clasped by a gold, bejeweled broach hung over his broad shoulders. He wore two rings of gold on his left hand and another on his right. A large shiny sword hung by his hip on a black leather belt.

Avar then signaled for the boy who bore the ring to come to the altar then. The child approached, and the Bishop made the sign of the cross over the ring before he took it from its pillow.

"Accipe anulum, fidei et dilectionis signum, atque coniugalis coniunctionis vinculum, ut non separet homo quos coniungit Deus. Qui vivit et regnat in omnia saecula saeculorum."

The Bishop handed the ring to King Christian.

"Despondeo te uni viro virginem castam, atque pudicam futuram coniugem, ut sanctae mulieres fuere viris suis, Sarra, Rebecca, Rachel, Hester, Iudith, Anna, Noemi, favente auctore et sanctificatore nuptiarum, ..."

Christian held his cousin's hand and put the ring on her third finger. Then the Bishop gestured for the couple to kneel on two pillows before him, and he made the sign of the cross over them and began the final prayer.

If the invasion did not come, Christian wondered, where should he and Kaith winter? The palace was the obvious choice. Kaith would feel at home there. There was also plenty of room inside the walls to house the troops as the rest of them assembled. However, the presence of so many idle men of arms might be more than the remaining serfs could bear. Also, if they were besieged, they would run out of food quickly.

Grey had invited them to his lands. His castle was large, had natural defenses, and housed over three hundred knights. He and Kaith would no doubt be well protected there, but Grey's lands were in the west. When Herryck attacked, Christian would be too far away from his own forces as well as the point of invasion to engage the invaders swiftly.

There were other invitations. Paschal wanted them to winter on his lands, and several other vassals had invited them to come to their castles.-

"Amen."

The King crossed himself and slowly stood back up. He bowed to the Real Presence and crossed himself and went back to his original place beside Bennet. Lady Kaithryn remained on her knees as the Bishop made the sign of the cross once again over her and began another blessing.

The Bishop then turned his back to Kaithryn and the congregation and bowed to the Real Presence and kissed the altar. He made the sign of the cross over the altar and the oil that was there. Then he turned back around and made the sign of the cross over her again.

"Domine sancte, Pater omnipotens, aeterne Deus, electorum fortitudo, et humilium celsitudo, qui in primordio per effusionem diluvii crimina mundi purgari voluisti…"

Julius, with a clean piece of linen draped over one arm, took the container of oil from the altar and handed it to the Bishop who poured some on Kaithryn's head.

"…iterum Aaron famulum tuum per unctionem olei sacerdotem unxisti: et postea per eius ungeuenti infusionem, ad regendum populum Israeliticum…"

As he read, the Bishop made a cross of oil on the girl's forehead and again on the skin just below the throat. Then Lady Kaithryn held out the palms of her hands while the Bishop slathered each one with oil. Then he placed her palms together and bound them together with the linen cloth and made the sign of the cross over them.

"…ut efferatum cor regis ad misericordiam, et salvationem in te credentium, ipsius precibus inclinares. Te quaesumus, omnipotens…"

When the Bishop finished the prayer, he smiled at her. He turned and picked up the crown from the altar and turned back to Kaithryn.

"Gloria et honore coronet te Dominus, et ponat super caput tuum coronam de spiritali lapide pretioso…"

Holding the circle of gold in the air above her as he read, the Bishop gently lowered the crown onto her head.

As the Bishop began the final blessing, King Christian noticed that, in her kneeling position with her hands clasped together as if in prayer and the golden crown upon her head like a celestial halo, Kaith resembled the painting of the saint on the walls of his new chambers. He glanced over to Bennet, wondering if his Chaplain saw the likeness as well.

Bennet was praying with the Bishop. Christian looked back and saw Avar and Julius helping the Queen to her feet. They bowed low to her, and then Avar unwrapped her hands and wiped the excess oil from them. Kaithryn rubbed the remaining oil into her hands, and Bishop Gildas smiled, bowed to her, and then helped her turn to the King and the congregation.

"People of Speyron!" Bishop Gildas called out loudly in Speyron's native tongue, "This is your Queen!"

Kaith's face was radiant with joy as thunderous cheering filled the cathedral, and the great church bells began their tremendous peals.

Van Necht turned. He stepped forward and bowed low on one knee before the King, and kissed Christian's hand. Then he rose and went before the Queen, knelt on one knee, and kissed her hand. He stood up then, turned toward the spectators, and drew his sword in a ceremonial, defensive posture. The church was noisy with celebration.

It was near deafening in the church as the cheers continued, and the organ and musicians began to play again. Acrida herself was in tears again. With a signal from the Bishop, the acolytes led the procession out in the order they had entered. King Christian of Speyron took the Queen's arm and brought up the very end of the procession as all of Speyron bowed in homage to them.

80

After several healths had been drunk to the Queen and the nuptial couple, a blessing was offered for the food and another for the table and a few more prayers were said in turn. Then, finally, everyone in the great, timbered feasting hall sat down at the long tables.

The great hall built especially for the guests of St. Benedict's Abbey was the largest in the land and could easily accommodate more than five hundred people. The walls were painted with a depiction of the seven corporal acts of almsgiving. The hall and tables were additionally decorated with evergreen branches and holly sprigs. Musicians in the gallery loft began to play as servants went about refilling goblets.

The King and Queen of Speyron sat at the center of the high table which, on its raised platform, afforded them a view of the entire hall. An enormous, pewter saltcellar in the shape of a castle had been placed before the King. Queen Kaithryn sat on the King's right side. Bishop Gildas sat to the King's left, and beside him, Lord Grey and his wife. Lord Paschal and Lady Manton were beside them and Lord Dewain and his wife next to them; Acrida sat at the table's end. Lord Olbert and his wife sat to the right of the Queen. The Abbot of St. Benedict's sat on the other side of them, beside the King's Royal Chaplain. The Abbess from a nearby convent sat beside Bennet.

The other noble guests sat with their families on either side of two, very long rows of tables that stood perpendicular to the high table. During the meal, the most prominent vassals would take turns serving the King and Queen.

"This is Lord Varick," Olbert told Kaithryn in her ear. "His lands are in the south."

The nobleman bowed before the King and Queen at the head table and offered them handwashing water.

Christian acknowledged the vassal with a smile and gesture, rinsed his fingers in the bowl, as did Kaithryn after him.

"Acrida-"

Acrida turned at Dewain's voice. Only then did she notice the servant waiting for her to wash her hands in the proffered bowl of water and rose petals, and another servant filling her goblet with wine. She smiled and quickly rinsed her fingers in the water.

A pair of trumpeters in the loft interrupted the musician's song with a fanfare signaling the first course was being served. The entire hall clapped and cheered in appreciation as the servants paraded past with five trays and set them on the dresser table. Five noblemen went to the dresser table and carried the platters to the King's table, setting the dishes before the King and Queen and then bowed.

Kaith smiled at the aldermen before her and forgot their names as quickly as Olbert introduced them. Her eyes moved hungrily to the beautiful dishes before her. The first was roasted boar cooked with an apple in its mouth. The second dish was baked haddock in butter. The third was roasted goose in sauce. The fourth was venison pie. The fifth was lamb in almond milk.

As the five noblemen left, Lord Van Necht and Sir Albern approached the high table next and bowed. Sir Albern set a sweetbread baked with dates before the couple. Kaith smiled at this familiar pair of vassals as the two men held their knives at the ready.

"Well, Kaith, what is your pleasure?" Christian asked, as he cut the large, golden trencher before him in half and gave one part to his wife to use as a plate.

"It all looks so delicious. What are you having, Christian?"

"Lamb and some boar-."

At once, Van Necht began to carve the lamb and serve the King.

"I will have some lamb too," Kaith said. "And some venison pie."

Sir Albern took his knife, cut a portion of the flaky pastry for the Queen, and placed it on her trencher.

"And the goose looks tasty also," Christian added, his stomach growling at the sight and smell of the meats.

Acrida was oblivious to the platters of food arriving in front of her. Her eyes did not stray from the carver before the King, her heart pounding at the glorious sight of Van Necht in his handsome clothes. Even as she watched his every move, she chided her feelings, reminding herself again that he had a love already and likely the lady was here in this very hall, admiring him even as she was.

When Van Necht had finished carving and serving the meats to the King and Queen, he and his vassal knight bowed again and took the carving knives back to the dresser table. On his return to the high table, as he passed by Acrida, Lord Van Necht stopped and bowed to the King's seer, his eyes locking onto hers.

Acrida's heart skipped a beat, then raced, and she blushed at the public acknowledgment. Then Van Necht proceeded toward the opposite end of the high table.

As the warlord left her sight, Acrida fought to possess herself again and to push down the feelings of elation that were already welling up inside of her. She looked around. Everyone was either eating, talking, or straining to hear conversations over the music. Perhaps no one had noticed his display.

Sir Albern was suddenly before her then, dressed too in splendid clothes, shiny spurs and sword. He bowed deeply before her and then boldly seized her hand and kissed it. Then, smiling and winking at her, the knight dashed after his lord; the two men took their places at the far end of the Queen's side of the high table.

Smiling and trembling, Acrida reached for the goblet in front of her, overwhelmed by the attention she was receiving. Dewain leaned toward her and yelled:

"Well, Acrida, it seems Lord Van Necht has missed thy company!"

Acrida went pale, but shook her head quickly.

"He is just showing courtesy, I assure you, My Lord."

"Is he? I find Lord Van Necht, unlike his vassal, Sir Albern, to be a very reserved man, particularly when the courtesy applies to women. Perhaps he thinks more highly of you than you are aware."

Although Acrida seemed alarmed by this, Dewain only smiled.

"What, My Dear, may I serve you? Do you prefer flesh, fowl, or fish?"

Acrida blinked at the food, suddenly aware of her loss of appetite. She shook her head.

"No?"

"My stomach-" she shook her head again. "I am too nervous to eat."

Dewain's wife smiled.

"Here, have some bread with butter and honey. It will help to settle it," she said, breaking off a portion of a loaf of sweet datebread and setting it on the seer's trencher.

She passed her the small containers of butter and honey. Acrida took the bread obediently, but only pinched off small bits to eat. Unsettled, she turned her attention to the entertainment at the center of the hall.

While the music played, three jugglers were throwing objects high into the air. One threw fruit of all sizes, another knives, and another eggs. Then they threw them to each other, mixing the items, and delighting the crowd with their abilities.

When they finished their act to much applause, a group of acrobats ran in and tumbled about the tables. After nearly hitting a servant with a tray of food, they began feats of balance. Standing on each other's shoulders or balancing on their heads, they towered over the feasters.

At the end of their performance, the acrobats bowed to the loud approval of the revelers. While the musicians continued to play, the servants returned to the tables, refilling the goblets, clearing away empty platters of food, and changing out tablecloths.

Christian observed that Kaith's attention seemed far away.

"Are you enjoying the entertainment?"

"Aye, Cousin," she smiled, but her gaze drifted again to the end of the hall.

"Well, have some more wine," he said, signaling to a winebearer.

She passed him her goblet, and then, with determination, the Queen stood up. The conversations near her stopped abruptly.

"Most Noble Lords!" she called out.

The servants immediately began hushing the crowd so she could be heard. The musicians put down their instruments and waited.

"Our Most Noble Vassals-" she began, her voice unsure, but strong and her face flushing red, "We thank thee heartily for coming to feast this happy day with Us."

She looked about the hall, noticing, apprehensively, the many, many eyes upon her and then at Lord Olbert who smiled encouragingly at her and then at her cousin who smiled with amusement at her. She smiled back helplessly. Then she continued:

"It is Our first wish as Queen to bestow favor on a merry soul. Know that Tate, old Fool to King Filberte, is Our Fool as well. And I ask all who love me to look after him as well. And if anyone treats him well for love of me -Us, they shall have Our thanks."

King Christian smiled and rolled his eyes. Lords Olbert, Grey, and Dewain laughed and applauded as did the rest of the revelers politely. Acrida smiled and clapped. Paschal just shook his head.

Kaithryn, who had been watching Tate in the shadows at the back of the huge hall for the past half hour, looked back to the old man now. His face wore a startled expression.

"Come and be your Queen's Fool, Tate!" she called.

Smiling broadly now, Tate, dressed in his commoner's clothes with his gray hair tied back, came forward to the high table and bowed low before Queen Kaithryn of Speyron, who smiled warmly at him.

"I have always been a fool for you, My Queen," he told her.

Kaithryn laughed, and in customary gesture, she picked up the scrap of lamb from her trencher and leaning forward across the table, offered the tidbit to the old man. Tate leaned forward and took the meat from her fingers with his very teeth and ate it. The guests laughed, applauded, and cheered.

"Beware, Kaith," Christian smiled, "for any fool who flatters his master is no fool at all."

Kaith laughed again and sat down once more.

Tate bowed again and rushed away.

With another fanfare from the trumpeters, the next course was served to the dresser table to the applause of the feasters. The first platter was quail. The second was beef in pepper sauce. The third was rabbit posset. The fourth was baked pears in syrup. The fifth offering was cabbage and leeks.

While the second course was being served, Tate returned to the high table followed by two servants who bore a huge chair between them. They set it at the very end of the Queen's end of the table as the Fool directed. Lord Van Necht and Sir Albern moved further up the table to make more room for him. Tate took his place then, and the servants brought him a green trencher and a cup. He immediately began serving himself food from the nearby platters.

81

The hall roared with laughter, applauded, and loudly cheered as the jester bowed to the high table and the crowd.

"He was wonderful!" Kaith exclaimed.

Christian agreed.

"I have never laughed so hard in my life!" Lady Manton declared ardently to Paschal.

While the guests had eaten the second course and the minstrels took a respite from their songs, a magician had delighted the crowd with sleight-of-hand tricks. The bard who followed him told a story using only bird calls. Each was a superb performer, renowned throughout Speyron and the surrounding kingdoms, but the most popular of all the entertainment was the jester who had just demonstrated the various sounds and varieties of farts.

As the jester withdrew, King Christian looked about. Everyone was enjoying themselves and the entertainment. The servants had begun clearing away empty platters of food and serving more wine. Another group was taking up the soiled tablecloths, replacing them with fresh.

They had not long finished when the trumpet fanfare again sounded, signaling the third and final course was being served. The first dish was partridge in sour sauce. The second was whiting in jelly. The third dish was glazed eggs. The fourth was apples in cinnamon. The fifth dish was swan neck pudding. The last group of nobles approached the high table, bowed to the couple, and offered to serve them.

"I can eat no more, Christian," Kaith said with a shake of her head.

Christian declined also.

The noblemen bowed and returned to their own tables, leaving the platters of food in front of the King and Queen. The new offerings fared as well at the other tables. Most of the guests had eaten their fill already and barely picked at the new offerings. The abbey's dogs and cats, however, had crept into the hall and now watched the untouched food hungrily.

Another bard approached the high table then, bowed, and cleared his throat.

"Your Graces, My Lords and Ladies, I bring you the tale of the Trials of Psyche in her search for her lover, Cupid."

"A strange story to tell at a marriage feast," Bennet commented.

"Think you so?" Lord Olbert asked.

"Does not the old, pagan, Romani tale warn that love can be gained when it is least expected, but once lost, is difficult to attain again? How is this appropriate for a royal wedding and coronation?"

Olbert laughed and shrugged.

"Methinks 'The Glorious Death of Hector, the Protector of Troy' or 'The Betrayal of King Arthur by his Queen Guinevere and Vassal Lancelot' would be less suitable selections for the occasion."

Bennet raised his eyebrows and had to agree.

As the audience listened to the long tale, some of the guests threw their scraps to the dogs, but many of the cats were on the tables already eating as much of the abandoned food as they could before being shooed away.

When the bard finished, the hall applauded him enthusiastically.

"That was good, but the farter was still the best," Lady Manton declared again. "We should invite him to entertain at our castle, Paschal."

The servants began to clear away the platters and some of the tables and benches at the far end of the hall so that dancing might commence. At this point, some of the guests rose from their places and began mingling freely among each other.

The Bishop, the Abbess, and the Abbott made their excuses therewith and took their leave of the royal couple, retiring for the evening. Lord

Dewain's wife went to see to the children, and Dewain moved closer to Acrida to speak with her.

"Are you enjoying yourself?"

"Very much, My Lord."

"The dancing will begin shortly. My son Jenkyn has told me he will request a dance from you."

Acrida smiled.

"No doubt your good ladywife has told him of my attempts to learn."

"Actually, I believe it was his youngest brother who told him," Dewain told her pleasantly.

Acrida smiled again.

"My Lord, I must again thank you for welcoming me into your household. Your family has been so kind to me."

"You have been a most welcome guest, Acrida, and we enjoyed having you. My wife tells me that the children complain daily of your absence."

Acrida smiled as she watched the various groups of nobles talking and laughing among each other.

Lord Olbert joined the pair then.

"Acrida, this morning I encountered Van Necht's vassal, Sir Albern. He inquired after you," Olbert told her.

"That was kind of him. Is he well?"

"The knight seemed quite well. But he told me a very interesting story about you. He told me that you saved Lord Van Necht's life."

The smile fell from the woman's face.

"Really?" Dewain said.

"Aye. And I am surprised, Acrida, that you did not tell me about this," Olbert added.

"Indeed, so am I," Dewain added, regarding her curiously.

A black cat leaped upon the high table then and began to eat from the abandoned platter of whiting.

"My Lords, the good knight overstates the truth of the matter," she said quickly, avoiding their gaze. She picked up the cat and dropped it to the floor, adding, "I did very little."

"He said that Van Necht was gravely ill for several days and that if you had not been there to tend him-"

The cat was immediately back on the table.

"I did tend him, but that was all. Anyone would have done the same," she said anxiously, picking up the cat again and dropping it to the floor. "It was God's will, no doubt, that he should live."

"Indeed, but Sir Albern says if it had not been for you and your aunt, *Deidre*, Lord Van Necht surely would have died."

Acrida grew pale at the mention of her aunt's name.

"He told me he had to travel all the way to Huntingdon's lands to find her," Olbert continued.

"Is she a well-known healer?" Dewain asked.

"No, My Lord," Acrida replied, completely panicked now.

She rose from her chair to escape her inquisitors as the cat returned again.

"Nor should she be known," she lied hastily, "for she has no special skills. -By your leave."

Olbert stopped her with his hand, and seeing her pale with alarm, he added, "My Dear, the King shall hear what you and your aunt have done. Van Necht is one of his most prized vassals. You both should be rewarded for your efforts."

"Pray, do not trouble the King over this little matter," Acrida entreated them. "No reward is necessary for my aunt, nor justified for me, I assure you. -'Twas a great risk to send for her when he lay so close to death and she lived so far away. It was chance alone that he survived at all. I acted foolishly. -I should have sent again for the physician in Leeds. -If anything, I deserve reproach for the risk I took with his life. -By your leave."

Abandoning the food to the cat, Acrida rushed away from them, careful to go in the opposite direction from where Van Necht sat. Olbert and Dewain watched her go, confused by her words and her overall unease.

As Acrida made her way through the great hall, she became even more flustered from having to stop several times and curtsy to knights and aldermen who greeted her.

Lord Van Necht observed Acrida leave the table, surprised that she had not come to speak to him yet. He watched as she made her way through the hall, flirting and curtsying to several men, both young and aged, who showed courtesy to her as she passed.

How well she looked, Van Necht thought. She was aglow with health and vitality, and she looked as if she had spent every day of her life at Court. The blue gown she wore was costly and fit her perfectly too.

When she disappeared from view, the warlord glanced at the hound across the table from him. Standing on its hind legs, its nose was just able to sniff at a platter; it licked at its edge. Van Necht stabbed a hunk of uneaten beef with his knife and tossed it to the floor for the dog, watching as it gobbled the scrap greedily.

Had she made the gown herself? he wondered. She had the skill to make it, but how had she attained such expensive cloth?

Van Necht refilled his goblet from a nearby pitcher and scanned the crowd for Sir Albern. He found him flirting with a group of young, unmarried ladies of about eleven years. He watched as Sir Albern bowed to one girl, kissed her hand, and led her to the dance.

"Excellent food."

Van Necht glanced at Tate who sat beside him at the high table; the Fool was surrounded by platters of food and was eating the breast of a partridge hungrily.

Lord Felix greeted and joined the pair then.

"I suppose congratulations are in order, Tate, now that your bread is secured again," Felix said.

"Thank you, My Lord."

"And for you as well, Van Necht. You were both employed by the Queen today. I suppose I shall be seeing you both regularly at the palace now."

Van Necht frowned.

Tate smiled, licking the sour sauce off his greasy fingertips.

"Not relishing the thought of returning to Court, I see," Felix said to Van Necht. "Aye, 'tis different now and *terribly dull* since the King returned from the monastery. Perhaps you have heard already: 'Tis Mass at dawn and to bed at dark. No drinking, no wenching, no sport at all! Likely it will be even more somber now that he has married."

Van Necht raised his eyebrows.

"Alas! What has become of our King Christian and the merry days of his Bachelor Court?" Felix lamented, then he turned and spoke to a passing lord.

Tate chuckled.

"The youth speaks the truth, My Lord. Perhaps you will find attendance at Court less of a burden now that the King has married."

The sour expression returned to Van Necht's face.

"-Still, at least you have lands of your own to retire to when you have had your fill of the gossip and intrigues at Court. 'Tis a most enviable asset. At times, even I have wearied of Court," the Fool continued, "but what must be endured, must be endured for patronage sake.-"

"I do not know why anyone attends Court," Van Necht said, "except that they are *forced* to do so."

Tate chuckled again.

"Even at its worst, Court is not as bad as the alternative, My Lord. Without a skill or a patron these past years, I have had to stay wherever I could *beg* shelter and a scrap of bread."

Van Necht smiled wryly.

"Somehow, it is difficult for me to believe that the good women of Speyron turned *you* away when you sought shelter under their roofs."

"Indeed!" Felix snorted, having returned to the conversation.

"The women- no. Their husbands and fathers? Aye. I have been constantly on the move. -Although I only recently returned from pilgrimage."

Both Van Necht and Felix raised their eyebrows in surprise.

"Two and a half years ago, I met a bishop journeying to Roma, who, favoring my wit, invited me to accompany him. He thought he even might be able to arrange an introduction with His Holiness, the Pope, for me, but that did not come about."

The noblemen listened with interest.

"And you went to Roma?" Felix asked, sitting down beside them in a vacant chair.

"Aye, eventually. It was a very long, meandering pilgrimage, I should say. I only returned this past summer."

"You must have seen many interesting things.-"

Tate laughed and wiped his hands on the tablecloth.

"Aye! 'Twas revealing in many ways! As you might expect, all along the journey we happened upon many devout laymen of the Church, including many pious priests, monks, and nuns. -But Roma is filled with prostitutes, and their main clientele are the celibates! The city itself is peopled with the bastards of bishops and popes!"

"You jest!"

"I do not," the Fool answered shaking his head. "The bishops, too, in all of Italia are utterly corrupt. They dine not on trenchers, but gold plate. They sleep in silk sheets in golden beds with a company of mistresses. After a while, I thought even *I* might like a profession in the Church."

They laughed.

"What of the monasteries?"

"We stopped at many."

Tate cut himself a piece of bread with his dagger. Scooping the butter out of the container with his pinkie, he spread it on the bread. Then he dipped his pinkie in the honey and drizzled it over the butter.

"Many of the monasteries we visited were full of drunken, quarreling monks; and several of the convents where we stayed the night, in Mercius especially, were nothing more than brothels, and a stopping point for every bishop traveling to or from Roma. The lords and knights of Mercius frequented many of those convents, not to mention a majority of monks from nearby monasteries."

"So those stories are actually true?" Felix asked.

"Aye-" Tate said, chewing a mouthful of bread, "though to participate in the most outrageous orgies on the Continent, we were told we had to journey to the monasteries among the Frankos where the lewdest kind of debauchery is supposedly common practice."

"Indeed, I will have to make a journey," Felix agreed, smiling.

Van Necht gave him a disgusted look.

Tate chuckled and stabbed a cinnamon-spiced apple off the platter before him with his dagger and plopped it down on his nearly empty trencher.

"But what of you, Van Necht? Have you still not remarried after all of this time?" the Fool asked.

"No, and I keep to myself and away from Court in the hopes that the King will not notice me- lest he tie me to some abominable woman for sport alone."

Felix laughed.

Tate looked at Van Necht questioningly.

"Believe you that the King would purposefully match you to a woman you despised solely to make you miserable?"

Van Necht smiled a small, bitter smile.

"What know I, Fool? When Christian first became king, I petitioned him for the appointment of Commander of Speyron's army, and he appointed me *Queen's Royal Guard* instead."

Tate raised his eyebrows and nodded.

"Truly, the King has dealt unjustly with you in the past."

"'Tis an honorable position, Van Necht," Felix shrugged. "And there is nothing Christian holds more dear than the life of his cousin. Truly he would not trust her life with just anyone."

Tate smiled at the youth for a moment, and then turned to Van Necht.

"Well, do not despair, My Lord. With any luck, the King may well still think your first wife lives."

Van Necht and Tate snickered at this.

"Why wait for the King to choose for you, Van Necht?" Felix asked. "Why not select a lady you find pleasing and present the match for his approval?"

"What have I need for a wife at all when wenches can be paid to lie down and then to leave?" Van Necht answered hotly.

Felix hooted in amusement.

"After all, what is more precious to a man than peace and quiet?" Van Necht continued.

"What, indeed?" Tate smiled, shaking his head.

Van Necht's eyes had drifted to Sir Albern again who had finished one dance and now made his way to three young widows in the company. They were in their early twenties and had full breasts and coy demeanors; and Sir Albern was all charm and smiles.

"I have been thinking for some time now that if I came into the means, I might take a wife myself," Tate said.

"Really?" Van Necht commented, as he watched Sir Albern escort one of the beauties to the dance. "Well, you certainly have the means now, though I can not imagine why you of all people would want a wife."

"Nor can I," Felix added.

"Can you not?"

"No," Felix said. "You have never lacked female companionship. It amazes me how, even now at your age, when you walk into a room, all the women watch you with hungry eyes- young and old, the beautiful and the hags."

"You flatter an old man, My Lord."

"'Tis true."

"Aye, 'tis," he grinned. "And I am a lucky man to be blessed by God with such a body that attracts the fairer sex."

The men laughed.

"Truly, what appeal do you find in marriage?" Van Necht asked again.

"There is hardly any appeal without the promise of lands," Felix commented.

"Spoken like a true nobleman," Tate smiled. "No, My Lords, -two things that my long life has lacked: female friendship and children."

Van Necht glanced at him skeptically.

"Well, children I may *publicly* claim as my own."

Van Necht nodded.

"I have been bedding women and girls since before you both were born, My Lords- all kinds. And it is a great pleasure. But when it is done with, and I have left her bed, or she, mine, I am alone again. -Now in the dusk of my age, I crave a companion who will be with me for the rest of my days, not simply one night-"

Felix and Van Necht raised their eyebrows.

"-and one I may keep company with openly. I tire of hiding from husbands and fathers. I want to wake up with a woman, and instead of hastily dressing and sneaking out of her chamber, I want to stay there and reap the benefits of her mind and spirit. I want someone I can confide in and tell my hopes and dreams to. I want one that will know me as well as I know her," Tate ended wistfully, his eyes on the bridal couple who sat hand in hand, both with a smile of contentment on their faces as they watched the dancers.

"Take care what you wish for, Fool," Van Necht warned, "you might receive it."

"I care not whom I marry," Felix commented, "as long as she comes with lands."

Tate smiled again.

The song ended then; and some of the guests sat down, and some stood up from the table to dance. The King and Queen rose as well, followed by Lord Grey and his wife, and Paschal and Lady Manton. Van Necht watched the couples make their way to the dance, his eyes falling on the happy and chubby, flat-chested bride in her grownup, purple gown.

"I would not be in the King's place for anything this night," Van Necht muttered.

Tate looked at the couple and at the happy face of Kaithryn.

"Why not?"

"She is too young for my taste."

"They say the younger the better," Felix replied. "They are supposedly easier to train. -I, too, will marry a young one."

Tate, gulping down another cup of wine, nodded.

"The last wife of Carolus Magnus was no older than she. -Besides, Kaith is mature for her age. If the King had not sent her to the convent, I warrant *I* could have been in her bed by now.-"

Felix raised his eyebrows and laughed in amazement.

"You jest-" Van Necht said.

"No, though that was never my intent," Tate said, stretching and leaning back in the chair. "But then, I have loved Lady Kaithryn since the day I met her in her infancy.- And you have seen the results of her affection for me," he gestured, referring to his new position. "'Twould be easily accomplished, -but I would never make the King a cuckold -at least not with his *bride*."

Felix grinned.

"-I am still surprised that I did not see that Christian intended Kaith for himself!" Tate said, refilling his goblet and finishing the pitcher.

Van Necht shook his head, wondering at the old man.

"How do you do it?" he suddenly asked.

"Do what?" Tate asked, sipping the wine.

"How do you bed all of these women?"

The question caught Tate off guard, and he nearly choked on his drink.

"My Lord, at your age, surely you should know how!" he laughed.

Felix snickered while Van Necht smiled dryly at the pair.

"What I mean is how do you get to their beds without force or money? And why do they not despise *you* afterward?"

"Aye, I have never been with a woman that did not *sulk* afterward," Felix sniffed, his attention back on the crowd of people before him. "'Tis part of it. After all, weeping, complaining, and being angry and resentful are what women do best."

Tate raised his eyebrows.

"Actually, My Lords, the easiest way to avoid being despised afterward is to take a woman to your bed who genuinely likes you."

The aldermen blinked.

"What does that matter?" Van Necht and Felix both asked.

Tate smiled and rubbed his eyes.

"The next important thing is not to frighten her.-"

"Frighten her?"

"Aye, intense passion on your part can overwhelm her. Try to have patience."

"Patience?" Felix asked. "You are talking about swyving?"

Tate chuckled.

"Truly, My Lords, if you can simply avoid bedding a woman when you are tired, drunk, upset or frustrated, -or in a hurry, all will be well," Tate said, finishing his drink.

"But Van Necht is always tired, frustrated, or in a hurry! When would he ever get any?" Felix teased.

"'Tis well that wenches can be paid to lay down-" Van Necht agreed.

The three men laughed; and Felix excused himself from the table and went to speak to Paschal.

"So how would you approach the Queen, if it were you?" Van Necht asked.

Tate cut into a baked pear that smelled strongly of cloves, stabbed a piece with his knife and popped the sweet fruit into his mouth.

"Well," he shrugged, "I would have no set plan to follow. I would just let things happen. But most likely I would play with her first."

"Play with her?"

"Aye, that works well, and Kaith loves to play. A pillow attack or a tickling fight are good. Both are physical games. And laughter tends to get people panting. The rest-" he shrugged and bit into another bite of pear.

"Is that it?"

Tate shrugged and nodded as he swallowed. Van Necht sighed and shook his head.

"My Lord, remember to always have fun in bed," Tate added. "Make certain *she* enjoys herself- lest a woman believe that bedding with you is all seriousness and dread and learns to hate it."

"Enjoy herself?"

"Aye, if you want to be invited back to her bed.-"

"Enjoy herself how so?"

Tate smiled and sighed, covering his eyes.

Sir Albern joined them then.

"How now, My Lord? What serious talk keeps you from the dance?"

Van Necht did not reply.

"The lord was just asking for some advice on swyving," Tate answered between mouthfuls of fruit.

Sir Albern smiled and slapped Van Necht on his back, saying, "Just relax and have fun."

Van Necht grimaced in embarrassment. He gave an annoying look to the Fool who only grinned.

A young girl all clad in green ran up to the table and curtsied.

"Sir Albern, come and dance with me and my sister."

"Duty calls," the knight told the men with a smile as he took the girl by the hand and returned to the dance.

Lord Grey then approached the pair with his goblet in hand.

"Congratulations, Tate!"

"Thank you, My Lord."

"Well, Van Necht, it has been a long time."

"Aye, it has, Lord Grey."

"I see you are not dancing."

"Indeed, I am not."

Grey gestured about the hall with his cup.

"The finest noblewomen Speyron has to offer are here. If I were you, I would take advantage of the situation as the bees do in the rose garden."

Van Necht smiled, but on the inside, he cringed.

"If I might point out one rare beauty that blooms near my own lands," Grey continued. "My brother has set a handsome amount on my niece who will be coming thirteen in a year's time. She is the one in the yellow gown sitting beside her brother at the far table."

"I am certain she is charming," Van Necht answered unenthusiastically, hardly noticing the girl, as he stood up from his chair.

"I do not believe that Lord Van Necht is ready for permanent female companionship, My Lord," Tate said. "Now that he has finally freed himself from Acrida's company, he is hard pressed to give up the peace and quiet that has been so hard won."

Van Necht paused at his words.

"What is thy meaning?"

"He meant no offense, Van Necht," Grey answered with a laugh as he signaled to a servant to refill his goblet. "He and Dewain have spent nearly two months with Acrida. I am certain they well understand how a lowborn woman with such a sharp tongue could try the patience of any man."

"Speak for thyself, My Lord," Tate answered. "The lass has been so reticent that I have hardly noticed her presence."

"Aye, 'tis very true also," Grey agreed. "Sometimes when she is so silent, I often wonder exactly what she is plotting in that head of hers."

"Oh, really, Lord Grey! Thou imagines the hounds under thy table are plotting to bite thee!" the Fool answered indignantly.

"Indeed, they very well may be!"

"I do not understand thee still," Van Necht interrupted. "She is welcome on my lands as pleases her and as her position permits. When she left two months ago, it was at the King's beckoning."

This time, Tate and Grey looked at Van Necht in confusion.

"No, Acrida was required to attend the King after his return from St. Brychan's only for these last three weeks."

"If not the King- then did not you or Olbert or Dewain send for her on the King's business?"

"No, we did not," Lord Grey answered.

"Aye," Tate said, "Lord Dewain and I were riding through your lands and by chance came upon Acrida in the village. When we told her we were going to Lord Dewain's castle, she asked to accompany us. She returned to your tent so that she could take her leave of you, and we departed. Did she tell you different?"

Tate and Grey watched as the expression on Lord Van Necht's face hardened.

With his heart beating very loudly in his ears, Van Necht numbly turned and walked away from the table, leaving the two men to stare after him.

"Apparently so," Tate commented.

Van Necht needed some air. She had not been called away! She had left on her own accord! He could scarcely believe it!

He pushed his way through the crowd of people toward the door, though he soon realized this was not the best way to get out of the hall. He kept encountering nobles and knights who greeted him and would then begin introducing either their daughters or their unmarried, younger sisters to him. Finally, Van Necht made it to the door and walked out into the quiet snowfall.

He took a deep breath as angry thought after angry thought went through his head. After all he had done for her, she had abandoned him on his deathbed! No wonder she looked so nervous when he had acknowledged her earlier. No wonder she was avoiding him! -And well she should, now that he knew the truth!

Van Necht's jaw clenched. Had she lied to her aunt about being summoned by the King? Had she lied to Albern? Or had her aunt simply lied to Albern in fear for her niece? Yet Deidre did not strike him as the sort that would bother to lie. The old crone would enjoy the antagonism that the truth would bring him.

But why? Why had C'sara left him? Clearly, she had believed that he would die. Had she feared she would be blamed for his death? Perhaps- but he had never seen her back down from anything she had done or said. Still, there were many who believed she was a witch, and if she thought that she would be accused and put to death if he died, then clearly she might have had the motivation to run. But why run to Dewain? Perhaps it had been simple convenience as the Fool had described. No doubt she had requested his protection until the King returned.

After thinking on this further, he decided her abandonment must have been born of fear. He could not explain her disloyalty any other way. C'sara had been ever dutiful and worthy of his trust. She had done all that he had asked of her. Dinner had always been ready when he had arrived home; the chores had always been finished. She had *sought* ways to serve him.

Truthfully, disloyalty was more of a trait of his first wife, than C'sara. If he had been on his deathbed, he doubted Gunhilde would have stayed with him at all, -lest he had bribed her to stay.

Van Necht stopped at this. The nobleman went cold as he remembered something he had long forgotten. He recalled how Acrida had haggled with the King's advisers for a position at Court and what had finally won her cooperation.

'You want the fine clothes of the softest, brightest cloth,' Grey had said, 'and the tasty meals that are prepared by others; and you want good wine, not watery ale. You want to live here- in the palace. *You want to live in such luxury as you have never imagined.*'

She had not even tried to deny it. She *had* desired riches and privilege more than anything else. *And she desired them still.*

Van Necht swallowed hard. If riches were what she desired, she would not have received them from him if he were dead. If she had thought him dying, she could have thought it to no real purpose to stay with him at all. He bristled at this thought.

So, she had left her aunt with him so that no one could accuse her of neglect, he realized, and then she had gone to find some other wealthy and prestigious sap to leech upon until the King summoned her. Van Necht's eyes narrowed and his lips grew thin as he positively seethed at these thoughts.

At least he had never given her anything to show his affection for her!

Now she found herself in a difficult position, he reasoned. He had survived, and she obviously was with another man already. Even now, she had likely rushed off from the festivities to meet him.

Van Necht could not recall if she was wearing a ring today, though, whoever her new admirer was, he no doubt had paid for the gown she wore. Likely, she had gone to his bed immediately on account of it. This thought made Van Necht livid as he remembered all those nights when he had longed to enjoy her, and he had held back, not wishing to sully her, despite her low birth. Cynically, he realized that she probably would have surrendered to him without hesitation if he had only given her some trinket.

The lord was so angry now that if Acrida had stood before him at that moment, he would have ripped her beating heart out of her chest. He had been wrong, he realized. He had thought, somehow, for some reason, she was different from other women. But she was not. All any of them wanted was wealth and prestige.

Van Necht struggled to contain his ire. This was neither the time nor the place for outrage. He looked around and noted the couples that were standing outside, their conversations peppered with intimate laughter. Taking a deep breath, Van Necht began to feel the cold air. He blew hot breath into his numbing hands and rubbed them together. Then he turned and made his way back into the warm hall, leaving the lovers to themselves.

Once inside, he made his way to a vacant corner where he could observe the entire hall. His eyes scanned the guests, searching. His gaze moved over the groups of talking nobles to the dancing couples.

He suddenly caught sight of her. Van Necht watched hotly as Acrida danced a delicate turn with a lad in a dark green tunic. He hated her as he observed her smile and the graceful way she moved about the floor with the youth who was not even of enough age for his first growth of whiskers.

As the dance ended, Van Necht fumed as he watched her curtsy smoothly to the gawky, skinny boy. The lad clearly wanted another dance, but he was forced to surrender his place and retreat when a knight, bowing shortly, offered Acrida his hand as the music began again. Van Necht's jaw set as he witnessed Acrida's flattered blush and coquettish smile in response to the knight's invitation.

"Lord Van Necht, it is good to see you."

Van Necht turned abruptly to see Sir Eldwin. He greeted the knight, and then his eyes fell to the troop of ten and eleven year old girls that followed him. Upon seeing Van Necht, the girls immediately smiled and giggled. From the look on the knight's face, the nobleman realized Sir Eldwin was trying to disentangle himself from the girls by providing them with a more interesting distraction.

"My Lord Van Necht," one girl addressed him with a curtsy which the rest of the four girls imitated in turn.

Then she held out her hand on which she wore a large emerald ring and waited.

Sighing internally, Van Necht stepped forward and took her hand and kissed it as manners required, muttering, "My Lady."

The girl smiled alluringly at him.

Lord Van Necht grudgingly smiled back at the entire group of girls, gave Sir Eldwin a tired look, and leaned back against the wall and crossed his arms.

The knight made a very quick retreat as the girls stood before the cornered alderman and tried to think of something to say.

"So, My Lord, we have all heard you have no castle," said this same bold girl.

"Aye, 'tis true," he answered politely.

"So, where do you sleep, My Lord?"

"In my tent, My Lady."

"A tent?"

And the girls giggled again and smiled at him and at each other.

"Why? A lord so noble as yourself should have a grand castle to match your station."

"And a grand lady to live in it-" another girl added.

Van Necht looked back into the crowd of people again as he yawned in his mind.

"How do you ever expect to get a wife if you live in a tent?"

Van Necht sighed.

"I live the life of a man of arms, My Lady. I am at the beck and call of the King and Queen day and night. I doubt it is the life that any wife would particularly enjoy."

The song ended then, and the musicians bowed to the applause, and then took a recess. The King and Queen returned to their seats as the other dancers left the floor. As Van Necht searched the moving crowd, he wished the girls would find some other bachelor to hound. Where was Sir Albern when he needed him?

"Still, now that the King is married, surely you will stay at Court-in order to protect the Queen. I am sure any *suitable* wife would find a chamber at the palace a most wonderful place to live."

Van Necht fought down the urge to inform the girls that a *suitable* wife in his opinion was one who would sleep out of doors without complaint, with only himself as a coverlet.

"And once you marry," this same bold girl continued, "surely you will have a new castle built. The *right* woman could make you want to build a grand one- *for her.*"

"You speak truly," Van Necht answered as a small smile floated across his features.

After all, he thought to himself, the *right* woman had made him burn the old one to the ground not so long ago.

"However," he continued, "the *right* woman, My Lady, is even rarer than a *suitable* one. If *she* is intelligent, such a lady will marry where she is appreciated and leave me to myself and my tent."

The smiles fell from the faces of the young ladies as they heard this remark and, curtsying slightly, they quickly sought other amusement. Van Necht breathed with relief as he continued scanning the hall.

Standing near the doorway fanning herself, Acrida felt a jealous pang as she watched the young and giddy highborn girls in their finery flirting so audaciously with Lord Van Necht. She watched him play his part, saying something witty and smiling so sweetly and contentedly at them. But this was where he belonged, she told herself sternly. They were of the same station.

She looked away then, suffering as she felt her very heart wrung out by feelings of hurt and envy. It had been harder to see him than she had expected.

She had watched him most of the night, wondering if she could spot his lady-love, but the nobleman had kept generally to himself the entire afternoon, though he seemed to always be looking through the crowd for someone. Was his lady here? Perhaps she had been delayed. Perhaps they were to meet this day, but the lady was unable to make the journey. -Only about half of the King's vassals had managed to come. Or perhaps she was here, Acrida considered, and they were to meet later, away from prying eyes.

She wondered again why he had acknowledged her earlier. Perhaps he meant it as a gesture of simple gratitude for saving his life. Still it was unnecessary. Any of his subjects would have done the same.

And it was cruel of him to openly give her a bit of attention when he was already pledged to another! She was like a dog that he was teasing with something to eat and then giving it nothing.

Why was she doing this? she admonished herself. She should be seeking an *attainable* man, one that wanted *her*, not pining after Van Necht.

Acrida winced as her heart ached; she feared she was going to cry amongst all these happy people. No, she would *not* embarrass herself or the King or Lord Dewain with such an outburst. With determination, she gripped her emotions forcefully and made her way through the people out of the hall into the cold air outside.

82

Christian rubbed his eyes and smiled as he watched his sated and drunken guests talk and laugh among themselves while others danced to the lively music. It was late afternoon, and although a few of his vassals who lived a short distance from the abbey had already departed for their lands, the revelries for the majority of the guests would continue long into the night.

A servant brought another pitcher of wine and tried to refill his goblet then. Christian smiled but refused it. The servant filled the Queen's cup and then moved further down the table. When he stepped aside, the King saw a man, tired, dirty, breathless, and ill-dressed for the occasion, standing before him.

The stranger bowed awkwardly before the high table and handed him a crumpled parchment. Christian took the parchment, broke the seal and read the contents, the pleasant expression falling from his face. He glanced at the man and then turned to his bride.

"Drink up, Kaith. I will be back in a moment."

Standing up from the table, he signaled to Paschal, Van Necht, and Grey to join him as he escorted the messenger outside the hall.

Acrida sat at one of the lower tables with Dewain's wife and youngest son and Olbert's wife and daughter-in-law, half-listening to the women as they discussed their children's activities and accomplishments. She watched Van Necht leave the hall with the King, Grey, and Paschal and, in a few minutes, saw them return again.

The King, Grey, and Van Necht returned to the high table. Paschal, however, went directly to Lord Manton and whispered in his ear. Then he went to a long table of loud, gregarious knights, and with not much more than a word and a gesture, they abruptly rose and followed the young nobleman out of the hall.

The King had not long returned to the table when the Queen's maid appeared, smiling.

"Come, My Lady, 'tis time to retire to bed."

"'Tis early!" Kaith protested.

The old serving woman smiled at the child.

"No! I am not tired! I want to stay up!"

"Kaith-" Christian chided.

She turned to her cousin and asked, "How is it I am Queen, and I still have to go to bed before everyone else?"

The nobles near her laughed.

"Kaith, it has been a long day-" Christian replied.

"But I do not want to go to bed! I have never had more fun in my life!"

"There will be other nights, Kaith. Be a good wife and do as your husband bids. Besides-" Christian consoled as he yawned and stretched for show, "I shall retire shortly myself- as soon as I make my excuses."

Christian's words seemed to placate the girl.

"Very well," she sighed, rising from her chair.

At this, a herald called out to the hall: "My Lords and Ladies, the Queen retires!"

At this announcement, the guests who were sitting all stood up. Van Necht groaned internally and went to stand near the Queen as all the unmarried girls, both those betrothed and those unpromised, hurried to the bride's side. The musicians immediately began to play and sing the traditional bridal song of blessing, comfort and joy. The entire hall joined the singing; the most enthusiastic of all were the young girls surrounding the bride.

"They are going to escort the bride to the bridal chamber. You should go with them, Acrida," Dewain's wife told her mildly.

Acrida smiled but shook her head as she looked at the crowd of young, highborn girls gathered around the Queen. She watched wistfully as the Queen, her maid, her Royal Guard, and the group of gaily singing girls passed through the bowing guests and left the hall, and the door shut behind them.

"A health to the Queen!" one of the guests called out, raising his cup.

"Aye!"

"Aye! A health!"

Dewain stood up behind the high table and waved his hand in the negative.

"No! Please!" he shouted, "No more drink for the King- lest it rob him of his-" then he gestured with a drooping finger.

The adviser's words were drowned out by a roar of laughter. The musicians abruptly ended the song of blessing and began enthusiastically playing and singing a lively and saucy song of swyving- much to the revelers' glee. All the men near the King immediately teased him with bawdy comments.

"Sire, if you will take some advice from an old fool-" Tate called out over the din of the crowd of guests. "If for some reason you forget what you are doing tonight, do not fear. Simply, remember the wise words of the dam builder: If you should find a hole, plug it up with whatever you find is handy.-"

The guests roared with laughter; even Christian chuckled.

"Never fear, My Lords," Grey called above the music to the guests. "If the reports from Gaulia are true, the King has been preparing for this night since he was a young lad.-"

"Aye, and if he has not learned it by now, he is no son of Filberte!" another vassal called out.

The guests laughed and cheered again. Christian himself reddened with embarrassment despite himself. The teasing and well-wishing continued from the growing number of men crowding around the royal bridegroom.

Then Christian held up his hands and signaled for quiet- even from the musicians. When he had everyone's attention, he spoke:

"We thank thee most heartily for coming today. -We regret that we must dampen this merry evening with grave news. We have just received word from Lord Walfrid that his castle is under attack."

"What is this?" Olbert and Dewain were asking.

Murmuring of alarm at once filled the hall, and Christian saw the fear on the faces of his guests. He caught sight of Bennet and many of the servants and guests crossing themselves.

"We have dispatched knights who even now ride to reinforce Walfrid and to intercept his attackers. Lord Walfrid's lands lie in the northeast of our kingdom," King Christian continued. "The invading force poses no immediate danger to this abbey. It would take them weeks to get here, if St. Benedict's is even their objective. The unfortunate consequence of this news is that the coronation festivities that had been planned and prepared for the entire week will end after this evening. At first light, We will lead the forces already assembled here to Medius and there gather the remainder of Our army.

"We ask any of you that are able to return to your lands this evening to go now- that you may organize your knights and supplies and so send them to Us shortly.

"For those of you who have come a great distance and had planned to stay the entire senight for the festivities, the monks have assured Us that you are welcome to stay however many days are necessary. The brothers have gone to much trouble to prepare food and drink for so many for the entire week; and it would be a pity if their efforts were wasted. -That is all."

After his announcement, the revelers were distressed and in turmoil. The King mingled with his startled vassals and guests, assuring them as he could. After about half of an hour, Lord Olbert collected him, his steady hand on his shoulder. Christian knew it was time, and reddening despite himself, excused himself from the conversation.

"My Lords and Ladies, the King retires!" the herald called out.

The musicians once again began to play, this time the traditional song of blessing for the bridegroom. Christian was instantly surrounded by his friends, close advisers, and favored knights.

Lords Felix, Olbert, Grey, and Dewain, Sir Ecktor, Sir Eldwin and Father Bennet, and the King's bodyguards, among the crowd, all sang cheerfully as they escorted the King through the bowing guests and through the door of the hall. Once outside, the cold, winter air of twilight sobered the group and the King even more; and the merry singing faded.

The group walked in silence through the snow ruined by hundreds of footprints toward the guestquarters where the King's chambers were.

How had the invaders made it so far within their borders so rapidly? Christian wondered again. Did Walfrid's castle still stand or had it already fallen? Did Paschal have enough knights to reinforce Walfrid's defenses or would they all be slaughtered? Had he dispatched his friend to certain death? Let Paschal for once be prudent and not rash! Christian prayed silently.

When would Herryck's main force invade or were they already invading? And where were they going? Where should he make his stand? Would Herryck's forces manage to secure a defensive position before his own army could respond? And why had there been no word from Lord Aistulf? His lands were closer to the border than Walfrid's. Had Aistulf's castle already been razed?

The group arrived at the guesthouse, entered, and at the bottom of the stairs, met the girls who had escorted the Queen to the chambers. Everyone wished the King a good night there and took their leave.

Christian continued up the stairs accompanied only by Bennet and his bodyguards. When they reached the chamber, they met Van Necht and the Queen's maid waiting outside with one of the priests from the abbey who had just finished blessing the bed. They bowed to the King and then stepped away from the chamber door.

"A good night to you all," Christian said quietly.

The group bowed again.

Then Christian opened the door. The chamber was lit with candles, and Kaith, dressed in a white sleeping tunic, lay in bed already. As he stepped into the chamber, she turned her face to the door and smiled at him. He smiled and shut the door behind him, leaving Bennet, the maid, Van Necht, his bodyguards, and the priest in the corridor.

83

As he emerged into the evening air from the guestquarters, Van Necht saw some of the guests departing the monastery for their homes. As he returned to the feasting hall, some noble families, now that the royal bridal party had retired, were heading for the guesthouses also. Those without sleeping accommodations there either had to find a place in the already crowded stables or else would end up sleeping on a bench or table in the hall itself.

Van Necht was glad to see the young, noble girls being escorted out of the hall by either maidservants or parents. The only people remaining in the hall were adults not burdened with parenting responsibilities- for this evening anyway. The drinking and merriment would continue in the great hall long into the night for anyone with the stomach for it, and already some of the wenches from the abbey's village had arrived and were mingling with some of the knights.

Van Necht caught sight of Albern talking in the shadows with the familiar woman whose well-known husband was at the other end of the hall laughing and drinking himself to oblivion with other friends. Van Necht frowned, knowing well that in a few hours when her husband was either passed out or asleep, the comely lady would sneak away to share the bed of his good friend and vassal.

Acrida stood with Tate, the King's advisers, and a group of knights as they talked of Herryck's attack on Walfrid Castle.

"-The King himself knows no more," Grey was saying. "The messenger was dispatched when the attack on the castle began. They were taken completely by surprise. Apparently the force was able to conceal itself by infiltrating the dense wood that borders Walfrid's lands."

Grey glanced at Acrida, who did not seem to be listening, and then continued.

"It is not the main part of Herryck's army, but only a small force of perhaps four hundred or so."

"Four hundred!" Sir Ecktor declared. "It *is* an army!"

"What has been done?" Dewain asked.

"The King dispatched Lord Paschal with fifty knights to Walfrid's castle."

"Or what remains of it-" Sir Eldwin commented.

"They should arrive in two days, weather permitting," Felix said. "Hopefully, Walfrid was able to rally help from the vassals nearer to him."

"Aye, but we will not know more for a few days," Grey surmised.

As the men continued to speculate about the strategy behind the attack, and Herryck's intended invasion point for his main force, Acrida's thoughts turned to Van Necht again against her will. She fought down her feelings of longing for him, telling herself she should retire for the evening.

"Van Necht, when do you depart?"

Acrida went cold, and her heart skipped a beat and then began to beat rapidly.

"The Queen will remain here for a few days. The King will send instructions when he knows more about the situation."

Acrida trembled as the familiar voice she so longed to hear answered the inquiry. To her alarm, the voice came from right beside her. Her breath became shallower, and the palms of her hands went damp at his close proximity. She could even smell his familiar scent that she knew so well. As her heart pounded hard and fast in her chest, she was helpless to the feelings of yearning and grief that overpowered her, but she would not allow herself to look at him.

He never cared for you, she reminded herself. *He only treated you with courtesy, as is his custom. He has made a pledge to his lady. You must forget him and seek a more suitable man.*

Her feelings, however, would not heed her head. They knew what they wanted, and it was Van Necht, no matter how. The shame or sin of it mattered little now, and Acrida knew she would surrender to him, if he but only bid her.

Struggling to keep control of herself and to fight down her desire to reach out to him, even here among his peers, she forced herself to be still and silent. She would not beg. She was a grown woman, not a lovesick child.

He loves a highborn lady and thinks nothing of you, she told herself again. Would she truly debase herself further by giving herself to a man who would bed her out of convenience and then cast her away at his whim?

He was not worthy of her love, she argued. He was not even worthy of her attention. In all likelihood, he was probably amused at her infatuation- an infatuation which she was certain this entire group of men must have some inkling of by now, as Tate did.

Her temper rose a notch at the thought of Van Necht and these other nobles laughing at her.

Still she would be civil to him, she told herself. He deserved civility. And she was at a royal party. If she wanted the nobles to continue to believe that she belonged among them, she was going to have to control herself.

Thus, she stood perfectly still, neither listening to the conversation nor allowing herself to look at the object of her affection. After a little while, the group began to disperse, and Acrida moved in step with the other advisers.

"Well, *Acrida,* it has been a long time."

Acrida stopped short, her heart beating madly. Van Necht had finally spoken *to* her. His greeting, however, was marred by the sarcasm he used in saying her name. Though she was curious, she dared not look at him lest her true feelings break free from her hold and she throw her arms about him and embrace him right there.

Lords Dewain, Grey, and Olbert turned back to him, however, as did the Fool. They all looked at her, expectantly. Acrida realized she was trapped, and slowly, she turned toward Van Necht. Staring straight at his wide, black velvet chest, she curtsied meekly.

"It has, My Lord. It is good to see you up and well," she said quickly, and then she turned to hurry away.

"Is it, indeed? Thou acts as if thou hast seen a spirit."

Acrida half-laughed, but stopped as she realized that his tone was not friendly.

"Aye, indeed she does, Van Necht," Dewain told him genially. "But we are all greatly relieved that thou art still among the living."

"Live, I do, thanks to the skill of her good aunt," Van Necht answered, his eyes watching her face carefully as she continued to avoid looking at him. "-I understand the King has kept you occupied since you left my lands, *Ac-rid-a*."

That drew her attention. She looked directly at him and wondered what he meant by both the comment and by the way he pronounced 'Acrida' in three distinct syllables. It was strange, particularly since he always called her Cinsara. As her eyes studied his face, she saw that his jaw was set and his eyes were intense with fury.

Although she was growing more nervous of the nobleman's mood, her reply was calm.

"I know not what you mean, My Lord. The King has been back from St. Brychan's monastery barely three weeks; before that, I was not engaged with the King's affairs."

Van Necht was surprised at her admission. -But then she could not lie in front of the advisers and say that she was sent for without being caught, he reasoned.

"Affairs of your own, then," he said, barely controlling his hostility.

Acrida again wondered what he could mean.

"She was a guest of my household for more than a month-" Dewain told him pleasantly, "the playmate of the children."

"Indeed? How was she received?" the warlord asked.

"Very well. We all found her to be very agreeable."

"And did the knights of your household find her so?" Van Necht asked.

"Aye."

"And what of your manservants and stable hands and squires?"

"Aye, they too found her very pleasant company," Dewain answered with an uneasy smile.

"Well, Acrida, that is high praise indeed," Van Necht said, "for most courtesans are never so well received-"

Acrida, the advisers, and Tate all looked at him in astonishment. "What?!"

"Usually there is a great amount of bickering over a wench- between those who have enjoyed her and those who want her next," Van Necht continued. "It is a wonder that your household has not been in utter chaos, Dewain."

Acrida gasped.

"What is this you are saying?!" Olbert and Dewain demanded.

"What nonsense is this, Van Necht?! She is not a courtesan!" Tate said.

"She will readily go to any man's bed if he will but present her a trinket," Van Necht argued.

Acrida's jaw dropped.

"That hardly makes her a courtesan," Grey said. "It only makes her- *a woman.*"

"Do I know you?" Acrida asked, hardly able to speak.

"Thou offendest her, Van Necht!" Dewain interrupted.

"Why dost thou abuse her?" Olbert asked.

"Abuse her? Howso? She can not seriously make a claim of chastity after residing in the King's Court, among the King's many vassals and servants, and seriously hope to be believed. But if there is a man in all of Speyron who will risk his life and honor defending her virtue, I will readily meet him."

The advisers, the Fool, and the growing group of spectators around Van Necht all gasped.

"Thou art a knave to insult me and issue such a challenge!" Acrida said through clenched teeth, all thoughts of civility and decorum abandoning her as her temper blazed. "Wilt thou call me unchaste when my virtue was truly at no greater risk than when I abided with you!"

"At no greater risk-?" Van Necht echoed in angry surprise, his hands making tight fists. "Dare you to complain about your treatment-"

Acrida swallowed.

Dewain laughed nervously, saying, "I am certain she has no complaints about thy hospitality, Van Necht."

"I should think not!" he agreed.

"Van Necht-" Olbert began.

"Perhaps you think I could do no better than the likes of you for a mistress!" Van Necht snapped back. "-You have neither the charms nor the skill to suit me!"

"Indeed, My Lord, I thought any sheep would satisfy you!"

"Acrida!" the advisers gasped.

The warlord grabbed Acrida's bare throat with his powerful right hand, so irate now he could strangle her on the spot.

"That tongue will be the death of you, I warrant," he snarled.

Acrida, her anger so roused now that she felt no fear at all, stared hotly back into his eyes, refusing to cower before him.

"Van Necht," Dewain said anxiously, "this is hardly the time or the place for such- a personal discussion! Clearly, you and Acrida have had some sort of-"

"This is my reward," Acrida said with short breath, while trying to pry his fingers off her throat, "for the days and nights I tended you while you lay near death-"

"'Tis likely the only reward I shall ever give you."

"Van Necht, the King will be unhappy if you kill his last seer!" Olbert was saying apprehensively, feeling like he was trying to talk some sense into the King, rather than this usually composed vassal.

"To think that I ever thought well of you! How happy am I that I escaped you-" she managed to snarl.

"It is I who have escaped, for you intended to use me well, I see! And I treated you above your birth, You Ungrateful, Peasant Bitch!"

In good spirits, Sir Albern pushed himself inside the tight huddle of people, curious to know what amusement had drawn the crowd of spectators in the center of the hall. To his astonishment, he found Van Necht with his death grip on Acrida, and she defiantly holding her ground.

"I never- needed- your good treatment!" she managed, struggling for breath under his tightening grasp.

"That much is obvious from the look of you, You Bloody Whore! I hope whoever he is, he is getting his money's worth!"

Acrida gasped, as did everyone. Sir Albern stood amazed.

"To think- that I wept- over you-" Acrida said angrily, hot tears rolling down her cheeks, wetting Van Necht's massive hand, "even after- I knew- you to be the beguiler- that you are."

"Me? A beguiler?"

"Aye, -beguiling a woman- who has been nothing but true- and trusting- into believing-"

Van Necht released her throat as suddenly as he had grabbed it. He wanted to hear this. He had never promised her anything, and they both knew it. He wanted her to speak and condemn herself.

"Beguile a woman into believing what? Tell me, *A-crid-a*, what did you hope I would give you?"

Acrida was silent as she caught her breath and as she noticed for the first time the crowd around her.

"Costly gowns? Jewels? Knowing you, I would not be surprised if even marriage was in the back of your mind, your aspirations lie so high."

Acrida was immediately shocked, humbled, and humiliated at the remark. And she suddenly felt her shame more than her anger as the tears streamed down her face.

Had she ever cared for him? No, she told herself, surely not! Nor would she ever, she promised.

"Well? Speak!"

"Now I understand what I truly mean to you," Acrida began, wiping her cheeks. "And I would say, My Lord, that my 'aspirations' were quite low to stay willingly so many days with you. The entire time that you coaxed my feelings, -you did not regard me enough to honestly confess your secret betrothal."

"Betrothal!"

"What?!" Felix and Tate stammered.

"Is this true, Van Necht?! Are you betrothed? Without the King's knowledge or consent?!" the advisers were immediately asking, stunned.

"What is this? A clandestine marriage?!" others were saying.

"The King will be livid!"

Van Necht's eyes widened in astonishment at the extent of Acrida's fabrication. He had never known her to lie, but now he saw it came easily to her. The eyes of everyone were on him now, and murmuring immediately began in the hall as word circulated.

"Who is the Lady?" Olbert, Dewain and Grey were demanding to know.

"Take him to the King at once!" Felix demanded.

"Aye! To the King!" others joined in.

"She is lying! I am neither married nor betrothed!" Van Necht shouted angrily over them all. "-You shall spend the night in the stocks for telling such a lie! Secret betrothal, indeed!"

"You are found out, My Lord! Why do you persist in denying it?" Acrida said.

"I deny it because 'tis a lie! Get the monks! Have they no stocks here?" Van Necht called out, grabbing her by the arm. "You will look well in that dress in the stocks!"

"Let her alone, My Lord!" Albern told him quickly.

"Take them to the King!" more were shouting in the hall.

"Enough! *No one* is going to disturb the King now!" Olbert shouted sternly to the crowd. "Release her, Van Necht! We shall look into this. If stocks are in order, we shall see to it."

Frowning at the Steward, Van Necht let go of Acrida's arm abruptly.

"By God in Heaven, I wish-" Acrida snarled with more tears gathering in her eyes, "I wish I had let you die- even as you were!"

Everyone gasped. All eyes turned to the warlord, but Van Necht could think of nothing to better this remark.

"I have no doubt of that," he said simply.

He turned and pushed himself through the crowd toward the door. He went directly outside into the cold air with his vassal knight following closely at his heels.

Seeing that the excitement was over, the revelers dissipated back to the tables as the three advisers and the Fool escorted Acrida to a corner of the great hall.

"I am *not* lying, My Lords! And you shall not put me in the stocks to appease him!"

"Remember your place, Woman! We may put you in the stocks for sport alone if it pleases us!" Grey told her.

"Grey!"

"Does he have a claim upon you, Acrida?" Dewain asked abruptly.

"No!" she answered indignant.

"What has come over Van Necht?" Olbert was asking. "He was in a good humor earlier."

"I care not!" Acrida answered.

"He seemed surprised," Tate answered, "to learn that Acrida left his lands of her own accord and not by summons from you or the King."

Lord Dewain looked at Acrida, who was standing against the wall of the hall, her arms crossed angrily.

"My Dear, when you took your leave of Lord Van Necht, did you tell him you were summoned?"

"No. I did not take leave of him, My Lord. When I left, he was still unconscious from his fever."

"You left him in such a condition? On his deathbed even?" Dewain asked, amazed.

"Why did you not wait until he had improved?" Olbert asked.

"I cannot believe this of you, Acrida! This was not well thought out," Dewain said.

"I was not his prisoner, nor his subject!" she argued hotly. "And I had stayed too long already!"

"Were you not his guest then?" Dewain chided.

She frowned.

"I admit I left hastily, My Lords, -but there was nothing more I could have done for him."

"Well, you may have thought so, Acrida. But you see, he did live."

"'Twas my intention that he should live! 'Twas my hope and my prayer, My Lords! I gave him the best care I could, but I had not the expertise to save him! He was at the foot of his grave, past hope, when my aunt arrived to tend him!"

The listeners raised their eyebrows.

"She was helping him; I could see that," she continued, wincing. "I was certain he would recover, and if he died, then, truly, it could be no fault of ours. My aunt is a very able healer, and it was in no way reckless for me to leave him with her. For if she could not heal him, no one but God could."

"But tell me, Acrida," Lord Olbert asked her compassionately, "what moved you to leave him at all? Despite your harsh words, clearly you care about him greatly."

She sighed.

"Because I could not bear to stay-" she admitted quietly on the verge of tears, "-not after I had discovered his secret love when he had concealed it so well from me."

"How did you discover it?" Grey asked.

632

"The fever freed his guarded tongue."

"I just supped with the lord, Acrida," Tate cut in. "We spoke at length of marriage, and his desire to *avoid* it. Are you certain-?"

"He declared his love to his noble lady!" she interrupted testily. "There could be no question of their *intimacy* or of his devotion *to her!*"

"But who is she?" Dewain asked.

Acrida frowned as she shook her head.

"I remember not her name, My Lords."

The men were silent, grasping the intensity of Acrida's feelings for the nobleman and both parties' injured pride. Whatever the relationship exactly had been between the two, clearly Van Necht considered it binding until he tired of her. Therefore, he was understandably angry to discover that she had left him on his deathbed of her own accord.

"Acrida, I believe you should retire for the evening," Olbert told her soothingly.

The other advisers agreed.

"I will escort her to her chamber, Ministers," Tate volunteered.

The advisers nodded in agreement, and Tate walked her out of the hall.

84

Albern walked briskly in the frosty winter air searching for his lord whom had gotten away from him in the dark. Finally, the knight made out the warlord's dark figure standing alone in the cloister walk of the monastery, looking out past the church.

Van Necht stood fuming in silence. How dare she make a complaint of imperiled chastity when he had shown so much restraint! How ungrateful she was! And to impeach his honor with the preposterous accusation of a secret engagement! What a liar she was! God's wood! How had he ever fancied her?

"How now, My Lord?"

Van Necht looked up to see his loyal vassal before him.

"Pray, what has happened? Why did you abuse Acrida so? -You who owe her so much!"

Van Necht gave one sarcastic laugh.

"*Never* speak that name in my presence again, I bid thee. She has proven herself to be a liar and a strumpet, and I regret the days I ever showed her a moment of regard."

Albern was stunned.

"I can scarce believe these words are thine own. I have never known you to be ungrateful for a favor done for thee, and this is how you repay the woman who hast saved thy life?"

"And 'twas I not struck down defending her? Methinks the debt is paid."

"I marvel at thee. I expected this to be a blessed and happy reunion for you both. But an hour ago, I expected that you would have the lass in thy bed by now, but instead I find the two of you hurling insults as I have never seen a man of equal honor to yourself do. Pray, tell me what has brought on this unhappy occasion."

Van Necht frowned, but answered grudgingly, "Truly, I had hoped for such a reunion as you have said, but then I began to be troubled by what I heard."

"What was that?"

"That she was not called away on the King's business as you told me. That she went to Dewain's lands of her own accord, no doubt for whatever benefits she could achieve, while I lay on my deathbed. See how she repays my kindness?"

The knight's face paled as he realized what had happened.

"Am I the cause of this? My Lord, I never told you that she was summoned by the King or his ministers to do his business."

Van Necht looked at him. Albern swallowed nervously.

"I said that she had gone to Dewain's *likely* to perform some business for the King."

"What is thy meaning?" Van Necht asked unamused, his eyes narrowing.

"I never said she was called away; I said she had *likely* gone to do the King's business," he repeated.

The blow sent the knight to the snow-covered ground. Albern moaned, his face hurting. Leaning up on his elbow, he put his hand to his cheek and confirmed that it was indeed bleeding. He looked up at Van Necht, but did not get to his feet immediately. He knew his temper too well.

Looming over the knight, Van Necht fought the urge to strike him again. He looked away toward the church again and tried to collect himself. Finally he spoke.

"Get up."

Albern got to his feet and prepared himself for another blow.

"Hast thou forgotten *thy* vow of honesty to thy lord? Do you think I will tolerate a liar to be my trusted vassal?"

"Perhaps I was not honest with you, Van Necht, *at the time*. Perhaps I should not have allowed you to assume what I knew you would. But *at the time*, I had my reasons."

"And they were?"

"You were ill, My Lord! Deathly ill! And I thought it unwise to burden you further with the melancholy that I knew the truth would bring."

"So you allowed me to assume that Acrida left to do the King's business when she left for no reason like that at all."

"Aye, that is the truth of it."

The blow that sent the knight to the ground was harder than the preceding one, and Albern's entire head ached with pain. Suddenly, Van Necht was pulling him back to his feet by his clothes, preparing to strike him again. The vassal cringed and set his jaw, preparing to take it and as many more that would follow.

"Why did you not tell me later? Why did you continue to allow me to believe this?"

"I meant to tell you, but you never spoke of her to me! You talked only of war and training the men! -And then there were the preparations for attending the coronation and bringing the men; and- I forgot."

Van Necht tightened his grip on the man, knowing well Albern had been engrossed these past days with thoughts of seeing his married lover. Yet, he also knew that Albern was speaking the truth. He remembered all the times that the knight initially had mentioned Acrida, and he himself had changed the subject, for fear that his vassal would guess how much he truly missed her.

"Why did she leave? Do you know? Did she fear I would die and she would be blamed? Or did she seek another man more to her fancy?"

"I know of no other man she cared for, save you. How could she?" Albern answered. "She feared you would die, but moreso she feared that you would live and n-"

"Speak clearly, Man! That is no cause to leave!"

"She believes you have a secret love, or so Deidre confided to me. -Clearly Acrida believes you are betrothed."

"You knew this, and you did not tell me?!" Van Necht exclaimed, his hand clenching into a fist again.

"Forgive me, My Lord! I meant to tell thee!"

Van Necht frowned, but opened his fist.

"Why would she think this?" he asked.

"Apparently, she heard you declaring your love either while you slept or while you were delirious. When Deidre told me of it, Acrida had already left. It was too late for me to tell her it was nonsense."

"When I was delirious? God's blood!" Van Necht swore, releasing the knight. "Who would believe anything a delirious man said?"

"As I have tried so often to explain to you, My Lord, women believe such things readily."

Van Necht turned back to Albern.

"Any idea what I might have said? Knowing me, it was probably something to Manda, or any of the tavern wenches."

"Not Manda, My Lord. -Most likely it was Gunhilde."

"*Gunhilde*-? What words of love would I have said to her? 'How, I hate thee, My Lady!' 'You Ungrateful Bitch, shut your shrewish mouth, 'Hilde!'"

Albern looked down at the ruined snow sadly as the words Van Necht used now sounded much like the words just spoken to Acrida.

"I know not, My Lord. But apparently, in your fever you swore your love to Lady Gunhilde. And if you have never told Acrida how you felt about her, 'tis only natural for her to lay down her arms to the victor."

Van Necht looked at his vassal evenly. So this was why she believed him betrothed. Although ridiculous, it made some sort of sense. Still, his doubts remained as well as his suspicions that since her abandonment of him, she had already taken up with some other rich nobleman.

"And you believe that?"

"Believe it?!"

"Aye, the 'Hilde part."

"Of course, I believe it! 'Tis the truth!" Albern declared.

Van Necht looked at him skeptically.

"Part of me suspects that she left because she knew that even if I lived, I would never give her the gifts or money that she -and *all* women-desire. -And she left to seek a man that would."

Albern blinked at him in surprise.

636

"Is that why you decried her?" he asked.

Van Necht made no reply.

"I cannot believe this of you, Van Necht!" Albern responded angrily.

Then he paused.

"What was it she asked you to give her?" the knight suddenly inquired.

Van Necht hesitated, surprised at the question. As he thought about it, he could not recall her asking him for anything specific.

Guessing at the answer to his question, Albern frowned at his lord.

"You are such a fool, Van Necht! You do not know anything about that woman, do you? And well you should not, for you are not worthy of her, or any woman worth having!" he said, outraged.

Van Necht glared at the outspoken vassal, but his look of warning was ignored.

"She saved your life! Do you think that if she was only interested in coin or gifts that she would have left at all before she had tried to collect them from you? She certainly earned them! Do you think that if she intended to milk you or any man for riches, and- as you say, she realized that they would not be forthcoming, do you think she would have even bothered to stay with you or send for her own family to heal you? What makes you think she would have cared if you lived or died? She could have easily sent me for the physician in Leeds who would have simply watched you die and then taken your fine stallion for payment of services rendered!

"I am so ashamed of you now and of the way you spoke to her in the hall that I cannot bear to look upon you any more this night! -If she has found a *generous* man who values her now, so much the better for her!"

And with that, Albern turned and walked away abruptly. Then he stopped and turned back to Van Necht.

"If you were not such a fool, you would see she did it all because she loved you, even to leave you rather than confront you about the love she thought you bore another woman! And if you were not such a fool, you would be seeking her now, swallowing thy pride, and apologizing to her before the wounds you have inflicted prove fatal to your- *friendship!*"

Then the knight turned and marched off, utterly disgusted, leaving Van Necht to himself.

Van Necht cringed, riddled with guilt. Albern was correct, of course. It was all so clear to him now. He was a fool. Reliving the display in the hall again, he berated himself harshly. Why had he not confronted her in private? Why had he not given her a chance to explain?

Once again he saw the look of disbelief on her face when he had challenged her virtue and then her humiliation as he accused her of desiring to wed him. He remembered again the agony in her eyes when he named her a dog and a whore. Finally he recalled her eyes full of tears of pain when she had uttered what was still ringing in his own ears, that she wished she had let him die with his sins upon his head. The memory tore at his very core.

Albern had given him good advice, but Van Necht knew it was too late. She would be with her lover now, and the warlord did not want to know who he was at the moment. In the morning, he would find her alone and apologize then. Perhaps, in a little time, after her present admirer dismissed her, he would have an opportunity to have her again. He turned to go to the guesthouse then where his chamber had been prepared for him.

The warlord had not walked five paces when he met Olbert, Grey, Dewain, and Sir Ecktor. Knowing what they were going to say, Van Necht spoke first.

"She is wrong. I am neither betrothed nor married to any woman, anywhere! -But, pray, do not put her in the stocks on account of her misunderstanding."

Van Necht then explained what his vassal Sir Albern had told him.

"And Acrida did not know that Gunhilde was the name of your former wife?" Olbert asked, perplexed.

"No, and there was no reason she should, for I have forbidden that shrew's name to ever be spoken on my lands."

The men raised their eyebrows.

"And you are just learning of this misunderstanding now?"

"Do you have a claim on Acrida, Van Necht?" Dewain asked directly. "-If so, she has not worn your ring."

"I have no claim on her," he admitted.

"Then pray explain to us why you issued a challenge to her virtue," Dewain said, "when in truth she has been as modest as any true woman of the Faith."

Van Necht shifted uncomfortably.

"Sir Albern also just admitted that he misled me into believing that she was summoned from my sickbed on the King's business. I admit I reacted poorly when I learned otherwise earlier at the feast. -I presumed the very worst about her."

The men raised their eyebrows and glanced at each other.

"Even so, word of your challenge has spread already, and, indeed, it may well be answered, My Lord," Sir Ecktor told him soberly.

"-By several knights in my own household. My eldest son threatens as well," Dewain grumbled.

"Indeed, 'tis best that your vassal knight publicly proclaim and bear his guilt in this so that this dishonor will pass from you," Grey said.

"No," Van Necht answered flatly, "I will bear it alone. I issued the challenge, and I must stand by it, though I admit I spoke rashly and out of passion. -But before I publicly proclaim her chastity and innocence -or before I am rushed upon by a gaggle of her would-be champions, someone should ask permission of her current paramour, for he may wish to seek satisfaction himself."

The advisers looked blankly at him.

"What paramour?"

"I know not," Van Necht answered. "Perhaps the one that gave her the blue gown."

"The King?" Olbert answered. "Oh, aye, he will definitely have a say in this."

"The King?" Van Necht echoed.

"Aye, when he arrived back from St. Brychan's, he commissioned the royal tailor to make her a livery," Olbert said. "She has an entire truck full of similar gowns."

"I doubt she has been to the King's bed," Sir Ecktor added. "He has not been near a woman since his return from the monastery. The King even returned the concubines to their own lands."

Van Necht looked at the knight, feeling utterly foolish then. He had never considered that King Christian had simply outfitted her as he had promised.

"I will publicly proclaim her innocence and apologize," Van Necht answered, "and do *whatever else* honor demands."

"Very good. We will inform her in the morning," Olbert told him.

The group of men turned and left.

Van Necht considered seeking Acrida out right then, and then thought better of it. It was too soon to apologize. If he went now, he would look weak. *And* he knew her temper. He would wait until it had time to lull a bit. He would go to her tomorrow- early and make it right again.

85

As the night spread out her dark cloak, the monastery glowed from the numerous burning torches that hung on the walls. Tate and Acrida walked by several groups of people gathered in the chill air. The sounds of their merriment as they laughed, drank, and exchanged stories in their friendly clusters only heightened Acrida's bitterness.

"No, this way," she instructed, shivering in the brisk wind as she pointed toward the cloister itself.

"You do not have a chamber at the guesthouses?"

"No, the *noble* families received chambers in the guesthouse. The King's *lowborn* seer stays in a cell."

"Really?" the Fool commented, impressed.

"Aye, one they save for visiting monks."

"How extraordinary!"

"It is cramped and sparse compared to my chamber at the palace!"

"I should hope so.-"

The pair arrived at a building attached to the cloister edge near the church. Finding and entering the cell, Acrida waited in the cold dark as the Fool retrieved a candle and lit it from the burning torch that hung on the outside wall. He returned after a moment, shut the door and looked about the chamber and at its contents.

The small, very narrow cell was quite plain; the walls were bare, and the stone floor was without a rug. A tall, frame bed with a straw mattress covered in sheets, feather pillows, and a woolen coverlet took up most of the space. In the far corner was a tiny, skinny bedside table; a pitcher of water set inside an earthen bowl and two more candles were set upon it. The door of the cell had a small window cut at eye-level into it covered by a dark cloth. Near the door was a medium-sized chest.

"You see it is little more than a hole in the wall!" she complained. "Indeed, methinks they have purposely made this chamber inside the wall!"

Tate raised his eyebrows and smiled.

"'Tis a fine little chamber," he commented as he lit the additional two candles on the table. "I have certainly passed the night in worse."

"I suppose it is better than sleeping in the stable," Acrida admitted grudgingly, rubbing her arms briskly for warmth.

"Indeed, Mary and Joseph did not fare so well," he smiled.

"I suppose I should be *grateful* for what I have been given."

"Truly."

"-Grateful to have an actual bed and a chamber at all! -Grateful that I am not spending the night in the stocks! -Grateful that I have survived to see another sunrise!"

Tate raised his eyebrows again and sat on the bed.

"Whore, indeed!" she muttered angrily. "-And after all I have done for him! What a fool am I to have ever wept one tear over him!"

Tate watched as the woman irritably propped her foot upon the chest, flipped up the skirt of her long, blue gown, and began to unlace her leather boot. Already the bruises were beginning to appear on her neck.

"*He* is the liar! He should spend the night in the stocks!" she fumed to herself. "-The nobles dispense justice to us. Who dispenses justice to the nobles?"

"The King," Tate offered, admiring the exposed leg in his view.

"Ha! What does *he* notice?" she snapped. "-Or care? I warrant he will do nothing about the lord's betrothal or the challenge to my virtue!"

She pulled her bare foot out of the boot, then changed feet, propping the other on the chest to unlace it.

"Likely not," Tate admitted. "Of course, you have the King's ear. You could petition him."

Acrida considered this for a moment.

"But most likely, even that will come to nothing," Tate continued.

"So what should I do?" she asked dismally, setting her boots beside the chest.

Tate shrugged.

"Forgive him."

"What?! Why should I forgive him?"

Atateo raised his eyebrows at the 'true woman of the Faith'.

"Because the Christ commands it, and the Church teaches it?"

"There could be no other reason," she replied testily, removing the linen headrail from her head.

"On the contrary, there are many reasons to forgive him," Tate scolded. "Van Necht is an honorable man, but a man, nonetheless, and vulnerable to all the temptations and weaknesses that plague men."

She looked at the Fool sourly and crossed her arms.

"-If that is not cause enough for you, then forgive him for your own sake. -You are a woman and have the divine gift of love flowing through you. It is the fate of women to be wronged and blamed for all matter of troubles and perplexities. But if you do not forgive, you will block that flow of love, and you will be bitter for the rest of your days."

She stood unmoved, her expression like stone.

"And Van Necht is not the only one, is he, *Acrida?* There are many you must forgive- lest you be 'acrid' all of your days," he accused sternly.

"Forgive those who have wronged *me*?" she scoffed. "Forgive the village neighbors who robbed me of my mother by chasing her off a cliff? Or the village children who teased and shunned me all the days I lived in Brackenbach? -Or King Christian who dragged me out of my home and very nearly put me to death? -Or Lord Huntingdon, who stood by and allowed him to take me and the other village girls? Ha! Never!"

"Acrida-"

"I will never forgive any of them! -Nor do I understand how anyone could forgive the King after the evil he has done! -Not after the innocents he has slain! -Nor after he unleashed three garrisons of knights upon his own serfs so that *his honor* might be avenged! -And certainly not after he desecrated the most precious Body of the Savior at the Mass! I will never forgive him!"

"He has repented, and God has forgiven him. If God can forgive him, can you not?"

"He does not deserve forgiveness!" she answered sourly. *"None of them do!"*

"But we all need it."

She gestured in exasperation.

"Truly, I can not comprehend your charity, Atateo! Have you never been falsely accused, scorned, hurt, or humiliated?"

"Aye, of course, I have," he answered mildly, "but I am a man who can look into the human heart and forgive all the pain, frustration, short comings, and bad decisions that cloud the goodness there."

"Goodness?" she scoffed again. "-Well, you are better than I. I do not want to forgive," she said, frowning. "I can not."

"'If I have the gift of prophesy, and understand all mysteries and all knowledge, et cetera, but have not love, I am nothing.'"

She shrugged indifferently at the Fool's paraphrase of the scripture.

"Acrida, if you will not forgive, you will lose the Bridegroom. You-"

"Bridegroom?! Have you no ears?!" she snapped. "Van Necht was never going to marry me! And I never hoped for it!"

Tate raised his eyebrows.

"We were never lovers, and he has no claim upon me!" she continued to fume. "Van Necht is the bridegroom of another! He has made a pledge to a noble lady!"

"As you say!" Tate smiled, bewildered and slowly shaking his head.

"-Does my humiliation amuse you?" she demanded.

"No, -but I find your jealousy quite entertaining."

"Jealous? I am not jealous!"

Tate laughed then.

"You are green with jealousy! You can see nothing but green! And not even over a woman, but the *possibility* of a woman!"

"I heard him declare his love to her!" she argued. "He is devoted to her!"

"To whom?" Tate pressed. "Who is she?"

"I told you I remember not!"

"Van Necht despises women! I can not fathom him speaking soft words to any woman. In truth, the only woman he has had any toleration for whatsoever in several years -is *you*."

"Aye! He tolerates me so well that he denounces me and challenges my virtue!"

"Because he too is jealous, Lass! What man complains whom a woman's bedfellow is except he who wants her in his own bed?"

"He can not be jealous, for he never loved me!"

"Perhaps not," the Fool shrugged, "but that does not mean he did not desire thee."

"No, he *never* did."

"Now thy contradict thyself. Did thou not just accuse him, claiming that thy virtue was in no greater peril than in his presence?"

Acrida flushed crimson and hesitated before she answered.

"'Twas as *he* said," she admitted quietly. "My chastity was never in real peril, for he was my desire; I was not his."

Tate smiled.

"The lord has always behaved- befittingly-"

The old man noted the disappointment on her face.

"-as he should since he is betrothed."

Tate looked at her, startled for a moment, and then laughed out loud.

"What are you saying, Woman? Are you suggesting he has made a pledge of chastity as a show of *devotion* to a woman?"

"Aye."

The Fool marveled at her naiveté and laughed again, shaking his head.

"Do you even know him, Acrida? Van Necht would never make such a pledge! I do not know a man that would! Most men, noble and common, fail to restrain their lust when they are out of earshot from their wives. Do you think any will deny themselves when they are only betrothed?

"I have known Lord Van Necht for years! He is an honorable man, but he is not yet a saint. 'Tis true, he will not touch a married woman, but he is a frequenter of wenches and a patron of brothels! -And I tell you as ever I have spoken a true word: That man desires thee!"

Acrida frowned.

"If he is not chaste; if he bedded wenches daily outside of my knowledge, then it only means he prefers them to me. He prefers *any* woman to me.-"

Tate sighed and made a gesture of exasperation.

"You still do not believe it-" he muttered, stretching out on the bed and propping himself up on one elbow. "Very well, how often did the lord visit you at the inn? Every day?"

Acrida looked at him in confusion.

"Did he make some excuse to visit?" he asked.

"The inn?"

"Aye, did you not lodge at the inn?"

"No, I stayed with him, as I always have."

Tate looked at her, astonished.

"You stayed with him at his tent?"

"Aye."

"-Had he any servants?" he suddenly inquired. "-For it has widely been said that he-"

"No, he keeps no servants."

Tate marveled at her.

"You spent those many weeks alone with him in his tent, without even a servant present?"

"Aye."

Tate was amazed.

"And he never touched you for all those weeks?"

"No."

"Where did you sleep? In his bed?"

"He does not have a bed."

"Answer the question!"

"I slept- near him," she admitted.

Tate was silent as he considered this. Acrida was a commoner and no doubt was completely accustomed to bundling with other family members for warmth along with the animals. Plainly, she did not realize how extraordinary the nobleman's behavior actually was.

"What is it?" she asked.

"And he has truly never touched you?" Tate asked again.

Acrida was silent.

"And he has never said anything?" he continued.

"Said what?"

The Fool said no more as he thought.

Acrida leaned against the wall, thinking of the night she too had mistakenly thought Van Necht desired her. Could there be any real harm in telling the Fool what had happened on the plateau? she wondered. Van Necht would likely only deny it anyway.

"Once- I thought as you do."

"Hmm?"

"The day before he was wounded, we traveled to the neighbor's land, and on the way back he stopped on the hillside and showed me where his castle used to stand and- something suddenly came over him and-"

Tate glanced at her.

"And?"

"He kissed me."

Tate smiled a small smile.

Acrida swallowed.

"But he was not himself.-"

"What happened then?"

"That was all," she shrugged. "It is hardly worth mentioning.-"

"What do you mean, 'That was all'?" Tate demanded. "What did you do?"

"Nothing."

"Nothing?"

"Aye."

"You did not kiss him again or yell at him or hit him or-?"

"No."

Tate looked at her skeptically.

"I was so stunned!" she shrugged again, helplessly. "-And then the horse was lame, and it began to rain, and so we stayed the night in the inn in his village. -He was in the foulest of tempers that night. I know not why."

"I bet he was!" Tate agreed, amused.

"What? Did I do something wrong?"

"Dear Girl, it was what you did not do! If you had but given him a smile- or, knowing him, if you had but fought him- he would have taken you."

Acrida was shaking her head. No, he would not have, for at no time had he truly desired her. He had simply not been himself on the plateau.

"'Tis true, Acrida! You might have gone up that hill a maid, but if you had given him the slightest encouragement on that hilltop, you would not have descended one for certain. He would have dispatched your maidenhead there and then."

Acrida stared at the old man, pale with horror.

"You are a lucky woman," Tate then chuckled and shook his head. "Perhaps the luckiest woman I have ever met! It is a wonder that Lord Van Necht did not strangle you this night, for he believes he has cause."

"What?!"

"Van Necht believes you have a lover, Acrida, perhaps several. And likely any man who knew the whole truth would feel him justified if he did choke the life out of you."

"What!"

"Van Necht spoke truly. His treatment of you has been *very high* above your birth. He has exercised remarkable self-restraint, and you dared complain about it! -And still you breathe!" the Fool laughed.

Acrida stared at the old man, still not understanding.

"-But he has done this for you, Acrida, not for another woman."

"No."

"Aye," Tate argued. "When the King initially sent you to Van Necht, he intended for you to be guarded, but also to be bedded as the warlord pleased."

Acrida swallowed.

"I know all about this, for it was a jest about the Court for several weeks. The joke of it was that Van Necht detests the company of women, and Paschal and the King thought it quite humorous to send a witch to his bed. The jest," he admitted with a snicker, "was even better than they could have guessed for they actually sent a *virgin* to him."

Mortified, Acrida gasped and turned away.

"No doubt it was always Van Necht's intention to take you to his bed, but when it became apparent to him that you were a maid, likely he did not know what to do with you. The warlord is no collector of maiden-gear."

Acrida sat down on the chest and covered her face with both hands, her humiliation brimming over. Was it obvious to everyone?

"Van Necht is a warlord," Tate continued. "To him, women are the spoils of battle or they are paid in brothels. They make two distinct sounds that are perfectly familiar to him: they cry and curse, or they engage in common tavern banter. He knows little else.

"As he spent more time with you and his fondness grew, likely he could not bear to hear either from you.

"Poor Bastard!" Tate laughed again. "How you must have vexed him! For months, he has probably pondered nothing but how to get in your lap with the least amount of blows to his dignity -and without *offending* you. Then, tonight, he learns you abandoned him on his deathbed, and he sees you adorned in an expensive gown and at the dance with many men."

Tate laughed.

"He must rue the day he did not bed you at his first whim! No doubt the poor man will be the joke of the Court for months again!"

Tate laughed hard again and then noticed that he alone was laughing. He looked at his companion and saw tears running down Acrida's face.

"My Dear, how now?"

"Do they laugh behind my back?"

"What?"

"Am I not the joke of the Court as well?"

Tate looked at her, not understanding.

"Am I not the 'Maid of the Court'? It must be obvious to everyone as it is to you! I can hardly bear the shame of it!"

"What shame?"

"What shame?! -I am of such age that I should have children nearly grown, but no man will have me! I shall die a maid! Was I cursed at birth that I should be alone? Was it not enough that my mother made me barren, but I must too live out my days unloved, undesired, and untouched? -What have I ever done to deserve this?"

"'Tis not so, Acrida! Thou art not cursed! The men at Court and, too, those in Lord Dewain's household, like you well. Give them time."

"Time?! I have done nothing but be patient and wait my entire life!" Acrida exclaimed, throwing up her hands in frustration.

"Very well. Van Necht certainly wants you. Dry your eyes and go to him now."

"What?!"

"Go to him! I know you want to!"

"After he called me a whore and challenged my virtue, you think I would go to him?!" she asked, getting to her feet.

"Aye! Take up your coverlet and go to him! -Tell him that it is all true, that you have been to every bed in Speyron for the lack of him."

"I will not!"

"Then go to him and say nothing, but take off your clothes. He will understand that even better."

"I will not! I can not endure more shame this night!"

"Shame if you go. Shame if you go not," Tate shrugged. "You will have to summon him. Shall I get him for you? He will never be able to find your chamber on his own. It is too far away from the guesthouses."

"I will not humiliate myself by begging-"

"You must-"

"No!"

"Why not?"

"Because I have gone to him before!"

Tate stopped and smiled, eyebrows raised.

"What happened?"

She turned away, embarrassed and flustered.

"I am going to bed," she announced, changing the subject.

"What happened?"

She swallowed. She did not want to tell.

"Acrida!"

She sighed with vexation.

"-That night at the inn in the middle of the night, it occurred to me that he might desire me -that he might have wanted me on that hillside, as you even now have said. -I knew it was wrong of me to think it," she added hastily, as she reached behind her neck and pulled at the laces of her gown.

"He is so noble.- He could have any woman. He could never truly want me.- But I went to his chamber anyway."

The Fool smiled.

"And when you opened the door, you found he was already *entertaining* a guest," he finished.

Acrida flushed red and yanked the lace.

"His chamber door was open, and he had two wenches in his bed- and they laughed at me."

"How angry he must have been!" Tate hooted, but upon seeing her pained look, added quickly, "You must forgive him, Acrida. He is a man! He has his pride!"

"As do I!" she said still struggling with the cords.

Tate sighed and shook his head.

With a moan of irritation, Acrida went over to the bed and turned her back to the old man.

"Tate, help me. My maid laced me into this gown, but she is not here to get me out of it."

"Very well, go to bed," he said, sitting up and examining the knot that she had made tighter. "Do not forgive him and do not go to him! Seek instead someone new. After your fine appearance tonight, someone will surely pursue you. You need only to encourage him."

"How?"

"Look at him. Smile at him. 'Tis not difficult," he shrugged.

"If that is all I had to do, I think I would be married by now."

Tate raised his eyebrows at this as he pulled on the laces. This was true, he admitted. Acrida was no seductress. Even if she did perceive a man who desired her, she did not know how to encourage him. -'Twas a pity that the King had not bedded her when he first took her from her home. She was quite possibly one of the few women who could have profited completely by the experience, no matter how disappointing it was.

The old man had the entire length of her back unlaced in less than a minute. Acrida stepped away from him, surprised at how deft he was with the laces. He was more adept even than her maid.

With a slight smile, Tate observed the bodice of the gown fall from her like an autumn leaf from a tree. He watched her push the material down over her hips to the floor. As she stepped out of the clothes at her ankles, the candlelight illuminated the soft curves of her body covered by the fine, thin undertunic she wore.

Acrida gloomily folded her gown and then her discarded headrail and placed them both inside the chest. As she began unbraiding her long, black hair, in the back of his mind, a little voice told Tate he should go now before it became any later so that he might still have his pick of the young widows to spend the night with. Images of the buxom women with bold eyes who had flirted with him earlier that day came to mind again, yet Tate continued to watch Acrida prepare for bed in silence.

He watched her retrieve a jeweled comb from the chest and then begin to comb out her hair that, unbound, flowed from her head like a dark waterfall down her back. After a few minutes, Acrida glanced over at the Fool. He was lying on his side, with his head propped up on his hand, this time with the oddest expression on his face and in his eyes.

"What?" she asked.

"What?"

"You look at me strangely."

"Do I?" Tate answered, musingly, with a small smile gracing his comely features.

"Aye, you are."

The old man's expression remained unchanged so Acrida returned her attention to her hair. She sat down on the chest and continued to comb her hair with long, slow strokes, the ends making a dark pool on the stone floor. After a minute, she looked back at Tate and smiled curiously at the man who wore the same bizarre look on his face and who seemed totally engrossed with watching her comb her hair.

Tate read her face like a familiar view, knowing she could not recognize the *come hither* look he gave her.

He smiled again.

"Acrida, do you want me to go now?" he asked carefully after a moment.

Having redirected her attention to the ends of her hair which she held tightly in one hand and combed vigorously with the other, she shrugged.

"Forsooth, I do not. I am not really tired, and I find you to be good company and the first, true friend I have been able to confide in -in months."

Hearing the old court jester beginning to chuckle quietly, Acrida looked at him for some explanation. Seeing her bewildered and vexed look, Tate stifled his mirth and explained as seriously as his sense of humor would allow him.

"No. I mean, *do you want me to go?*"

Acrida watched him speak these words, noting carefully his tone and inflection on certain words and the look in his eyes as they glittered by the candlelight. The blood in Acrida's body suddenly turned cold as she realized the meaning of his question: He was not asking her whether she wanted him to go, but actually whether she wanted him to stay- the night.

As Acrida's face went blank, Tate smiled again. She understood him. He waited patiently, trying not to laugh as he watched her consider what he had asked.

After her initial shock passed, Acrida's heart pounded, and her mind raced. She stared at the man that age and experience had made even more handsome, lying so invitingly on her bed, like he belonged there. The amused smile he wore on his face made her feel reckless. There was something about him that had always caught her attention, that had always made her watch him whenever he was near, though she was not certain what it was.

Perhaps it was just that he was blessed with good looks that improved with each passing day. His smooth, shaven face, which was besieged with its deep wrinkles, allured her. She was lost in it, entranced. His gray hair, which bordered the edges of the slick, abandoned field on the crown of his head and hung down loose to his shoulders, showed signs that it would soon begin to turn silver. In her mind, Acrida could not imagine his hair any other way; indeed, she would not have had it any other way. The rest of him was also unexpectedly appealing. He was not frail or weak in his age, nor did he possess a large belly that so many old men had. The Fool was a tall, good-sized man and powerfully made. He still had a broad chest and wide shoulders. He did not possess the musculature of Van Necht, but he was clearly strong.

Acrida looked away from him, her palms perspiring, as she acknowledged her attraction to him. Then her head caught up to her and took control again. Cold fear gripped her as her mind informed her in specific detail just what they would do if he did stay.

She glanced back at him anxiously only to see him still smiling mildly at her. She realized she must say something.

"I - I do not know," she managed with a blush.

"Well, you will have to decide."

Acrida swallowed, remembering Van Necht's kiss on the ridge again and how his pure might had overpowered and frightened her. Her heart pounded in her chest as she felt it all again just as she had then -especially her fear.

She was not ready, she knew. It would be better to wait.

In the back of her mind, she heard her own words once more: '-I am of such age that I should have children nearly grown, but no man will have me! I shall die a maid! Was I cursed at birth that I should be alone? -What have I ever done to deserve this?

-I have done nothing but be patient and wait my entire life!'

Acrida paused. Tate was correct, she admitted. It was not what she had done, but what she had failed to do. If she truly wanted her life to change, she would have to act. If she was unwilling, then there was no one to blame except herself.

"I want you to stay," she suddenly heard herself say.

Acrida stood shocked, not believing she had said it. She wanted to take it back, but it was too late.

Instead, she added, "But- I am afraid."

"Of what?" he was asking, his eyes dancing in amusement.

She looked away.

"Are you afraid of me?" he asked her, speaking slowly like one speaks to a cornered bird that has flown in a house.

"No. Not of you."

"Of swyving then? -Why?"

Acrida looked away.

"Did someone hurt you? Or did you see someone hurt?"

"No-" she admitted. "My aunt and uncle were always -quiet."

"Perhaps you are just nervous. Well, do not be anxious, I have had a bit of practice over the years," Tate said with a teasing smile.

She looked at him blankly. Acrida knew this was meant as a joke, but she just could not bring herself to laugh. Then she became quite alarmed as he climbed off the bed and came over to stand in front of her.

Acrida's eyes went to the old man's blue ones. As he approached her, she began to tremble, but her reaction was not completely from fear of what he would do. In fact, surprisingly, Tate had a calming influence on her. She looked deeper and deeper into his eyes, getting lost in them. She saw no ferocity, actually nothing besides genuine interest, except perhaps amusement.

Tate stood very close in front of her, invading her personal space, all the while looking down into her blue eyes, his fingers clasped casually together in front of him, a simple smile gracing his features. Acrida realized then he was waiting.

Waiting for what? Was she supposed to do something? And then it occurred to her that he was giving her time to run for the door- if she wished it. She realized then that he did not intend to force her, that this really would be her decision.

Lost in his blue eyes and the disarming wrinkles on his face that deepened as he smiled, Acrida felt so odd. She felt so comfortable with him, so safe, almost like they had known each other forever. Her heartbeat quieted as she felt the energy and strength and self-assurance that poured from him. In that moment, she knew that she would follow this man to the edge of the world if he but beckoned her.

He was still standing patiently before her, still waiting on her to do something. This made her smile.

"I am not going anywhere. I want you to stay, truly."

He chuckled and then reached out his hand, putting it behind her head into her black hair, stroking it gently. Then he abruptly bent down and kissed her on the mouth.

His romantic assault was so unexpected that Acrida jumped backward a little in reflex, her body quaking with the effects of his touch.

It was not a brief kiss. Tate put his other arm about her to brace her and softly changed the pressure on her lips. This sent another wave of pure sensation through her, so much so that Acrida suddenly felt every muscle in her body give out on her.

He felt her go weak, too. He broke off the kiss at once and held her securely in his arms. He moved her smoothly toward the bed where, rather than setting her down gently on the edge of it, he shoved her backward into the midst of it. The unexpected tumble into the bed disarmed her and made her smile in spite of herself.

As he removed his faded and worn, woolen cloak from his shoulders, Tate turned and went and bolted the door and then pushed the heavy chest in front of it. Then he came back to the bed and put out one of the candles, leaving two still lit.

"Acrida, My Sweet," he said in the cheeriest of tones as he pulled his tunic over his head, "I must warn you: I am a thorough taskmaster. You shall get little sleep tonight, I fear."

Acrida's heart fluttered as the gray-haired paramour spoke these words. As she watched him remove his knife and shoes and begin to unwrap his leg bandages, part of her wondered what she had gotten herself into; the other part, still reeling from the sensations stirred within her from his kiss, could not think at all.

Author's Note: The following three chapters contain graphic descriptions of sexual activity which some readers may find offensive. To skip these chapters, please go to page 678.

86

are-chested, Tate climbed into the bed beside Acrida with his braes still on. His undressing had prompted a new surge of fear in Acrida, and she had fixed her eyes on the bare wall. Feeling the bed sink under his weight, she did not dare to look toward him or to breathe.

Tate observed the telltale signs of her raw fear with a frown, knowing if it was not relieved, fear would be her lover, not him. A woman could lie seemingly lifeless during avowtrye, completely surrendering her body while her spirit separated itself from the labor. He hated bedding women who did it. While most men did not particularly care or notice what a woman felt as long as she lay still, he found the swyve perverse and distasteful. Over the years, he had met a few women that did it every time, no matter what man came near them, and Tate had a good idea of when they had learned to do it.

And seeing Acrida stiffen as he moved toward her and keep her eyes turned away from him, he knew this was going to take some effort. He would have to slow down a bit.

"What? *Now* you are suddenly at a loss for words?" Tate teased in the lightest of tones.

Lying on his side, he wrapped her in the wide circumference of his bare arms and held her close to him, her back to his chest. He said nothing more for the moment. What he wished to tell her, he communicated through the strong arm that held her while his other hand smoothed her long, luscious, shiny hair that covered the coverlet and pillow.

Acrida did not know what she had expected, but finding herself enveloped in his embrace was an unforeseen comfort to her. She felt warm and safe, and the tension drained from her until she was like a rag doll in his arms.

As he held her, Tate relaxed, letting go of all his cares, allowing his consciousness to drift into a state of pure, physical sensation. His mind relented readily as he was still intoxicated by the taste of Acrida on his lips and the smell of her lavender-scented hair mixed with the scent of the burning candles. He was ushered further into that blissful state of mind by the warmth of her body pressed against his, her thin, linen tunic the only barrier separating her from his own flesh. The feel of the flimsy material against his chest proved to excite him as much as the flesh promised to which it hid from him. The Fool lay still for a long while, savoring the delicious feeling the intense blood flow to his groin brought with it.

Only when he was certain Acrida was quite calm did he begin. Sweeping her copious hair away from her neck, he began to kiss her lightly there. As he laid his trail of kisses, Acrida gasped and could not help but hold her breath as goosebumps ran up and down her body. His kisses were so light that she could hardly detect them on the surface of her skin. Somehow her body registered them, and Acrida felt the effects of his feather touch and warm breath deep inside her body, instead of where the man set them.

Acrida's whole body came alive and shuttered and tingled as it never had before. Every light brush of his lips translated to pure sensation inside her; she was defenseless against it, as well as to her own body's immense physical reaction to it.

Tate slowly worked his lips and the tip of his tongue up and then back down the side of her neck that was exposed to him. He smiled as he noted the changes in her breathing and the frequency of the shivers that he caused to run through her body. The quivering he caused and the taste of her skin under his tongue served to fuel his own excitement as well. As was his custom, he would continue building his own desire slowly as he built hers until he was nearly delirious with excitement.

'Twas a pity that so few men ever practiced the technique, Tate thought. The self-discipline, as well as the self-knowledge required, was character building in his opinion.

While he contemplated this, Tate went to Acrida's ear and kissed her lobe and underneath. Even as she squirmed in urgent, reflexive reaction and tried to put her ear to her shoulder to ward off his attack, by her giggling, Tate knew he was doing the right thing. He continued to assault the ear just to hear her protest and laugh unrestrained, as she wriggled against him to escape. He laughed too.

Finally, he let her ear alone. He renewed his offensive by nibbling on her neck again with light bites from his teeth, and by the way she cooperated instinctively, he knew she liked it.

Then the Fool allowed his hands to roam. Staying on the outside of her tunic, he caressed her softly around the navel and then his hand went lower to her abdomen, where it rubbed large, soft circles.

Acrida could feel his touch all the way through her body. This man had the gentlest touch, she found herself thinking, and God's eyes, what was he doing to her? He was turning her body to mush. She had never known she could feel this way.

Tate ceased his caresses and shifted a bit then, easing Acrida onto her back. She sank into the coverlet on the soft, loosely stuffed mattress. Once there, Tate kissed her on her forehead, then on her nose, then softly kissed her trembling lips. Although she was expecting this, Acrida could not stop herself from involuntarily jumping as his lips brushed hers. However, she forced herself to keep still, and she settled quietly against him cooperatively, as his mouth's gentle but persistent pressure continued to soften her mouth to his. Even after she became accustomed to this touch, Acrida was still amazed at the shivers that swept through her body in reaction to his kiss and at the stirrings taking place in her abdomen. His hand stroked and clutched her hair that lay in a heap by her face, and even this touch sent waves of pleasure to her scalp.

Then she felt the tip of his tongue brush her lips with a little force during the last, long kiss. Tate broke off the kiss abruptly.

"Open your mouth."

When she tried to ask him why, Tate kissed her again, dominantly. It was an odd sensation, but hardly anything compared to the next- of something touching and then rubbing her tongue. It was so unexpected that she wrenched herself away from him.

Was that his tongue? she wondered. She looked up bewildered and found Tate's laughing eyes and amused expression peering down at her. Tate smiled at her, while wiping the sides of his mouth dry with his hand.

"Like that? 'Tis very popular among the Frankos."

"I think it very odd."

Tate chuckled and kissed her again, allowing her no time to protest if she had wanted to, his saliva mixing with hers. Her mouth tasted of sweet wine. His tongue charged deeper into her mouth than before as his arms, sliding around behind her back, held her close so there could be no escape. Tate held her young, soft body snugly to his own, fully possessing her mouth as he conquered her spirit and will.

With his mouth completely controlling hers and his tongue rubbing her tongue, Acrida found that the way he kissed her so deeply made her feel totally secure, even more so than when he had just held her alone. In a way, he was forcing her tongue to submit as well. Despite the kiss, Acrida could not help grinning slightly at the humor of it. She slipped her arms around Tate's neck and shoulders then and concentrated on this new feeling which even now did not feel as strange to her as it first had.

Gradually, his tongue retreated from her mouth, and he began to pull away from her; and Acrida felt a wave of disappointment. Determined that he should not escape, she pressed her mouth even harder to his lips, and plunged her tongue into his mouth. Following his movement, she shifted her weight against the Fool, further unbalancing him, and managed to tip him over so that he landed flat on his back, and she over him.

Still she kissed him. He tasted of cloves and pears and wine. Acrida was totally mesmerized by the tactile feeling and the relaxation she felt as she rubbed her tongue roughly against his: all her mind and energy was directed there. She was entirely oblivious to the saliva that leaked from their interlocked mouths or how provocatively her body rubbed against his. Still focusing on the explorations of her tongue in his mouth, Acrida's hands began to wander under Tate's back and shoulders, one floating up to stroke his soft gray tresses.

Finding himself suddenly overpowered and lying beneath his quarry, Tate surrendered himself momentarily to the beauty's terms. The Fool was surprised by how suddenly uninhibited Acrida had become, how hard and passionately she kissed him, and how eagerly she made him her prisoner in her embrace. His body burned with excitement as she maneuvered herself with wanton abandon to straddle his body so that she could better position herself for complete possession of him. It was almost too much for the old man. As he moved his hands up her smooth sides to rest on her waist above him, he trembled involuntarily, desiring only to be inside her now. He fought this urge successfully until Acrida, in her zeal, pressed her soft, inviting flesh a little too firmly against him. Tate moaned and pushed away from her mouth and embrace.

"What is wrong?" Acrida asked, looking down at him.

Tate, sweating now, laughed self-consciously.

"Nothing at all. You are too good at this is all."

He pushed her off of him, and he rolled over onto his side again; and while his mind gained control of his body once more, with one hand he worked her long tunic up. With her eyes lost in his wrinkled, handsome face which she touched lightly with the back of her fingers, Acrida let her head sink into the mattress, simply surrendering to the series of chills she felt as Tate uncovered her. After several tugs, he pulled the material above her navel, leaving the young woman naked from the waist down. Tate admired her soft, well-made form, the smoothness of her flesh that shivered at its exposure to the cool room and the triangle of dark, course hair that hid her secret garden: the garden that would not remain undiscovered for very much longer, he told himself with relief.

Tate proceeded to run his hand up Acrida's leg, but then changed his mind. He sat up, his erect yard pressing uncomfortably against the confinement of his braes. Looking at his dark-haired companion whose eyes were locked onto his own, Tate guessed she was as of yet unaware of him. He pulled the young woman to a sitting position between his own bent knees. Acrida scarcely breathed as the man grasped a couple of folds of her tunic in both hands. With a practiced motion, he lifted it quietly and gracefully removed it, letting it fall to the floor. Acrida blushed crimson, and looked away, embarrassed, as she sat completely naked in front of the handsome, mature man.

Amused by her blush and embarrassment that were traits unique to maids alone, Tate was struck by how lovely and fresh Acrida was. He gently brushed the long, black hair that had fallen in disarray over her breasts and belly back over her shoulder, and then he took a moment to enjoy the view of her naked body in the soft candlelight. Her shoulders and upper arms were meaty and round, but smooth. Her breasts, though not large, were ample, cone-shaped handfuls. Her hips were pleasantly wider than her waist, and her legs were agreeably long and supple. But it was her face with its simple appeal and those penetrating, blue eyes that had caught Tate's attention- even from the first day he had seen her as the King's prisoner.

He eased his left hand behind the girl's shoulders to support her as his other hand moved her chin so that her face was turned to him again, and his eyes locked back onto hers. Then he bent forward a little, and his mouth found hers once more, her lips immediately parting. As he sucked gently on her full lips, his right hand slid from her chin and jaw down her smooth neck, and then slowly down over her breasts.

Acrida jerked away reflexively at his intimate touch, breaking from the kiss, laughing and shivering as the gooseflesh covered her. The old man held her firmly in his arms and knees as she squirmed.

"That tickles," she giggled, unconsciously lifting her arm to protect her chest.

"I know," he smiled.

He softly cupped the fullness of her left breast, and in so doing, sent Acrida wriggling and giggling uncontrollably. Tate laughed with her, good-naturedly dropping his hand from her breast to her thigh. They laughed together for a moment, letting the laughter melt the tension away.

After a moment, the Fool readied himself for the new raid on her sweet, unspoiled breasts with a slight, wicked smile and a tilt of his head. When, however, he turned to focus his seductive gaze into her eyes again, he was momentarily startled by the look of genuine affection in the young woman's eyes.

Tate's smile wavered: for the first time that night he was uncertain of how he felt. Her look, in fact, was so honest and unexpected, that Tate's defenses completely dropped, and with it, his smile altogether. Becoming lost in her lovely eyes that held him captive, the old man's face was filled with seriousness, as he was suddenly inundated with his own powerful feelings of attraction, admiration, and fondness for this young woman.

Very carefully, Tate regained control of his feelings, and swallowing the uncomfortable lump in his throat, he leaned forward again slowly and kissed her chin, then moved to kiss her throat, and then lower, working his way down her chest, easily moving away her guarding arm. He pushed her down to the mattress as he descended.

Tate's touch and kisses sent a whole series of new goosebumps and quiverings through Acrida, particularly as he began to concentrate his attention on her breasts. She gasped in pleasure, overcome with the sensations the old man created as he gently took the left tit into his mouth, caressing it softly with his tongue and lips. For the first time in her life, she came to the conclusion that her body had a mind of its own and a language- and Tate was talking to it; and her body was answering him with every tremble. She felt all kinds of stirrings, particularly in her abdomen; it was as if her very heart was beating down there.

Once Acrida had grown to accept his touch at her breasts, Tate expertly moved to her right nipple and began to circle it with his tongue, softly and gently. Holding her down just a bit to keep her still, Tate reveled in the pleasure that shot through his body as he explored the smooth texture of the nipple with his tongue. Taking the tip between his lips, he sucked very gently, feeling the blood course to his groin with new energy. After her nipple hardened under his administrations, he moved back to the other one.

As he continued to lick her, Acrida's mind slowed even more, overcome with the fantastic sensations that swept through her. Her only reoccurring thoughts were amazement at what she felt and the hope that no matter what the man did, he would not stop what he was doing.

As the other nipple hardened, Acrida was surprised and a little alarmed as she became aware that the top of her inner thighs were wet.

Tate finished with the breast, his own breath coming short and quick, mirroring Acrida's. He put his hand on her left calf, and trying to keep his touch as light as a feather's, slowly ran his hand up her leg, little by little, his efforts rewarded by the woman's gasp. Acrida held her breath as Tate touched her, every part of her being completely focused on his hand and how he caressed her leg. Her body ran wild with trembling and ripples of excitement. And all she wanted was for him to go on.

Tate sat up impatiently and stroked her other leg, though a little faster and a little more carelessly than he had done the first one. As he reached the top of her leg, he slid his hand to the inside of her thigh which was slippery with her juices. She was ready, and that was good because he was so excited now he could not even feign to be calm. His breathing was short, and he was in a sweat. The only lasting thought among all the other fleeting ones in his mind was a command to take her, and he knew better than to ignore that command too long.

Needing no more prompting, he deftly untied his braes, releasing his standing yard.

Acrida's heart raced as she realized what the Fool was doing, and her fear came bounding back to her. She turned her head to the wall then, watching the flickering shadows of the candlelight; and Tate, seeing her face, saw that she was fighting her fear again.

Working swiftly, he pushed his breeches down a bit so that his privy parts stood unhampered and immediately moved back to her. He climbed over onto her as surely and carelessly as he would have mounted his own horse, noting, agreeably, how her legs fell apart, making room for him to lie between them. Lying on top of her, he steadied himself on his forearms, trying to keep most of his weight off of her.

She felt like a rock beneath him; she was so suddenly tense and nervous. Tate, with an immense amount of self-control, forced his excitement down and willed himself to relax, though it was difficult. Taking a deep breath, he made himself count. As he lay on top of her, concentrating on his numbers, he combed her hair with one hand and watched her face, waiting for her to relax in return. She would eventually, he knew.

After a moment had passed, and when Tate did nothing more than lie on top of her, and not very heavily at that, Acrida turned her face back to him.

… twenty-six, twenty-seven, twenty-eight…

Tate's lips were curled into a mysterious, but encouraging, smile; and the eyes that regarded her seemed to dance with some secret that they were desiring to share. A feeling of security swept over Acrida, despite her fear. She could not help but smile back; she relaxed a little.

…thirty-one, thirty-two…

He lowered his head the few inches separating their faces and gave her a soft kiss that turned quite passionate almost immediately, and sent his tongue directly to hers. He felt her body relax a great deal then against the pressure of his mouth on hers.

Swiftly, he removed his tongue, breaking the kiss, and in one motion brought his hips forward, pressing his throbbing yard inside her. Tate moaned quietly with intense pleasure as the swollen head of his hardened prick gained access to the warm, wetness inside her. At the same time, he felt her body immediately tense up, but this did not stop or even slow the man's entry. Fighting the urge to seize her and hold her down while he entered her, he gripped the coverlet and sheets of the bed instead in his hands and pushed himself inside her warm, slick, tight crevice, forcing her reluctant flesh to allow him admission. Neither did Tate slow or falter his thrust at the first wince of pain he felt from her, nor when he felt her maidenhead refuse him further passage, nor even as she cried out in pain when he breached that barrier. He did not stop until he was completely lodged inside her.

Once there, the Fool looked at the young woman to survey the damage. Acrida's face was a study in pain: every line on her sweet face attested to it. Tate was sorry for her pain, but she had to be open to receive him.

After the initial surprise of feeling something enter her queynt, Acrida had experienced some friction, great pressure, then pain, and then a very sharp pain. All that registered after that were expressions of that pain. Acrida wanted the pain to stop and that thing that caused it to be out of her.

And like some answer to a prayer, she felt it withdrawing. It still hurt, but it was being removed slowly and that was the important thing. But to her surprise and immense disappointment, just before it left her and was done with, she felt the pressure and pain increase again as Tate pushed himself fully back inside her.

"Owh," she protested.

"Easy now," Tate breathed to her in soothing tones.

He paused in his motion for a moment, giving her time to become accustomed to the novel feel of the whole length of him inside her.

Though he knew no words he could say would take away the pain she now experienced, he said, "You are doing well," keeping the tone of his voice both warm and cheerful.

His hands having released the sheets a little before, the right one moved back to Acrida's hair and stroked it gently. He watched the young woman's lovely face as she looked mutely at the ceiling. He smiled as he saw her swallow and then to breathe more deeply.

He started to slowly move inside of her again. With determination and patience, he fought down his own desire to drive into her as fast and deeply as possible.

After several slow strokes in and almost out of her, the Fool began to build his tempo to one that was a little faster and a little more comfortable for him to maintain. The warmth and tightness of Acrida's queynt served to excite him even more. And his excitement rather than his exertion brought his breathing on harder.

After about three or four minutes of actual penetration, Tate said, "This should not hurt as much now. Does it?"

The pain *had* subsided under his rhythmic thrusts into a dull, achy pressure that was very uncomfortable.

"Not so bad now," Acrida replied, her words strained.

"Good."

And with that, Tate withdrew completely from her.

Acrida did not think she had ever felt anything so marvelous in her life as him removing himself from her.

Tate climbed all the way off of her then and off the bed, and Acrida took a deep breath with relief and slowly eased her knees back together from where they lay spread wide apart against the mattress. Her thighs ached as she moved them. She realized she was going to be as sore as she had been when she had first ridden astride Van Necht's horse.

Occupied with these thoughts, she was quite surprised when the Fool, standing at the foot of the bed now, caught hold of her under the knees and dragged her toward him across the coverlet to the end of the bed. He maneuvered her until her ass alone rested on the mattress edge; her legs hung over the side. She watched incredulously and with a little horror as Tate, a pleased smile gracing his features, said in response to the bewildered look on her face, "Not done yet, Acrida. You must be patient."

She watched in disbelief as he parted her knees and held them. Standing between her legs, he brought his hips to her, and slowly inserted his yard back into her. Acrida cringed as the pressure returned.

A small gasp of pleasure escaped the Fool as his member was surrounded again by wet, warm, tight pressure. Once inside her, however, Tate assumed his normal coupling rhythm. Dropping her left leg, he placed his hand on Acrida's breast and caressed it firmly. After a moment, he leaned over more and took the nipple into his mouth to suckle roughly. He did not do this for her pleasure, but for his own, as reward for his own earlier patience.

As his need grew stronger with each stroke he made, he let her breast alone, straightened up, and held Acrida's thighs firmly to him. Tate ravaged the naked, young woman beneath him with his eyes even as his yard ransacked her queynt. As he pumped into her vigorously, each thrust of his powerful hips pushed Acrida a little farther back on the bed, despite Tate holding her in place. He was still careful though not to allow his pelvis to bang completely against Acrida's cunt, allowing the edge of the bed to receive most of the impact from the blows of his thighs. His prick alone was the only part of him that made contact with her with any force.

Acrida completely yielded to the dull, painful ache that engulfed her and lay still, watching the shadows dancing on the ceiling and listening to the heavy bed rasp against the stone floor in perfect time with Tate's thrusts into her. She put all her concentration on lying perfectly still, finding the discomfort greatly lessened when she did not move.

As Tate concentrated on his work, his gaze went to Acrida's face occasionally. Defying reason as it always did, after a while, he saw, as well as could feel, the girl gradually become more relaxed and accustomed to the steady but quick rhythm he set.

Acrida was surprised as the uncomfortable pressure began to slacken and wane, and, as it did, she relaxed even more. The more relaxed she became, the less uncomfortable she found the invasion. After several minutes, most of the discomfort was gone, leaving behind a new, but equally strange feeling she had never felt before. It did not particularly feel good, but it was not an uncomfortable feeling.

Panting above her, Tate involuntarily tightened his jaw as felt his end approaching. His hands gripped her legs even tighter.

Tate began moaning, and Acrida watched his face above her, his eyes tightly shut, his face contorted. She winced as he began to stab into her harder and faster then, the pressure on her thighs and pelvis increasing, his buttocks flexing mightily with each fierce stroke, the scraping of the bed against the floor keeping pace with him. Then suddenly, his rate dropped to slow, deep strokes. And with the change in tempo, he moaned loudly. Then the Fool shoved himself deeply inside of her one final time. And he stopped.

The only sound in the suddenly quiet room was each of them catching their breath. After taking a moment to savor his pleasure, Tate looked down at the young woman pinned beneath him. Comprehending the look of question on her face, he smiled and leaned down and kissed her cheek. Straightening back up, he slowly pulled his yard out of its hot shelter and released the young woman; and, again, Acrida thought there was no better feeling in the world. Her queynt throbbed painfully in the cool air of the room as the Fool removed his warm body from her, but her legs were too weak to move back together.

Turning her head to the side, she watched the old man stretch slowly, his gray hair flowing smoothly to his shoulders. Her eyes followed him as he walked around the bed and put out the two candles on the table. The room went pitch black, and the smoke from the extinguished candles scented the air. Then she felt Tate climb in bed beside her. She felt him pull the coverlet and sheets down, and then his strong hands hooked her beneath her arms and pulled her across the coverlet, up higher in the bed. Then he was beside her, his naked knee against her side testifying that he had removed his braes. He snuggled close to her and covered them both with the sheets and coverlets to protect against the cold in the chilly room.

Acrida lay quietly in the man's arms in the dark, listening to Tate's heartbeat and bearing witness to the new aches and pains registering in her body. She was suddenly aware of the steady stream of ooze running out of her onto her legs and the bed.

"I am wet," Acrida muttered in surprise.

"Aye," Tate answered, amused. "Breeding is messy business."

He kissed her on the shoulder sweetly.

"Was it as terrible as you feared?" he asked, his breath warm on her damp skin.

Acrida thought for a moment before answering.

"No, but it hurts quite a bit."

"Only the first time. -Never again like that anyway," he yawned.

He was asleep shortly. Completely entwined in both his arms and legs, Acrida felt strangely safe in the old man's warmth. She lay in the darkness for a long time listening to his even breathing as she waited for sleep to come to her.

87

𝕬crida opened her eyes slightly, sleep still heavy on her and her mind a blur from drowsiness. She was vaguely aware that her bedmate was biting her neck and telling her quietly to wake. As consciousness returned, she was assailed with the petitions of complaining, strained muscles in her inner thighs and a painful, throbbing suit from her privates. Ignoring the grievances of her body as easily as any lord ignores the pleadings of the subjects he rules, Acrida peered through heavy eyelids and summed that it must be the middle of the night. -And there was singing coming from somewhere.

"Wake, Acrida."

Acrida blinked slowly and turned her face toward the voice that spoke beside her, her skin awakening to the touch of the hand that now moved lusciously around the fullness of her breast.

"Huh?" she murmured, lifting her eyebrows even as her eyelids shut again.

"Wake," Atateo said. "Time to work, and there is much to do."

She must be dreaming, she told herself; after all, surely the man was too tired to want to swyve again. She was exhausted, and she had done next to nothing compared to him.

"Wake."

"What kind of work?" she muttered drowsily.

She heard him chuckle.

"-We can begin with some of the corporal acts of charity."

She smiled.

"Is there someone here who is hungry?" she teased. "Or naked?"

"Aye, and definitely in need of shelter."

She giggled sleepily.

Her body tingled under Tate's hand as it moved from her breast down to her belly and stroked her there, even as she registered another aching throb from her sore queynt. She also seemed to be lying in something wet.

"Are you not fatigued?" she asked with a mumble as she rolled away from her companion and the wet spot, her mind alone still foolishly doubting the man's seriousness.

She heard Tate laugh and felt him kiss her cheek in confirmation of his intention.

"What is that singing?" she asked half-asleep.

She snuggled against Tate's warm, firm, naked body that was once more pressed against her back, all the while attempting to give herself to sleep again. She had lain restless long into the night before she had finally drifted off for what seemed like a few minutes of sleep.

"Nocturns. The songs of the night."

The monks- Acrida sleepily remembered, while acknowledging that her body was undoubtedly responding to Tate's love bites on her shoulder and his light caresses on her belly.

Tate kissed the young woman's cold, bare upper arm which was outside the coverlet in time with the pitch changes that seeped into the chamber from the church. As he nuzzled his cold nose against the warm flesh of her neck, he concentrated on the smooth feel of the woman's skin under his fingertips. He was quickly becoming stimulated from inhaling her scent, intermixed with the musty remnant odor of their previous swyving.

He could barely discern her form in the darkness, and this visual fast served only to heighten the Fool's gathering excitement. For in being denied the sight of her body, Tate was forced to recall it vividly to mind- and to relearn her shape with his hands. This he did by placing his right hand on her face and gently exploring all the contours and indentations his fingers came across. He felt the fluttering of eyelashes against his palm and fingers, the soft, fullness of her lips, the sudden, sharp decline as his hand moved over her chin and down her neck and then under the covers, across the smooth, low mounds of her breasts and on down her whole front.

He wanted to kiss her, but knew it was futile since Acrida was still not fully awake. He settled for nibbling her uncovered shoulder again and then moved to bite her neck lightly while his right hand stroked her breasts beneath the coverlet, all the while urging the lovely woman from the grip of sleep.

Tate was uncertain what he wanted to do exactly; his desire was so ravenous. He wanted to take her fiercely, possess her completely, and frighten her with the enormity of his passion, but at the same time, he wanted to do nothing but just hold her, soothe her, and melt into her.

He started kissing her ear again, licking and nibbling the lobe, but this time, he stuck his tongue inside her ear.

Acrida woke abruptly with a complaint.

"Agh!"

Squishing her ear to her shoulder and pushing her elbow against his chest, she shoved the old lecher away from her and her ear. Hearing him chuckle at her, she realized that he had been in earnest when he had told her that she would suffer from lack of sleep.

Amused, she rubbed her ear while rolling over to face him. Immediately, his strong arms surrounded her and pulled her closer against his naked body, his right leg migrating between hers. Then his lips found hers, and her mouth opened to receive his kiss eagerly. Wide awake now and her body beginning to feel fluid under his caress, Acrida matched his hard kiss with her own passion, forgetting quickly the aches and pains that her body had registered just a moment before. Her arms encircled his neck and back and pulled him fully against her own bare flesh.

Completely at ease, Tate kissed her more passionately than before, knowing now he could take her anyway he pleased, the hard part finished. As he kissed her deeply and boldly, he rolled and pulled her half-way onto him, one hand firmly clinging to her young, smooth back, while his other hand roamed across her left breast, lightly and then firmly, squeezing the nipple between his fingers.

Leaving a trail of chills with it, Tate moved his hand from her breast down her stomach and abdomen over her left hip. He ran his hand slowly up over the soft curve of her buttock, thrilled by the reflexive tightening of the muscle he felt under his hand, before sliding both his hands down over the back of her firm thighs. Tate returned his attention to Acrida's fine ass and caressed both her cheeks, firmly, even roughly, in his strong hands.

Gasping from pleasure, Acrida fell from his kiss. Hearing her appreciative moan, Tate intensified his touch and stroked her ass with even more force, until he thought she must feel some pain. But Acrida only moaned ecstatically.

Drunk with the pleasurable sensations, Acrida felt a flood of juices flow from her queynt. She moved her bent knee over the man's stomach to almost straddle him. She bent her head down and began kissing Tate's neck and ear as he had done to her, tasting his salty skin, while Tate continued stroking her back and buttocks.

She stopped kissing him after a moment.

"Am I squashing you?"

"No," he smiled, quite pleased.

Then he kissed her again, his tongue deep in her mouth.

Overcome with wonderful sensations, and still attempting to respond to the new desires of her own body, Acrida could not help but press her pelvis against him, undaunted even as she felt his yard raised to readiness above his lower hair against her thigh.

Tate had not expected Acrida to be so willing so quickly, and the feel of her soft, supple body being pressed against him made the demands of his member even more intense. Tate broke off the kiss and hesitated for a moment, estimating he could hold out a little longer if he really tried. But then Acrida pressed her pelvis to his body even harder and smeared some of her wetness on his hip and abdomen; and Tate changed his mind.

He immediately ripped away the coverlets that entangled them, and in an instant, he had Acrida on her back again and two pillows beneath her bottom. As Acrida shivered in the cold air and the goosebumps covered her skin, the Fool sat on his knees between her bent legs and scooted closer to her until his knees were on either side of her slightly raised hips.

Acrida knew what was coming and involuntarily tensed up; she forced herself to listen to the songs drifting into the room, rather than give herself over to dread.

Tate took a moment and slid his hands sweetly and slowly from her knees down the inside of her thighs. Feeling her tension rather than seeing it, the Fool stroked her wet hair and lips gently with his fingers.

"Acrida, relax," he said in a tone that was slightly admonishing, but more friendly than anything else. "You have been through the worst of it already."

And giving her about two heartbeats to comply or not, Tate leaned forward and plunged his impatient, throbbing prick inside her warm and slippery, swollen flesh. Tate moaned as he shoved his yard deeper inside the delicious snugness.

Acrida breathed a sigh of relief. It had not hurt just as he had said that it would not. There was just pressure. His hands were on her breasts again; he caressed them for a moment and then slid his hands slowly down her belly and abdomen and around her hips, coming to rest underneath her ass.

As he stroked and held her ass, waves of pleasure lapped over Acrida, and she began to relax. Then Tate's grasp on her buttocks tightened; and she was surprised when he pulled her buttocks off the pillows and held them in the cool air.

Balancing on his knees, Tate sat up straight once more and pulled her buttocks to his groin and began driving into her at his usual coupling rhythm. He matched his pelvic thrusts simultaneously with the pull of his arms, forcing Acrida's cunt to slide forward and backward on his yard, their pelvises clashing in mid-air. Tate found the sensations the position generated and the exertion it required nothing less than euphoric. He moaned with every stroke.

Lying with her head and shoulders on the mattress while her queynt was assaulted at least a foot above her, Acrida found herself in immense pain.

"Owh-" she whimpered, tears brimming in her eyes.

Tate frowned as he heard her. With all the pleasure he was receiving, he knew his climax would not be far off. Determined to continue, he instructed through grit teeth:

"Relax! -Even more! -Go -with -the motion-" he managed, his words labored like his breath.

Acrida, panting, tried hard to focus on relaxing and, most of all, tried not to resist his violent stabs into her tender queynt or the tremendous and painful grip he had on her buttocks and hips, as he yanked her onto him in fierce, jerking motions. But it was no use.

She whimpered again, and Tate internally groaned in exasperation. He could feel his climax building within him, but he was tiring and his own hands were numb now from their odd position and fierce grip on her buttocks.

Reluctantly, he pulled his yard all the way out of her and set her ass down swiftly. Breathing hard, he pushed her at once over onto her belly, knocking the pillows out of the way onto the floor. Acrida, relieved, went willingly where he maneuvered her. Climbing between her parted legs, he pulled Acrida back onto her knees rapidly. Pulling her backward against his own thighs, he shoved his prick back into her hastily and gasped. He began thrusting into her wildly again, his hips ramming her soft ass, while he kept her hips fixed by holding the front of her thighs firmly. Despite his passion and urgent need, Tate would not allow himself to grip her hips or her shoulders now as he wanted or as, indeed, he would have done with any woman who was accustomed to swyving.

Acrida was a bit bewildered to find herself suddenly on her knees with her face and chest sunk in the mattress, but at least the earlier pain was greatly lessened in this position; she pushed herself onto her forearms and rested her forehead on the bed, relenting to the Fool's rapid thrusts into her. She could see nothing and was now quite hot in the chilly room, her face completely shrouded by her long, disarrayed hair. Making a great effort to relax to the invasion as she had been instructed, Acrida felt the remaining discomfort in her pudendum depart from her as it had before, leaving only the oddest feeling. Moving her hair out of her face so that she could breathe, Acrida occupied herself then by listening to Tate pant and the song of the monks that came through the walls.

Suddenly, Tate's thrusts became even harder and more violent as his hips pounded full force against her. He grunted hoarsely almost in what Acrida perceived as frustration, and then he groaned and shoved his member as deeply into her as it could go as he pulled her backward against his groin, impaling her with his length, her thighs slightly spread around his.

They remained there, panting for a moment, neither moving. After a moment, Tate released her carefully and leaned her forward, unsheathing himself. With relief, Acrida felt the pressure withdraw, and she slumped down onto her stomach.

After taking a moment to rest, Tate picked up the pillows from the floor and then collapsed by Acrida's side, his chest still heaving. He could just barely make out her form in the darkness. He gathered the woman in his arms and pulled her close and securely to him, then leaned up once more to gather the discarded sheets and coverlets back over them.

When he was settled, Acrida laid her head on his gray-haired chest then and listened to his breathing and his still rapid heartbeat, while her own breathing and heartbeat slowed. They lay quietly in the dark; the Fool exhausted, but blissful, fell asleep immediately. Acrida was tired too, but her body was still alert and stirred up like leaves on hot coals.

The monks continued to sing.

88

When Acrida woke, the monks were still singing. She was lying face down, draped across the old man's gray-haired chest like a coverlet. Tate was stroking her long hair inattentively, his mind adrift. She stirred quietly.

"Are the monks yet singing?" she asked drowsily.

"I am sorry. I must have awakened you," Tate answered softly, his voice gentle. "I intended to let you sleep," he told her wistfully with a smile, still stroking her hair in the same way.

"'Tis well," Acrida mumbled, snuggling comfortably against his warm body and the pillows surrounding them. "How long have I slept?"

"A long time. The brothers have been to bed and are up again to sing morning praise before the sun rises. 'Tis Lauds you are hearing."

"Oh, not dawn yet?" Acrida asked, yawning.

"Not yet."

She ran her hand down his thick arm then and asked teasingly, "And what is the matter with you? You are not weary, are you?"

Tate chuckled.

"Not particularly, but I had thought to let you rest," he said, while wrapping his hand around and around her loose hair and inhaling deeply her scent.

They were silent for a while, listening to the harmony straying into the room, but Acrida, disarmed of her usual reserve and propriety by fatigue, spoke what came in her mind.

"There are some things I do not understand-"

Tate grinned.

"Like at the end," she continued, "-before you stop, you seem to-"

Acrida stopped, horrified and embarrassed at what she had caught herself about to say.

Tate chuckled and looked down at the woman in his arms. In the darkness he could still only make out the barest of outlines.

"When I find my pleasure, you mean? Aye, it usually ends the coupling," he told her with a wide grin, enjoying immensely the combination of the young woman's curiosity and embarrassment.

He observed her with amusement as she, struggling to gather herself, ended up covering her face with her hand as she asked the next question that she could not help but ask.

"It feels good then?"

Tate laughed.

"Aye! Better than words can describe!"

"Do all men find it so?"

Tate chuckled at this question, but only briefly.

"Aye, all men- and some women, too."

"Women -like this?" she double-checked, her eyebrows coming together skeptically.

Tate grinned, loving her naiveté.

"Some women who know how to find their pleasure like it."

"Obviously, I have not found it then," Acrida muttered, while cuddling back against him comfortably.

Hearing her, Tate smiled. He stroked her hair again, feeling her warm breath against his chest. Then deciding, he moved her off of him.

"Here, roll over."

Acrida went onto her side obediently as he positioned her, sinking a little into the lumpy mattress. She felt him curl up to her back as he had earlier, this time pushing his top knee between her legs. After rearranging the covers over them, Tate leaned up on his left elbow and draped his right arm over her, his fingers gently stroking her breasts. Acrida pulled a pillow underneath her head and enjoyed the feel of the man against her and his soft caresses. She wondered what the Fool was like when he *was* tired.

Tate bent his head down a little and kissed her salty shoulder. Then he ran his hand down her belly, brushing over the light-colored scar at the base of her abdomen. His hand stopped on the triangle of coarse, black hair that covered her loins. Resting the heel of his hand on that hair, he stretched out his fingers and gently stroked the lips of her pudenda softly. He felt rather than saw Acrida go completely tense. He eased his hand away from her loins and adjusted her top leg slightly in order to open her legs wider so his hand would have more room to maneuver. Then returning his hand to her open garden, Tate allowed his fingers to trace around the sides of those lips, creating little fires of sensation for her. Although he could tell that she was clearly holding her breath to be still, Tate felt her begin to fidget.

Acrida was amazed at the sensations the Fool could create in her. Now what was he doing to her? She did not know, but her body seemed to, and it liked it.

Very dimly, Tate could make out Acrida's face in the dark chamber. His fingers delved inside the lips then, and slowly circled there, tracing the inner edge delicately. Acrida gasped as her heart pounded, and she could not lie still as hard as she tried. God's wood, his touch was driving her mad!

Tate gradually worked his way around and around down inside her lower lips until he was circling the heart of her. He allowed his fingers to graze gently the small lump there, and then he immediately circled it several times. Acrida had gone from holding her breath to panting; all her attention was focused on his fingers and where and how they stroked her.

Tate increased his finger pace somewhat around the lump, and fluctuated the pressure, knowing full well that he was driving Acrida into a bittersweet agony. His fingers were gooey with her juices, and she held her thighs even wider apart for him without even realizing it.

Observing Acrida become overwhelmed with these sensations affected the Fool as well. His yard was erect and waiting, but for the time being, Tate put his own desires aside. He concentrated completely on his manipulations.

After a while, he leaned back against a pillow and, in so doing, was less precise with his fingers. He let them stroke where they might, sometimes around the heart and sometimes on it itself. As his fingers fluttered and stroked her most intimate place in the most teasing way possible, Acrida experienced various intensities of pleasure, and if he touched the heart too hard, pain along with that pleasure.

After a while, she was breathless with some physical need she did not understand; with each stroke, Tate awakened an itch that had to be scratched, and each scratch brought on another itch. Acrida was sweating now and moaning uncontrollably, but from sweet agony, not pleasure. His touch was torture, which promised with every stroke an even better pleasure, but did not, in itself, deliver it.

"Oh, Tate, please, stop. -I cannot bear this."

Surprised, Tate looked down at her face to be certain he had heard her correctly. She had not begged for anything until now, not even sleep, and she certainly had not asked him to stop before, not even when he had hurt her. Seeing the lines on her face, he realized she was quite serious.

"Not just yet, My Sweet. But I will give you something else to think about," he told her, as he moved his hand away from her cunt.

And with that, he inched his pelvis closer to her and slipped his engorged member inside her. Acrida, whose queynt was already raw and sore, cringed at the discomfort that accompanied the unwanted invader. After a moment of his yard being once again inside her, her body relaxed instinctively.

Tate nuzzled her shoulder again and bit her gently, while his hand returned between her thighs and began circling her heart once more.

The feel of Acrida's hot, wet, swollen flesh clutching his yard again egged on Tate's desire. He forced himself to begin slow; she had been through enough already for one night, particularly the *first* night. His hips began the motion back and forth as gently as possible. Tate's other hand held her securely against his chest, which reminded Acrida to make herself relax. After a minute or two, the discomfort again abandoned her completely, and her attention was solely on the sweet sensations that sprung from the caresses of Tate's fingers.

They moved quietly together, only breathing hard, while the songs of the choir flowed into the chamber, until Tate purposefully began to touch the lump more often and to apply a firmer pressure around it. He began to stroke it in time with the motion of his hips as his yard moved back and forth a little faster inside her.

Acrida, in torment, lay writhing against Tate's hand, her pelvis arching to meet his fingers. Her eyes were tightly shut; her whole consciousness centered on his touch; occasionally a gasp escaped from her lips. She was oblivious to everything else, even his yard. Then she felt it, the first, faint sensation of real, carnal gratification under his fingers. It was there only a second, but it caused her to catch her breath as she waited to see if there would be another. Gradually, another flash of pleasure went through her, causing her to gasp and then hold her breath again. The sensations began to arrive more frequently, and with greater intensity. And then there was a strong one, and the flash of pleasure snatched a moan from her throat. She gasped and moaned again and then again as the sensations came closer and closer together.

Having leaned back up on his elbow, Tate watched her face, noting it was neither smooth nor marred with lines, but completely contorted in desperation in her search. Her moans were quite close together, and Tate knew her pleasure would soon be upon her. He broke off the stimulation immediately and removed his hand from her. As he expected, he saw this disappointed her tremendously. But he knew what he was doing. He had given her a taste of gratification, but he would not teach her to find it in this way. Very few men in the entire of Christendom knew how to give pleasure to a woman like this, and even fewer had the patience.

With her heart pounding in her ears, Acrida lay still, facing the wall, surprised and disappointed that Tate had stopped when it had begun to feel so good, and she herself was too utterly ashamed to protest.

Tate withdrew his yard from Acrida then and yanked the coverlet away once more. He pulled her down on her back and climbed on top of her. He was back inside her before she hardly knew he had been gone. Using one hand at a time, he shoved her knees up and out to the side, way up as far apart as they would go. Then settling on top of her, he began thrusting fiercely into her at his normal pace.

Though she did not resist, Acrida caught her breath from the sudden change of peace to violence. Back to this already? she thought, disappointed.

Balancing on both forearms, Tate shoved himself as deep as possible within her. He put all his weight on her hips and pelvis and rammed his pelvis against hers. This time, however, he withdrew very little, but instead stayed deep and rolled his hips, so that their loins ground together.

Acrida lay quiet, overcome for a moment by the pain invoked by his forceful attack against her tender queynt. Breathing hard and still wondering why the Fool had stopped with what he had just been doing, she forced herself to relax. Then, suddenly, she felt it. The same familiar pleasurable sensation she had had before. After so many strokes of his yard, Acrida felt the pleasant sensation again and stronger, and she moaned. It took fewer and fewer strokes between each time; and each time it came, the sensation tore a moan from her throat. Each time, the pleasure built on the last, growing stronger until suddenly the pleasure was there with every stroke, and Acrida was writhing and moaning and groaning helplessly, a prisoner of the pleasure.

Tate sweated as he worked over her, his buttocks and back flexing strongly with each thrust he made into her, all the while keeping her privities pinned beneath his pelvis in the soft mattress. His whole mind concentrated on his strokes into her, while paying strict attention to each gasp and moan that escaped her so that he might repeat the motion of the previous thrust that had pleased her. As she began to writhe and moan beneath him, he cheered her on in his thoughts. Then he felt her queynt tighten around him, one of the sure signals that spasms would soon follow.

Knowing nothing except what she suddenly experienced, Acrida grabbed Tate to her, clutching his buttocks to her groin, forcing them to thrust into her even harder; and with each powerful stroke, her pleasure intensified. Acrida panted with Tate and rolled her hips and pelvis to meet his and his thrust. Then it was there, wave after wave of intense pleasure hitting her. She moaned ecstatically and wept an affirmation, as if to answer God Himself who had asked her some question, all in time with the powerful, rhythmic meeting of their hips. As the pleasure ravaged her, Acrida felt her womb open wide with spasms, even as spasm after spasm racked her body. Acrida thought nothing and knew nothing except that she wanted this sensation to go on forever.

She clutched Tate tightly to her, continuing to try to force him harder, deeper inside her. She moaned and whimpered with every stroke, even as she felt the tide of pleasure ebb, and felt it leave her as it had come: at every other thrust, then at every third, and then it was gone as suddenly as it had come, taking all her energy with it.

Tate suddenly shoved himself deep inside her one last time and groaned in triumph and ecstasy as his seed exploded from his yard, as oblivious to her in his pleasure as she had been to him during hers. After a moment, he opened his eyes, and taking a deep breath, removed his yard and rolled off of her, but he immediately pulled her to him.

Acrida eased her legs back together slowly, her body weak, still amazed at what she had just experienced and how she had responded. She looked up at Tate, who read the look on her face quickly. He smiled at her and kissed her sweetly on the mouth, and then, to her surprise, he hugged her. Then he let her go a little, but still held her securely to him, while pulling up the covers.

Entangled in each other, they fell into weary sleep while the monks continued singing their songs of praise.

89

Bam! Bam! Bam! Bam! Bam!

Acrida jerked from sleep at the fierce pounding on the door.

"Wake and open! Wake and open!"

Acrida squinted unhappily at the noise and moaned. What was happening? God's wood, was it noon already? -It seemed that her eyes had only been shut for a moment.

"Acrida! You are summoned! Rouse yourself and open the door!"

Acrida groaned again in pain as she attempted to move.

"Coming!" she answered loudly and was rewarded with the cessation of the pounding on the door.

Reluctantly releasing his hold of her, Tate yawned, stretched, and raised up on one elbow. He rubbed his eyes and face with his hand and looked at the dim light seeping in from the edges of the cloth that covered the window, trying to guess the time.

Acrida slid from the warm bed slowly, her skin still damp with sweat, her body relaxed but sore, her queynt aching with every move she made. Finding her undertunic on the floor, she slipped it over her head and went and uncovered the window of the cell door.

"Who beats upon the door?" she asked, squinting at the face of the messenger who held the brightly burning torch.

"Acrida, the King is up and departs even now."

"The King? It is not even light yet. -And what has that to do with me?"

"You depart with the King's forces, Woman! Make haste and collect your things."

"What?!"

Tate chuckled. What luck that she would be summoned to accompany the King before dawn on this of all mornings!

"Acrida, unbolt the door!" came the voice of Dewain. "The King has summoned you!"

Acrida sighed and pushed the trunk out of the way and unbolted the door. Lord Dewain immediately entered the chamber, followed by Lord Olbert and a maidservant.

"Make haste and get her dressed!" Olbert ordered the girl.

The maid at once went to the trunk and removed the blue gown and shook it out.

The advisers stopped short in surprise then, espying the Queen's Fool in the bed in the dark chamber. They looked again at the disheveled, exhausted seer.

"Good morrow, My Lords," Tate greeted them pleasantly.

Dewain and Olbert nodded dumbly in greeting; the knight holding the torch grinned.

"We will await you in the courtyard," Dewain said hastily, shaking his head, and then he left with Olbert and the knight.

After retrieving her silver mirror from the chest, Acrida poured water into the basin and splashed her face with water. Then the maid helped her into the gown and proceeded to lace up the back while Acrida combed her hair quickly and then began to braid it.

In a few minutes, Acrida had her boots and headrail on, and the chest packed. The Fool had risen and put on his clothes as well. Acrida opened the cell door and pulled her woolen cloak about her, and she bid the waiting knight to take her chest as she hurried off to the monastery's latrines. The maidservant and the Fool left the chamber after her, leaving the disarrayed bed with its coverlet and sheets laying amiss, one still partially wet and marked with a spot of blood.

"Make haste and prepare, all who would go with the King!" the watchmen were calling.

With the edge of his black fur mantle flapping in the cold wind, Lord Van Necht stood with arms crossed, observing in silence the commotion in the courtyard as sleepy squires, knights, and servants scrambled about, saddling horses, collecting weapons and armor, and checking supplies by torchlight. Attired in royal purple with a heavy fur mantle about his shoulders and his sword at his hip, the golden-haired King strode toward the warlord, trailed by Olbert, Dewain, and Cedd.

"But would she not be safer with you, Sire? With an entire army to protect her?" Olbert asked.

"We have made Our decision."

King Christian paused beside Van Necht.

"We regret We have not had time to consult with you at length, Van Necht, but We entrust the Queen to your care. When We know where Herryck's army will make its stand, We will send word of where to take the Queen."

Van Necht bowed obediently.

Christian turned as he saw Grey approaching.

"Are the forces outside ready to depart, Grey?"

"Aye, My Lord, they are mounted and packed."

Christian nodded.

A serving woman approached Van Necht then and curtsied.

"My Lord, the Queen summons you."

Van Necht glanced at the woman, surprised.

"Is the Queen astir so early?"

"Aye, My Lord, and she summons thee."

The warlord sighed, but followed the woman to the guesthouse.

King Christian bowed to the Abbot of St. Benedict's Abbey.

"We thank thee for thy hospitality, Lord Abbot. With reluctant feet, We take Our leave."

"Go with God, My Son," the Abbot replied. "You are in our prayers during this time of testing and always."

"Thank you, Father Abbot. -Will you bless our company as we ride?"

"Of course, Your Grace."

In the steadily brightening darkness of predawn, Acrida, trying to ignore her aching body, hastened passed the open doors of the banquet hall where a few revelers and knights were sprawled about on the tables and benches and floor, sleeping off their drunkenness. Evading a collision with a servant loaded down with his master's supplies, she hurried toward the group of noblemen at the center of the courtyard.

Once with the group, she curtsied quickly and slipped in quietly beside the Fool who stood beside the knight and Lord Olbert.

"Ah, here she is, Sire," Dewain said pleasantly, gesturing toward her.

"Have you dreamt?" Christian asked her abruptly.

"What?"

"Did you dream last night?"

"No, Sire," Acrida answered self-consciously.

"The better question is did she sleep at all," the knight muttered with a smirk.

Tate and Lord Olbert smiled.

Christian then noticed the woman's ashen face, the bruises on her neck, and the dark circles under her eyes.

"You look affright," he told her. "Are you well?"

"I am, Sire."

"Indeed, she is," Tate said under his breath, to the grin of the knight beside him.

Acrida glanced at the Fool with a bewildered smile. Tate only smiled back innocently in response. She yawned and rubbed her eyes again, and casually watched as the stable boy helped Brother Bennet onto a horse.

"Bring the seer's horse," Dewain instructed the stable boy.

The boy bowed and hurried off to get it.

The pleasant expression fell from her face as she realized *she* was going to have to ride also. She was already sore just from walking.

Lord Felix approached the group then.

"We are ready to depart, Sire."

Christian nodded.

"Your Grace," Acrida began, "forgive me, but I cannot ride today."

Tate snorted and smiled, but managed not to laugh, and the knight and Olbert and Dewain covered their mouths to hide their amusement.

"Cannot ride? What mean you?" Christian asked irritably.

"I can walk! I prefer to walk! Or perhaps I could simply come to the camp in a few days."

"Walk? Woman, We are in haste! Get thee to thy horse!"

Christian noticed Tate snickering behind his hand and the knight beside him too, and Acrida's look of annoyance towards them.

The King turned and went to the stableman who held his saddled and waiting, luminous, white charger. The group followed him.

"But Sire-" Acrida tried again.

Sir Ecktor approached Lord Olbert and bowed and then bowed again to the King. Then he glanced at Acrida.

"Merry, you look wretched! You look as stiff and tired as a mount that has been ridden the entire night!"

Acrida blinked at the youth as the men about her broke forth in laughter. Despite herself, she could do nothing but smile helplessly with them.

Christian and Felix looked at them curiously.

"Oh-" King Christian smiled, surmising the truth. "Very well, Acrida. You may walk behind with the infantry."

He mounted his horse; then he pulled one of the rings from his gloved hand and gave it to her.

"Wear Our ring, so that all will know you are in Our service and will not accost you."

At a loss for words, Acrida took the large, gold ring and slipped it onto her thumb. She smiled and curtsied to the King.

Christian glanced at the knights.

"Olbert, wilt thou allow thy good knight, Sir Ecktor, to accompany Our Royal Seer and bring her safely to Us?"

"Aye, Your Grace," he smiled.

Sir Ecktor bowed dutifully.

Van Necht cleared his throat. The young Queen and one of her serving women were sitting on a bench at the window of her chamber, watching the activity in the courtyard below. She still wore the plain sleeping gown, but her golden hair was braided and wrapped about her head in the style of a married woman.

"Ah, Van Necht, you are here to comfort me," she said with a fragile smile, rising from her seat and turning to him.

"My Lady?" he asked, bowing.

"I am so sad that my cousin is so soon departing. He goes to meet our enemy," she explained with a slight smile as she wiped her teary eyes. "I complained that I would surely cry if he left me so soon, and Christian made me promise not to come down and see him off, for he feared my tears would dishearten him and his vassals. He made me promise to sit at the window and only smile and wave."

Van Necht regarded her curiously, marveling at her sweet disposition after her wedding night. He glanced uncomfortably then about the candlelit chamber and at the smiling, serving women near him.

His eyes fell on the bed, still disarrayed and with a small spot of blood on one of the sheets.

"Oh, I nearly forgot to tell you!" she said. "He gave me a gift before he took his leave this morning! You will never guess! He gave me lands and chattel! And he gave me another ring!"

She held out her hand and showed the warlord the signet ring that was too big for her finger.

"You see the raised design? You can press it in the wax when you seal a letter."

Van Necht forced himself to smile and to look interested. His morning gift to Gunhilde had also been the lands she arrived with plus a horse his family had raised. The horse soon colicked and died, surely a sign of all the trouble and pain that was to come.

"My Lady!" the maidservant called from the window.

The Queen hurried back to the large window, her servants and Van Necht behind her, and looked down into the dark at the torchlit spectacle of the King's going forth.

King Christian on his gleaming, white charger led the great procession of knights out of the abbey. In the distance, the pinkish-gray hues of dawn colored the sky, bearing the promise of light and the new day. The Abbot stood high above, on the tall abbey wall near the gate, making the sign of the cross repeatedly as the riders rode out of the entrance beneath and turned their horses toward the sunrise.

Author's Notes

1) I have done my best to faithfully research and incorporate into this story all aspects of Medieval life in general, including the beliefs and teachings of the Catholic Church. I apologize for any errors that I have made.

2) I wanted to give the reader a sense of where they might have been on the social scale in the Medieval world, which is why I did not include any translations for the Latin in the book. In Medieval society, Latin was the language of correspondence and the Church. The common people who had no education would have only picked up Latin from hearing it during the Mass. Some nobles who had the benefit of some education might be able to read and write some Latin, and perhaps their use of it was fairly elementary. However, those with the best understanding of Latin were of course clergy or monks or nuns.

3) It is with mixed emotions that I include what may be termed loosely as "graphic and gratuitous" sex in this story. I was tempted to "tame" it down or to not include it all together. However, sex in reality is almost always graphic, gratuitous and problematic. And as the book examines and attempts to reflect life back then (and in comparison to now), and as so much of the book is about sex, or the pursuit of it, as well as its uses and abuses, I felt in the end it had to be included in its raw bluntness. Ultimately, after all, sex is God's invention, not man's.

The Medieval Church was confounded by the sex issue also. The Church grudgingly condoned it in marriage for the sake of children. They too saw that the withholding of sex by one spouse encouraged infidelity and sin in the other; thus they promoted the policy of the "marital debt" that must be paid, i.e. neither spouse could refuse coition to the other if the other wanted it.

However, the Church did withhold communion to marital couples who had engaged in sex the day or night before. The Church further instigated a policy of abstinence during certain Church seasons, particularly Lent, and also on certain days of the week. Furthermore, the Church taught the "proper" position for intercourse and also strongly encouraged spouses *not* to disrobe when having intercourse.

Although it took many years, the Church eventually was able to demand celibacy from their clergy, refusing to allow the priests to keep concubines and finally forbidding them to marry.

Although I include sex in this story, I neither condone nor recommend sexual activity in our modern times. This story is set in a time before most sexually transmitted diseases existed or were widespread and conveniently in a kingdom that is cursed with infertility. These lack of consequences leads the subject of sex to be treated casually in the story. In stark contrast, today we live in a world plagued with sexually transmitted diseases, including syphilis, gonorrhea, genital herpes, HIV, Aids, etc., and where having either an abortion or an illegitimate child is considered acceptable and even routine; these modern phenomena are a direct consequence of treating sex casually in real life.

Helpful Sources

Augustine, St. First Catechetical Instruction (De Catechizandis Rudibus). Trans. Rev. Joseph P. Christopher. Westminister, MD: Newman Bookshop, 1946.

Benedict, St. The Rule of Saint Benedict. Ed. Timothy Fry, O.S.B. NY: Vintage Books, 1998.

Biller, Peter and A. J. Minnis. Eds. Handling Sin: Confession in the Middle Ages. York: York Medieval Press, 1998.

Brundage, James A. Sex, Law, and Marriage in the Middle Ages. Collected Studies, Vol. 397, Ashgate Pub. Co, 1993.

Burford, E. J. Bawds and Lodgings. London: Peter Owen Limited, 1976.

Cawthorne, Nigel. Sex Lives of the Popes. Prion, 1996.

Cosman, Madeleine Pelner. Medieval Wordbook. NY: Facts on File, Inc., 1996

—-. Fabulous Feasts: Medieval Cookery and Ceremony. NY: George Braziller, Inc., 1976.

Durant, Will. The Age of Faith. NY: Simon & Schuster, 1950.

Edge, David. Arms and Armor of the Medieval Knight: An Illustrated History of Weaponry in the Middle Ages. Diane Pub., 2000.

Fielding, William J. Strange Customs of Courtship and Marriage. NY: The New Home Library, 1942.

—-. Strange Superstitions & Magical Practices. Philadelphia: Blakiston Co., 1945.

Fischer, Andreas. Engagement, Wedding & Marriage in Old English. Heidelberg: Carl Winter Universitatsverlag, 1986.

Fossier, Robert. Peasant Life in the Medieval West. Trans. Juliet Vale. Oxford, UK: Basi Blackwell LTD, 1988.

Gueranger, Prosper. Religious and Monastic Life Explained. St. Louis, MO: B. Herder Publishing, 1908.

Goetz, Hans-Werner. Life in the Middle Ages from Seventh to the Thirteenth Century. Trans. Albert Wimmer. Ed. Steven Rowan. USA: University of Notre Dame Press, 1993.

Hadley, Dawn. Masculinity in Medieval Europe. London: Longman Publishing, 1999.

Jackson, Richard A., ed. Ordines Coronationis Franciae: Texts and Ordines for the Coronation of Frankish and French Kings and Queens in the Middle Ages. Vol. 1. Philadelphia: University of Pennsylvania Press, 1995.

Jaeger, C. Stephen. Origins of Courtliness. Philadelphia: University of Pennsylvania Press, 1985

Kenyon, Sherrilyn. Writer's Guide to Everyday Life in the Middle Ages. Cincinnati, OH: Writer's Digest Bks, 1995.

Krehbiel, Edward B. The Interdict: Its History & Operation with Especial Attention to the Time of Pope Innocent III, 1198-1216. Merrick, NY: Richwood Publishing Co., 1977.

O'Brien, John A. Understanding the Catholic Faith: An Official Edition of the revised Baltimore Catechism No. 3 Confraternity of Christian Doctrine Edition. Notre Dame, Indiana: Ave Maria Press, 1965.

Parsons, John C. Ed. Medieval Queenship. St. Martin, 1993.

Piponnier, Francoise and Perrine Mane. Dress in the Middle Ages. Trans. Caroline Beamish. Yale University Press, 1997.

Price, Lorna. The Plan of St. Gall in Brief. Berkley, CA: University of California Press, 1982.

Riche, Pierre. Daily Life in the World of Charlemagne. Trans. Jo Ann McNamara. USA: University of Pennsylvania Press, 1996.

Russell, Jeffry Burton. Witchcraft in the Middle Ages. London: Cornell University Press, 1972.

Scaglione, Aldo. Knights at Court: Courtliness, Chivalry, and Courtesy from Ottonian Germany to the Italian Renaissance. USA: University of California Press, 1991.

Schramm, Percy Ernst. History of the English Coronation. Trans. Leopold G. Wickham Legg. Oxford: Clarendon Press, 1937.

Scullard, H. H. Roman Britian: Outpost of the Empire. London: Thames & Hudson Ltd, 1979.

Searle, Mark and Kenneth W. Stevenson. Documents of the Marriage Liturgy. Collegiate, Minnesota: Liturgical Press, 1992.

Southworth, John. Fools and Jesters of the English Court. Gloucestershire: Sutton Publishing, 1998.

Stafford, Pauline. Queens, Concubines, and Dowagers. UK: Leicester University Press, 1983.

Stenton, Sir Frank M. Anglo-Saxon England c.550-1087. 3rd ed. Vol. 2. Oxford: Clarendon Press, 1971

Thompson, Michael. The Medieval Hall: The Basis of Secular Domestic Life, 600-1600 AD. England: Scolar Press, 1995.

Time Life Books Eds. <u>What Life Was Like In the Days of Chivalry:</u> <u>Medieval Europe AD 800-1500 A.D.</u> Alexandria, Virginia: Time-Life Pub., 1999.

Turner, Ralph V. <u>King John.</u> England: Longman Group, 1994.

Waugh, Scott L. <u>The Lordship of England: Royal Wardships and Marriages in English Society and Politics, 1217-1327.</u> Books Demand, 1988.

Wemple, Suzanne F. "Consent & Dissent to Sexual Intercourse in Germanic Societies from the 5th to the 10th Century." <u>Consent and Coercion to Sex and Marriage in Ancient and Medieval Societies.</u> Ed. Angeliki E Laiou. Washington, DC: Dumbarton Oaks Research Library & Collection, 1993.

Helpful Internet Websites

The Catholic Encyclopedia Online
http://www.newadvent.org/cathen/13181a.htm

The Life of St. Patrick:
http://www.ireland-now.com/heritage/myths/historpatrick.html

Medieval Sourcebook: Mass of The Roman Rite [Latin/English]
http://www.fordham.edu/halsall/basis/latinmass2.html

Organ of the Middle Ages:
http://panther.bsc.edu/~jhcook/OrgHist/history/hist002.ht

About the Author

Fletcher King is from East Texas, is a member of MENSA, and holds a Bachelor of Arts in English Literature from the University of the South in Sewanee, Tennessee.